Praise for *KUSHIEL'S DART* and *KUSHIEL'S CHOSEN*

'The author's sensual prose, su~~itable~~ ~~for~~ readers,
should appeal to fans ~~of~~ ~~~~ stantine,

'Superbly detai~~led~~ ~~~~ and sometimes
unbearably i~~n~~ ~~~~, deeply satisfying and
alt~~ogether~~ remarkable debut'
Kirkus Reviews

'*Kushiel's Dart* takes fantasy into shadowy, exotic
corners it rarely dares to tread. The standard of the
writing is so high, it's hard to believe this is a first novel.
There are some genuinely shocking moments, but even
the darkest of them are written with a skilful elegance.
The characters are captivating and the plot cleverly
convoluted. I read many new writers, but few of them
capture my imagination as Jacqueline Carey has. A writer
to watch – as the cliché goes – but more importantly a
writer to read'
Storm Constantine

'A powerful narrative, with savage action balanced
by exquisite characterisation. The best fantasy I've read
in years'
Piers Anthony

Kushiel's Chosen

Jacqueline Carey was born in 1964. After receiving BA degrees in psychology and English literature from Lake Forest College, she embarked on a writing career. An affinity for travel has taken her to countries as far apart as Finland and Egypt. She currently resides in west Michigan. Her previous publications include various short stories, essays and a non-fiction book. *Kushiel's Dart* was her first novel, and the final book in this trilogy is *Kushiel's Avatar*.

KUSHIEL'S
CHOSEN

JACQUELINE CAREY

TOR

First published 2002 by Tor, Tom Doherty Associates, New York

First published in Great Britain 2003 by Tor

This edition published 2004 by Tor
an imprint of Pan Macmillan Ltd
Pan Macmillan, 20 New Wharf Road, London N1 9RR
Basingstoke and Oxford
Associated companies throughout the world
www.panmacmillan.com
www.toruk.com

ISBN-13: 978-0-330-41277-3
ISBN-10: 0-330-41277-9

3 5 7 9 8 6 6 4 2

A CIP catalogue record for this book is available from
the British Library.

Typeset by Intype Libra Ltd
Printed and bound in Great Britain by
Mackays of Chatham plc, Chatham, Kent

Acknowledgments

To all my friends, kith or kin, near or far—for understanding the struggle, for forgiving the lack of time, for space given and grace granted, for sharing in the joy (and *joie*), for asking, for listening, for notes written and sent, for evenings on the porch, for champagne drunk and toasts given, for reading, for letting the wings of story soar, for spreading the word: Thank you. A thousand times, thank you.

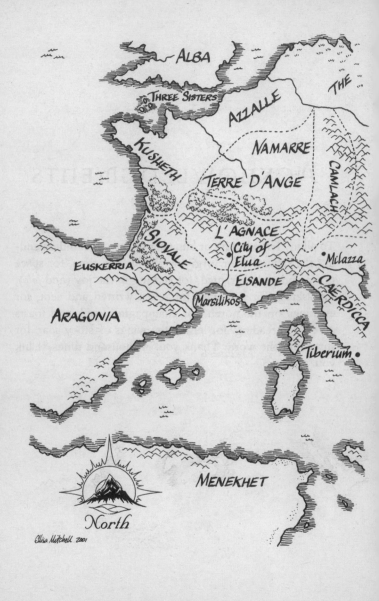

Dramatis Personae
– Kushiel's Chosen

Phèdre's Household

Anafiel Delaunay de Montrève – mentor of Phèdre
  (*deceased*)
Alcuin nó Delaunay – student of Delaunay (*deceased*)
Phèdre nó Delaunay de Montrève – Comtesse de
  Montrève; *anguissette*
Benoit, Gemma – household staff
Fortun, Remy, Ti-Philippe – chevaliers, a.k.a. Phèdre's
  Boys
Eugènie – kitchen-mistress
Joscelin Verreuil – Cassiline Brother (Siovale)
Purnell Friote – seneschal of Montrève
Richeline Friote – wife of Purnell

Members of the Royal Family:
Terre d'Ange

Ysandre de la Courcel – Queen of Terre d'Ange; wed to
  Drustan mab Necthana

Ganelon de la Courcel – former King of Terre d'Ange; grandfather of Ysandre (*deceased*)

Isabel L'Envers de la Courcel – mother of Ysandre (*deceased*)

Rolande de la Courcel – father of Ysandre (*deceased*)

Barquiel L'Envers – brother of Isabel; Duc L'Envers (Namarre)

Baudoin de Trevalion – son of Lyonette and Marc; Prince of the Blood (*deceased*)

Bernadette de Trevalion – daughter of Lyonette and Marc; wife of Ghislain de Somerville

Lyonette de Trevalion – great-aunt of Ysandre; a.k.a. Lioness of Azzalle (*deceased*)

Marc de Trevalion – husband of Lyonette; former Duc of Trevalion (Azzalle)

Nicola L'Envers y Aragon – cousin of Ysandre

Members of the Royal Family: La Serenissima

Benedicte de la Courcel – great-uncle of Ysandre; Prince of the Blood

Maria Stregazza de la Courcel – wife of Benedicte (*deceased*)

Etaine de Tourais – second wife of Benedicte de la Courcel

Imriel de la Courcel – son of Benedicte and second wife

Marie-Celeste de la Courcel Stregazza – daughter of Benedicte and Maria; Princess of the Blood; wed to Marco Stregazza

Severio Stregazza – son of Marie-Celeste and Marco; Prince of the Blood

Thérèse de la Courcel Stregazza – daughter of Benedicte and Maria; Princess of the Blood; wed to Dominic Stregazza (*deceased*)

D'Angeline Peerage

Isidore d'Aiglemort – son of Maslin; Duc d'Aiglemort (Camlach) (*deceased*)

Marquise Solaine Belfours – noble; Secretary of the Privy Seal

Cecilie Laveau-Perrin – wife of chevalier Perrin (*deceased*); adept of Cereus House; tutor to Phèdre and Alcuin

Roxanne de Mereliot – Lady of Marsilikos (Eisande)

Quincel de Morhban – Duc de Morhban (Kusheth)

Lord Rinforte – Prefect of the Cassiline Brotherhood

Edmée de Rocaille – betrothed of Rolande (*deceased*)

Faragon Shahrizai – Duc de Shahrizai (Kusheth)

Melisande Shahrizai – noble (Kusheth)

(Tabor, Sacriphant, Persia, Marmion, Fanchone – members of House Shahrizai; Melisande's kin)

Ghislain de Somerville – son of Percy; wed to Bernadette de Trevalion

Percy de Somerville – Comte de Somerville (L'Agnace); Prince of the Blood; Royal Commander

Tibault de Toluard – Marquis de Toluard (Siovale)

Gaspar Trevalion – Comte de Forcay (Azzalle); cousin of Marc

Apollonaire and Diànne – joint holders of the Marquisate de Fhirze

Vivienne Neldor, Marie de Flairs – ladies-in-waiting to Ysandre

Lord Amaury Trente – Captain of the Queen's Guard
Lady Denise Grosmaine – Secretary of the Presence

NIGHT COURT

Moirethe Lereux – Dowayne of Eglantine House
Favrielle nó Eglantine – seamstress
Raphael Murain nó Gentian – adept of Gentian House

THREE SISTERS

Master of the Straits – controls the seas between Alba and
    Terre d'Ange
Hyacinthe – apprentice to Master of the Straits; Phèdre's
    friend; Tsingano

ALBA AND EIRE

Drustan mab Necthana – Cruarch of Alba, wed to
    Ysandre de la Courcel
Eamonn mac Conor – Lord of the Dalriada (*deceased*)
Grainne mac Conor – sister of Eamonn; Lady of the
    Dalriada
Necthana – mother of Drustan
Breidaia, Moiread (*deceased*), Sibeal – daughters of
    Necthana

LA SERENISSIMA

Cesare Stregazza – Doge of La Serenissima
Marco Stregazza – eldest son of the Doge

Ricciardo Stregazza — younger son of the Doge
Allegra Stregazza — wife of Ricciardo
Benito Dandi — noble, member of the Immortali
Orso Latrigan — noble, candidate for Dogal election
Lorenzo Pescaro — noble, candidate for Dogal election
Bianca — Priestess of the Elect; Oracle of Asherat
Vesperia — Priestess of Asherat; Oracle-in-training
Giulia Latrigan — noble
Magister Acco — astrologer
Serena Pidari — wife of Phanuel Buonard
Felicity d'Arbos — former lady-in-waiting to Maria
  Stregazza
The Warden of La Dolorosa
Constantin, Fabron, Malvio, Tito — prison guards

İLLYRİA

Vasilii Kolcei — Ban of Illyria, a.k.a. the Zim Sokali
Zabèla Kolcei — wife of the Ban
Pjètri Kolcei — middle son of the Ban
Czibor — commander of the Ban's Guard
Kazan Atrabiades — pirate captain
(Epafras, Gavril, Lukin, Nikanor, Oltukh, Pekhlo,
  Spiridon, Stajeo, Tormos, Volos, Ushak — Kazan's
  men)
Daroslav — Kazan's brother (*deceased*)
Glaukos — Kazan's man, former Tiberian slave
Zilje — wife of Glaukos
Marjopí — Kazan's housekeeper
Njësa Atrabiades — mother of Kazan
Janàri Rossatos — Ambassador to La Serenissima

Kriti

Oeneus Asterius – Hierophant of the Temenos
Pasiphae Asterius – the Kore of the Temenos
Demetrios Asterius – Archon of Phaistos
Timanthes – noble, Archon's lover
Althaia – noble, sister of Timanthes

Others

Maestro Gonzago de Escabares – Aragonian historian;
    Delaunay's former teacher
Thelesis de Mornay – Queen's Poet
Quintilius Rousse – Royal Admiral
Emile – member of Hyacinthe's former crew
Jacques Brenin – Phèdre's factor
Nahum ben Isaac – the Rebbe
Hanna – Yeshuite woman
Micheline de Parnasse – Royal Archivist
Tarren d'Eltoine – Captain of the Unforgiven, Southfort
    (Camlach)
(Octave, Vernay, Svariel, Fitz, Giles – soldiers of the
    Unforgiven)
Phanuel Buonard – guardsman of Troyes-le-Mont
Louis Namot – Captain of the ship *Darielle*
Brys nó Rinforte, David nó Rinforte – Cassiline Brothers
Gregorio Livinius – Principe of Pavento
Duke and Duchess of Milazza
Gilles Lamiz – apprentice-poet
Micah ben Ximen, Sarae, Teppo – Yeshuites; Joscelin's
    allies
Cervianus – attendant in Temple of Asherat

⦿ONE

ΠꙨ ꙨΠE would deny that I have known hardship in my time, brief though it has been for all that I have done in it. This, I think, I may say without boastfulness. If I answer now to the title of Comtesse de Montrève and my name is listed in the peerage of Terre d'Ange, still I have known what it is to have all that I possess torn from me; once, when I was but four years of age and my birth-mother sold me into servitude to the Court of Night-Blooming Flowers, and twice, when my lord and mentor Anafiel Delaunay was slain, and Melisande Shahrizai betrayed me into the hands of the Skaldi.

I have crossed the wilds of Skaldia in the dead of winter, and faced the wrath of the Master of the Straits on the teeming waters. I have been the plaything of a barbarian warlord, and I have lost my dearest friend to an eternity of lonely isolation. I have seen the horrors of war and the deaths of my companions. I have walked, alone and by night, into the vast darkness of an enemy encampment, knowing that I gave myself up to torture and nigh-certain death.

None of it was as difficult as telling Joscelin I was returning to the Service of Naamah.

It was the *sangoire* cloak that decided me; Melisande's challenge and the badge of my calling that marked me as an *anguissette*, Kushiel's Chosen, as clearly as the mote of scarlet emblazoned since birth in the iris of my left eye. A rose petal floating upon dark waters, some admirer once called it. *Sangoire* is a deeper color, a red so dark it borders upon black. I have seen spilled blood by starlight; it is a fitting color for one such as I, destined to find pleasure in pain. Indeed, the wearing of it is proscribed for any who is not an *anguissette*. D'Angelines appreciate such poetic niceties.

I am Phèdre nó Delaunay de Montrève, and I am the only one. Kushiel's Dart strikes seldom, if to good effect.

When Maestro Gonzago de Escabares brought the cloak from La Serenissima, and the tale by which he had gained it, I made my choice. I knew that night. By night, my course seemed clear and obvious. There is a traitor in the heart of Terre d'Ange, one who stands close enough to the throne to touch it; that much, I knew. Melisande's sending the cloak made it plain: I had the means of discovering the traitor's identity, should I choose to engage in the game. That it was true, I had no doubt. By the Night Court and by Delaunay, I have been exquisitely trained as courtesan and spy alike. Melisande knew this — and Melisande required an audience, or at least a worthy opponent. It was clear, or so I thought.

In the light of day, before Joscelin's earnest blue gaze, I knew the extent of the misery it would cause. And for that, I delayed, temporizing, sure in my reasoning but aching at heart. Maestro Gonzago stayed some days, enjoying the hospitality I was at such pains to provide. He suspected somewhat of my torment, I do not doubt. I saw it reflected in his kind, homely face. At length he left without pressing me, his apprentice Camilo in tow, bound for Aragonia.

I was left alone with Joscelin and my decision.

We had been happy in Montrève, he and I; especially he, raised in the mountains of Siovale. I know what it cost Joscelin to bind his life to mine, in defiance of his Cassiline vow of obedience. Let the courtiers laugh, if they will, but he took his vows seriously, and celibacy not the least of them. D'Angelines follow the precept of Blessed Elua, who was born of the commingled blood of Yeshua ben Yosef and the tears of the Magdelene in the womb of Earth: *Love as thou wilt*. Alone among the Companions, only Cassiel abjured Elua's command; Cassiel, who accepted damnation to remain celibate and steadfast at Elua's side, the Perfect Companion, reminding the One God of the sacred duty even He had forgotten.

These, then, were the vows Joscelin had broken for me. Montrève had done much to heal the wounds that breaking had dealt him. My return to the Service of Naamah, who had gone freely to Elua's side, who had lain down with kings and peasants alike for his sake, would open those wounds anew.

I told him.

And I watched the white lines of tension, so long absent, engrave themselves on the sides of his beautiful face. I laid out my reasoning, point by point, much as Delaunay would have done. Joscelin knew the history of it nearly as well as I did myself. He had been assigned as my companion when Delaunay still owned my marque; he knew the role I had played in my lord's service. He had been with me when Delaunay was slain, and Melisande betrayed us both — and he had been there that fateful night at Troyes-le-Mont, when Melisande Shahrizai had escaped the Queen's justice.

"You are sure?" That was all he said, when I had finished.

"Yes." I whispered the word, my hands clenching on the rich *sangoire* folds of my cloak, which I held bundled in my arms. "Joscelin . . ."

"I need to think." He turned away, his face shuttered like a stranger's. In anguish, I watched him go, knowing there was nothing more I could say. Joscelin had known, from the beginning, what I was. But he had never reckoned on loving me, nor I him.

There was a small altar to Elua in the garden, which Richeline Friote, my seneschal's wife, tended with great care. Flowers and herbs grew in abundance behind the manor house, where a statue of Elua, no more than a meter tall, smiled benignly upon our bounty, petals strewn at his marble feet. I knew the garden well, for I had spent many hours seated upon a bench therein, considering my decision. It was there, too, that Joscelin chose to think, kneeling before Elua in the Cassiline style, head bowed and arms crossed.

He stayed there a long time.

By early evening, a light rain had begun to fall and still Joscelin knelt, a silent figure in the grey twilight. The autumn flowers grew heavy with water and hung their bright heads, basil and rosemary released pungent fragrance on the moist air, and still he knelt. His wheat-gold braid hung motionless down his back, runnels of rain coursing its length. Light dwindled, and still he knelt.

"My lady Phèdre." Richeline's concerned voice gave me a start; I hadn't heard her approach, which, for me, was notable. "How long will he stay there, do you think?"

I turned away from the window that looked out at the garden loggia. "I don't know. You'd best serve dinner without him. It could be a good while." Joscelin had once held a vigil, snow-bound, throughout an entire Skaldic night on some obscure point of Cassiline honor. This cut deeper. I glanced up at Richeline, her open, earnest face. "I told him I am planning to return to the City of Elua. To the Service of Naamah."

Richeline took a deep breath, but her expression didn't change. "I wondered if you would." Her voice took on a compassionate tone. "He's not the sort to bear it easily, my lady."

"I know." I sounded steadier than I felt. "I don't chose it lightly, Richeline."

"No." She shook her head. "You wouldn't."

Her support was more heartening than I reckoned. I looked back out the window at the dim, kneeling figure of Joscelin, tears stinging my eyes. "Purnell will stay on as seneschal, of course, and you with him. Montrève needs your hand, and the folk have come to trust you. I'd not have it otherwise."

"Yes, my lady." Her kind gaze was almost too much to bear, for I did not like myself overmuch at this moment. Richeline placed her fist to her heart in the ancient gesture of fealty. "We will hold Montrève for you, Purnell and I. You may be sure of it."

"Thank you." I swallowed hard, repressing my

sorrow. "Will you summon the boys to dinner, Richeline? They should be told, and I have need of their aid. If I am to do this thing before winter, we must begin at once."

"Of course."

"The boys" were my three chevaliers; Phèdre's Boys, they called themselves, Remy, Fortun and Ti-Philippe. Fighting sailors under the command of Royal Admiral Quintilius Rousse, they had attached themselves to my service after our quest to Alba and the battle of Troyesle-Mont. In truth, I think it amused the Queen to grant them to me.

I told them over dinner, served in the manor hall with white linens on the table, and an abundance of candles. At first there was silence, then Remy let out an irrepressible whoop of joy, his green eyes sparkling.

"To the City, my lady? You promise it?"

"I promise," I told him. Ti-Philippe, small and blond, grinned, while solid, dark Fortun looked thoughtfully at me. "It will need two of you to ride ahead and make arrangements. I've need of a modest house, near enough to the Palace. I'll give you letters of intent to take to my factor in the City."

Remy and Ti-Philippe began to squabble over the adventure. Fortun continued to look at me with his dark gaze. "Do you go a-hunting, my lady?" he asked softly.

I toyed with a baked pear, covered in crumbling cheese, to hide my lack of appetite. "What do you know of it, Fortun?"

His gaze never wavered. "I was at Troyes-le-Mont. I know someone conspired to free the Lady Melisande Shahrizai. And I know you are an *anguissette* trained by

Anafiel Delaunay, who, outside the boundaries of Montrève, some call the Whoremaster of Spies."

"Yes." I whispered it, and felt a thrill run through my veins, compelling and undeniable. I lifted my head, feeling the weight of my hair caught in a velvet net, and downed a measure of fine brandy from the orchards of L'Agnace. "It is time for Kushiel's Dart to be cast anew, Fortun."

"My lord Cassiline will not like it, my lady," Remy cautioned, having left off his quarrel with Ti-Philippe. "Seven hours he has knelt in the garden. I think now I know why."

"Joscelin Verreuil is my concern." I pushed my plate away from me, abandoning any pretense of eating. "Now I need your aid, chevaliers. Who will ride to the City, and find me a home?"

In the end, it was decided that Remy and Ti-Philippe both would go in advance, securing our lodgings and serving notice of my return. How Ysandre would receive word of it, I was uncertain. I had not told her of Melisande's gift, nor my concerns regarding her escape. I did not doubt that I had the Queen's support, but the scions of Elua and his Companions can be a capricious lot, and I judged it best to operate in secrecy for the moment. Let them suppose that it was the pricking of Kushiel's Dart that had driven me back; the less they knew, the more I might learn.

So Delaunay taught me, and it is sound advice. One must gauge one's trust carefully.

I trusted my three chevaliers a great deal, or I would never have let them know what we were about. Delaunay sought to protect me — me, and Alcuin, who paid the ultimate price for it — by keeping us in ignorance. I would not make his mistake; for so I reckon it now, a mistake.

But still, there was only one person I trusted with the whole of my heart and soul, and he knelt without speaking in the rain-drenched garden of Montrève. I stayed awake long that night, reading a Yeshuite treatise brought to me by Gonzago de Escabares. I had not given up my dream of finding a way to free Hyacinthe from his eternal indenture to the Master of the Straits. Hyacinthe, my oldest friend, the companion of my childhood, had accepted a fate meant for me: condemned to immortality on a lonely isle, unless I could find a way to free him, to break the *geis* that bound him. I read until my eyes glazed and my mind wandered. At length, I dozed before the fire, stoked on the hour by two whispering servant-lads.

The sense of a presence woke me, and I opened my eyes.

Joscelin stood before me, dripping rainwater onto the carpeted flagstones. Even as I looked, he crossed his forearms and bowed.

"In Cassiel's name," he said, his voice rusty from hours of disuse, "I protect and serve."

We knew each other too well, we two, to dissemble.

"No more than that?"

"No more," he said steadily, "and no less."

I sat in my chair gazing up at his beautiful face, his blue eyes weary from his long vigil. "Can there be no middle ground between us, Joscelin?"

"No." He shook his head gravely. "Phèdre . . . Elua knows, I love you. But I am sworn to Cassiel. I cannot be two things, not even for you. I will honor my vow, to protect and serve you. To the death, if need be. You cannot ask for more. Yet you do."

"I am Kushiel's chosen, and sworn to Naamah," I whispered. "I honor your vow. Can you not honor mine?"

"Only in my own way." He whispered it too; I knew how much it cost him, and closed my eyes. "Phèdre, do not ask for more."

"So be it," I said with closed eyes.

When I opened them, he was gone.

Two

WHEN LAST I entered the City of Elua, it was riding in triumph in the entourage of Ysandre de la Courcel, fresh from victory over the Skaldi, with the Royal Army and Drustan mab Necthana and the Alban contingent at our side. This time, my return to the city of my birth was considerably less dramatic, although it meant a great deal to me.

It is a powerful thing, homecoming. I had come to love Montrève, with its green mountains, its rustic charm; but the City was my home, and I wept to see its white walls once more. My heart, a year and more accustomed to the sedate pace of the countryside, stirred within my breast and beat faster.

We had been long days on the road, while the brisk weather of autumn turned to the chill of impending winter. When I had travelled before, it had been with no more than my companions and I could carry on sturdy mounts. Now, we were accompanied by laden wagons of wool, product of the last shearing of the season, with an entire wagon for my goods, which included the volumes and scrolls of Yeshuite research I had accumulated within a year.

It was a goodly amount, for the followers of Yeshua were a prolific folk. Their history is ancient, reaching back long before the time when Yeshua ben Yosef, the true-gotten son of the One God, hung upon a Tiberian cross, his blood mingling with the tears of the Magdelene to beget blessed Elua. I had not yet discovered in their writings a clue to unravel the *geis* that bound Hyacinthe, but I was yet hopeful.

Also in our train was a wagon for our gear, tents and foodstuffs, and pack-mules for my retainers' possessions. There was even a pair of saddle-horses we led unridden, fresh mounts for Remy and Ti-Philippe, who dashed back and forth between our slow party and the City.

"You'll need a carriage," Fortun said pragmatically as we drew near to the City. "It won't do for the Comtesse de Montrève to ride astride, my lady. But I reckon it can wait until we've sold the wool."

"It will have to." I had supposed, before Ysandre's Chancellor of the Exchequer had informed me that I was the inheritor of Delaunay's estate and never-claimed title, that all D'Angeline nobles had coin in abundance; in truth, it was not so. I drew a modest income from my holdings at Montrève, and I had funds from the recompense of Delaunay's City house. It had been seized upon his death, when I was judged in absentia to be his murderer. Now, my name was clear, thanks to Ysandre's intervention. In the City of Elua, it is known that I loved my lord Delaunay well and had no part in his death; as he named me his heir, so did I inherit. Still, I had no wish to dwell in the place where he died.

So, his estate of Montrève I inherited, and I accepted recompense for the sale of his home in the City; but the proceeds from the former went toward the payment and equipage of my retainers, and the latter toward the purchase of a home for us. Of the small amount that remained, I confess, a great deal went into my library.

Those purchases, I did not regret. All knowledge is worth having, Delaunay used to say; and I had every intention of putting what I garnered to good use. But it left me with little in the way of capital.

I had a diamond, once, that would have financed the beginnings of a salon any courtesan might envy. Thinking on it, I touched my bare throat where it used to hang. I would rather have starved than profit from that gem.

As we rode nigh to the southern gate, Fortun raised the banner of Montrève; green, a crescent moon in argent upper right, and sable crag lower left. The City Guard hoisted their spears in answer, a shout sounding from the white walls — Ti-Philippe, dicing with the Guard, had been awaiting our arrival. I heard a ragged chant arise, all too familiar: the marching-song of Phèdre's Boys, born out of our desperate quest to Alba.

Glancing at Joscelin, I saw his shoulders set with resignation.

So we entered the City.

In some parts, it was small, and in others, vaster and more lovely than I remembered, gracious and proud. Ti-Philippe scrambled down to meet us, and led us inward, along the winding course of the river toward the Palace. In the street, citizens paused and watched curiously, marking our passage. I could hear the rumors begin to spread. To the east, the hill of Mont Nuit sloped upward. The Night Court was there, with its Thirteen Houses, where I had received my earliest training; in Cereus House, First among the Thirteen. At its foot lay Night's Doorstep, my refuge, where Hyacinthe had established himself as the Prince of Travellers.

That was the past. The future lay before us. In sight of the Palace, at the juncture of a narrow street, Remy met us. After a hurried conference, Ti-Philippe took stewardship of the wool-wagons, leading them to the worsters' district.

"My lady." Remy grinned, and swept me a bow from the saddle, rising to point down the street. "Your quarters await you!"

If anyone might question the wisdom of allowing my wild sailorlads to seek out lodgings for us, their fears would be mislaid; they were jealous of my honor, Phèdre's Boys, and no one was allowed to mock it save they themselves. Hidden away in the shadow of the Palace, it was a charming house. It had a tiny courtyard near overgrown with shade vines, a stable and a deceptively generous layout, being narrow, but deep. There was ample room for our party.

"I contracted a kitchen-mistress," Remy said anxiously, "and a daymaid. There's a lad to help with the stables, and I reckon between the three . . . four of us . . ." he shot a glance at Joscelin, ". . . we can do what else needs doing. Will it suit, my lady?"

I stood in the entry, where the winter light filtered cool and green through the hardy vines. "It will suit," I said, catching my breath in a laugh. "It will suit most admirably, chevalier!"

Thus did I take up residence as the Comtesse de Montrève in the City of Elua.

My first invitation arrived before I'd scarce gotten settled; no surprise, for I'd written to Cecilie in advance that I was returning. We had maintained a steady correspondence during my time at Montrève, for in addition to being one of my oldest acquaintances — and one of the few I trusted nearly as much as I did Joscelin — she was a delightful correspondent, her letters laden with bits of news and gossip that I relished to no end. I accepted her invitation at once.

"Phèdre." Meeting me at her door, Cecilie Laveau-Perrin enfolded me unhesitatingly in a warm embrace that I returned without reserve. Her light-blue eyes, set in a face no less beautiful for encroaching age, glowed as she held me at arm's length. "You look well. Country living must suit you." Smiling, she gave Joscelin the kiss of greeting. "And Joscelin Verreuil! I am still jealous of Cassiel's claim upon you."

Joscelin flushed to the roots of his hair and murmured something in reply; he had been more gracious, the last time. "With your permission," he said stiffly to me, "I'll see if I can find the scholars' hall that Seth ben Yavin spoke of, and return for you in a few hours' time. I'm sure you and the Lady Cecilie have much to discuss."

"As you wish." It was awkward, this formality between us; I could have bitten my tongue at the tone of my voice, though it was no cooler than his.

Cecilie raised her eyebrows, but said nothing until we were seated in her lesser parlour, the cozily appointed room where she received her intimate friends. A maid-servant poured wine and brought a tray of delicacies, withdrawing with the immaculate discretion of one trained to serve an adept of Cereus House. "So did the strain of your star-crossed union prove too great, my dear?" she asked then, kindly.

"Not in Montrève, no." I shook my head and took a sip of wine, then drew a deep breath. "I am returning to the Service of Naamah."

"Ah." Cecilie rested her chin on her fingertips, regarding me. "And Messire Joscelin grieves. Well, I did not think Naamah had done with you, Phèdre," she said, surprising me. "You were born to be one of the great ones, not to waste your youth on sheep-shearings and barn dances. How old are you? Twenty?"

"Twenty-two." A touch of indignation in my tone made her smile.

"You see? Scarce out of girlhood." She toyed with a strand of pearls, but her pale blue eyes were shrewd. "Although I'll allow that you've seen and done things no Night Court adept could survive. Still, in ten years, you might come into your prime. Is it only that, my dear, or is it Anafiel Delaunay's game you seek to play?"

I should have known she would suspect it. Cecilie had been the one to train us, Alcuin and me, in the arts of love; she had also been one of the few who knew what Delaunay was about. For a brief moment, I considered confiding in her. I trusted her discretion. But it would worry her; and it could endanger her, too. And unlike Joscelin and my chevaliers, Cecilie was no warrior sworn to my protection, skilled in the arts of defense. It cast Delaunay's dilemma in a different light, and for the first time I sympathized with his desire to shield me in ignorance.

"I'm sworn to Naamah, and not to House Courcel," I said lightly. "Unlike my lord Delaunay. But you may be sure, I've not forgotten what I learned in his service. I will keep my ears open and my wits about me. If I learn aught that Ysandre should know . . ." I shrugged. "So much the better."

Not entirely convinced, Cecilie leveled her gaze at me. "Be careful, Phèdre."

As an adept of Cereus House, she had cause to know. In the Thirteen Houses of the Court of Night-Blooming Flowers, Naamah's Service was an item of faith. As Naamah had lain down with strangers on blessed Elua's behalf, so did we; but we were mortal, and where power intersects with pleasure, there is danger. Adepts of the Night Court dabbled with great caution in political intrigue. As a peer of the realm, I risked all the more. No one living had done it.

Placing a candied rose petal on my tongue, I let it melt in a wash of sweetness. "I will," I promised. "What news have I missed?"

"Ah, well!" Her eyes danced. "Despite the Cruarch's visit this summer, it grows obvious that the Queen is not with child. Now that winter stares us in the teeth, speculation mounts as to whether or not she will take a lover; and if so, whom."

"Does it indeed?" I murmured. "Do you think she will?" We were D'Angeline. *Love as thou wilt.* She would not have been the first, nor the last.

"No," Cecilie said decisively, shaking her head before sipping her wine. "Ysandre was raised as a pawn on the playing field of marital alliance; she knows how to play the game and commit to none. Any mind, I hear she is committed to him. If House Courcel provides an heir, he or she will be half Picti."

It was true; I had reason to know it. Against all odds, the marriage of the Queen of Terre d'Ange and the

Cruarch of Alba was a love match — and the Strait that divided them was nigh as deep as the one between Joscelin and me.

"Still," Cecilie continued, "it is open season on the position of Queen's paramour, and contenders abound."

"If Ysandre is not troubled, I'll not trouble myself." I took up the wine-jug and refilled our glasses. "What of the Skaldi? Have the borders been quiet?"

"As the grave." There was satisfaction in her tone. "Somerville was awarded a duchy, you know; sovereign in L'Agnace. No one disputes it. The Royal Army's been approved to stand down, now. Camaelines hold the border."

"D'Aiglemort's men?" I glanced up, surprised. Cecilie nodded.

"The Unforgiven, they call themselves," she said softly. "They bear black shields."

We were both silent a moment, remembering. Only a few of the Allies of Camlach had survived the battle of Troyes-le-Mont, where the Skaldi warlord Waldemar Selig had united his people, leading an invasion against Terre d'Ange. He had had reason to believe he would prevail, encouraged in his endeavors by Melisande Shahrizai, who played a deep-laid game. I know, for she sold me into slavery among the Skaldi when I learned her plan. I do not think she meant me to survive. I did, though. In the deepest winter of Skaldia, I survived to become Selig's mistress, and I learned his plan, escaping in time to warn Ysandre. It was enough, by the nearest of margins. Ysandre sent me to Alba, and I brought the Cruarch's army to my country's aid. In the end, only Melisande escaped unscathed.

I could have done none of it without Joscelin.

The Allies of Camlach had been vassals of the traitorous Duc Isidore d'Aiglemort, Melisande's ally, whose fatal conspiracy had opened the door for the Skaldic invasion and nearly brought ruin on the nation. Isidore d'Aiglemort is dead now, and he died a hero at the end.

I was there, watching from the parapet, when he led the charge against Waldemar Selig's army. It was the Allies of Camlach who had driven a wedge into the massed Skaldi, and d'Aiglemort himself who slew Selig. He didn't live to tell of it; not many men of Camlach had survived that charge. Those who had lived had vowed themselves to driving the invading Skaldi far beyond D'Angeline borders.

The Unforgiven. It was a disturbing name.

"Did you hear?" Cecilie changed the subject, poring over the tray of dainties. "Prince Benedicte has remarried."

"No!"

"Oh, yes." She looked amused. "Do you suppose the passions of the flesh wither with age, my dear?"

"But he must be . . ."

"Only sixty-aught," Cecilie said complacently. "And twelve years a widower. Ganelon was his elder, by a considerable amount. He took a Camaeline lass to wife, whose family was slain in the war. Tourande, Tourais, something like that. They're expecting a child, come spring. I didn't tell you?"

"No," I said absently. "What does it betoken, for the throne?"

"Naught that I know of." She nibbled at a bit of marchepain. "As Ganelon's brother, Benedicte is still formally next in line, but he has two daughters to succeed him, although I understand Thérèse is imprisoned for her part in Isabel L'Envers' death."

"And Barquiel L'Envers?"

"The Duc L'Envers." Cecilie set her piece of marche-pain down unfinished. "If you're wary of anyone, be wary of him, Phèdre. Ysandre is thick with her uncle – and I do not say it is wrong, for blood calls to blood. But House L'Envers was ever ambitious, and he was your lord's enemy, you know. Ysandre may be Isabel's daughter, but she bears Rolande's blood."

I knew; I knew it well. The Duc Barquiel L'Envers was high atop the list of peers I mistrusted. As it happens, I also owed him my life.

"Well," I said reflectively. "A proper hornet's nest, it seems."

"When were politics aught else?" Cecilie gave me a long, evaluating glance. "If you're going to do this, we'll need to set you up properly, Phèdre nó Delaunay de Montrève. In living memory, no peer of the realm has chosen to follow Naamah's service. You're going against fashion, my dear."

"I know," I said. "But Naamah's arts are older than Terre d'Ange itself, and her service is ancient among us. I was her Servant before I was a peer. There was honor in both, once, and neither precluded the other. I swore an oath, Cecilie. I made the dedication and released a dove in Naamah's name. Do you say I should gainsay it?"

"No," Cecilie sighed. "Nor will the Queen. Do you plan to maintain a salon?"

"No." I smiled. "I never did, in Delaunay's service. My . . . patrons

. . . prefer to set their own terms, on their own territory. I am an *anguissette*, after all."

"Well, if anyone can restore the lustre to Naamah's service, it's you, child." She cocked her head. "You'll at least need the services of a proper attendant. Have you a seamstress in mind? If you've not, I've word of a lass in Eglantine House who might do." I shook my head. "Have you registered with the Guild yet? You'll need to do that, now that you've made your marque. Oh, Phèdre!" Cecilie clapped her hands together, eyes sparkling. "We've so much to do!"

THREE

"İ FOUND the scholars' hall. The yeshiva."

We had not spoken of it on the ride back from Cecilie's; Joscelin had not offered, and I pushed him on little these days. Pouring more tea, I raised my brows and waited.

"I met the Rebbe." He cleared his throat and sipped at his tea. "He's . . . a rather formidable figure. He reminded me of the Prefect."

"Did you speak to him of studying there?"

"I mentioned it." Joscelin set his cup down. "He thought I was interested in converting," he said dryly. "Mayhap I should consider it."

The Cassiline Brotherhood had a peculiar relationship to the followers of Yeshua; in many ways, they held the same beliefs. I felt a creeping sense of alarm, which I hid. "You didn't tell him about Hyacinthe, then."

"No." Rising, Joscelin wandered the study, running his hand over the newly built shelves and cubbyholes. "I thought it best to wait. Phèdre, do you really think there's a key?"

"I don't know," I answered honestly. "But I have to look."

Somewhere, far to the west, on a lonely island, my Prince of Travellers spun out his days in apprenticeship to the Master of the Straits, condemned to serve out the terms of Rahab's curse. It was a sacrifice he had made for us all, a bitter bargain. If he had not, the Alban army would never have succeeded in crossing the Straits, and the Skaldi would have conquered Terre d'Ange. But, oh! It was a cruel price to pay. For so long as the One God punished the disobedience of his angel Rahab, the curse would endure; and as the Master of the Straits had said, the One God's memory was long.

Elua disobeyed the commandment of the One God, but he and his Companions were aided by our Mother Earth, in whose womb he was begotten. Silent these many long centuries, She did not seem inclined to intervene once more – and this affair was none of Hers. No, if there was an answer, a means of breaking an angel's *geis*, it lay in the ancient doctrines of the Yeshuites.

It had been done, I knew; there were tales of heroes who had defied the will of the One God's emissaries, outwitting them with guile and scholarship. But those were in the days when angels walked the earth and the gods spoke directly to their people. Now the gods kept their counsel, and only we lesser-born mortals, whose bloodlines bore faint traces of ichor, were left to the stewardship of the land.

Still, I would try.

"Well, I will speak to him, if he will hear me."

"He'll be amused at the novelty." Joscelin's tone was dry again. "A D'Angeline courtesan speaking Yeshuite. He had a hard enough time hearing it from me."

I have a gift for languages, but that wasn't what he meant. I closed my eyes against the pain; Joscelin's, mine, piercing at the core and welling outward in misery. Elua, but it was sweet! The pain of the flesh is naught to the pain of the soul. I bit the inside of my lower lip, willing the tide of it to subside, horrified in some part of me that I could take pleasure in it. Melisande's face swam in memory behind my closed lids, sublimely amused. True scion of Kushiel's line, she would have understood it as no other.

"Remy found a carriage." Joscelin changed the subject. "I sent him to Emile, from Hyacinthe's old crew. He still has the stable in Night's Doorstep."

"How much did he spend?"

He shrugged. "He got it for a song, he said, but it's in dreadful shape. They think they can repair it. Fortun's grandfather was a wheelwright."

I ran my hands through my hair, disheveling the mass of sable curls. I didn't care for this penny-counting, necessary though it was. My father had been a spend-thrift, which was how I came to be bond-sold to Cereus House as a child; it made me wary of debt. Still, I didn't have to like it. Joscelin watched me out of the corner of his eye. "How long, do they think? I should send word to Ysandre."

"Three days, mayhap. Less if they've naught else to do." He made an abrupt movement, gathering the tea tray. "It's late. I will see you in the morning, my lady."

There were barbs on the words, his formal address. I endured them in silence and watched him go, leaving me alone with the remorseless pleasure of my pain.

It took only two days to restore the carriage to a

presentable shape, sufficient to arrive at the Palace in a style befitting the Comtesse de Montrève. I sent word to Ysandre, and had a reply by royal courier that afternoon, granting an audience on the morrow. He stood waiting while I read it, elegant in blue Courcel livery, and bowed graciously when I told him to tell the Queen I would be honored to attend. There was a trace of curiosity in his eyes, but he didn't let it show in his manner.

That there were stories about me, I knew full well. Thelesis de Mornay had included my tale in earliest drafts of the Ysandrine Cycle, the epic poem documenting Ysandre's tumultuous ascension to the throne in the midst of war. There were other stories, too, passed about by word of mouth. Most of my patrons were discreet, but not all.

So be it. There is no shame in being a Servant of Naamah, nor an *anguissette*. We are D'Angeline, and we revere such things. Other nations reckon us soft for it; the Skaldi found otherwise. But too, it is as I have said – our blood has grown thick with mortality, and one such as I, marked by a celestial hand, was a rarity.

It is not a thing, I may say, in which I take pride; I grew up in Cereus House, where the crimson mote in my eye marked me not as Kushiel's chosen, but merely as one flawed beyond the canons of the Night Court. It was Delaunay who changed that, and named me for what I was. And in truth, I have no special gift beyond the transmutation of pain, which has been as much curse as boon to me. If I am skilled at language and logic, it is because I was well taught; Alcuin, who was a student with me, was better. It is only a quirk of fate that left me alive to exercise them, while he and Delaunay perished. Not a day passes but that

I remember it. I would give up all that I have gained to change that past. Since I cannot, I do the best I can, and pray it does honor to their memories.

It was strange to have the Queen's Guard bow at the Palace gates, to be met by liveried servants and enter the halls with an entire entourage in tow. If Joscelin was grave, Phèdre's Boys were on their best behavior, trying hard to look dignified. I didn't worry about Fortun, sober by nature, but Remy and Ti-Philippe had a talent for mischief.

Ysandre received us in the Hall of Games, a vast, colonnaded salon where the Palace nobles liked to gather for gaming and conversation. I spotted her with two of her ladies-in-waiting, pausing to observe an intense game of rhythmomachy. Her own Cassiline guard, two Brothers clad in ashen-grey, stood a discreet distance away. Not young, either of them, but their straight backs defied age. Few of the Great Houses follow the old traditions any more, sending their middle sons to serve Cassiel.

"The Comtesse Phèdre nó Delaunay de Montrève!" our escort announced loudly.

Heads turned, a few murmurs sounded. Ysandre de la Courcel came toward me with a smile. "Phèdre," she said, grasping my hands and giving me the kiss of greeting. There was genuine pleasure lighting her violet eyes when she drew back. "Truly, I am happy to see you."

"Your majesty." I curtsied. Ysandre looked much the same; a little older, worn by the cares of the throne, but with the same fair beauty. We were nearly of an age, she and I.

"Joscelin Verreuil." She rested her fingertips on his

arm when he finished his sweeping bow. "I trust you have been keeping my near cousin safe?"

It was Ysandre's jest, to name me thusly. Of a surety, there were ties of neither blood nor marriage between us, but my lord Delaunay, who had taken me into his household, had been dearly beloved of her father Rolande. Indeed, that love had gone deeper than many suspected, and Delaunay had sworn in secret an oath to ward Ysandre's life as his own.

"I protect and serve, your majesty." Joscelin smiled, warmth in his words and not irony. Whatever lay between us, his loyalty to the Queen was undiminished.

"Good." Ysandre looked with amusement at the bowed heads of Remy, Fortun and Ti-Philippe, who had all dropped to one knee before her. "Well met, chevaliers," she said kindly. "Does your service still suit, or does the sea beckon you back to my lord Admiral Rousse?"

Remy grinned up at her. "We are well content, your majesty."

"I am pleased to hear it." Ysandre looked back at me. "Come, Phèdre, tell me how you have been keeping. I am sure your men will find ample entertainment in the Hall of Games, and I am eager to learn what has brought you back to the City of Elua."

If it had been strange to enter the Palace as a peer, stranger still to stroll the Hall at Ysandre's side, her Cassiline guards trailing us. It had been different, after the war, when everything was still in a jumble, Albans and Dalriada everywhere, and my services in constant demand as translator. This measured order was like the Palace of my youth, which I had attended only at the behest of noble patrons.

"Matters proceed well, it seems," I observed to Ysandre.

She smiled wryly. "Well enough. We are fewer than before, I fear, but our alliance with Alba has given us new strength. Drustan will be sorry to have missed you."

"And I him." There had been a strong sympathy between us, the Cruarch of Alba and I.

"Come spring, he'll be back." There was a faint trace of longing in Ysandre's voice; I doubt it would have been evident to anyone not trained to listen for such things. "So tell me, was Montrève too rustic for your liking?"

"Not entirely," I answered honestly. "It is very pleasant. But there is a matter I am pursuing that I cannot follow from the isolation of a country manor." Ysandre looked at me with interest, and I told her of my research into Yeshuite lore, my dream of finding a key to unlock Hyacinthe's prison. I could not help but mark, as we walked, how all eyes in the Hall of Games followed the Queen, and a hum of speculation followed in her wake. Nobles contrived to place themselves in our path, moving aside with a bow or curtsy; I could see the offers plain in their faces, men and women alike.

Ysandre handled it with an absent grace. "Your Tsingano lad, yes. I wish you luck with it. They are a strange folk, the Yeshuites." She shook her head. "I do not pretend to understand them. We welcome them openly in Terre d'Ange, and they accept our hospitality on sufferance."

"There is no room in their theology for Blessed Elua, my lady. They cannot reconcile our existence, and it troubles them."

"Well." Ysandre's fair brows arched. "They have had

some time to grow accustomed to the notion. Have you come to a decision on the other matter?" she asked then, changing the subject. "You are still vowed to Naamah, unless I am mistaken."

"Yes." Unthinking, I twisted a ring I bore on the third finger of my right hand; black pearls, given me as a patron-gift by the Duc de Morhban. I smiled. "If I bare my marque," I said, "you will know my answer, my lady."

Ysandre laughed. "Then I shall have to wait and see." She swept her hand about the Hall. "They will be wondering, you know. They've naught better to do."

"I have heard as much," I said reservedly.

"Majesty." A man's voice spoke, deep and silken; from the corner of my eye, I caught a swirl of black and gold, intricately patterned, as a figure rose from a deep-backed chair. He bowed, then straightened, and I caught my breath. His blue-black hair hung in plaits like tiny chains, and eyes the hue of sapphire were set in a dangerously beautiful face, skin like ivory. He smiled, showing white teeth, and fanned an ornate deck of cards. "You promised me a game of batarde."

I knew him; I had last seen him in the company of his cousin, whom he had betrayed.

"I did, my lord Marmion, but I did not say when," Ysandre replied lightly.

"I shall await the day." His deep blue gaze rested on my face. "My lady Phèdre nó Delaunay de Montrève," he said, caressing my name. My knees turned to water. "For a short life, you have a long history with House Shahrizai."

Along with his sister Persia, Marmion Shahrizai betrayed his cousin Melisande, mayhap the most dangerous act any of their House could undertake, giving her unto the custody of Duc Quincel de Morhban, the sovereign Duc of their province of Kusheth. I watched them bring her into Ysandre's impromptu court at the fortress of Troyes-le-Mont, after the battle was won. I was there at the hearing, where Melisande was accused of treason.

I gave the testimony that condemned her.

"My lord Shahrizai." With all the willpower I could summon, I made my voice cool. "Your loyalty to the throne has prospered you."

He laughed, and bowed. "How not, when it has such a lovely occupant?" he said for Ysandre's benefit. "Her majesty is wise beyond years, to recognize that the treachery of one member of a House does not taint all born within it." With one last florid bow, he turned away.

I let out a shaking breath.

"I should have warned you." Ysandre gave me a compassionate glance. "He's been a great help, actually; we uncovered several of Melisande's allies thanks to Marmion. I'd forgotten about your . . . long history with his House."

"Allies." I wrestled my thoughts into order. "But not Melisande?"

"No." Ysandre shook her head. "She's gone well and truly to earth, Phèdre, like a fox; and I suspect she's far beyond the borders of Terre d'Ange. Wherever she is, her power here is broken. What allies she had, have been executed, and no one, I think, would be fool enough to trust her with a bounty on her head. I promise you, you've naught to fear from Melisande Shahrizai."

Once upon a time, I was young and naïve enough to have thought a Queen's reassurance beyond question.

Now, I merely smiled and thanked Ysandre for her concern, holding my fear in check and gazing about the Hall of Games, wondering where the traitors lay.

Of their presence, I had no doubt.

FOUR

THE KEY to finding the traitor in the Queen's inner circle was hidden in that night at Troyes-le-Mont. Of that much, I was certain. Melisande Shahrizai had vanished from a well-guarded chamber in a fortress on high alert, and someone had helped her do it. If I could figure out how it was done, I would have the beginning of a trail to follow.

It was Fortun, the steadiest of my chevaliers, who hit upon the notion of mapping out the route of Melisande's escape. "Do you know where she was held, my lady?" he asked thoughtfully. "The ground floor, or the second?"

Joscelin gave me a long look.

"It was the second floor," I said.

Melisande had sent for me that night and, like a fool, I had gone, meeting with her in her royal prison-cell. What had passed between us was of no account, save that it left me shaken. Afterward, I retired to the high walls, wishing to be alone with my tangled emotions, awaiting her execution at dawn. For all that she deserved it – there was no doubt, in the end, that Melisande Shahrizai had conspired

with the Skaldi warlord Waldemar Selig to overthrow the
throne of Terre d'Ange – I couldn't bear to watch. She had
been my patron, once.

It had never come. Instead, daybreak found two guards
dead outside her chamber, and a third at the postern gate.

"So if the corridor was here . . ." Kneeling beside the
low table in my sitting room, Fortun plucked a long-
stemmed iris from a vase and laid it lengthways atop the
table. "How far from the stairs?"

I counted on my fingers, remembering. "Three doors.
No, four. Her chamber was the first door past the corner."

"Here, then." He broke the flower's stem, bending it at
an angle, then setting an empty cordial glass at one end.
"And the stairs, here."

"Yes." Leaning over the table, I studied it. "Near
enough."

Across the room, Joscelin shoved himself to his feet.
"Phèdre."

"Yes?" I glanced up from the table.

"Leave them out of it." His expression was unreadable.
"If you insist on playing dangerous games, so be it. Don't
drag these poor, besotted boys into your intrigues. I can't
protect the lot of you."

"Did I ask you to?" I felt my ire rise. "If it disturbs you
so greatly, then leave. Throw yourself at the feet of the
Prefect and beg forgiveness. Or go tell Ysandre I release
you from my service, and beg leave to attend her. She's
used to having Cassilines around."

Joscelin gave a short laugh. "And let you go hurtling
into peril with three half-trained sailors to ward you? At
least allow me to keep from dishonoring the last vow I've
kept, Phèdre."

I opened my mouth to reply, but Fortun cleared his throat, intervening. "Quintilius Rousse does not pick half-trained soldiers for his flagship, brother."

"It's not the same." Steel glinted from Joscelin's vambraces as he shifted in frustration. "You're trained to battle, not to protect and serve. It's not the same at all."

"I am learning." Fortun's voice held steady.

Their gazes locked, and I held my tongue. What would it profit, to come between them? Joscelin had to choose freely, or not at all. After a moment, he threw up his hands with a sound of disgust.

"I wish you the joy of them," he said harshly to me, and left the room.

I hadn't thought he would go. I stared after him.

"He'll be back," Fortun said calmly. "He cares too much to leave you, my lady."

"I'm not sure," I whispered. "I didn't think he'd go at all."

"Here." Without looking at me, Fortun bent back to the table, his broad hands moving objects. "If this is the lower level and the postern gate is here . . ." he placed a vase at one corner, ". . . and this the passage . . ." he moved a lacquered coffer, ". . . there would have been guards here and here." He marked the spots with his finger. "Whoever led Melisande to the postern gate had to pass these points. So did others, no doubt, but still . . ."

I rubbed my aching temples, trying to concentrate, trying not to think about Joscelin. "They were questioned. We were all questioned, Fortun. If there were anything there, believe me, Ysandre would have seized on it."

"What if they weren't the right questions?" he asked.

"What do you mean?" I frowned at the table,

remembering. As one of the last people to see Melisande alive, I'd been questioned at length. In the end, I was exonerated, if only because it was my testimony that had condemned her. Ysandre was looking for treachery, or evidence of treachery. No one questioned admitted to seeing anything of the kind. But what *had* they seen? "You're right. There was a guard at the foot of the stair, too. And someone had to pass them all, to get to her chamber. Melisande couldn't have killed those guards herself. One, mayhap. Surely not two." I began rearranging the pieces on the table. "If we had a list of who passed them, that night, to compare to the other . . ."

"We would have a shortlist of suspects." Fortun's eyes glowed. "My lady, this is somewhat that we can do for you. For you to question the Queen's Guard, it would seem amiss. Even my lord Joscelin is not on . . . easy terms, if I may say it, with the rank and file. But three ex-sailors, former soldiers of Admiral Rousse . . . we could ask. Drinking, dicing; these are things we know, things that loosen men's tongues. He is trained to protect and serve, and not to battle. It is not the same thing, not at all."

He looked smug enough with it that I laughed, then sobered. "Truly, Fortun, this *is* a dangerous business. If anyone suspected what you were about, you would be in grave danger."

"My lady, if you think any of us sought security in your service, you are mistaken." His brows knitted in a dark scowl. "We are sailors, after all, and bound to adventure. If we have deemed you a star worth setting a course by, do not belittle our decision."

"Why did you do it?" I asked him. "Why me?"

"I saw you on the battlefield of Bryn Gorrydum,

carrying water to the wounded and dying. And after, when you made us chevaliers. I know the Admiral asked it of you. His sword was nearly as long as you're tall." One corner of his mouth crooked at the memory. "Queen's emissary. You looked like someone had hit you over the head. How could I choose otherwise?"

I sighed and rumpled my hair. "All right, then. Learn what you may. But never . . ." I poked his chest for emphasis, ". . . *never* let them suspect you are aught but simple chevaliers, eager to relive your moments of glory and pore over the mysteries of nobility."

"Don't worry. I have a good-luck name, my lady." Fortun smiled. "My mother swore it on my name-day."

FIVE

JOSCELIN DID return, late that evening; I did not question him, and he did not offer an explanation. We greeted each other in the morning, courteous as two strangers. He performed his exercises in the secluded rear garden, flowing gracefully through the Cassiline forms, steel blades weaving, breath frosting in the crisp air. I watched him, and felt my heart ache within my breast.

How strange, how compelling a pain; to cause injury to a loved one.

One thing else I did, when driven to it: I ran away.

Properly speaking, I rebelled. I used to do it at Cereus House, and I did it Delaunay's. Although I will say, if I may, that there was more in it than simple rebellion. It was a game, with my lord Delaunay; if I succeeded at it, there would be no repercussions.

I was no child, now, to run to Night's Doorstep and the comfort of Hyacinthe's antics. Still, it was a comfort to slip unnoticed from under the eyes of my well-meaning guards, go to the stable and convince the simple lad,

Benoit, to saddle a horse for me. I led the gelding cautiously into the street, where Benoit considerately latched the
gate behind me.

Once astride, I was free.

I rode away from the Palace, exhilaration singing in
my veins, hard put to remember the last time I was well and
truly on my own. It is an oddity, how having retainers
binds one. Without their concerns to think of, I had only
my own. I made my way to the river, and followed it to the
market square, where criers hawked their wares.

It was the doves that put it in my head, dozens upon
dozens of them, caged offerings huddled against the cold.
Choosing the smallest out of pity, I paid for a gilt cage.

"My lady has an eye," the vendor said obsequiously,
transferring the bird. "This one, he is small, but he has a
will to survive."

"Elua hear you, and grant it is so." I smiled, leaning
down from my mount to take the cage in hand. The
gelding snorted and tossed his head. "This one is for
Naamah."

The vendor performed an elaborate bow, smiling at me
sidelong. My dove rattled his wings against the gilded bars
and the gelding shied, shod hooves ringing on the cobble-
stones; people cheered as I kept my seat. I was a dreadful
rider, once. That was before I fled Waldemar Selig's
steading on pony-back, through the direst winter. I have
spent a good bit of time astride, since then. Strange, to look
back and see how skill was acquired; at the time, I only
thought to stay alive.

With my head up despite the snapping cold, I rode
through the streets to the Temple of Naamah. If people
called out and saluted me along the way, it was not because

I was the Comtesse de Montrève or Phèdre nó Delaunay —
they could not see, from the street, my tell-tale gaze — but
only because I was young, and beautiful, and I rode without care, bearing a dove for Naamah.

The Great Temple of Naamah in the City is a small
structure, but lovely with gardens; even now, with winter's
breath in the air, it held warmth and bloomed. I gave my
mount over to a stable-lass who met me with lowered eyes,
and walked alone to the temple, carrying the birdcage. An
acolyte met me at the door.

"Be welcome," he said, bending in his scarlet surplice
to give me the kiss of greeting. His lips were soft, and I
knew, in a way, I was home. He looked at me out of eyes
the color of rain-washed lupine, eyes that studied my own.
"Be welcome, *anguissette*, and give honor to Naamah."

I took his arm in one hand, carrying the gilded cage
within my other, and entered the Temple of Naamah. Up
the long corridor we walked, to the vast statue that awaited us at the end: Naamah, her arms spread wide in greeting
and embrace. There, beneath the oculus, we awaited the
priest.

Priestess, it was; I knew her when she emerged, attended by acolytes. Long hair the color of apricots, and green
eyes tilted like a cat's; she had been an acolyte herself,
when I was dedicated. The priest who had dedicated me
had died of the fever during the Bitterest Winter, as so
many had done. "Well met, sister," she said in a mur-
murous voice that nonetheless carried to every corner of
the temple, and kissed me in greeting. I gripped her elbow
with my free hand, steadying myself; it had been a long
time, and the presence of Naamah's Servants was a heady
thing. "You wish to rededicate yourself?"

"Yes," I whispered, holding aloft the gilded cage. "Can you tell me if it is Naamah's wish that I do so?"

"Ah." The priestess fingered the collar of her scarlet robe and turned to gaze up at Naamah's face, welcoming and benign above us. "In the City alone, there are many hundreds of Naamah's Servants," she said softly. "Three hundred at least in the Thirteen Houses of the Night Court, and for every one who serves at that level, there are others who aspire to lesser heights. In Namarre, they number in the thousands. No village throughout the land, I daresay, but has one or two called to the Service of Naamah. You would be surprised at how many ask that question. Is it the will of Naamah that I serve her? To each one, I give the same answer: It is your will that matters. No less than any other, the Servants of Naamah keep the covenant of Blessed Elua. *Love as thou wilt.* Naamah's path is sacred to us, for she chose of her own will to win the freedom and sustenance of Blessed Elua with the gifts of her body. It was her choice, and she does not compel her Servants to follow." With that said, she turned back to give me a long, considering gaze. "To you, I answer differently."

Her acolytes murmured, drawing near to listen. I set down the birdcage and waited. The priestess smiled and reached out to touch my face, tracing a line along the outer curve of my left eye.

" 'Mighty Kushiel, of rod and weal/Late of the brazen portals/With blood-tipp'd dart a wound unhealed/Pricks the eyen of chosen mortals,' " she quoted, citing the very verse with which Delaunay had identified my nature. "I cannot chart your course, *anguissette*; your calling lies beyond Naamah's purview alone. You are Kushiel's chosen, and he will cast you where he will. Only Elua, whom even the Companions follow, knows the whole of it. But you are Naamah's Servant as well, and under her protection, and to that I may speak. You ask, is it the will of Naamah that you serve her? I say: Yes." Wrapping her robe about her, the priestess gazed into the distance. "Tens of thousands of Servants of Naamah," she mused aloud, "all following a sacred calling. And yet our stature diminishes across the land. Whores, catamites, trulls . . . I have heard these words, spoken with harsh tongues. Not by all, but enough. Too many."

It was true, for I had heard it myself. Such words had not existed in our tongue when Elua and his Companions trod the earth, and peers and commoners alike delighted in Naamah's service. It was different, now, and the customs of Terre d'Ange were tainted by those of other nations. I had not chosen an easy course.

"How long has it been since an enthroned ruler summoned the Dowayne of Cereus House for counsel?" The priestess' sharp green eyes measured my thoughts. "Four generations or more, I think. Too long. It is not my place to restore the glory of the Court of Night-Blooming Flowers, but the glory of Naamah . . . yes. I know who you are, Phèdre nó Delaunay." She smiled, unexpectedly. "Comtesse de Montrève. Your story is known, and it is told, a *sangoire* thread woven deep into the tapestry of war and betrayal that nearly sundered our nation. Because of you, the Scions of Elua and his Companions have returned to the Houses of the Night Court, playing at fashion, grasping at secondhand glory with thoughtless ardor. But you are a peer of the realm, now. Is it Naamah's will that her presence breach the

Palace walls to shine once more at the heart of Terre d'Ange? To you I say, yes."

I met her eyes and held them. "Politics."

Her smile deepened. "Naamah does not care for politics, nor power. Glory, yes. What does your heart say, sister?"

I shivered, and had to look away. "My heart is torn," I murmured.

She touched my face again, gently. "What does Kushiel say?"

It burned this time, her touch, heating my blood so that it rose in a warm blush. Priests and priestesses, they have that damnable surety about them. I wanted to turn my face against her palm, taste the salt of her skin. "Kushiel's will accords with Naamah's."

"Then your question is answered." The priestess took her hand away, calm and undisturbed; I nearly fell yearning against her, but kept myself steady. "And I will pose mine again. Is it your wish to be rededicated unto the Service of Naamah?"

"Yes." I said it strongly this time, and stooped to open the birdcage. I took the trembling dove in my hands and straightened. "It is."

The acolytes stumbled against one another in confusion, then one bearing a basin of water came forward to offer the aspergillum to the priestess. I stood, the dove's quick-beating heart racing against my palms, as she flicked a few drops of water over me. "By Naamah's sacred river, I baptize you into her service." So I had stood, scarce more than a child, while Delaunay and Alcuin waited proudly behind me. No one awaited me now. I opened my mouth obediently for the portion of honey-cake, the sip of wine.

Sweetness and desire. Elua, but I ached with it! And chrism at the last, oil upon my brow, for grace. When I was a child, I'd no notion of what it meant; now, I prayed I might find it in Naamah's Service.

It was done, and the priestess and her acolytes stepped aside. I knelt before the altar, the statue of Naamah, holding the dove in closed hands before me. Opaque, those sculpted eyes; we find in her service what we bring to it. "My lady, be kind to your Servant," I whispered, and released the dove.

I did not watch, this time, as it launched free of my hands and winged its way to the oculus. The priestess and her acolytes did, tracking it smiling. I did not need to watch to know my dove found its way. With bowed head, I knelt until I felt the priestess' hands at my shoulders, bidding me to rise.

"Welcome back," she said and kissed me; I felt the tip of her tongue dart between my lips and had to keep myself from clutching her wrists as she released me. The priests of Naamah are not quite like any other. Her long green eyes glinted in the slanting light of the temple, wise and knowing. "Welcome back, Servant of Naamah."

Thus it was done, and I stumbled twice leaving the temple, leaning hard on the arm of the acolyte who had admitted me. A dam may hold for a hundred years, but once it develops a chink, the rushing tide comes after. Thus did I feel, having dammed the terrible force of my desires for a year and more. The dam had cracked when I opened Melisande's parcel and found my *sangoire* cloak; the flood was not far behind.

I do not mean, if I may say it, that I loved Joscelin the less, nor desired him less for it. From the first, even when I despised him, I found him beautiful. And to those who think a Cassiline, unschooled in the arts of love, no fit match for a trained courtesan, I may say they are wrong. When he surrendered to it — and he did — Joscelin brought to our bed a desire wholly untutored, but as pure and wonder-struck as Elua's first wanderings on mortal soil. That is a treasure no one else has ever given me, nor ever could. What I taught him, he learned as if he were the first to discover it, eager and natural as a new-minted creature.

It was enough, for a time.

No longer.

So it was that I rode home, torn between exhilaration and guilt. Dusk was falling when I reached the house, and by the stable-lad Benoit's downcast gaze, I knew he had been chastised for permitting me to leave alone.

"Benoit," I said, causing him to lift his head with a jerk. "*I* am mistress of this house."

"Yes, my lady," he mumbled, taking my reins. I couldn't blame him for it; if I hadn't felt the same, I'd not have regarded my escapade as an escape.

Nonetheless, I told him firmly, "You do no wrong in obeying my wishes. I will tell them as much."

He mumbled something else, hurrying toward the stable and leading my horse at a trot. Chin upraised, I swept into the house.

They were all there, waiting. The day-maid sketched me a quick curtsy, and whisked past to make her escape. Remy and Ti-Philippe would not meet my eyes; Fortun gazed at me expressionlessly. In the background, my kitchen-mistress Eugènie waited nervously.

And Joscelin strode forward to grasp my shoulders. "Phèdre!" My name burst from his lips, harsh with anxiety;

he shook me a little. "Blessed Elua, where in the seven hells have you been?"

His fingers bit into my flesh and I closed my eyes. "Out."

"Out?" The white lines of rage stood out on his face, so close to mine. His hands clenched hard. "You idiot, one of us should have gone with you! Whatever it was, there is *no* reason for you to go unescorted, do you understand? Whoever Melisande's allies are, they know damned well who you are!" He punctuated his words with hard shakes. "Never, ever go out unattended, do you promise me? What on earth would possess you – ?"

Hard, his hands on my shoulders; my head rocked with the force of his fury as he shook me. Ah, Elua, it was sweet! The violence of it was spark to tinder for me.

Whatever was reflected on my face, Joscelin saw it; his hands fell away. "Blessed . . ." he whispered in disgust, turning away from me, his voice trailing off. When he spoke, it was without looking at me. "Don't do it again."

"Joscelin." I waited until he turned. "You knew what I was."

"Yes." His voice was brief. "And you what I was. Where does that leave us, Phèdre?"

I had no answer, so gave none, and presently he went away. Remy released a long-held breath and fingered the dagger at his belt.

"My lady, if he harms you, Cassiline or no . . ."

"Let him be." I cut him off. "He is in pain, and it is my doing. Let him be."

"No." It was Fortun who spoke, slow and thoughtful. "It is Cassiel's doing, my lady. And even you can do naught about that."

"Maybe." I pressed the heels of my hands against my eyes. "But I chose my course, and it is Joscelin who bears the price of it."

"Stupid to speak of blame when the wills of the immortals are involved." Ti-Philippe, irrepressible as ever, fished a pair of dice from his purse and tossed them high, grinning. "Let the Cassiline stew, my lady; I am told they thrive upon it. Fortun says we have questions to ask, and quarry to pursue!"

"Yes." I dropped my hands and gazed at their open, eager faces, steeling my resolve. "We do. And I must plan my debut."

Six

I∏ THE end, my decision was made for me. There are patterns which emerge in one's life, circling and returning anew, an endless variation of a theme. So musicians say the greatest sonatas are composed; whether or not it is true, I do not know, but of a surety, I have seen it emerge in the tapestry of my life.

I received an invitation to the Midwinter Masque at the Palace.

The first such event I attended was as a child not quite ten, at Cereus House. It was there that I saw for the first time Baudoin de Trevalion, Prince of the Blood. He is dead now, executed for treason, along with his mother Lyonette, who was sister to King Ganelon and called the Lioness of Azzalle. I used to spy upon her for Delaunay; there was a Marquise among my patrons who answered to the Lioness of Azzalle. It wasn't Delaunay who brought down House Trevalion, though. That was Melisande's doing, Melisande and Isidore d'Aiglemort. None of us guessed, then, why Melisande would do such a thing;

Baudoin ate from the palm of her hand, or near to it. He gave her the very letters that condemned him, correspondence between his mother and Foclaidha of Alba, plotting to seize the throne of Terre d'Ange.

I know, now; everyone knows. Melisande knew Baudoin would not have defied his mother openly for her sake, and she had a greater target in mind. Terre d'Ange and Skaldia combined, an empire the likes of which no one has seen since the days of Tiberium's rule. D'Aiglemort was only a pawn, though he didn't know it until the end. I know, I'm the one who told him.

Thus my first Midwinter Masque. And my last . . . my last had been the last assignation I ever took as Delaunay's *anguissette*, and the only time Melisande Shahrizai ever contracted me as sole patron. I earned my marque, that Longest Night, with the patron-gift she made me. It is the only time, in a hundred assignations, I ever gave the *signale*, the code word of surrender that requires a patron to cease. I gave it twice that night, and the second time for no reason beyond the fact that Melisande ordered me to speak it.

Well and so, that is my history with the Midwinter Masque. When Ysandre's invitation arrived, I took it for a sign — which is how I came to stand frowning at my wardrobe.

"I have nothing to wear." Irritated, I flung the doors of the wardrobe closed and sat with a flounce upon my bed. Gemma, the day-maid, set down her feather-duster and stretched her eyes at me; by her standards, I had gowns aplenty.

"My lady," she said timidly. "What of the grey velvet? It is passing lovely, and I . . . I have a brother who is apprenticed to a masquer, he could make somewhat to match; a diadem of stars, mayhap, or a mistmaiden . . ."

"No." I dismissed her suggestion, but kindly. "Thank you, Gemma. If I were going anywhere but the Palace, it would do nicely, and you are good to offer. No, I need somewhat else. If I am to debut as a Servant of Naamah among my peers, it must be somewhat no one has ever seen." Chin in hands, I mused. "Cecilie is right. I need a seamstress." Gemma ran for paper — she had been quick to discern my ways — and I penned a swift note.

As a former adept of Cereus House and one of the great courtesans of her time, Cecilie Laveau-Perrin's status was undiminished within the Night Court for, within a day, I had an appointment to meet with Favrielle nó Eglantine, and if I thought my own standing had aught to do with it, I was disabused of the notion within minutes of meeting my prospective seamstress.

All of the Thirteen Houses claim different strengths; as all of the Thirteen hold to different versions of Naamah. Eglantine is the artists' House, and her adepts are skilled in a dozen disciplines: players, poets, artists, musicians, dancers and tumblers. And, it would appear, clothiers. Even so, all adepts must make their marques before dedicating themselves to their artistic pursuits, and I was puzzled as to how a young clothier had risen to renown while still under the aegis of her House.

I was not puzzled for long.

"Comtesse," Favrielle nó Eglantine greeted me briefly, sizing me up in one wry glance. "You realize you've chosen the worst possible time to request my services? I have two dozen adepts clamoring for masque attire, and this is scant notice."

Taken aback, I blinked. She was no older than I; younger, perhaps, by a year or two. Wide grey eyes and a mop of red-gold curls, a charming sprinkle of freckles across the bridge of her nose – there is a limit, within the canons, of the number allowable for beauty. Favrielle's met it. What did not was the scar that marred her upper lip, twisting it slightly.

She saw me take notice. "Shall we get it out of the way? I am flawed goods, Comtesse," she said in a voice laden with irony. "Unfit for patrons, with a marque to meet nonetheless. This compels me to take commissions, when my Dowayne allows it. And inconvenient as it is, I cannot bypass this opportunity. So shall we do business?"

"How did it happen?"

Favrielle sighed. "I slipped in the bath," she recited tone-lessly, "and split my lip." Glancing at a note, she raised her eyebrows. "The Palace masque, yes? Is that what you want?"

"Favrielle." I touched her arm. "I understand, a little. I grew up in Cereus House, flawed, unfit to serve."

"And now you are Kushiel's chosen, the Comtesse de Montrève, bringer of the Alban army, heroine of the Battle of Troyes-le-Mont and the Queen's pet courtesan." Her scarred lip curled. "Yes, Phèdre nó Delaunay, I know. And when you can transform me into the same, let me know. Until then, tell me what you want to wear."

Stung, I lifted my chin and made my reply coolly. "Something fitting for the first peer of the realm in a hun-dred years to debut as a Servant of Naamah at the Royal Masque."

"Fine." Favrielle crossed her arms. "Strip."

It had been, I found, a surprisingly long time since I subjected myself to the critical gaze of a Night Court adept. I stood naked in the fitting-room of Eglantine House, surrounded by mirrors while Favrielle paced around me, grey eyes narrowed, measuring me here and there with an impersonal touch, draping bolts of various cloth over my shoulders to study the lie of it.

"You could be taller," she said grudgingly; there was not much else for her to criticize. I may have been absent from Naamah's Service for a year and more, but I had not let myself go. "It makes for a better line. At least you're proportioned well." Satisfied, she nodded curtly. "Put your clothes on and I'll tell you what I think."

Obediently, I dressed and waited in the draping room. A blushing apprentice brought mint tea, pouring gracefully. Favrielle emerged to join me, taking an unceremonious gulp of tea.

"Costuming will be ornate this season," she said abruptly. "Heavy brocades, layers of skirts, lacework and trim, triple-slashed sleeves, masques an arm-span broad. Prosperity on the heels of war and all that. If I tried to outdo for you what I've already begun for others, I'd have you in so many layers you'd scarce be able to move. So." Her cup clattered on the tray as she set it down and reached for a length of fabric. "You want to stand out, *anguissette*? We go the other way. Simplicity."

I fingered the fabric; a silk jersey spun so fine it flowed like water through my fingers. "On what theme?"

"You know Mara's Tale?" Favrielle raised her brows inquiringly. I shook my head, and she made a sound of disgust. "Kushiel's chosen, and ignorant as a pig. Livia . . ." she turned to the apprentice, ". . . run to the library and fetch me Sarea's *History of Namarre*. The illustrated version."

I opened and closed my mouth, deciding discretion was the wiser part of couture. Ignorant as a pig! I spoke five languages with passing fluency, and had unravelled the riddle of the Master of the Straits. But it was true that Eglantine House was a repository of more lore and learning than the academies of Siovale, and much of it unknown outside their bounds.

"Here." Favrielle opened the leather-bound book and pointed to a glowing illustration; a slender, dark-haired woman clad in a crimson gown that flowed like flame. Her hair was upswept in an elaborate coif of ringlets, and a sheer black veil hid her eyes. " 'In the fifth year of Elua, Naamah lay with a man condemned for murder,' " she read aloud, " 'and his skin was fair and his eyes as black as coal. And he was hanged by the neck until dead, but Naamah had taken his seed unto herself, and she was with child. Unto Naamah was born a daughter in the sixth year of Elua in Terre d'Ange that was, and that daughter she named Mara. And Mara bore the curse of her father's blood, and went with her eyes veiled. In atonement for the curse she bore, she went unto Kushiel, and in pity he granted her penance and made her his handmaiden.' " Over my faint sound of protest, Favrielle closed the book. "You see?"

I did. "You think she was an *anguissette*."

"It's a likely story." Favrielle shrugged. "We're not supposed to tell it," she admitted grudgingly. "Beggars, princes and shepherds are all right, but the Night Court doesn't like it known that Naamah lay with a murderer. Still." Biting her knuckle, she regarded me. "Some know it. I thought you might. You'd make a good Mara."

It was true; more than true, it was brilliant. I eyed the

closed volume. "Is there any chance I might have a copy made of that?"

"No." Favrielle's reply was curt. "You're interested in the *book*?"

" 'The fruit of the future is rooted in the soil of history,' " I said in flawless Caerdicci, quoting the historian Calpurnius; the look of surprise on Favrielle's face was deeply gratifying. "Never mind. I'll speak to the Dowayne. Tell me your idea for my costume."

Taking a deep breath, she did, sketching it out in swift, elegant lines on a piece of foolscap. It was gorgeous, and it was perfect. I wished it had not been, for I did not like her overmuch, but once seen, I could not forget it.

"We'll need to leave a seam open, there . . ." she pointed, ". . . and stitch it closed once you're wearing it. If your maid is handy, she might do. It's the only way, with the back so low. But with your marque, it would be a crime not to." Favrielle tapped the stylus absently against her teeth and gave me a skeptical look. "I'd have expected to find you welted from stem to stern, from the stories I've heard, but you've skin like cream."

"I heal clean," I said briefly; it is the only blessing to being an *anguissette*. Kushiel's chosen would not last long were it not so. "What would be the cost?"

"Five hundred ducats." Her words were blunt.

It is a tribute, I think, to my self-control that I did no more than blink. It was an outrageous amount. It was also an amount I did not possess. "I beg your pardon? I thought you said five hundred ducats."

"The fabric will have to be dyed to order. It's a rushed job." She shrugged. "You will recoup it in a night, if you well and truly intend to enter Naamah's Service, Comtesse.

And I have my marque to think of. What I do for the House is reckoned my upkeep. The Dowayne has granted me leave to take your commission. I cannot afford to charge less."

"If the costume is a success, you will have patrons from the Great Houses of Terre d'Ange knocking at the gates of Eglantine House for your services," I observed. "And your Dowayne will not turn them away. Three hundred, no more."

"The design is sound," Favrielle said flatly. "Whether or not it succeeds depends wholly on your fortitude, and I would sooner put my faith in my coffer. Four hundred."

"If you find another *anguissette* whose fortitude you like better, I would be interested to hear it. Three hundred fifty." I didn't have that either, but I would find a way.

"Done." The young seamstress gave a faint smile. They do not drive so hard a bargain as Bryony House, who know well the erotic power money holds, but they are no slouches in Eglantine. None of the Thirteen Houses are. "I will send for the Chancellor to draw up the contract. Livia, bring my pigments. I must match the color of your marque, Comtesse."

We were some time concluding our business. I hoped that Favrielle would warm to me once our bargain was struck, for I felt a reluctant sympathy for her and I misliked such animosity in one my own age, but her manner was unchanged.

It would be a stunning costume.

I found Remy awaiting me in the outer sitting room. A bronze-haired boy clad in the green and white of Eglantine House leaned on his knee, watching agape as Remy showed him the trick of walking a copper coin across his knuckles.

"My lady," my chevalier greeted me, making the coin disappear, and seemingly pulling it from the boy's hair. "Here," he said to the lad. "You keep it, and practice."

The boy giggled; darting forward, he planted a kiss on Remy's lips, then slithered away, skipping out of reach and doing a handspring out of pure high spirits.

Remy watched him wonderingly. "Truly, were you like that as a child of the Night Court, my lady?"

"No." I shook my head. "It would have been reckoned brazen, in Cereus House." Night-Blooming Cereus prides itself on offering beauty of a most ephemeral nature; I was taught delicacy of conduct, there. "My lord Delaunay made me learn tumbling, though," I added, "and Hyacinthe taught me some sleight of hand."

"You can turn handsprings?" Remy asked it straight-faced, glancing at me out of the corner of his eye with the scarcest hint of amusement.

"And pick locks." I daresay he didn't believe me; it made me laugh. "Come. I need to visit my factor, to see if he'll advance me a loan. I've just signed a contract I can't pay, chevalier, and I need to do somewhat about it."

My factor in the City of Elua was a man named Jacques Brenin. I'd been referred to him by no less than the Chancellor of the Exchequer himself, and his reputation was stainless. Unfortunately, the very stringency that made him an irreproachably honest agent rendered him reluctant to make me the loan I requested.

"My lady," he said, clearing his throat, "I can only advance funds for goods vouched in kind. I cannot indulge in speculation against your. . . probable income . . . as a

Servant of Naamah any more than I can next spring's shearing. Certainly there are factors willing to do so, but I tell you, I do not advise it. If you wish to pledge a portion of the acreage of Montrève as surety, or the house in the City . . ."

"No," I said firmly. "I will not barter with my lord Delaunay's inheritance, nor the roof that houses my retainers. In conscience, I cannot do so."

Jacques Brenin spread his hands in a gesture of help-lessness. "If you are not willing to take these risks . . ."

"Messire Brenin." I cut him off. "I do offer goods in kind." Slow and deliberate, I rose from my chair and began to unlace my bodice. He wet his lips with the tip of his tongue and stared as I slid the sleeves from my shoulders and let my gown fall to my hips, turning as I did so.

I had seen, in the mirrors at Eglantine House; I did not need to see to know how my bare skin glowed in the dim lamplight of my factor's office. And rising from the dim-ples at the small of my back to the final at my nape was my marque, the bold, intricate design etched in black, with crimson accents. It had been inked by Master Robert Tielhard, the greatest marquist of his day.

My factor swallowed audibly. Without haste, I drew my gown back up and laced my bodice. When I turned around, his face was pale. "You offer your services as surety if you should default on your loan." He kept his voice even with commendable effort.

"I do." I smiled. "But I do not think I will default."

"Neither do I," Jacques Brenin muttered, scribbling out a receipt. Licking his lips again, he handed it to me. "Take this to my treasurer, she will advance you the funds.

Repayment within sixty days at a rate of twelve percent. And Elua help your patrons."

  I laughed. "Thank you, Messire Brenin."

  "Don't thank me," he said dryly. "I find myself hoping you default."

SEVEN

IN THE days that followed, there was little enough to
do in preparing for the Midwinter Masque. I went once
to Eglantine House for Favrielle to check her measure-
ments, but the draping proper awaited the arrival of the
fabric.

A good time, then, to meet with the Rebbe.

It was Joscelin who arranged the meeting; he had
become friendly with this grand Yeshuite scholar — Nahum
ben Isaac, his name was — insofar as Joscelin became
friendly with anyone in those days.

The day was cold and sharp, and I was glad of the
carriage affording protection from the wind. We did not
linger in the courtyard, but hurried into the hall.

Knowing some little bit about Yeshuite sensibilities,
thanks first to our friends Taavi and Danele, who gave us
succor on our flight from the Allies of Camlach, and
latterly to Seth ben Yavin, the young scholar who had
tutored me in Montrève, I dressed modestly. It is not my
way to flaunt myself as a Servant of Naamah — whatever
certain prudish Cassilines may think — but I have my

vanity. Nonetheless, I put it aside to meet the Rebbe, donning a gown of brown worsted which I used to wear travelling, and a thick woolen shawl. Well-made, but the sort of stuff a rustic noblewoman might don for common-wear. With a woolen cap on my head, my hair coiled in a braid, and sturdy boots, surely, I thought, I was the very picture of drab modesty.

That is what I thought at home, anyway. When we entered the hall of the yeshiva, where charcoal braziers battled the chill and the sound of children's voices murmuring filled the air, it was another matter.

In a sea of foreign faces, a D'Angeline stands out like a beacon, flashing that deadly beauty that cuts like a blade. In the City, among my own kind, I forgot; here, as voices fell silent and Yeshuite children raised wondering eyes, I remembered. What must it be like, for them? I had offered Cecilie an apology on their behalf, but still. To see the blood-lineage of an errant branch of their own mythology stamped in the faces of the folk who surround them; it must be a strangeness. Yeshua ben Yosef walked the earth, and died, and was risen. So they believe, with enduring stub-bornness; he is their Mashiach, the Redeemer and the King-to-Come. But Blessed Elua, whom they do not acknowledge, walked the earth as well, and he and his Companions peopled a nation. There is no D'Angeline peasant, no matter how mean his origins, but has a tale in his heritage of a celestially begotten ancestor; mayhap it is only that Azza tumbled his thirty-generations-ago grandmother in a haystack, but there it is.

So the children stared, and the young woman leading them. Joscelin cleared his throat. "We are here to see the Rebbe," he told them, blushing — although they were not staring at him. Only me. "I am sorry, we are early. Please continue."

To my surprise, the young woman colored too. "Caleb, tell the Rebbe his friend Joscelin Verreuil is here," she said to one of the boys in charmingly accented D'Angeline. "And . . . I am sorry," she said to me, "who shall I say is with him?"

"I am Phèdre nó Delaunay," I said, remembering to add, "the Comtesse de Montrève."

"Oh!" Her color deepened, and she clapped a hand over her mouth. Removing it hastily, she pushed the boy gently toward the door. "Make haste, Caleb."

He must have done so, for a tall man of middle years and a solemn face emerged in short order. "I am sorry, Comtesse," he said, giving a brief bow. "We expected you at three bells, but the Rebbe will see you now." He allowed a small smile for Joscelin. "Brother Verreuil. A pleasure, my apostate friend."

"Barukh hatah Adonai, father." With an answering smile, Joscelin gave his Cassiline bow. "This way," he said to me, gesturing.

How often had he been here since the first visit? It had not been long, and yet he was familiar with the passages, striding surely along at the rear as our escort guided us. There were small cubbyholes for study; I heard the murmuring voices of older scholars reciting passages that were half-familiar to me.

The Rebbe's quarters were larger, though poorly illumed. He kept us waiting a moment in the hallway, before our guide ushered us into his study.

Joscelin had spoken truly; Nahum ben Isaac cut a formidable figure indeed. Despite the withering effects of age, one could see he had been doughty in his youth, and his broad shoulders still strained at the black cloth of his jacket. He must have been nearly eighty; his hair was almost wholly white, shot with a few strands of black. He'd not lost a whit of it, either – his side-locks almost hid the dangling ends of his prayer shawl and his square-cornered beard fell midway to his waist. Fierce eyes glowered at me from a face like crumpled parchment.

"Come in." His voice was as strongly accented as the young teacher's, but harsh with it. Joscelin bowed, murmuring the blessing again, and took a seat on a low stool at his feet; to my surprise, the Rebbe patted his cheek. "You're a good lad, for an apostate." The pitiless gaze came back to me. "So you're the one."

"Phèdre nó Delaunay de Montrève, father." I inclined my head. I did not curtsy, though it cost me a good deal of effort. Comtesse or no, I am trained to be subservient to authority, and the Rebbe had it in abundance.

"A Servant of Naamah." The words fair curdled on his tongue. "Call it what you will, I know what you are, girl, fancy titles and all. Why would one such as you want to study Habiru and the teachings of the Mashiach?"

We call them Yeshuites; so they call themselves, now. Before, they were the Children of Yisra-el. But before that, even, they were a tribal folk on the outskirts of Khebbel-im-Akkad, and Yeshuite scholars still call their ancient language by that name. If the Rebbe thought I would blink in confusion, he was mistaken. I am still one of the few D'Angelines who understands the divisions of the Cruithne, whom Caerdicci scholars name the Picti. Delaunay made me learn such things, and I have not lost the trick of it. I took a seat on a second stool, spreading my skirts carefully about me.

"I have some knowledge of the teachings of Yeshua ben Yosef, father," I said, drawing a deep breath. "All the descendants of Blessed Elua and his Companions know the tale of the Mashiach, for it is, too, a part of our history. But it is the older teachings that interest me; the Tanakh, and most especially such midrashim as have been recorded in writing or passed from ear to ear. And for that, I must study Habiru."

The Rebbe *did* blink; I daresay he never expected to hear such words from the mouth of a Servant of Naamah. Nonetheless, he repeated his question relentlessly; although there was a crafty gleam in his fierce old eyes now. "Why?"

I answered with a question. "What do you know of the Lost Book of Raziel, father?"

"Bah!" Nahum ben Isaac made a dismissive gesture. "You speak of the book of all knowledge, that Adonai gave to Edom the First Man? Tales to entertain children, no more."

"No." I shook my head, surety giving me strength. "What of the Master of the Straits, father? Is he a tale to frighten children?"

He chewed thoughtfully on a corner of his beard. "Sailors say he is not. Sailors lie. But a schism eight hundred years long across a piece of water I could shout across does not lie." Yes, it was definitely a crafty light. "You say it has somewhat to do with the Sefer Raziel?"

"Yes." I leaned forward. "And the angel Rahab, who begot a child on a mortal woman. For this, the One God punished him; but Rahab brought up pages — scattered pages, from the Lost Book of Raziel – from the deep, and gave them to his son, and bound him to endure the length of his punishment as the Master of the Straits, unless someone could penetrate his mystery and take his place."

The Rebbe chewed fiercely; I don't think he was aware of what he was doing. Not with his beard, at least. "You tell a good story," he said grudgingly. "But it is only that."

"No." Joscelin intervened quietly. "Not a story, father; I was there too. I have seen the Face of the Waters, and been carried on the crest of a wave that never breaks. And I know the Tsingano who penetrated the mystery. He was . . ." He hesitated, then finished the thought firmly. "He was a friend of mine."

I was grateful to hear him say it. Joscelin caught my eye and smiled ruefully; for a moment, it was as if nothing had changed between us.

"A *Tsingano!*" The Rebbe seemed horrified; no one but holds the Tsingani in the lowest of esteem, I fear.

"He was a prince of his kind," I said sharply, "and gifted with the *dromonde*, that looks backward as well as afore. He was my friend, and I beg you do not mock him to my ears, father."

"Pay it no mind." The Rebbe waved his hand dismissively again. "So." He fixed me with his gimlet stare. "Do I understand, Naamah's Servant? You wish to study Habiru and learn a secret to unlock the chain that binds this Tsingano friend of yours. You seek a means to force the messengers of Adonai Himself to obey."

"Yes." I said it simply.

To my great surprise, the Rebbe began to chuckle. "Well." Shaking his head, he picked strands of his beard from the corner of his mouth. "Well, well." Perhaps he did know, after all, that he chewed his beard. "I am compelled by the word of Yeshua to give succor where I may," he said mildly, "and it seems you make a case for it after all, Naamah's Servant. You claim to have studied with Seth ben Yavin of L'Arène, and he writes to me that you are not a bad pupil, despite the fact that you would make the Magdelene unrepentant blush. But he is a young man, and I do not trust the word of young men any more than I do sailors. Tell me, what does this mean?" From within the depths of his beard, he brought forth a pendant, worn close to the heart on a chain about his neck.

I had only to glance at it once; the symbol, wrought in silver, was known to me. A broad, flat brush-stroke atop two legs, it looked like, with a tail squiggled on the left. "It is the word *Khai*, father, combined of the Habiru letters Khet and Yod."

"And what does it mean?" He looked cunningly at me.

"It means 'living.'" I made my voice firm. "It is the symbol of the resurrection of Yeshua, a pledge that the Mashiach rose from death and lives, and will return as the King-to-Come and establish his reign on earth."

"So." Nahum ben Isaac tucked away the pendant beneath his beard. "Seth did teach you something, it seems. And yet you do not believe."

I offered the only answer I had. "Father, I do not believe or disbelieve. I am D'Angeline."

"Even a D'Angeline may be redeemed." The Rebbe adjusted his prayer shawl. "There is no sin, of the blood nor of the flesh, so great but that the Mashiach's death may not redeem it." He glanced at Joscelin as he said it, and Joscelin did not meet my eyes. "So be it, then. I will teach you, Naamah's Servant, insofar as I am able." I opened my mouth to thank him and he raised a finger, gesturing me to silence. "This I ask. For so long as you choose to live a life of indecency, you will come only when I summon you. You will heed our ways, and speak to no one. Our children shall not lay eyes upon you. Do you agree to these terms?"

I made to retort, stung, and thought better of it. Hyacinthe's face rose in my memory; alight with merriment, black eyes shining, his teeth flashing in a white grin. Eight hundred years, condemned to a lonely isle. "Yes, father." It bears saying that I can sound very meek when I choose to do so. "I will abide as you say."

"Good." The Rebbe clapped his hands. "Then for the next week, you will study the Be'resheith, the first book of the Tanakh. We will begin, as it is written, 'In the beginning.' And when I summon you, you may be sure, I will question you." His glare returned. "In Habiru! Do not speak to me of this language you call Yeshuite, is that clear?"

"Yes," I murmured. "Thank you, father."

"Barukh hatah Yeshua a'Mashiach, lo ha'lam," the Rebbe intoned, and waved his hand. "Now go away. And wear something decent, when you return."

Outside, Joscelin looked sidelong at me and fidgeted with the carriage-team's harness. It was quiet in the courtyard, no children in sight, Elua be thanked. I did not want to give offense on the heels of our agreement. "He is a very great man, Phèdre," Joscelin said with restraint. "He does not mean to insult you."

"And I am a living insult to all that he holds holy," I replied calmly. "I understand, Joscelin. I will do my best not to tax him with it. If he can help us find a way to free

Hyacinthe, that is all that matters. Unless you fear I will intervene in your redemption."

It was hurtful, my last words, and I knew it. He shuddered as if they pained him. "I am not seeking *redemption*," he said, his voice low and savage. "It is only that the Rebbe is the first one to tell me that I need neither share Cassiel's damnation nor discard my vows as facilely as if they were naught but some outmoded convention!"

"Joscelin!" I took a step back, startled. "I never said that!"

"No. I know. But you have thought it." He shuddered again, turning away to needlessly check the harness buckles. "Get in the carriage," he said, his voice muffled. "I'll drive you home."

It was a long ride home, and quiet and lonely in my carriage.

EİGHT

İT WAS on the following day that Thelesis de Mornay called upon me, and I greeted her visit with unfeigned delight. The Queen's Poet was an unprepossessing woman with features that might almost have been homely, were it not for her luminous dark eyes and musical voice. When she spoke, one heard only beauty.

"Phèdre." Thelesis embraced me with a smile, eyes aglow. "I'm sorry I've not had a chance to see you sooner. Forgive me for coming unannounced."

"Forgive you? I can't think of anyone I'd rather see," I said, squeezing her hand. It was true. Once, when I thought I was suffering the gravest sorrow of my life, Thelesis had drawn me out of it; it had been nothing more than childish jealousy, I know now, but I have always treasured her kindness and tact.

And Delaunay treated her as an equal, and trusted her. When Joscelin and I escaped from Skaldia and made our return to the City, only to find ourselves condemned in absentia of Delaunay's murder, it was Thelesis who aided us in secrecy and won us an audience with

Ysandre. I trusted her with my life, then, and I would again.

"Here." She turned to her footman, dressed in the livery of House Courcel, and nodded. He held out a large wooden box. "I brought a gift."

"You didn't have to do that," I protested. Thelesis smiled.

"I did, though," she said. "Wait and see."

We adjourned to the sitting room, and Gemma brought glasses of cordial. Thelesis sipped hers and coughed once, delicately.

"Your health still troubles you?" I asked sympathetically. She had caught the fever, that Bitterest Winter, that killed so many.

"It will pass." She pressed her hand briefly to her chest. "Go on and open it."

The box sat on the low table before us. I pried the lid loose and peered inside, pulling out wads of cotton batting to find it concealed a small marble bust. Lifting it out, my hands trembled. I held the bust aloft and gazed at it.

It was Anafiel Delaunay.

The sculptor had caught him in the prime of his thirties, in all his austere beauty; the proud features, a faint wryness to his beautiful mouth, irony and tenderness mingled in his eyes and the thick cable of his braid coiling forward over one shoulder. Not the same, of course, in its marble starkness; Delaunay's eyes had been hazel, shot with topaz, his hair a rich auburn. But the face, ah, Elua! It was him.

"Thank you," I murmured, my voice shaking; grief, unexpected, hit me like a blow to the stomach. "Thank you, oh, Thelesis, Blessed Elua, I miss him, I miss him so much!" She looked at me with concern, and I tried to shake my head, waving it off. "Don't worry, it's not . . . I love this, truly, it's beautiful, and you are the kindest friend, it's only that I miss him, and I thought I was done with grieving, but seeing this . . . and Alcuin, and Hyacinthe, and now Joscelin . . ." I tried to laugh. It caught in my throat, thick with tears. "Now Joscelin wants to leave me to follow his own path, and thinks even of becoming a Yeshuite, oh, Elua, I just . . ."

"Phèdre." Thelesis took the bust gently, setting it on the table and waited quietly throughout the sudden onslaught of sobs that wracked me. "It's all right. It's all right to mourn. I miss him too, and he was only my friend, not my lord and mentor." It didn't matter what she said; she might have said anything in that soothing voice of hers.

"I'm so sorry." I had buried my face in my hands. I lifted it, blinking at her through tears. "Truly, this is the most wonderful thing anyone has ever given me, and I repay you like this." I said it politely, though I couldn't help sniffling.

"I'm glad you like it. I commissioned it from a sculptor who knew him well, once." She touched the bust, stroking it with a rueful touch. "He had an effect on people, Anafiel Delaunay did."

I nodded, scrubbing at my tear-stained face. "He did that."

"Yes." Thelesis regarded me with her quiet gaze. "Phèdre." One word, naming me. It is a poet's gift, to go to the heart of things in a word. "Why?"

With anyone else, I might have dissembled; I had done it already with Cecilie, and indeed, with Ysandre de la Courcel herself. But Thelesis was a poet, and those dark eyes saw through to the bone. If not for illness, she would have gone to Alba in my stead. I owed her truth, at least.

"Wait," I said, and went to fetch my *sangoire* cloak. Returning, I gave it to her, a bundle of velvet folds the color of blood at midnight. "Do you remember this?"

"Your cloak." Her head bowed over it. "I remember."

"It saved my life, in a way." I found I was pacing, and made myself sit. "Ysandre's man-at-arms remembered it too, the day Delaunay was killed; an *anguissette* in a *sangoire* cloak and a member of the Cassiline Brotherhood, seeking an audience with the Princess. It proved our story. But I never saw it, after that day. I took it off in Melisande Shahrizai's quarters, where she poured me a glass of cordial." Remembering my own, I picked up my glass and drank, grimacing. "I woke up in a canvas-covered wagon, halfway to the Skaldi border, wrapped in woolen blankets and no cloak in sight." There had been considerable more between, but Thelesis had no need to know it. It involved Melisande, and the razor-sharp blades they call flechettes, and a good deal of me screaming. Everything but my *signale* and Quintilius Rousse's message for Delaunay. I have dreams about it still, and Elua help me, some of them are exquisite. "I got it back this autumn."

"How?" Thelesis asked carefully.

"Gonzago de Escabares." I rested my chin on my hands and gazed at the bust of Delaunay. "A friend of his met a woman in La Serenissima; a beautiful woman. She gave him a parcel to carry for his friend, who was going to meet the Comtesse de Montrève." I gestured at the cloak. "That was the whole of it."

"Melisande." She breathed the word. "Phèdre, have you told the Queen?"

I shook my head. "No one, except Joscelin and my boys. They know. I asked Ysandre when she received me, if she'd heard of Melisande's doings. She has sent word to every major city from Aragonia to Caerdicca Unitas, and no one has seen her. Benedicte de la Courcel is in La Serenissima, Ysandre is sure he'd clap her in chains if she showed her face. Nothing."

"Benedicte de la Courcel," Thelesis said tartly, "has a D'Angeline child-bride and is preparing to become a father again in his dotage. By all accounts, he'd not notice if Melisande kicked him in the shins."

"Mayhap." I shrugged. "Be as that may, she's hidden herself well. But one thing I know, and that is that someone helped her walk out of Troyes-le-Mont alive. And whoever it was, it was someone powerful enough that none of the guardsmen posted that night even questioned him. Or her. The guard at the postern gate was killed by a dagger to the heart. Whoever did it, got close enough to do it unchallenged." I spread my hands. "You weren't there, Thelesis. I was. I can count the number of people that would have included on my fingers. And this cloak?" I plucked at it. "That's Melisande's message, the opening gambit in her game. Whoever it was, I have a chance of finding them out."

The Queen's Poet looked sick. "You have to tell Ysandre. If not her, then at least . . . at least tell Gaspar. He would help."

"No." I said it softly. "He's one of the ones I count, Thelesis."

"*Gaspar?*" She looked incredulous; well she might.

Gaspar Trevalion, the Comte de Forcay, was one of the few people Delaunay had trusted unquestioningly. He'd even stood surety for Gaspar when the net fell on House Trevalion.

"Gaspar," I said relentlessly. "Thelesis, whoever it is, they *fought* on our side, don't you see? It had to be someone we trusted, beyond thought. Those guards, they wouldn't have let the Duc de Morhban through unchallenged, sovereign of Kusheth or no. Promise me you'll say nothing. Not to Gaspar, nor Ysandre . . . not to anyone. Whoever it is, if they know what I'm about, it will silence them, sure as death."

"So you think," she said wonderingly, "you truly think that they will hand it to you, as a Servant of Naamah, in careless pillow talk."

"No." I shook my head. "I am not as foolish as that, I promise you. But I think the threads are there, and if I am lucky — Naamah willing, and Kushiel — they may let a loose end dangle, that I might discern the pattern they are weaving. It is a long chance, I grant you. But it is a chance, and the only one I have. Melisande plays fair, by her own rules. If the chance were not there . . ." I hoisted a fold of the cloak, ". . . she would not have sent the challenge."

"I think you are mad." Only Thelesis de Mornay could have made the words gentle. "Madder than Delaunay, and I thought he was mad for honoring that ridiculous vow to Rolande de la Courcel." Well she might, for Delaunay had suffered a great deal from the enmity of Rolande's wife, Isabel L'Envers; but my lord Delaunay kept his promises. Now all of them are dead, and it is the living who must bear the cost. Thelesis dumped the *sangoire* cloak back into my lap, and sighed. "But I will honor your request just the same, because you are Delaunay's pupil, and you bear the mark of Kushiel's Dart, and it is in no poet's interest to cross the will of the immortals. Still, I wish you would reconsider it. The Duc L'Envers, at the least, has no interest in seeing Ysandre dethroned."

"Barquiel L'Envers," I said, "is high on my list of suspects."

Thelesis de Mornay laughed ruefully. "Anafiel," she said, addressing the bust of Delaunay, "you should have been made King's Poet in my stead, and left this one to the mercies of Valerian House." If I had not gone to serve Delaunay, it is true, Valerian would have bought my marque. It is their specialty to provide adepts who find pleasure in pain. But they did not find me. Delaunay did. "Well, so," Thelesis said, changing the subject. "What is this about Joscelin Verreuil joining the Followers of Yeshua?"

I am not ashamed to admit that I poured the story out to her, and she listened unjudging, as only a truly good friend may do. When I was done, she pressed my hand in sympathy.

"He is in pain," she said gently, "and you have wounded him deeply, meaning or not. His choice is his own, Phèdre, and you cannot make it for him. Allow him this space, then, to choose. When the One God sent his messengers to summon Elua back, it was Cassiel handed him the dagger to make his reply. But I have never heard Elua asked it of him."

She was right, and I could not speak against it. I fiddled with my cloak instead, folding its luxurious mass. "Do you think it's true?" I asked presently. "That Yeshua has the power to redeem sin?"

"I don't know," Thelesis said thoughtfully. "The ways of gods are strange, and Yeshuites do not reckon sin as we do, any more than Cassilines. I cannot say. The Hellenes claim the descendents of the House of Minos have the ability to cleanse a man of a blood-curse; it is a gift of Zagreus, after they atoned for . . . well, you know the story." I did, for I bore the ill-starred name of a Queen of that line. "But I have heard, too, that few mortals can bear the process at less than the cost of their wits."

I shuddered; it was a frightening thought. "Well, Elua grant that neither of us need find out. I will heed your advice, and give Joscelin leave to choose. So a priest foretold for him, once, that he would ever stand at the crossroads, and choose and choose again. But I am fearful, that this Rebbe presents him with a third path."

"All paths are present, always," Thelesis de Mornay said philosophically, "and we can but choose among them." She stood. "Phèdre, thank you for your hospitality, and for your . . ." she smiled, ". . . for your trust. I will honor it, with the promise you have asked. Promise me in turn that you will have a care, and divulge to Ysandre aught that you learn." She raised her eyebrows. "I take it that you do not suspect her, at least?"

"No." I laughed. "Not Ysandre. Other than myself, and probably Joscelin, Ysandre de la Courcel is the one person I am sure had no interest in seeing Melisande freed. And if I'd not been there, I'd likely suspect myself as well. Thelesis, thank you." I rose to embrace her. "I'm sorry to have made a fool of myself. Truly, I will cherish this gift beyond words."

"You are welcome." She returned my embrace. "Phèdre, please know that you have a standing invitation to call upon me at the Palace. For any reason."

"I will," I promised, escorting her to the door.

When she had gone, I returned to my sitting room, gazing at the bust of Delaunay. Ah, my lord, I wondered, what would you tell me if you could speak?

Beautiful and silent, his marble face kept its oblique, secret smile.

I was on my own.

Nine

THE FABRÍC for my costume had arrived, and a courier had sent word from Favrielle nó Eglantine that I was to come for a fitting. One matter, however, pertaining to the Queen's Masque remained unsettled.

"I would like you to come," I said to Joscelin, "but if you want to maintain your vigil, I will understand."

We had made peace, after a fashion; he had brought me a silent offering of apology, a beautifully wrought plinth of black marble on which Delaunay's bust now stood. Where he had gotten the monies for such a thing, I did not know, nor did I ask. Later I learned that he had pawned a jeweled dagger for it, a gift of Ysandre.

"I think it might be best if you took one of the lads," Joscelin murmured. "I don't . . . It's been a long time since I held Elua's vigil on the Longest Night, Phèdre, and I think I am better suited for it than sharing *joie* with nobles right now." He gave a faint smile, to remove any hurtfulness from his words. "Let Fortun escort you; he's more sense than the other two."

"All right." I stooped to kiss his brow on my way out; he shivered under it.

So it was that Fortun accompanied me to Eglantine House, where Favrielle eyed him with approval. "Asmodel," she said, measuring the breadth of his shoulders with the span of her arm. "One of the seven courtiers of hell, who served under Kushiel. We'll put him in a black velvet doublet and hose, and a great bronze key on a chain about his neck. A simple horned domino, I think; black satin. A fitting attendant for Mara. Noreis!" Raising her voice, she beckoned to a tailor. No adept, he hastened to obey. "Will you see to it? Something elegant, not this season's forsaken nonsense."

"Of course." He bowed his head. Genius rules in Eglantine House. If Favrielle was unfit to serve Naamah, she clearly reigned over the fitting-room.

"Very well." With a sigh, Favrielle turned back to me. "Let's see what we have."

Once I had stripped and donned the half-sewn gown, I had to admit a grudging acknowledgment of her skill. Truly, it was splendid. The scarlet of the silk jersey-cloth matched the accents in my marque perfectly, and it flowed on my skin like a living thing. Standing on a stool while Favrielle grumbled about me, gathering and pinning, I gazed wideeyed at my reflection in the mirror.

"Favrielle, my sweet!" The door to the fitting-room swung open to admit a tall adept in his mid-thirties, with merry eyes and a handsome, mobile face. "Where's my three-layered cloak for the Troubador of Eisande? I'm commissioned for Lord Orlon's fête tonight, and the Dowayne *promised* him a private performance!" Catching sight of me, he stopped and swept an elaborate bow.

"Forgive me, gentle lady . . ." His resonant voice trailed off, and the merry gaze turned sharp as it swept up the length of my marque. His eyes met mine in the mirror, looking for the scarlet mote. "My lady, indeed. Phèdre nó Delaunay de Montrève, if I am not mistaken."

"Roussillon nó Eglantine." I smiled. His satires were famous in Night's Doorstep; I'd heard him declaim, once. "Well met."

"And me without an ounce of doggerel!" He made a dismayed face, then struck a pose. "Waldemar Selig was a warlord," he declared. "Waldemar Selig had a big sword. But his plan fell apart, thanks to Kushiel's Dart, and Waldemar Selig got Isidore'd."

Across the room, Fortun gave a snort of repressed mirth. He had been there, on the battlefield, when Isidore d'Aiglemort slew Waldemar Selig. It cost him his life, but I reckoned Terre d'Ange's greatest traitor won his redemption in destroying her greatest enemy.

Still, it was good to be able to laugh.

"I'm not done," Roussillon said mildly, and cleared his throat. "Mighty Selig turned his back, when he divulged his attack, to the men of his barbarian horde. His loins, how they burned! Too late, Selig learned, a skilled *anguissette* is not safely ignored!"

I laughed aloud, clapping my hands; Roussillon swept me another bow, and Favrielle muttered in disgust. I winced as a carelessly wielded pin scratched me.

"The trim needed stitching," she said crossly to the satirist. "I'll have it sent to your room on the hour. Now get out, and stop distracting me with your wretched verse!"

He mimed fear convincingly, and I was hard put to keep from laughing again. "Thank you," he said then to

Favrielle. Catching up her hands, he kissed them despite
her best efforts to swat away his grasp. "You are a very
angel of clothiers, precious one, and I shall light a candle
to your name." Releasing her, he smiled at me, this time
without any artifice. "May I say that it is an honor to meet
you, my lady. Naamah's Servants are in your debt."

"Thank you." I returned his smile gravely. He
laughed, gave one last swirling bow, and departed.

"Blathering *jackass!*" Favrielle muttered, picking up a
dropped pin and driving it hard through the silken fabric.
The fine stuff gave easily, and she buried the pin nearly an
inch deep in the flesh at the base of my spine. I barely had
time to gasp.

Pain, fiery and radiant, burst outward in concentric
circles, pulsing and contracting. It washed over me in
ripples, acute at the core, sweet as it spread. A red haze
occluded the vision in my left eye, blurring my reflected
image. Somewhere, behind it, I sensed the bronze visage of
Kushiel, rod and flail crossed on his chest, stern and
approving.

When it cleared, Favrielle knelt staring up at me in
blank astonishment, holding the pin she had withdrawn.
She blinked and closed her mouth. "That must be . . .
inconvenient."

For once, her voice held no censure, just a certain wry
sympathy. I drew a long, shuddering breath. "Yes." I
released my pent breath. "An *anguissette* is not exactly a
convenient thing to be." Through long discipline, I made
my tone match hers. "It doesn't mean I like you any
better."

Against her will, Favrielle nó Eglantine laughed.

When I returned home, I found Joscelin agitated and

the Rebbe's solemn pupil awaiting me. He rose as I entered the room. "It is suitable for the Rebbe to see you now, Comtesse," he said. "Will you come?"

I sighed. "He really means *when* he summons me, doesn't he? All right." I brushed the front of my gown; it was a finespun blue wool, less drab than what I'd worn before. "Give me a moment to change into something the Rebbe would find suitable. Fortun, tell Benoit not to unhitch the team."

The Rebbe's pupil gave a slight smile. "Your attire is fine, Comtesse. You mustn't take everything he says to heart. He may disapprove of Servants of Naamah, but I believe he was having a jest."

I made a face, which was probably not an appropriate response for a peer of the realm. "The Rebbe's humor leaves somewhat to be desired."

"Perhaps." The Yeshuite ducked his head, hiding another smile. "But he is a very great man, and he has earned the right to his small jests, I think. Shall we go?"

He had spoken truly; Nahum ben Isaac made no comment on my clothing, but merely sat me down at a desk and brought forth a scroll from the cabinet in his study. Joscelin sat quiet on a stool. "Now," the Rebbe said decisively. "We will see." Unfurling the top of the scroll, he revealed the opening words of the Be'resheith. With a pointer, he indicated the first sentence. "You will read until I tell you to stop. And then you will tell it to me again, in your own tongue. And we will see."

Following the pointer – it was a holy scroll, one used for services, which may not be touched by human hands – I read aloud in Habiru, smoothly at times, faltering at others. Each time I stumbled, the Rebbe corrected me;

impatiently, I thought, but then he would gesture for me to continue. When at last he motioned for me to stop, I took a deep breath, and recited the entire tale in D'Angeline, all the way through the covering of the earth with the great flood.

The Rebbe leaned back and listened, chewing thoughtfully on his beard. Periodically, he nodded with something resembling approval; periodically, he winced.

When I was done, he looked grudgingly at me. "You studied a translation, I suppose."

"No." I shook my head. "I've read it in translation before, father, in the past. But you told me to study it in Habiru, and I did."

He gave me a suspicious glare. From the corner, Joscelin spoke up. "Phèdre is a gifted linguist, father. The Queen sent her to Alba because of it."

"Hah. I have heard that story." The Rebbe plucked a few strands of beard from his bottom lip, and gave me his cunning look. "Well, then. You will read it again, child, line by line. First in Habiru, then in D'Angeline. And perhaps – *perhaps* – if you make it through without too many mistakes, I will tell you a tale my own master told me, about the Sefer Raziel and the disobedience of Rahab."

On this stool, Joscelin settled and prepared for a long wait. I sighed, and began again.

Nahum ben Isaac was an exhausting teacher. If I thought young Seth had taught me well, I was disillusioned that day. A great many of the mistakes I made in pronunciation and translation, he had allowed me, slight as they were. No surprise, I suppose; for the first weeks, he could not even look at me without blushing. But slight mistakes accumulate, and grow to gross errors if unchecked. The Rebbe allowed me no mistakes, and halted me repeatedly during this last reading to correct some minor point until both of us were irritable with it.

"Blame!" he said crossly, correcting me a third time; it was a mistake in translation I'd got lodged in my memory. "Not sin, blame! Blame! Only Yeshua was without sin!" Emphasizing the point, he rapped my knuckles smartly with the pointer.

With a faint scraping sound, Joscelin surged to his feet, daggers half-drawn before he realized what he was doing. When he did, he looked mortified. "Forgive me, father! I . . ."

"Are still more Cassiline than anything else." Looking up at Joscelin, the Rebbe chuckled into his beard. "Well, apostate, we will see." Fingering his *khai* pendant, he nodded at me. "You did not embarrass the Tanakh. Master these verses, and next time I will tell you of Rahab and the Lost Book. Maybe there is somewhat in these children's tales you may use."

"Thank you," I said gratefully, standing. My muscles had grown cramped from sitting so long, and my mind felt taxed. Oddly enough, it was not a bad feeling. So it had been when I was a child in Delaunay's household, and he used to push Alcuin and me to cram our minds full of history and politics and language. I had fretted at it, then, though I learned. Now I knew the value of it. "I will come at your summons, father, whenever I am able."

Joscelin, still red-faced, made his Cassiline bow. "Ya'er Adonai panav elekha, father, please accept my apology. I was half-drowsing, and did not think."

"So like a child, you rest safely in the presence of

Yeshua, hah!" The Rebbe gave his cunning smile, and poked a finger at Joscelin. "There is something to think about." He made a wave of dismissal. "Now go."

Outside, Joscelin moved like a man in a dream, hitching the team and making ready to drive. I longed to say a word to draw him back, but what that word might be, I did not know.

Arriving at home at dusk, all three of my chevaliers were clustered in the reception salon, with Gemma hovering over Ti-Philippe and pressing a cool, moist cloth over his right eye.

"Don't tell me," I sighed. It had been a long day.

"It's not what you think, my lady." Ti-Philippe pushed Gemma's hand away and grinned at me, revealing a bruised and swollen visage. "We didn't get caught, or any such thing. We were dicing in quarters with the Palace Guard, like you said."

"One of 'em accused Ti-Philippe of cheating," Remy said helpfully, "and we quarrelled. Then he said somewhat about you that we didn't take kindly. So we showed him the error of his ways."

I flung myself into a chair. "And how much trouble are you in?"

Remy coughed. "Not much. The Captain of the Guard agreed we had the right of it and put the fellow under reprimand. We're allowed back, all right. But there's, um, a small fine for causing a disturbance in their quarters."

"How small?"

"Twenty silver regals." He squirmed. "We promised you'd send it around."

"Fortun?" I looked imploringly at him.

"I'll take it tomorrow," he said calmly. "And you can

dock our retainers for it, if need be. But my lady, there's somewhat else you should know. The lads learned a few things that might explain how Melisande Shahrizai escaped."

Ten

AT FORTUN'S words, a sharp excitement seized me, and my weariness fell away. I'd as soon have heard their news right there and then, but for the habit of discretion. Delaunay's servants had been hand-picked and trusted; though I liked them, mine were not. "Gemma." I turned to the day-maid. "Would you see if Eugènie has aught prepared for dinner? 'Tis early, but I'm fair famished. If you would be good enough to serve whatever is ready, that will be all."

Gemma pouted, but did as I bid. Happily, there was a lamb stew with fennel ready to serve, and loaves of warm crusty bread. I thanked the kitchen-mistress and dismissed her for the evening, over her grumbles; Eugènie did not trust that a D'Angeline noblewoman could get along without at least one trained servant. I would have laughed at that, another time. In the Skaldi wilderness, I boiled pottage with melted snow and survived. I'd not have thought I could either, before I had to. Of course, I'd not been a peer of the realm, then, but highly prized courtesans are not exactly known for woodcraft. I learned to build a fire in a blizzard with naught but a flint and damp tinder on that dreadful flight with Joscelin. No adepts of the Night Court can claim as much, I daresay.

At any rate, we were soon enough seated at the dining table, and Remy and Ti-Philippe told their story over bites of rich stew and warm bread, washed down with plenty of wine.

"So," I asked directly, "you found the men who were on guard the night Melisande escaped?"

Ti-Philippe, his mouth full of stew, shook his head vigorously. "No, my lady," Remy answered for them both, pulling a rueful expression. "That, no one seems to know, exactly; we have a couple of names, but no one knows where they're posted, and we dare not ask too closely if you don't want us to arouse suspicion. It may be that they're not attached to the Palace Guard. If they were among the men the Royal Commander sent to Camlach, they've been ordered to stand down, and it will be a hard job finding them. But we found somewhat almost as good."

"Go on," I said, intrigued.

"House Shahrizai is at war with itself." Ti-Philippe grinned lopsidedly. "The two that betrayed Melisande? Marmion and Persia? Well, Persia's dead."

"What?"

"Oh, yes." Remy took a long drink of wine, eyes sparkling. "It was an accident, in Kusheth, my lady; a fire in her manor-house. Only a few of the Lady Persia's men-at-arms, they did not think it an accident. And neither did two of her kin. So they have sponsored them, three men-at-arms, to the Palace Guard, where they could keep an eye on Lord Marmion."

"They think Marmion did it? Her own brother, and an ally at that?" My mind began to tick over the possibilities. A dreadful thing, yes, but dreadful things have been known to happen even in the Great Houses of Terre d'Ange.

"This fellow," Ti-Philippe said, "Branion, his name was, he said it was the Lady Persia that the Duc de Morhban approached first. She was the one who persuaded Lord Marmion to join her in giving over their cousin. This Branion, he thinks Lord Marmion only went along with it so he could set her free. Now Melisande holds him in high regard, all the while he holds the Queen's trust. Only Persia must have known something, or guessed. And now the House is split over it, but they don't dare accuse him without proof."

"Marmion might have got past the guards at Melisande's chamber," I said thoughtfully. "They knew he was her cousin; they'd have let him in to speak with her on the eve of her death. They did me. Joscelin." I turned to him. "Ysandre questioned the Shahrizai. There was talk about that, at least; they were under a lot of suspicion. Didn't one visit Melisande that night? After . . . after I did?"

He tore off a hunk of bread, frowning. "Yes. But it was Persia, not Marmion. She needed to beg Melisande's forgiveness, she said." He shrugged. "I don't know if it's true. But she did leave, and well before daybreak. The guard at the stairs backed her story, or Ysandre would never have let it go. He saw her coming and going." Joscelin paused, then added, "Ghislain de Somerville said he saw her leave the audience hall in tears, after Ysandre was done questioning her. He said it was the only time he'd ever seen one of House Shahrizai cry."

"But not Marmion." Deep in thought, I rapped my spoon against my empty stew bowl. "Well. Even if he did visit Melisande, the guard at the postern gate would have challenged him. So if he was involved . . ."

"There still had to be someone else," Fortun said, finishing my thought. "Someone the guard would have trusted."

"Yes." I set down my spoon. "Which gives us a new question: Who is in league with Lord Marmion Shahrizai, and why? And the answer to those questions . . ." I smiled, ". . . lies in my purview."

"Phèdre," Joscelin murmured, gazing into his wine-glass. "Have a care with the Shahrizai."

"He's not Melisande." I did not need to add that Marmion Shahrizai was as the pale moon beside the blazing sun next to his cousin. Joscelin knew it. Poets wrote odes to Melisande Shahrizai, although I never heard one that did her justice. They still sing them; they just change the names. Even inadequate verses were too beautiful to sacrifice to politics.

"No." He gave me a hard look. "But a viper is no less dangerous for being small. And if Marmion Shahrizai arranged the death of his own sister, he'll scruple at naught."

"I'll be careful."

"Ysandre favors him," Ti-Philippe announced. "So the guards say. He makes her laugh."

Well he might; from time out of mind, House · Shahrizai has produced deadly skillful courtiers. None of them have ever held the throne – nor even the sovereign duchy of Kusheth – but they have amassed tremendous amounts of wealth, and a network of influence rivaled by none. If Marmion was in league with Melisande, then he had sacrificed some of his allies in gaining Ysandre's trust. If any survived, they must be nervous.

"Well," I mused aloud. "If the Captain of the Guard allows it, maintain contact with these disgruntled Shahrizai retainers, and learn what you may. More than ever, it's important that we find the men on guard that night at Troyes-le-Mont."

"Yes, my lady!" Grinning, Remy gave me a crisp salute. "We didn't do too badly, though, did we?"

"No," I said. "Not badly at all. Except for the fighting part."

"My lady!" Ti-Philippe protested. "He said we were lackeys to a——"

"Stop," I said mildly, cutting him off. The words died in his mouth. "Philippe, you have pledged your service to an *anguissette* and a Servant of Naamah. If the jests you hear are no worse than the ones you have made yourself, then you will be quiet and swallow them."

Muttering, he subsided into some semblance of acquiescence.

"What if they are worse?" Remy inquired.

"They couldn't be," I answered him dryly.

It may seem at times as if a riddle has been chased to ground, all possibilities exhausted, all avenues of inquiry covered. So it seemed to me that night, but in the morning, a new thought struck me. Thelesis de Mornay, the Queen's Poet, had interviewed many of the survivors of Troyes-le-Mont, taking copious notes for her epic of the Ysandrine Cycle. Mayhap there was somewhat in her notes that might prove useful.

I voiced my suggestion to Joscelin as he came in from

his morning's exercises, and he nodded agreement. "It's worth a try, at any rate." He smiled. "I missed her visit, the other day. I'd not mind seeing her."

We arrived at the Palace at midday, and were swiftly granted audience. Thelesis' rooms in the Palace were spacious and well-appointed, with an elegant mural of Eisheth at her harp on the eastern wall and a lovely bronze statue of the Tiberian poet Catiline. For all of that, they were a mess, strewn about with books stacked in teetering piles, carelessly heaped scrolls and half-scratched parchments. Truly, a working poet's quarters.

"Phèdre, Joscelin!" The ink smudged on her cheek took nothing away from her glowing welcome. "I'm pleased you've come. Joscelin Verreuil, let me look at you." Thelesis took his hands, regarding him with pleasure. "You look splendid," she declared. He bent to kiss her cheek. Thelesis de Mornay was one of the few people for whom Joscelin felt unalloyed affection.

"So do you," he said fondly. "I hope you've been keeping well."

"Well enough." Thelesis gestured to her blazing fireplace. "Ysandre makes certain there's no chance of my taking a chill," she said, amused. "It's hot enough for a steam bath in here, most of the time. I hope you don't mind. So tell me, what brings you here?"

I told her, and watched her expression turn keen and thoughtful.

"I took some notes, I remember that much. Ghislain de Somerville was dreadfully upset; his father had entrusted the watch to his command that night."

Joscelin and I exchanged a glance. He shook his head slightly.

"You don't suspect——" Thelesis began, then stopped. "Ghislain. You do."

"I don't want to," I said. "We travelled under Ghislain's command from the banks of the Rhenus to the mountains of Camlach. He could have laughed in my face, when I proposed we offer Isidore d'Aiglemort a chance at redemption, and he didn't. But still."

"Not Ghislain," Joscelin said firmly. "I don't suspect Ghislain."

I shrugged. "What did he tell you?"

Thelesis moved stacks of paper and books, unearthing a bulky folio tied with leather thongs. "I think this is the right one," she said ruefully, glancing at a marking scratched hastily on an upper corner. "This may take a moment."

We sat quiet, waiting while Thelesis de Mornay shuffled through sheaves of parchment.

"If it were verse," she murmured, "I'd have it committed to memory, you know, but I chose in the end to give scant play to Melisande's disappearance . . . let her be a footnote in the annals of history, after all, it is better than she deserves . . . here it is." Holding her notes at arm's length, she read aloud. " 'And the night passed fair quiet, with the solemnity appropriate to an eve whose dawn brings the execution of a member of D'Angeline peerage. I made my rounds at one bell, and three, and five, and all was quiet. Then with the changing of the guard at dawn, all seven hells broke loose, when Phanuel Buonard made to relieve the guard at the postern gate and found him dead of a knife to the heart. He ran shouting through the lower halls for my father, and I caught him to ask what was the matter. By the time he had told me, half the guard had mustered in the lower quarters, and I had to order many back to their stations. By now, my father had emerged, and assumed command unthinking. He wasted no time in ordering a detachment to the second floor, to Melisande Shahrizai's chamber where she was confined. There, he found her guards slain; one with a dagger to the ribs, and the other with his throat cut. The chamber itself was empty.' " Thelesis cleared her throat and looked up apologetically. "That's all, I'm afraid. It's not much help."

"Nothing we didn't know, at any rate," Joscelin observed.

"That's not true." Pinching the bridge of my nose in thought, I glanced up to meet their surprised gazes. "We know that it didn't happen before five bells. We know that Ghislain commanded the watch that night, and not his father Percy. We know that the death of the gatekeep was discovered before the disappearance of Melisande, and we know the name of the man who discovered it. And we know that the gate-keep and the guards at Melisande's door were not killed in exactly the same manner."

"Phèdre, there are a dozen different killing strikes with a dagger," Joscelin said reasonably.

"Mayhap." I shrugged. "But it is worth noting, nonetheless." I turned to Thelesis. "Thank you, indeed. Was there anyone else you spoke to about that night?"

"No." She shook her head, regretfully. "Would that I had, now. If you'll trust no one else, I still think you should speak to Ysandre."

"I will," I said. "When I know somewhat more."

ELEVEN

İ HAD learned no more by the day of the Midwinter Masque. It would have to do, for now the time was come to devote my energies unto the Service of Naamah.

Everything was in readiness. My costume and Fortun's attire had been delivered by an Eglantine House courier. After making certain that no final adjustments were wanting, I began my preparations by luxuriating in a hot bath fragrant with scented oil, with half a dozen candles set about to illuminate the wreathing steam.

"Phèdre."

It was Joscelin's voice at the door; I started, splashing water over the edge of the tub. "Come in."

He let himself into the room, closing the door carefully behind him. I leaned my arms on the rim of the tub, looking up curiously. "What is it?"

"I just wanted to see you one last time," he said quietly, kneeling opposite me and taking my hands in his. A rueful smile hovered at the corner of his mouth. "Before the rest of the world did."

"Oh, Joscelin." I squeezed his hands; mine were

slippery with water and oil. His face by candlelight was heartbreakingly beautiful. "Can you forgive me, a little anyway?"

"If you can me." He stroked my damp hair. "I love you, you know."

I nodded. "I know. And I you."

"Elua have mercy on us." He rose, and stood looking down at me. "You'll dazzle them. They won't reckon the tenth part of your worth, but you'll dazzle them, Phèdre." Tears stung my eyes; I'd no reply. After a moment, he gave his faint smile. "I've got to leave now if I'm to be at the Temple of Elua before dark. Naamah hold you in her hands and keep you safe."

Somewhere, I found my voice. "Thank you," I whispered.

With an unwontedly awkward bow, he nodded in return, and left.

I closed my eyes and let myself wallow in the bittersweet pain of it for a moment. At least he *had* come to see me, and given me his blessing, after a fashion. Naamah's Servant and a Cassiline; Elua have mercy, indeed. But there was too much at stake to linger overlong in the intricacies of my relationship with Joscelin. After a moment, I set it reluctantly aside and emerged from the bath to pat myself dry, calling for Gemma to assist me.

In truth, I could have used a coterie of attendants to make ready for the Masque. Since I didn't have them, I made do. My hair, I twined carelessly atop my head; it would have to wait until the last. First, came the gown.

Finespun as a whispered prayer, the scarlet jersey slithered over my head and fell like water about me, fitted close to the hips and then falling in immaculate folds to sweep the floor. It had a high neckline, rising like a crimson flame to clasp around my throat, belying the daring nature of the low back; and low it was, skimming the very base of my marque.

"Oh, my lady!" Gemma cried, wide-eyed, biting her knuckles.

"Not bad, considering the cost." I surveyed myself in the mirror. "Here." I pointed to the seam along my left side, which gaped open. "This is where you'll need to sew it. Are you sure you're up to the task?"

"Ye . . . yes." Her voice trembled, and her fingers shook with nervousness as Gemma endeavored to thread the needle Favrielle nó Eglantine had provided. After a minute, I sighed.

"Here, let me — no, wait. Gemma, fetch Remy, will you?"

She brought him in a trice, and he entered grinning, caught sight of me, coughed and promptly tripped over his feet.

"Remy." I eyed him impatiently. "If I remember right, all of Rousse's sailors are handy with a needle and thread, and you in particular, yes?"

"Elua!" He breathed it. "You really *do* notice everything! What do you need sewn, my lady?"

I told him. His grin grew enormous.

If things had gone otherwise in my life, I reflected, this would have been a very different evening. I could have made a fortune working under Delaunay's patronage; by the time I opened my own salon, I'd have been well settled. I would not have been the Comtesse de Montrève, with most of my monies tied to the welfare of my estate and its inhabitants, begging funds, at the mercy of a surly young clothier for my costume, with a war-seasoned sailor as my chief attendant.

It is a good thing Blessed Elua saw fit to endow me with a sense of humor.

As it happens, Remy did a neat job of it, and when he had finished, the scarlet gown clung to my upper body like it was painted there. That damnable Favrielle was a genius. "Thank you," I said to Remy, dismissing him; he grinned once more, and left chuckling. "Gemma, bring my cosmetics."

I do not use a great deal; I am young enough that it would be vulgar. A hint of kohl to accentuate my eyes, which would be mostly hidden behind the veil, and carmine for my lips. When that was done, I set about styling my hair. One must learn such things, in Cereus House; happily, I had not lost the touch. It took some time, recreating the elaborate coif I'd seen in Favrielle's illustration of Mara, but I was well satisfied when I was done.

The half-veil, I secured with hairpins topped with glittering black jet, and when it was in place, a stranger's face gazed back at me from the mirror. My veiled gaze was lustrous and mysterious, for once not betrayed by the scarlet mote in my left eye. The elaborate coif of my dark hair added an archaic elegance, and my fair skin glowed against the black gauze of the veil. And the gown – I rose, and it swirled around my hips in a crimson glissade.

"I think that will do," I said softly.

"My lady." Gemma held up a tangle of scarlet ribbons. "For your wrists."

I had forgotten, that was the final touch to the costume of Mara; silk ribbons bound about the wrists, hanging gracefully and fluttering. Deft enough now that her nerves had settled, Gemma tied them in place with elegant knots. I caught my breath, feeling them tighten around my wrists. That settled it, then. If there was any truth to old legends, Naamah's child Mara was truly an *anguissette*. I turned, ribbons trailing, surveying my reflection one last time. From the rear, the entire expanse of my back was bare, ivory skin framed in scarlet silk and bisected by the dramatic black lines and crimson accents of my marque.

"That will do, indeed." It was Fortun's calm, deep voice. He stood leaning in the doorway, surprisingly elegant in black velvet. The bronze key glinted dully on his chest, emblem of Asmodel's calling, and the black domino made his features mysterious. It peaked in twin horns, piercing the dark locks that fell over his brow. "Are you ready, my lady? Ti-Philippe has the carriage waiting."

I drew a deep breath. "I am ready."

He bowed, and held out his arm. "Then let us depart."

Perched in the driver's seat, Ti-Philippe wore an imp's mask shoved high on his forehead, the better to see. When I emerged on Fortun's arm, he gave a sharp whistle and stamped his feet, making the horses skittish.

"Enough," I said, laughing. "You're to be on your best behavior tonight."

"Much like yourself, my lady." With an irrepressible grin, he leapt down to throw open the carriage door. "Though it may mean somewhat different!"

Fortun handed me into the carriage and followed after, and in short order we were on our way.

Unaccountably, I found I was nervous. It had been a long time – two years, exactly – since I had appeared in public in the formal role of a Servant of Naamah. A great deal had happened since Melisande Shahrizai had paraded me before the peers of Kusheth on a velvet lead. Thinking on it, I reached instinctively to touch my throat where her diamond had lain. I had been a slave, an ambassador, and inherited a noble title; what I was about now was a far cry from my days as Delaunay's *anguissette*, where I had naught to do but that which my own nature dictated and to recount the observations of my faculties to my lord Anafiel Delaunay.

I had no master, no patron to whom to report, and I knew altogether too well the stakes for which I played.

"My lady." Fortun interrupted my thoughts. "There are bound to be inquiries. How do you wish me to handle them?"

He was right, of course; every D'Angeline past the age of five knew what it meant to see a Servant of Naamah bare his or her marque publicly. "Tonight," I said, "is the Longest Night, and I am attending the Queen's Midwinter Masque by her invitation as the Comtesse of Montrève. To conduct business, even Naamah's business, on this night would be unseemly, and you would do well to remind them of that — courteously, of course. As of tomorrow, however, if they wish to propose an assignation, they may send around a courier with a written offer."

Fortun cleared his throat. "Would I be right in assuming that no promises are to be made, as you are highly selective in the assignations you choose, but no one is to be discouraged, as your tastes are notoriously eclectic?"

"Yes." I smiled. "You would at that."

"Have you chosen already, my lady?" he asked curiously. "Who will be the first?"

"No." I brushed my fingers along the edge of the window-curtain. "My lord Delaunay cast out his bait, and fished accordingly. I will do the same. I don't know, in truth, who will bite."

"What if it's Marmion Shahrizai?"

"If it's Marmion," I said, "we will see." I ran the curtain through my fingers. Melisande had known me almost eight years before she had contracted me, excepting for Prince Baudoin de Trevalion's pleasure. It nearly drove me mad. I doubted her younger cousin could play her waiting game with the same devastating patience, but it would be interesting to see.

We rode for a time in silence. "It should be Joscelin here with you," Fortun said presently, his voice low. "He's right, I'm not trained to serve as a bodyguard. And he's the only one of us permitted to wear arms in the Queen's presence."

I leaned my head back against the cushion of the carriage-seat. "Joscelin is doing what he needs must do," I said, "as am I. Go where you are invited, listen and learn what you may. Don't grieve me on that score, Fortun."

"I'm sorry, my lady. Only . . ." He leaned forward, his gaze intent behind the eyeholes of his mask as he looked at me. "Begging your pardon, but anyone who does not choose to be at your side this night of all nights is a fool."

I smiled. "Thank you, chevalier. That is exactly what I needed to hear."

TWELVE

WE ENTERED the ballroom as the bells were striking nine.

"The Comtesse de Montrève!" shouted the crier, his voice half-lost in the din of music and conversation.

Nonetheless, it caused a stir.

It took some time, for eyes to see and rumors to spread. Favrielle had spoken truly, the costuming for the Midwinter Masque that year was ornate. Women, flounced and layered in swathes of fabric turned slowly, moving like galleons beneath the weight of their attire; the men were scarce less laden. Masked faces turned in my direction.

I felt it, the brunt of a hundred stares, as a path opened across the marble floor. In Cereus House, we were taught to move like a swaying willow, limbs disposed to grace, heads high with pride. I drew on all the strength of my training to make that passage, gazing at the crowd from behind my veil, feeling half-naked in my scarlet gown, ribbons trailing from my wrists. At my side, Fortun was a model of austere decorum.

And behind me, in the wake of the sight of my bared marque, the murmurs rose.

Truly, the Palace ballroom was a splendor that night. It is a vast, open space, pierced by a double row of slender columns. Wrapping around three walls is Le Cavaillon's gorgeous fresco of Elua and his Companions at banquet, and overhead, the ceiling is painted a midnight blue with gilded stars. In the very center of the hall stood a tree cunningly wrought of bronze, and from its branches hung a dozen fruits on silken threads; apples, pears, dates, figs and persimmons, plums and nectarines and others whose names I knew not.

At the far end, beneath the wall on which Elua, Cassiel and Naamah disported themselves, stood a small mountain crag and in it a grotto in which musicians struck a tableau as Hellene muses and played sweet tunes. Here and there stood false columns, hollow to the core, holding in niches clear glass lamps that gave a mellow light. Elsewhere, from the ceiling, hung chandeliers of glass lamps floating in colored waters, giving the illusion of fairy lights. Braziers burned sweet incense, and garlands of evergreen added its clean, resinous odor.

"Phèdre!" Ysandre de la Courcel, Queen of Terre d'Ange, cleaved a path through the revelers, her two grey-adorned Cassiline guards incongruously in tow. As was fitting, she was clad as the Snow Queen, in layers of frothing white gauze aglitter with diamonds. She wore the swan mask of House Courcel, an elaborate hood curving over her head, violet eyes behind the white-feathered mask. "I might not have known you with your veil, but with that marque, my dear! You did give warning. May I ask the nature of your costume?"

"Mara," I said, lifting one arm so the scarlet ribbons trailed from my wrist. "Naamah's daughter, gotten by a murderer, and Kushiel's handmaiden."

"Very apt." Ysandre's eyes looked amused behind her mask. "Well, near-cousin, I have greeted you properly and given sanction to your purpose here; let it not be said that I failed to give Naamah's Service its proper regard." With the effortlessness of one born and raised to command, she turned to find a servant exactly where she expected him, offering a salver with small glasses of cordial. *"Joie,"* Ysandre said, raising a glass in toast. "May the Longest Night pass swiftly and the light return."

"Joie." I took a glass and raised it in turn, drinking. The servant lingered as Ysandre moved on, proffering the tray to Fortun. He accepted a glass and drank, gasping at its clear, fiery taste. "To the Longest Night, chevalier!" I laughed, feeling the blood in my veins tingle with excitement. "Do you dance, Fortun? I never asked."

"Try me and see." Taking both our glasses, he set them on a passing servant's tray and bowed, escorting me to the dancing floor.

He did dance, and passably well; I am trained to follow anyone's lead. We looked well together, with the scarlet fabric of my gown swirling against the sober black velvet of his doublet and hose. I saw heads turn as we passed, puzzled whispers at my half-veiled face giving way to dawning recognition at the sight of my marque. I could feel it, almost, the intricate pattern etched the length of my spine, burning as if the ink were fresh-pierced into my skin by the marquist's tapper.

As our dance ended, I espied a figure clad as the Eremite of Seagrove making his way toward me, unrecognizable in flowing blue-green robes with a half-mask of the Eremite's features and a false beard of white curls that spilled down his chest. "Phèdre nó Delaunay," he said, and his tone, though formal, was warm with affection. "Your costume leaves you at a disadvantage to conceal your identity."

I smiled. "As your voice does you, my lord de Forcay."

Gaspar Trevalion, the Comte de Forcay, chuckled and embraced me. "Elua, child, but it's good to see you well! How does your peerage sit with you?"

"It would have sat better on Delaunay, my lord, but I do my best," I said honestly. Disowned by his father, Anafiel Delaunay de Montrève never held the title to which he was born; it was ironic that it had passed to me. And while I could not eliminate him from those I must suspect, I never doubted that Gaspar Trevalion's friendship with my lord Delaunay was genuine – nor, indeed, his affection for me. "Tell me, how have you been keeping?"

As we spoke, a tall woman costumed as an elegant shepherdess – with flounces enough to terrify any flock, I daresay – invited Fortun to squire her in a dance with a subtle beckon of her gilded crook. He glanced inquiringly at me, and I nodded.

"Your Cassiline is not with you," Gaspar observed.

"He is maintaining Elua's vigil on the Longest Night."

"A pity. Ghislain will be sorry to miss him. He has a great respect for that young man." He smiled. "As do I, although I'll admit, I thought Delaunay was mad when he told me he'd contracted one of the Cassiline Brotherhood to ward a Servant of Naamah."

"So did I," I said absently, scanning the costumed

crowd. "My lord de Somerville is here? No, wait, don't tell me." I spotted a tall, broad-shouldered figure in an osprey mask, a smaller mate in similar garb at his side, speaking to someone I didn't recognize at all. "There, beneath the fresco of Azza; that must be Bernadette with him."

"Indeed." Gaspar Trevalion sounded surprised. "I didn't know you'd met her."

"I haven't. I saw her at the trial." It was something of a delicate subject; Bernadette de Trevalion had been exiled for treason, though she'd had no part in her mother's machinations. It was Ysandre who had restored her, mending the breach through marriage to Ghislain de Somerville, the Royal Commander's capable son. Lent discretion by my veil, I stared, trying to place their companion by virtue of shape, stance or demeanor, but he evaded recognition. Even his costume, an elaborately striped affair with puffed sleeves, parti-color hose and a longnosed mask, defied placement. "Gaspar, who is that with them?"

"Ah." He smiled. "That, my dear, is Severio Stregazza, eldest-born son of Marie-Celeste de la Courcel Stregazza, grandson of the Doge of La Serenissima. Would you like to meet him?"

"Yes." I took his arm, resting my fingertips on his sleeve. "Very much, my lord."

Gaspar Trevalion was as good as his word, escorting me over forthwith. After exchanging fond greetings with Ghislain and making the formal acquaintance of his wife — I did not tell Bernadette that I had seen her sentenced to exile — I was introduced to the young Serenissiman lord.

"Charmed, Comtesse." Severio Stregazza's surly tone, in faintly accented D'Angeline, said otherwise. He tugged at the stiff ruff of lace at his neck. At close range, he had a sheen of sweat on his features, and he looked uncomfortable in his costume. Severio had been born and raised in La Serenissima. No more than a year or two older than me at best, he was clearly ill at ease in his surroundings and awkward at the evidence of his mixed blood at a D'Angeline fête. His hot, irritable gaze took my measure. "You're very beautiful," he said abruptly. "I suppose we're related somehow?"

"No, Prince Severio," I said, shaking my head. "My lord Anafiel Delaunay de Montrève of Siovale adopted me formally into his household, and it is his title that I inherited. We are no kin, you and I."

"That's a relief." He tugged harder at his collar, scowling. "Damn nigh every noble I've met claims kinship to the throne one way or another. I can't keep it all straight in my head."

"It is not easy, cousin," Bernadette commiserated kindly. "I grow confused myself, trying to sort out the tangled threads of Blessed Elua's descendants."

Severio Stregazza gave her an ungracious glance. I could not blame him for his anger and discomfort, in truth; in this, of all gatherings, his coarse curls and the ruder cast of his features showed clearly the dilution of Elua's lineage, brought to La Serenissima in the person of Benedicte de la Courcel, great-uncle to Ysandre. "Your inheritance seems clear enough, *cousin*."

"Looks can be deceiving." Ghislain slid his arm protectively about her. Although he remained calm, one could tell he was heated; a scent of apples hung in the air, hallmark of House Somerville, scions of Anael's lineage. "My wife has known betrayal and exile, Prince Severio, and the sovereignty of our duchy hangs on our offspring. I daresay you cannot claim the same."

"Blood tells, though, here." Severio shrugged. "Scions of Elua and his Companions!" He made a mockery of the words. "It means nothing, in La Serenissima. You can't know what it's like."

"Perhaps you will tell us, my lord," I offered.

"And will you pretend interest, for a price?" Harsh-voiced, Severio caught my wrist and gripped it hard, leering. "I have heard, Comtesse, whom you have sworn to serve! In La Serenissima, we keep our courtesans in their proper place, where they belong."

His grip pained me, and in the roughness of his hands, I felt his anger and frustration commingled, his need to strike out at all things D'Angeline and their attitude of implicit superiority toward all that was not. My blood beat quicker, responding to his anger, and I held his gaze steadily through the haze of my veil. "I serve Naamah, my lord, it is true. And for a price, I will pretend absolutely nothing."

There was a little silence around us; Gaspar, Ghislain and Bernadette, I daresay, did not know what transpired. But I knew, and the young Stregazza. If I have one pride in my calling, it is that I have never judged a patron wrongly – and I have never failed to recognize a patron upon meeting. Severio Stregazza was one of mine. After a moment, he released my wrist with a disgusted sound.

"I need a glass of cordial," he said, dismissing himself rudely.

Gaspar Trevalion stared after him. "What a strange young man," he observed. "Phèdre, what on earth is your interest in him?"

I could not explain to him the compulsions of an *anguissette*, and of a surety, I dared not discuss my suspicions concerning Melisande Shahrizai and the deadly coils of intrigue within the Stregazza family. Instead, I smiled. "I have a fancy," I said lightly, "to learn somewhat of La Serenissima. Surely he can tell me that much, at least."

"If you say so," Gaspar said slowly, eyeing me doubtfully.

What I would have said to allay his suspicions, I do not know; Gaspar Trevalion had been one of Delaunay's closest friends, and he was no fool. But happily, at that moment, a woman's hand touched my bare shoulder, and I turned in answer to see a drunken couple clad as Diana and Apollo, the twin moon-and-sun deities of the Hellenes.

"Tell me, Servant of Naamah," the woman said laughing, her silver mask askew on her lovely face, "Who does your costume represent? We have a bet, my brother and I."

I inclined my head to them, raising my arms so the scarlet ribbons trailed from my wrists. "Mara, my lady; Naamah's daughter, and Kushiel's handmaiden."

"I told you!" he said to her in drunken triumph.

The woman laughed again, brushing my veil with her fingertips. She was close enough that I could feel the heat of her body and smell *joie* sweet on her breath. "Then I shall have to pay the penalty for losing," she whispered. "We already agreed upon the settlement. When you receive my proposal, remember there is a debt of honor at stake."

"My lady," I said, struggling against dizziness. "I will remember it."

They laughed and moved on. Gaspar Trevalion in his

Eremite's costume shook his mock-bearded head at me. "Delaunay would be proud," he said wryly. "I think."

"Mayhap." Would that Mara's accoutrements included a fan, I thought; I could use a cool breeze. "My lord, the Serenissiman has the right of it, and there is *joie* to be drunk this night. Will you call upon me before you leave the City of Elua? It would please me greatly to offer you my hospitality ere you return home."

"I would be honored," Gaspar promised, bowing.

By this time, *joie* and wine flowed freely and the fête had reached the height of gaiety. I cannot begin to count the number of lords and ladies of the realm with whom I danced, bantered and flirted, nor the number of inquiries, discreet and overt, I received. I heeded the advice I had given Fortun, and made promises to none. It was a good hour before my diligent chevalier found his way back to my side, looking somewhat disheveled for his absence.

"My lady," he greeted me, a touch out of breath. "It seems the interest you incite rubs off on your companions!"

I laughed, and smoothed his rumpled hair. "Whose clutches did you escape, Fortun?"

"A gentleman does not tell," he replied, grinning. "Let me say only that there are some few D'Angeline nobles who think their suits may be heard clearer if I plead for them. They are laying bets on who will be your first patron, my lady."

"Let them," I said with satisfaction. "For now, do you think you might secure us a place at the banquet table?"

"Consider it done."

No formal dinner is served on the Longest Night, but the Queen's table was heaped high at all times and a steady stream of servants came and went, bearing away the empty trays and platters and bringing an endless array of foods. Plates and silver clinked and rattled, gleaming by candlelight, and guests ate and chattered incessantly, lifting wineglasses, dipping fingers in bowls of rosewater to rinse. I dined on pheasant glazed with honey and thyme, so tender and sweet it near melted in my mouth; I daresay Fortun sampled five dishes to my every one. There was a contingent of Cruithne at the table, representatives of Drustan mab Necthana, and we had a lively time conversing once they discovered I was in their midst, for many of them were awkward still with the D'Angeline tongue, and I had not forgotten my sometime role as translator.

It was during one such conversation that the musicians struck up a lively Caerdicci tune, and I felt a presence at my shoulder. Turning, I gazed up to see Severio Stregazza.

"Comtesse." He bowed curtly and extended his hand. "Will you dance?"

"It would be my great pleasure." Taking his hand, I rose gracefully and followed to join him on the dancing floor.

For all that I had boasted of my skill, the Serenissiman led awkwardly, and I was hard put to follow him in such a manner as to conceal it. Still, I managed — we are taught to do no less, in Cereus House. The long nose of his mask bumped against my bare shoulder, and his gaze burned through the eyeholes.

"I heard the King of the Dalriada went to war for one night in your arms," he said abruptly. "Is it true?"

"Yes, my lord." Anticipating a swift turn, I followed. "After a fashion." It was no more and no less than the truth; I did not deem it necessary to mention that Eamonn mac Conor had gone to such lengths out of jealousy of his sister as much as desire for me. Eamonn is dead now, slain on the field of Troyes-le-Mont, and at any rate, he would rather have the latter believed than the former, I think.

"Terre d'Ange is at peace." He steered us through a crowd, then out. "What cost, then, for a Prince of La Serenissima?"

"My lord," I said mildly, raising my head to meet his gaze. "I have set no price, save what Naamah's honor demands. When the Longest Night has passed, I will entertain offers, and we shall see. But this much, I will say." I smiled, and felt his heat rise at it. "Naamah's interests were ever . . . eclectic. And you are the only Serenissiman prince in attendance upon my debut returning to her service."

Severio's arms, holding me, tensed, though he did naught but nod. When the Caerdicci air was ended, he released me with a stiff bow, and stalked away. I would hear from him. I had no doubt of it.

The pause following the end of the tune stretched into silence, growing slowly apparent to the crowd. The musicians in their mountain grotto took up their instruments and slipped away. One by one, the revelers fell back from the dance floor. In the silence, the tocsin began to beat. The horologists had proclaimed the hour, and Night's Crier made his way through the hall, sounding his brazen gong with a steady beat. I felt a touch at my arm as Fortun joined me, glancing swiftly at me. On the far side of the colonnade, I saw Ysandre de la Courcel, resplendent in her costume as the Snow Queen, surrounded by a coterie of admirers, her gaze fixed on the false mountain.

When the Night's Crier reached its base, he sounded the tocsin one last time.

All at once, darkness fell. There must have been servants at every candle, to snuff them with such utter thoroughness, and where the lamps hung suspended in chandeliers, they lowered rows of silver cones strung on ropes to extinguish them in all swiftness. Only the lamps in the hollow columns continued to glow, and a single lamp above the mountain crag.

With a dreadful, grinding sound, the mountain itself split open to reveal a hollow core, a stair and a promontory; and on it, the Winter Queen, aged and hobbled, bearing her blackthorn staff. I have friends who are players, I know how such things are done. Even so, I gasped. Everyone bowed their heads, even Ysandre; I was hard put not to kneel, the habit deeply ingrained. From the far end of the hall, where the great doors were closed, came a measured pounding of a spear-butt. Once, twice, thrice.

"Let the doors be opened to admit the return of the light!" Ysandre cried imperiously, and the great doors were flung open at her command.

Through them drove a splendid chariot, hung with lamps and drawn by a matched pair of white horses. In it rode the Sun Prince, gloriously garbed in cloth-of-gold, his mask that of a beautiful youth, surrounded by gilded rays. A murmur of awe arose in the hall. Its team moving at an impeccably matched pace, it drew nigh to the foot of the split-open crag. Standing in the chariot, the Sun Prince pointed his gilt spear at the Winter Queen.

She seemed not to move, and yet her garment was riven, falling away to reveal the slender form of a maiden within. In a single, bold gesture, she drew off her aged mask and showed herself to be in the flower of youth, shaking out golden tresses that fell to her waist. And light returned to the hall, tongues of flame snaking up long oil-soaked wicks strung to countless lamps, igniting them all at once. Suddenly, the hall was ablaze in light, seeming twice as bright for the darkness that had preceded it.

We cheered; we all cheered. One cannot help it, at such a time. From the far corners of the hall, the musicians returned, playing with redoubled vigor. The Sun Prince leapt from his chariot, and the Winter Queen, now a Spring Maiden, descended from her mount to join him on the dancing floor. In a trice, they were joined by a dozen couples, and at the corner of the floor, Ysandre's coterie began to break up, vying for the honor of procuring her next glass of *joie*.

I exhaled a breath I'd not known I held, leaning on Fortun's arm. It was a greater spectacle than the one at Cereus House, which is famed throughout the City, although I daresay they lay no odds on the players in Night's Doorstep. These were professionals, performing at the Queen's behest, with scores of artisans to assist them.

"Shall we dance, my lady?" Fortun inquired.

"And it please you, Comtesse de Montrève," a man's silken voice insinuated, "I would beg that honor."

Turning, I espied my latest suitor clad as Hesperus, the evening star. His doublet and hose were of a deep twilight blue, and over them he wore a surcoat of a deeper blue silk, the shade of encroaching night. For a rarity, the cut was elegant and simple, flattering his well-made form. His coat was adorned with intricate brocade, and in it were set myriad bits of mirror, so that he glimmered with the subtle light of the evening sky, and a silver star mask obscured his features. I knew him by his voice, his grace and his black hair, that fell in a river of finelinked braids down his back.

"My lord Shahrizai," I said, keeping my voice cool. "Let us do so."

With an immaculate bow, Marmion Shahrizai escorted me onto the dancing floor.

If I had had a dozen or more partners that night, and I had, not a one approached his skill. One trains as hard to be the perfect courtier as courtesan, I think, and the Shahrizai are without peer. Marmion swept me over the floor, one hand holding mine, one placed with surety low on my back, and I needed no more think to follow his lead than I need think to breathe. Indeed, I heard murmurs of admiration as we passed, for it is in the D'Angeline nature to admire beauty in all its forms. We were well-matched, he and I.

In the scant inches that separated us, it was another matter.

"So tell me," he said, smiling pleasantly, "have you heard from my cousin?"

I smiled back at him, my movements flowing effortlessly with his. "It is strange you should ask, my lord; I was wondering the same about you."

Marmion Shahrizai bent his head tenderly beside mine. "If I heard from Melisande," he murmured in my ear, "the message would likely be delivered at knife-point. But I have been thinking, little Comtesse." He held me at arm's length as we executed a complex series of steps, then drew me in close again as the music slowed. "Someone reached the postern gate unchallenged at Troyes-le-Mont, yes? And who was better trusted and less feared than the Queen's pet *anguissette*." His expression never changed, smiling down at me. Only I would have caught the cruelty in it. "You have been in league with my cousin from the first, Comtesse; do not think I am blind to it. I assure you," he whispered, his grip tightening on my hand, "I am watching."

It brought me hard against him, my loins pressed firm against his, my breasts brushing his chest. I craned my neck back to gaze at his implacable, smiling star-masked face. "Do you pretend loyalty to the Queen, my lord Shahrizai?" I asked him breathlessly, struggling to match his composure. "I hear you set the fire that killed your sister, lest she reveal the complicity with which you betrayed her."

Marmion's smile hardened and his hand splayed on my back, pressing me harder against him. I could feel his fingertips digging into my flesh, and beneath his breeches, his phallus rising, rigid and pressing against me. His other hand clenched hard on mine, grinding the small bones together. "Do you?" he asked. "I hear a great many things about you, too, Comtesse. I trust not all are slanderous lies, as is this thing you have heard."

Kushiel's Dart strikes where it will; my body betrayed me, yearning toward his. He danced with consummate grace, and no one but I knew that his hips moved with the subtlety of a skilled tribadist, moving against me as his iron grip held me in place. I fought unsuccessfully against the flutter in my loins, the surging warmth. "Lord Shahrizai," I said, my voice taut, "I beg you release me."

"Will you make a scene?" He smiled remorselessly; my left hand was numb from his grip and I moved helplessly against him, rippling with desire. "Or give your *signale*, perhaps, *anguissette*? I know all about you, and I am watching. Understand that nothing will come between me and the Queen; not some tattooed barbarian princeling, not my cousin and, surely, not you!"

The musicians ended their air with a flourish, hiding my gasp as Marmion Shahrizai released me, nigh on the verge of climax. He gazed down at me superciliously from behind his mask. "When you think to cross me, little *anguissette*," he said with amused contempt, "I pray you remember this dance."

"My lord," I said, drawing myself up with difficulty. "The Aeolian harp sounds at each passing breeze, but that does not mean the tune is masterfully played."

A moment's pause, and then he gave a cynical laugh and bowed. "You put a good face on it, *anguissette*. I should expect nothing less from one of Melisande's creatures, and you are an exceptional one at that." He touched my face lightly in warning. "I have said it once; do not make me say it twice. Whatever game you play, keep it far from me."

As I watched him take his leave, Fortun made his way to my side once more. "My lady," he asked anxiously, "do you wish me to speak to him?"

"No," I murmured, watching the candlelight diffuse in a thousand shifting points from the Shahrizai's mirrored coat. "Either he's a fool, to overplay his hand thus, or he's more subtle than I credited, to make me think as much. And I rather doubt it is the latter. Let us keep our eye on Lord Marmion Shahrizai, to see what else he may reveal. But for now, I think we must seek our traitor elsewhere." I sighed, my body throbbing with desire unfulfilled. "Fortun, if you care for me, stay at my side the remainder of this Longest Night, and see that I do naught I will regret come dawn."

"I promise," he vowed stoutly.

Somewhat to my dismay, he did.

Thirteen

"ELUA HAVE mercy!" Gemma entered the sitting room staggering under the weight of the parcels and letters she bore. "My lady, how many more . . . oh!" A neatly ribboned missive dangling a small, stoppered bottle slid from her grasp and struck the floor. The spicy scent of cloves filled the air as the wax seal cracked and oil leaked from the bottle.

"Never mind," I said absently, setting aside a pile of opened proposals to make room for the latest. "Put them here, thank you."

"You'll need a larger house, at this rate." Ti-Philippe carefully detached the leaking bottle from the letter and placed it upright on the table, licking oil of cloves from his fingers and making a face. "Too strong."

"It's not supposed to taste good, exactly. It sweetens the breath." I picked up the missive, glancing at the seal. The Baron d'Eresse, an Eisandine lord with interests in the spice trade. "Good for toothaches, too. If I were in the market for imports, I'd consider him." Since I wasn't, I put his letter on the likely-to-decline pile. "Here, help me sort through these latest."

Happily, for there had been a great many proposals delivered in the past days, all three of my chevaliers found the prospect amusing enough that none minded playing at secretary. For a time, there was no sound in the sitting room save the faint crack of seals breaking and the rustle of paper.

"Ah!" Remy laughed aloud. "A brother and sister, my lady; who hold jointly the Marquisate de Fhirze. Shall I put them on the decline pile?"

"I should think – oh, wait." I caught sight of the seal, twinned masks of Diana and Apollo. "No, I liked her. I'll see it."

"As you wish." He grinned, eyebrows raised.

"My lady," Fortun said quietly, looking up from the missive he scanned. It was unopened, a scroll of thick vellum tied with a gold cord and sealed with red wax. "I think you will be interested in this."

"Whose is it?" Accepting the scroll, I glanced at the seal; too crudely drawn for D'Angeline work, it depicted a Serenissiman carrack at harbor, a tower in the background. The insignia of the Stregazza family. "My lord Severio," I mused, cracking the seal and sliding off the cord. "I wondered how long he would wait." I skimmed the contents of his letter.

No one noticed when the scroll fell from my nerveless fingers.

"Phèdre?" Joscelin, entering the room, checked at my expression. I looked blankly at him. "Are you all right?"

"Yes." I blinked, picked up the scroll and handed it to him. "Look."

He read it quickly – it was only a couple of lines – and looked bewildered. "Does he jest?"

"No." I shook my head. "I don't think so. He didn't seem much for humor."

" 'No one outbids the Stregazza,' " Joscelin read aloud in a flat tone. " 'Twenty thousand in gold to be the first.' " Ignoring the collective indrawn breath of my chevaliers and a faint squeak of astonishment from Gemma, he tossed the scroll on the table. "No poetry, no protestations of desire and no pretty sentiments in honor of Naamah," he observed. "But you can't argue with the price, if that's what matters."

I looked coolly at Joscelin. "Severio Stregazza is three-quarters Caerdicci, and raised in La Serenissima. If he lacks the grace and polish to compete with half the royal D'Angeline court, at least he has the wit to know it. I promised him no pretense. He has taken me, I think, at my word."

"He's a boor," Fortun murmured.

"Yes," I said. "He is. And I am going to accept his offer."

"What — " Gemma was still wide-eyed at the figure. "My lady, what will you do with all that money?"

I smiled. "You will see."

As it happened, they learned sooner rather than later what I intended with the sum. It took the better part of two days to hammer out the terms of the assignation, with Remy serving as my representative. He had a knack, it seemed, for such things. It was necessary to explain to Severio the guild-laws that bound the terms of our contract, and the penalties for breaching them. It is a serious business in Terre d'Ange; to violate the rights of one of Naamah's Servants is to violate the precept of Blessed Elua, and is the gravest form of blasphemy.

Elsewhere, I am told, courtesans are largely dependent on the whims of their patrons. It is not so among D'Angelines.

The nature and purpose of the *signale* needed also be explained to the Serenissiman Prince, for although I heard a group of young gallants had taken him to the Night Court, it was to Orchis House they went, for lovemaking and merriment. Valerian and Mandrake alone among the Thirteen Houses use the *signale*, and at Mandrake, it is for the benefit of the patrons. In the arts of pain, protestation is a part of the game; it is therefore important that a *signale* be established. I should know, having gone to extreme lengths without speaking mine.

Choosing the word itself was simple, for I have had the same one since first I was an adept: Hyacinthe. He was the truest friend I ever had, and my refuge and sanctuary from childhood onward. If I chose his name in part to annoy Delaunay all those years ago – and I did – I chose it now for Hyacinthe himself, who made the greatest sacrifice of all of us on that fateful journey.

My plans kept me busy, and by the time Remy returned with the signed contract and a nervous clutch of Palace Guardsmen surrounding two laden mules, I had an appointment waiting.

"Half on signing," Remy called, grinning. "As you asked, my lady."

"Good." Standing in the doorway, I fastened the clasp of my *sangoire* cloak. "Now bid them take it to Eglantine House. I've a meeting with the Dowayne."

His mouth fell open and he gaped at me; the Guardsmen grumbled. "You're not – "

"It's my fee, and I'll do as I please with it," I said

mildly, then raised my voice. "Joscelin! Will you do me the honor of beholding how I disperse this money that so offends you?"

If I thought to find him apologetic, I was wrong; he came at my call with an amused expression, adjusting his vambraces. "Will it please you if I admit to curiosity?"

"It would please me if you admitted to rather more," I said, "but I will settle for that. Come and see."

The Dowayne of Eglantine House was one Moirethe Lereux, a stately woman in her middle forties, without the madcap streak that marks so many of that house; which, I suspect, was a large part of how she came to be its Dowayne. I have heard also that she played the harp so beautifully that warriors wept and criminals confessed at the sound of it, but I never had the pleasure of hearing her play. No adept of the Night Court is easily swayed by the sight of money and a Dowayne less than most, but even Moirethe was hard put not to look twice as the Palace Guardsmen deposited clinking sack upon sack on her desk. I could see the Chancellor of the House itching to count it after I thanked the Guardsmen and dismissed them. They left posthaste, shaking their heads at the madness of Naamah's Servants.

"Are we agreed, then?" It felt strange, sitting and facing the Dowayne as a D'Angeline noblewoman fair swimming in gold, with a Cassiline and a chevalier attendant behind me. "Four thousand for her marque, and four thousand against the House's loss of her art and labor in the time she would have made it."

"And a balance of two thousand toward the purchase of materials and a year's patronage at Eglantine House should she so desire; hers clear if she does not," Moirethe

Lereux agreed, glancing over our written agreement. "I am in accord, Comtesse. Shall we sign?"

We did, and it was witnessed and approved by the Chancellor after he had opened and peered into each of the sacks, weighing Severio's coinage with sensitive fingers.

"Done," the Dowayne proclaimed. "Anselme." She beckoned to an apprentice, who knelt quietly *abeyante*. "Will you bring Favrielle, please?"

He fetched her as quickly as he could, I think; still, we had a time to wait. Moirethe Lereux bided patiently, serving us chilled wine and sugared almonds, of which Remy ate a great many. When Favrielle nó Eglantine entered scowling, it was clearly at her own pace.

"You," she said without pleasure, beholding me. "I've got half the petty lordlings in the City plaguing me on your account, Comtesse! I didn't ask you to tell *everyone* who made that gown."

"I didn't," I protested.

"Fortun told them," Remy volunteered helpfully. "They daren't ask you, my lady."

Moirethe Lereux cleared her throat. "Favrielle, for your services in designing a costume for the Midwinter Masque, the Comtesse Phèdre nó Delaunay de Montrève has chosen to bestow a patron-gift upon you. The balance of your marque as established prior to your . . . accident . . . is paid in full, and the balance of funds from the loss of your services. To you is remanded the sum of two thousand ducats, which you may apply toward materials and a year's patronage in Eglantine House if you so choose. You may retain such assistants as you have trained, and all profits in that time would be your own. If you do not wish to remain here," she added, "it is yours clear, but we would be pleased to have you."

Sharp-tongued as she was, Favrielle was at a loss for words, staring at me. "Why would you do that?" she asked me finally, her voice sounding young and bewildered without its customary edge. "You don't even *like* me!"

Cocking my head, I regarded the seamstress, her pretty face with its scattering of golden freckles marred only by her scarred lip now that astonishment had smoothed away her habitually cross expression. "You told me to let you know when I could transform you as surely as Kushiel's Dart unmade my flaw," I said. "Well, I cannot make you into an *anguissette*, and I do not think you would like it if I did. But I can give you the means to transform yourself from an unfit adept indentured to years of service in Eglantine House to a woman of independent means and the foremost couturier in the City of Elua."

Still staring, Favrielle gave a short laugh. "You're mad!"

"Mayhap." I shrugged. "So too have been the proposals I have received, and your genius may well have doubled their insanity. That much, then, do I give back, and we are at quits, you and I."

Biting her lower lip, she turned to the Dowayne. "That's it, then? I'm free?"

"Yes." Moirethe handed her a document. "By the tenets of the Night Court, of course, you are forbidden to bear Eglantine's marque on your skin, as you have not, properly speaking, been engaged as a Servant of Naamah. But the amount of your marque is paid in full, and your contract is returned to you."

Favrielle accepted the contract absentmindedly, her

gaze distant as she calculated. "I'll stay," she said abruptly
to the Dowayne. "Two thousand's not enough to do it
properly, not with the costs of lodging and materials. In a
year's time, I can earn enough to set up my own lines of
credit with merchants and hire my own assistants. But I'll
not work free for Eglantine House."

"Of course." Moirethe Lereux spread her hands. "Any
arrangements you make with adepts of the House will be
strictly on commission. Provided, shall we say, that you
continue to train such assistants as you choose and allow
them to work on the House's behalf when precedence
requires. We can negotiate such occasions as they arise."

"Done." Favrielle nodded. Regarding me once more,
she knit her brows in a scowl. "I'll not work free for you
either, Comtesse. You chose this, not I. There is no debt
between us."

"I agree," I said mildly.

She narrowed her eyes gaugingly. "Do you have any
money left?"

Remy coughed, and I could hear a faint sound as
Joscelin's elbow dug into his side. "I will," I said, ignoring
them. "Once the assignation is completed, and I have
repaid my debt to my factor. Why?"

Her scarred lip curled wryly. "I've set a high tidemark
with you, Comtesse. The City will look to you, now, to set
the mode. It will serve us both well if I continue to design
your wardrobe. Anyway, whether I like you or no, you're
interesting to dress."

"Then," I said, rising, "I will call upon you again,
Favrielle nó Eglantine, when my coffers are full again."

So it was that we took our leave, and Joscelin waited
until we were in the courtyard before bursting into rueful

laughter. "Phèdre," he said, shaking his head. "Will you never be done with surprising me?"

"If you thought better of me," I retorted, "you would not be so surprised."

No longer laughing, he looked at me with sorrow in his summer-blue eyes. "You don't make it easy," he said quietly. "It would be simpler, if it were only about money."

"Yes." I sighed. "You'd have fled back to the Cassiline Brotherhood long ago. But I'll not pretend to simple greed, Joscelin, just to ease your conscience. Stand at the crossroads if you will, but if you'll not choose, I'll move on without you."

"I know," he murmured, and we spoke no more of it.

FOURTEEN

ON THE day of my assignation with Severio Stregazza, a summons came from the Rebbe to meet with him for another session. In truth, I had been somewhat remiss in my studies, but he had promised to tell me tales of the Lost Book of Raziel, and I did not want the opportunity lost. Gauging the hour to a nicety, I determined I had the time to spare.

Unprepared as I was, there are times when distraction serves better than focus, and this proved one such; half-unthinking, I rattled through the verses of the Tanakh he'd assigned me without an error. Expecting to have my knuckles struck, instead I was rewarded with one of the Yeshuites' apocryphal tales, such as are passed from mouth to mouth and not recorded in their books.

"It is commonly said," the Rebbe told me, "that Sammael and others among Adonai's servants were jealous that He had given such power to Edom the First Man; power even to master the *Malakhim*." (For so, I may add, did the Yeshuites name angels in the Habiru tongue.) "And Sammael stole the Sefer Raziel, and cast it into the waters."

"I have heard as much, Master," I replied politely.

"I am not done." The Rebbe glowered at me. "There is another tale, of Lilit, Edom's first wife, whom Adonai wrought before the mother of all, Ieva. Out of dust He made them both, equal to equal, and blew the breath of life into their flesh — and sorry enough He was, for Lilit disdained to serve beneath Edom and fled, taking with her the Sefer Raziel. And when Adonai sent his *Malakhim* to retrieve her, she laughed, and opened the book and read aloud a word, commanding them by the Sacred Name to return empty-handed."

Intrigued, I rested my chin in my hand. The One God had sent his servants to bid Elua to return, too. The first, who came with a sword, Blessed Elua charmed with his sweetness; the second, who came with a plea, Elua answered with his own red blood, piercing his flesh and bleeding onto the rich soil of Terre d'Ange. So are we bound to this earth, we who are D'Angeline; even the followers of Cassiel, for it was he who handed Elua the dagger. But for all of that, I never heard that Elua and His Companions knew a word that could compel the One God's servants. "And?" I prompted.

"And Mikael, the commander-in-chief of the Lord's Host, strove with her and wrested the Sefer Raziel from Lilit, but he was bound by her command, and threw the book into the ocean, returning empty-handed to the Throne of the Lord," the Rebbe finished. "So it was that Adonai bid Rahab, Prince of the Deep, to retrieve the tome. If you say truly, perhaps it is that Rahab obeyed but in part, keeping back some few pages." He shrugged. "These are stories that are told. I do not know."

"What became of Lilit?"

The Rebbe fingered his *khai* pendant. "She wed Ashmedai, the Prince of Demons, and spawned six thousand children of darkness, who haunt our dreams at night, or so it is said. Until Yeshua ben Yosef was born, and they dared to tempt him, and he changed them into the likeness of black dogs, chaining them beneath Mount Seir, where they fester and howl until the Mashiach shall return, and put an end to their suffering."

"A lot of good that does me," I murmured. "Well, then, what became of the Lost Book of Raziel after Rahab brought it up from the deep?"

"Would you run before you walk?" the Rebbe asked sternly, pointing at the Tanakh scroll. "Next time, you study the Sh'moth. Perhaps then I will tell you more."

"Yes, Master." I sighed, and made ready to leave. "I will await your summons."

Keeping to the letter of our agreement, I smiled pleasantly at such folk as I saw upon departing the yeshiva, but made no effort to engage them in conversation. I was hard-put to ignore Joscelin's exemption from this charge, as he exchanged smiles and murmured greetings with half a dozen Yeshuite folk. Indeed, the young woman I had seen teaching schoolchildren on our first visit caught him back as we left, whispering something urgent to him and blushing as she reached up to slip a chain about his neck.

I would have asked him about it the moment the door closed behind us, were it not that a disturbance in the courtyard distracted me. Near to where our carriage awaited, a handful of Yeshuites stood arguing in Habiru; young men, all of them, ganging up on the youngest of the lot. I daresay I'd not have paid it much heed, were it not for the fact that all save the youngest were clad in D'Angeline fashion, eschewing their sober attire and sidelocks for such garb as soldiers might wear. Indeed, two of them bore swords at their sides.

" '. . . giveth snow like wool,' " one of them was saying, face thrust aggressively forward, " 'he scatters hoarfrost like ashes.' How do you take that to mean, Simeon, if it is not northerly? I tell you, we are not meant to sit idle, when Adonai bids us build a kingdom for Yeshua's return! Do you doubt? 'He sendeth forth his word and melts them.' It is the craven fear of old men and mewling women that keeps the Chosen of Terre d'Ange homeless as Tsingani!"

I glanced at Joscelin, who stood frowning thoughtfully at them. "What do they mean?" I asked him; one of the Yeshuites looked over, hearing my voice.

"You should join us, brother apostate!" he called to Joscelin. "We could make good use of a blade such as yours."

Joscelin shook his head politely, smiling, and opened the carriage door to hand me inside. I caught the door and held it ere he could close it. "Will you tell me?" I asked, and caught sight, unexpectedly, of a *khai* pendant hanging on his doublet, a small silver disc with the KhetYod symbol graven in black. "And this?" I added, lifting it from his chest.

"A gift," Joscelin said firmly, plucking it from my hand. "It is not your concern."

Pain, unexpected, lanced through my heart; his face was closed and shuttered to me. "Well, then," I gasped, catching my breath at it. "Will you tell me why they spoke of blades?"

For a moment, he only frowned at me, then answered reluctantly. "There is a prophecy that the Kingdom of Yeshua will be established to the north; further even than the Skaldi territories, and eastward. It is said that Yeshuites in other nations have left already to found a new homeland. Some of the younger ones wish to follow. They believe that they will need carve it out with steel."

"Very well." Regaining such composure as I could, I strove to keep my voice from trembling. "I did not know that. Thank you."

He nodded, expressionless, and made to close the door.

"Joscelin," I said, halting him once more, unable to help the spite that crept into my tone. "My lord Delaunay contracted you because his man Guy was slain by a creature of the Stregazza. Will you allow me to go to this prince of the Stregazza attended by a, a half-trained sailor," I cited his words maliciously, "or do you propose to attend me yourself, O Perfect Companion?"

His face might as well have been a mask as he bowed, the *khai* medallion swinging forward to clink against his crossed vambraces. "In Cassiel's name," he said coldly, "I protect and serve."

With that, he closed the carriage door firmly, leaving me alone to grit my teeth against the threat of tears. Against all odds, I heard Melisande's voice in my memory, melodic and amused. *Oh you protect well enough, but I'd ask better service, were you sworn to attend me, Cassiline.* Elua, I thought, stifling a despairing laugh, I wish she were here! No one else could appreciate the perverse anguish of my situation. I wondered if she had known, when she sent the cloak, the havoc it would wreak between Joscelin and me.

Most like she had, when I considered it; Melisande had been the first to perceive his feelings, long before I thought it possible. She had laughed out loud, the first time she'd seen him attendant upon me; it was the only time one of Delaunay's ploys truly caught her by surprise. Even at the end, when I stepped forward to reveal myself alive and give the testimony that condemned her, she had betrayed less.

Well, done was done, and I could not go back. In many ways, it was Melisande who united Joscelin and me, selling us together into slavery to the Skaldi. Now her game thrust us apart, the cloak a gambit I could not ignore. And the winding trail by which it had reached me led inevitably back to La Serenissima, and the coiled machinations of the Stregazza. I had a chance, now, to tease out some thread from that tangled coil in the person of the young Prince Severio. If I stood any chance of regaining Joscelin, it was on the far side of that mystery.

I could only hope he would still be here when I found my way clear.

I had come to such resolution as I could, and set the matter behind me. Cassiline guilt and Yeshuite prophecies would wait; I had a patron to attend. But the memory of Melisande's amusement stayed with me as I bathed and made ready, and whether I willed it or no, a slow eagerness heated my flesh as I considered this evening's entertainment. Elua, but it had been a long time! If Severio Stregazza lacked the skill to play me as I deserved, still, his blunt anger would suit my mood.

"Are you ready?" Joscelin asked curtly when I emerged at length, clad in a gown of deep blue velvet that made my skin glow like cream, my dark hair bound low at the nape of my neck with a fillet of gold. Ti-Philippe, who had offered to drive the carriage, stood nervously by. None of my chevaliers liked it when Joscelin and I quarreled; but I had gone well beyond that, in my mind.

"I am," I said softly, settling my *sangoire* cloak upon my shoulders.

"Let's go, then."

So much the same, and so different, walking with Joscelin through the Palace, en route to an assignation. I did not think I would ever become accustomed to the inclined heads, the murmured greeting, "Comtesse." The whispers, though, after I passed; those were the same. And Joscelin, austere and disapproving – that was the same. It was only the reason that was different. That, and the fact that instead of the ashen-grey garb of his former brethren, he wore sober livery of black and green, the Montrève crest wrought small over his heart, and hung about his neck, a *khai* pendant on a silver chain.

No one, though, would mistake him for aught but a Cassiline. It was not only the traditional arms he bore – twin daggers low on his waist, the longsword at his back and steel vambraces buckled on his forearms – but the sternness of his mien, the odd combination of rigid dignity and fluid grace that marked members of the Brotherhood. In Montrève, he'd all but lost the habit of stiffness. It had returned, here.

Idiot, I thought, and felt guilty at it.

As the grandson of the Doge, Severio had brought a retinue of Serenissiman servants, and I was ushered into his quarters with respectful greetings and sidelong glances. Ysandre had granted her cousin fine lodgings indeed, I thought, gazing around. I did not wonder at it, for Severio was the first emissary from her Serenissiman kin to acknowledge her since her coronation; due to the intervention of war or the bad blood between her uncle the Duc L'Envers and her great-uncle Prince Benedicte's descendents, I could not say, although doubtless the latter played some part in it.

"Contessa." A servant in Stregazza livery bowed low to me, speaking in softly accented Caerdicci. All the city-states of Caerdicca Unitas speak the Caerdicci tongue, but it varies from place to place, and in La Serenissima, the faint, fluid accent of the ancient Phoenician seafarers who founded her endures. "Master Severio will receive you presently," he said, taking my cloak and folding it over his arm. "Does your man wish aught while he awaits?"

They did not call him Prince, then; his own servants. I marked that as worth remembering and glanced at Joscelin, who declined the offer courteously. Serenissiman or no, as a direct descendent of Benedicte de la Courcel, Severio was a Prince of the Blood in Terre d'Ange. It seemed his status as the Doge's grandson, while noble enough, meant somewhat less in La Serenissima.

Strange to remember how little I knew, then, of Serenissiman politics.

Another servant, higher-ranking to judge by his chains of office, entered the antechamber and bowed. "Master Severio will see you now, Contessa."

He did not meet my eyes, and I wondered what awaited me. Well, I would know, soon enough. I commended myself to Naamah's grace, and turned to bid Joscelin farewell. "Be at ease," I said softly. "I will return anon."

Joscelin nodded briefly and bowed, vambraces flashing. "I will abide, my lady." His jawline was taut and there was misery in his gaze. "Elua keep you."

Taking a deep breath, I turned back to the servant. "Lead on," I said.

Fifteen

WHAT I had expected of Severio Stregazza, I cannot say; in truth, I had too little knowledge of the Serenissiman to hazard a guess. If I had, though, I daresay it would have been wrong.

He wore the guise of an ancient Tiberian magistrate.

It should not have surprised me, when I reflected later, from the benefit of greater knowledge; the structure of governance in La Serenissima dates back to the glory days of Tiberium, indeed, prior to the empire. It is the pride of La Serenissima even now that she is the sole republic among the monarchic city-states of Caerdicca Unitas. If I had known then what I know now of her, it would not have startled me in the least that this son of hers chose to remind a D'Angeline courtesan that La Serenissima was a civilized nation while we were living in thatched hovels and scratching cheerfully in the dirt. Until Elua and his Companions set foot on D'Angeline soil and called it home, bringing ichor in their veins and arts and sciences ransacked from Heaven, we were no different than the Skaldi.

Well, I did not know, then, the envy that other civilized nations held toward Terre d'Ange, although I had learned well enough the covetousness of barbarian realms. But I am Night Court–raised and trained by Anafiel Delaunay, and I do not need to be told to follow a patron's cue. When I beheld Severio Stregazza seated in an ivory chair, wearing a Tiberian toga and a laurel crown on his dark curls, I bowed my head and knelt.

"Come." His voice was resolute, hiding only a trace of uncertainty as he gestured with the *fasces* he held, a bundle of birch rods bound with a scarlet thread. I knew it, from my readings, as a symbol of the authority of Tiberium. "Approach the dais and kneel, supplicant."

He had had a length of carpet laid before his chair, dyed a rich crimson. I crossed it obediently, feeling my heart beat faster at laying my welfare in his hands. Truly, there is nothing like the exquisite submission of surrendering one's will to one's patron! I sank down once more to kneel before him, *abeyante*; a supplicant's pose indeed, that I had learned as a child in the Night Court. It had been a long time indeed since I had knelt to a patron's whim, and the feeling of it was like a homecoming.

"What do you wish of me?" His voice was harsh, striving to overmaster his uncertainty. I raised my head and met his eyes.

"My lord," I whispered, not needing to feign nervousness. I must needs guess at his innermost desire, and if I guessed a-wrong, I would fail in Naamah's Service. "My lord, you have been grievously treated by my countrymen, and they fear they have incurred your displeasure. I am here to make amends."

My words and the tremor in my voice pleased him

greatly; like spark to tinder, I saw the eager light of cruelty kindled in his gaze. "You are here, then, to please me?" Severio leaned back in his ivory chair and smiled unkindly, keeping his sandaled feet placed just so, as statues of Tiberian magistrates would have them; one back, one placed afore. "Well, then." He gestured with the *fasces* bundle. "Rise, then, and let me behold you."

I stood before his avid gaze, trembling as he measured every inch of me. Pressure beat upon my ears, and I heard from afar the rustling sound of great bronze wings stirring. If Naamah had sent me, my lord Kushiel would have his due. A flush arose on my skin as Severio stared, heat rising in my veins.

"Disrobe," he said curtly.

It is a monstrous thing, to find pleasure in such treatment; tears stood in my eyes as I undid my laces and shed my gown, letting it slip from my shoulders and pool at my feet until I stood before him naked. By now he had taken my measure, and his lip curled with scorn as he realized I had, indeed, spoken truly – I pretended nothing.

"What do you wish, D'Angeline?" he asked, taunting.

"To please you, my lord," I murmured.

Severio Stregazza's eyes gleamed with the knowledge of his power. "Beg me for the privilege," he said, "and I may allow it."

To my mingled shame and relief, I did, the words coming faltering at first, and then spilling from me in a veritable torrent, until my voice grew thick with desire at my own abasement. I knelt unbidden to kiss his sandal-shod feet; there is a Bhodistani caress called "teasing the eel," a wriggling of the tongue between the toes . . .

"Enough!" Severio's hand closed on my hair, yanking

my head upward. "Let us see," he said, breathing heavily, "how repentant your people are." With his free hand, he twitched aside the folds of his Tiberian toga, revealing his engorged and swollen phallus.

Kneeling between his knees, I performed the *languisement* upon him, putting the whole of my art into the process. I daresay the young Stregazza had the benefit of his deal, that day; it had been a long time since I had served Naamah, and with lips and tongue and throat, I took him in as the fields drink in rain after a long drought, playing him for all I was worth. Twenty thousand ducats? It was a bargain. His body arched hard as he came to his climax, his hand clamped hard on my neck.

"Ah!" Severio cried out harshly, thrusting me away, his tangled grip pulling my hair loose from the fillet that bound it. I fell sprawling on the carpet as he caught up the bundle of birch rods. "Do you think I am so easily swayed to mercy?" he demanded.

"No, my lord." Gasping for breath, I licked my lips, salty with the taste of him. "I sought only to please . . ."

"If you wish to make amends for your folk," he said grimly, slapping the *fasces* against his palm, "I require somewhat more. Do you say so, still?"

I stared at the bundle of birch-rods, supple and cruel, smacking against his palm, and my breath came short until I had to close my eyes. "Yes, my lord. Please, my lord."

"Turn, then, and place your hands behind your neck."

I did it, shivering, my eyes still shut, gathering up my unbound hair. I heard him draw a long, shuddering breath at the sight of my naked back, my marque in its full glory against my fair skin. I heard the sound of him rising, and the faint swish as he drew back the birchrods. Even with my eyes closed, I could see the red haze spreading, and behind it Kushiel's face, stern and bronze. The bundled switches cut through the air as he swung his arm, and a crimson burst of pain slashed across my skin. I could not help it; I cried aloud in pleasure.

"Asherat!" A curse or invocation, the word exploded from Severio's lips and the birch-rods cut the air again, flailing my back. "You . . . D'Angeline . . ." Again, and again, his voice, breathless; the pain, sublime. Locked behind my neck, my hands clutched each other, whiteknuckled. "You . . ." again, "will . . . acknowledge . . . my . . . sovereignty . . ." Ah, Elua, Naamah, Kushiel! I drew breath, shaking, and heard myself plead for him to stop, meaning it and not meaning it. "You like this, don't you?" Severio taunted, flogging mercilessly. "You want it to end? Ask me again . . ." Again, and again, lashings of pain, bursting exquisitely over my consciousness. My vision reeled, swimming in a red fog of pain, threaded by my pleading voice and the slashing sound of the birch-rods. "Again!" His voice, harsh and panting. "Tell me again . . . how you want . . . to please me . . ."

What I said, I do not remember, only that I felt his hands on me then, shoving my knees apart as he thrust himself into me and I wept at the release of it, hanging my head until his fingers tangling in my long hair and drew my head back hard, so I was bent like a bow. "Show me," his voice grated at my ear, and I did, in a long, shuddering climax that milked the length of him as he pounded into me, my haunches thrust back hard against his loins.

"Again." His voice was merciless, his hands relinquishing my hair, grasping now at my breasts, squeezing and pinching. He was tireless, I had taken too much from him with the *languisement*. "Again!"

Despairing, I obliged.

Thus was my first assignation since my rededication to the Service of Naamah concluded, and when it was done, I felt calm and languid, my mood as soft as the warm, moist air of a summer evening after a thunderstorm has passed. So it has ever been, since I was a child at Cereus House, whipped for disobedience, a delicious languor suffusing my aching flesh.

For his part, Severio Stregazza was lamb-meek, purged of his youthful rage and full of wonder at what had transpired. Solicitous as a lover, he laid a silken robe across my shoulders, mindful of the fresh weals that marred my skin, and aided me to his couch, calling for wine.

"It is true, then," he marveled, laying a hand upon my face and gazing at my eyes, the scarlet mote in the left. "That you are an, an *anguissette*."

"Yes, my lord." I laughed softly. "It is true. Are you sorry to find it so?"

"No!" His eyes widened, and he took a seat at the opposite end of the couch, laughing. "No, not hardly, my lady. Tell me, are there others?"

"Not now." I shook my head. "There have been, in the past. Master Robert Tielhard, who inked my marque, heard stories from his grandfather."

"What happened to them?"

I arranged the folds of my robe about me in a more pleasing fashion. "The last living *anguissette* I know of was Iriel de Fiscarde of Azzalle, who went willingly into a marriage of servitude to the Kusheline Duc de Bonnel to avert war between their Houses. A matter of D'Angeline politics." I smiled at the servant who brought wine, ignoring his look askance at the deserted ivory chair and *fasces* bundle as he poured for us. "Tell me, my lord," I said to Severio, sipping my wine as his servant departed. "Do you truly despise us so?"

He sighed, running his hands through his hair and dislodging his laurel crown, which sat rather askew anyway. "Yes. No." Regarding the wreath, he tossed it on the floor. "Say rather that my hide, rough Serenissiman stuff as it is, has grown thin in this regard," he said wryly. "I have been too often reminded of my inadequacies in comparison to full-blooded D'Angelines."

"I thought my lord acquitted himself rather well in comparison." I smiled, watching him flush with pleasure. Flattery is headier stuff than wine, to young men. "Who is it dares say otherwise?"

"Not honest Serenissimans." He drank half his wine at a gulp, wiping his lips. "And not anyone here, in truth; it's all looks and glances. No, if it comes from anywhere, it comes from the Little Court, in La Serenissima." He caught my inquiring gaze. "That's what they call it, you know; my grandfather Benedicte's palazzo and the D'Angeline holdings in the district." Severio's mouth twisted. "It didn't used to be as bad when my grandmother was alive."

"Your grandfather remarried, did he not?" I asked.

He nodded absently. "Etaine de Tourais, she is called; a noble-born D'Angeline refugee from the Camaeline hills. Husband, father, even her brother, all killed in the first wave of Selig's invasion. Her family had a quit-claim on House Courcel. Somewhat to do with her father taking arms at Benedicte's side in some ancient battle against the Skaldi."

"The Battle of Three Princes," I murmured; I had cause to know it well. My lord Delaunay's beloved, the dauphin Rolande de la Courcel, had died in it.

"That's the one." Severio drank off the rest of his wine. "She's all right, I suppose; it's not her fault. She even took the Veil of Asherat, to thank the Gracious Lady of the Sea for offering sanctuary where Elua and his Companions failed her." He gloated a little, saying it. "But whatever store of courage she had, I'm afraid she used in fleeing the Skaldi. I'm sorry for her losses, but all the same, she wed the old man, and now there's rumor in the Little Court that he's prepared to throw over the rest of us for a true-born heir. An heir untainted by base-born Stregazza blood, that is." He looked bitterly into his empty glass. "Did you know we trace our line back to Marcellus Aurelius Strega?"

"An honorable lineage, to be sure," I said automatically. "Your ancestors would be proud. Severio, if your father stands to inherit the Doge's throne, what do the machinations of the Little Court matter?"

"The office of the Doge is an elected one," he said simply. "For a lifetime, aye, but the succession is never sure. If my father is not elected and Prince Benedicte withdraws his patronage from the Stregazza, well, I'm just another Serenissiman lordling scrabbling for position. I'll be little better off than Thérèse and Dominic's four children, with their father slain and their mother imprisoned. Benedicte countenanced that, you know. My own cousins, and no hope of a future among the lot."

It gave me a chill to hear it. I was responsible for that, Alcuin and I.

"Surely you have some inkling of how the election will fall out?" I asked him.

Severio shrugged. "My father is well loved among the clubs of our Sestieri, my lady, but it is no guarantee, and less for me. He must needs court the approval of Prince Benedicte, and that has been a shaky thing since Dominic and Thérèse's treachery was exposed. Meanwhile, my uncle Ricciardo plots against him, rousing the craft-guilds. It is important, therefore, that I win some regard for my family on this visit. D'Angeline trade-favor has prospered La Serenissima." He refilled his wineglass, looking rueful. "I've not made a good job of it, thus far. And a good portion of the funds my father allotted me to win favor among the nobles, well . . ." Gazing at me, Severio cleared his throat and flushed. "My father was very generous, but I do not know that he will consider his monies well spent."

When I took his meaning, I laughed out loud. "You bought *me* with your father's goodwill purse?"

"Ah, well. Not the whole of it, no." He fidgeted with a fold of his tunic. "A goodly portion," he admitted.

"Severio." I leaned forward, my eyes dancing. "Do you realize there's naught else you could have done with that money that would impress D'Angeline nobles more? They were laying odds on who my first patron would be! In one grand gesture, you have acquired a status no D'Angeline will ever hold. It is not my place to advise you, but believe me, if you make it known, you will be admired and envied by the Palace entire."

His face lit up, making him look younger and handsomer. "You truly think so?"

"I know it." I did, too. The stakes were different, when I was Delaunay's *anguissette*, a delightfully decadent secret to be shared among peers with certain vices. The Comtesse de Montrève was a hotly sought prize.

"Why did you choose me?" A thought struck him, and he frowned. "Was it only the money? I thought it would be. That's why I made the offer so high."

"No." I gazed at his scowling face and smiled. "I liked your anger."

"Did you really?" Reaching for me, he drew me onto his lap so that I straddled him and began to open my robe, hands laying claim to my flesh. "Do you like me still, now that I am not so angry?" he asked curiously, tugging his toga half-off. The blunt head of his rising phallus probed between my nether lips as his hands, inside my robe, slid up my welted back.

"Yes, my lord," I managed to gasp before he entered me, his nails digging into my skin.

Young men.

Sixteen

SEVERÍO STREGAZZA took my advice, although I did not hear the whole of it until I returned to court. As had been my wont in Delaunay's service, I took some few days' leisure to recover from the assignation, after being tended by an Eisandine chirurgeon.

It had been my intention to contract the Yeshuite doctor who had tended Alcuin and me in prior days, but Joscelin objected adamantly. I gazed at his beautiful, implacable face, the *khai* pendant gleaming silver on his chest, and gave way, too tired to do battle with his conscience. Let no Yeshuite be offended by my nature; I would be tended by one of our own. Eisandines are mayhap the most skilled healers in the world, and I had no objection on that score. Delaunay had trusted the Yeshuite's discretion; they do not gossip about their clients. I resolved the matter by setting Fortun to contract the dourest Eisandine he could find.

Joscelin had said naught when I returned to him in Severio's quarters; I daresay only we two knew the unspoken shoals that loomed beneath the surface of our cordial greeting. He had bowed, I had inclined my head, and perforce kept from wincing as my heavy cloak brushed against my freshly-lashed skin. I have had far worse than I endured at the hands of the young Stregazza and walked away with a steady gait.

What Joscelin felt, I did not ask, knowing it well enough. The pain of the flesh is naught to that of the heart.

Severio had come forward as my first patron, and allowed the amount of the fee he paid for our assignation to be whispered in the corridors. This I learned from my chevaliers, who had it from the Palace Guard – nothing escapes the Guard's ears – and from Cecilie Laveau-Perrin, who paid me a visit during my time of recuperation.

"Twenty thousand ducats, they say," she related, eyeing me speculatively. "Is it true?"

"True enough," I said, laying aside another stack of proposals. The offers had risen considerably with this batch; some were outlandish. One L'Agnacite lordling promised me a vineyard. "Do they say what I've done with it?"

"No." Cecilie eyed me shrewdly. "I heard, though. I've ears still in the Night Court. You paid Favrielle nó Eglantine's marque. Did you know it's said she was pushed?"

"In the bath, when she split her lip?" I raised my brows. "No, but I guessed as much. I grew up in the Night Court too, remember. When she said she fell, she recited it like a Yeshuite catechism."

"It was a fortnight before the eve of the new-made adepts' debut. They have leave to design their own costumes, at Eglantine." Cecilie picked up one of the proposals and glanced absently at it. "There was some dissent over the advantage it gave her, I heard. Jealousy is a cruel mistress. Who's the Baroness de Charlot and what do you want with a team of matched blood-bays?"

I took the parchment away from her. "Nothing. But House Charlot breeds very fine horses. In Kusheth. And blood-bays . . . oh, never mind, Cecilie, I'm not accepting it. What else have you heard?"

"Are you feeling quite well?" Cecilie looked mischievously at me. "I think you should pay a visit to the Palace."

More than that, she would not say, leaving me to learn it for myself. I bethought myself of visiting Thelesis de Mornay, but an opportunity came quicker than I reckoned when Ysandre sent an invitation to attend a concert held in honor of a tentative reconciliation between her uncle, the Duc L'Envers, and the Stregazza family. Echoing the theme of liaison, an Eisandine composer — music and medicine are among the gifts of Eisheth — and a Siovalese engineer had collaborated on a concerto involving a cunningly wrought instrument of Siovalese design that used a bellows-and-pedal system to force air through myriad pipes of differing pitches.

It made for a strange and haunting sound that was not displeasing, full of odd harmonics. Seated toward the rear of a half-dozen rows of chairs, I listened with half an ear, my attention on the principles at the front of the salon. Tibault, Comte de Toluard — Marquis, now, as reward for his role in defending against Selig's invasion — sat beaming; an avid Siovalese scholar himself, he was also the engineer's patron. Many of Shemhazai's line are interested in such things. I daresay if Delaunay had been here, he would have wished to examine the instrument too. Severio Stregazza was seated between the Queen and Duc Barquiel

L'Envers, and I noted how Ysandre leaned toward him and whispered from time to time. She was as anxious, I thought, to have this rift mended as Severio was to acquit himself well.

Barquiel L'Envers managed to lounge in his stiff chair, stretching his long legs before him. One might take it for irreverence, or not; I never knew with him. He had been a long while posted in Khebbel-imAkkad, and claimed to prefer its cushioned comforts. For all that, I would never make the mistake of reckoning him soft.

Beside L'Envers, I was surprised to see Percy de Somerville, the Royal Commander, his son Ghislain and daughter-in-law Bernadette beside him. The last I had known, he had been reviewing the strengths of the border guard in Camlach – the remnants of d'Aiglemort's men who called themselves the Unforgiven. No one had a stronger motive for dedicating themselves to the protection of the Skaldi borders, having once betrayed our nation; but then again, Ysandre was wary enough to keep them under watch.

If Percy de Somerville had returned, perhaps then so had those men posted on guard the night Melisande escaped from Troyes-le-Mont, I thought hopefully. I would have to dispatch my chevaliers for a scouting expedition to the barracks.

Less cheering to my eyes was the sight of Marmion Shahrizai in the second row, near enough to the Queen to murmur in her ear, as I saw, twice, he did. There was a youngish woman seated next to him whom I knew not at all, slight, with an upswept mane of bronze-gold curls. She treated Marmion coolly, I saw, but I saw too a faint, amused smile on her face as she watched him address the

Queen. Barquiel L'Envers turned once and said somewhat to her, grinning. I thought that she laughed.

When the concert was done, we applauded politely. The musicians — it had taken three to operate the instrument — bowed, and then the composer and the engineer bowed, and the engineer invited the audience to inspect the instrument. Tibault de Toluard, for all that he must have known it better than any noble there, was first on the dais, his face aglow with pleasure.

For my part, I mingled among my peers, making pleasant conversation as servants circulated with wine and chilled fruits. I kept my eye on Severio, and marked how he greeted the assembled D'Angeline nobles with unfailing courtesy.

"Phèdre!" Ghislain de Somerville hailed me cheerfully. "What on earth did you do to that boy?" he asked, laughing. "I swear, you've transformed him! Five days ago, he was scarce fit for polite company; now, he's well-nigh a court darling. How did you do it?"

"Naamah's Servants keep her secrets," I said, smiling. "I'm pleased to hear it, though. How is your father? He looks well."

"Hale as ever." Ghislain threw an admiring glance toward his father, a stalwart figure with golden hair turned mostly grey. "He rode the length of Camlach himself, midwinter, to inspect the garrisons there. I hope I've half his stamina at his age."

"You've his gift of command, my lord," I said. "No doubt you've inherited his constitution as well."

Ghislain flushed, smelling faintly of apples. "You're kind to say so, but I fear I'm a pale imitation of my father on the battlefield."

I do not think it was true, although I am no judge; father and son had headed the armies that formed the hammer and anvil between which we caught Selig's forces, enabling the Allies of Camlach to breach their might. Neither would have succeeded alone. Of a surety, Percy's brilliant plan had held the Skaldi at bay long enough for the Alban army to arrive — but without Ghislain's leadership, I daresay we never would have reached Troyes-le-Mont. "Say what you will, my lord," I said diplomatically, "but it is the two strong branches of House Somerville that upheld Terre d'Ange in her direst hour."

"Well." Ghislain looked gravely at me. "It was a near thing. Do not think I forget, Phèdre, your part in it. I would have tied you to a tree, had I known what was in your mind that night, but if you'd not broken Selig's lines to warn the fortress . . ." He shook his head. "You saved a great many lives in that battle, and mayhap our victory in the bargain."

"Mayhap," I said softly; I do not like to remember that night. If I never have to live through its like again, it will be too soon. I felt the ghost of remembered pain, the delirium of agony as Waldemar Selig's dagger-blade sheared my skin from my flesh, and shuddered. Even I had my limits. "Kushiel's blessing is a dubious gift, my lord. I spent it as I thought best."

"And I am glad you are here to say it." Smiling, he patted my shoulder — setting off a fresh wave of remembered pain — and left me.

Blinking away the scarlet haze that threatened my vision, I accepted a glass of wine from a passing servant, sipping it to calm my nerves. I nearly missed seeing Severio coming to intercept me, his face lit with pleasure.

"Comtesse de Montrève," he said with elaborate formality, bowing; his dark eyes danced as he straightened. "I stand indebted to your wisdom!"

The memory of Troyes-le-Mont faded; I collected myself and returned his smile. "It worked, then?"

"Every bit as you said it would." Severio laughed. "It is a different land, this Terre d'Ange! I am grateful to you for playing guide in it, as well as . . . other things."

"As for those, my lord magistrate," I said teasingly, "I am equally grateful to you, and we owe thanks to Naamah, if anyone, for the diverse gifts she shares with lovers."

"So you say, here." He took my hands. "In La Serenissima, we do not speak of such pleasures. Truly, I thought my spirit malformed, for entertaining such desires. For that alone, I am grateful — " Severio broke off his sentence mid-thought, gazing over my shoulder. "I wish he wouldn't look at me like that," he said, annoyed.

I turned and looked to see Marmion Shahrizai staring at us, a sickly cast to his ivory skin. He gave an ironic smile and moved onward, but not before I caught the look in his eyes. It was fear. "You mean Lord Shahrizai?" I asked, keeping my tone light.

"Oh, he's always about the Queen. I played batarde with him the other day, in the Hall of Games," Severio said, frowning. "When I made an outrageous bluff, he said the strangest thing . . . what was it? 'If she's sent you to threaten me, tell her I'm not frightened.' When I asked him what he meant, he brushed it off. What on earth did he mean by it?"

I swear, my heart skipped a beat, and when it resumed, it pounded at double time. "Oh, it was rumored that his cousin Melisande was in La Serenissima, under the protection of the Doge," I said casually, horribly aware of the risk I was taking. It *wasn't* rumored, not in the slightest. The only incident to even hint at such a thing was a parcel that had made its way to my doorstep, in Montrève. "So it is not so, then?"

"If it is, I've never heard of her." Severio shrugged. "It could be. I don't know the name of every D'Angeline noble to seek refuge in La Serenissima's arms."

"You would know this one, my lord," I said conservatively. "She resembles Lord Marmion, insofar as the sun resembles a star. And if Prince Benedicte caught word of her presence, he would surely have her extradited, for she stands condemned of treason in Terre d'Ange. It was Lord Marmion who betrayed her unto the Queen's justice."

"Ah." Severio nodded understanding; he had, it seemed, a fair grasp of internecine intrigue. "Well, I understand his fear, then, but his suspicions are misplaced. If his cousin is in La Serenissima, it's naught to do with me. Nor, I think, my grandfather the Doge. He is too canny to risk displeasing the D'Angeline Queen."

"Doubtless you are right," I said automatically, watching Marmion make his way to Ysandre's side. He *knew* Melisande was in La Serenissima! And he lived in fear of her retribution. It had been no act, that night at the Midwinter Masque; he truly suspected me of being in league with her. Marmion was playing a guessing game, the same as I. Wherever she was, it had somewhat to do with the Stregazza. Not Severio; I'd no doubt his ignorance was genuine. I'd seen him reveal his innermost self, and he didn't dissemble well enough to play the innocent. But Marmion didn't know that.

Who, then? Lost in thought, I bit my lip and wondered.

"I must greet his grace the Duc de Somerville," Severio observed, pulling a face. "I am charged by my mother on behalf of Prince Benedicte to thank him for the company of D'Angeline guardsmen he sent to attend the Little Court. It seems my maternal grandfather grows chary of protecting his pure-blooded heir." He gave me another bow. "Phèdre, may I call upon you before I must needs return home? Just to converse," he added with a self-conscious laugh. "I have come in these few days to hold a great regard for your advice. Truly, it would please me."

"You would honor my household," I said, smiling at him and curtsying. "Now go forth and be politic, Prince Severio."

He laughed delightedly at that, kissing my hands before taking his leave.

"You must be considerably pleased with yourself." Leaning against a column, Barquiel L'Envers pitched his voice to reach my ears without bestirring himself.

"Your grace," I murmured, curtsying and wondering how long he had been there and how much he had heard. "It is a pleasure to see you once more. I think often on my debt to you." It had to be said, even if it took me back to the field of Troyes-le-Mont. I could not forget that, either. How I had swayed, on my knees, blood-soaked and awaiting death, gazing at the terrible love in Joscelin's eyes as he broke away from Selig's men to perform the *terminus* that would end both our lives mercifully. How that look had changed as he saw the portcullis raising beyond me, and Barquiel L'Envers and his Akkadian horsemen racing out to attempt a wildly daring rescue.

"Save it for your patrons," L'Envers said. "You've made quite an impression on the young Stregazza, I hear, Phèdre. He was even gracious enough to allow the possibility of peace between our Houses, for all that his kin murdered my sister. Gracious, indeed. How do you think your lord Delaunay would like this day's work?"

"I don't know, my lord." I tried to read him, and failed. Barquiel L'Envers smiled at me, revealing even white teeth. His pale blond hair was cropped short as ever, defying fashion for D'Angeline noblemen, and his eyes were the same dark violet as Ysandre's.

"Neither do I," he said pleasantly. "On the one hand, the Stregazza disposed of his nemesis in the form of my sister Isabel; on the other, they posed the greatest threat to his sworn charge, his darling Rolande's Ysandre. It must have galled him dreadfully to turn to me to set the balance aright."

"If it did, he never said so."

"And now we are all in bed together, so to speak." Barquiel flashed another grin at me. "Some of us more so than others. Ah, poor Anafiel! I do wonder what he would have thought."

"So do I, my lord." In the face of his prodding, I drew on the dignity of my grief, thinking with sorrow of my lord Delaunay. "I wonder it every day."

"Well, we'll never know, will we?" Shrugging, the Duc straightened. "Come here, Phèdre nó Delaunay; I've someone you should meet."

Obediently, I followed him through the salon to Ysandre's side, where a small knot of folk were gathered. The bronze-haired young woman I had seen earlier turned, giving him the kiss of greeting as if it had been days, and not minutes, since she had seen him. Scarce taller than I, she was some five years older and very beautiful.

"Cousin Barquiel," she said in a naturally sultry voice, linking her arm with his and looking at me with interest. "Who have you brought me?"

Barquiel L'Envers favored me with his white smile, gazing down at me with those lovely violet eyes; like the Queen's, like the woman whose fingers wrapped familiarly around his arm. "Phèdre nó Delaunay de Montrève," he said, sounding amused. "Nicola L'Envers y Aragon."

I made a curtsy without thinking, the response automatic upon hearing the names of two of the Great Houses of Terre d'Ange and Aragonia jointly linked.

"Impressive, isn't it?" Nicola had the same unreadable smile as the Duc. "Too bad my husband is a minor lordling, and a drunkard at that. But one does what one can for one's House, even if one is a minor offshoot." Releasing Barquiel's arm, she took a step toward me, standing a little closer than courtesy dictated. I felt the familiar dizziness of being in the presence of a patron, and her violet gaze held awareness of it. "Still," she said softly, "I think I might have an interesting time here at court, should I choose to stay a while." Patting my cheek, she moved away in Ysandre's direction.

I watched as Marmion Shahrizai struggled to choose between entertaining the Queen, and engaging the interest of this new-found cousin Nicola, who treated him so coolly. No mistake about it, what I had seen during the concert. She was playing him, and playing him well. I turned to look at Barquiel L'Envers.

"What can I say?" He smiled and shrugged, opening his arms. "House L'Envers is an ambitious one, and I made

a bad marriage for Nicola some years ago. It gained me ties
to the House of Aragon, but she's not prospered by it. Her
husband is a fool. Who can blame her, if she wishes to try
her luck at home now that Ysandre is Queen?"

The first and greatest lesson we learn in Cereus House
is silence. I looked at Barquiel L'Envers and did not
answer, until his smile faltered.

"Anafiel Delaunay didn't do you any favors when he
trained you to spy, little *anguissette*," he said in a low voice,
and no one would mistake him now for anything but a
deadly opponent. "He died through dabbling in the affairs
of state when he shouldn't. Don't you make the same
mistake."

I made my voice mild. "My lord Delaunay was
murdered by traitors plotting to overthrow the throne,
your grace. Do you threaten me with the same?"

L'Envers laughed harshly, wagging his finger at me.
"Don't even think it, Phèdre. I have a great deal of forbearance for you, for what you've done, but it only goes so
far. There are questions unanswered in my mind, and I
hope, for your sake, you don't hold the answers." With
that, he made me a curt, dismissive bow and stalked away,
dangerous as a hunting leopard.

Staring after him, I thought of the questions
unanswered in my own mind.

SEVENTEEN

"YOU'RE SURE." Joscelin frowned at me.

"I'd stake my life on it. He's terrified."

"Well," he reflected. "If Lord Marmion Shahrizai conspired to free Melisande, why should he fear her?"

"He wouldn't." Chin in hand, Fortun sat staring at the two-story plan of Troyes-le-Mont spread and weighted on the table; markings indicating Melisande's room, the postern gate, the guards' positions. "Because he didn't." He looked up at me. "Does it make sense any other way?"

"No." I shook my head.

"Then why did he kill his sister?" Fortun contemplated the map again as if it held answers. "That guardsman Branion, I tell you, my lady, he was sure of it. Remy and Ti-Philippe made no mistake about it."

Joscelin and I exchanged a glance.

"There are two possibilities," I said, holding up a forefinger. "One, your guardsman is mistaken, Fortun. And since this is the simplest explanation, it is the likeliest. But two . . ." I held up a second finger, ". . . 'Twas the other way 'round. Marmion killed Persia because *she* helped Melisande escape."

"So?" Fortun frowned, puzzling it through. "If she did, and he learned it, why kill her? He gained the Queen's trust by betraying Melisande's allies, for Elua's sake. Why let this coin slip through his fingers? To kill his sister? He's torn House Shahrizai apart, with the rumor of it! Unless . . ." He glanced up at us. "Unless he had no proof, that's why."

"No." Joscelin leaned forward, folding his arms over his knees. He looked at me like in the old days, when our survival depended on our ability to think and act together as one. "That's only part. You're right, he's no proof of it, but there's still somewhat more. Marmion or Persia, either one, the same premise holds true. The guard at the postern gate would have given challenge. There's still the unknown ally, the trusted one. Whatever Marmion learned, if he threatened Persia with it, she would have threatened back, with somewhat he feared."

"Melisande," said Fortun.

"He's scared of Melisande now," I observed. "It can't be that. It's got to be someone whose reach is closer. Someone Ysandre trusts implicitly, whose mere word would be enough to condemn him. If Persia threatened him with that . . . well, mayhap."

"If he knew who it was," Joscelin said simply, "he could tell the Queen."

"But if he didn't," Fortun observed, "he'd be left with the choice of calling her bluff, or – "

"Or killing her," I finished. "He doesn't know. If he did, he'd not suspect *me*. And he does, believe me. He warned me at the Masque, and he turned grey seeing me talking with Severio. I don't think he's playacting. He's feared for his life."

"How does he know Melisande is in La Serenissima?" Joscelin asked reasonably. "We only do because . . ." He eyed me sidelong. "That damnable cloak."

"Which means a patron," I murmured. "If I knew which one, I promise, this would be much simpler. Well, if Marmion confronted Persia, who knows what she told him? Enough to know that Melisande is well protected, here and in La Serenissima. Enough to threaten him, so that he was moved to kill her. But not enough for proof."

"Why would Marmion suspect his sister?" Fortun asked.

I pressed my temples and stared at the plan of the fortress until it swam in my vision. There, marked with her initials, were Melisande's quarters on the second floor. So little space in Troyes-le-Mont, we all slept two and three to a room, except for Melisande. Ysandre had allowed her that much, on what was to be her final night on this earth: A room of her own. Thelesis de Mornay's voice echoed in my memory, repeating the words she had recorded when she interviewed Ghislain de Somerville about that night. *By now, my father had emerged, and assumed command unthinking. He wasted no time in ordering a detachment to the second floor, to Melisande Shahrizai's chamber where she was confined. There, he found her guards slain; one with a dagger to the ribs, and the other with his throat cut. The chamber itself was empty.*

A piece of the puzzle fell into place, with a satisfying sense of rightness and surety I'd nearly forgotten.

"She never left Melisande's room," I said, lifting my head.

"You think . . .?" Joscelin stared at me. "Melisande."

"Yes," I said. "Remember Selig's steading? People see what they expect. You put a wolf-pelt over your head and muttered a few words of Skaldi, and Selig's folk saw one of the White Brethren. It would take less than that for the guardsmen of Troyes-le-Mont to see Melisande as Persia. The Shahrizai are all cast from the same die. They saw a daughter of House Shahrizai enter alone, and they saw her leave. They saw what they expected."

"Well, but how would Marmion guess it?" Fortun asked.

I shrugged. "Look to the wolf-pelt. Whatever his sister wore into that chamber, she didn't have it afterward. They rode into Troyes-leMont cloaked and hooded. I'd be willing to hazard a guess that Persia Shahrizai somewhere mislaid that garment, and her brother Marmion took note of it. He's not stupid, no matter if he's a match for Melisande or not. He'd guess well enough to confront his sister with it." I stirred. "Elua! We need to talk to those guardsmen. Did the lads have any luck at the barracks?"

Fortun pulled a glum face. "No one who served that night was with de Somerville in Camlach, my lady, but most of his men are quartered in outlying L'Agnace. Do you want us to pay a call?" His face brightened at the prospect.

"I think so," I said decisively. "I need to hear from Phanuel Buonard, who found the slain guard at the postern, and anyone else on duty that night. Anyone! Unless I miss my guess, Melisande was at large from three bells onward, and Persia simply slipped back to her own quarters when the alarm sounded, before anyone thought

to check Melisande's rooms. Whoever thought they saw
Persia in that time, saw Melisande. Ghislain de Somerville
made no report of it, but *someone* must have seen!"

"Who killed the guards at Melisande's door, then?"
Joscelin asked softly. "Did she do it herself, then, with
never a sound to alert the guard at the stair?" He placed a
finger on the map of the fortress, raising his eyebrows. "Is
she so skilled with a dagger, think you? Or was it the
unknown ally?"

"I don't know," I murmured. "Melisande uses people
well; it is her gift. I have never known her to dirty her own
hands." I met his eyes. "What do you think?"

Gazing at the plan, he bit his lip. "I think," he said
slowly, "I think it was someone very skilled with a
dagger, to dispatch two of Percy de Somerville's hand-
picked guardsmen without a sound. If I were you . . ."
His voice shook; he cleared his throat and steadied it, holding my gaze. "If I were you, my lady, I would ask who
among the Cassiline Brethren attended Ysandre de la
Courcel during the siege of Troyes-le-Mont. Because . . .
because that is a possibility so impossible we never even
considered it. But there were Cassilines there. And we are
human."

Fortun sucked in a hissing breath. "Cassilines! If I
were posted on guard by Admiral Rousse, in the old
days . . . my lady, I'd never think to question a Cassiline! I
don't know as I'd even mark one's passing."

"They carried intelligence," I said, sick at remembering. "The length and breadth of the nation, working on
Ysandre's behalf. Lord Rinforte, the Prefect, pledged as
much, because no one would ever suspect the Cassiline
Brotherhood of politicking." I saw the same sickness

reflected in Joscelin's eyes. "Joscelin, you were one of them. Is there any Cassiline, for any reason, who would support Melisande?"

"No." He sank his face into his hands. "I don't know. The training, oh, Phèdre! It goes bone-deep. But stranger . . . stranger things have happened, I suppose."

"I will try to find out," I said gently. "But will you write to the Prefect, and ask him? All I need are the names. We will do the rest."

Joscelin raised his stricken face. "I'll ask," he whispered. "You said . . . do you remember? Even if . . ." He made his voice stronger. "Even if it is so, you said you didn't think the same person killed the guard at the postern gate, do you remember?"

"Yes." My heart ached for him. "It may be . . . it may be another blind alley, Joscelin," I said slowly, not pointing out the fact that he himself had been first to disabuse me of the notion. "But we need to know."

"I will ask," he whispered.

Fortun had resumed staring at the plan of Troyes-le-Mont, a formidable scowl on his face. "The question remains," he said. "Why?"

None of us could answer.

True to his word, Joscelin wrote to the Prefect of the Cassiline Brotherhood, though I knew it cost him to go begging for information not rightly his to the man who had condemned him as a vow-breaker. Whether for spite or other concerns, no answer was forthcoming.

Remy and Ti-Philippe rode to Champs-de-Guerre, where the Royal Army was quartered, with funds enough for a three-day carouse. This they did to the fullest degree, returning to the City of Elua with aching heads, empty pockets and no more knowledge than before. The guardsmen of Troyes-le-Mont had as good as vanished.

I checked with Thelesis de Mornay, who had no record of the Cassiline Brothers attendant on Ysandre during the siege; indeed, she looked at me with mild surprise, having never considered the matter. At length, I found an opportunity to query Ysandre herself, broaching it in a sidelong manner.

The Queen frowned, pale brows knitting. "Honestly, I don't recall. There have always been Cassilines about, ever since I was a child; I don't think I ever saw my father without a pair of them hovering in the background. One comes to forget their presence. Lord Ignace d'Avicenne was Secretary of the Presence, he might remember. Or you could ask the Royal Archivist. May I ask why?"

Her tone changed, with that last question; Ysandre de la Courcel was nobody's fool, and most certainly not mine. I murmured something inadequate about Joscelin having an interest in the matter. Ysandre was sensitive enough to the troubles in our relationship not to pursue it, but her gaze rested thoughtfully on me. And beyond her, just out of earshot, I saw that same interest mirrored in another pair of violet eyes.

Nicola L'Envers y Aragon, whose presence at court troubled me.

Taking leave of the Queen, I went to bespeak Lord Ignace d'Avicenne, and found him old and feeble in his wits. He had been Ganelon's Secretary of the Presence; Ysandre had allowed him to retire gracefully after the war. He remembered the names of every nursemaid he'd had as a child, and not a one of the Cassiline Brethren who'd attended the Queen.

I went then to Micheline de Parnasse, who was the Royal Archivist. She had ten years on Ignace d'Avicenne if she had a day, but her mind was as sharp as Cassiel's dagger. She peered at me and spoke a few sharp words to one of her assistants, a lanky young Siovalese lordling who grinned when she wasn't looking, and treated her with the utmost deference.

One might expect dust and disarray in the Royal Archives, where the records of a thousand years of D'Angeline royalty are housed, but the place was spotless, smelling of sweet beeswax and organized within an inch of its life. Micheline de Parnasse's assistant followed her orders unerringly; and halted, stock-still, in astonishment.

"It's not here, my lady," he said. "The pages are missing."

Her brows beetled furiously. "What! You must be looking in the wrong place. Let me see." Moving with the aid of a cane, she came to scan the shelf. He passed her the hide-bound ledger he'd withdrawn, and she examined it carefully, tilting it to and fro in the lamplight. At length, she looked soberly at me. "He's right. Three pages have been excised." Balancing the ledger, she showed me the sharp edges buried in the spine where the pages had been cut. "Five years of Cassiline Brethren attendant on House de la Courcel, recorded there. Someone's taken them out."

Oh, Joscelin! With an effort, I kept my voice level. "My Lady Archivist, who has access to these records?"

"Directly?" Micheline de Parnasse frowned, absently stroking the ledger as one might comfort a wounded child. "Myself, and my two assistants, who'd sooner murder a babe in the cradle than tamper with the archives! The Queen, of course. And the Secretaries of the Privy Seal."

I had been out of the City too long. "Who holds those posts?"

She gave me three names, and I startled at the third.

"Solaine Belfours? I did not know she held the honor still." Hastily, I gathered my wits. "My Lady Archivist, it is needful that these records be complete."

"Yes." Distraught, she held the ledger close to her. "Yes, I will write to the Prefect of the Cassiline Brotherhood, and ask him to supply the information. Rinforte will know, they keep records of their own. 'Tis a grave thing, to desecrate the Royal Archives!" She scowled, and I'd not have liked to be held accountable for the crime. "Rinforte will know. Do you want me to send notice when it comes, young . . . Phèdre, was it?"

"Yes, my lady," I murmured. "If you please."

I wrote out my name and address for her Siovalese assistant, who held the bit of parchment on which I'd written like it was a precious thing, and grinned at me. "Don't worry," he said. "We'll find it."

So I left them, the Royal Archivist muttering in a fury, and her smiling assistant.

I had learned a great deal in the pursuit of knowledge that eluded me.

EIGHTEEN

GASPAR TREVALION heeded my invitation shortly thereafter, paying a visit.

A confederate of Delaunay's from the beginning, he was the closest thing to an uncle I had ever known. I received him warmly, and bid Gemma fetch out our finest wine to serve. After I had poured for him and we were seated, after he had suitably admired the bust of Delaunay that ever watched over my sitting room, I asked him the question that had been burning in my mind.

Gaspar Trevalion, the Comte de Forcay, frowned into his wine. "Ysandre kept Solaine Belfours on because I interceded on her behalf, Phèdre."

Sipping my wine, I nearly choked. "Why?"

It is a vivid memory for me, kneeling forgotten in a corner at Solaine's country estate, while the Marquise paced the room with gleaming eyes, switching her riding crop, and deciding to accept the offer of the Lioness of Azzalle to commit high treason and put the imprimature of the Privy Seal on a forged letter to the Khalif of Khebbel-im-Akkad.

"Because she begged me to." Gaspar met my eyes firmly. "Yes, I know. She was Lyonette's creature, and nearly acted treasonously on her behalf. But it never happened, Phèdre. You know it and I know it. Solaine knew it wouldn't when she asked Baudoin's escort as surety. Lyonette de Trevalion would never have risked her son thusly." He spread his hands. "Lyonette was her sponsor, and a powerful one. What could she do? She dared not risk a flat rejection. So she said, and I believe her."

I stared at Delaunay's marble face and wondered what he would have thought.

"Phèdre." Gaspar's voice was gentle. "She was less complicit than my own cousin in Lyonette's scheme. I convinced Ysandre to reinstate Marc as Duc de Trevalion in all but name, with his grandson's inheritance clear. I would have been remiss if I'd let Solaine bear the punishment House Trevalion evaded. She was *fostered* at Trevalion, do you understand?"

"Yes." I did, though I didn't like it. The ties of noble fosterage were complex and binding, second only to marriage; and maybe not even that. The bonds of matrimony could be dissolved easier than the bonds of childhood debts and loyalties. "I understand."

"Good." His expression cleared. "Now, why is it that you ask?"

This, at least, I could answer honestly without throwing suspicion on the present. "She was one of my patrons, my lord. And Delaunay did not trust her, but bid me watch her carefully. He stood ready to intercept that letter to the Khalif, you know, had it been sent."

"I know. And I stood with him. But it wasn't." His tone put an end to the matter, and we turned our conversation to more pleasant topics. I put a good face on it, talking lightly of affairs of the Palace. But I could not shake my deep unease, as I did not think it was conscience that had moved Solaine Belfours.

I did not know if it was conscience that had moved Gaspar Trevalion.

That night, I told Joscelin all that I had learned, and his face grew tight and drawn, the white lines forming. He paced the room like a caged tiger, splendid in his wounded anger. I sat quiet and watched him. Whatever I thought of the letter of Cassiline vows, I respected their nature. Joscelin, outcast and anathema, in violation of the vows of obedience and chastity, had never, in his darkest hours, violated the central precept of Cassiel: To protect and serve.

When at last he sat down and buried his face in his hands in despair, I stroked his hair, the wheat-gold strands that fell loose and shining over his strong hands where they covered his face.

"Don't," Joscelin muttered, shuddering hard. He lifted his face, taut with rage and anguish. "Phèdre, don't. I can't bear it."

Neither could I, so I did the only thing I could, and left him alone.

I was drowning, and no hand would reach out to clasp mine. I slept ill, and dreamt, plagued by nightmares, waking with a stifled cry, my mouth half-stopped with gasping fear. I do not know what my lord Delaunay did at such times, when he was cast adrift in a sea of intrigue, bits of information all around like flotsam and jetsam, but none he could grasp, none that would bear his weight, no vessel to assemble. I was Naamah's Servant and Kushiel's

Chosen. I cast myself on their mercies, and accepted another assignation.

It has never been my wont to service more than one patron at a time, but I suppose I could not help thinking of the Twins, Eamonn and Grainne, when I accepted the proposal of the joint rulers of the Marquisate de Fhirze. What might it have been like, had the Lords of the Dalriada shared me? Would it have balanced them all the same? I did not know; I had never even wondered, before then. And I would never know, for Eamonn was dead, slain on the fields of Troyes-leMont, and his sister had carried his head home to Alba, preserved in quicklime. Well, and they were barbarians, but all the same, noble in heart and deed.

Apollonaire and Diànne; no idle jest, the Hellene masks of sun and moon, but a play on their names, a long history in House Fhirze. They were not twins – Diànne was elder by a year – nor barbarians, but quintessentially D'Angeline. The de Fhirze estates lay in Namarre near the Kusheline border, where the blood of their House had mingled freely with that of Kushiel's scions, but they were creatures of the Palace and wintered in the City of Elua. It was a tall, narrow house with many stories, and multiple windows on every one, so peering sun and moon alike could illuminate its interior.

One story entire was given over to their pleasures, and in truth, it was as well stocked with toys as any seraglio of the Night Court. There was a flagellary with whips and crops and tawses, pincers and feathered ticklers, trusses and trapezes and suspension harnesses, and *aides d'amour* sheathed in leather and carved from ivory.

And all of these things Apollonaire and Diànne de Fhirze used on me, trading off in a well-orchestrated game, so that I must needs please the one while the other tormented me nearly beyond bearing. It was she who commanded the game, I quickly discerned, but she reckoned on him to carry it, for though he seemed quiet and bashful beside her, his stoic strength and endurance and prodigious endowment were near as obdurate as rock.

Well, I am what I am, and after many hours, Apollonaire de Fhirze sank trembling and exhausted to the cushions strewn about the chamber, his handsome face slack and empty, small muscles jumping in his strong thighs.

"No more, Diànne," he murmured, his once-awesome phallus damp and limp against his groin. "Enough."

"Elua!" His sister jerked hard on the pincers clamped to my nipples, joined with a leather thong; a fresh wave of pain lanced through my body, doubled and suspended as it was. "Do *you* say it is enough?" she asked ominously, trailing a pinion-feather along the soft skin of my inner thigh, between my legs, parting my damp and swollen nether lips with the tip of it.

One would think, after hard usage, the nerve-endings would grow dull to such finesse. Mayhap it is true with others. It is not true with me. I whimpered and closed my eyes, breathing the words of my response. "As you wish . . . my lady."

"Pfaugh!" With a disgusted sound, Diànne de Fhirze tossed aside the feather and loosed the catch on the pulley that held me suspended; I dropped with a soft thud onto the cushions. "You disappoint me, Apollonaire," she said, going matter-of-factly about unfastening the leather shackles that bound my wrists and ankles, and the pincers as well.

Recumbent on cushions, he smiled at her with sweet contentment. "Do I?"

She ignored him, laughing and toying with my hair. "You, though . . .

No one, man or woman, has ever outlasted my brother. No wonder the Dalriada went to war for you!"

Catching my breath a bit, I drew myself up to kneel and compose myself. "The story is somewhat exaggerated, my lady."

"All the best stories are," she said idly, reclining and eyeing me. "Tell me, Comtesse, what will you choose as a patron-gift? We have thrown open the coffers of Fhirze for this assignation, but I would not slight the traditions of Naamah." Diànne gestured with one languid arm. "Anything you wish, in this house, is yours. Only you must name it. It is something indeed, to ride Apollonaire de Fhirze to exhaustion."

I gathered up my tumbled locks, raising my arms to lift my bare breasts, tossing my hair back so it fell dark and serpentine down the length of my back, obscuring my marque. "If you would honor Naamah in my name," I said, "make a gift to her Temple. For myself . . ." I smiled, ". . . I will bear the marks of your remembrance on my skin."

"Is it true that you were a spy?" Apollonaire asked suddenly. "Even in Naamah's Service?"

"Yes." Sitting on my heels, I looked gravely at him. "It is true."

He leaned on one elbow, face alight with interest. "What would you do, then, if you were spying on us?"

"Well, my lord." The question amused me, coming from a patron I had chosen wholly without regard to the arts of covertcy; which is likely why I answered it honestly. "I know of no intrigue coming out of Fhirze, but you are well-placed at the Palace, and like to hear gossip, especially since there are the two of you, and no doubt you mull over each day's gleanings together. If there was somewhat I wished to know, like as not I would sound you out."

"Such as what?" Diànne looked as interested as her brother. I had never reckoned, till now, the erotic potential my former — for all they knew — calling held for my patrons. I smiled and shrugged, turning my hands palm-up on my thighs.

"Nicola L'Envers y Aragon," I said casually. "Her interest in Marmion Shahrizai is passing strange, is it not? He set himself for the Queen, but she has turned his head."

"Nicola!" Diànne and her brother exchanged glances, and she laughed. "She hasn't a centime to her name, did you know it? It all went to her husband, through Aragonian law, and what he's not drunk, he's squandered. Whatever she's about, the Duc L'Envers put her up to it, and no mistake. 'Tis rumored that he's invested heavily in the tin trade everyone says will come out of Alba. It's in his interest to keep the Queen and her Pictish King sweet, with no scheming Shahrizai between them."

If I thought Barquiel L'Envers' schemes boiled down to mere commerce, I'd have slept easier at night. "Coin for her, and tin for him. Well, then, I would have learned somewhat." I shrugged again, and smiled ruefully. "But it would take my lord Anafiel Delaunay to make sense of it."

"I could tell you somewhat." Apollonaire sat up cross-legged, heedless of his own magnificent nudity. Though I

knelt demurely, I could not help but eye him. I had chosen
well, with these two. "The Comte . . . the Duc, that is,
Percy de Somerville, is not so happy as he seems with
the Queen's trust in the Unforgiven. I overheard him
quarrelling with Ghislain. He is not so inclined as his
son and the Queen to trust in the loyalty of the Black
Shields!"

"My lord Delaunay would have found that interesting," I murmured. It *was* interesting. Would Ghislain
plot with the former Allies of Camlach? Would Percy plot
against them? Or was it naught but father-son rivalry?
Ghislain had ridden with Isidore d'Aiglemort, the consummate traitor and ultimate hero of Troyes-le-Mont. So had
I. Percy had not. It was interesting. So was the Marquis de
Fhirze, who beamed at me, proud of his revelation, his
sizeable phallus beginning to stir to life.

I felt my arms caught from behind in an unexpectedly
strong grip, elbows drawn together. Diànne's breasts
pressed against my back, her voice laughing at my ear. "It
seems," she whispered, "my brother is not so tired as he
thought. Your Delaunay's machinations are an inspiration
to the scions of Naamah!"

So it seemed, for I continued to inspire them for a good
while longer.

One does not reckon, at such times, the cost to one's
limbs and joints; there is a limit to the pliancy of the mortal form. I daresay I surpassed it that day, although I have
kept myself limber, ever since Delaunay first ordered
Alcuin and me to study as tumblers. Still, it was a fine time,
for brother and sister alike were wholly without shame in
the arts of Naamah, and had honed their desires on the fine
edge of Kushiel's cruelty. Some things I learned, and it

accomplished what I set out, purging my mind for a time of its endless workings.

For all of that, my bed was still lonely when I went to sleep at the end of the day, and I still woke shuddering from nightmares.

Nineteen

WINTER SPUN out its length in grey, dreary days, chill wind and bluster, and only sometimes a snow that transformed the City into a vista of pristine whiteness, shining towers and icy minarets. I had become quite the fashion by this time, and I accepted assignations as readily as my swift-healing flesh allowed, choosing sometimes at whim and sometimes out of covert interest, so that no pattern might be discerned in my choices. My patrons were noble-born, scions of Elua and his Companions, diverse in their desires, and not a one displeasing to me.

Everything I had dreamed of having as a young adept in Delaunay's service, I had. Poets wrote odes in my honor, praising my beauty and charms; indeed, one slept three nights on my doorstep, nearly dying of cold and exposure, until Fortun dragged him bodily to his home. My patrons sent me gifts unbidden, curiosities and trinkets of varying value. Of money, I had no want; it flowed like a river. I paid my retainers and servants generously, and my debt to my glumly unsurprised factor. I invested in a Serenissiman enterprise, on the strength of a vague foreboding. I gave, quietly, considerable sums to Naamah's Temple, and made certain a portion of it went to sanctuaries in Namarre devastated in the war, where a captive priestess had once given her body to win me a few precious minutes of freedom in which to warn the fortress of Troyes-le-Mont.

I paid visits to Favrielle nó Eglantine, who had taken to freedom like a fish to water and designed for me any number of spectacular gowns with the fierce, focused joy of a genius at work. And when I was not doing any of these things, I met with the Rebbe Nahum ben Isaac and bent my mind to the difficult tasks he set me, droning Habiru verses for hour upon hour, while he chewed his beard and glowered at me.

And I was, quietly, unhappy.

No more pieces of the puzzle fell into place, no matter how I juggled them in my mind. No matter how diligently my chevaliers drank and diced and delved, not a single guardsman from Troyes-le-Mont was found. No word was forthcoming from the Prefect of the Cassiline Brotherhood; not in answer to Joscelin's query, and not in answer to the Royal Archivist's. I gave myself up to violent ecstasies at the hands of patron upon patron, all the while waiting and watching and listening in that tiny, Delaunay-trained corner of my mind I held back, but none divulged the key to make sense of it all.

Joscelin and I spoke less and less.

Somewhere, Melisande was laughing.

I thought a great deal of Hyacinthe in those days, and sometimes I missed him so terribly I ached with it. It had been our youthful dream, he and I: The Queen of Courtesans and the Prince of Travellers. Well, I was living it, but a shared dream half-lived is a hollow thing. I used to tell him everything. I could not even count the hours we spent in the Cockerel, puzzling out the mystery of Anafiel Delaunay, putting the pieces together, trying to guess at the patterns that emerged. He had always wanted to hear it all, my guesses and speculations; and the tales of my patrons, their wants and foibles, listening while his black Tsingano eyes danced merrily, his white grin flashing at the good parts.

Sometimes I felt as alone and islanded as he.

I had my chevaliers, it is true, and their ever-burgeoning, swaggering pride; Remy and Ti-Philippe, at least. Fortun was always steadier. I used to gaze at him, sometimes, and the way his dark hair curled on his brow, and thought of taking him as a lover. Thought, and chose not to, time and again. I liked Fortun, very much, and trusted him not a little.

But he did not make me laugh. And there was Joscelin.

One day our paths crossed at the yeshiva, although he knew it not. The Rebbe had sent for me, and Ti-Philippe had driven me; I gave him leave to dally at a nearby wineshop while my lesson was concluded. It was a long ordeal and draining; I saw in the Rebbe's eyes the mingled pride and despair, that a pupil of his should exceed so well, and have so little faith. And, too, I was hearing tales by then spoken openly in D'Angeline circles of the schism among the Yeshuites. I had not forgotten what I saw in the courtyard, the young men with swords at their hips, arguing fiercely in Habiru for harsh glory to be won in a far-off land.

The Rebbe dismissed me that day, lowering his hoary old head with weariness. I went quietly, stooping to kiss his withered cheek and seeing myself out of the yeshiva to await Ti-Philippe's return. I knew the way well, by then.

Impossible to mistake a D'Angeline voice in that place, even in hushed tones.

I have not forgotten my earliest training. I can move silently when I choose, and make myself as unobtrusive as a shadow. With noiseless steps, I followed the thread of Joscelin's voice, until I came nigh upon them, conversing in urgent tones in an empty study chamber. I had heard her speak before; it needed only once, for my memory. A young woman's voice, speaking softly accented D'Angeline. She taught the children, and had given him a *khai* pendant.

Hanna, her name was. It meant "grace." I knew, because I studied her mother tongue.

"Don't you see, Joscelin," she pleaded in her charming voice, "this pain, this *pain* you suffer, you cling to it; it is the pain of separation from Adonai, who is Lord of us all! You have only to make an offering of this pain, lay it upon the altar of Yeshua, and He will take it away. Can you not see it?"

Joscelin's voice was tense. "You speak of it as if it were a thing separate from me. It is not. I am Cassiel's, and vowed to his service. It is all that I am, this pain."

"Do you think Adonai would demand less?" Her voice took on passion, the shaking passion of a true believer. "Your pain is your pride; do not think He does not see that! But He is compassionate, and loves you all the more for it. I tell you, the Mashiach lived and suffered, to redeem the pain of us all. Would you belittle His sacrifice? Even so, He loves you, and awaits you like a bridegroom. There is a place prepared for you at His table, I tell you! And it

awaits us, so close we might touch it, not even beyond the
gates of death, but here and now, if only we dare seize it!
The Diaspora has begun, Joscelin, and Yeshua's kingdom
lies to the north. Will you deny, even now, your place in
it?"

"Yes." His voice was harried, and I heard his
vambraces rattle against his dagger-hilts. If he had bowed,
it must have been with unwonted awkwardness. "No. I
don't know, Hanna! I must think on it."

Another rattling bow, and the quick rush of his long
strides departing, carrying him away. I sank back against
the dim-lit wall, and he never saw me; all the turmoil he felt
reflected in his face. I heard her sigh, and make ready to
leave.

I stepped into the hallway in front of her.

Hanna's face changed when she saw me; guilt and
defiance and passion all at once. A Yeshuite and a teacher,
she was, but a woman too, and one in love. I had heard as
much, in her voice. I am versed in such things. "My lady
Comtesse," she said defensively, drawing back a step and
clutching her shawl at her throat. "We were but talking.
Joscelin Verreuil is not your servant, when all is said and
done."

"No," I said softly, tilting my head to gaze at her.
"When all is said and done, he is Cassiel's servant. And the
gods are jealous of those they have marked their own. I
ought to know."

"Gods!" The young Yeshuite teacher's eyes flashed,
and her hand dropped from her throat, clenching into a fist.
"Whom Joscelin worships as a god is but the least of
Adonai's servants. Will you condemn me for telling him
so?" When I did not answer, but shrugged, turning away,

she raised her voice. "Comtesse!" Despair made her harsh. "The Rebbe has no knowledge that will save your friend. He plays you for a fool, knowing that where you are tied out of hope, Joscelin will be bound out of loyalty. You may be a lost cause; but he is nearly one of us, now. It is said that if ever Cassiel the Apostate returns to the throne of the Almighty and bows his head to the Mashiach, Elua's Companions will follow. All rivers flow to the ocean in time, Comtesse. Adonai is the sea, and one mortal soul may turn the tide."

Though her words struck like arrows betwixt my shoulder blades, I did not turn back, but walked steadily away from her. She had told me nothing I did not know, where the Rebbe was concerned; he had never pretended to have the answer to Hyacinthe's riddle. All I required of him was the knowledge to pursue it myself, and that, he taught me fairly.

As for Joscelin; well. Now I knew in full why the Yeshuites courted him. It was his choice, still. Cassiel's Choice, they call it, when a member of his Order chooses banishment rather than abandon his once-sworn word. He had made it for me, though I had not asked it of him. I had warned her. I could do no more. And perhaps, truly, it would be different, when a god demanded the choice. I could not know, but only grieve at the necessity of it.

In the small courtyard, there was no sign of Joscelin, and three sword-bearing young Yeshuite men set upon Ti-Philippe as he drew up in my carriage; laughing in Habiru, catching at the horses' bridles and snatching at the long reins, mocking Ti-Philippe as he perched in the driver's seat. Wrapping the reins about his wrist, my chevalier scowled and hurled a D'Angeline insult at them;

one of the Yeshuites drew his sword and prodded Philippe's boot with the point of his blade.

An anger I'd not known I was suppressing overcame me.

"Gentlemen!" My voice rang out across the courtyard with an icy contempt I didn't know I could muster. I stood motionless, wrapped in my cloak, as they turned guiltily. "Let him be." Lest they were unsure, I added in flawless Habiru, enunciating each word with chill precision. "Leave him. Do you understand?"

Swords were sheathed, the carriage abandoned. The young men walked past me, sullen. The last turned, his face full of loathing. "You would not speak to us so, in Adonai's country!"

Mayhap he was right; I do not know. But this was Elua's country, and free by the grace of soldiers like Ti-Philippe, who had risked his life to beat back the Skaldi invasion. If not for him and ten thousand like him, we would all be equally on our knees, baring our necks for Waldemar Selig's yolk and offering praise to All-Father Odhinn. I thought these things, and did not say them. The Yeshuite glanced quickly from side to side, to be sure no one saw, and made a gesture, poking forked fingers at my face.

"A pox on your witch-marked eyes!" he jeered, spitting at my feet.

Men mock what they fear. I looked at him without answering, until his belligerence turned to unease and he shuffled, jerking away from me and hurrying to rejoin his companions, his walk turning to a swagger as they neared the yeshiva.

Ti-Philippe came down from the driver's seat in a fury,

swearing a blue streak as he yanked open the carriage door and threatening vengeance.

"Let it be," I said wearily, climbing inside. "Yeshua's House is divided against itself; I will not add to their sorrows. I owe a debt to his children." Remembering Taavi and Danele, the Yeshuite couple who had been so kind to Joscelin and me in our dire flight, I wondered if they were caught up in this schism, and prayed not.

I had money; I bought books, and read them, tracing with my finger the lines of Habiru text. I slept ill at night and tossed in my sheets, waking fevered from dreams I could not remember. I read, and studied, and learned, and came no closer to answering the riddle.

Hyacinthe.

Elua, but I missed him!

I suppose that my rootless sorrow made me reckless, although it may have been in part the slow-wearing frustration that arose from my stalled inquiries. Whatever the source, it was recklessness that led me to accept an assignation with Nicola L'Envers y Aragon.

It was in the Hall of Games that she approached me, where I watched Fortun engaged in a game of rhythmomachy with the Baronesse de Carvoile, whose mother had been an adept of Bryony House. It is a game for which I have no especial gift, being the province of those whose strength of wit lies in dealing with numbers; I can play it, if I must, but I do not do it well. Fortun, who had never once laid hand to the board ere becoming my chevalier, showed considerable skill at it.

Back and forth they went, placing their different-shaped counters in varying progressions, according to varying mathematical formulae, until I was well-nigh lost.

"Ah!" murmured a watching connoisseur, as Estelle de Carvoile laid down a sequence with surety. "A Fabrisian series!"

I blinked, bewildered, seeing no correlation in the numbers she played; Fortun merely frowned and countered with something called a Tertullian set. I can see patterns in events, and behaviors — in mathematics, I follow slower. Still, I added my voice to those lauding Fortun's play.

"A dull game," murmured a nearby voice, "for those who would rather dally with somewhat other than numbers." I turned to meet the violet gaze of Nicola L'Envers y Aragon, who gave me the lazy smile of a stalking leopardess. "Your chevalier is skilled, Comtesse."

"Yes," I said automatically. "He is." I eyed her sidelong. "Where is your companion, Lord Shahrizai, my lady?"

"Oh, Marmion." Nicola shrugged. "Sulking, no doubt. I told him I'd not divorce on his account, and he is wroth with me. It will do him good, in time. Meanwhile, I grow bored." She laid the tips of her fingers on my arm and smiled at me. "Do you know there is a term for your dalliances, Phèdre? Hunting hyacinths, they call it, those peers who have enjoyed your favors."

"No." With an effort of will, I kept my voice steady. "I did not know there was a term for it." I did not need it explained. Every patron knew my *signale*.

"Oh, yes." She smiled again, lazy and dangerous. "And no one has plucked one yet, I am told. Tell me, if I made you a proposal, would you accept it?"

Something happened at the gaming table; a good-natured cheer arose. Fortun had won. I stared at Nicola's violet eyes – so like her cousins', Duc and Queen – and weighed the risks, making my decision in spite of them. "Yes," I said, calculating. What was it worth, to Barquiel L'Envers? "If it was fitting."

The proposal came the next day by courier.

Twenty

A LONG white cord sturdily-wrought of silken threads hung around my neck.

"I knew a man in Aragon," Nicola mused aloud, drawing the ends of the cord beneath my arms and crossing them at my back, "who had travelled the spice routes to the uttermost east; the Empire of the Sun, they call it. They have arts of the bed-chamber as would interest even Naamah, he said." She wrapped the cord about my waist and moved behind me, using it to secure my wrists together. "Of course, I'd not time to learn them all. But what I did was most interesting. Ah, yes, that's nice."

Stepping back, she regarded her handiwork. I stood, docile, halfbound and naked as she took up another length of cord and set about securing it, from nape to waist and through my thighs, binding it to my wrists. I shifted my shoulders experimentally, feeling the friction of the cord between my legs.

"I'm not done," Nicola L'Envers y Argon said mildly, taking hold of the back of my neck. "On your knees, if you please."

I knelt, bowing my head automatically; the tension on the cord caused the silken length working its way between my nether lips to tighten, making me gasp. I raised my head, forced to kneel with back arched and breasts out-thrust.

"Now," she said, satisfied, "you begin to understand."

And then she set about finishing her work, binding my ankles tight together, and running the cord to knot it at my wrists. No matter how I moved, the cord grew taut between my legs, slipping back and forth. Lest I mistake it for chance, she had cunningly tied a knot there, a small, hard protuberance in the soft cord that taunted me, rubbing against Naamah's Pearl every time I shifted, causing me to bite my lip.

It pleased her; it pleased her a great deal. I could not help but gaze at her, on my knees, my chin upraised by virtue of the cord's necessity. Nicola prowled around me, smiling, violet eyes alit with pleasure, a finely-made deer-skin flogger in her hand. There were steel tips at the ends of it.

"Do you like this?" she asked, almost tenderly. "Hmm?"

"No."

Her arm moved in a swinging, sidelong gesture, and streaks of pain burst across my buttocks, my lower back, and my tied hands. I cried out and jerked against my bonds, causing the cord to saw into me, making my breathing ragged.

"You lie, don't you?" Nicola brought the flogger across me in a backhanded blow, raking across my breasts; the pain was so vivid I saw stars, and Kushiel's red haze. "Don't you!" She struck me again. I tossed my head involuntarily to avoid the blow, and the cord tautened against my efforts, tightening at the wrists, the knot between my thighs riding up and down against the sensitive node of flesh there. Nicola laughed, and trailed the flogger over my flesh; like an idiot, I struggled, bound tighter each time I writhed. The cords bit into my flesh everywhere, and a throbbing tide of pleasure rose in me. "Fight it, then, and see if you may free yourself," she taunted, striking me again. "Fight it!"

Half-obedient, half-defiant, I did, until the cord drew so tight my hands were numb, and that knot, that little knot, rode up and down, up and down against Naamah's Pearl, slick with moisture against my swollen flesh, pleasure mounting higher the harder I struggled against it, until I surrendered and cried out at the waves of pleasure that overwhelmed me.

When I opened my eyes — for I had closed them involuntarily — I saw the rich weave of Nicola's woolen carpet inches from me, and felt it scratch against my cheek. I'd not known, till then, that I'd fallen on my side.

"You may struggle all you like, but the result will never change," Nicola's voice said far above me, rich with amusement. "What I learned, I learned well. What will you give for your release, Phèdre nó Delaunay?"

"Anything you want," I whispered, trying not to move. The least gesture set off fresh ripples of ecstasy, giving me further into her hand.

Nicola crouched down, flogger in hand, her lovely, amused face close to mine. "What I want," she said, "is your *signale*. You have only given it once, I am told. To Melisande Shahrizai. Or was that only because you loved her?"

Before the moment those words left her mouth, I swear, I was not thinking of it at all — politics, betrayal, the game of covertcy, and Nicola L'Envers y Aragon's part in it all. These things I relegate to a small part of my mind, the only part I hold back from a patron, and think on afterward. But when she spoke, a connection formed, and I did something I had never done before with a patron. I could not help it. I did not mean to laugh, but I did; soundlessly, barely shaking, lest the very act of it trigger further arousal. Nicola regarded me with startled displeasure.

"Do you find it such a matter for laughter, Phèdre nó Delaunay?" she asked irritably, sitting back on her heels and giving me a flick with the flogger. "Do I *amuse* you so?"

"No." I sobered, lying quiescent in my bonds and rolling my eyes to look up at her beneath my lashes. "My lady, you tie a very skillful knot, and I am like to expire of involuntarily pleasuring myself if you do not release me from these bonds. If it please you to watch it, then you may do so. But I will not give you my *signale*." Power is a relative thing; she had been unwise, in letting me know what she desired to learn. "Tell me." I moved my legs and winced, as the knot shifted against me. "Was it Lord Marmion bid you ask that, or the Duc?"

With a disgusted sound, Nicola L'Envers y Aragon threw her flogger to the floor. "I *told* him I was overmatched with you!" she exclaimed, rising to her feet and pacing in annoyance.

Cautious to the utmost, I tucked my knees to my belly and rolled to a kneeling position, legs doubled beneath me, buttocks resting on my calves. Moving stiff fingers, I plucked at the knots that bound my ankles together. "The Duc," I said, as if I were certain; I was, fairly.

Nicola paused to cast a wry glance in my direction. "You could do me the courtesy, at least, of sounding surprised. And I thought you said I tied a skillful knot," she added, watching me kick off the cords that had bound my ankles.

"You do." I wriggled my hands and shrugged my shoulders, very carefully. "I can't get the rest on my own." I probably could, in time, but the pleasure it would provoke would cause a distraction I didn't wish to afford just now. "Why is it worth my patron-fee to Barquiel L'Envers to know if I once loved Melisande Shahrizai?"

"Once?" Nicola raised her eyebrows.

I knelt and regarded her. "My lady, she is indirectly responsible for the death of Anafiel Delaunay, whom I loved, admired and adored. Beyond that, she betrayed me and sold me into slavery among the Skaldi, and committed treason of the highest degree. Whatever I may have felt for her as my patron, I assure you, it pales beside that."

If we were in the Hall of Games, I would say that she hesitated, before laying the hand she had been dealt upon the table. No matter; I had guessed rightly, when I guessed who conned her into the game. "She spared your life, once," Nicola said.

"Does his grace wonder if I returned the favor in kind?" I asked, watching her face closely. I could hear Delaunay's voice, in my mind. *What are the telltales of one who conceals information?* Nicola exhibited several of them; eyelids flickering, her hands moving restlessly, busying herself picking up a flagon of cordial and pouring a drink. "I did not. But if he suspects me . . ."

"He didn't do it," Nicola said brusquely, tossing off her cordial and setting the glass down hard. "And yes, he wonders who did. Marmion Shahrizai was his first suspect. You were his second."

I might have laughed, though I didn't. "And you have established Lord Marmion's innocence?"

"I have established that Lord Marmion Shahrizai lives in covert terror of his cousin's retribution." Retrieving her flogger, she examined its braided thongs. "While you, who gave the very testimony that condemned her, do not seem particularly concerned at the prospect. You know, I told Barquiel to let me play you a time or two, but no, he was impatient."

"It wouldn't have mattered." The loops around my wrists really were cunningly tied.

"Probably not." Amusement returned to Nicola's voice. "But I would have enjoyed it, all the same. And he's not likely to fund another such excursion, now that I've botched this one."

I gave up on the knots. "My lady, the fault is mine, and I will remand your patron-fee. My laughter was inappropriate and inexcusable, and I can only beg your forgiveness."

Nicola looked at me a long time without speaking, her gaze thoughtful. "You *did* suspect him, didn't you? Cousin Barquiel."

"Yes." I didn't add that I was not entirely convinced of his innocence. If there was anyone on my list clever enough to throw off suspicion by turning the tables, it was Barquiel L'Envers.

"Why not Marmion?"

"I did, for a while. But . . ." I shook my head, forgetting

the ropes, and drew in my breath sharply at the
resulting friction. "You're right, though," I said when I
recovered myself. "He's truly afraid." I shifted, trying in
vain to ease the cord's tension. "Nicola, I swear to you,
on Elua's name, I did not conspire to free Melisande
Shahrizai."

Her purple gaze continued to regard me. "Do you
know who did?"

"No." In one reckless phrase, I cast the dice. "Not
yet."

Why I risked trusting her with that much, I cannot say;
it was born in part out of my abiding frustration and loneliness, of that much I am sure. Then too, it is a matter of
pride to me that I have never yet misjudged a patron.
Whatever her motives, Nicola was that — she'd had me
well in hand indeed, before mentioning Melisande's name.
I watched her full lips curve in a smile.

"I knew it would be interesting," she said softly,
caressing the flogger, "crossing wits with you, Phèdre
nó Delaunay. It is worth the price of losing, to see how it
is done." Nicola circled me, letting the lashes trail over
my skin, making me shudder. "This is what your patrons
see, isn't it?" she mused. "This beautiful, abject flesh,
trembling in supplication. Forgetting all the while . . ."
pausing, she raised my chin with her fingertips, ". . . that
behind those great dark eyes, shining with tears, lies a
subtle, calculating mind. It's so, isn't it?"

"Yes," I whispered, trembling.

"I like to see you cry." Cupping my cheek, Nicola
brushed her thumb along my eyelashes, then licked the
glistening, salty wetness from her skin; Elua, I could have
died! She truly was good. House L'Envers was Naamah's

lineage, but there must be Kusheline blood in there somewhere. I'd always wondered why their arms featured the
bridge over the river of Hell. It was a good thing it was
sufficiently diffused in Ysandre; House Courcel was
descended in a straight line from Blessed Elua. "But,"
Nicola said, jerking my attention back to her, "I will
always wonder what else you are thinking when you do."

In truth, I did not think a great deal after that; not
then, and not for a time to come. I daresay Nicola got her
fee's worth after all. It is a considerably difficult thing, to
thoroughly please a patron when one is constrained to
suffer unbearable pleasure at the slightest movement – and
it is harder, too, to please women than men, who are
simpler to gratify. On this, Naamah's Servants agree; one
is trained half again as long for it in the Night Court. Well,
I have never disgraced my training, with man or woman,
and I did not that day. But there were a few times when I
had to pause, writhing in my bonds, and Nicola's laughter
rang in my ears. She punished me with the flogger, then,
which only made it worse.

So it is, with patrons of mine. Naught pleases them so
well as the exercise of power; and by virtue of Kushiel's
Dart, I am the perfect instrument for their desires.

"Take it." Nicola laughed and pushed the purse back
across the table. "You earned it, in the end. I have no
complaints of you, Phèdre; and it's Barquiel's money, after
all."

"I know." I smiled, but shook my head. "No, my lady.
If I have made amends for my misstep, I am pleased. But I
cannot in conscience take this fee."

Toying with the purse-strings, she frowned. "You
know I contracted you under false circumstances."

"Well." I shrugged. "That may be, but I am Naamah's Servant still, and in her service, I erred. Naamah cares naught for politics and espionage. I cannot accept this fee."

"You really mean that?" She sounded surprised; I nodded. "Well, I would scarce say you failed her!" Nicola smiled, her eyes heavy-lidded. "Nonetheless, if I keep it, I will have your patron-fee still. Would you accept, if I offered?"

I glanced involuntarily at the silken cords lying coiled and harmless on the carpet. "Yes," I said, my voice rough-edged with desire. "You do . . . you do tie a skillful knot."

"Good." Nicola took back the purse, the matter settled. "Ramiro likes to be tied. My husband," she added, catching my puzzled glance. "But it's not nearly so pleasing a sight. You're a great deal more fun, and considerably more skilled. Besides, I never have the slightest interest in knowing what he's thinking. And when you come to it, he's probably cost me more than you."

I had to ask. "My lady . . . you didn't tie Lord Marmion, did you?"

"No." She laughed. "I can play Valerian as well as Mandrake, if I have to. Anything, to get out of Aragonia for a time." A non-D'Angeline wouldn't have known what she meant; I did. They are the houses of pain, in the Night Court. Where Valerian receives, Mandrake gives. "I'd rather the latter, but . . ." She shrugged. "I am interested by variety. And the Shahrizai are . . . well, you know."

I knew. "I wondered," I said aloud.

"Yes, well." Nicola looked down, frowned, and met my eyes. "I'm quite sure he killed his sister," she said softly. "Why do you suppose he would do that, if he were innocent?"

I could have dissembled; I thought about it, an expression of shock at the ready. In the end, I didn't. "She wasn't," I said bluntly. "I think she played a part in Melisande's escape, and Marmion knew it. His mistake was confronting her. He didn't know who her ally was; I think she threatened him, and he killed her rather than call her bluff. Now he's well and truly isolated himself. He's right, to be frightened; I don't blame him for that. But he's an idiot to think it's me. I don't hold that kind of sway."

"Mmm." Nicola looked speculative. "I don't know about that. Ysandre rallied her nation for invasion and civil war, on your bare word — if Marmion thinks she'd trust your condemnation, he may not be wrong. Nonetheless . . ." She chuckled. "You and cousin Barquiel, all at cross-purposes, suspecting each other. It's Anafiel Delaunay all over again, with him! Just think, if they'd made peace earlier. All they ever wanted was the same thing; Ysandre de la Courcel on the throne."

"Mayhap," I said slowly. "But there was blood between them, bad blood. Edmée de Rocaille was a friend of Delaunay's. And not even the Duc denies his sister Isabel was responsible for her death."

It was an old story, that one; a portion of the puzzle Hyacinthe and I had spent so many hours piecing together. I was not even born when Edmée de Rocaille died, who was betrothed to Prince Rolande. A hunting accident, it was said — but the girth of her saddle had been cut, and Edmée had a bitter rival in Isabel L'Envers, who bore no love for the Prince's poet-consort, Anafiel Delaunay. Edmée de Rocaille had been his friend since childhood.

Although it cost him the favor of the court and nearly Rolande's regard, my lord Delaunay wrote a deadly satire about Isabel L'Envers, blackening her name. Since then, he and her brother Barquiel had been dire enemies. I was but a babe in arms when Rolande was slain in battle. As for Isabel, whom Rolande had wed in the end, I remembered her death; I'd been a child, in Cereus House.

It meant as little to Nicola as to me: She shrugged. "And your Delaunay's verses named Isabel a murderess on everyone's tongue," she concluded. "Well and so, it's naught to do with you, Phèdre, nor with me. What would you say, if I offered to help you? What would you have me do?"

It was tempting; Elua, it was tempting! "Why?"

"Because." Nicola frowned. "Because you're damnably good at what you do, so good that I daresay no one else within fifty leagues of the City even knows you're doing it. When this is over, Barquiel will ship me back to Aragonia, whether I will it or no, and my only hope of gaining stature lies in intrigue. That, and the fact that my cousin Ysandre de la Courcel retains her seat on the throne of Terre d'Ange. Is that reason enough?" She smiled, then, that heavy-lidded smile. "Besides, it may afford another occasion for dalliance. And that would please me for its own sake. So tell me, what might I do?"

I had been thinking, all the while she spoke. "Do you know the Marquise Solaine Belfours?"

"Tall and haughty? Secretary of the Privy Seal?" Nicola laughed. "I know her. Why?"

"I need occasion to question her, without her suspecting. If you were to hold a fête and invite us both . . ."

"I can do that." Nicola cocked her head at me and

jingled the purse with my erstwhile patron's fee. "With this. Will you tell me why?"

"No." I shook my head.

"Well, then." She glanced at the white cords, such simple objects, lying in limp and dormant coils on the rich-toned carpet. "If you will not trust me, Phèdre, I will not do it for free, I think. Such are the lessons of intrigue I am learning. If I do as you ask, will you give me leave to question you about it? In a manner of my choosing?"

I have bartered myself for aught other than money before; it was not the first time. I gave myself to the Duc de Morhban in exchange for passage across his land. I would like to say that I thought it over carefully, and weighed the gain; in truth, I followed her gaze and looked once more at those damnable ropes. "You may question me to your heart's desire, my lady," I murmured.

"Oh, good," Nicola said cheerfully. "I was hoping you'd say that."

TWENTY-ONE

NICOLA'S FÊTE was considered a success all-round.

My patron-fee was a considerable amount, though less than the twenty thousand Severio had paid. Still, it was enough to throw an outstanding gathering. I learned, in the course of the evening, that Nicola was renowned in Aragonia for her hostessing skills. I'd not have guessed it, ere that.

The fête took place in one of the salons in the diplomats' wing of the Palace, and it had an Aragonian flavor, with a leisurely meal featuring course after course of spicy delicacies, and a goodly amount of hearty red wine poured with a free hand by servants in Aragonian attire. Afterward came music and dancers, fiddles and timbales marking the beat, while women danced in flounced skirts; I daresay among the guests, only Joscelin and I recognized a strong Tsingani influence.

The highlight of the evening was a quartet of players Nicola had hired to stage a pantomime. Skilled performers to a man, they played out a D'Angeline version of the Aragonian bull-fight. It gave me a shiver, when the "bull" emerged; clad all in padded black, hose showing his well-shaped legs, but above the neck, a towering bull's head with long, wicked horns curving high into the air. The picadors in their gilt-threaded jackets danced with the bull, prodding and whirling away, setting their barbed picks in cleverly placed padding while the bulldancer's steps grew slower and more deliberate, massive head lowering.

And then came the matador, the death-bringer, carrying cape and sword, bowing and flourishing. I gasped along with all the others as the matador's blade flashed toward the bull's neck. The shining edge of the sword cut clean, shearing through the papier-mâché bull's head, which fell tumbling to the floor. Out spilled an abundance of candies and trinkets, and the player's own human head poked grinning from the truncated bull-neck of his costume. Everyone applauded, then, and skirmished good-naturedly for the spoils. Nicola smiled, and ordered casks of sweet, nutty Aragonian brandy to be breached and poured all around, and we laughed and toasted her cunning entertainment, while the players bowed to considerable accolades.

Amid the dancing and mingling that followed, I nodded a cue to Joscelin, who nodded in reply and waited as I made my way to greet Solaine Belfours.

Her demeanor had changed not a wit since I had first encountered her at Alcuin's debut; a little older, perhaps, but no less arrogant. Her golden brows arched, and she looked down her nose at me as I greeted her.

"Phèdre nó Delaunay . . . de Montrève, is it? You've come a long way from scrubbing my floors, little Comtesse," she said coolly. I could not help but flush a little at that; she had always known, the Marquise Belfours, how to gall me. Among my old patrons, she was one I did not miss, and I was glad she had made me no proposals.

"My lady," I said with all the sincerity I could muster, "we are both in service to her majesty Ysandre de la Courcel, and it does not become us, this ill will between us."

Solaine Belfours gave a rather delicate snort of laughter. "I would be more like to believe you, Comtesse, if you had not counseled her majesty to replace me."

At that moment, Joscelin joined us, tripping over someone's leg and staggering a little, sloshing the glass of brandy he held, his face open and guileless. I swear, if I'd not known better, I'd have believed him half-drunk. Somewhere, my Cassiline had missed his calling as a player of no little renown. Hyacinthe had guessed better than he knew, when he put a Mendacant's cloak on Joscelin Verreuil. "Forgive me, my lady!" he exclaimed, offering a sweeping cross-armed bow and spilling brandy on her shoe. "Oh, oh! Twice over, I beg your forgiveness!"

Blessed Elua, but he was good! I would have kissed him, if he'd have let me; as it was, I bit my lip and made a courteous introduction.

"Oh!" Joscelin said, widening his gorgeous summer-blue eyes at her and swaying on his feet. "You would know, then, my lady of the Privy Seal . . . my lady, I am writing a treatise on the history of the Cassiline Brotherhood and House Courcel, very interesting stuff, to be sure . . ." Swaying, he placed one hand clumsily on her arm and peered at her. "Pray, my lady, mayhap you would help me gather information?"

Solaine Belfours shook him off, profound irritation

reflected in her mien. "Love of Elua, man, ask the Royal Archivist if you've need of that hoary old history! I've no time for Cassiel's nonsense."

"Pardon, my lady." Joscelin blundered backward a step, catching my eye for the merest second, a flicker of amusement come and gone so fast I might have imagined it. I would have held on to that flickering instant if I could; caught it and held it tight to me. "A thousand pardons!"

Solaine stared after him as he went weaving into the crowd, shaking her head. "I never thought," she said unpleasantly, "that left to your own devices, your taste would run to dumb and pretty, Phèdre. Do yourself a favor, and root around in the archives, if you will, but stay out of politics."

Nicola was right; my patrons failed, time and again, to pay heed to what I saw, what I witnessed. And I had seen enough to know that the Marquise did not dissemble. Her irritation was unfeigned; howeversomuch I mistrusted her – and I did – there was naught she feared to have uncovered in the Royal Archives or the history of the Cassiline Brotherhood.

Still, she had been a patron once, and I could not resist pushing. "As my lady bids," I murmured, curtsying; she did, after all, outrank me. "I did not mean to offend."

"I swear, sometimes, you live to give offense." Solaine Belfours looked sourly at me. "But I will forgive your intervention with Ysandre, if you swear to leave well enough alone. As you say, our interests lie in the same sphere. All the same, you ought to have a care, Phèdre." A curl of contempt shaped her lips. "If you think all of Lyonette de Trevalion's secrets died with her, you're twice the fool I reckoned."

It was an empty threat, made for the sake of taunting; I'd have staked my reputation on it. I knew Solaine Belfours, and I knew it rubbed her on the raw that Delaunay had played her for a fool, and I the bait on his hook. Still, a threat is a threat, and I noted it well, bethinking myself of Gaspar Trevalion, who had stood surety for her.

He had disavowed all knowledge and escaped all blame, when Lyonette de Trevalion's plan to put her son Baudoin on the throne was revealed; and indeed, it was my lord Anafiel Delaunay who stood surety for him, then. If Solaine had blackmailed Gaspar into aiding her, surely it was to do with that. I put two pieces together and thought: Gaspar knew. He knew of the plot, and said naught, even to Delaunay. Once, then, Gaspar Trevalion would have been content to see his kinsman Baudoin crowned in Ysandre's stead. His loyalty did not run as deep as my lord Delaunay had believed.

Satisfied with my conclusions, I made her another curtsy and withdrew, finding Joscelin. He kept up his pretense well, unsteady on his feet with another glass of brandy. "They will be gossiping tomorrow about Phèdre's Cassiline," he murmured. "And Solaine Belfours knows nothing."

"Well, that in itself is something," I retorted. "And I have never known you to care for gossip."

Joscelin smiled wryly, swirling his brandy and lowering his head as if to drink. I daresay no more than a sip of it had passed his lips. "They talk about you, you know," he said into his glass. "They say you are somewhat taken with the Lady Nicola L'Envers y Aragon, so much that you refused her payment. Your friend Apollonaire de Fhirze was passing jealous." Raising his head, he gave a short laugh. "And of me." His lips twisted bitterly. "He thinks I am the most fortunate man alive, it seems."

"You would be," I said. "If you had his tastes."

"Or his sister's."

Why is there ever this perverse cruelty in humankind, that makes us hurt most those we love best? Mayhap there is time and world enough, in the blessed Terre d'Ange-that-lies-beyond, to play these games out to their conclusions, but for us, on mortal soil, there is so little time! And I, of all people, was the least equipped to answer this riddle; I, who even now, in a hidden part of my soul, savored the deep ache of the words Joscelin and I threw at each other, the pain of a lovers' quarrel magnified by the deliberate act of hurting each other. Who knows how long we would be bound to the wheel of life by these acts, doomed to live again and again in mortal flesh, until we freed ourselves to pass through Elua's Gate? Yet even so, we do it, time and again.

"Come." Barquiel L'Envers' voice, light and mocking, slid between us like a blade. "Trouble among the Companions' chosen twosome? Say it is not so!"

With an effort, I erased my thoughts from my face to smile pleasantly; Joscelin, forgetting himself, gave a smooth Cassiline bow, hands settling watchfully over his dagger-hilts.

"Your grace," I murmured to the Duc, curtsying.

"If Ysandre doesn't stand on ceremony with you, I'll not." He smiled, showing his teeth. "And of a surety, Nicola is not minded to! She'd not be the first beholden to me I'd lost to your charms, would she, Delaunay's *anguissette*?"

In truth, she would not. There had been Childric d'Essoms, before, and a minor lordling named Rogier Clavel. Delaunay had used me to get to them, and them to get to the Duc L'Envers. Neither of us had forgotten. "I do not think the Lady Nicola is lost, my lord," I said carefully. "Say rather she thinks we are about the same business, you and I."

L'Envers rubbed at a scar on his chin, a souvenir of Khebbel-imAkkad, if rumor spoke truth. "And you doubt it."

I raised my eyebrows at him. "Don't you, my lord?"

He laughed. "Ah, Phèdre! I begin to think Anafiel Delaunay named a worthier heir than any of us suspected. I thought Ysandre was mad, when she sent you to the wilds of Alba as her emissary. If I'd thought it was aught else than a fool's errand, I'd have done somewhat more to halt it. But you did it, didn't you? And yet." His thoughtful gaze measured me. "Could you truly have watched her slain?"

I didn't have to ask who he meant.

Melisande.

I didn't have to answer honestly, either, but I didn't trust myself with a lie. I returned his gaze squarely. "No. No, my lord, if you must know; I could not have watched it. Which is why I passed the night on the battlements of Troyes-le-Mont. If you do not believe it, question those men who stood guard that night, and learn it for yourself."

Barquiel L'Envers gave me a wry expression and ran a hand through his short, fair hair. "I've tried, actually; or my men have. They are singularly difficult to locate, the guardsmen of Troyes-le-Mont."

Joscelin started, and I glanced sharply at him. L'Envers didn't miss it, looking from one to the other of us.

"So you, too, have looked. Have you found them? Or," he asked, pleasant and dangerous, "or have you hid them, hmm?"

"Your grace." With an effortless motion, Joscelin stepped between us, and his hands rested lightly on his hilts. "I swear to you, on Cassiel's Dagger, that my lady Phèdre nó Delaunay de Montrève had naught to do with the disappearance of Melisande Shahrizai, nor any knowledge of the guardsmen of Troyes-le-Mont." His voice was even, and deadly. "If you would be her ally, then be so; if you would not, then do not impugn her."

He had a couple of inches on the Duc, and the training of a Cassiline warrior-priest, begun at the age of ten. But Barquiel L'Envers was a battle-seasoned D'Angeline warleader whose prowess had won the admiration of the Khalif of Khebbel-im-Akkad; and there are no fiercer warriors on earth than the Akkadians, ever since Ahzimandias, the Spear of Shamash, led his people out of the deserts of the Umaiyyat to reclaim the rights of the long-fallen House of Ur.

"Don't swear on your daggers, Cassiline," he said calmly, "unless you mean to use them. And if you do, strike quickly, because I'll have your head if you don't. Well, we are at an impasse, it seems; perhaps allies, perhaps foes. Shall we bargain, then, Phèdre nó Delaunay? I know one place no one has looked for the guardsmen of Troyes-le-Mont. What do you offer?"

I touched Joscelin's arm lightly, and he stepped reluctantly back. "What does his grace the Duc de Somerville say of his guardsmen?" I asked thoughtfully. "You are friends, my lord. Have you not inquired?"

Barquiel eyed me. "Yes, of course; do you take me for an idiot? He had given their command unto Ghislain, who gave them leave to expiate their failure by pursuing the Skaldi. That much is clear. Their return, howsoever . . ."

"The Unforgiven." I bit my lower lip, unmindful of L'Envers' amused glance. "Whom Percy de Somerville does not trust, and where no one has inquired."

"Even so." He opened his hands. "What will you give me for it in trade?"

"Phèdre," Joscelin murmured.

Sometimes, one must play at hazards. "A speculation, my lord; do with it what you will. Persia Shahrizai paid her cousin a visit that night, but it was Melisande who left in her stead. This is the knowledge with which Lord Marmion confronted his sister. What she threatened him with in return . . ." I shrugged. "I cannot say, except that I think he killed her for it."

His violet eyes narrowed. "Mayhap I will ask him."

"And mayhap I will join the Unforgiven," I said dryly. "Unless I think of a better way to question them."

"Your usual methods seem fairly effective." He gave me an amused glance. "I am given to understand you've made a bargain with Nicola as well, in exchange for this night's entertainment. I might even claim it myself, Phèdre nó Delaunay, as 'twas my purse funded it in the first place, if you'd not convinced me to be wary of you."

With that, he bowed and took his leave; I hastily closed my mouth on my astonishment, in time to find my arm caught tight in Joscelin's grasp.

"No," he said, his voice taut. "Not him. Phèdre, if you love me at all, promise me, not him!"

I thought of Melisande sending the cloak and laughed

despairingly, my voice cracking on it. "And if he were the one? Oh, Joscelin!" I shook the tears from my eyes and caught the front of his doublet, a handful of velvet and the *khai* pendant bunched in my fist. "What will you give me for it in trade? If you love me at all, will you promise what I might ask?"

"Don't. Phèdre, don't ask." With infinitesimal gentleness, Joscelin pried my hand loose; turned, and walked away.

Watching him go, I whispered the words, knowing he wouldn't hear.

"I promise."

TWENTY-TWO ⊙

AFTER NICOLA'S fête, I prevailed on Remy to serve as my carriage-driver and ventured out to pay another visit to the Royal Archives. As it transpired, Micheline de Parnasse was abed that day with an ague in the joints, and I spoke to her assistant instead, the Siovalese lordling.

"Bernard." Having learnt his name, I smiled at him. "Tell me, truly; are no others than the Queen and the Secretaries of the Privy Seal allowed admittance to the archives?"

Ducking his head, he blushed and mumbled. It took some doing, but eventually he confessed that at those times when the Royal Archivist's steely gaze was elsewhere, various peers of the realm had been known to badger her assistants for access. I made him give me names, and from what he could remember, it was a long list.

Barquiel L'Envers was on it; so was Gaspar Trevalion, and Percy de Somerville. He remembered them well enough. None, however, had been near the ledger recording members of the Cassiline Brotherhood attendant on House Courcel. Indeed, Bernard swore up and down that no one — no one! — had ever desecrated the archives on his watch.

"What did they want to see?" I asked him. "Do you remember?"

He nodded, swallowing hard; the apple in his throat bobbed with it. "Some one of them at least asked after the folios on the trial of Lyonette and Baudoin de Trevalion."

Nothing for it then but that I must look through the folios, poring over transcribed records and supplementary materials. The letters were there — all there, insofar as I could tell. Letters written by Foclaidha of Alba to Lyonette de Trevalion, the Lioness of Azzalle, plotting the invasion that would have put Baudoin on the throne.

Baudoin, infatuated, had showed them to Melisande; even worse, in extravagant, idiotic proof of his love, had given several of them to her. And Melisande used them to destroy him, and any claim to the throne House Trevalion may have held.

She gave him a farewell gift, though.

Me..

Well, and so; it was the past, and should have been over and done, if not for the endless intrusions of old quarrels, old betrayals, into the present. Whatever was there, if it could incriminate one of those three, it was gone now, the allegedly watchful eye of Bernard of Siovale notwithstanding. Some one of them, he said; mayhap others. More than one person had asked to see these folios. I had a good guess about Gaspar's apprehensions; about the Duc L'Envers and the Royal Commander, I could only wonder. And, of course, there were eight or nine others Bernard had named whom I hadn't even begun to suspect.

"Thank you," I said to him, making ready to leave.

One last thought struck me. "Bernard, my lady de Parnasse said the Queen visits the Archives, sometimes. Does she bring her Cassiline attendants, when she does?"

"Of course!" His eyes widened. "Not that she'd come to harm, here, mind, but . . . she is the Queen. It is their sworn duty to protect and serve the scions of Elua."

"Have any ever come alone?" I asked.

Bernard shrugged. "Oh, once or twice, mayhap, the Queen has sent one of her Cassilines on an errand. One must make allowances for royalty, my lady; even the Archivist herself would not turn away the Queen's Cassilines!"

Alas, his description of the Cassiline Brothers he had seen in the archives was predictably vague; of middle years, dour, grey-clad. In short, it fit nearly every Cassiline I'd ever seen, save for Joscelin. "So you do not keep watch over them," I said, discouraged.

"No." He blinked at me, puzzled. "Why would we watch over Cassiline Brethren? They're . . . Cassiline! They, they . . . you know. Protect and serve."

"Yes," I sighed. "I know."

Since there was no more to be learned in the Royal Archives, I collected Remy from the wineshop where he was awaiting me and returned home in a pensive mood.

"You're back," Joscelin said flatly. "I was worried."

"If you're so damnably worried," Remy said, eyeing Joscelin, "you should have gone yourself, and left off your hang-dog sulking, Cassiline."

Joscelin smiled tightly. "Should I not worry, then, that Phèdre nó Delaunay entrusts her safety to dice-playing sailors without the sense to remain sober when warding her?"

Remy swore once, and swore again, with a sailor's eloquence, and threw a punch at him. Joscelin shifted his balance, turning at the waist, and Remy's fist struck the wall of the entryway. Cursing and shaking his bruised knuckles, Remy drove his left elbow backward into Joscelin's ribs, forcing him back a step. Catching himself against the wall, Remy turned to face him, spitting out an epithet. "Sour-faced, vinegar-sucking cleric!" He threw another angry blow. With the ease of long training, Joscelin slid out of its way, caught Remy's arm between crossed wrists, grating the small bones together, and with an effortless twist brought him to the floor, not disdaining to thrust a knee hard in his midriff on the way down. I stared open-mouthed, scarce able to credit the outbreak of violence within my own walls. When I gathered my wits, I shouted.

"Joscelin!"

He froze, and stepped back, raising his hands in surrender. Remy, swearing furiously, struggled to his feet, shaking his head like the dancer in the Aragonian bull-masque, ready to attack again.

"Enough!" I was angry, truly angry. "Remy, I granted you the title of chevalier at your Lord Admiral's request; if you wish to hold it, act the part. Joscelin . . ." Glaring at him, I rapped the daggers at his belt, then flicked the *khai* pendant on his chest with my finger. "Live by one or the other, if you must, but don't break faith with both."

He drew himself up at that, but I stood my ground.

"This is my household," I said softly. "And I will not countenance violence within it, least of all from you. If you do not like it, you may leave."

Joscelin muttered something – I could not hear it – and

stalked off. And even as I watched, Remy gathered himself to follow.

"Don't." I made my voice flat and emotionless. "Have I ever given you an order? I order it now: Let him be, Remy."

He stared at me and shook his head, his auburn queue moving fiercely. "You're mad, my lady. I know you care for him, I do. But he'll break your heart, that one, grind it to bits against his cursed Cassiline pride."

"Mayhap," I murmured. "And mayhap his pride will break first. It is between Cassiel and Naamah, who make our mortal flesh their battleground. Either way, let be."

Remy paused, then bowed stiffly to me. "My lady."

I would have spoken to Joscelin afterward, and told him aloud what I had whispered unheard, in the matter of Barquiel L'Envers' interest, had somewhat else not arisen. We learned of it in the morning, from the lips of a runner sent by Nicola L'Envers y Aragon, racing so quickly with the news that he needs must double over on my doorstep, breathing hard.

"Comtesse," he gasped, trying to straighten. "My lady bids me . . . my lady bids me tell you Marmion Shahrizai is charged with murder!"

I ordered water brought him, and by the time he had the story out, Fortun had quietly made ready the carriage. It seemed that Barquiel L'Envers had wasted no time in pursuing his investigation. Where House Shahrizai quarrelled among itself and feared to risk Ysandre's displeasure while Marmion stood in her favor, the Duc L'Envers had no such fears. Putting all his considerable resources to the task, he sent his men-at-arms on swift Akkadian horses to ruthlessly question Shahrizai retainers and survivors of the fire, and gathered enough evidence to confront Marmion, within a scant fortnight of our conversation. When he played his trump card — my guess at Persia's role in Melisande's escape — Marmion turned pale as death, and Barquiel L'Envers ordered him taken into custody.

All of this, I learned, and more. Outraged at L'Envers' inquiry, Faragon, Duc de Shahrizai, the patriarch of House Shahrizai himself, had left his estates for the first time in fifteen years, riding toward the City of Elua the moment he'd heard word of it, with a large retinue. And if *that* were not trouble enough, Quincel de Morhban, the sovereign Duc of Kusheth, had gotten wind of the matter, and elected to lead a delegation of his own.

It all converged at once, and Ysandre de la Courcel, Queen of Terre d'Ange, was furious.

"What," she said succinctly, pacing the floor of her chambers and fetching up before Barquiel, "were you *thinking?*" Her eyes flashed violet with anger. "If this is a matter of state — and I have heard no evidence that it is so — you should have informed me, uncle! And if it is not, then it is most certainly *not* in your purview!"

To his credit, Barquiel L'Envers never flinched; and Ysandre's was scarce the only fury cast his way. In the center of the room, surrounded by the Palace Guard, stood Marmion, glowering and shackled. Clustered to his right were the representatives of House Shahrizai, their Duc Faragon at the forefront. A black-and-gold brocade coat masked a barrel chest, but his face had that unmistakable beauty, like something carved of ancient ivory. His hair fell like rippled silver, caught below the nape in a gold clasp, and despite wrinkled lids, his eyes were the deep blue of sapphires. A half-dozen Shahrizai faces, male and female, were sprinkled among the retainers massed behind him.

No less menacing was Quincel de Morhban, a lean wolf of a man with a watchful look in his grey eyes. Despite the machinations of House Shahrizai, he retained sovereignty over Kusheth, and was no one to be toyed with lightly – and Barquiel L'Envers had done just that, with his investigation. De Morhban's men stood at ease, as watchful as their lord.

In the face of all this, Barquiel L'Envers gave a lazy smile. "My apologies for the irregularity of my methods. But it *is* a matter of state, Ysandre, and your Lord Marmion Shahrizai is involved in it up to his eyeballs. He's been concealing knowledge of Melisande's escape and whereabouts, which you . . ." he bowed ironically to her, ". . . chose not to believe. Since I cannot prove that, I have proven instead that he was complicit in his sister's death, which matter neither his House nor his sovereign Duc thought worthy of pursuing."

There were murmurs all around at that; a couple of the Shahrizai surged forward. Duc Faragon raised one hand, and they subsided. Quincel de Morhban narrowed his eyes. For my part, I stood unobtrusive as I could behind Nicola. How Ysandre had learned it, I do not know – never underestimate a ruler's network of informants within their own demesne – but when I arrived at Nicola's quarters in the Palace, there was already a curt order awaiting that I attend the hearing with her.

"I've done nothing!" Marmion declared angrily, shifting so his chains rattled. "You've proof of nothing, for there's nothing to prove!"

Barquiel L'Envers raised his eyebrows, and gave a cool

nod to one of the Palace Guardsmen. Opening the door to Ysandre's private hearing room, the guard ushered in the first in a long line of witnesses.

There must have been over a dozen of them, all told; the guardsmen my chevaliers had questioned were among them. But too, there were maidservants and kitchen staff, stewards, hostlers, and most telling, a daring poacher's boy who'd espied two figures fleeing the burning manor-house and riding west on horses they'd concealed in the wood. It had taken him two days, but he'd tracked them to Lord Marmion's estate. If it had been aught but an internecine affair, he'd have sought an award for the information, but he feared to come forward among quarreling Shahrizai, who were as like to string him up for poaching as reward him. How Barquiel had found him, I'd no idea.

Ysandre sat formally to hear the testimony, and her face turned unreadable as it wore on. Two Cassiline Brothers flanked her, upright and motionless, hands on daggers, nearly identical in their ash-grey mandilion coats and clubbed hair. They were fixtures, part of the trappings of royalty, as much as the gilded sconces and the elegant tapestries. Small wonder, I thought, Bernard could not describe them individually; I was hard put to do it myself.

I could consider such things, because it had grown evident, long before the testimony ended, that Marmion Shahrizai was guilty. After the poacher's boy, his shoulders slumped, chains hanging slack from his wrists. I glanced at the Duc de Shahrizai, and saw an implacable sentence writ in his gaze.

When it was done, Ysandre spoke, her voice cool and measured. If ever she had cared for him, no one would know it to hear her. "What do you say, my lord Marmion?"

His answer, by contrast, was strained. "I didn't intend it." He gave her an agonized look. "I sent them, but only to search the manor! When yon steward summoned the guard, they panicked and fled, throwing down their torches." Marmion Shahrizai turned out his elegant hands, shackles clanking. "I never intended a fire," he whispered.

One by one, beginning with Duc Faragon, the members of House Shahrizai turned their backs upon him. I pitied Marmion his fear, a little.

Ysandre's expression never changed. "And why, my lord, should we believe you, when you have done nothing but lie to us? It is far easier to credit that you set fire to your sister's manor to silence her, lest she reveal your complicity in the matter of Melisande's escape. Of a surety, she is not alive now to gainsay you."

"No!" The word burst from Marmion's lips. Staring around the room, he gave a wild laugh. "Who is it? One of you here? You, your grace?" He indicated Barquiel L'Envers with a jerk of his chin. "You've done for me, sure as death! Or you, my lord." He laughed despairingly as Quincel de Morhban raised an eyebrow. "I trusted you! I betrayed my own cousin into your hands, for the promise of the rewards my loyalty would bring. Did you and Persia use me as your stalking-horse? Was it naught but a plot within a plot all the while?"

It could not have been de Morhban, I thought. He delivered Melisande as a pledge of his loyalty, but he hadn't fought on the battlefield. Ysandre never trusted him wholly, nor would the garrison of Troyes-le-Mont. The guard at the postern gate would have challenged Quincel de Morhban, Duc or no.

So I was thinking, when I realized Marmion's stare had picked me out of the gathering. "Or you," he said softly. "How high you have risen, little Comtesse! To think, so short a time ago, you were but a runaway bondservant convicted of murdering her lord. Now, commoners bow in the streets, nobles vie for your favors and you conspire openly with a scion of the Stregazza. But I, I have not forgotten you were Melisande's creature."

"Enough." Ysandre did not raise her voice, but the tone of command silenced him like a hammer. "Then is it your claim, my lord Marmion, that your sister Persia conspired with an unknown ally to achieve Melisande Shahrizai's escape from Troyes-le-Mont?"

"It is," he said grimly. "She told me as much, and that it was worth my life to breathe word of it within ten leagues of the throne."

"And you sought proof of this from her manor-house?"

Marmion licked his lips. "A courier had come from the east. Unmarked livery, but there was . . . there was a stable-lad, who brought me information in exchange for silver. He saw the insignia of the Stregazza on the courier's bags. I thought if I could learn somewhat . . ." He gave that laugh that was no laugh, tears standing in his eyes, and raised his shackled arms. "I thought," he gasped, "I might not end like this, Ysandre!"

She looked at him without remorse, without pity. "You should have told us, Lord Marmion. We would have protected you."

"Would you?" he whispered. "From whom?"

Having no answer, Ysandre gave him none. "Your grace," she said crisply to Quincel de Morhban. "I am satisfied with Lord Marmion's confession in the matter of withholding evidence in an affair of state. As for the crime of arson leading to death, that is a matter for Kusheline justice, and I remand him unto your jurisdiction."

"Your majesty." Quincel de Morhban bowed, and turned to Duc Faragon. "Your grace, these crimes fall within the demesnes of House Shahrizai. I am willing to give Lord Marmion over unto your custody, do you wish it."

Silver-grey hair rippled as the patriarch of House Shahrizai shook his head, never glancing at Marmion. "From this day forth, he is no scion of my House," Faragon de Shahrizai said in a deep voice. "Pass sentence as you deem fit, cousin."

"Very well." Quincel de Morhban took a breath, and in a formal tone, gave his judgement. "Marmion of Kusheth, for the crime of arson leading to death, you are herewith stripped of your title and estates. Your possessions shall be sold, and the proceeds distributed among the survivors of your actions and the families of the deceased." Pausing, he continued in a different voice. "Whether or not you sent your men to fire the manor, I cannot say. I don't suppose you can produce them to testify on your behalf?"

A distant look in his eyes, Marmion shook his head. "I dismissed them from my service and told them I never wanted to see them again."

"Then I shall do the same." Quincel de Morhban pronounced his final sentence. "Exile."

At a nod from Ysandre, her Captain of the Guard produced a key and struck Marmion's shackles. No one spoke.

He stood alone in the center of the room, rubbing his chafed wrists. The guards formed a double line leading to the door, giving him a cue to exit. After a moment, Marmion gave a soft, despairing laugh, and I thought I had never seen a man more alone in the midst of a throng. He turned to Ysandre, and bowed. She inclined her head once, briefly, and Marmion turned, walking away. A pair of guards fell in behind him. They would see him, I knew, to the gates of the City.

Beyond that, he was on his own. I gazed at Barquiel L'Envers, lounging against a column; at the keen hatred on the Shahrizai faces scattered here and there. I did not think Marmion Shahrizai would live long.

Ysandre turned her expressionless gaze on Barquiel L'Envers. "I am still wroth with you," she said, although she abandoned the royal pronoun for the personal. "And you." The violet eyes turned my way. "I want to talk to you, Phèdre."

TWENTY-THREE

İ WAS some time cooling my heels, waiting on the Queen's indulgence, imagining all the while the most dreadful things — foremost among them that Ysandre had taken Marmion Shahrizai's accusations to heart. Indeed, Ysandre may well have intended it, bidding me to wait in an antechamber without so much as a foot-servant for company. A nervous silence loosens tongues; I knew that much from Delaunay's teaching.

When one of her Cassilines came to fetch me, it was not to one of her receiving rooms that he escorted me, but a room in the Palace I'd never seen before; the Hall of Portraits, it is called. The scions of House Courcel were prominently displayed. I walked past a long line of them, to find Ysandre gazing at a small portrait hung in an out-of-the-way niche, near to the images of Prince Rolande and Princess Isabel, her parents.

"Pretty, wasn't she?" Ysandre asked by way of absent greeting, ignoring my curtsy.

"Yes, your majesty." Unsettled, I glanced at the portrait; a young woman with kind brown eyes and a gentle smile, rich brown hair coiled at the nape of her neck in a pearl-studded mesh caul. "Who was she?"

"Edmée de Rocaille. She was to have married my father." Ysandre touched a brass plaque at the base of the frame that gave Edmée's name. "Imagine," she mused, "how different matters would have fallen out, if she had. I would not have been born, and Anafiel Delaunay would have stood at my father's left hand as his sanctioned Consort. You and I would not be standing here having this conversation, Phèdre."

"Your father," I said, "would still have been killed in the Battle of Three Princes. And Skaldia would still have given birth to Waldemar Selig, uniting for the first time under a leader who thought."

"Mayhap." Ysandre looked directly at me. "My mother was responsible for her death, you know."

"I know." I glanced involuntarily at the portrait of Isabel L'Envers de la Courcel, a fair, blonde beauty with her daughter's violet eyes and a cunning mouth like her brother Barquiel's. A cut girth-strap, a riding accident. Ysandre resembled her a great deal more than her father.

"And now I have allowed Marmion Shahrizai to be sent to his death," Ysandre murmured. "Or at least, I'd not give a fig for his chances. Would you, near-cousin?" She glanced at me, and I shook my head slowly. She sighed. "If he dies, and I learn the cause of it, I'll have to mete out justice, and there's another blood-feud in the making. It never ends. And the awful irony of it is, Marmion *was* loyal, after a fashion. 'Twas fear sealed his lips."

"He did what he did," I said automatically. "Loyalty does not make right of it, nor fear."

"I know that," Ysandre said impatiently. "Elua! Do

you think I *wanted* to rule as I did? One has no choice, when the law is clear. But I think Marmion spoke the truth nonetheless. Phèdre. I am neither stupid nor blind. Did Persia Shahrizai aid in Melisande's escape?"

I nodded, slowly.

"Good." Her voice was hard. "Did she have an ally?"

I nodded again.

"Do you know who it was?"

I shook my head. "No," I whispered.

"Neither do I." Ysandre gave a short laugh and pressed the heels of her hands against her eyes. "Marmion always suspected you, but he wasn't there, when you and that half-mad Cassiline staggered out of the wilds of Skaldia onto my doorstep, while my grandfather lay dying, to give me worse news than I could have dreamt in my darkest nightmares. I gambled everything on your bare word, Phèdre, and rewarded you by sending you into even direr circumstances. I want, very badly, to trust you. And yet I am afraid."

At that, I fell to my knees and protested my loyalty, tears standing in my eyes. I could not help it, then. What I said, I scarce remember; not everything, but it was a great deal more than I'd intended. Ysandre listened, and gradually a semblance of calm came over her features.

"You should have told me." It was what she had said to Marmion. I daresay she was right, on both counts. "Why did you tell my uncle instead? I did not think there was much love lost between Barquiel L'Envers and the household of Anafiel Delaunay."

"It was scarce more than he knew," I murmured. "Nicola already suspected Marmion was responsible for killing his sister. He plays at some game with me; I wanted to see what he would do. I didn't think it would be . . . this."

"My uncle," Ysandre said reflectively, "had, to the best of my knowledge, Dominic Stregazza assassinated on suspicion of killing my mother. He is not a temperate man. Exactly how deep in it is my charming cousin Nicola?"

"Not very." I shook my head, settling back to sit on my heels. "He uses her as Delaunay used Alcuin and me, only she does it for amusement and money, and the experience of the thing. I don't think Marmion guessed it."

"You trust her?"

I shrugged. "I trust it is no more than that, with her."

"And my uncle?" When I didn't answer, Ysandre gave me a hard look. "You suspect him, don't you?"

"My lady." I spread my hands. "Barquiel L'Envers claims to be protecting your interests, and I owe him my life. But it is someone we all trusted." In the distance, but not out of earshot, Ysandre's Cassilines stood on guard, features impassive, at ease in the familiar stance, hands crossed above their dagger-hilts. I thought of saying more, and closed my mouth.

"*Why?*" Ysandre asked aloud, frustration in her voice, staring at the portraits of her family line. Rolande, Isabel, Ganelon, Benedicte, Lyonette. House Courcel, in all its tumultuous history, and off to one side, Edmée de Rocaille, who had been caught up in it and died because of it. So had my lord Anafiel Delaunay, keeping a promise. Ysandre was right. It never ended. "Why would anyone who risked their life to save the realm risk everything to betray it?"

I heard the Marquise Solaine Belfours' voice in my

memory. *If you think all of Lyonette de Trevalion's secrets died with her, you're twice the fool I reckoned.*

A desecrated ledger in the Royal Archives; a folio perused by unknown eyes. Condemning letters, written to Lyonette de la Courcel de Trevalion. Letters provided by Melisande Shahrizai. When had Melisande ever played the whole of her hand? Never, I thought. Melisande had held somewhat back, and whatever it was, it sufficed for blackmail.

The more I learned, the less I knew.

At the far end of the Hall of Portraits, the door opened.

"Your majesty!" The Captain of the Guard stood bowing in the open doorway. "Forgive my intrusion, but I thought you would wish to know. The outriders from Azzalle have arrived. The flagship of the Cruarch of Alba has been sighted crossing the Straits."

"Drustan!" Ysandre breathed his name, and her entire countenance lightened, violet eyes fair glowing. For a moment, she looked not like a Queen, but only a young D'Angeline woman in love. "Blessed Elua be thanked." All thoughts of intrigue temporarily forgotten, she looked down at me in puzzlement. "Phèdre, what on earth are you doing on your knees?"

I wasn't sure myself. "Asking forgiveness?"

"Name of Elua." Ysandre considered me. "All right, Phèdre. I need candour, not apologies. Fail in it again, and I'll consider my trust misplaced. Now get up, and help me plan to welcome the King. And while you're at it," she added, asperity returning to her voice, "you may tell me exactly what you were about with that young Stregazza lad."

"Yes, my lady," I murmured, rising with the fluid motion drilled into every prospective adept of the Night Court and casting a dubious glance at her Cassiline guards. "As you wish."

I made a fair job of evading her questions, after that; it was not so hard, with the news of Drustan's incipient arrival distracting her. Ysandre had not forgotten – she missed little and forgot less – but she was more than willing to set it aside for the moment. For that, I could not blame her; her path to the throne had been a difficult one, and the crown lay heavy on her head. Lest anyone doubt that Ysandre de la Courcel cared for her Pictish lord, I may say, the Palace never knew such a scouring as it received in the days that followed.

My skills as a translator were much in demand in those days, for naught would do but that diverse entertainments were to be staged in Drustan's honor, given in D'Angeline and Cruithne alike. It was sweet, after the long winter months of wrestling with Habiru, to turn my tongue to a language I knew well.

Ysandre planned a procession to begin a full league outside the City, and I rode out as part of her delegation to make arrangements. Her Master of Ceremonies came himself, fussing over plans for a series of pine bowers to arch over the road. My part was easier, and I had Nicola L'Envers y Aragon to help me. Accompanied by a Guardsman bearing a great satchel of coins, Nicola passed out silver centimes to children and youths along the way with the injunction that they gather flowers to throw in Drustan's path, while I instructed them in shouting, "Long live the Cruarch of Alba!" in Cruithne. In truth, we had a great deal of fun doing it, and the day passed in laughter.

Even so, I slept fitfully, plagued by nightmares, which had worsened since Marmion Shahrizai's exile. In an effort to take my mind from such matters, I took an assignation with Diànne and Apollonaire de Fhirze, for between the two, nothing passed at Court nor in the City but that they heard of it. Most of their talk was of the coming arrival of Drustan mab Necthana; in those days, it was on everyone's tongue. But they heard other things, too.

"There's a rumor Tabor Shahrizai has sworn blood-feud against Marmion for the death of Persia," Apollonaire said lazily, winding a lock of my hair about his fingers. "Our Marmion hit the gates of the City and started running, they say. Some say south," he added, eyeing me, "toward Aragonia. Of course, some say he set out dead east, for Camlach and the Unforgiven. I heard there are Shahrizai hunting parties riding both routes. What do you say, sweet Phèdre? Did our fine Lord Marmion please cousin Nicola well enough that she would offer him asylum in Aragonia?"

"I've no idea," I answered honestly.

"Oh, I daresay Phèdre has other things on her mind," Diànne said cheerfully, snapping a bullwhip for the sheer amusement of watching me twitch. "Arranging for the Cruarch's processional and all. Not to mention the Yeshuite fracas. Your Cassiline's been seen with them, I hear tell." She examined the tip of the bullwhip. "A quarrel on the outskirts of Night's Doorstep, and a Yeshuite lad of no more than sixteen dead; the Baron de Brenois ran him through himself. He went to Kushiel's Temple to be purged of it, they say." She cracked the whip again, and I jumped half out of my skin. "What are armed Yeshuites doing wandering around Night's Doorstep, anyway? Let 'em go north, if that's what their prophecy demands! Why cause trouble here?"

That, I didn't answer, though I could have. They were testing their blades and their courage, reminding themselves of D'Angeline iniquities, summoning the resolve to split away from the greater Yeshuite community. Summoning the resolve — and forcing the reason.

And these were the folk courting Joscelin.

It worried me considerably; enough so that I dared broach the subject with the Rebbe when he sent for me a day later. We read from the *Melakhim*, the Book of Kings, and he told me the tale of the enchanted ring of the glorious King Shalomon, that compelled the demon Ashmedai to build a temple at his bidding. A word, a ring; tokens powerful enough to compel. Somewhere was a key to free Hyacinthe, I thought. For now, a tale only. When he was done, I spoke, couching my words respectfully in Habiru.

"I heard a boy was killed, Master."

The Rebbe sighed heavily, exhaling through his copious beard. "Yeshua weeps."

"I am sorry." I was, too.

Rolling the scroll from which we'd read, Nahum ben Isaac stowed it carefully in its cabinet. "You are a member of the D'Angeline nobility, yes? Do they seek justice against us?"

"No." I shook my head. "It was a quarrel; the Baron de Brenois was provoked, and acted rashly. He is to blame, though there was no legal fault. The boy drew first. He is doing penance for it," I added, meaning the Baron.

"It is not enough for these children." The Rebbe lowered his head, resting chin on fist. "They are eager, and fearful. They seek to rouse their anger, that it might make them less fearful, and daring enough to break us in pieces. For two thousand years, the Children of Yisra-el have endured as a people." His deepset eyes measured the distance. "I fear for the soul of my people, Naamah's Servant. There is blood on our hands, ancient blood. Yeshua ben Yosef bid us sheathe our swords and turn our cheeks, awaiting his return. Now these children, these hasty children, would carve out a place with steel to await him. It is not right."

"No," I murmured. "Master, you say the Baron's penance is not enough. Do they blame us for the boy's death?"

"Your D'Angeline pride, your arrogance, your lustful ways." Nahum ben Isaac looked gravely at me. "Yes, Naamah's Servant, they blame you. And yet you — " His laugh was sad. "To me, they will not listen, and you; you come, at my bidding, to sit at my feet and learn the *Tanakh* and dream only of freeing your friend. What you do, the patrons you serve . . . I know of it. We hear such things, even in the Yeshuite quarters. It is an abomination to me. And yet." Reaching out, he laid his aged hand against my cheek. "You are a good child, Phèdre nó Delaunay, and a good pupil. I have pride in you."

No one had spoken to me so since Delaunay had died. "Thank you, Master," I whispered, leaning against his hand. "I do not wish to grieve you."

The Rebbe withdrew his touch, tucking his hands into his sleeves and smiling sadly into his beard. So old, and so mortal, he looked to me. "Ah, perhaps even Adonai says the same, when he considers his ill-begotten son Elua. I do not know, Naamah's Servant. But I fear in my heart, when

I think on the fate of my people. If your Queen will hear wisdom, counsel her to temperance. They are but children, who draw their blades."

"I will." Rising, I curtsied to him. Still seated, he looked up at me.

"Your . . . your Cassiline, the follower of the Apostate." He cleared his throat. "He comes no more, to sit at my feet and hear the teachings of Yeshua. When he comes, he listens now to the others, these children of steel." His eyes were deep with sorrow. "It is true, what they tell him; it is prophesied, that if Cassiel should return, Elua's Companions will follow. But in my heart of hearts, I do not believe it was meant to happen at the point of a blade."

"No." Swallowing hard, I made myself ask. "Rebbe . . . was Joscelin involved in what happened the other night?"

"No." He looked at me with pity. "Not this time. But next — who knows? If you love the lad, heed my words, and marry him."

I could have laughed at that, or wept. Instead, I thanked him, and left.

TWENTY-FOUR

IT WAS a splendid day when Drustan mab Necthana rode into the City of Elua.

Ysandre met him outside the gates, and I was part of the vast receiving party. All the banners of Terre d'Ange were flying, uppermost the golden lily on a field of green, surrounded by seven gold stars, sign of Blessed Elua and his Companions. Below it, side by side, flew the silver swan of House Courcel and the black boar of the Cullach Gorrym, Drustan's line, Earth's eldest children in Alba.

We saw them coming a long way off, and heard the cheers. An honor guard of D'Angeline soldiers flanked them on either side, riding helmetless and crowned with wreaths of violets and irises, parade-trained mounts prancing and arching their necks, violets braided into their manes. There were Alban war-chariots in the procession, covered in chased gold-work and shining in the bright sun, driven by men and women both.

And in the lead rode Drustan on his black horse.

He wore the trappings of the Cruarch of Alba; the scarlet cloak that spilled over his mount's hindquarters, the gold torque at his throat and a simple circlet of gold pinning his straight black hair. Intricate spirals of blue woad decorated his features, entwined his bare brown arms. Drustan mab Necthana was unquestionably Cruithne, whom scholars call Picti and name barbarians. I could not help but hear murmurs among the gathered nobility.

But along the way, the D'Angeline people threw a flurry of spring petals and shouted themselves raw in adoration, because Drustan mab Necthana had brought an army of Cruithne to our aid when the civilized folk of Caerdicca Unitas wouldn't even muster a delegation to cross our borders. And he married Queen Ysandre de la Courcel, who loved him.

We waited as the Alban procession made its way to the very foot of the gates, and the crowd fell silent. Ysandre stood tall and slender in the colors of House Courcel, backed by her Palace Guard. Astride his black horse, Drustan sat motionless, and the Albans lowered their banners as King and Queen gazed at one another, their eyes speaking silent volumes.

Ysandre broke it first, opening her arms. "Welcome, my lord!" she cried, and her voice caught a little at it. A clarion blast of trumpets rose skyward and Drustan mab Necthana laughed like a boy, swinging down from his mount and taking Ysandre in his arms. We cheered as they kissed, cheered and cheered again, and I prayed that the tears in my eyes and lump in my throat were due more to joy than envy.

In the days that followed, there was feasting and celebrating sufficient to delight even the most libertine of souls. No talk of Naamah's Service now; I was at Ysandre's bidding, and busy enough for two. There were far more translators now than before, but Drustan had brought two hundred Cruithne in his entourage, and my skills were sore needed.

We had greeted each other, Drustan and I, and I was surprised to find how deeply glad I was to see him. Our eyes met in that familiar understanding; his dark and quiet in his tattooed face, like those of his sisters and his mother, who saw true things in their dreams. We both smiled a little, and then he took my hands and I gave him the kiss of greeting. There were murmurs at that, too, but Ysandre's calm mien silenced them. When he greeted Joscelin as a brother, I saw Joscelin smile for the first time in days.

For all that, I had precious little time to speak to Drustan mab Necthana, and I fretted at it, longing, as I never thought I would, for the fearful days when he was a deposed heir unable to move his allies, and I the terrified emissary of an embattled Queen, wholly unsuited for my role. It is a time I never thought I would wish to revisit — and yet, it seemed to me in retrospect, I had friendship and companions about me, instead of pageantry, court politics and dire intrigue.

I'd had Hyacinthe . . . and Joscelin. One I had lost, and the other, I was losing.

At night, I had nightmares still. I woke bathed in cold sweat and could not remember.

At the Palace, I attended court functions and watched, while those I suspected — Barquiel L'Envers, Gaspar Trevalion, Percy and Ghislain de Somerville — surrounded Drustan, speaking to him sometimes as a companion of war, sometimes as the Cruarch of Alba, feeling him out for trade, attempting to discern the hierarchy of power that supported his rule and forge alliances therein. Drustan handled it with deceptive skill, masking a calm intellect behind his woad markings and less-than-fluent D'Angeline; and little passed between them that was not heard and noted by Ysandre. Still, they played the game, and all the while before the impassive faces of the Queen's Cassiline attendants. I watched them all, and never a flicker of interest crossed the features of the latter. It did not allay my fears.

I tried to delve into the buried secrets of Lyonette de Trevalion, and got nowhere.

It was Drustan himself who took notice of my condition, hearing me stumble over a simple translation for one of his trusted lieutenants, a high-ranking lord of the Cullach Gorrym. We were at a state dinner, and he drew me aside.

"Phèdre." His voice was concerned. "You look unwell. I think maybe Ysandre asks too much of you."

He spoke D'Angeline, though my Cruithne was better. My eyes welled at the simple kindness and I bit my lip against tears. "No, my lord," I said when I was sure my voice was steady. "I am troubled by ill dreams, is all. I've not been sleeping well."

Drustan frowned slightly, brows creasing where a line of blue dots bisected them. "Breidaia wanted to come, but I asked her to stay. Would that I had let her. She is skilled in the speaking of dreams."

"I remember," I murmured. She was his eldest sister, who had dreamt of Hyacinthe on an island. Moiread had been the youngest, but she was gone now, slain in the fighting outside of Bryn Gorrydum. We both remembered, silent, and then I gave myself a little shake. "It doesn't matter, my lord. I don't remember them anyway."

"You have no D'Angelines gifted in the matter of dreaming?"

"No," I said automatically, then laughed. "There are, actually. It's not a quarter where I would think to seek aid, but yes."

"Your dreaming self seeks to tell you something your waking ears will not hear." Drustan's tone was serious. "You should go to them."

"I'll think on it," I said.

I did think on it, and dismissed the idea; and woke again that night with my heart racing, cold sweat on my skin and my mind a perfect blank.

Dispatching Ti-Philippe to the Palace to send word to Ysandre that I was ill, I went instead to Gentian House.

Although I was raised in the Night Court, of the Thirteen Houses, Gentian was the one I knew the least. Mystics and visionaries number among her adepts, and many of them join the priesthood of Elua when their marques are made. Indeed, the priest who taught me as a child was a former Gentian adept. What her patrons sought, I never knew until then.

Fortun looked askance at me as we stood before the entrance on Mont Nuit, bearing a subtle bronze relief with the insignia of the House; a gentian flower circumscribed by a full moon. "You are certain of this, my lady?" he asked doubtfully. I didn't blame him. 'Twas passing strange indeed, for one of the foremost courtesans of the realm to go seeking solace at the Night Court.

"Yes." A hint of coolness in the spring breeze made me wrap my arms around myself and shiver. It had gotten worse, since the day Marmion was exiled; I couldn't remember the last time I'd slept through a night. "Drustan is right. I can't go on thusly."

"As you wish." Fortun gave a bow, and knocked upon the door.

Inside, I met alone with the Dowayne, a tall man with greying hair and leaf-green eyes. He had a trick of gazing at one out of the corner of his eyes, as if he saw more on the periphery of his vision than straightward.

"Comtesse Phèdre nó Delaunay de Montrève." He gave my full name and title in a melodious voice, no trace of surprise in it. "Gentian House is honored by the presence of Naamah's esteemed Servant. How may we please you?"

I told him about the nightmares, while he gazed at a sunbeam slanting across the open air. "Can you help?" I asked when I had done.

"Yes." He looked remotely at me, face upturned to the slanting light. "Any adept of Gentian House is trained to aid a patron in giving voice to night's visions. What manner of adept would please you? I will have a selection arrayed for your pleasure."

I blinked, startled; I hadn't thought that far. "It matters not. Naamah's Servants have no preferences," I added with a faint smile.

"Every patron has a preference." Wrenching his attention from the sunbeam, the Dowayne looked me in the face without smiling. "Male or female, young or old, fair or dark."

I shook my head. "My lord, I have known all these things, and none pleases me any better than the other. I am here for my dreams. Choose whom you think best."

"Very well." Rising, the Dowayne went to the door

and murmured something to an apprentice. The lad went running, and presently returned with a young man in tow.

All the adepts of the Night Court are beautiful, and Raphael Murain nó Gentian was no exception. He was near to my own age, with straight ash-brown hair that fell shining almost to his waist and long-lashed grey eyes. He smiled at me with a sweetness that put me in mind of Alcuin, and I felt the sting of tears. That was another thing; with this lack of sleep, I was altogether too near to crying in my waking hours.

"Does he please you?" the Dowayne asked, watching me carefully with his sidelong gaze.

"Yes," I murmured. Raphael Murain bowed, shining hair falling forward over his shoulders, and took my hands, raising them to his lips to kiss them. I felt his breath play over my knuckles, a warm exhalation of pleasure at my acceptance.

It is very effective, the training of the Night Court.

The Dowayne told him of my nightmares and my wish to recover them and discern their meaning; Raphael listened as grave as a physician, and turned to me when he was finished. "It is needful that you pass the night in Gentian House, my lady," he said softly. "Such dreams will not come when bidden, but as the course of their nature dictates. I must needs sleep beside you, and breathe the air of your dreams. Is this acceptable to you?"

"You will inform my man-at-arms?" I asked the Dowayne.

He nodded. "He may reside in comfort in the retainers' quarters, or depart and return in the morning. The choice is yours."

"Bid him return in the morning." I took a deep breath,

and turned to Raphael Murain. "I place myself in your hands."

Raphael bowed again, solemn as a priest.

So it was that I signed the Dowayne's contract and made arrangements for the payment of the fee, and afterward, I was escorted to the baths. One does not hasten pleasure, in the Night Court. I luxuriated in the hot waters and the attentions of a skilled apprentice, while a pair of House musicians played softly on harp and flute. When I was done, I was given a robe of heavy silk to don, and served a light meal with wine. There was some whispered discussion outside the door, and then Raphael Murain came in to join me, and two apprentices appeared to dance for our pleasure, a boy and girl no older than fifteen, clad in veils of filmy gauze.

"It is a part of their training," he told me in his soft voice, a glimmer of amusement in his grey eyes. "But they are nervous, I think, at performing for Phèdre nó Delaunay."

"Are you?" I asked, a little reckless. He shook his head and smiled. It made me like him better, for some reason.

It was strange indeed, to be a patron of the Night Court, and I struggled to relax. I, who could surrender my will in an instant to a patron's desires, was hard put to accept indulgence. Raphael watched me and cocked his head, hair falling to one side, and beckoned to an apprentice to issue a request. In this place, his soft voice commanded. Taking my hand, he led me to his quarters, where silk hangings swathed the walls in dim colors and lamplight flickered on a rich, velveted pallet. A boy sat cross-legged in the corner playing a lyre, and a young

female adept knelt *abeyante* beside the bed, warming a bowl
of scented oil on a brazier.

"My lady," Raphael whispered, undoing the sash of
my robe with skilled, gentle hands and sliding it from my
shoulders, kissing me softly. The robe pooled around my
feet, and for a moment, his eyes gleamed. I could hear the
adept draw in her breath. He loosed my hair, gathering it
up in both hands, the rich, dark mass of it. "Naamah's
blessing is upon her servants." Kissing me again — he had
lips as soft as a woman's — he urged me gently to the pallet.
"It is not yours only to give, but to receive."

I lay down, obedient, and felt the young adept's hands
spread warmed oil over my skin, fragrant and pleasing. I
had not known, until then, how much tension my body
held; even the bath had not assuaged it. Bit by bit, it eased
beneath her skillful massage, muscles easing one by one,
until I lay upon my belly, loose-limbed and languorous,
watching Raphael move gracefully about the room. He
opened a coffer on his nightstand and withdrew a lump of
resin, placing it in a small brazier, and the sweet scent of
opium filled the room, a thin line of blue smoke redolent
with visions. The music slowed, the lyricist's fingers
wandering dreamily. Growing light-headed, I sprawled at
ease beneath the adept's slow-kneading hands; she bent
low, when Raphael was not looking, to place a kiss at the
base of my spine where my marque began, and I could feel
her breath warm against my skin.

When her hands bid me turn over, I made no protest. I
lay languid and waiting, watching Raphael Murain remove
his clothing as the adept — I never learned her name —
performed the arousement, hands slick with oil sliding
over my body; my breasts, nipples taut and upright, my

hipbones and the flat hollow of my belly, clever, oiled
fingers exploring the valley between my thighs, parting me
as one would open the petals of a flower. All the while, he
smiled at me, undressing slowly to reveal a body lithe and
boyishly muscled, the tip of his erect phallus brushing his
belly. When he turned, I saw the marque of Gentian House
limned on his spine, complete even to its moon-and-flower
finial. As young as I, and as experienced. He took a long
time with the *languisement*, until I could not tell where my
flesh ended and his mouth began.

By the time he knelt over me, I was ready and more,
and I cried out at the pleasure of it as he entered me, oil-
slickened body sliding up the length of mine. There are
those who think an *anguissette* knows pleasure only
through pain, but it is not so. Though any one of my
patrons would have seized his pleasure or forced mine,
thrusting hard, Raphael Murain was an adept of the Night
Court. He braced himself on his arms above me, smiling
and moving in slow, languorous strokes, lowering his head
to kiss me. Elua, it was sweet! His hair fell around my face
in shining curtains, and I returned his kisses as only
another of Naamah's Servants might, an intricate dance of
tongues, slow and unhurried. His hard, slender chest
brushed my breasts. I could hear my breathing, and his,
and that of the young adept, who knelt watching.

One surrenders, as a patron; I never understood that
before. I surrendered that night, to Raphael and Gentian
House, the fragrance of scented oil and the sweet blue
opium smoke, letting pleasure mount in slow-building
waves, while we rocked on it as on the breast of the sea. It
seemed to come from a very great distance when it broke,
moving in a great tidal surge, vaster and slower than any

climax I had known. I closed my eyes, feeling it spiral outward from our conjoined bodies to the vast reaches of
time, wave after wave breaking on the outermost shoals of
my awareness, distant and ponderous.

"May I?" Raphael Murain whispered when my eyes
opened.

I felt him still moving inside me, and whispered back,
"Yes."

It was his eyes that closed, then, long lashes curled like
waves breaking; I gasped as he inhaled sharply, drawing in
the very breath of our commingled pleasure. His body
went rigid against me as he spent himself, a sweet, hot
throbbing deep inside of me.

Afterward, we slept, and I dreamed.

Not since Joscelin had foresworn me had I spent a
night's slumber with any other living soul; I could
have grieved, to realize how much I had missed it. After
all his careful grace, Raphael slept with a child's abandon,
fine silken hair spilling across my face, limbs slack
with spent pleasure. The lamps had burned low, the
opium expired. The lyricist and the adept had discreetly
withdrawn. Because I had given myself no choice, I
welcomed Raphael's weight, his even breathing, and
slept.

Slept, and dreamed.

I dreamed I was a child once more in Delaunay's
household. Alcuin was there, and our old study, in
Delaunay's home. We sat across a table from one another,
he and I, poring over scrolls, pursuing the mystery of the
Master of the Straits. I was near to grasping the key, when
an adept of Cereus House wearing a snow-fox's mask
poked his head in the door, and I bid him crossly to leave

me. "You're late," the snowfox said, voice muffled. "The *joie* has already been poured."

With the shock of horror one feels only in dreams, I realized that I was not in Delaunay's home at all, but Cereus House; not a child, but an adept, late for the Midwinter Masque. My costume was unfinished, and I had no mask. Despairing, I hurried to join the fête, thinking I might find Favrielle nó Eglantine and beg her to loan me a mask.

The Great Hall of Cereus House was filled with light and gaiety, and all the adepts of the Thirteen Houses in their finery, and I had come in time to see the Sun Prince revealed. I was laughing, then, thinking everything would be well, and wondering what foolishness had possessed me to imagine I should have been studying with Alcuin, when this, yes of course, this was my life, laughing and cheering as the Winter Queen was unmasked as the beautiful Suriah, who had always been kind to me.

That was when I realized the Sun Prince was Waldemar Selig.

No one else noticed, as he took off his mask, smiling, half a head taller than anyone there; no one noticed, as he ran Suriah through with the Sun Prince's gilded spear and she sank to the dais, mouth open and eyes blank, hands clutching around the haft as a dark stain spread across her breast. Waldemar Selig stepped down, wolfskin cloak swinging from his shoulders, and the D'Angeline revelers smiled and bowed and moved out of the way, while the musicians struck up a merry reel.

My scream caught in my throat, struggling for air; dancers swept past me, bright and glittering – and Delaunay, my lord Delaunay was among them. Almost, I

got out his name; then he turned, and I saw he held
Melisande Shahrizai in his arms, smiling down at her.
And Melisande looked past him, over his shoulder, across
the crowded hall, to meet my eyes, and the shock of
her beauty turned my knees to water. And she smiled at
me.

I knew. She knew. And I was too late.

The voice that woke me, reciting the details of the
dream, ragged with panic, was my own. I took a deep,
gasping breath, half-choking on it, and knew myself to be
awake in the chambers of Gentian House. Like an echo in
my memory, I could hear Raphael Murain's soft murmur
winding through the dream, drawing the account of it
from my unwilling lips. I sat upright in the bed, willing the
pounding of my heart to slow and waiting for my vision to
clear.

When it did, I saw Raphael kneeling at the bedside, his
face quiet and composed. "Do you want me to tell it to
you?" he asked gently.

"No." I passed my hands blindly over my face and
shuddered. "I remember."

"It is often so, when the dream is caught in the making." Rising gracefully, he turned open the shuttered
lamps, letting their soft glow brighten the room, and
poured me a glass. "Watered wine. Drink it, it will do you
good."

I obeyed unthinking, gulping the cool liquid, which
soothed my throat and nerves. Raphael sat back on his
heels and regarded me.

"It is an easy dream to interpret," he said in his soft
voice. "You are putting off a hard choice, Phèdre nó
Delaunay, and only ill can come of it. If you wish, we may

explore this dream together, and learn what is this choice you fear."

"That won't be necessary." I laughed shortly, and felt myself tremble a little. "I already know." It was not so much easier, after all, to face it waking. I did, and knew fear, smiling crookedly at Raphael Murain nó Gentian. "You see, I have to go to La Serenissima."

TWENTY-FIVE

THOUGH I did not think I would be able to sleep after that nightmare, in time, I did; and that, too, was due to the gift of Raphael, who bid me stay when I would have gone, using his calm presence and soft voice to weave a spell to catch slumber. I slept without dreaming, and in it regained a measure of the ease the night's pleasure had afforded. In the morning, I was glad I had stayed.

Before I left, I knelt before him, placing two fingers against his lips. "Naamah's Servant, in her name, I bid you keep her secrets. Do you understand?"

Raphael nodded against my fingers. There were violet smudges of weariness beneath his eyes; this process took a toll on him. "It is a sacrosanct law of Gentian House. You need not fear. I have taken an oath." His expression changed, lightening a shade as he smiled at me. "Anyway, I would never betray your dreams. It must be difficult," he added gently, "to have feelings for a patron that conflict so deeply."

I did not need to ask who he meant. "Yes," I said, a tremor in my voice, more grateful than I could say. There was a tremendous relief in uttering the words, in the one place it would not draw suspicion upon me. "Yes. It is." And to that, Raphael Murain said nothing, but merely understood. "Thank you." I kissed him lightly, and went to leave a purse of coin, my patron's gift to him, on the nightstand. There is an item they use in the Night Court for the purpose — Naamah's Hands, we called it, a sculpture carved to resemble a stylized pair of cupping hands. Raphael's was of pale, translucent jade. He had prospered in Naamah's Service, I was thinking as I set down the purse, and well he should.

"My lady!" His voice rang like an untuned lyre, and I turned to see a stricken look on his face. "Please. I cannot accept a patron-gift from you!"

"Why?" I asked curiously. "You have opened my dream to me like a book."

Standing, Raphael Murain nó Gentian shifted and ran a hand through his shining hair. "You paid the fee of the House," he said awkwardly. "For the rest, it was gift enough to serve." Seeing me hesitate, he gave that sweet smile so reminiscent of Alcuin. "I will only give it in offering to Naamah. Better you should do it, and speak my name. I would have her hear it from your lips."

"Then I will," I promised.

In the courtyard of Gentian House, Fortun glanced at my face and asked me no questions, which was well. Freed of the oppressive weight of my nightmares, I felt my mind keen and sharp again. Upon returning home, I went immediately to my study and drafted a note to Ysandre, begging a meeting with her and Drustan, sealing it with a blot of red wax and the impress of the official signet of Montrève. I dispatched Remy with it forthwith, giving him explicit instructions. "If you cannot gain access directly to the Queen, try the Cruarch. Drustan's guard will make allowances for a veteran of Troyes-le-Mont. Only to her or him, mind! No one else, not even one of her Cassilines."

"I understand," Remy said solemnly, bowing; when he raised his head, his eyes gleamed. "Are we bound for trouble, my lady?"

"We will be, if you don't do exactly as I say, and quietly," I threatened him. He just laughed, bowed again and left. I don't know why I worried about Raphael Murain's discretion, with retainers like Phèdre's Boys.

For all my concerns, Remy carried out my instructions faithfully. I daresay Ysandre was intrigued; at any rate, she granted my request almost immediately, making time in her schedule and sending a royal coach to escort me into the joint presence of the regents of Terre d'Ange and Alba. A private audience in truth, neither servants nor guards nor Cassilines in attendance.

"Well?" Ysandre asked, raising her eyebrows.

Taking a deep breath, I began, telling her the whole story, beginning with Gonzago de Escabares bringing me the *sangoire* cloak, and leaving out none of the details I had omitted in the Hall of Portraits. Melisande's challenge, and all my quest thereafter, all the suspicions I harbored, and the winding path I'd taken in pursuing them.

When I had done, both of them were troubled and thoughtful.

"It would ease my mind," Ysandre said slowly, "if you had some proof of your suspicions, Phèdre. If there were cause, I would not hesitate to pursue it . . . Trevalion, the de Somervilles, even my own uncle. I would summon the Prefect of the Cassiline Brotherhood before the throne if I thought there was cause. But what you tell me is guesswork, and nothing more. I will not act on supposition, not even yours."

I had not expected her to; only to heed my warning. "There is the cloak."

"Yes," Ysandre said wryly. "There is. I should tell you, I have had a correspondence from my great-uncle, Prince Benedicte de la Courcel. Did you know I dispatched couriers to him after Marmion's hearing?" She looked sharply at me, and I shook my head. "I did. And he has scoured La Serenissima, and found no trace of Melisande. Indeed, he invites me to make the Caerdicci *progressus regalis* ere winter, that the city may receive me as Queen of Terre d'Ange."

"Why doesn't Benedicte come here to acknowledge you?" I asked.

Ysandre rested chin on hand and gazed at me. "It is customary for the D'Angeline ruler to make a *progressus*, to renew alliances with the Caerdicci city-states. My grandfather did it as a boy; it's not been done for decades. Not in either of our lifetimes. Mayhap if it had, they'd have been quicker to aid us against the Skaldi. Benedicte is right, I can't afford to let those ties lapse. At any rate," she added quietly, "his new wife has just been delivered of a son, and he's not minded to travel."

"My lady," I said, "that may all be true, but from what Severio told me, La Serenissima is a knot of intrigue. Even Prince Benedicte didn't know his own daughter and son-in-law were guilty of poisoning your mother."

The Queen's eyebrows rose again. "And did Severio Stregazza tell you Melisande Shahrizai was in La

Serenissima?" she asked with deceptive mildness. It made my blood run cold.

"My lady," I whispered. "I would have told you if he had. No. He did not know her, and I believe he spoke the truth. Marmion plagued him, and he didn't know why. I promise you, if I had the least corroborating proof of any of this, I'd have come to you."

Drustan kept his silence, watching us both.

Ysandre sighed. "So. You suspect the Lord Commander, his son Ghislain, Gaspar Trevalion – whom even Delaunay trusted – and my uncle the Duc, who saved your life. Also the Cassiline Brotherhood, whose service has been beyond reproach for centuries. You believe Melisande Shahrizai is in La Serenissima, despite the fact that you received this information at third hand, obviously by her own devising, and no Serenissiman has laid eyes upon her."

"Yes." I had to admit, it sounded insane to my own ears. "My lady . . ." I said reluctantly. "I cannot ask you to believe me. But I *know* Melisande. If she wanted me to think she is in La Serenissima, it is because she is in La Serenissima. I have come to a blind alley, here. It is there I need to go."

It was Drustan who spoke at last, frowning. "I do not like it either, Phèdre nó Delaunay. But it is in my thoughts that this is the voice of your dreams you feared to heed."

I nodded.

Ysandre looked dourly at me. "Last time, you brought me a heap of stinking hides, a Skaldi dagger and a Tsingani fortune-teller. This time, a velvet cloak and a dream. What next? A kerchief and a worrisome feeling?" I bit my tongue and did not answer. "Very well. It is my profound hope that you're wrong this time, but I'm not fool enough to wager on it, nor to try and stop you. What do you want of us?"

I told them my plan. Drustan looked amused, although Ysandre did not. Nonetheless, she agreed to it.

When I made my obeisance and would have left, she called me back in a different tone. "Phèdre." I turned and met her violet eyes, dark with concern. "Anafiel Delaunay was my ally when I had no other around me who did not seek to use me. I called upon his oath, and he died of it. We are at peace, now, and I hold the throne unchallenged. The army is in my hand, and no province but that acknowledges my sovereignty. Drustan mab Necthana is my acknowledged husband and brings with him the sovereign might of Alba. Skaldia's reign is as divided as ever it was before the ascendance of Waldemar Selig, Aragonia gives alliance, and no single Caerdicci city-state has the might to challenge us. When I sent you to Alba, I was desperate; now, Terre d'Ange is in a position of great strength. Yes, I would rest easier if Melisande Shahrizai were dealt with, but whatever she is about, it cannot pose a threat so grave it is worth risking your life."

I paused. "Mayhap. But whoever aided her stands close to the throne."

"And if they did it for blackmail's sake, like as not they pray every day to Elua that I never find it out," Ysandre said grimly. "I am telling you, it is not worth the risk. There is enough blood spilled at the doorstep of House Courcel. I don't want yours added to it."

Like as not she was right; but there was the dream, and the bone-deep terror of it. Would that Hyacinthe or his mother had been there, or any Tsingani who could speak the *dromonde*, because I knew, in my heart of hearts, that I was not wrong. "I will be careful," I promised.

"Good." Ysandre settled back, and added one last codicil. "If you will not let me give you an honor guard, you will at least take your men-at-arms, and that stubborn Cassiline."

I opened my mouth, and closed it, swallowing. "I . . . am not sure if Joscelin will go."

Drustan started at that, but Ysandre's look turned flinty. "He swore his sword unto my service when he renounced Cassiel's. He will go, or be forsworn. And I do not hold lightly with oath-breakers."

"I will tell him," I murmured, wondering how he would take it.

With that, I was dismissed.

I did not tell Joscelin or my chevaliers immediately, but set about making the arrangements. I paid a visit first of all to my factor, to explain my desire to travel to La Serenissima to oversee firsthand my investments there. After some searching, he found for me an interest in a shipment of Alban lead, bound from Marsilikos to La Serenissima in a fortnight's time, which suited my needs perfectly. One part of my plan I had withheld even from Ysandre.

Thelesis de Mornay, who had known what I was about from the beginning, did what Ysandre had requested, and I met with her to review the list of Cassiline Brothers on active duty at the Palace. "Etienne de Chardin, Brys nó Rinforte, Lisle Arnot, David nó Rinforte, Jean de Laurenne . . ." Scanning the list, I glanced up at Thelesis. "Why so many adopted into Lord Rinforte's household?"

"I asked." As the Queen's Poet, Thelesis could ask

nearly anything without being questioned; it would be presumed research for some work of poesy. "Orphans taken
in by the Cassiline Brotherhood always take on the
Prefect's name. Rinforte's been Prefect for a long time."
She turned her head away to cough, and looked back
apologetically. "He's had a wasting sickness these past
months, one of the Brothers told me. That's likely why
neither Joscelin nor Micheline de Parnasse received a
reply."

"Ah." I finished reading the list and set it down.

"Nothing?" Thelesis' dark eyes were sympathetic.

I shook my head. "No. Or if there is, I don't see it."

"I'm sorry." She rose to embrace me, and her bones
felt light and frail; it unnerved me, on the heels of the news
of the Prefect's health. "Kushiel is not gentle with his
chosen," Thelesis whispered. "Have a care, Phèdre, and
come home safe." She drew back and smiled gently at me.
"Blessed Elua keep you."

"And you," I murmured, gripping her hands. "And
you."

On the night the first part of it was to be implemented,
I told my chevaliers of my plan. Would that Joscelin had
been there, too, but I had played my game too closely; he
had gone out that afternoon and not yet returned. I had no
choice but to tell them, first dismissing my servants for the
evening and swearing Phèdre's Boys to secrecy.

Predictably, they were overjoyed – even steady
Fortun's eyes gleamed with excitement. Not two minutes
was it out of my mouth but they were already planning the
excursion, dividing up responsibility among themselves.
Amused, I let them have at it.

I chose Fortun to escort me to the natal festivities of

the Duchese de Chalasse that night, and left the others with two cautions. "Whatever you hear said of me," I said, looking especially at Ti-Philippe, "do *not* bely the underlying truth of it, mind? And when Joscelin returns, do not tell him. Let him know I would speak to him first thing, and leave it to me."

They promised, albeit reluctantly on the latter point. I threatened to leave whomever broke his word in the City of Elua, and left satisfied that they would obey.

Of that night, I will say little, save that it went as planned. Vivianne de Chalasse held great sway in L'Agnace; indeed, hers had been the sovereign duchy in the province until Ysandre had raised Percy de Somerville to the rank of Duc, and granted him ascendance. There was little ill-feeling over it – no one questioned that de Somerville had earned it, for commanding the defense against the Skaldic invasion – but enough that the Queen and Cruarch were impelled to attend the fête, smoothing any feathers that might remain ruffled.

I do not have a player's skill, but I daresay I dissemble well enough; and it was no hardship, to flirt and dance with Drustan mab Necthana. He played along with it with surprising grace, smiling and returning my banter in a mix of D'Angeline and Cruithne, and dancing with an elegance that belied his misshapen right foot. It was not difficult, finding a rhythm that accommodated his halting gate. He had lived with it since birth; one easily forgot that Drustan was lame. I remembered Delaunay's words, so long ago, light and amused. *And Ysandre de la Courcel, flower of the realm, shall teach a clubfoot barbarian prince to dance the gavotte.*

For her part, Ysandre did not overplay her role, but

when I heard her voice, cold as the Bitterest Winter, ask if I were finished with her husband and would mind returning him to his wife, the Queen of Terre d'Ange, I swear, I felt the chill on my skin, and my flush was genuine. If Drustan's sudden gravity was feigned, no one would ever know it. All around us, D'Angeline nobles stepped back several paces as I made myself answer with studied indolence, a favored young courtesan trading on her stature.

"Phèdre nó Delaunay," Ysandre said coolly, omitting my title. "Your presence is no longer pleasing to us. We ask that you remove yourself from it."

With that, she turned her back on me, and even though it was as we had planned, I could not but help feeling my heart sink within me. Insolence to patrons is one thing, when it fans the embers of their desire, but the instinct for obedience is deep-rooted in me, and I was hard put not to throw myself at her feet and beg forgiveness. Thankfully, Fortun hurried to my side to take my arm, tugging me away, and in a corridor of silence, we left the fête.

Behind us, I could hear the eternal murmurs rising.

Twenty-six

"YOU WHAT?" Joscelin's voice rose incredulously. "Phèdre, what were you thinking?"

"Done is done." I looked steadily at him. "I would have told you last night, but you weren't to be found. By now, the City will know that I am out of favor with the Queen. And on the morrow, we depart for La Serenissima. After what transpired last night, no one will think it strange. And no one will think me Ysandre's agent in this."

"I can't believe Ysandre agreed to it," he muttered.

I looked down at my plate and toyed with a quartered pear. "It does not please her," I admitted, "but she agreed. Joscelin, I won't compel you. Will you go or not?"

He rose without answering, and paced the dining hall to gaze out a window that overlooked my tiny rear courtyard, where Eugènie had planted the beginnings of an herb garden. I sat watching him, his tall figure drenched in sunlight. "And if I say no?" he asked, not turning around. "What then?"

"Then you say no." My voice sounded like it belonged to someone else, someone whose heart was not shattering into piercing splinters. Even as Joscelin turned around, one hand clenched around the *khai* pendant at his breast, my voice continued calmly. "You will stay, and play out your part in leading the Yeshuites to this prophesied homeland in the far north, if that is what your heart commands."

"My heart!" He laughed harshly, a tearing sound; it might almost have been a sob. He wrenched at the pendant as if to break its chain. "Would that I could make of heart and soul something other than a battleground!"

I ached for him, and yearned to go to him; since I dared not, I closed my eyes instead. "If that is your choice, then tell the Rebbe that I did as I promised. The Queen will treat as lightly as she dares, but if they break the law, they will be punished under it." I had spoken to Ysandre of it, before we were done laying our plans. She had agreed, bemusedly, to take my words under advisement.

Joscelin was staring at me when I opened my eyes. "What else does Ysandre say?"

It seemed he cared more for the Yeshuites than for me, and it turned my pain to anger, making me reply sharply. "That you are sworn into her service, and she orders you to accompany me to La Serenissima. And that she does not hold lightly with oath-breakers."

It is perhaps the worst thing one could say to a former Cassiline. His head jerked back as if I had slapped him, nostrils flaring, white lines etching themselves on his face. "Then it seems I must go," he said, biting off the words, "unless I am to break faith all at once with Cassiel, you and the Queen."

"Yeshua's forgiveness is absolute," I retorted. "If you seek it for one oath broken, why not three?"

Joscelin's summer-blue eyes held a look very close to

hatred. "My lady Phèdre nó Delaunay de Montrève," he said with cruel, deliberate courtesy. "I will see you to La Serenissima, and fulfill my liege's command. And after that, I remand you to Naamah's custody and Kushiel's, since you are so ardent to serve them. Let them have the joy of you."

"Fine," I said grimly, rising from the table and tossing down my linen napkin. "Speak to Remy about the travel arrangements. He will tell you all that is needful. You remind me, I have an obligation yet to fulfill."

I was not even certain, after last night's enactment, that Nicola L'Envers y Aragon would receive me; I'd not intended on this visit, before my unfortunate conversation with Joscelin. But Ti-Philippe returned posthaste from bearing my message: The lady was indeed most anxious to see me. So it was that I went one last time to the Palace, and in part, I was not sorry. I did owe Nicola the assignation I had promised in barter, and it would not have been well-omened to leave with my Service to Naamah incomplete.

I would have foregone it, though, if Joscelin had come willingly.

The Palace Guard admitted me without comment, cool and perfunctory. They had no orders to keep me out, though I daresay I'd have been turned away if I had asked to see Ysandre. But Nicola was the Queen's cousin, and they allowed me passage on her explicit order.

Mayhap it would have been wiser to seek solace in Kushiel's temple, but it was a relief, after all that had gone before, to surrender to a patron's whim. This time, Nicola's bindings held true to a knot, and there was not the least I could undo. Eyes bright with mingled curiosity and cruelty, she wielded the flogger unmercifully until it drew blood, moving me to violent pleasures, which I repaid with all the ardor with which Joscelin had accused me, until she was sated.

Afterward, she had chilled wine and fruits served, until I said it was time for me to go.

"No," Nicola said thoughtfully. "I don't think so. You have called the day and time of repaying your debt to me, Phèdre, and I would claim a forfeit for it. I had your promise that I might question you, but I've not done it yet, have I?"

"No, my lady." I met her L'Envers eyes and hid a frisson of fear. She was, after all, Barquiel's ally, and I ran a risk in coming here.

Nicola smiled lazily. She knew; patrons almost always do. "All the Palace says you have fallen out of favor with Ysandre," she said softly. "But I do not believe it. Think of us what you like, but House L'Envers does not break faith with her followers for less than a mortal offense, and my cousin the Queen is as much L'Envers as she is Courcel. What game do you play now, Phèdre nó Delaunay?"

I did not answer, but said instead, "One rumor says Marmion Shahrizai rode straight for the Aragonian border, and has not been seen since. Did you offer him sanctuary?"

Her brows creased in a frown, then she laughed again, ruefully, and shook her head. "I should know better, after the first time. All right, then. Yes. I did." Nicola gave me a long, level look. "Marmion had word of what Barquiel was about, and he came to me the eve before, and told me the truth about the fire. I believed him. I do not disagree with my cousin the Duc's motives, but his methods . . ." She shrugged. "He threw Marmion's life away, at that hearing. I told him if the worst fell out, the House of Aragon would receive him, if he made it there alive. I gave him Ramiro's name, and my word as surety. That, and no more."

"Your husband would take him in?" It surprised me, a little.

"Marmion likes to drink, and gamble. He's an excellent courtier. Why not?" Nicola gave another shrug. "Ramiro knows the merits of indulging my whims, and it does not cross de Morhban's edict. Aragonia *is* exile. Believe me, I know. Will you answer me now?"

I shook my head, slowly.

"Blessed Elua!" She spat out the words like a curse, rising to pace restlessly about the room. "You and Barquiel . . . Phèdre, you're on the same side, only you're both too mistrustful to see it. Can't you see that with his resources and your wiles, you'd get a lot further working together?" She shot me a frustrated look. "Why would I lie? Any influence I hold in Aragonia is wholly dependent on Ysandre's retaining the throne of Terre d'Ange."

"Not exactly," I murmured, glancing at her. "Your cousin the Duc would do just as well, I think. And if he wishes me out of the way, he would be indebted to you for aiding him in the process. He's already disposed of Marmion, and Elua help me, I gave him the means to do it. Would I be wise, you think, to trust?" I shook my head. "Barquiel is more enemy than ally, and Ysandre has withdrawn her favor. Our debt is settled, and in Naamah's eyes, I owe you naught. I am not fool enough to linger here, my lady."

"So I heard. One of your chevaliers was reported buying travelling stores in the marketplace this very morning." She said it matter-of-factly; I hadn't doubted that the eyes of the City would be on my household, after last night.

Nicola's gaze lingered on my face, and it was decisive. "Phèdre, listen to me," she said, her voice low and urgent, stooping in front of my chair to grasp my hands. "I don't know what you're about and when you come to it, I don't blame you for not telling me. But what I do know for truth, I know all the same. Cousin Barquiel is not a traitor." She drew a deep breath, paling slightly, and continued. "The password of House L'Envers is 'burning river.' If you need aid — mine, Barquiel's, even Ysandre's — any scion of the House is honor-bound to give it unquestioning."

"Why are you telling me this?" My voice shook asking it.

"What does it matter?" Releasing my hands, Nicola stood and smiled wryly. "Whatever I told you, you'd only come up with half a dozen reasons, each more sinister than the last. As it happens, I've seen my House torn apart by suspicion and enmity once, and I don't care to see it again. Your lord Delaunay and my cousin Isabel pulled Rolande de la Courcel in twain; I don't need to watch you and Barquiel do the same to Ysandre. But it doesn't matter what you believe. Just remember it."

I wanted to believe her; I wanted to question her. In the end, I dared do neither. At the door of her quarters, she gave me the kiss of farewell, and kept me for a moment, one hand on my arm, a peremptory touch that stirred my desires.

"Cousin Barquiel would have my tongue for what I told you," Nicola said quietly. "But he'll answer to it all the same. Do me a favor, and don't put it to the test unless you're truly in need."

"If you will do me the kindness of nursing your suspicions in silence," I murmured.

Nicola laughed at that and kissed me again, this time as a patron rather than a peer. "If you hold to that bargain as well as this one, I will promise it." Releasing me, she cocked her head as I regained my composure. "I like you, Phèdre," she said with regret. "For whatever reason you're going, I'm sorry for it. I'll miss you."

"So will I," I said, and meant it.

I made the rest of my farewells that day, which were few; 'tis an astonishing thing, how quickly one's friends diminish with a Queen's disfavor. That it meant we had succeeded made it no less painful to find doors closed which had once opened eagerly to my name. Even Diànne and Apollonaire de Fhirze would not see me. It served to make me mindful that Nicola had meant what she said. Either she was foolish enough to risk Ysandre's displeasure — and I did not think she was — or she was sure our roles were but a deception. It gave me no ease, when I thought of Barquiel L'Envers, and the fresh welts on my skin, painful beneath my gown, reminded me of how rash my actions had been. I would pay for it, riding tomorrow.

Nonetheless, I locked the words in my memory: Burning river. If I dared, I would have asked Ysandre to verify it, but there was no way I dared risk contacting her without giving the lie to our falling-out, and I was dependent on that perception to gain access to anyone who might be her enemy. At any rate, I thought, there was no way I would entrust my fate to the password of House L'Envers; not even if I trusted Nicola wholly, which I did not.

My last visit was as my first had been: Cecilie Laveau-Perrin, whose door opened with alacrity. Indeed, she embraced me on the doorstep, heedless of whatever gossips might be watching. "Oh, Phèdre," she whispered in my ear. "I'm so sorry!"

Her unquestioning loyalty touched me to the core, and I struggled to hold back tears; as luck would have it, she thought I grieved at my disgrace. It is the most dire thing of all, among Naamah's Servants, to incur the displeasure of a sovereign. I spent an hour or better in her home, enduring her kindness with all the squirming unease of a guilty conscience, and at last fled, before I gave voice to the entire deception, which lay the whole time on the very tip of my tongue.

So it was done, and my farewells all said. When I returned home, all was in readiness for our departure. I spoke with Eugènie, and confirmed that she would maintain the house in my absence, giving her a purse of money and a note for my factor, should further funds be needful. I promised to write her with an address, to forward any urgent communication, as soon as we were established in La Serenissima. To my surprise, she burst into tears in the middle of our discussion, clutching me to her bosom. I had not known, until then, that she regarded me with such fondness; indeed, mothers have wept less, bidding farewell to their children.

At least, mine certainly did.

Whether it be through exhaustion, pain, pleasure or fear, I laid my head on the pillow and slept that night like the dead, a deep and dreamless sleep, and woke alert and ready at dawn. After strong tea and a light breakfast, our party assembled in the courtyard, Remy still yawning and knuckling his eyes. Five mounts, and three packhorses; enough, for my purposes. My chevaliers wore the livery of Montrève, black and green with my personal insignia at the

breast bearing the moon and crag of Montrève, to which
Delaunay's sheaf of grain and Kushiel's Dart had been
added. Joscelin wore his own attire, dove-grey shirt and
trousers with a long, sleeveless mandilion coat of the same
drab color over it. It was close, very close, to the ashen
garb of the Cassiline Brotherhood, save that his hair was
braided, and not clubbed at his nape. I looked at him, his
vambraces glinting in the early morning sun, daggers at his
belt, sword strapped to his back, and made no comment.
He looked back at me, equally expressionless.

"Let us go," I said.

Twenty-seven

AS THE white walls of the City of Elua fell behind us, I felt my spirits begin to rise with the freedom that comes of action after long confinement. It was a glorious D'Angeline spring day, a blue vault of sky and the sun bright and young overhead, the earth surging eagerly into bloom. Our horses were plump and glossy from winter's long stabling, restless with energy too long unspent. Remy sang aloud as he rode, until I had to regretfully bid him to silence; there were other travellers on the road, headed toward the City, and my household was supposed to be in disgrace.

Still, we were travelling light and making good time, and it was hard to suppress our excitement. After several hours, even Joscelin's expression grew less severe, although he took care to remain stoic when I glanced at him. No child of the City, he, but Siovalese born and bred; he thrived in the open air. I daresay if there had been mountains, he might even have smiled.

At least, until we reached the crossroads of Eisheth's Way, where it curves to within a half-day's ride of the City of Elua.

"Smell that?" Ti-Philippe stood in his stirrups, sniffing conspicuously. "Salt air," he declared, grinning at me; I knew full well he couldn't smell the sea at this distance. "A sailor's nose never lies! Two days' ride to the south, and we're in Marsilikos, my lady, with ten days' leisure in harbor."

"So we would be," I said, drawing up my mount and shifting my shoulders so that the fabric of my gown rubbed my skin. Kushiel's chosen may heal swiftly, but 'tis betimes an itchy process. "If we were going straight to Marsilikos."

They stared at me, all of them; I hadn't told them this part. I'd not told anyone. It was Joscelin who sighed. "Phèdre," he said in a tone of weary resignation. "What have you planned?"

I rested my reins on my pommel. "If we move quickly," I said, "we've time enough to reach the southernmost garrison of the Allies of Camlach and ask after the missing guardsmen."

Joscelin looked at me without replying, a strange expression on his face. "You want to query the Unforgiven."

I nodded.

"Bloody hell and damnation!" Ti-Philippe grumbled, fiddling with a purse at his belt. "I bought a set of new dice for this journey. Azzallese staghorn, guaranteed lucky. You mean to tell me we're riding all the way to Camlach, just to turn around and race for Marsilikos?"

"You can gamble from Marsilikos to La Serenissima," I told him, "and if your stakes hold out longer, it will be lucky indeed. Unless you'd rather not go?"

"No, my lady!" Eyes widening, he took up the reins and turned his horse's head to the north. "Whatever the seven hells you're about, I'll not be left behind. Camlach it is."

Fortun and Remy laughed. I glanced at Joscelin, who was looking away, and identified at last his odd expression. I had seen it before; he was trying not to smile.

Unaccountably, my heart lightened, and I laughed too. "To Camlach!"

The truth of Ysandre's parting words to me – her real words, in our audience – was more than evident in this journey. Terre d'Ange was at peace, and prosperous. Eisheth's Way, built by Tiberian soldiers over a millennium ago, was solid and well tended. More than once, we saw teams of masons and bricklayers at work, repairing winter's damage. There are no major cities in Camlach, but the road wends through myriad villages, and in each one, we saw the signs of contentment and prosperity – open markets, with the first fruits of spring for sale, and the last of winter's dried stores; poultry, mutton and wild game; fabrics, threads and necessities. Once we saw a Tsingani *kumpania*, outfitted with a travelling smithy. There was a line of villagers waiting, with horses to be shod, pots to be mended. I thought of Hyacinthe and all that he had sacrificed, and swallowed hard.

And flowers; there were flowers. "You see that, my lady?" Fortun asked, nodding toward a stand where a young woman buried her face in a nosegay, eyes closed with pleasure. "When common folk have coin to spare for flowers, it bodes well for the land." He laughed. "Though they say in Caerdicca Unitas that D'Angelines will buy flowers before food."

That first evening we reached the village of Aufoil, which had an inn large enough to lodge our party. If my purposes had been different, I would have been carrying letters of invitation to half a dozen noble holdings, and we would have been welcomed and feasted in style, but 'twas better this way. No one would be looking for the Comtesse de Montrève on the road to Camlach, and if they were, they'd not look in common travellers' inns.

For their part, the villagers made us welcome. The innkeep rushed about to procure fresh bed-linens, ordering a cask of their finest wine breached. We sought to repay their hospitality with courtesy as well as coin, and Phèdre's Boys surely excelled at that, remaining in the common room to take part in revelry and drink into the small hours of the night.

It was not wasted time, either. In the morning, a bleary-eyed Fortun sketched for me a map to the closest garrison of the Unforgiven, some few days' ride away. One more day on Eisheth's Way, and then we needs must turn aside, on less travelled paths.

"I wondered why you wanted camping gear," Remy muttered. "Thought you'd never sleep on aught but silk sheets, after campaigning with the Cruithne."

I smiled. "Now you know better." In truth, I'd sooner have slept under a silk coverlet on a down-stuffed pallet, but the pursuit of knowledge makes all manner of hardship worthwhile.

And I had known worse. I could not help but remember, as we travelled deeper into the forests of Camlach, how Joscelin and I had staggered, half-frozen, windburned and exhausted, out of the Camaeline Mountains and into shelter in this land. How the men of the Marquis de Bois-le-Garde had found our meager campsite, and that awful, terrifying flight through the benighted woods.

Travelling by day, golden sunlight slanting through the pines, it seemed harmless, but we had come near to death in this place.

Different times, those; Isidore d'Aiglemort's treacherous Allies of Camlach held the province, and there was no telling who was friend or foe. Now those same men guarded the borders and the Duc d'Aiglemort was dead, slain on the battlefield of Troyes-le-Mont, spending his life to thwart the very enemy he'd invited onto D'Angeline soil. Kilberhaar, the Skaldi had called him; Silver Hair. I had watched it all, from the parapets of the fortress. Seventeen wounds d'Aiglemort had taken, battling his way across the field to challenge Waldemar Selig. They counted, when they laid him out and gave him a hero's funeral.

I had been there, at the end, when he died, carrying water to the wounded and dying. *I am afraid of your lord's revenge,* he said to me, lying in a welter of his own gore. At first, I thought he meant Delaunay – and then I knew better. It was Kushiel he feared; Kushiel, who metes out punishment.

For that, I could not blame him. I fear Kushiel myself, for all that I am his chosen. On the whole, Naamah's Service is a great deal more pleasant, but I do not think it is Naamah whose hand placed me on the battlefield that day.

So I mused and remembered as we travelled, and the time passed swiftly.

On the fourth day, we came upon the stream that Fortun had recorded on his map, and a broad, well-trodden trail that led out of the woods and toward the foothills of the Camaelines. The first garrison lay to the south of the southernmost of the Great Passes. It was but early afternoon, and the woods were cheerful with birdsong.

"I don't like this," Joscelin said, frowning at the serenity of our surroundings. "Why isn't there a guard posted?
If Fortun's directions are right, we're inside the perimeter
of the garrison."

"Mayhap they thought it wiser to guard against the
Skaldi," Remy offered sardonically.

"No," I said absently. "Joscelin's right; any Camaeline
corps this close to the border would mount a guard on all
sides. They're not likely to let themselves be flanked."

"There's been a large party riding through here,"
Fortun observed, pointing to the myriad hoofmarks churning the soft loam. "Not long past; these are fresh since it
rained this morning. A scouting party, mayhap?"

In the distance, we heard a sudden shout, and then the
distinctive metal-on-metal sound of swordplay.

"Mayhap not," Joscelin said grimly, and wheeled his
horse. "Whatever trouble it is, we're best away from it."
He nearly clapped heels to his mount's sides, before he saw
me motionless in the saddle, head cocked to listen.
"Phèdre, you brought me to keep you safe!" he snapped,
jostling his mount next to mine and grabbing at my reins.
"At least do me the kindness of heeding my advice!"

The chevaliers were milling, uncertain. I met Joscelin's
eyes. "Listen."

Biting back a retort, he did; and he heard it too. Rising
above the clash of arms and shouted orders, a faint cry,
ragged and defiant. "Yeshu-a! Ye-shu-a!"

Joscelin quivered like a bowstring, his face a study in
anguish. With a sound that might have been a curse or a
sob, he let go my reins and jerked his horse's head around
and set heels to it, riding at a dead gallop toward the
garrison.

"What are you waiting for?" I asked my staring cheva-liers, turning my own mount after Joscelin. "Go!"

I daresay we made for a strange sight, bursting from the forest trail to fan out across the narrow plain; a D'Angeline noblewoman, three men-at-arms and trailing packhorses chasing someone who looked very much like a Cassiline Brother riding hell-for-leather toward an entire garrison. If the Unforgiven corps had not been occupied, they might have laughed – but occupied they were. Thirty or more encircled a party of Yeshuites, who numbered in the dozens. There were two wagons at the center, and I could discern the figures of women and children on them, while the men grappled with the Unforgiven guardsmen, calling on Yeshua with fierce, exultant cries.

For all of that, they were outfought and losing.

Until Joscelin slammed into the garrison's perimeter.

Two of the Unforgiven he took down with main force, checking his mount into them. The soldiers went down, as did Joscelin's horse; and then he was on his feet, vambraced arms crossed, daggers in his hands.

I lashed my horse's rump with the ends of my reins, gasping a quick prayer of thanks that Joscelin hadn't drawn his sword instead. Cassiline Brothers do not draw their swords unless they mean to kill, and he was Cassiline enough for that. He was only trying to protect the Yeshuites.

Of course, that didn't matter to the Unforgiven, who knew only that the garrison was under attack.

"Blessed tears of the Magdelene!" I heard Remy's shocked voice close to me, his horse drawing briefly on a level with mine, before I urged it to even greater speed.

I had forgotten that none of Phèdre's Boys, Rousse's

wild sailorlads, had ever seen Joscelin Verreuil fight. No one but I had seen the terrible splendor of his battle in the midst of a Skaldic blizzard. At the battle of Bryn Gorrydum, he had stayed at my side; when the campsite was ambushed, he fought almost single-handed to defeat an entire party of Maelcon's Tarbh Cró. At Troyes-le-Mont, he crossed the battlefield at night to follow me, and challenge Waldemar Selig to the holmgang.

We are alike, Joscelin and I, in that what we do, we do very well.

And with the aid of a few dozen Yeshuites, I might have given him odds, against any other company; but these were the Unforgiven, scions of Camael, born to the blade, and survivors of the deadliest suicide charge in D'Angeline history. Plain steel and leather armor they wore, and carried unadorned black shields. By the time I reached the battle, seven or eight of the Unforgiven had him isolated, surrounding him with careful swordwork and waiting for an opening, steel blades darting past his guard to score minor wounds. In truth, despite his skill, Cassiline training is not meant for the open battlefield; it is designed for efficiency in tight quarters. The Yeshuites and the remaining Unforgiven battled in knots, the skill of the latter slowly prevailing, and from one of the wagons rose a child's scream, endless and unremitting.

Three Yeshuite dead already; it would be more, in a moment. It would be Joscelin.

"Stop!" I drew up my horse, shouting, pitching my voice to carry over the battle, even as I realized the idiocy of it. "Stop the fighting!"

Enough to give them pause; Joscelin redoubled his

efforts, and nearly broke free. Unfortunately, it was at that moment that the Captain of the Guard and another two dozen reinforcements, all mounted, reached the plain. He gave a series of sharp commands, and his men split in two, one group surrounding the Yeshuites and calling on them to throw down their swords or die, the other moving to intercept me and my three chevaliers, who came ranging and panting up behind me.

They were gentle, and firm. I struggled with the young corporal who blocked my view, moving me forcibly back from the fighting, his battle-trained mount pressing hard against mine, his companions separating us, containing my chevaliers. "You don't understand!" I said wildly, trying to see around him; Joscelin had not surrendered. "Love of Elua, *stop* it! He's a Cassiline, he's just trying to protect them . . . I swear, if you kill him, I'll have your head!"

"M'lady," he muttered, flushing beneath his helmet, "We're trying to protect you, please get *off* the field of battle!"

A bellow of pain, distinctly Camaeline in tone, and the Captain's voice rose ringing. "For Camael's sake, just *kill* him!"

I could hardly see for the tears of fear and frustration that blurred my eyes; after all we had been through, for him to die like this! Shoving at the corporal, I drew a great breath and loosed it. "Joscelin! No!"

The corporal caught at my arm, wrenching me around in the saddle to stare into my face. His eyes widened, and his hand fell away. "Captain, hai! Company, hai! Black Shields, hold!" he shouted, his voice loud and frantic. "Hold, hold, if you love your honor, hold!"

It made absolutely no sense to me, and even less when he dropped his reins and dismounted, going down on one knee and bowing his head over his unadorned shield. I looked in bewilderment to the next-closest soldier, and saw him swallow visibly, hurrying to dismount and kneel. In seconds, every one of the Unforgiven near me had followed suit. From this center of stillness, a hissed whisper spread, and stillness followed, battle abandoned. I sat atop my horse open-mouthed, while the entire Unforgiven garrison knelt, until no one was standing but Joscelin, and the Yeshuites.

One of whom raised his sword over the neck of a kneeling Unforgiven soldier.

"No!" I flung out my arm, pointing at the man. He glanced at me, then away, and made to swing the blade. I could see the muscles quiver in the bowed neck of the kneeling Unforgiven; and yet, he never raised his head. From the corner of my eye, I saw Joscelin moving, turning, a terrible despair in his face, switching his right-hand dagger to grasp its hilt. I knew, beyond a shadow of a doubt, that he would throw it at the Yeshuite if he had to; and I was afraid, very afraid, that he held the hilt of the other dagger in his left hand, and meant to bring it across his own throat. A fine idea, this side trip of mine. A film of red veiled my vision, and my blood beat in my ears, a sound like great bronze wings clapping about my head. Somehow, I spoke, and my voice seemed distant and strange, edged with blood and thunder. "*Drop your swords!*"

He did; they did. All of the Yeshuites, weapons falling with a clatter. Joscelin halted, in the middle of executing the *terminus*, that final move that no Cassiline Brother in living history has performed. If it was that. In the wagon, the child continued screaming.

None of the kneeling Unforgiven even looked up.

"Fortun," I asked, bewildered, "what's happening here?"

TWENTY-EIGHT

"YOU ARE Kushiel's hand."

That was how the Captain — whose name was Tarren d'Eltoine — explained it to me in the garrison keep as he poured me a generous measure of very good Namarrese red wine, of which I drank a long draught. "My lord Captain," I said, shuddering and setting down the glass, "forgive me, but I do not understand."

Tarren d'Eltoine sat opposite me and fixed me with an intent gaze. "My lady Phèdre nó Delaunay de Montrève, you bear the mark of Kushiel's Dart. You are his chosen. And we who name ourselves the Unforgiven, scions of Camael, in our pride and arrogance, conspired to open our borders to the Skaldi, betraying the sacred trust of Elua and his Companions." He smiled grimly. "We have thrown away our honor, in bright-bladed Camael's eyes. For this, there is no forgiveness; only the hope of redemption. It is you who brought us that hope. Do you now understand?"

I gazed into the hearth-fire, burning merrily against the evening chill that fell during spring in Camlach. "Isidore d'Aiglemort," I said presently.

"Even so." Captain d'Eltoine nodded. "You gave him a chance to die a hero, and he took it. He did. Those of us who survived, we will not sway from the course you set, not until we die. What you have given us is a chance to endure Kushiel's punishment here on earth, and expiate our sins."

I looked reluctantly at him. "My lord . . . I am grateful for the lives you spared. But I didn't ask Isidore d'Aiglemort and the Allies of Camlach to fight for the sake of their souls. I asked because I was desperate, and I could think of no other way we stood to defeat the Skaldi."

"That doesn't matter." He gazed at his wineglass and lowered it untasted. "Kushiel's hand need not know its master's mind; it does his bidding all the same. We are the Unforgiven. We have a debt we must honor unto death, should you command us. That is all you need know."

"You could have notified me," I murmured. D'Eltoine blinked; my humor was lost on him. It was true, most Camaelines do think with their swords. Isidore d'Aiglemort was an exception, but then, he was fostered among the Shahrizai. "Never mind." My head was reeling. It is not every day that one learns an entire militia has sworn unbeknownst to obey you. "My lord," I said, gathering my thoughts. "Why did your men attack the Yeshuites?"

"We sought to question them." He shrugged apologetically. "A party of that size, seeking to cross into Skaldia? There can be no good reason for it, my lady, save espionage. But when we sought to detain them for questioning, they drew steel. So my men say, and I have no reason to doubt them." He eyed me. "Though if you demand it, I will put them to questioning."

"No." After what had passed in the City, it rang altogether too true. "They seek to cross Skaldia, and find refuge in lands further north, my lord. They mean us no harm."

"You know this to be true?" Firelight washed his face, etching in shadow the severe Camaeline beauty of his features. Some of us live closer in the hand of those we serve than others; this Captain was one such. Whether he had broken faith or no, I could see the bright edge of Camael's sword hovering over him.

"Yes." I said it firmly. What he was asking for, I could well guess; the stern truth of Kushiel's chosen, a terrible justice. I did not think it wise to tell him I was as much Naamah's Servant as Kushiel's, that the immortal hand that pricked my left eye with a crimson mote had led me not to pass sentence on the errant scions of Elua and his Companions, but to find luxuriant pleasure in enduring pain. But I thought of the Rebbe, and the depth of grief in his eyes, and I did not doubt the truth of my response. "Yes, my lord, I know it to be true."

"Madness." He shook his head, then looked squarely at me. "We will allow them passage. My lady, what else do you ask of us?"

Ah, Elua; such power, and so useless to me! If I could have put a name to an enemy who could be fought with cold steel, I would have. The ancient Hellenes claimed that the gods mocked their chosen victims. I never quite understood, until then, the double-edged curse of my gift. Melisande, I thought, would have relished the irony of it.

There remained, though, that which I had come for. "My lord," I said, leaning forward. "I am in search of the garrison of Troyes-leMont, those guardsmen who were on duty the night that Melisande Shahrizai escaped. I am given to understand that some number of them requested service among the Unforgiven, pursuing the remnants of Selig's army. What can you tell me?"

"Ghislain's lads." Tarren d'Eltoine surprised me with a fierce, bleak grin. "You're hunting traitors. I knew you would be about Kushiel's business, my lady. Yes, I've two under my command, and there are some few others, I think – three or four – scattered among the garrisons of Camlach. Would you speak with those here at Southfort?"

"Yes, my lord Captain. Please." After so long, I nearly felt dizzy with relief at tracking down at least two of the missing guardsmen. Barquiel L'Envers, I thought, I owe you for this tip. Pray that I use it better than you used my information regarding Marmion Shahrizai.

"They're loyal lads, to the bone, and I'm willing to swear as much, but mayhap they'll point your trail for you. I'll arrange for it first thing in the morning." The Captain stood and bowed. "Is there aught else?"

"No," I said automatically, then, "Yes. Do you promise me that no one of your men will seek vengeance against Joscelin Verreuil for his actions?"

"Do you jest?" His eyes gleamed; he did have a sense of humor after all. It was simply a uniquely Camaeline humor. "If I am not mistaken, they are badgering him even now to show how he managed to hold off half a dozen of the Black Shields."

"Seven," I said, meeting his amused gaze. "It was seven, at least."

Tarren d'Eltoine laughed. "He should have been born Camaeline."

High praise, indeed. I mulled over in my mind whether or not to tell Joscelin.

That night, I slept in the Captain's own quarters, listening to the wind out of Skaldia blow through the pines. It made me shiver in my marrow, and wish I were not alone beneath the fur-trimmed covers. I think, sometimes, I will never shake the cold of that Bitterest Winter. Though the lash-marks of my final assignation had faded, my shoulder ached; the old wound, where Waldemar Selig's blade had begun to carve my skin from my flesh. 'Twas but a memory, but even so, I felt it. I heard the sounds of a nightbound garrison, the call and response of guards, the occasional staccato beat of hooves, and saw light streaking against the darkness as a torch was handed off. I didn't guess what they were about, then. There was a watch set on the Yeshuite encampment, an uneasy truce.

I had gone to speak with them, along with Joscelin, and explained the nature of the misunderstanding. They were holding funeral rites for the slain, and though I spoke in their own tongue, most would not even look my way.

At length, one of the men came to address me, a barely contained rage in his face. I knew this man. He was the one who would have slain the kneeling guard "Yes, we hear what you say, D'Angeline," he said, making a term of contempt of it, not deigning to address me in Habiru. "Do you not see that we sit in grief for the dead?"

"You could have *told* them!" I listened to the keening of women and children, and a cold anger filled me. "You sought to cross a hostile border into enemy land – an enemy who well-nigh conquered us not two years past! They had a right to question you. Is it Yeshua's way to answer questions with steel?"

The man's eyes shone in the firelight, and he spat at my feet. "When the Mashiach returns, he will come bearing a sword, and He will separate out the goats from the sheep, D'Angeline! It is the faithful who lay His path. Are we prisoners here? Must we suffer for your pride, your wars?"

Those Unforgiven maintaining a watch stirred uneasily, and Joscelin twitched at my side, torn. I held up a hand, stalling them. "No," I murmured. "Will you make your people suffer for yours?"

The Yeshuite looked at me, uncertain. I thought with grief of the needless death I had witnessed, the lives thrown away on the battlefield. What stakes are worth that cost? I did not know then; I do not know now. What prize he sought, I could not even fathom. A promise gleaned from a dead prophet's words. In the end, all I could do was sigh.

"I have secured you safe passage through the mountains," I told him. "Captain d'Eltoine's men will see you to the pass on the morrow, and your weapons will be returned to you. Beyond that, I can only pray that you are right, and Yeshua keep you safe."

Joscelin gave his Cassiline bow, putting a seal on my words. His *khai* pendant flashed in the firelight, but he made no comment, and the Yeshuite offered him no thanks for the intervention that had surely saved lives. I turned to make my way back to the garrison.

"Tell me," I said to Joscelin as we reached the well-guarded entrance to the keep. I stopped and looked him full in the face. "Was it the *terminus*?"

He hesitated, and did not meet my eyes. "No. I would have thrown, that's all. He was going to kill a man in cold blood."

"You did as much, once." I said it softly.

"Yes." Joscelin did look at me, then, hard. "I haven't forgotten."

It had been my idea, my plan. I had not forgotten, either. I will never forget, until I die. Who is to measure cause? It may be that Terre d'Ange stands as a sovereign nation and not a Skaldic territory because Joscelin Verreuil throttled an unsuspecting thane. It was still murder. Are the stakes the Yeshuites seek any lower? I cannot say; only that we gauged the need and the profit better. And what had been the cost to Joscelin's soul? He bore the guilt of our deed, and his own broken oaths. I could not see his left hand, on the field today. I would never know if he meant to bring the second dagger to his own throat.

He'd done that once, too.

Thus for the wisdom of Kushiel's chosen. I wish sometimes that the gods would either choose better, or make their wishes clearer. Small wonder, that my sleep was restless. Still, sleep I did, alone in my cold and borrowed bed, and awoke to find that the Unforgiven had planned a show of arms for my benefit.

There were no women in the garrison of Southfort, only Camaeline lads eager to apprentice, for whom the taint of the Unforgiven held the glamour of the doomed, and a few grizzled ex-soldiers, who kept the lads in line. They made a considerable fuss over arranging for my toilet that morning. It would not do for me to visit the baths, oh no, but a great bronze tub must be hauled into the Captain's rooms, and bucket after bucket of steaming water to fill it. A guardsman, blushing, apologized for the lack of attendants; it disturbed his sensibilities that I must scrub myself and dress my own hair.

I bore it with good humor, glad my restless night was ended. Cereus House may have trained me, but I am no night-blooming flower to wilt in broad daylight. Still, it impressed upon me that the Unforgiven took this matter seriously, and I dressed accordingly. I'd had most of my wardrobe shipped ahead, two trunks already boarded in Marsilikos, but I had kept back one of Favrielle's creations, a travelling gown in black velvet with a bodice and sleeves that hugged the form, and flowing skirts designed for riding astride.

Over that, I wore my *sangoire* cloak.

So it was that we rode out onto the practice-field at Southfort, and Captain Tarren D'Eltoine barked out commands while his corps of Unforgiven executed a smooth series of maneuvers. Worn armor was oiled and polished to a high gleam, black shields fresh painted. His pikemen advanced before the line of horse, knelt and held, then broke away smoothly as the cavalry simulated a charge, lances held low. Then they too split away, and the pikemen regrouped in their place, swords drawn. Spaced far apart, they advanced; and the wheeling cavalry turned and charged through the gaps, baring naked steel.

When it was done, Tarren d'Eltoine raised one hand, and to a man, the Unforgiven knelt in that same uncanny motion; swords sheathed, shields lowered to touch the earth and heads bowed. Elua forgive me, but it made me uncomfortable. He beckoned, before giving the dismissal. Five infantrymen stayed.

I took their measure as they approached; L'Agnacites all, by the look of them. Broad, earnest faces, handsome in their way, bearing the sweat of their toil and smelling of the earth. Joscelin and my chevaliers drew close as they

came, especially Fortun, who had studied most the maps of
Troyes-le-Mont. He had brought one of our renderings
with him, and drew out the scroll from its cylindrical
leather casing, spreading it over his horse's withers.

"Five?" I asked Tarren d'Eltoine. "You said you had
two."

He gave me his bleak smile. "We sent our fastest riders
out last night, to the garrisons of Camlach. There are pas-
sageways through the mountains, known only to us. Three
other of Ghislain's men, you see before you. The last, at
Northfort, was too far to reach."

I remembered hoofbeats, and the torches. "Ah."

The men saluted and gave their names. Octave,
Vernay, Svariel, Fitz, Giles . . . Fortun had it all recorded,
once. All from L'Agnace; I'd been right about that. They
gave their positions, each one, the night of Melisande's
escape, and Fortun noted them carefully on his map.

"Tell me," I said, leaning forward in the saddle, "all
that you saw that night."

They did, with earnest voices and open countenances,
evincing not one of the telltales of evasion I might have
noted; indeed, they fair spilled over one another, eager
to say what they had seen. I kept my expression serene
and gnashed my teeth inwardly. Vernay, from the north-
ernmost garrison reached, gave willing testimony to what
his friend and comrade Luthais of Northfort had seen,
tendering his comrade's sincere regrets at his absence:
The distance had been too great. Vernay swayed on his feet
saying it, eyes bloodshot with exhaustion. I did not like to
guess how far he had ridden, nor how fast – nor how many
horses it had taken, and whether they lived. I had not asked
the Captain for this.

And these were the folk they saw abroad that night in Troyes-leMont: the chirurgeon Lelahiah Valais; Barquiel L'Envers; Gaspar Trevalion; Tibault de Toluard; Ghislain and Percy de Somerville. No more than I knew before, and two I had already discarded as suspects. I could have wept. Instead, I asked about Persia Shahrizai.

"Yes, my lady," replied Svariel of L'Agnace, who'd stood guard on the stairway of the second floor. "One of her majesty's Cassilines escorted her to the prisoner's chamber and back."

I closed my eyes. "Did you look closely as she left?"

He shook his head, reluctantly. I heard it all the same.

"When the Queen questioned you, did you tell her the Lady Persia was accompanied by a Cassiline?" I asked, opening my eyes.

He looked surprised. "I must have done, my lady. Don't remember as anyone asked. Well, she'd have known it, any mind, right? They're hers, the Cassiline Brothers."

"Yes." I gazed at him. "What did he look like?"

Svariel of L'Agnace looked uncomfortable, darting glances between Joscelin and me. "Well, like . . . like a Cassiline. I don't know. Grey togs, daggers and whatnot. They're all more or less the same, saving Lord Joscelin, aren't they?"

"More or less." I regarded Joscelin. He looked sick. "A young man? Old?"

"Middling." Svariel shrugged. "Tallish. Well, most of 'em are, aren't they? Not fair, and not grey. Dark hair, like; or brown. Or reddish, mayhap." His face creased. "I'm sorry, my lady! I'd have paid closer heed, but Cassilines . . . well. I'd as soon question one of Camael's priests. I should have, I know. S'why I'm here, and sworn to serve the Unforgiven. I don't forgive myself, I swear it."

"It doesn't matter," I told him gently. "You did all that duty required, and very well indeed, to remember that much. What of the others?" I glanced round at them all. "There must be ten or more of the guardsmen of Troyes-le-Mont not numbered among the Unforgiven."

"There were." It was the Captain's voice, cool and incisive. "We had two dozen among us, when we chased the remnants of Selig's men past the Camaelines. Some chose to stay; those men you see here before you. The rest returned to their duties in the regular army."

I thought about that. "To whom did they report?"

Tarren d'Eltoine shrugged. "The Lord Commander, I suppose, or mayhap the Captain of the Palace Guard. I concern myself with the men under my command, not those who've chosen dismissal."

"Not the Palace Guard," Remy said certainly, and Ti-Philippe nodded vigorously. "Believe me, my lady, we've haunted the barracks long enough! If Captain Niceaux knew aught of their fate, he'd have told us for the pleasure of seeing our backsides."

I could not help but smile. "Well, then. Percy de Somerville claims no knowledge of them; but then, it is Barquiel L'Envers who told me as much, so I do not know if I can believe it. My lord Captain, messires soldiers, might they have reported to Ghislain de Somerville?"

"Who knows?" Tarren d'Eltoine flicked dust from his sword-hilt. "I heard Lord *Percy* . . ." his lip curled, ". . . would fain see his son succeed him as Royal Commander. That's why he gave Ghislain command of the garrison in Troyes-le-Mont. Then again, Ghislain has his hands full holding the northern borders with Marc de Trevalion."

"I'd as soon report to Ghislain as the old man," Fitz of L'Agnace said stolidly. "He's the one gave us leave to join the Unforgiven. The old man would've had us digging irrigation ditches in his appleyards if he thought we needed punishing."

"Kerney and Geoff went back because they were ready to dig ditches instead of graves," Octave reminded him wearily; he had ridden far in the last twelve hours too, I could tell. He shook his head. "I don't know, my lady. We're L'Agnacites, we muster to the Comte . . . excuse me, the Duc . . . de Somerville's banner. If his lordship doesn't know, one of his subcommanders should."

I gazed at him. "And if no one knows? Mayhap they went home, without reporting."

"Mayhap." He said it reluctantly. "But they were owed pay in arrears. I don't think any of 'em would have foregone that. After all, the army's been ordered to stand down."

Fortun consulted his map of Troyes-le-Mont. "What of Phanuel Buonard?" he asked.

The L'Agnacites exchanged glances. "No," one of them said eventually. "I remember him. He's the one found poor Davet at the gate. He's Namarrese, he is. He didn't have the balls to become a Black Shield." Glancing at me, he coughed. "Begging my lady's pardon."

"Certainly," I murmured, wracking my brains for further questions. None availed themselves to me. I glanced at Fortun, who shook his head. So be it. "Thank you, my lord Captain, messires soldiers. You have been most helpful."

Tarren d'Eltoine gave the order for dismissal. As one, the L'Agnacites knelt, bowing their heads, then rose and departed at a fast jog toward the keep, even the most exhausted among them squaring his shoulders. "They serve well, these farmers' sons," d'Eltoine mused, watching after them. "I must say, it is notable."

"Anael's scions love the land," I said softly, "as Camael's love the blade. So they say." I did not add that for this reason, no Camaeline had been named Royal Commander in six hundred years. Tarren d'Eltoine would have known what the kings and queens of Terre d'Ange had held true for centuries: Battle for the sake of honor may be a fine thing for bards to sing of, but it is no way to preserve one's homeland. I gazed toward the base of the mountains, picking out the Yeshuite party in the distance, wending its way toward the southern pass, sunlight glinting off the steel plates of their Unforgiven escort. "My lord Captain." I turned back to him. "I am grateful and more for your aid. You have given more than I could ever have required. But now, I fear, we must depart. There is a ship sailing from Marsilikos that will not wait for us."

He bowed to me from the saddle, then dismounted and went down on one knee, bending his head briefly. "As you must, my lady. I wish you good hunting." Rising, he mounted smoothly, guiding his horse with his knees. "Remember," he said, raising his shield. Like his men's, it was dead black, save a single diagonal stripe of gold to mark his rank. "If you have need of the Unforgiven, we will answer to you. Commend us to your lord, Phèdre nó Delaunay de Montrève!"

With that, the Captain of Southfort thundered after his

men. We sat, Joscelin, my chevaliers and I, gazing after him.

"Well," I said thoughtfully. "Shall we go to Marsilikos?"

Twenty-nine

WE PUSHED hard that day and talked little, making good time. Once or twice Fortun glanced at me, thinking to speculate on what we had learned from the L'Agnacites, but whatever he saw writ on my face kept him silent. Time enough, on a long sea journey, to discuss it. He had the maps, and he would not forget.

A great deal occupied my mind as we rode. It is a startling thing, to find one has been made a legend unaware, even in a small way. It is a burdensome thing. *A whore's unwanted get.* So the ancient Dowayne of Cereus House named me, long ago; my earliest memory of identity. 'Twas bitter, indeed, but simple, too. Delaunay changed all that, putting a name to Kushiel's Dart, making me somewhat other. Then, I reveled in it. Now . . . I thought of the Unforgiven soldier kneeling beneath the Yeshuite's sword with his bowed head, neck muscles quivering, willing to die for an *anguissette*'s desperate plea.

Now, I was not so sure. And there was Joscelin.

The weather held fair and balmy, and we made camp in a pleasant site surrounded by great cedars. A spring burbled from a cleft in the mossy rocks, dark and cold, tasting faintly loamy. Remy, who had begun his service with Admiral Quintilius Rousse as apprentice to the ship's cook, made a passing good stew of salt beef and dried carrots, seasoning it with red wine and a generous handful of thyme. The Unforgiven had made certain our stores were well stocked ere we departed.

Afterward, as dusk fell, coming swift beneath the canopy of boughs, Joscelin volunteered quietly to take the first watch, and my chevaliers wrapped themselves in their bedrolls and slept. For some time, I lay awake on my fine-combed woolen blankets, watching the stars emerge one by one in patches of black sky visible through the trees. At length, I gathered up my blankets and went to sit beside him near the fire, which had burnt low.

"Phèdre." He looked sidelong at me, poking a long branch into the core of embers.

"Joscelin." It was enough, for now, to say his name. I sat gazing at our campfire, watching a thin line of flame lick at the underside of the branch. He fed it carefully, twig by twig, branch by branch, until it blazed merrily and sent sparks into the night air. So we had done in Skaldia, the two of us, with numb fingers and prayers on our half-frozen lips. 'Twas all so different, now. "Do you remember—"

Joscelin cut me off with a mute glance, and I held my tongue until he spoke, fiddling with a bit of tinder. "You know, I didn't want to believe it," he mused, throwing the debris into the fire. "You think it's true. There is a Cassiline Brother involved."

"I don't know." I wrapped my arms around my knees. "I found nothing to suspect in the list Thelesis gathered, but I think it is likely, yes, based on what we heard today." I stole a look at his brooding profile. "Even if there is, Joscelin . . . too many strings have been pulled, by someone with influence. A Cassiline could not have arranged for so many guardsmen to go missing. It cannot be only that."

"But it's part of it." He tipped his head back, gazing at the stars; I saw his throat move as he swallowed. "Despite it all, the training and the oaths, one of my own Brethren. We *are* human, Phèdre. Elua knows, we are that. But to break that faith, that training?" Joscelin drew a shaky breath and let it out slowly. "I never even went home. I promised my father, at Troyes-le-Mont, do you remember? And Luc. We were going to go to Verreuil."

"I remember." Sorrow rose, inexorable as the tide, and mingled with it, guilt. It was my fault. I had dragged him with me to the City instead, compelled by the strength of his vow. The Perfect Companion. "We were going to go this spring, you and I."

"Yes." He rubbed his eyes absently, his voice rough. "Almost fifteen years, it's been. My mother must be like to kill me."

I remembered his father, a stern Siovalese lordling, with the same austere beauty as his son, one arm bound in a stump after that terrible battle. I remembered his elder brother Luc, with those same summer-blue eyes, wide and merry. What must his mother and sisters and younger brother be like? I could not even guess. "Joscelin." I waited until he looked at me. "For Elua's sake, go home! Go see your mother, raise sheep in Siovale or lead the Yeshuites across Skaldia, I don't know. It doesn't matter. You were ten years old, when the Brotherhood claimed you. You don't owe them a debt of service to me! Even if you did, that bond was dissolved, by the Prefect's own words, years ago. It is killing you," I added softly. "And I cannot bear to watch it. If I could change what I am, I would. But I cannot."

"Neither can I," he whispered. "I swore my vows to Cassiel, not the Prefect, and the one I've kept is the only one that matters in the end. Phèdre, if I could be as other D'Angelines, I would. Mayhap it is killing me to stay, but leave you?" He shook his head. "They laid down their swords. You ordered it, and they did. Not the Unforgiven, I know what they hold true. Kushiel's hand. They have their redemption to think of. But the Yeshuites . . . they despise you, and yet, they obeyed."

I had forgotten it, until then; forgotten the ringing in my head, the bronze edge of power that shaded my desperate words. I ran my hands blindly over my face. "I know," I murmured. "I remember."

Until he took me into his arms, I did not realize my body was trembling. I laid my head on his chest, and the worst part of a long-pent fear and tension went out of me with a shudder, grounding itself in his warmth. Joscelin tightened his arms and stared over my head into the fire. "It scares me too, Phèdre," he said. "It scares me, too."

I fell asleep curled in his arms, and knew no more that night, wrapped for once in Joscelin's protection and the sound of his steady breathing. Would that it were always so, though I think I knew better, even then, than to hope for as much.

In the morning, Fortun shook us carefully awake and Joscelin disengaged himself from me, limbs stiffened by long inaction. I knelt in my blankets and dragged my fingers through my disheveled hair, watching him rise to commence his morning exercises, movements growing increasingly fluid as his muscles loosened and blood flowed, reinvigorating his limbs. His face was calm and expressionless.

Whatever had passed between us, nothing had changed.

We were four more days on the road, riding swiftly for Marsilikos, and I was heartened once we passed beyond the bounds of Camlach and into the province of Eisande. Elua forgive me, but I had too many bad memories that lay close to the Skaldic border, and the fealty of the Unforgiven had unnerved me. My chevaliers watched Joscelin and me as warily as they might the weather, but he was closed once more, cordial and distant. I daresay they held him in a greater degree of respect, having seen him do battle. Once we regained Eisheth's Way, we made our lodging in travellers' quarters, and I had a room to myself and a great empty bed.

A funny thing, that; I have been a courtesan all my life, and yet, I never passed a night entire in another's company, not until I was a slave in Skaldia. My patrons are not the sort to desire their beds warmed after pleasure.

Well, I have endured worse hardships than a cold bed, and I was not going to press the matter. Let Joscelin stand at the crossroads as long as need be, for while he stood, he stood at my side, and when all was said and done, for all the guilt I felt, I was grateful for it. One day, he must choose, and I was not so sure as I had been what path it would be.

Nor where mine would lead without him.

So we rode onward, and this time, when Ti-Philippe sniffed the air, 'twas no jest; we could smell it, all of us, the salt tang of the sea.

We had reached Marsilikos.

Of all the cities in Terre d'Ange, it is one of the oldest – a rich port from time out of mind, since the Hellenes began to conquer the sea. Tiberium held it, too, but since that mighty empire fell, it has belonged to us. It has a deep, protected harbor, and by tradition, the Royal Fleet anchors along the northern coast, warding off the threat of piracy. Ganelon de la Courcel ordered the fleet to the Straits after Lyonette de Trevalion's rebellion, fearing to trust to the loyalty of Azzalle. Ysandre, who restored peace in the province, had returned the Royal Fleet to its proper berth. Small wonder that my chevaliers were excited. For them, it was somewhat akin to returning home.

Indeed, they knew the city well, and pointed out its marvels to me as we rode, skirting the bustling quai, where a fish-market to fair boggle the mind was held. There, the Theatre Grande, where players and musicians flocked every season of the year, and competitions were staged in Eisheth's honor. There, the ancient Hellene agora, where orators and Mendacants still held forth, and people gathered to listen. There, just off the shore, a tiny, barren island, sacred to Eisheth and dedicated to fishermen. And all the length of the harbor, galleys and cogs were at dock, cargos loaded and delivered, the sound of shouting and the groaning wheels of oxcarts and the crack of whips snapping filling the air.

Above it all, on a high hill overlooking the harbor, stood the Dome of the Lady.

Sovereignty of the province of Eisande has passed from hand to hand with the whims of politics, but one thing has never changed: Marsilikos. It is ancient and wealthy, and it is ruled by the Lady of Marsilikos. If the heir to the city was male, no mind; his wife or consort was styled by the people the Lady of Marsilikos, and acknowledged as such, sharing equally in his power. I daresay there have been Lords who have challenged this, but none, to my knowledge, have succeeded in breaking the tradition. Eisheth herself was the first Lady of Marsilikos, and her precedent stands. So long as Terre d'Ange remains a sovereign nation, there will be a Lady in Marsilikos.

In this instance, it happened that I knew her.

The Duchese Roxanne de Mereliot was one of the few peers of the realm that Ysandre de la Courcel had trusted in those dark, precarious months before the war, when first she had ascended the throne – and she had proved a faithful ally.

If she was still, she would be expecting me.

I sent Remy and Ti-Philippe in advance, racing unburdened up the hill to announce our arrival, while Fortun bargained with a pair of shrewd dock-urchins to aid us with the packhorses. In truth, I was not certain what welcome we would find; I had been too long with my own suspicions, and too short a time a member of the peerage to expect the best. It is something to inspire awe, the Dome of the Lady, towering walls of white marble rising far above the city, gold leaf gleaming atop the dome. Siovalese architects were hired to build it, and there is a story about a lost ship being saved by seeing it shine on the far horizon like a second sun, a hundred leagues at sea.

At any rate, I was soon to be shamed by my own doubts.

The golden Dome reared up against a blue sky as we made our approach, flanked at its base by white minarets. It is a splendid structure, and highly defensible, walled fortifications encircling the peak of the hill. The standard of the Lady of Marsilikos fluttered from the minarets and the crenellated tops of the gate-tower; two golden fish, head to tail, forming a circle on a sea-blue field. It is ancient, too, by our reckoning – Eisheth's sign.

This day, the gates stood open, and a guardsman sounded a long trumpet blast to herald our arrival. They bowed as we rode through, a double line of guards, clad in light shirts of chain-mail over sea-blue livery.

In the courtyard, smiling, stood Roxanne de Mereliot, accompanied by her retinue of guardsmen and retainers, and another figure I knew well; red-haired, burly as a bear and half again as elegant, a broad, lopsided grin splitting his scarred face.

"My lord Admiral!" My exultant cry rang in the court-yard, and before I thought twice, I dismounted and ran to him, flinging both arms about his neck.

"Easy, child!" For all that he protested, Quintilius Rousse chuckled and enfolded me in a great embrace, crushing me against his brawny chest. "Sweet tits of Naamah, you're a sight for sore eyes, Phèdre nó Delaunay!" Resting his hands on my shoulders, he grinned down at me, eyes a bright blue in his weather-beaten face. "The Lady thought you might be pleased to see me. Glad to note she wasn't wrong."

"Your grace!" Appalled, I turned to Roxanne de Mereliot, dropping into a deep curtsy and holding it, my head lowered.

"Comtesse de Montrève, be welcome to Marsilikos," her voice said above me, rich with amusement. "And please, do rise."

I did, reluctantly meeting her gaze. No longer young,

the Lady of Marsilikos retained an abundant beauty, deepened with the passage of years. Her coal-black hair was streaked with white, her generous mouth smiled easily, and kindness and wisdom lit her dark eyes. "Your grace," I said. "Pray forgive my rudeness."

"Rudeness?" She gave her warm smile. " 'Twould have spoiled my surprise if you'd acted otherwise! I miss my own children, who pursue their studies in Tiberium and Siovale. Spontaneity is the province of youth; indulge me my delight in it, young Phèdre."

Over her shoulder, I saw Remy and Ti-Philippe, grinning like idiots, while behind me, Fortun and Joscelin exchanged hearty greetings with Quintilius Rousse. I could not help but smile, too. "By all means, my lady," I said, and meant it.

That night in the Dome of the Lady, Roxanne de Mereliot held a feast for us. It was a closed affair, for it would not do to have it gossiped about Eisande that the Lady of Marsilikos had received me in state so soon on the heels of my disfavor at the Palace, but splendid nonetheless. I have a fondness for seafood, and Marsilikos is renowned for it. We ate course after course, all plucked fresh from the sea — mussels in their own salt juices, terrines of lobster, sea bream in ginger, filets of sole and salmon, whitefish in flaky pastry. I daresay nearly all of us ate until we were fair groaning; cuisine is reckoned one of the great arts in Terre d'Ange, and we would too soon be at the mercy of Caerdicci cookery.

Afterward, bowls of warmed water scented with orange blossom were brought round, and we dipped our fingers and wiped them on linen towels, and then sweet almond pastries were served, and a dessert wine from

Beauviste that lingered on the tongue with a taste of melons and honey, and Roxanne de Mereliot bid her servants leave us until further notice.

"Ysandre has written to tell me what you are about, Phèdre," she said without preamble. "From her courier's haste, I thought to see you in Marsilikos some days past."

"My apologies, my lady," I replied. "I had other business to attend to." 'Twas not for lack of trust that I did not share with her and Rousse what had passed among the Unforgiven. In truth, I had learned naught of use to anyone, and I was uncomfortable enough with their regard to remain silent. To their credit, not a one of Phèdre's Boys even blinked.

"No matter." She dismissed it with a wave of her hand. "Would that we'd had more time, is all. But I have taken the liberty of confirming your arrangements, and clearing their security through Admiral Rousse. The *Darielle* sails on the morrow, late afternoon; she'll be loading cargo all morn. Your shipment of lead has safely arrived, and your trunks as well. You've passage booked for five to La Serenissima." The Lady of Marsilikos frowned. "Would that there was ought else I could do, Phèdre."

" 'Tis but a sea voyage, my lady." I shrugged. "A thousand others have done the same, and a thousand shall after me."

"I have been on one of your sea voyages," Quintilius Rousse rumbled, "and scarce lived to tell the tale, child. I know better. Whatever else Delaunay taught you, he made you an apt compass for trouble. I'm minded to send an escort with you. Three ships, no more."

Joscelin, Remy, Ti-Philippe, Fortun — all looked at me, while I shook my head slowly. "No, my lord Admiral.

I thank you; but no. If I'm to harbor any illusion in La Serenissima that I'm *not* Ysandre's creature, I can scarce arrive with an escort culled from the Royal Fleet."

"La Serenissima," Rousse said mildly, "fields a navy which is second to none, child; even to my own. They hold the entire length of the Caerdicci coast, aye, and Illyria too, with fingers stretching into Hellene waters, and eyes that gaze beyond, toward Ephesium and Khebbel-im-Akkad. Peaceful now, aye, but La Serenissima hungers for power, and we have Prince Benedicte de la Courcel alone to thank that her eyes do not turn west. Those who do not fear her are land-locked fools."

I flushed at that. "My lord, it may be so. If it is, will you defend me with three galleys?"

"Nay," he growled. "But I can remind them that they do not control the waters yet, and any Serenissiman fool enough to harbor Melisande Shahrizai will answer to Terre d'Ange, with blood if need be!"

"Admiral." It was Fortun's voice, quiet and even. "Do, and you'll warn every enemy of the nation before we've even set foot on dry land. My lady Phèdre is right. If there is aught to learn, and we stand any chance of learning it, we must rely on the arts of covertcy."

"You've been at the lad," Quintilius Rousse sighed, leveling his blue gaze at me. "Child, Anafiel Delaunay was my friend, and I never had better. For his sake, let me afford you such measure of protection as is in my ability to grant. For surely, if he knew the road on which he'd set you, he'd ask no less."

Roxanne de Mereliot did not speak, but her dark eyes pleaded with me, those of a sovereign and a mother alike. I should have guessed she had a stake in it.

"My lord." I spread my hands helplessly. "It is too much, and not enough. Fortun is right, your aid would but tie our hands. And if my lord Delaunay were alive to say it, he would surely agree." I summoned my resolve and held his fierce gaze unblinking. "Time passes, my lord Admiral, and I am no child to be ordered. Her majesty has agreed to my plan. Let it stand."

"Bah!" It was Rousse who looked away first, beseeching Joscelin and my chevaliers for assistance. "Will none of you talk sense to the girl?" he demanded. In truth, I was not sure. But all of them, even little Ti-Philippe, shook their heads, one by one. At last, Quintilius Rousse heaved another sigh, more massive than the last. "So be it," he said heavily. "But if you've need of aid, Phèdre nó Delaunay, know this. Do you but send word to the Lady of Marsilikos or myself, I will come. I will come with ships, and I will come in force. I have seen the Face of the Waters, and I do not fear anything at sea born of mortal flesh. Do you understand?"

"Yes, my lord," I murmured, flinching away from the ferocity of his stare. "I understand." It brought somewhat else to mind, and I bit my lip. "My lord . . . my lord Admiral. Do you have any word of the Master of the Straits?"

Joscelin stirred, alert at that. He knew what I meant: Hyacinthe.

"Nay," Rousse said softly, his expression turning compassionate. "Tamed they are, child, and all manner of craft cross at will. But I swear to you, every three-month, storm or calm, I have sent a ship to dare the Three Sisters. None has drawn within a league; the seas themselves rise against us. I am sorry," he added with unwonted gentleness. "I liked that Tsingano lad, I did. But whatever fate he's bought himself, the Master of the Straits holds him to it."

I nodded. "Thank you."

It was meant to be my fate, Hyacinthe's. The Master of the Straits had posed us a riddle. I had guessed the riddle first, and I had guessed it right. He drew his power from the Lost Book of Raziel. But Hyacinthe had challenged my answer. He had used the *dromonde*, the Tsingani gift of sight, and seen further into the past, answering the riddle to its fullest and naming the terms of Rahab's curse. His was the answer the Master of the Straits had accepted. If not for that, it would have been me, chained for eternity to that lonely isle. It should have been me.

"I will keep trying," Quintilius Rousse said roughly, and reaching across the table, took my face in both massive hands, planting a kiss on my brow. "Elua keep you, Phèdre nó Delaunay, and heed my promise, if you'll not heed my advice. We went to the ends of the earth together, you and I."

"Yes, my lord," I whispered, grasping his hands and kissing them. Alone among all the others, all I suspected, I trusted Quintilius Rousse. 'Twas true, we *had* gone to the ends of the earth together, he and I; gone and returned.

Roxanne de Mereliot shook her head fretfully. "I was hoping you would see reason, Phèdre. But you will do what you will, I suppose. I will pray to Eisheth for your safe return," she said, and added her voice to Rousse's. "And if you've need of aid, send word, and I will send it."

"I will," I promised.

THIRTY

THE NEXT day, we said our farewells to the Lady of Marsilikos, and made our way to the quai to board the *Darielle*. She was a three-masted galley, one of the newest and finest merchanters D'Angeline traders had afloat, and not even my chevaliers had a word to say against her.

The last thing we did, before boarding, was conclude the sale of our mounts and packhorses to one of the many horse traders who provide for and profit from travellers in Marsilikos. We had not arranged for their portage, and I was minded to start anew in La Serenissima, unencumbered upon my arrival. Still, it was a frightening thing, to commit ourselves to the bowels of the ship, knowing we would arrive without home or transport. I prayed that my factor's arrangements held good, and the sale of the shipment of lead would go through without difficulty.

Quintilius Rousse had accompanied us to the quai, and whatever it was he said to the captain, hauling him aside and muttering ungently in his ear, I daresay it went a long way toward explaining the careful, courteous treatment I received throughout our journey.

When he had done with the Captain, he turned to me, and his blue eyes were canny in that unhandsome face. "Phèdre nó Delaunay," he mused. "Off to chase a will-o'-the-wisp. Well, you have my pledge, and I have your promise. Now hear me, for I've one last piece of advice for you to heed." He laid his calloused hands on my shoulders and gripped them hard, staring down at my upturned face. "Your lord Delaunay might not have died had he toyed less lightly with Melisande Shahrizai. If you're right, lass, and you find her in La Serenissima, don't play at her game. Go straightaway to Prince Benedicte, and tell him. Royal-born he may be, but Benedicte's a soldier from olden days. He rode with Rolande de la Courcel and Percy de Somerville, and aye, Delaunay too, before you were born. He'll know what to do."

"Yes, my lord," I promised him. "I will."

"Good." One last squeeze of my shoulders and a rough embrace, his coarse red hair tickling my ears, and then Quintilius Rousse released me, turning to Joscelin. "You, lad!" he said gruffly, shaking him. "You're travelling with the most beautiful courtesan in three generations of Naamah's Servants! Try to look a little less as if it were a death sentence, will you? And keep her safe, for if that prune-mouthed Cassiel doesn't have your guts for bowstrings, I surely will, if she comes to harm."

To his credit, Joscelin grinned. "I will remember, my lord!" he said, giving a sweeping Cassiline bow, his steel vambraces flashing in the sunlight.

Rousse merely grunted, and turned away. He brooked no foolishness, the Lord Admiral, and he knew whereof he spoke; one does not command the seas and face down the Master of the Straits without learning to take the measure of a man. He gave a seaman's salute to Fortun, Remy and Ti-Philippe, crisply returned by all three, then strode away, his rolling gait carrying him swiftly the length of the quai.

A fair breeze sprang up past the noon hour, and all was in readiness. Sailors on board the *Darielle* shouted to and fro with those on the docks; knots were undone, ropes tossed on deck. My chevaliers were restless, eager-eyed, clinging to the railings. This had been their lives, once. The rowers set to, and the galley moved ponderously away from the dock, into the narrow harbor, where the breeze briskened. At a shout from the Captain, the mainsail dropped. The stiffened canvas filled slowly, bellying in the wind, and the ship glided toward the mouth of the harbor, prow nosing toward the open seas.

We were on our way.

In truth, a lengthy and uneventful sea voyage makes for a poor tale; and, by Elua's grace, that is what we were granted. Laden with cargo, our ship rode low in the water, but for all of that, the winds blew fair, and we made good time.

For the first two days of the voyage, Joscelin Verreuil, my Perfect Companion, spent a great deal more time than was seemly hanging over the railings and disgorging the contents of his stomach. No born sailor, he.

My chevaliers, for their part, were at home in an instant, and it did not take long for the crew of the *Darielle* to ascertain that they had expert sailors aboard ship. They took turns at manning the rigging, or the oars, when we rounded the Caerdicci point and the winds turned against us. I daresay I could have bartered their aid against the price of our passage, if I'd been minded to, but it kept them out of trouble and the Captain's nature sweet, so I held my tongue.

As for me, I had a cabin in the aft castle; a narrow berth, to be sure, but my own. The hempen strands of my hammock cradled me securely, and I slept soundly therein.

The winds held steady and we surged ahead of them, a froth of white water where our prow cut the seas, keeping in sight of the coastline for the most part. The Captain, whose name was Louis Namot, was quick to summon me, pointing out such sights as might be seen from shipboard. I have learned, since, that there are sailors who think a woman's presence aboard ship to be a sign of ill luck. Elua be thanked, D'Angelines are spared such idiotic superstitions.

There is a certain peace to it, committing one's fate to the seas, even as there is in surrendering to a patron's will. I thought often of Hyacinthe on that long journey, wondering if he had come to gain mastery over the scudding waves, and how such a thing might be accomplished. I wondered, too, how far his dreadful inheritance extended. Rahab's realm lay everywhere on the deep, if Yeshuite teaching was to be believed; but the Master of the Straits was born of a D'Angeline woman, who loved a mortal Alban, and I never heard of his dominion extending beyond the waters that bordered our two lands.

With such things were my thoughts occupied during our journey, and I daresay it passed quickly enough. White-winged gulls circled our three masts as we travelled, always within a half-day's sail of land. I thought them pretty; 'twas Remy who told me that they followed the wake of offal left by our galley, descending to pluck the waters clean of fish entrails and other such discarded matter.

Day by day, we made our way northward up the length of the Caerdicci coast. We passed tiny islands; barren rocks thrusting into the ocean, fit only for gulls and the poorest of fishermen. 'Twas another matter, according to Louis Namot, on the far side of the sea, the Illyrian coast, which was fair riddled with islands, rich and fertile and a veritable breeding ground for pirates. Indeed, his men kept a keen watch once we'd rounded the point, sharpening their swords and manning the trebuchet mounted atop the forecastle, but we passed unmolested. Illyrian pirates are notorious, but their country is caught between the hammer of La Serenissima and the anvil of Ephesium; they have no quarrel with Terre d'Ange.

On our twenty-third day at sea, the watcher in the crow's nest atop the midmast gave a shout, and we passed the isle that marks the outermost boundary waters of La Serenissima. Unlike the others, this was no barren grey hummock; a sheer cliff faced the sea, black basalt crags towering angrily above the waves, which broke hard on the rocks below. I didn't know why, as we passed, the sailors all whistled tunelessly, and had to ask the Captain.

"La Dolorosa," he said, as though it explained everything; even he averted his eyes from the black isle. "It is a Serenissiman superstition, my lady. They say that when Baal-Jupiter slew Asherat's son Eshmun, the Gracious Lady of the Sea wept and raged and stamped her foot, and the floor of the sea rose up in answer, spewing forth La Dolorosa to mark her grief."

I am always interested in such things, and leaned upon

the guardrail as we sailed by, giving the black isle a wide berth. There was a fortress nestled amid the crags, and I could make out the faint, spidery lines of a hempen bridge suspended high in the air, swaying and sagging betwixt the isle and the mainland. "But why do they whistle?" I asked, intrigued.

"To mimic the grieving winds, and turn aside the wrath of Asherat-of-the-Sea, who is wroth still at the death of her son." Louis Namot shuddered and took my arm, drawing me further in deck. "My lady, if you ask me on dry land, I will say it is an old quarrel between the descendants of the Phoenicians and the conquering Tiberians cast in terms to explain a volcanic phenomenon, but we are at sea, and I do not want the Gracious Lady to think we mock her grief with staring. I pray you, turn away!"

"Of course, my lord Captain," I said politely.

His manner eased the moment I obeyed, and he wiped his brow. "Forgive me, my lady," he said, apologizing. "But the currents around La Dolorosa are strong and uncertain, and no one is wise who mocks the superstitions of a place, most especially not a sailor."

"No." I remembered Quintilius Rousse tossing a gold coin to the Lord of the Deep upon reaching safe harbor in Alba. "I should say not."

"I heard tell of a rich merchant," one of the sailors offered, "who laughed at the ship's crew for whistling, and no sooner had he done, than a great wind came up and the ship heeled hard about, and he was thrown over the side and dashed on the rocks of La Dolorosa."

"No," said another. "I heard it too, only they never found his body."

"And I heard," Louis Namot said grimly, "his corpse

was washed ashore on the isle of Kjarko a hundred leagues south, on the Illyrian coast. And that, lads, is no Mendacant's tale. My uncle served aboard a trireme under Admiral Porcelle, and they chased down a band of Illyrian pirates who were raiding D'Angeline ships along the point. Their captain was wearing the merchant's signet. He pled clemency and told how they found the body. My uncle had to return it to the merchant's widow."

I turned back and gazed at the black isle, dwindling in our wake, the fortress towers silhouetted against the sky. "Who would live in such a place?"

"No one, by choice," the Captain said shortly. " 'Tis a prison."

"The worst prison," a sailor added, and grinned. "If *I'm* ever accused of aught in La Serenissima, I'm taking refuge in the temple of Asherat, I am! I'll take the veil myself, like Achilles in the house of Lycomedes, and give all her priestesses a nice surprise!"

One of his fellows hushed him quickly, with a furtive glance in my direction. I paid it no heed; I'd been three weeks at sea, and had heard worse. Sailors must make do with one another aboard ship — those who favor women are notoriously eager upon making landfall.

Still, it made me think on what I knew of La Serenissima. Women do not hold offices of power in most of the Caerdicci city-states, that much I knew. It is men who built them, and men who rule, by dint of toil and iron. Asherat-of-the-Sea holds sway, still, because she is the Gracious Lady of the Sea, and men who live by the grace of the sea are wise enough to fear her wrath, but this was not Marsilikos, where Eisheth's living blood runs in the veins of the Lady who rules there.

In La Serenissima, it would be different.

Soon the lookout cried again, and presently we saw before us the long, low line of the spit that bars the great lagoon of La Serenissima; the Spear of Bellonus, they call it, another legacy of the Tiberians. It extends nearly all the way across the vast, wide mouth of the lagoon, some seven leagues long, forming a natural barrier well guarded by the Serenissiman navy.

As we drew near to the narrow strait that breaches the spit, there were a great many more ships to be seen, of all makes and sizes, flying all manner of colors: cogs and galleys and triremes, and the low, flat-bottomed gondoli and gondolini with the curving prows and sterns that are ubiquitous in the city, propelled by skilled rowers at tremendous speed. And, too, there were craft I had never seen before, small ships with masts canted forward, bearing odd triangular sails – of Umaiyyat make, the Captain told me. It did not look as though they could carry much in the way of cargo, but they moved swiftly and agilely across the waters, tacking back and forth before the wind while larger vessels must needs go to oars.

A fleet of Serenissiman gondolini surrounded us at the mouth of the straits, their insubstantial menace backed by manned watchtowers on either side and the presence of the navy within the lagoon. Namot's papers, his writ of passage, were all in order, and in short order, they waved us through.

Thus we entered the lagoon.

Joscelin had come to stand beside me in the prow of the *Darielle*, and I was glad of his presence as we gazed together on our first sight of La Serenissima.

Serenissimans claim she is the most beautiful city in the

world, and I cannot wholly begrudge them; 'tis indeed a splendid sight to see, a city rising up from the very waters. I had read what I could find prior to our journey, and I knew it was an ever-ongoing work of tremendous labor that had built La Serenissima, not on dry land, but on islands and marshes, dredged, drained and bridged, oft-flooded, always reclaimed.

If I sound unpatriotic in acknowledging the city's beauty, I may add that a great deal of the engineering and building that had made her splendid had come in recent decades, under the patronage of Prince Benedicte de la Courcel, who brought with him Siovalese architects and engineers when his fate was wed to the Stregazza family, exiling him from his homeland.

The sun shone brightly on the waters as we crossed the lagoon and made for the Great Canal, the sailors cursing good-naturedly as they took to the oars. Ahead of us, galleys and darting craft were everywhere on the vast waterway. Ti-Philippe, who had been once to the city during a brief apprenticeship aboard a merchanter, took it upon himself to point out the sights.

"The Arsenal," he said reverently, nodding behind us to a vast, walled shipyard hugging the lagoon. "It houses one of the finest navies in the world, and they can build a ship faster than you can cut timber." As we curved along the vast quai, he simply pointed. "The Campo Grande. There lies the Palace of the Doge. At the end, the Temple of Asherat-of-the-Sea."

The Great Square; it was that, indeed, a vast, marbled terrace simply opening onto the sea. In the center, where it verged the water, stood a tall column, and atop it a statue of the goddess, arms outspread, gazing benignly over the lagoon. Asherat-of-the-Sea, bearing a crown of stars, waves and leaping dolphins worked into the plinth. To her left stood the Palace of the Doge, a long, tiered building worked in white marble, with a level of striated pink, surprisingly rich in the glowing light.

It is the seat of all politics within La Serenissima, and not merely the Doge's home; within those walls was housed the Judiciary Hall, the Chamber of the Consiglio Maggiore, indeed, the Golden Book itself, in which were inscribed the names of the Hundred Worthy Families deemed fit to hold office in La Serenissima.

Beyond, at the far end of the square, sat the Temple of Asherat, with its three pointed domes; an Ephesian influence, that, for they ruled La Serenissima for a time and worshipped the goddess under another name. I could see little of the temple, as the square itself was crowded with a vast market, stalls occupying preordained spaces marked in white brick, and, in between, a throng of people. Serenissimans and other Caerdicci, most of them, but I saw unfamiliar faces – proud Akkadians and hawk-faced Umaiyyati; Menekhetans, dark-eyed and calm; Ephesians; even an entourage from Jebe-Barkal, ebony and exotic.

And here and there, fair, brawny Skaldi, which gave me a shiver.

Then we were past it, and entering the mouth of the Great Canal itself, and Ti-Philippe pointed to the left where stood the Temple of Baal-Jupiter on the island's tip. It had clean, straight lines in the Tiberian style, and before it stood a statue of the god himself, one foot striding forward, thunderbolt in hand.

He had slain Asherat's son, according to myth.

I knew what the Captain had meant; 'twas but a translation of mortal history into divine terms, the faith of the conquering Tiberians mingling with the beliefs of those inhabitants they found here. Still, I thought on the black isle of La Dolorosa, and shuddered.

Great houses rose along the canal after that, splendid and magisterial, with balconies and winding stairs leading down the quai; along its length were docked craft like the gondoli, only larger and more luxurious, canopied, painted in bright colors and rich with gilt and carving. I did not need Ti-Philippe to tell me we were among the homes of the Hundred Worthy Families.

I did not need Ti-Philippe to point out the Little Court, although he did.

I daresay it was nearly as large as the Doge's Palace, although not quite. Three tiers tall, with long, colonnaded balconies, rippling waterlight reflected along the marble length of it. Fluttering pennants hung from the balconies, bearing the silver swan of House Courcel.

Deserving of its name, I thought.

And then we were beyond it, and sailed beneath the cunning, peaked bridge of Rive Alto that linked the largest islands of La Serenissima, tall enough to admit a galley to pass, and on our right stood the vast, elegant structure of the Fondaca D'Angelica, the D'Angeline warehouse. Already the Captain was shouting to men on the quai, and the rowers heaving to all on one side, as our ship wallowed in the deep green waters of the canal and sailors tossed ropes ashore, bringing us to port at last.

I had reached La Serenissima.

THIRTY-ONE

AFTER SO long at sea, 'twas strange setting foot on solid land, and I was hard put not to stagger, unnaturally convinced that the quai moved beneath me. Around us was the bustle of the *Darielle*'s docking and laborers working to unload her cargo, and all at once I felt weary and salt-stiffened and in dire need of rest and a bath.

Thanks be to Blessed Elua, my chevaliers were solicitous and capable, quick to swing into action. Joscelin was no help; having finally gained his sea legs, he was twice as queasy as I on solid ground. But my factor's man in La Serenissima was present as arranged, and Remy and Ti-Philippe rounded him up in no time. Once he was done gloating over the quality of our shipment of lead, he greeted me unctuously.

"Well met, well met, Contessa!" he said in fluid Caerdicci, punctuated with many bows. "All your requests have been seen to, and we have arranged for most elegant lodgings during your stay in the Serene Republic, most elegant indeed!"

Out of the corner of my eye, I could see Fortun

examining the papers acknowledging receipt of the shipment. "Thank you, messire," I said in the same tongue, grateful that matters were well in hand. "If I might be conducted to them . . .?"

"Of course!" He hurried to the edge of the quai, beckoning to the steersman of one of the large, gilded craft, returning presently. "It was the house of Enrico Praetano," he explained to me, "who has defaulted on a loan to the Banco Grendati. They were most eager to arrange for a seasonal lease."

"Ah." So long as I was not displacing an orphanage, I thought, I did not care. In short order, my chevaliers had my trunks brought up from the hold of the *Darielle* and placed in the craft; bissone, they are called, longer and broader than the simple gondoli. The oarsmen grumbled at the number of trunks, and then they caught sight of me as Joscelin aided me carefully aboard.

I was tired, unwashed and not at all at my best.

"Asherat!" one of the crew muttered in awe, then grinned, standing up to execute a bow and kiss his fingers. "A star has fallen to earth!" Moving with an alacrity that set the bissone to rocking, the others scurried to arrange the cushions beneath the canopy for greater comfort.

Joscelin looked unamused; I couldn't have cared less. I settled into the cushions with a sigh of relief. My chevaliers leapt aboard, the steersman pushed off, and we were on our way, gliding over the green waters.

So it was that I came to be ensconced in an elegant house along the Great Canal, rubbing shoulders with the Hundred Worthy Families. My factor's representative in La Serenissima – whose name was Mafeo Bardoni – might be an unctuous fellow, but he was a skilled businessman, and I never had cause to fault his dealings. If I did not like him, it was no fault of his own; he reminded me overmuch of Vitale Bouvarre, who had been Alcuin's patron, his first and last. 'Twas Bouvarre who gave up the name of Dominic Stregazza as Isabel de la Courcel's killer. He is dead, now, though he tried first to kill Alcuin for his silence.

Though it was but late afternoon when I gained my lodgings, I ordered first a bath, and then went straightways to bed, and slept for some twelve hours. My sleeping-chamber was directly off the balcony, and 'twas a strange and wondrous thing to awake not knowing where I was, with the shifting light off the waters of the canal playing over the walls of my chamber.

A pity I had to wake to it alone, I thought.

My maidservant was a shy young girl named Leonora, who trembled and spilled the tray when she brought me tea and pastries, and blushed every time I looked at her. Still, my garments were unpacked and neatly pressed, and she buttoned my gown adeptly when I dressed. On my first day in La Serenissima, I wore a gown of apricot silk, with a fine gold brocade woven with seed pearls; another of Favrielle nó Eglantine's creations, marked with the simple, elegant lines so deceptively hard to mimic.

"Please tell Signore Joscelin and the others that I am awake," I said to her in Caerdicci, when I was properly attired and had tucked my hair into a gold mesh caul, donning a pair of dangling pearl earrings. "Oh, and bring me paper and ink, if you would be so kind."

At this, Leonora's chin rose with a surprised jerk and she gazed at me wide-eyed. "Does my lady wish the services of a secretary?" she asked tentatively.

"No." I frowned. "My lady wishes to write a letter."

"Oh!" Blushing once more, Leonora hurried out. I shook my head and waited. Presently she returned, breathless, clutching a sheaf of paper and holding the inkpot gingerly, as if it would bite her. I sat down at a little table near the balcony and penned a note to Severio Stregazza, sealing it with taper wax and the impress of the Montrève insignia.

I thought of asking one of the house servants to deliver it, and thought better, descending to find Joscelin and my chevaliers assembled in the parlor.

"Do you think you could find your way to deliver this to Severio Stregazza?" I asked Ti-Philippe, who fair bounded out of his chair.

"Aye, my lady!" he said promptly.

I let him go; I let all of them go, Phèdre's Boys, in the end, to take the city's measure. I knew Fortun would oversee the sale of our shipment, and all of them had become adept at scouting the sort of information I needed. It left Joscelin and me alone in the house together.

When they had gone, he gave me a long, level look. "Now that we are here," he said, "exactly what is it that you propose to do, Phèdre?"

It was a fair question, and a good one. It was astonishing that he'd waited so long to ask it, and a pity I had no answer. I met his eyes and shrugged. "Wait," I said. "And see."

Joscelin sighed.

In the matter of Severio Stregazza, I did not have long to wait. A reply came even before my chevaliers had made their way back to the house, scrawled in Severio's impatient hand. I smiled to read it, remembering how terse his initial proposal to me had been; by contrast, this was a jumbled missive expressing his undying affection, his enormous joy at learning of my presence and, as an afterthought, a pleading invitation that I attend a celebration that night in honor of his friend Benito Dandi's natality.

"Will you go?" Joscelin asked coolly.

"No." I shook my head, and sent once more for writing materials while Severio's manservant waited. "I asked him to present me to his grandfather the Doge and to Prince Benedicte. I'll wait on that answer before I plunge into Serenissiman society — 'tis the Doge's Palace I need to access. Anyway, it does no harm to keep him anxious."

To that, he made no reply.

Ere nightfall, my chevaliers had returned, full of high spirits and useful information, which they related to me over dinner. Careful to take no chances, I had the household servants dismissed while we dined; knowing no better, they put it down to some D'Angeline oddity.

"The chiefest rumor," Ti-Philippe announced eagerly, "is that the Doge himself, Cesare Stregazza, has plans to step down come year's end." He looked at me to continue, and I nodded. " 'Tis well known he has the shaking-sickness, and rumor says the Oracle of Asherat has proclaimed he will die of it, if he does not cede the throne."

"Rumor says too," Fortun murmured, "that there is pressure from the Consiglio Maggiore, who fear his illness weakens their position in negotiation."

"It has not been formally announced?" I inquired.

"No." Ti-Philippe shook his head vigorously. "But *everyone* says it, and we went over half the city, pretending to be drunk, after Fortun found out how much profit you made on that lead shipment, my lady!" He grinned. "I always liked Drustan mab Necthana, but I like him better now that I know how cheap he's selling Alban goods for D'Angeline trade!"

Fortun cleared his throat. "I arranged to put it on account at the Banco Tribuno," he said apologetically. "Messire Brenin said it was the best."

"Fine," I said. "And what does La Serenissima say about the Doge's imminent retirement?"

Remy laughed, then sobered at my quizzical look. "Pardon, my lady, but it's a dogfight, or near enough. There are six Sestieri to the city, and each one's the right to put forward a candidate, though it must be one whose family name is inscribed in the Golden Book – and that's by popular election. When the Doge is elected, 'tis the Consiglio Maggiore who does the choosing among 'em. Right now, it's all rumor and chaos, with the districts fighting among themselves and with each other over who they favor. I mean really fighting," he added. "Mobs of young gallants in striped hose, beating each other over the head."

"We saw a splendid fight," Ti-Philippe said cheerfully. "On the bridge, with staves. I wanted to join it, but Fortun threatened to throw me in the canal."

"Thank you," I said to Fortun, who nodded gravely. To Ti-Philippe, I said, "La Serenissima lacks a proper sewage system, you know. They use the canals." I knew, I'd seen Leonora empty the chamber pot.

"Well, that's why I didn't, isn't it?" he asked logically. "Anyway, two of old Cesare's lads are in the mix, it seems. Marco's the elder of the Stregazza; your Severio's father, that's wed to Prince Benedicte's daughter. He's got the Sestieri Dogal's vote, all the clubs are behind him, and they love him well, only he's fallen out with Prince Benedicte, they say, since the old boy remarried, so his people are nervous that the Consiglio's going to turn against him. And the other's Ricciardo, his younger brother, who's going for the Sestieri Scholae, where all the craft-guilds are quartered, and getting them all up in arms over some tax."

Severio had told me as much, I remembered; it hadn't meant anything to me at the time. Now, I struggled to encompass it. "Six Sestieri," I said. "Six districts. There are four other candidates, then?"

"Not yet," Fortun told me. "We heard Orso Latrigan has a lock on the Sestieri d'Oro, and what he can't win, he'll buy. But there are three others where candidates are still vying." He shrugged and gave a quiet smile. "I like Lorenzo Pescaro for Sestieri Navis, myself. They say the ink's still wet in the Golden Book where his family name was entered, but I've heard of him; he made a reputation chasing Illyrian pirates. He's a good commander."

"I'll be sure to note that." Having heard more than I hoped I'd ever need to know about Serenissiman electoral candidates, I asked the one question that really mattered. "And Melisande?"

One by one, my chevaliers shook their heads.

"My lady," Fortun said reluctantly, "we asked. We played at being drunken D'Angeline sailors up and down the length of the Grand Canal, and too many byways to count, and some of us—" he scowled at Ti-Philippe "—were not exactly playing. Remy sang that song, you know the one? 'Eyes of twilight, hair of midnight.'" I knew it; it had been written for Melisande, though they sing it now with a different name. "At any rate," Fortun continued, "he sang it over half the city, beseeching everyone in sight for news of his beloved, who abandoned him for his lack of station." He looked gravely at me. "What we learned, you heard. But no one – no one, my lady – had word of a D'Angeline noblewoman answering to Melisande Shahrizai's description. And I do not mean that they were reluctant to betray her to a drunken sailor, my lady. I mean that they have not heard of her, ever. You taught me to recognize the signs of evasion and dissemblage. We talked to oarsmen, porters and nobles alike. Not a one knew of her, and not a one lied."

A little silence fell over our table.

"Phèdre," Joscelin said, his voice unexpectedly gentle. "You think Melisande is in La Serenissima because she *wanted* you to think it. It stands to reason, therefore, that she is not."

Ysandre had said as much, and as rightly. I could not explain to Joscelin any more than I could to the Queen my unreasoning certainty, because, ultimately, whether I liked to admit it or not, it was rooted in the belief that I knew Melisande Shahrizai's deepest nature better than anyone else alive or dead, even Delaunay.

As she knew mine.

I took a deep breath. "Gonzago de Escabares' friend was contacted after he paid a visit to the Doge's Palace. If the answer is here, surely it lies within those walls, and if Melisande took shelter within them, it may well be that no one outside them knows of her existence. Think on it," I added, gazing round at them. "We know the Stregazza capable of treachery, and, even now, they fight among themselves for a throne not even vacated. At least let me gain entrance within the Palace, before we conclude that this journey has been for naught."

"Well," Ti-Philippe said optimistically. "It's not for naught if we profit by it."

With that, no one of us could disagree. Money, after all, is a valuable thing to have.

Indeed, I was to find that it was a great greaser of locked doors, before the sun set on the following day. In the morning, Leonora shook me awake to murmur anxiously that another courier awaited, once again clad in Stregazza livery. I kept him waiting while I washed and dressed, and then read his missive to learn that Severio had secured for me an audience with the Doge that afternoon, which he was most impatient that I should attend, that he might speak with me afterward.

As to Prince Benedicte, Severio wrote, he had written his maternal grandfather with no response to date, but that was to be expected, with the strain betwixt their houses.

Ah well, I thought; I tied my own hands, when I insisted on the appearance of a falling-out with the Queen. If I'd wanted entrée into the Little Court, Ysandre would have been happy to provide it. But it was the Stregazza with whom I needed to deal, and no royal writ from House Courcel would obtain their trust. If I needed aught from Prince Benedicte, there were other names I could invoke — such as Quintilius Rousse, or even Anafiel Delaunay, if need be. I had made my promise to Rousse and I meant to keep it, but not until I knew somewhat worth the telling. And surely not while it posed the risk of jeopardizing my semblance.

I wrote out a reply for Severio's courier, promising to arrive on the appointed hour.

To my surprise, Severio sent his own bissone, a splendid affair with a canopy of midnight-blue, the Stregazza arms worked in relief on the sides, depicting a carrack and the tower I now recognized from the Arsenal. In the prow stood a gilded wooden statue of Asherat, extending her arms in blessing over the waters of the canal.

By their attire, I saw that the oarsmen were noble-born; parti-color hose striped in blue and saffron, affixed by points to overtunics of velvet slashed to show the white damask of their shirts. One wore a short mantle of green fastened with a gold brooch, and it was he who stood and gave a sweeping bow as I descended the stairs to the quai, calling out, "Contessa Phèdre nó Delaunay de Montrève, the Immortali welcome you to La Serenissima!"

"That's one of the noblemen's clubs," Ti-Philippe murmured behind me. "Your Severio's, I'll warrant."

I had chosen him and Joscelin both to accompany me that day; the latter for his sober presence, and the former for his quick wit and knowledge of the city. I nodded briefly, and made the rest of my descent smiling.

"Thank you, my lord," I greeted the Serenissiman, inclining my head and giving him my hand to aid me onto the bissone. "You know my name, but I confess, I am at a disadvantage."

"Benito Dandi." He grinned and swept another bow. "You would not come to my birthday party, my lady, but I confess, the mere sight of you is a gift nonetheless precious for its tardiness! I thought Severio was boasting, but it seems he spoke the truth."

"For once," one of his fellows added impishly, pretending to stagger when I glanced at him. "Ah! It's true! She wounds me with her bloodpricked gaze!"

I could not help it; I laughed. Serenissimans do not worship Elua and his Companions, but they know our religion well by virtue of a long-standing D'Angeline presence in the city. Obviously, Severio's boasting had added to the lore. Another of the Immortali dropped his oar and fell to the bottom of the boat. "Bells and chimes!" he groaned, rolling and clapping his hands over his ears. "The D'Angelines seek to invade us with beauty and destroy us from within; Baal-Jupiter, forgive me, I worship the sound of my enemy's voice!"

It was enough of a spectacle to gather an audience, figures appearing on the balconies of neighboring houses, gazing down with amusement.

"My lady," Joscelin said in a flat tone. "You have an audience with the Doge."

"Ah." Benito Dandi eyed him warily. "The chaperone. You'll have to leave those arms with the guards ere you enter the Palace, fair Sir Gloom. Well, never mind us, Contessa; we're an unruly lot, but the fastest rowers on the water, and only the Immortali are fit to carry you! Summon your pretty squawking grey-crow aboard, and yon maiden-faced boy, and we'll be at Old Shaky's doorstep before you can blink!"

I raised my eyebrows at Joscelin and Ti-Philippe, waiting to see if they would balk at the insults, but both gave way – Joscelin with stiff dignity, and Ti-Philippe with a glint in his eye that told me he would take full advantage of their erroneous perceptions. Yon maiden-faced boy, I thought, would fill his pockets at the Immortali's expense once their play turned to dicing.

We were off to see the Doge, whom the scions of the Hundred Worthy Families, I had just learned, called Old Shaky. It didn't augur well for the level of respect he commanded.

Along the way, folk in passing craft and on the bridges and quais cried out greetings to the Immortali, who shouted in response. Admiration, aspiration, adversity; I heard it all, in the ringing shouts. There was no small curiosity about me, and I took care to keep my features serene, even when Benito Dandi shouted my name to a group of his fellow Immortali atop the Rive Alto bridge.

Not until we passed the bustling center of the Campo Grande did my unsolicited escort sober, under the unamused gaze of the Dogal Guard. Benito Dandi handed me ashore, and I brushed off my gown, a rich blue satin inset with velvet panels; Serenissiman blue, the color is called. It had a fretted silver girdle with jet beads and a caul to match; somber, nearly. Except for the elegance of the fit.

I looked away as the Guard confiscated Joscelin's arms.

The Immortali trailed behind, laughing and jesting as a pair of guardsmen escorted us along the serried colonnade, through alternating patterns of light and shadow, and thence through the old triumphal arch into the inner courtyard, where statues of ancient Tiberian statesmen and heroes stood in niches along the façade of the building and a marble well stood in the center of the courtyard. We mounted the broad stairway, flanked by tall statues of Asherat-of-the-Sea and Baal-Jupiter, and were met at the top by Severio Stregazza.

"Phèdre!" His voice caught echoes in the courtyard. Smiling, he bowed and greeted me in my own tongue. "My lady Phèdre nó Delaunay de Montrève, welcome to La Serenissima."

I curtsied, and answered in Caerdicci. "Well met, Prince Severio."

The Immortali elbowed each other and made jests, while the guardsmen remained stoic; for his part, Severio glowed with pleasure. I had not forgotten that his own attendants acknowledged him as noble-born, not royal — but I was D'Angeline, and by our reckoning, he was of the lineage of House Courcel and a Prince of the Blood.

In Terre d'Ange, the evidence of his Caerdicci heritage had set him apart. 'Twas different, seeing Severio here, where his D'Angeline blood dealt him a measure of grace lacking in his comrades. He took my arm, leaning to murmur in my ear. "You've no idea how much I've longed to see you. Promise you'll speak with me afterward?"

"Of course, my lord."

"Good." He straightened, adding, "Father would like to meet you, too. He's a mind to discuss trade or some such thing. But I thought perhaps I could show you the city."

"That would be lovely," I said politely, and Severio's brown eyes lit at my reply. I should not have, but I stole a glance at Joscelin, who stood impassive, strangely vulnerable without his daggers and sword, clad in mute grey. Even so, there was no mistaking him for aught but what he was: a pure-blooded D'Angeline from one of the oldest families. I sighed inwardly and smiled up at Severio Stregazza, resting my fingertips on his velvet-clad arm. "Shall I be presented to your grandfather the Doge, my lord?"

"By all means," Severio said gallantly, sweeping his free hand before us.

Thirty-two ☉

Ì WAS received in the Room of the Shield, where a great fireplace roared even in the heat of summer, and on the opposite wall hung the arms of the reigning Doge's family, the familiar tower and carrack of the Stregazza.

Beneath them stood the throne, a modest wooden affair, and in it sat the Doge.

Rumor had not lied; Cesare Stregazza had the shaking-sickness. His flesh was frail-seeming and sunken, and his entire body trembled with the palsy. The ancient dome of his skull looked vulnerable beneath the peaked crimson cap he wore, silk earflaps covering thinning wisps of white hair; terrible and strange to see. The hair of D'Angeline men does not diminish with age, as I have noted with other peoples. Mortality is more pronounced in other lands.

"The Contessa Phèdre nó Delaunay de Montrève, grandfather," Severio announced.

I curtsied and sank to kneel before the wooden throne, gazing with lowered eyes at the Doge's slippered feet. Cesare Stregazza's hand descended to rest on my head, tremorous and gentle but for the weight of the signet it bore. "I have heard your name, child," he said in quavering Caerdicci. Startled, I glanced up to meet his eyes, dark and canny behind hooded, wrinkled lids. For all that his head bobbed perceptibly, those eyes were steady. "Benedicte sent a harpist last winter, with the latest D'Angeline lay. The Battle of the Skaldi. You brought the Alban army."

"Yes, your grace," I said simply.

"That's good." The Doge withdrew his trembling touch, folding his hands in his scarlet-robed lap. The dogal seal flashed gold, a signet bearing the Crown of Asherat in relief. "We need young people of courage, even mere girls, to fight something more than each other," he added in his thready voice, looking past me to Severio, and I saw a flash of somewhat in those dark eyes. "The Serene Republic!"

Contempt and frustration; I am trained to read voices. Severio flushed, but before he could reply, another man came forward — of middle years, handsome in the Caerdicci fashion, with the same dark, hooded eyes as the Doge. "Contessa," he said in smooth intervention. "Well met. I am Marco Stregazza, Severio's father." He took my hand and drew me to my feet, bowing as I rose. "And this," he added, turning, "is Marie-Celeste de la Courcel Stregazza, my wife."

"My lady," I said, curtsying to her.

"Oh, don't!" Marie-Celeste said impetuously, grasping my hands. "Phèdre, I'm so glad you're here! I've been fair *dying* to hear the latest gossip and styles from the City, and I've scarce seen a D'Angeline face since I quarrelled with Father. Promise you'll tell me everything, do!"

"Of course, my lady," I said, faintly bemused. Benedicte's elder daughter — who was, indeed, niece and daughter-in-law alike to the Doge — was attractive in her own right, plumply rounded, in the fullness of her years. I could see traces of House Courcel's lineage in her dark-blue eyes, the graceful curve of her brow.

"I have tried to explain," she said confidentially, leaning toward me, "about Naamah's Service, and what it means to a D'Angeline. But you understand, they are all provincial here."

"Customs differ," I murmured. "La Serenissima is not the City of Elua."

Severio muttered something under his breath.

"Come," Marco said expansively, opening his arms. "Phèdre, I pray you, take a glass of wine with us! Severio, surely you and your madcap Immortali can entertain the Contessa's men for an hour or two. Father, if you've naught else to say . . .?"

I glanced instinctively at the Doge. The motion of his head could have been taken for a shake of denial; certainly his family chose to take it as such. But my lord Delaunay always taught us to look twice. I saw it was but the palsy, and knelt before him.

Deep in his hooded eyes, I saw a flash of approval.

"Courage, and vision." The Doge laid his trembling hand against my cheek, and I felt the hard press of his signet. "You remember what I said. And come sing for me, girl! Benedicte doesn't send singers any more, since this idiot's quarrel. Do you sing?"

"Yes, my lord," I said, confused.

"Good." Cesare Stregazza leaned back, satisfied. "D'Angelines always made the best poets and whores. And singers. I want to hear a D'Angeline voice sing again, before Asherat's bitches prophesy me into my grave."

"Uncle!" Marie-Celeste hissed, mortified.

"I'm old," he retorted querulously. "And you're fighting over the throne before I've even left it. I can ask for what I want. Can't I?"

Look twice, I thought, remembering the gleam in those sunken eyes. Whatever game he played, 'twas best I played along. I rose smoothly, inclining my head. "My lord, I was trained in Cereus House, First of the Thirteen Houses of the Court of Night-Blooming Flowers. It will be my honor to sing for you whenever you desire it."

"That is well." The Doge waved one crabbed hand, gold signet flashing. "You are dismissed."

"Shall we go, then?" Marco Stregazza inquired impatiently.

I glanced at Ti-Philippe and Joscelin, my silent retainers; the latter's face had a mutinous set. Severio looked impatient, but obedient to his father's wishes. "Yes, my lord," I said aloud to Marco. "I'm sure my men will welcome the reprieve."

The private quarters of Marco and Marie-Celeste Stregazza were generous, with an elegant mosaic inlaid in the floor depicting their purported ancestor, Marcellus Aurelius Strega, seated on an ivory stool and bearing the bundle of *fasces*, in much the pose his young descendant had once adopted. The rooms intersected a loggia which overlooked the mouth of the Grand Canal, a slice of the lagoon itself within their view. We sipped our wine and strolled its length, taking in the vista in the clear midday air.

"Do you see that?" Marco Stregazza asked rhetorically,

gesturing with his wine-cup at the hundred vessels working their way up and down the harbor. "Trade! Lifeblood
of the Republic!"

"It is most impressive, my lord," I replied honestly.

"Yes," Marco said. "It is." He beckoned brusquely for
a servant to refill my cup. "Severio tells me interesting
things about you," he said obliquely.

I set down my brimming cup untouched and raised my
brows. "Such as?"

"Such as the fact that he spent twenty thousand ducats
of my money on you," Marco answered nonplussed, "and
never invested a penny wiser."

The blood rose to my cheeks, but for Naamah's honor
– and my own – I kept my voice level. "In D'Angeline
society, what your son purchased was beyond price, my
lord. It made his fame. Do you wish the money unspent?"

"Were you listening?" Marco grinned, looking
younger and boyish. "Not a copper centime! Our customs
differ indeed. Here, we'd die of shame rather than let a
courtesan hold title; but there, it bought him admirers and
influence. In fact, one such reports that you have fallen out
with the Queen, over a certain matter of the Cruarch of
Alba. And yet my own reports tell me you shipped Alban
lead and made a nice profit in the bargain." Setting down
his own cup, he steepled his fingers. "What I am thinking,
Contessa, is that Terre d'Ange will grow fat acting as
middleman between Alba and the rest of the world. But
such a thing need not be. Alba does not have a merchant
fleet. La Serenissima does. If someone with, shall we say,
entrée, to the Cruarch himself were to arrange it, there is
great profit to be made in trading directly."

This was a repercussion of our staged falling-out I had

never considered, though I had known well that overland
couriers would bring news before my arrival, and mayhap
gossip as well. I rephrased carefully, to make certain of it.
"You wish me to approach the Cruarch regarding trade
with La Serenissima?"

Marco shrugged, picked up his winecup and sipped. "I
wish you to consider it, no more. I admit, Contessa, I am
ambitious. You have seen my father; he is a little mad, I
think, and grows more so with each day that passes. Prince
Benedicte is enamored of his war-bride and his pure-
blooded D'Angeline son, and withdraws his support from
our family, fearing we are tainted since Dominic and
Thérèse's treason. It may pass, but well and so; I am
Serenissiman, and I will woo my city in the manner to
which she is accustomed. Yes, I seek trade, but on honest
terms. You have the Queen's enmity. Like Benedicte's
infatuation, it too may pass, but you have a life to lead, and
it need not dance at the whims of D'Angeline royals. Will
you not consider my request?"

"My lord," I said slowly, "I will consider it. But there
must be more in it for me than mere profit, to circumvent
the interests of my own nation."

"My son adores you," Marie-Celeste offered candidly,
Serenissiman shrewdness in her half-Courcel face.
"Phèdre, my dear, you may hold sway in your own nation,
but in La Serenissima, courtesans do not marry into the
Hundred Worthy Families. For free trade with Alba . . .
exceptions may be made."

I nearly had to bite my lip to keep from laughing, and
made a show of swirling my wine to disguise it. I liked
Severio well enough, but to wed him — Elua preserve me!
Still, I appreciated the Stregazzas' naked candour, their

ambition and the offer plain on the table. And I had an idea. "My lady," I said, inclining my head to her. "There is somewhat that interests me. I seek an old acquaintance, Melisande Shahrizai by name. I heard it rumored you had knowledge of her."

"Oh, dear!" Marie-Celeste Stregazza turned pale. "I know that name. Father — Prince Benedicte — was looking for her too, not two months' past. Some sort of traitor to the nation, is she not?"

How our concerns encompass us! It seemed astonishing to me that all the world did not know of Melisande's treachery — and yet, small wonder. I have ever known that Melisande played a deep game. She was convicted in an impromptu court in the garrison of Troyes-le-Mont, and those who witnessed it, I could count on my fingers. Of those who had proof . . . there was only me. I had seen the letter, in her writing, to Waldemar Selig of the Skaldi. No other trail existed.

Now, I would use that to my advantage, and pray the Stregazza knew no more of my history than Severio had related.

"So it is said, my lady," I replied cautiously; there is an art to phrasing matters just so, that listeners may hear what they will. "And, of course, it might be just the thing to retain my place in the Queen's good graces—" I cleared my throat delicately, "—whatsoever might happen with Alban trade. But she is an old acquaintance, and would see me, I think."

"No." Marco shook his head forcefully. "Benedicte gave us a description, and there is no one fitting it in our knowledge. Believe me, young Contessa; trade is one matter, and court politics quite another. If I had any knowledge of a D'Angeline traitor within these walls," he said grimly, "I'd not hesitate to buy my father-in-law's gratitude with it."

I opened my mouth to reply, but a ruckus at the entrance to their quarters cut me short. Even as I turned to look, a Serenissiman with the hooded Stregazza eyes, a neat dagger-point beard and a soft cap perched on his curly hair made his way onto the loggia.

"Marco," he said peremptorily. "Why am I hearing about a ten percent tax being added to the Saddlers' Guild on festival days? We had an agreement!"

Marco Stregazza's lids flickered. "Ricciardo," he said briefly. "We have a guest."

"Charmed." Ricciardo Stregazza offered dismissively, giving me a perfunctory glance, which changed quickly to a startled double take. "Asherat! What pretty fish do you have on your line this time, Marco?"

"This," Marie-Celeste intervened, speaking in dignified D'Angeline, "is the Comtesse Phèdre nó Delaunay de Montrève. Phèdre, my husband's brother, Ricciardo Stregazza."

"Contessa." Ricciardo took my hand and bowed. "You are far too beautiful to be party to my sister-in-law's petty intrigues with the Little Court," he said cynically, straightening. "Pray do me the honor during your stay of accepting an invitation to dine, that my wife and I might show you that not all Serenissiman hospitality comes with strings attached."

"The honor would be mine, my lord," I replied politely in Caerdicci.

"Your wife!" Marie-Celeste gave an inelegant laugh. "A jest to the end, Ricciardo."

His expression grew cold. "Whatever poison you spew, leave Allegra out of it, sister. Marco." He turned back to his brother. "The Scholae were promised there'd be no additional taxes after the Treaty of Ephesium was signed. This is an end run around our agreement."

"If they don't want to pay the taxes," Marco said reasonably, "they needn't come to market on festival days."

"And lose a third of their trade?" Ricciardo tugged at his curling locks with one exasperated hand. "As well tell them to throw half their goods in the river! I gave them my word, Marco."

"Take it up with the Consiglio Maggiore," Marco said wearily. " 'Tis their legislation, and they passed it."

"At whose behest?" Ricciardo asked dangerously.

"Not mine." Marco shrugged, and spread his hands. "Ask, if you don't believe me, brother. You courted Sestieri Scholae, not I. If they're like to lynch you for making promises you can't keep, I cannot help it. The problem is yours."

It is never a comfortable thing to find oneself in the midst of a family squabble, and all the less so when political intrigue is involved. Murmuring something innocuous, I withdrew to gaze out over the lagoon, while Ricciardo Stregazza struggled to get his temper in check.

"We'll speak of this later," he said shortly, and then, to me; "My lady Phèdre, you swim in dangerous waters when you dally with the Stregazza, but I pray you, remember my invitation kindly. My lady *wife* — " he cast a venomous glance at Marie-Celeste, " — would be pleased to speak with one such as yourself."

With that, he made his exit, and Marco Stregazza

sighed, passing his hands over his face. "Forgive the intrusion, Contessa," he apologized. "My brother . . . is rather intemperate. So it has been since our father declared him a disgrace to the family. He courts the Scholae out of desperation, and makes rash promises to these rough tradesmen, then needs must fear their anger when he cannot deliver." He shook his head ruefully. " 'Tis an ill match if ever there was one, but Ricciardo is determined to contest for our father's seat. I would do what I could to protect him, if I did not fear he'd repay me with treachery."

Marie-Celeste fanned herself and sipped her wine, making a face. "It's gone warm," she complained. "Marco, send them for a fresh-cooled jug." When he had left to summon a servant, she leaned in confidentially. "Ricciardo has the D'Angeline sickness, I'm afraid. It didn't sit well with his father when the scandal broke."

"The D'Angeline sickness?" I repeated, feeling foolishly ignorant.

"You know." She raised her brows. "He likes boys."

"Ah." One undercurrent of their bitter exchange suddenly came clear to me. I turned my empty wine-cup in my hands, looking across the busy lagoon. "You name this a sickness, in La Serenissima."

"Yes, well, I told you, they are all provincial here." Lowering her voice, she added, "I do not say this to Marco, for when all is said and done, he loves his brother, but if I were to seek out someone with ties to a D'Angeline traitor, I would start at Ricciardo's doorstep. His . . . proclivities . . . have led him to stranger places, and he has no love for the Little Court, whereas we still hope to make peace." Marie-Celeste patted my arm in a motherly fashion as

Marco returned, exclaiming in a different tone. "Come inside and sit, my dear! I must know who made your gown. Are such plain lines the fashion this season?"

Still pondering her comments, I thought of Favrielle nó Eglantine and wondered what she would make of Marie-Celeste Stregazza's attire, which, from what I had seen, was the height of Serenissiman style – a long, sleeveless overdress gaudily adorned with appliqués and cutouts, bound beneath the breasts with gold net and worn over a fine silk tunic with tight-fitting sleeves. The whole ensemble, dreadful to my eyes, was topped with a gauze turban and finished at the bottom with a pair of wooden-soled sandals – pattens, they are called – a full four inches in height.

"Not exactly, my lady," I said diplomatically. "My seamstress is very particular."

"Well." Marie-Celeste de la Courcel Stregazza smiled. "You must tell me everything."

THIRTY-THREE

IT WAS late afternoon when Severio returned to usher me out of the Doge's Palace, and the Square was awash in golden sunlight. I left Marie-Celeste with sufficient advice to ensure that her knowledge of current D'Angeline fashion was competitive with the Little Court — not that I saw her inclined to take it — and Marco with a final promise that I would consider his proposal.

The Immortali were waiting, and Ti-Philippe and Joscelin with them. I would have preferred a chance to speak privately with my retainers, but it was not to be, not yet.

"My lady Phèdre," Severio said gallantly, extending his arm. "Shall we promenade about the Square? It is a most pleasant afternoon for strolling."

"Of course." Hiding my impatience, I smiled at him and took his arm, ignoring Joscelin's look of silent disapproval. At least, I thought, his Cassiline arms had been restored to him; that should please him. Ti-Philippe, by contrast, was in good spirits, trading jests with the Immortali.

I daresay I might have enjoyed it, if not for the pall
Joscelin cast. Like a pair of young noble-born lovers,
Severio and I strolled about the Square, observing the
goods for sale and the colorful throng of buyers and
sellers. The Square itself was inlaid with paving stones of
white marble etched with guild-markings for the various
Scholae, delineating the allotted market stalls for each
guild.

It was strange and exotic to me, seeing such vigorous
commerce take place cheek-by-jowl beside the Doge's
Palace and the Temple of Asherat. In Terre d'Ange we are
more reserved, separating our royal seats and sacred places
from the common milieu. But it was true, what Marco
Stregazza had said; trade was the lifeblood of the Republic,
and I supposed it was meet that its beating heart lay at the
center of La Serenissima.

Hosiers, clothiers, glovers – a separate guild for each,
and that was merely a beginning. There were stalls for
shoemakers, coopers and carpenters, jewelers and soap-
boilers, farmers and spice merchants, fishermen and
butchers, barbers, smiths and saddlers. Commonfolk in
rough fustian and shawled women bartered alongside
silk- and velvet-clad nobles. Here and there, we saw other
strolling lovers, though I noted that the young women who
appeared unwed covered their hair in modest silk head-
scarves and were attended by stern-looking dowagers.

Well and so, I thought, I will have to be wary of how
I am perceived.

It came to a crux faster than I guessed, when we paused
before a merchant from Jebe-Barkal, who was displaying
birds of astonishingly bright plumage in wicker cages. I
had seen a few women carrying them, and guessed they

were a popular novelty as a lover's token; for that, I would not have lingered, but that the Jebean merchant intrigued me. His skin was a brown so dark it made the whites of his eyes vivid, and his teeth when he grinned. This he did readily, when I tried, laughing, to converse with him – his Caerdicci was so broadly accented that I had trouble comprehending it, and mine is the formal scholar's tongue and not the soft Serenissiman argot he was used to. Still, we made ourselves understood, and I gathered that the birds had come from his homeland.

How vast is the world, I was thinking, and how little of it I have truly seen, when Severio's voice cut through my reverie, his hand closing urgently on my wrist.

"Phèdre." His tone was low, and I glanced up to meet his hot gaze. "Phèdre, I will buy you a parrot, I'll buy you a horse, an Umaiyyat camel caravan if that's what you want. A gilded bissone, a house on the Great Canal, a country villa! Name your price, and I will meet it; set your terms, and we will draft the contract. Only promise me I may see you again."

For once, I could have used my overprotective Cassiline's attention; Joscelin's glower has a quelling effect on patrons' ardor. As luck would have it, he was engaged with dissuading Ti-Philippe from poking his finger through the wicker bars of one of the cages. I was on my own.

"My lord," I said gently, "you flatter me. But I do not think it wise that I pursue Naamah's Service here. You yourself said to me, when first we met, 'In La Serenissima, we keep our courtesans in their proper place, where they belong.' "

"I did, didn't I?" Dropping my wrist, Severio flushed a

dull red. "Gracious Lady of the Sea, I was a prig," he muttered. "But you see, don't you, what it's like to live here, to be caught in the middle of this never-ending intrigue? And how out of my depth I felt in the City of Elua. Phèdre." He looked earnestly at me now. "I have never known such pleasure with a woman, but I swear to you, it's not only that. My very nature is changed because of you, and I have made peace with a side of myself I did naught but revile. Pleasure I can find elsewhere, if I must; there are always women who will do anything for coin. Only you do it because it is your glory."

"In Terre d'Ange, it is," I whispered; I hadn't expected him to make such a compelling argument. "My lord, in La Serenissima, it would be my shame."

"Was it Naamah's shame when she bedded the King of Persis?" he asked cunningly. I had forgotten, too, that he was one-quarter D'Angeline and knew the tales of that legacy. "Was it her shame when she lay down in the stews of Bhodistan that Elua might survive?"

"No," I murmured. "But Severio, I am not Naamah, only her Servant. I need to think."

"No? Think on this, then." Taking me in his arms, he drew me against him; I could feel the heat of his body and his rigid phallus straining against his velvet hose, pressed against my belly. My knees grew weak. "If you will not have me for a patron," he said softly, his breath brushing my hair, "accept me for a suitor. There are ways to accomplish anything. With your guile, your beauty and your title, and my father's money and position, we could rule La Serenissima together one day, you and I."

I have never aspired to power beyond a role as the foremost courtesan in the City of Elua; I do not think, if

Joscelin and I had not been estranged, that I would have considered Severio Stregazza's offer for an instant. On D'Angeline soil, I could have handled it with grace. But 'tis a dangerous thing to be courted in a strange city, and I was isolated and lonely on this wild-goose chase even my closest companions thought a folly. Yes, for a few scant seconds, I entertained the notion of conjoining my life to his.

And spending a lifetime playing supplicant to his Tiberian magistrate.

No, I thought; if Kushiel has marked me, surely it is for some greater purpose than this.

"My lord," I said lightly, extricating myself from his grasp with a subtle, flirtatious twist that every adept of the Night Court practices to flawless perfection, "you will fair dazzle me with speed! As to Naamah's Service, I have given my answer. For the other . . ." I touched his cheek with my fingertips and smiled, ". . . if you would court me, why then, 'tis romance, and a different game altogether! You will not win the hand of the Comtesse de Montrève by the same means that you gain the services of Phèdre nó Delaunay. I have heard that Serenissiman men are among the most romantic in the world. I would hope that means somewhat more than grappling in the marketplace."

Severio groaned aloud, accompanied by the sound of bells. It took a full moment to realize that the two were unrelated.

I had not seen, until then, that the priestesses of Asherat were offering a daily libation of wine unto the waters of the lagoon beneath the vast statue of the goddess at the end of the Square. Now I saw them making their way back, six of them forming two neat lines, flanked at each corner by a beardless male figure carrying a barbed silver spear and ringing a bell. Later I learned that these were eunuchs, who had voluntarily unmanned themselves to serve the goddess.

The priestesses themselves wore robes of blue silk, overlaid with silver net. Unlike the rest of the women I'd seen in La Serenissima, they did not wear tall wooden pattens on their feet, but went unshod, bare ankles encircled by silver chains from which tiny bells jingled, bare feet treading the marble pavement. Also unlike other women, the priestesses wore their hair loose and flowing; but over their faces, they wore veils.

And such veils! Gauze silk, I have seen aplenty; I have worn it in my guise as Mara, and I have worn it too in the Service of Naamah, where the Pasha and the Hareem Girl is a common fantasy for male patrons. These veils were not gauze, but the finest silver mesh, glittering in the sun and strung with clear beads of glass that caught the light and flashed. It was, in all truth, a lovely conceit, and would it not have been blasphemous, I've no doubt that it would have been taken up as a fashion in Terre d'Ange long ago.

Such were the priestesses of Asherat-of-the-Sea, whom every good Serenissiman worshipped. In Terre d'Ange, we do not; yet she is an aspect of Mother Earth herself, in whose womb Blessed Elua was begotten, and thus we honor her customs. Following Severio's unthinking lead, I touched my fingers to brow and heart, then bowed my head as the priestesses' entourage passed. From the corner of my eye, I could see that Joscelin and Ti-Philippe had followed suit; indeed, so had everyone within my vision, even the Jebean merchant.

My field of vision did not include the Yeshuite. Unfortunately, one of the Immortali's did.

"Heya!" His voice rose in a shout before the crowd had scarce closed behind Asherat's procession. "What are you staring at? Turn your eyes away, damn you!"

I glanced up to see several of the Immortali surrounding an innocuous-looking man in commoner's garb, a yellow cap atop his dark hair. "I meant no offense," he said, a touch of uneasy defiance in his voice. "I do not worship Asherat-of-the-Sea. By our commandments, it is unlawful for me to lower my gaze before false idols and prophets."

Until then, I hadn't known him for a Yeshuite; then, I did. I didn't know yet that Serenissiman law required all followers of Yeshua to identify themselves with yellow caps, but I knew the accent – and I knew their sacred precepts. The Rebbe had made sure of that; I could quote Moishe's Tablets verbatim.

"And by *our* commandments," the Immortali said menacingly, "you should have your eyes put out!" He drew his belt-knife and nodded to his companions. "Grab him!"

The crowd scattered back, abandoning the Yeshuite; the Immortali charged. They got so far as to snatch the cap from his hair, and I heard, ringingly, the sound of two daggers clearing their sheaths in precise simultaneity.

"My lady." Ti-Philippe appeared at my side and spoke in irritated D'Angeline. "It is Southfort all over again, and I do not wish to die for that idiot's heroics, but if you ask me to, I will."

"No." I sighed, looking across the Square to where Joscelin stood before the Yeshuite, crossed daggers forming a deadly barrier of protection against the Immortali, bright steel blazing in the sunlight. I had taken the measure of Severio's comrades, and I did not think they meant to do aught more than scare the Yeshuite. "My lord," I appealed to Severio "if you would woo me, pray bid your companions not spill the blood of my men in my presence."

No coward, Severio Stregazza; he waded amid the Immortali, shoving down raised arms. "Enough, enough! You've given him a fright to remember, now let my lady's guardsman be! What are you, noblemen or thugs?"

It was over in seconds, the Immortali giving way good-naturedly, forgetting their quarrel; two of them clapped Joscelin on the shoulder, which he bore with frigid tolerance. Ti-Philippe retrieved the Yeshuite's cap and brought it to me. I made my way over and spoke to the poor man. "Are you all right?" I asked in Caerdicci, handing him his cap.

"Yes, thank you." He replied absently in the same tongue, settling the yellow cap atop his curls, his gaze fixed intently on Joscelin. He lacked the traditional sidelocks, I noted, and his hands clenched into fists with the undissipated force of his anger. One of the schismatics, I thought; even so, his interest in Joscelin was peculiar. All the more so when he murmured beneath his breath in Habiru, "And he shall carve out the way before you, and his blades shall shine like a star in his hands."

Like a secret code, a shared tongue carries over a crowded space. I saw Joscelin turn, eyes wide and startled as the murmured Habiru reached his ear. The Yeshuite made a bobbing bow in his manner, and stepped back, the milling throng closing around him. I met Joscelin's wide-eyed gaze and wondered.

"So the Immortali bear insults to the Gracious Lady of the Sea," spoke a taunting voice from somewhere behind me; I spun about to see us surrounded by another noblemen's club, its fellows clad in green-and-white striped hose, their leader wearing a blue chlamys over his tunic. He gestured, making the short cloak swirl. "You have grown fearful, since losing the support of the D'Angeline Prince. The Perpetui of Sestieri Navis would not abide such a slap in the face to the Dea Coelestis!"

"Pietro Contini," Severio said through clenched jaws, "I am in the mood to kick in someone's teeth today, and it might as well be yours. If you don't want to pick them up from the Square, go tell Lorenzo Pescaro I said so!"

"And miss such a glorious opportunity?" The leader of the Perpetui smiled and drew a short truncheon from his belt. "I think not."

And with that, he swung hard at the head of Severio, who ducked with an oath and planted a punch in his midsection. The Perpetui leader grunted, and in short order, fists and bats were flying, and the crowd was scattering anew. I saw some of the strolling lovers watching, one of the young women clapping her hands in glee at the entertainment. A horde of Perpetui descended on Severio, scion of their Sestieri's greatest enemy; he struggled against them, shielding his head. Pietro Contini had caught his breath and was roaring for blood. The Immortali flung themselves into the fray, and I heard Ti-Philippe's voice call out my name like a paean as my chevaliers waded into battle. "Phè-dre! Phè-dre!"

Bodies surged, and the dull thwack of wood and knuckles on flesh resounded. Benito Dandi had gotten hold of a Perpetui truncheon, and laid about him fiercely.

Somewhere in the fray, Fortun surfaced at Severio's side, broad shoulders heaving as he thrust attackers aside by main force, his expression calm as Remy and one of the Immortali defended him from behind, clubbing down attackers with a sickening crunch. Young men fought, and blood flowed freely on the marble squares of the Campo Grande.

I watched the whole fracas at the side of the Jebean bird merchant, whose merriment was erased by concern for his feathered charges. He need not have worried. Cursing in a most un-Cassiline fashion, Joscelin stood guard before his stall, and fought without drawing his daggers. One spinning kick to the head of a would-be assailant sent one of the Perpetui staggering away, and an unceremonious chop with a vambraced forearm caused another to measure his length on the paving stones of the Great Square; after that, they stayed well away.

"Now *that*," Ti-Philippe enthused later, lying with head tilted back in the Immortali's bissone, "was a good fight!"

"Shut up and press," Joscelin muttered, shoving a wadded kerchief beneath my chevalier's spurting nose.

There were bruises and lumps all around, and I was not even certain who had won. The Immortali could not have been in better spirits. "Your men look like girls, Contessa," Benito Dandi said to me, "but they fight like tigers. Like ten tigers! No wonder Lord Marco has not tried to settle with the Little Court by force."

"Benito," Severio murmured futilely. "We should not talk politics."

"My lord," I addressed him. "At Midwinterfest, you were fearful that your father would lose Prince Benedicte's support, and with it his bid for the Doge's Seat, should election prove imminent. Well, and from what I hear, the first has proved true, and the latter is likely. What has come to pass?"

Severio sighed, but he answered candidly; I had guessed aright, he had no secrets from the Immortali. "Benedicte's son by the Tourais woman was born this spring," he said bluntly. "And my grandfather named him heir to all his D'Angeline titles and holdings. My mother . . ." he searched for words, ". . . took exception, and they have not spoken since. You see, my father was counting on the leverage that gave him, to influence the Consiglio Maggiore. Without the promise of D'Angeline support . . ." He shrugged. "His election to the Sestieri Dogal is secure, but the Consiglio might just decide that a naval commander could do more for La Serenissima."

"Or a banker," one of the Immortali added, spitting over his oar into the green waters.

"Or a banker," Severio agreed glumly. "Or even my damned Uncle Ricciardo, if he makes good on his threat, and rouses the Scholae to strike. I don't think anyone's reckoned how much damage that would do, if it includes the salt-panners."

For all that she is built on trade, La Serenissima is primarily a gateway; her greatest commodity is and has always been salt. I knew that much from my reading.

"Why not make peace with Prince Benedicte?" I asked. "It seems to me your father has little to lose, and much to gain."

"My mother will not swallow the insult, that her own father should cut her off, and he is adamant in leaving his D'Angeline properties to this, this . . . puling infant, this Imriel de la Courcel, they named him." Severio made a wry face. "My half-uncle, as it were. Mother has not spoken to Grandfather since the day he announced it. And she has a right to her anger," he added reluctantly. "By Serenissiman law, my grandfather cannot name a woman his successor. Mother cannot inherit the Little Court."

"*What?*" The question, happily for me, came from Ti-Philippe, struggling to a sitting position, kerchief clamped to his nose. If he'd not asked it, I would have, and just as incredulously. "What do you mean he can't appoint a woman his heir?"

"It is Serenissiman law," Severio repeated patiently. "He could cede it to my father's custody in her name, but he is loathe to do it since Dominic's betrayal. Don't worry, though." He caught up my hand and toyed with my fingers, smiling. "Grandfather will come 'round in the end. Sestieri Angelus has no viable candidate; he must endorse someone, or lose all influence in La Serenissima. If Father cannot persuade Mother to swallow her pride and beg forgiveness, then perhaps a D'Angeline love-match will do the trick."

And if it does not, I thought, smiling back at Severio, mayhap a D'Angeline malcontent dropping Alban trade in Marco Stregazza's lap will do the same. Well, my young lord, you are not so canny as your parents, but you play well into their scheme. And this is all very interesting, but it does not answer me one thing.

Where in the seven hells is Melisande Shahrizai?

THIRTY-FOUR

I THOUGHT myself skilled in court intrigue, but after a day — one day! — in La Serenissima, my mind fair reeled. I have always thought that the notion of a Republic is a noble one, dating back to the glory days of Hellas, which all D'Angelines regard fondly as the last Golden Era before the coming of Elua. Now, seeing it in action, I was not so sure. At any rate, I took to my bed at an unwontedly early hour. It has been my experience, faced with a bewildering perplexity of information, that sleep is an excellent remedy for confusion. My recent excursion to Gentian House only confirmed it.

Whether it is true or not, I awoke feeling refreshed, and better able to face the tangles of La Serenissima. Over the breakfast table, we plotted our strategy.

"Fortun," I said gravely. "Of you, I ask the hardest chore. I have dropped word into the ears of Marco and Marie-Celeste Stregazza, and I am minded to see if it spins out any thread that might lead to Melisande. It may be too late, indeed, but I would be pleased if you would keep an eye on the Doge's Palace, and follow any Stregazzan retainers where they might go."

"Of a surety, my lady," Fortun said quietly. I had chosen him because I knew I could rely on him, for obedience and discretion alike.

"Philippe." I eyed Ti-Philippe thoughtfully. His nose looked rather like a burst strawberry, which didn't seem to bother him in the slightest. "The Immortali seem passing fond of you. Learn what you may of these clubs, and the candidates they endorse. If any espouse enmity to Prince Benedicte and the Little Court, it would be worth knowing. He is the only force in the city who would seek to oust Melisande on principle; for the rest, it is a matter of benefit. Anyone seeking to bring down the Little Court might well be her ally."

"And what benefit might a hunted D'Angeline traitor offer?" Joscelin asked quietly.

I knew he was merely trying to offer the voice of reason; nonetheless, I looked hard at him. "Joscelin, I saw Skaldi in the Great Square the day we arrived. Marco Stregazza is ready to sell his son into wedlock if it will secure him trade with Alba; what price would you set on Skaldia? If Melisande had an agreement with Waldemar Selig, like as not she had other contacts in Skaldia as well. I would not be surprised to learn she could deliver a trade agreement with one or more of the southern tribes."

"Mayhap," he said gently. "And mayhap you are haunted by ghosts of the past."

I could bear anything but compassion from him. It was hard enough, believing I was not wraith-ridden, without Joscelin's quiet censure. I turned to Remy. "You," I said, "I will send to the Little Court, to gain admittance if you may, with a request for audience with Prince Benedicte. He may not entertain it, if gossip has reached him — it had obviously reached the Stregazza — but learn what you may of the Little Court nonetheless."

"Aye, aye, my lady!" Remy grinned, and gave me a crisp salute.

Would that I could have accepted it at face value, but I saw the glances they exchanged when they thought I was looking elsewhere; I knew full well that my chevaliers were of the same opinion as Joscelin. They were merely less open in voicing it, and more willing to go through the motions of a hunt for the sport of the thing.

"One more thing," I said, more sharply than I'd intended, playing my trump card. "This is a matter I did not wish to press with the Stregazza, lest I give our hand away. Find out for me who is the astrologer to the family of the Doge. Whoever he is, he is the conduit. Gonzago de Escabares' friend called upon this man; on the following day, he was visited by Melisande. All of you, inquire as you may. When we find the astrologer, we find the trail."

It did as I intended, giving them a tangible quarry. I wrote out the letter for Remy to carry — shocking Leonora yet again with my perverse literary quirk — and dispersed my chevaliers to their various errands.

"So." Joscelin looked at me. "You have the lay of the land, and a Serenissiman lordling begging for your hand. What shadows will you set me to chasing before you wed him, Phèdre nó Delaunay?"

"I'm not going to wed Severio Stregazza," I said irritably. "I've no mind to wed anyone."

"You let him court you." Joscelin got up from the table and walked to the window overlooking the balcony. "Is it because he can give you what you desire?" he asked, his voice muffled.

"No." I sat gazing at his back, broad-shouldered and graceful, bisected by the cabled length of his wheat-gold braid. Kushiel's gift is cruel; I have never, ever, found any man so beautiful to me as Joscelin Verreuil, and no man has ever caused me such pain. One does not, I suppose, reign over hell without a well-developed sense of irony. There were no living *anguissettes* with whom I could compare notes, but surely, I thought, Kushiel must be pleased with this arrangement. Nothing else could have ground my heart so fine. "Joscelin, it is because that is the game Marco Stregazza and his wife Marie-Celeste de la Courcel Stregazza have decreed, and I see no way out of it but to play along and stall, if I wish to learn anything."

Back to me, he shuddered, but when he spoke, his voice was hard. "And if there is nothing to learn?"

"If there is not, then there is not," I said equitably. "There is another option where this talk of marriage is concerned, and you know it as well as I. If I were to declare you my consort, by D'Angeline law, that is binding. So it was before, and even the Queen acknowledged it. The Stregazza will abide by that without ill-will, they know the ways of Terre d'Ange. It is you who have closed that door, not I."

"*I can't!*" This time, the shudder that wracked him was profound. Clenching his fists, Joscelin turned to stare at me, wild-eyed. "To think of you, on your knees to the likes of that, that overgrown *juvenile*, Phèdre, it sickens me! And don't tell me you weren't, because I know you, I know you were. It was all the talk of the City, how for twenty thousand ducats Phèdre nó Delaunay made a man of the grandson of Prince Benedicte and the Doge of La Serenissima!"

I do not anger easily, but somehow, Joscelin Verreuil has ever had the trick of it. I stared back at him coldly, and answered colder. "A pity," I said contemptuously, "I could not do the same for you."

It was enough and more to send him storming out of our rented house, and I sat as coolly as if the broken shards of my heart were not grinding each other to bits and watched him go, knowing, of a surety, where he went. Ten centuries later, the blood of Yeshua ben Yosef was claiming its due. *And he shall carve out the way before you, and his blades shall shine like a star in his hands.* Joscelin had heard it, and so had I; what were the whims of a single Servant of Naamah against the will of an entire people?

Whatever they believed of him, it was true, I thought; when Joscelin made ready to defend with his daggers bared and crossed, they really did shine like a star in his hands.

"My lady," Leonora said tremulously; she had caught the tail end of our exchange. Though we had spoken in D'Angeline, the sense of it needed no translation. "There is, um, another message from my lord Severio Stregazza."

She proffered his letter on a silver salver; I took it impatiently and cracked the wax seal, scanning the contents. Severio, it seemed, thought I might be amused by touring the Temple of Asherat; indeed, he had taken the liberty of arranging an audience with the Sovereign Priestess at an hour past noon.

Well, as it happened, I did find the notion amusing; moreover, I found it intriguing. I have ever been curious about the faith of other peoples, and this was a chance to experience it firsthand; and, too, I was curious about this Oracle. At any rate, it was better than moping alone in my chambers. Beginning to know my ways, Leonora had brought a pen and inkwell, and I dipped the pen recklessly, scrawling a hasty reply – although, I must add, only an astute observer would have known my mood and the speed with which I answered.

When the appointed hour arrived, I descended the stairs from my balcony unaccompanied. Severio did not fail to note it, rising to his feet and rocking the craft; a simple gondola today, and not the gilded bissone. Only a few of his Immortali were in attendance. "No Cassiline chaperone?" he cried, spreading his arms. "My lady, your trust heartens me!"

"Be worthy of it, my lord," I said, stepping into the vessel. "I have placed my honor in the keeping of the Immortali; I pray they will not fail me."

"Not a chance," retorted Benito Dandi, manning the tiller with a sharp eye as we surged into the water traffic of the Great Canal. "In fact, we took a vote, to elect you to the rank of *compagne*, my lady, for holding your ground in a skirmish. Severio may be our prior, but it took two councillos, the secretary and the notary to pass this motion. Now he impugns you at his own expense."

For all of that, Severio looked delighted, and for his sake, I accepted the honor with good will. Joscelin would be upset that I had gone out without a D'Angeline guard, but then, Joscelin was already upset. And I did not think I erred in my estimation of Severio's character. Rude he might be, by our standards, but wise enough to know that what he desired of me could only be given freely. If I was not safe with Severio and his Immortali, I was not safe anywhere in La Serenissima.

A light rain had fallen early that morning, and the Square glistened like a vast mirror. Severio and I went alone into the Temple of Asherat, while his comrades lounged outside, idly baiting the impassive eunuchs who stood guard at the doors. I must confess, Asherat's Temple was a splendid place.

There is not much painting in La Serenissima, but they are skilled at the art of mosaic. The vast ante-chamber of the Temple was filled with tiled images, exquisitely rendered. A veiled priestess, young and slender, wearing the white robes of an acolyte, assisted us in removing our shoes and washing our hands in the ritual basin. Afterward, we wandered the ante-chamber and Severio pointed out to me the various images of Asherat. My favorite was an Ephesian image that showed the goddess erect and gracious, holding fronds of date palms in both hands, flanked by an ass and a bull. In La Serenissima, they worship her as Asherat-of-the-Sea and the Dea Coelestis, the Tiberian Queen of Heaven, but she is an ancient goddess and has taken many forms.

"There she is grieving her son Eshmun." Severio pointed to a mosaic that depicted Asherat kneeling over a male figure in a field of scarlet flowers. I did not like it so well as the others, in part because the lines lacked the fluidity necessary to make the scene poignant, and in part because it reminded me of La Dolorosa, the black isle. "And there is the Peace of Asherat and Baal-Jupiter, which they made when the people implored them."

"A terrible story." I shivered. "We passed La Dolorosa on our way here."

"The place of no hope." There was an edge to his voice. "That's what the shorefolk call it. Grandfather Benedicte wanted my aunt Thérèse imprisoned there, when it was found she was complicit in the poisoning of Isabel de la Courcel."

"Is she?" Awful as the crime was, I couldn't help but be disturbed.

"No." He shook his head. "The Stregazza rose up in arms at the prospect. That's probably when this whole quarrel began. She's banished to the Villa Conforti, which is an island prison of sorts for disgraced nobility." He grinned. "Actually, I'm told it's quite pleasant. Nonetheless, she's bound not to leave its shores while she lives."

I thought of Hyacinthe, and could not muster an answering smile. Sensing my mood, Severio changed the subject.

"There's a lovely Temple of Eshmun on the Isla Maestus," he said. "Where the anemone blooms crimson in the spring. We'll have to visit; it's good hunting, as well. Look, Phèdre, I brought honey-cakes. Would you like to make an offering?"

His kindness touched me, and I was able to smile. A strange business, this having a suitor! I was accustomed to grand gestures from my patrons, but these homely courtesies were something altogether different. "Yes," I said. "I would."

The great statue of Asherat loomed beneath the high, pointed central dome, and it took only a glance for me to see that she was old, very old. Unlike the benign countenance of the statue on the harbor, this goddess had a wide-eyed stare. Instead of stars, a crescent moon crowned her head. She stood upright, leaping waves about her feet, her open hands touching the waters.

Brackets of candles lit the dome, and two priestesses flanked the stone altar before the goddess, attending to the sacrifice — for sacrifice it was. A commoner stood before the altar, cap in hand, and on the slab in front of him, a bound lamb.

I must have made an involuntary sound, for Severio shushed me. "We'll have to wait a moment," he murmured. "I should have warned you; I forgot, you don't have blood offerings in Terre d'Ange, do you?"

"No." I watched, horrified, as the elder priestess lifted the sacrificial knife; bright-edged and tiny, with a curving blade. The lovely, shimmering veil hid her face, but her motions were serene. I had to look away as she brought down her arm. Even so, I heard the lamb bleat once, a strangled sound.

And silence.

I didn't know I was shaking until Severio put his hands on my shoulders to still me. "Phèdre," he said gently. "I'm sorry, I made a mistake. You needn't stay. Go back to the antechamber, and the acolyte will conduct you outside. I'll meet you in just a moment, I promise. But I cannot cheat Asherat, having brought her offering."

"No," I said stubbornly, watching him blink in surprise. I don't think he knew, before that, how much will I had. I summoned a measure of composure. "I've come too, and one doesn't turn one's back on a goddess. I will go through with it."

"As you wish," he said, bewildered.

Eunuch attendants had removed the lamb's carcass —
the Temple would dine on it that night, Severio told me
later — but the altar still reeked of fresh blood as we
approached and I could see, drawing near, traces of ancient
blood blackened in the crevices. I held the honey-cake in
my hands, gazing at the statue's face.

Long ago, I knew, Asherat-of-the-Sea had another
name, and a consort, too; El, who ruled the sun and skies as
she ruled the earth and sea. So said the most ancient of
Habiru myths, the ones the Rebbe pretended did not exist.
But they quarreled, and divided, and took on different
names and faces, as deities have done through the ages. El
became the One God, Adonai of the Habiru; he begot a
son named Yeshua.

And Yeshua's blood and the tears of his mortal
beloved mingled in the womb of the earth, the great
Mother Goddess, who took their semidivine spark and
nurtured to life Blessed Elua. If she wore in La Serenissima
the face of Asherat-of-the-Sea, 'twas not for me to turn
away.

"Gracious Lady of the Sea," I whispered in
D'Angeline, my mother tongue. "Pray accept this gift
from your many-times-removed daughter, and grant me
your blessing." With trembling hands, I broke the honey-
cake in half and laid it on the bloody altar.

High above me, the face of the statue was unchanged,
but I saw in it now somewhat different, a terrible and
impassive mercy. Severio made his offering, murmuring a
Caerdicci prayer. The priestesses nodded grave acceptance, and we turned to go.

"Wait." It was the elder priestess, putting out a hand
to stop me. Through her veil, I saw her eyes, dark and

curious, searching mine. "Some god has laid his hand upon you, child. Will you not seek the counsel of the Oracle?"

I glanced at Severio, who gave a faint shrug. "It is not wise to turn away the gifts of the goddess," he said neutrally.

So it was that we were conducted by silent eunuchs into the lefthand chamber, beneath one of the two lesser domes. It was dark and smoky, and the walls were unadorned; indeed, the chamber held naught but a stool and a table, on which lay a large, deadly-looking cleaver that filled me with apprehension. Like the altar, the table was stained a dark red, though I could not detect the stench of blood, even with eyes closed. The eunuchs set about lighting tapers, and left us. The chamber brightened somewhat and presently an ancient priestess shuffled out, carrying a simple woven basket of pomegranates.

"Some god-touched child, they say, and time to summon old Bianca," she said querulously, setting down her basket and lifting one crabbed hand toward my face. "Well, and why not, I've given counsel to a thousand and a thousand before, from altar and balcony alike, and never missed a day, except the one I had the grippe, when His Grace sought advice. Young Vesperia, she handled it well enough, they say, and why not, I trained her. Well, don't dawdle, child, let me see you!"

Belatedly, I realized that her eyes behind the light-shot silver mesh of her veil were milky and blind, and bent my face to her searching hand. Crimson-stained fingertips soft with age drifted over my features, and old Bianca grunted with satisfaction.

"D'Angeline, are you?" she asked. "No, don't tell me, I know it. Skin like a babe's arse, and the echo of a hundred fingers touched you before, men and women alike, kind and cruel, hard and soft. A rare beauty, yes? And marked, so plain even the blind can see it. Well and so; you don't belong to Asherat, but she takes an interest in all Her children, whether they like it or no. You have a question for the Gracious Lady. Choose, and I will tell Her answer."

I hesitated, unsure of what to do. Severio was frowning, half in awe; he hadn't planned for this. I daresay it unnerved him somewhat. I hoped so, because it surely unnerved me.

"You *do* have a question?" the old woman asked impatiently.

"Yes, my lady," I murmured. "I wish to know—"

"Asherat! Don't *tell* me, child. It taints the answer." Old Bianca gestured at the basket of pomegranates, the sleeves of her blue silk robe hanging loose and voluminous on her bony arm. It was nearly a mockery, such gorgeous fabrics adorning so wizened a form. "Choose, and I will tell."

With no better guidance, I gazed at the heaped basket and selected a large, ripe fruit, its outer rind a rich maroon hue. I placed it on the table before the ancient priestess. Groping for the stool with one hand, she took up the cleaver in the other, then grasped the fruit firmly.

I am not ashamed to say that I gasped when Bianca brought down the cleaver with unexpected swiftness, the deadly blade splitting the pomegranate a mere hairsbreadth from her fingertips. And I was not alone, for I heard Severio wince involuntarily.

The old woman merely grunted again, dividing the halves and setting them upright. The deep red seeds shone in a radiating pattern against the rigid white inner pulp, as vivid as the mote of Kushiel's Dart within my left eye. Scarlet juice oozed onto the table and stained her skin anew as she read the pattern of the seeds with her questing fingertips.

"What you seek you will find," she said matter-of-factly, "in the last place you look."

I waited for more. Bianca levered the cleaver cautiously this time, divided one of the pomegranate halves into quarters. Bending it to expose the glistening ruby seeds, she lifted the quarter to her mouth beneath her veil and deftly gnawed at the tart fruit.

"That's all there is to tell," she said, chewing and turning her head to spit out the pips. "You can make an offering to the treasury before you leave, if you like. Silver's customary."

Outside, with the bright Serenissiman sun reflecting on the rainwashed Square, it seemed almost a dream. Severio related the tale to the Immortali, who took it in stride.

"That's an oracle for you," Benito Dandi said, shrugging. "Common sense, tricked out in smoke and mirrors. I mean, of *course* you're going to find what you're seeking in the last place you look, aren't you? Because after that, you stop looking. Heya," he said, distracted by the sight of a Serenissiman approaching the temple. Clad in a noble-woman's attire and swaying on tall wooden pattens, she nonetheless wore the Veil of Asherat, silvery mesh and gleaming beads obscuring her features. "Bet I know what *she's* looking for!" he exclaimed, and let out a whistle. "My lady, if it's male heirs you're seeking, no need to become a supplicant. If the field doesn't bear, change plowmen, I say!"

I smiled faintly at his ribaldry, pitying the poor
woman. After what I had seen today, I was of no mind to
mock Asherat's powers.

Common sense, indeed; but I had not told the priestess
my question.

Thirty-five

TO MY surprise, all my chevaliers and Joscelin as well had returned by the dinner hour — and with the exception of the latter, who was quiet and indrawn, all gave a good accounting of their day. Unfortunately, there was little to be gained from it. Remy had been turned away at the entrance of the Little Court; the guards had accepted my letter and sent him on his way, warning him pessimistically that the D'Angeline Prince held few audiences these days, and there was a long list of requests. He had haunted the perimeter for the better part of the day to no avail. Prince Benedicte's guards were strict on duty, and housed within the Court itself, so he had no access within.

Fortun had spent a fruitless day trailing couriers in Stregazzan livery, although he described to me with great relish the inner workings of the Arsenal, the great ship-yard. There was an ongoing negotiation, it seemed, between Sestieri Dogal and Sestieri Navis. Well and fine, it might influence the election, but it meant little to me.

For his part, Ti-Philippe had been carousing with those of the Immortali who had not accompanied Severio and me. He had lost nearly a purseful of silver denari, but he had to show for it somewhat more valuable; to me, at any rate. The mother of one of the Immortali attended the Doge's wife – I'd not even known she yet lived, such was the role of women in La Serenissima – and regularly sought the services of her lady's astrologer, although the man had been disgraced and no longer served the Stregazza.

"Good," I said to him. "Find out how I might make an appointment with the man." I gazed at Joscelin. "Do you have aught to report?"

He gave an awkward shrug. "I found out the Yeshuite quarter. 'Tis much the same here as at home; they argue among themselves, and speak of a northern destination. Worse, though. Yeshuites here are confined to their own quarter, yet forbidden to own property. The men may have no congress with Serenissiman women, and those hats, they must wear at all times to identify themselves."

What he did there, I did not ask. I was sorry for the plight of the Yeshuites, but I could not afford to worry over whether or not Joscelin Verreuil had become a part of their grand prophecy. I related instead my own day's adventure.

Predictably, Joscelin was irate. "You should not have gone out without an escort! Bad enough it's soldiers and sailors, and not respectable women, like the Serenissimans have – to venture out on your own, without a single companion! Phèdre, it's folly."

"Well, and I would not have," I retorted coolly, "if you'd not left in a temper. But I did, and no harm done."

"It's stupid." Ti-Philippe scratched his healing nose. "The prophecy, I mean. You always find what you're

looking for in the last place you look, don't you? Why
keep looking after you find it?"

"I know," I said patiently. "The thing of it is, I never
asked the question aloud, which makes me believe the
answer worth considering. If I might guess, I think the
meaning is more subtle. I think we will find Melisande in
the place we least expect her."

"Selling fish at the market," Remy offered in jest.

"Or wiping gruel from the Doge's chin," Ti-Philippe
added.

"Changing the swaddling clothes of Prince
Benedicte's infant son," suggested Fortun with a trace of a
smile.

I could not stop them, once they were off and running
– driving mules along the salt-pans, blowing glass on Isla
Vitrari, tanning hides, teaching archery. With each new
proposed location, it grew more and more absurd, until I
begged them, laughing, to desist.

It was Joscelin, oddly enough, who took the prophecy
most seriously; though not so odd, when I thought on it.
After all, he had been a priest himself, and would be still,
were it not for me. "What you seek, you will find," he
murmured, glancing at me. "Blessed Elua grant it is so,
since you're damnably single-minded about it. I never
thought you'd desist, no matter what I argued." Propped
his chin in his hands, he gazed at the lamp in the center of
the table, its flickering light casting his face into shadow
and making a mask of it. "Prophecy is a dangerous thing.
But I'll say naught to dissuade you, for now."

"Thank you," I said simply.

We left it at that, for the evening. If nothing else,
Joscelin's words had lent the prospect of believability to

our quest, and I was grateful for that, although I did not
know how far I could count on his aid. We had declared a
peace by default, and I was glad he had returned, but our
harsh words earlier lay like a sword between us, and
neither of us willing to take it up or cast it aside.

In the days that followed, I came to see a great deal of
La Serenissima and became accepted into the society of
Severio's peers. A season of truce-parties had begun,
where young gallants of all the Sestieri's clubs held extravagant fêtes, and no quarreling was allowed on the host's
estate. Strange affairs, to a D'Angeline mind, where the
young men gathered to discuss politics and the women to
discuss romance and fashion, under the watchful eyes of a
half-dozen chaperones. Married women had some freedom; maidens had little. More often than not, I was bored,
except when there was dancing and entertainment. When
the fête dwindled to a close, the revelers would straggle
homeward in torchlit processions – and there the truce
ended. Any gallant escorting his lady's party was reckoned
safe from harm, but unaccompanied clubsmen set upon
each other in the sort of gleeful skirmishes I'd witnessed in
the Square.

It goes without saying that a great deal of match-
making went on at these truce-parties.

For his part, Severio displayed me like a jewel, and his
pride in it was nearly enough to offset his impatient desire.
The gallant sons of the Hundred Worthy Families, sport-
ing the colors of a host of vividly named clubs – Perpetui,
Ortolani, Fraterni, Semprevivi, Floridi – flocked to me like
bees to honey, and I was glad of the Immortali's zealous
protectiveness, both for my person and my reputation. The
young women of La Serenissima treated me with a certain

jealous awe, and if I made no friends among them, at least they were wary of maligning me where the Doge's grandson might get wind of it. Most of them, I was shocked to learn, were illiterate. Only priestesses and a few rare noblewomen learned to read and write.

Although I must say, they did know how to cipher. A shrewd mind for trade was reckoned an asset in a wife. Giulia Latrigan, whose uncle was one of the richest men in La Serenissima and stood as the likely candidate for Sestieri d'Oro, could add and deduct whole lists of figures in her head in the blink of an eye. She was clever and funny, and among all the young women, kindly disposed toward me; I think we might have been friends, if not for the rivalry between her family and the Stregazza. But there was talk of an engagement between Giulia and a son of the Cornaldo family, who held great sway among the Consiglio Maggiore, and Severio said bitterly in private that Tomaso Cornaldo would take six votes with him if the rumors regarding the size of Giulia's dowry were true.

Amid the whirl of activity, Ti-Philippe tracked down the Doge's astrologer.

I went to see the man with Remy and Ti-Philippe, and I was glad I'd taken both, for I saw another side to La Serenissima, winding through the smaller canals in the poorer quarters of the city. Here, the work of building this city on the sea was evident. Brackish water flowed sluggishly in the narrow canals and ramshackle wooden houses crowded together, built on ill-drained marshland that stank of rot and fish. When we paid the hired boatman and dismounted, I quickly understood where pattens had originated, the teeteringly high wooden platforms women of style wore as footware. It had begun on the muddy, unpaved streets of La Serenissima.

We were attracting enough curious glances already; I refused Remy and Ti-Philippe's laughing offer to carry me. As a result, I was mired to the ankle by the time we had trudged through a murky labyrinth of back alleys into a mean little courtyard, strung with crisscrossing lines of drying laundry. One closed door onto a windowless dwelling bore a rude painting of the circle of the Zodiac.

"Quite a comedown for the Doge's astrologer," I remarked, holding up my skirts and trying in vain to stamp the worst of the mud from my finely made heeled slippers, which were likely ruined.

"He read the stars for His Grace's wife when she was ill," Ti-Philippe said philosophically, "and prescribed a philtre of sulfur to cure her. It's a wonder it didn't kill her. My friend Candido said Prince Benedicte sent his own Eisandine chirurgeon, who gave her a purge that likely saved her, though she's been sickly ever since. But his mother's superstitious; she thinks someone played foul with Magister Acco's potions, and is yet devout to his advice."

I gave up on the mud. "Lucky for us we're not seeking him out for his medical acumen."

Remy chuckled and rang the bell outside the astrologer's door. Presently it opened a crack, and a sallow face peered out. Weary eyes sized up our persons and our attire, and the astrologer's face took on a cunning look. "Adventurers from the Little Court, yes? Does the fair lady want her stars charted?" Magister Acco stepped back and opened his door wide. "Come in, come in!"

We entered the dark and frowsy interior of the

astrologer's dwelling. He bustled around, lighting additional lamps. I gauged him to be some fifty years of age, lean, streaks of iron-grey in his black hair, atop which perched a fraying cap of velvet. The satin robes of his calling, decorated with celestial symbols, had been fine once, albeit unsubtle. Now they were stained with food-stuff and worn about the hems. Still, there were books and scrolls strewn about his rooms. One, obviously well-thumbed, was in Akkadian script, which I could not read. Obviously, he'd had some learning. I should have guessed as much, since he had been a friend of Maestro Gonzago's.

"Sit, my lady, I pray you." With some embarrassment, Magister Acco cleared the picked remains of a chicken leg from his worktable. Covering his shame, he asked in passably good D'Angeline, "Shall we conduct the charting in your maiden tongue, my lady?"

"Caerdicci is fine, my lord astrologer," I said politely, sitting opposite him, the table between us. Remy and Ti-Philippe took a stand on either side of me. "But I'm afraid—"

"Ah, yes, of course." Magister Acco steepled his fingers, nodding wisely. "My lady, have no fear, your coin buys my utmost discretion. I ask only that if you find my advice sage — and you shall, you shall! — you drop a kind word in the ear of Prince Benedicte. It is not meet that I should be without a royal patron, being trained to serve kings."

I leaned forward and held his eyes. "My lord astrologer, if you have the knowledge I seek, believe me, Prince Benedicte will reward you. I seek not counsel, but information." The astrologer drew back, a veiled look coming over his face. I smiled disarmingly, changing my tactic. "Forgive me, I did not mean to alarm you. You are a friend of the Aragonian historian Gonzago de Escabares, are you not?"

Magister Acco relaxed. "Yes, Gonzago, of course. Did he send you? I know he's ever had a fondness for Terre d'Ange and . . . " he chuckled, ". . . its fair cuisine. Pray, send the old rascal my greetings."

"I shall," I said, and paused. "Magister, I know Maestro Gonzago visited you last year, and after he left, an acquaintance of his, Lucretius by name, came seeking him too late. You sent him on to Varro, whence the Maestro was bound, and gave him the name of a reputable inn in La Serenissima."

"Yes." His dark eyes grew wary again. "I have some vague recollection of such a man. But I've no idea what became of him, if that's what you're seeking."

"No." I shook my head. "I'm looking for a D'Angeline noblewoman who contacted him at that very same inn, the following morning." I smiled, shrugged, spreading my hands. "She is an old acquaintance of mine, my lord, and gave him a gift for Maestro Gonzago to carry for me. Alas, she left no address, and I would thank her for it."

"I don't know what you're talking about." The astrologer's voice was tight, and even by the dim lamp-light, I could see a sheen of sweat on his brow.

"Surely you would remember the Lady Melisande Shahrizai," Remy offered, giving his sailor's rowdy grin. "A face to make men weep for beauty, black hair like waves of the sea at night, eyes like twin-set sapphires and a nightingale's voice? I saw her at fifty paces, and have never forgotten it!"

Magister Acco gave a convulsive shudder. "No," he

said hoarsely. "I've never seen such a person. If she found out Gonzago's friend, she must have gotten it from a servant. I'm sorry, I don't know anything about it."

Compulsive motions, perspiration, altered tone, repetition — he wasn't merely lying, he was lying out of fear. I spoke to him in my gentlest voice. "My lord astrologer, I did not jest with you. Prince Benedicte would pay dearly for this knowledge. And whatever you fear, I promise, he will take you under his protection." Though I had no authority whatsoever to make that kind of pledge, I was reasonably certain Benedicte would agree; and if he wouldn't, I'd summon Quintilius Rousse if I had to.

But 'twas to no avail.

"I know nothing," said Magister Acco, desperation making him bold. "Do you hear? Nothing! Not even if you were to offer me the post of Royal Astrologer to the D'Angeline Queen herself! Now get out and leave me be, and don't come back!" He trembled with mingled fear and anger. "Do you people think I can't chart my own fate? Do you think I don't see the thread will cut my lifeline short if I cross it? Get out, I tell you!"

"Magister Acco . . ."

"Out!" He screamed the word with corded throat, one shaking hand pointing at the door. There were veins throbbing at his temples, and I feared we'd give him a seizure if we stayed. I beckoned to Remy and Ti-Philippe, and we went quietly. The astrologer's door slammed behind us and I heard the sound of furniture being dragged within, something heavy thudding against the door.

We stood in the muck of the little courtyard and stared at one another.

"Well," Remy said thoughtfully. "There's a man that's tangled with Melisande, all right. Only what do we do about it?"

"We go to Prince Benedicte." The voice that spoke those words was so quiet and reasonable it didn't sound like Ti-Philippe. He met my eyes reluctantly, rubbing at his nose, which no longer resembled a fruit. "My lady, I'd follow you to the ends of the earth, whether you chased a will-o'-the-wisp or no, but if there's any merit to that man's fear, this business is too serious for us to handle alone. We've good reason to believe the astrologer knows somewhat about Melisande, somewhat that put the fear of Kushiel into him. It's a matter of state, and you gave the Admiral your word. Let Prince Benedicte handle it."

"You're right," I said slowly, and sighed. "I'd rather we had proof, a great deal more of it. But he won't talk of his own accord, and I don't think we can afford to let him go. Remy, if you'll stay and keep a watch, we'll go straightaway to the Little Court, and pray that Rousse's name opens doors there as quickly as he thinks it will."

"Aye, my lady." Remy saluted, taking up a post leaning against the wall outside the astrologer's door. "Elua grant you luck."

That was when we heard the second thud, and this one didn't sound like furniture.

It sounded very like a falling body.

Ti-Philippe swore and put his shoulder to the door, shoving hard. Remy set to beside him, and between the two, they forced open the door, which was blocked by a large trunk. I would have gone inside, but they made me wait while they went first.

"It's safe, my lady," Remy called back, his voice disgusted. "But so much for going to Prince Benedicte. You may not want to look."

I went to see anyway, and found the astrologer's body lying in a pitiful heap on the floor of his pitiful lodging. His eyes were open and staring, and there was a little foam about his mouth. At his side lay a shattered phial. Magister Acco was very much dead. Ti-Philippe stooped and sniffed at his foam-spattered lips, touched one finger to the glass shards of the phial and sniffed that as well.

"Laugh at my nose all you like," he said, wiping his finger on his trousers, "but it smells just like the rat poison my Da used to set out, my lady."

"He poisoned himself." I pressed my hand hard to my breast, shaking. "Oh, poor man! And we drove him to it. I should have seen he was that terrified."

"My lady." Remy took my arm and urged me turn away. "I think mayhap he was a little bit mad," he said softly. "That business he spoke at the end, about crossing threads cutting short his lifeline? I think whatever fear he had of Melisande was jumbled in his mind with his expulsion from the Palace, and he drove himself mad with it rather than face his own guilt. The man nearly killed the Doge's wife. Surely it haunted him."

"Mayhap." My head ached. "But if he stood at the verge, Remy, I am the one who pushed him. I wonder if he knew what we meant to do."

"How could he?" Ti-Philippe asked rhetorically. "Lucky we didn't, now. I'd hate to have dragged out the Prince's Guard to visit a corpse. You can still tell Benedicte, and let him investigate it."

"No." I rubbed my temples. "There's naught to learn

here, with the astrologer dead. Whatever else is true, he did violence by his own hand, and there's no one Benedicte could question that he hasn't asked before. It would only alert Melisande, if she's tied to him in any way. And if she's not, 'twould only embarrass us, and give away our game in the bargain. I'll go to Benedicte when I've proof, not speculation and bodies."

We made a cursory search of Magister Acco's lodgings, turning up naught but the tools of his trade, texts and charts. A few Serenissimans began to gather outside the door, and Remy went out somber-faced to report the news and send for the undertaker, telling them only that the astrologer had bid us leave in a temper, then suffered a seizure.

No one seemed surprised, and a few nodded solemnly, as if they'd expected no less. Magister Acco, it seemed, had a reputation for having an uncertain temper and occasional fits of raving.

He also had a reputation for unerring prognostication.

I thought about that, during the silent trip back to our rented house, the gondola emerging onto the Great Canal to glide softly over water tinted lavender by the setting sun, the boatman dipping his long oar in mesmerizing rhythm, singing absently to himself. I did not think the astrologer was mad, any more than I thought a tincture of sulfur would kill in small doses. If the Doge's wife had died, if Benedicte's chirurgeon had not intervened, Magister Acco would likely have been executed. Whether or not Melisande had done it, I did not know; if she had been in the Doge's Palace, and that close to his astrologer, someone else had known it, someone who had lied to Prince Benedicte — and it had never been her way to use her own hand. Mayhap it was different, now that she was more desperate.

One thing I did know. Magister Acco had seen her, and if he was not merely raving, he had seen in the stars that his death lay in crossing her. He had taken control of his fate in the only way he saw.

And I had led him to it.

Thirty-six

UPON OUR return home, I found an invitation awaiting me. I had nearly forgotten Ricciardo Stregazza's promise, but he, it seemed, had not. I was invited to visit their country villa two days hence.

I daresay I might have politely refused, were it not that the invitation itself captured my attention. It was not from Ricciardo, but his wife, Allegra. It had a warm, open sentiment that surprised me, and in the note she spoke of her interest in hearing my perspective on Serenissiman society.

"Will you answer, my lady?" Fortun asked quietly. His manner was gentle; he had heard the day's tidings from Remy and Ti-Philippe.

"Yes." I sighed. "I should. For all I know, I might learn somewhat."

"I'll escort you, if it please you." It was a kind offer. He was steadier than the other two, and we both knew it. I wouldn't have replied as I did if I hadn't been weary and disheartened.

"I want Joscelin." It was a child's response, petulant and sulky; I saw the hurt on his face the moment I spoke, and would have bitten back the words if I could have. "Fortun, I'm sorry, I didn't mean it like that. It's only that it's isolated, we'll be on the mainland, among folk I dare not trust, and he's trained best for it."

"Well, he's not here." Fortun flushed at his own bluntness, dropping to kneel beside my couch. "My lady," he murmured. "I know you miss him. I know how you have quarreled, we all do. If I could drag him back to your side by his heels, I swear I would do it."

I set aside the invitation. "Where is he? Among the Yeshuites?" I saw the answer in his face and gave a short laugh. "You know what he's doing there, don't you?"

"Yes." Fortun looked away. "My lady," he said, his voice scarcely a whisper. "Forgive me. But you heard the Unforgiven, as well as we. That night in Troyes-le-Mont, there was a Cassiline Brother escorting Persia Shahrizai. I know you would never suspect him, in a thousand years, but he keeps disappearing, and we talked about it, we three. It's not right, with him sworn to protect and serve you. We drew lots, and I got the short straw. I've followed him, more than once."

I passed my hands blindly over my face. "Joscelin Verreuil may be a poor excuse for a Cassiline, but he'd as soon dance naked for the Khalif of Khebbel-im-Akkad as conspire with Melisande Shahrizai. What's he doing?"

"Um." Fortun cleared his throat. "He's training Yeshuite lads to Cassiline arms."

"*What?*" My voice rose.

"I told you, he's training them to fight like Cassilines." He glanced about to make certain no servants were near. "I asked about, in the taverns. I found one fellow willing to talk. Seems they've been trying to teach themselves, but it's unlawful for a Yeshuite to bear arms in La Serenissima. They're allowed a single temple; he trains them in the catacombs below."

"What are they going to do?" I asked wearily. "Storm the Doge's Palace?"

"No." He shook his head. "Go north, in accordance with some prophecy. There's rumor of a warlord, Hral, Vral, somewhat like that, has converted to the Yeshuite faith, and seeks to forge a single nation among the tribefolk of the northern wastes."

"Well, I wish them the joy of it," I muttered. "Fortun, forget what I said. I would be very pleased indeed to have you attend me."

"I'll send him to you when he comes," he said quietly, leaving me.

What passed between them, I never knew, but it fell out that Joscelin accompanied me to the Villa Gaudio, where Ricciardo and Allegra Stregazza made their home. We travelled from the linked islands of the city proper by boat, forging some little ways up the Brenno River, along which several villas lay. In the true Tiberian style, these were working farms as well as gracious estates, and it surprised me, from what little I knew of him, that Ricciardo Stregazza chose to live on one.

Joscelin and I spoke little on the journey, except to discuss the death of Magister Acco. Like Remy, he was minded to think that the astrologer had been unstable in his wits and his death none of my fault. Nonetheless, I think it unnerved him somewhat, that I had been so close to a man's death, and my Perfect Companion nowhere in sight.

Well, and it should, I thought, remembering him coming in from the garden the day I had told him. *I protect and serve,* he had said. *No more, and no less.* No matter what anyone said, his vow was between him and Cassiel – not me, and not even Ysandre. But in my opinion, he'd done considerably less than more.

That, at least, I kept to myself. After all, no one was telling *me* it was my destiny and salvation to lead a people to a nation of glory in a far-off land.

Ricciardo Stregazza had lookouts posted, and we were met at river's edge. He and his family met us in the gardens between the dock and the villa, a modest, gracious affair with marble columns to the fore.

"Welcome, Comtesse," he said in D'Angeline, and gave me the kiss of greeting; I returned it unthinking. His demeanor seemed easier, and he looked younger than I'd thought before. "This," he said, turning, "is my lady wife, Allegra Stregazza, and these . . ." he indicated a shy girl of some seven years, and a merry, curly-headed boy of five or so, ". . . are our offspring, Sabrina and Lucio. My dears, this is Phèdre nó Delaunay, Comtesse de Montrève."

We had greetings all around, and I introduced Joscelin, who gave his Cassiline bow. Allegra Stregazza embraced me warmly.

"I'm so pleased you came," she said in Caerdicci, smiling, faint lines crinkling at the corners of her grey-green eyes. I guessed her to be some ten years younger than her husband; twenty-seven or eight. After the city, her attire seemed elegantly simple, and she wore her waving brown hair unadorned. "We don't get many visitors here, as it's not fashionable, although I daresay it will be one day. And since . . . well. It's a pleasure."

"You honor me," I replied politely, slightly bewildered.

"Signore Verreuil," Allegra began to greet Joscelin, then gasped, gazing at his daggers and vambraces. "Oh! You're a *Cassiline!*"

It sounded exotic, from her lips. Blinking, Joscelin gave another bow. "I had that honor once, my lady Stregazza," he said. "I beg your pardon, for wearing arms into your presence." Straightening, he plucked his daggers free and dropped them neatly at her feet, beginning to unbuckle his baldric.

"Oh, no, no! Pray, keep your arms!" Allegra clapped her hands together like a girl, and then bent to explain to the children how no matter what the circumstances, the King or Queen of Terre d'Ange was always attended by two members of the Cassiline Brotherhood. The boy stooped to pick up one of Joscelin's daggers; the girl dug her toe in the grass and peered at him through her hair.

"Lucio, no, leave it for Signore Cassiline," Ricciardo scolded, catching one arm about the boy's middle and hoisting him, giggling, onto his shoulder. "Shall we go inside? I nearly think Cook's outdone herself with a fine repast."

It was a pleasant stroll through the gardens, which were mostly yew and cypress, with some few patches where roses were cultivated. "Prince Benedicte had promised me the loan of his court gardener," Ricciardo said ruefully, "before the quarrel began. Still, he's a fair man, and I think we might come to some arrangement, if my dear sister-in-law hasn't poisoned his ear against me." When I protested that his gardens were lovely, he shook his head at me. "Thank you, Comtesse, but I know better. Still, Allegra's done wonders with the roses."

"You grew those?" I asked. "They're lovely."

She blushed. "My mother had some skill with plants. I wish I had more time."

As they moved on ahead of us, Joscelin and I exchanged glances behind their backs. For once, he looked as bewildered as I felt, and I was glad of it.

Inside, the villa was both elegant and comfortable, airy, sunlit spaces offsetting the dark weight of the gilt-trimmed wooden furnishings. A few Akkadian rugs and bowls of blooming roses added a note of color. We had, indeed, a very fine luncheon. The children were allowed to dine with us and took on the guest-duties of serving Joscelin and me with a charming, well-coached solemnity. It was all very much as one might find at the country estate of a noble-born D'Angeline family.

Our hosts made light conversation, but 'twas never dull. I found Ricciardo surprisingly well-informed regarding poetry, and we discussed in detail the latest verses of Thelesis de Mornay's Ysandrine Cycle. Allegra, in turn, was keenly interested in the role of education in D'Angeline society, and I realized in short order that Allegra Stregazza was one of those rare Serenissiman noblewomen trained to read and write. The invitation had been written by her own hand. All of them were fascinated to learn of the ten-year regimen of training the Cassiline Brethren underwent, which Joscelin obligingly described. When we had done, the children were dismissed unto the custody of their nursemaid, leaving us with a hastily bobbed bow and curtsy and beaming approval on the part of the parents.

It was, on the whole, a delightful performance – and I did not think it was only that. There was genuine affection and respect between Ricciardo and Allegra, and an abiding warmth for their children. But he was the Doge's son, and I was not naïve enough to believe that this pleasant visit was not about politics.

So it proved, over a dessert cordial. Ricciardo toasted our health, then spoke bluntly. "My lady Phèdre." He set down his glass. "Please do not take it amiss when I say I know who and what you are. I didn't recognize the name when we met, but I remembered it later, from the Ysandrine Cycle. I say this not to embarrass you, because I think in your own land you must be reckoned a heroine, and I admire that, as I do many things about Terre d'Ange, but because I know my brother. Whatever he may have promised you, no matter what the religious significance in your homeland, Marco Stregazza will not let his son marry a courtesan."

I did not protest that I had no desire to do so, but said instead, "Severio thinks he will." To his credit, Joscelin made no comment.

"Severio." Ricciardo grimaced. "Severio has done no more than dip a toe in the bottomless pool of intrigue that is his birthright. He's not a bad lad, though he can be short-tempered and cruel. Less so, I hear, since meeting you, for which I owe you thanks. Nonetheless, he doesn't know the tenth part of his father's schemes."

I raised my eyebrows. "He seems to know a tenth part of yours. And he actually has a good grasp of what a strike by the salt-panners could do to La Serenissima."

"Does he?" Ricciardo paused, startled. "Well, if he knows that much, I wish he could see that the Consiglio is breaking the back of the workers and tradesfolk who support them with these damnable taxes, all to build this glorious navy." He shook his head, adding bitterly, "But I suppose he believes his mother and father, who tell him that his uncle is rousing the Scholae in a desperate bid for political gain."

"It's plain folly!" Allegra said indignantly. "Anyone with half a wit to study the annals can see that the Consiglio Maggiore has never elected a Doge from Sestieri Scholae. If all Ricciardo wanted was gain, why he'd, he'd be better off courting Sestieri Angelus' vote!" She blushed at her own words, but her expression remained no less indignant.

"Marie-Celeste said you have no love for the Little Court," I said neutrally to Ricciardo.

"My sister-in-law doesn't know a damned thing about it!" His eyes flashed. "Yes, I sided with my family, out of respect for my father. I think Benedicte was wrong, blaming the entire Stregazza line for the treachery of Dominic and Thérèse. And I think he was wrong to set the son of this second marriage above his firstborn children, especially knowing that Marie-Celeste may inherit naught of his holdings in La Serenissima. But if she hadn't been so suspicious, if she hadn't reacted like such a termagant . . ." He sighed, gathering his composure. "Comtesse, your Prince Benedicte languished twenty years in a loveless marriage, sold into the bonds of political matrimony by his brother Ganelon. When Maria Stregazza died, he mourned her as much as was seemly. But now he is an old man with an adoring young bride, a refugée from his beloved homeland, who has given him a son. I believe he declared this infant Imriel his heir out of sheer exuberance, with no thought for his actions. Given time and a tactful approach, he would doubtless revise his words and divide his territories between children. If my father would only see reason, he would send a suitable emissary to Prince Benedicte and resolve this foolish quarrel."

"Such as yourself?" I inquired.

Ricciardo shrugged. "I have friends, still, among the Little Court. I think Benedicte would listen to me. It is my father who will not." He looked at me. "I trust Marco and Marie-Celeste told you there was a scandal."

"Yes." I glanced at Allegra, but she was watching her husband, compassion on her face.

"Yes, well." Ricciardo's mouth twisted. "You may as well know it. My father gave me the task of entertaining the son of a D'Angeline ambassador from the Little Court. I was caught out at performing my duty rather too well, and my father has held me in contempt ever since, no matter how hard I labor to win his admiration." He let his eyes close briefly, and said, "Yes. I know what you're wondering. The youth was of age, and willing. I'm not that much a fool; but fool enough."

"I'm sorry, my lord," I said politely, not knowing what else to say. Ricciardo's eyes snapped open, his gaze sharp and canny once more.

"I tell you so that you know," he said, "what my family is capable of, and how little they will bend on certain matters. My brother dangles Severio before you as bait, but once he has whatever he's asked of you – and I know him, there's somewhat he wants – he'll snatch his son away and leave you gaping."

"And he'll turn you to his own purposes if he may," Allegra murmured, "even if 'tis against your own loyalties. Meanwhile, the Doge will hear naught of reason, the silence draws on between the Stregazza and House Courcel, and Prince Benedicte grows fearful for his son

and wife and increases the number of his guard at the Little
Court."

Her words struck me like a blow, triggering a
memory. *I must greet his grace the Duc de Somerville,*
Severio had said to me in the concert hall. *I am charged by
my mother on behalf of Prince Benedicte to thank him for the
company of D'Angeline guardsmen he sent to attend the Little
Court. It seems my maternal grandfather grows chary of protecting his pure-blooded heir.*

For the first time in months, I felt the satisfaction of a
piece of the puzzle falling into place.

The missing guardsmen of Troyes-le-Mont.

"My lord Ricciardo," I announced, coming out of my
reverie. "Let us not toy with one another. Your brother has
asked me to approach the Cruarch of Alba regarding trade
rights, and if you know who I am, you know there is a
chance Drustan mab Necthana would hear me. For reasons
of your own — and mayhap concern for my welfare — you
ask that I do not. Very well, I will consider it, but there is
somewhat I want. You say you have friends in the Little
Court. I want access therein, without troubling Prince
Benedicte."

Ricciardo was staring at me; they all were, even
Joscelin. But it was the Doge's son who spoke, wondering.
"You don't have any intention of marrying my nephew, do
you?"

He was clever; I should have been more circumspect. I
shrugged, opening my hands. "I enjoy Severio's company.
In Terre d'Ange, that is enough. Beyond that, my business
is my own."

"Not if it affects La Serenissima," he said flatly.

I met his dark, hooded gaze squarely. "It doesn't."

"My lord," Joscelin said unexpectedly, leaning forward at the table. "We are looking for Melisande Shahrizai."

I wouldn't have dared say it so baldly, but coming from Joscelin – it took them by surprise. I saw Ricciardo blink, considering Joscelin, who bore it with stern Cassiline calm. "Benedicte's traitor," he said thoughtfully. "Yes, he looked for her too, not two months ago. I daresay it's one of the reasons my father is wroth with him and will not extend his hand in peace, that Prince Benedicte would suspect the Palace of harboring traitors. I'm sorry." He shook his head. "I know no more of it than that."

He evinced none of the signs of lies and evasion I knew to look for and had seen in such abundance in Magister Acco the astrologer; but then, he was a Stregazza, and trained to guile. Still, I thought he had dealt fairly with me, and if his motives were no less ambitious than his brother's, I could not fault him for it.

"Enough of this!" Allegra pushed her chair back from the table and stood. "Ricciardo, we invited the Comtesse here to show her hospitality, not to intrigue," she said, chiding him, then turning to me. "My lady Phèdre, would you do me the kindness of seeing the library? I would see that my children – *both* my children – are well versed in an education befitting their station. If you would recommend texts, I would be grateful."

"Of course," I murmured.

Their library was small, but not ill-furnished. I glanced over the tomes available and spoke well of several D'Angeline volumes, recommending the addition of key Hellene philosophers and a handful of Tiberian historians. Allegra sat at the desk and made notations in a graceful hand, then took a fresh sheet of parchment and wrote out a brief letter, folding and sealing it with a blot from a wax taper and the familiar Stregazza signet.

"Here." She handed it to me. "It is a letter of introduction to Madame Felicity d'Arbos, who was a good friend to my mother when she served as lady-in-waiting to the Princess-Consort Maria Stregazza de la Courcel in the Little Court. She will remember me kindly, I think, and be pleased to hear my greetings."

"Thank you, my lady." I didn't know what else to say.

"You are welcome." Allegra smiled ruefully. "My husband is a good man, Comtesse, and I think you would come to see it in time. I did. If he is suspicious, he has been given reason for it, too often to count. But he struggles very hard to do what is right, and is rewarded with scorn." She sighed. "If the Doge were not ill, it might be different. Once, he would entertain the captains of the Scholae thrice a year, and hear their complaints. If he could talk to them, he would know that Ricciardo labors honestly on their behalf, and they regard him with respect. Tradefolk do not care for the petty intrigues of nobility so much as the bread on their table. But his father . . ." She shook her head, and gave me a direct look. "Would it be different in Terre d'Ange, do you think?"

"Mayhap," I said gently. "Many things are. But not of a necessity, my lady. My own lord, Anafiel Delaunay, was shunned by his father for choosing to pledge his life to our Prince Rolande rather than marry and beget a family of his own. It ended in tragedy, and the title I inherited, he never lived to bear. The laws of love are different, but the entanglements of family and betrayal are the same."

Allegra nodded. "I see. Thank you." She rose from the desk and went to gaze out the window overlooking the rear of the estate, rich with farmlands. "Ricciardo has done his duty by his family. And we have been happy after our own fashion. Let his brother and sister-in-law mock if they will. For me, it is enough."

I thought of their merriment in the garden, Ricciardo swinging his son astride his shoulders. His affection, her compassion. And I thought of my bitter quarrel with Joscelin, the hurtful words, yet unrecanted. We had been granted imperfect happiness in love, Allegra Stregazza and I, but where I squandered mine, she nurtured hers, cupping her hands about the embers and blowing to life a flame warm enough to sustain them all.

"You have a lovely family, my lady," I said softly. "I envy you."

Thirty-seven

İ WASTED no time calling upon Madame Felicity d'Arbos.

For this excursion, I took with me my three chevaliers. I doubted I'd come to harm within the Little Court, well-guarded as it was, and they were more adept than Joscelin at ferreting out the sort of knowledge I sought.

Fortun had smacked his forehead when I put my theory to them, for not having thought of it himself. He dragged out the carefully crafted maps of Troyes-le-Mont and we marked afresh in memory the knowledge we had garnered before, including the positions and reports of the guards I'd interviewed among the Unforgiven.

Thus armed, we went forth.

The guards at the canal gate of the Little Court greeted me with deference, examining the seal of Allegra's letter and granting us admittance, summoning a servant lad to run to Madame d'Arbos' quarters and announce me.

It was strange, after the bustling familiarity of Serenissiman society, to be in D'Angeline territory once more, surrounded by D'Angeline faces, hearing my native

tongue spoken. There was a measured elegance to the pace,
a hush in the presence of nobility. The very marble seemed
whiter, the ceilings higher, the halls wider, and all the little
grace notes I had missed were present – musicians playing
in the salons we passed, unexpected niches holding vases
of blooming flowers, graceful frescoes on the walls and
ceilings.

All of these we passed en route to Madame d'Arbos'
quarters, the lad having returned to report that she would
be most pleased to receive me. A young guardsman was
delegated to escort us, tugging his blue-and-silver House
Courcel livery straight and blushing every time he glanced
my way. At the doors, I suggested that we need not trouble
Madame with the presence of my chevaliers, if he would
be so kind as to entertain them, showing them, mayhap, to
the guards' common room, where they might while away
the time.

To this, he acceded with another blush.

I must say, although it accomplished no end in itself,
my visit with Madame Felicity d'Arbos proved delightful.
A widow of some fifty-odd years, she was one of the
D'Angeline noblewomen sent with Prince Benedicte to
attend his Serenissiman wife; Allegra's mother had been
one of the native Serenissimans so appointed, many
years ago. It explained, I thought, a good deal about
her education. Felicity's rooms were small, but well-
appointed. She had retired from her position when Maria
Stregazza had died, but chose to remain at the Little Court,
and Prince Benedicte had seen that she was given a
generous pension. We sat sipping tea while she told me of
her life and her fond memories of the young Allegra and
her family.

"And the Princess-Consort?" I asked politely. "What was she like?"

"The Serenissiman wife." Her grey eyes looked shrewdly at me over the rim of her teacup. "That's what they call her, now. 'Twas not so bad, for a time. Oh, she dabbled in intrigue, on behalf of her family, but Benedicte knew how to handle it. No love lost between them, but we all got on well enough. After . . . well, he should never have married his daughters into the Stregazza. That family's too close-bound as it is. The King wanted it, to cement ties, but all it did was breed suspicion, if you ask me. And resentment."

"So I've heard," I murmured.

" 'Tis true enough." She set her teacup down carefully. "They hate us a little, you know. You won't have seen it, yet, with your youth and beauty. They'll be fresh-dazzled with it yet. But when it wears on, year after year, the dazzle-ment grates. Maria Stregazza came to hate her husband, while her beauty faded, and his did not. She came to hate the sight of D'Angeline faces around her. It's a hard thing."

"I can imagine," I said, thinking of the unspoken enmity of many of the young noblewomen I'd met. "But it must be different, now, with . . ." I smiled. "Do they call her the D'Angeline wife?"

"The Serenissimans do." Felicity d'Arbos smiled back at me. "It was good, at the beginning. She pleased them, taking the Veil of Asherat. 'Twas well-considered. Now, well, there is a bit of a tempest, but it will pass soon, I hope. Do you wish to see her?"

"Is she receiving visitors?" I asked, surprised. "I've not yet received a response to my request for an audience with Prince Benedicte."

"Oh, no." She laughed. "He's busy with affairs of state, and she with the young one. I'll put in a word for you, if I may, to see your request granted. It might do her good to see a fresh young face, the poor thing. But she is like to stroll on the balcony over the Queen's Garden at this hour, with the babe. And I have leave to wander the garden, as I helped plant it many years ago."

Since I wished to give my chevaliers as much time as possible, we adjourned to the Queen's Garden and spent a pleasant time therein. It was wholly enclosed by walls, with a single gate to which Felicity d'Arbos had a key. A tiny fountain burbled at its center, and an abundance of roses bloomed, in profusion of color and scent. She pointed out various hybrids to me, and I'd no doubt of where Allegra's mother had acquired her skill.

"Ah," Felicity murmured presently, and nodded. "There."

Attended by two pages and a single guard, a figure strolled the balcony above the garden, tall and slender, clad in an elegant gown of creamy white, overlaid with silver brocade, complimenting the shining silver net of Asherat's Veil. In her arms, Benedicte's young wife held their infant son; I could make out chubby fists waving, and a riot of dark curls. Madame d'Arbos and I both made deep curtsies and held them until they had passed back inside.

"Poor little lad," Felicity d'Arbos said sympathetically, straightening. " 'Twill be a mercy when he's of an age to foster, and I pray Benedicte has the sense to send him to court in the City of Elua. Maria's kin won't like it, but truth, there's naught for him here in La Serenissima, D'Angeline-bred as he is."

Having seen what I had of Serenissiman politics, I

could not help but agree. Indeed, I remembered my momentary consideration of Severio's proposal with somewhat of a shudder. La Serenissima was a beautiful city, to be sure, but it was not home to one of Elua's line.

We said a cordial farewell after our stroll, and I promised to send her greetings on to Allegra Stregazza, and urge her to visit with her two young ones. I daresay I should have sent a page in search of my chevaliers, but it had been a long time since I'd had the liberty to go anywhere unaccompanied, and instead assured Madame d'Arbos that I would meet my attendants by the gate.

So it was that I wandered the halls of the Little Court on my own, guessing rightly that the guards' quarters would be found in the vicinity of the kitchens. Inside the common room, a dozen and more guardsmen laughed and jested, leaping to attention when the sentry on duty announced me.

My three chevaliers were there, and I could tell by the gleam in Ti-Philippe's eyes that they had learned somewhat. They fell all over themselves offering me a seat, a cup of wine, a bowl of barley stew, all of which I declined.

"My lady," Fortun said soberly, bowing. "We have been reliving times of old, which you will well remember. This is Geoffroy of L'Agnace, who served at Troyes-le-Mont. And Ignace, and Jean-Vincent, and Telfour, all veterans of the same. You missed Kerney and Meillot, I fear, who were called to duty, but I am told there are others here, as well. Meillot promised to send them if he might."

Six or better of the missing guardsmen? I exclaimed in partially unfeigned surprise, and did take a seat, then — and since I'd no idea what had already been said, I kept my mouth closed on the topic of Melisande's escape. For the better part of an hour, they rehashed the fateful battle. My role in it – crossing the Skaldic encampment to alert the fortress – was related with especial glee. I smiled as if flattered, and ignored the phantom pain that flared on my left shoulder, where Waldemar Selig had begun stripping my skin from my flesh. All in all, that escapade was one I did not like to remember.

"Raimond!" The entry of another guardsman was hailed by his fellows, and he was introduced all around as another of the survivors of Troyes-le-Mont.

"Well met, soldier!" Remy rose to clap him on the back, laughing. "Come, we're fighting the battle over, and trying to settle somewhat besides. Tell us, what did you see, the night of Melisande Shahrizai's flight?"

"Ah, well." Glancing at me, the new arrival bobbed a nervous bow. "Begging your pardon, my lady, to speak of such unhappy things."

"Pray, speak freely." I smiled, and took a gamble. "It is a matter of many outstanding wagers at home, in the betting-houses of Mont Nuit. We might all be the richer for your perspective."

Raimond the guard accepted a full mug of wine and quaffed half its contents before sitting. "Naught out of the ordinary, I'm afraid. I was on duty when young Lord Ghislain came 'round at five bells, outside the war room on the first floor. Afore him, I saw naught but Lord Barquiel, the Queen's uncle. Escorting the Lady Persia, he was, her what turned in her cousin."

Others murmured agreement.

My heart beat faster within my breast and I felt dizzy and short of breath. "Duc Barquiel L'Envers. You're sure?"

"Sure, I'm sure." He drank off the second half of his wine and looked straight at me. "I served next to him, didn't I? Him with that scarf wrapped round his head, like the Akkadians do, and eyes like the Queen. Never saw aught else, until the alarm sounded."

I glanced round at my chevaliers. Remy and Ti-Philippe were vibrant with triumph; Fortun wore a different look, somber and watchful. He shook his head a little when I caught his eye. "Well," I said lightly, "you're like to make his grace the odds-on favorite, although it's no help to me. Whatever happened to the poor fellow who found the sentry at the gate? The one who sounded the alarm?" Snapping my fingers, I glanced at Fortun. "What was his name?"

"Phanuel Buonard," he supplied. "From Namarre."

Raimond shrugged; all the veterans of Troyes-le-Mont shrugged. It was one of the others who said thoughtfully, "Wasn't he the one as resigned his commission? Scarpered to marry a Serenissiman lass, I recall."

Another laughed. "He resigned without permission. Captain Circot was like to track him down, I think, only he wed into an Isla Vitrari family, and those glassblowers protect their own. Likely he's still there, tending the oven-fires and watching his bride grow a mustache."

Amid the jesting that followed, Fortun asked Raimond, "What made you choose to take a commission in the Little Court?"

"I'd a mind to see somewhat beyond the bounds of Terre d'Ange," the guardsman answered promptly. "Anyway, it pays well, and the Old Man asked for volunteers."

I heard it with half an ear, my mind reeling. Barquiel

L'Envers with Persia Shahrizai! If it was true, and my suspicions and Marmion's confession held good, 'twas not Persia at all, but Melisande — and the Duc L'Envers himself the traitor. Ysandre's uncle. I kept my countenance serene as I rose, summoning my chevaliers, bidding farewell to all and concealing the dull, terrified thudding of my heart.

It was a short journey homeward along the Great Canal. Remy and Ti-Philippe were exuberant, and I had to caution them to silence in the boatman's presence as they laid plans to bring this knowledge to Prince Benedicte's attention. All of the missing guardsmen, it seemed, had spoken the same.

Only Fortun was silent and withdrawn.

When we had gained the security of our rented home and secluded ourselves against servants' listening ears, Remy and Ti-Philippe recited to me in a litany the guardsmen's testimony. A full half-dozen, each cited by name — and all had seen the same thing. Duc Barquiel L'Envers, escorting Persia Shahrizai. Dizziness threatened again as I wondered how to convince Ysandre, and I had to grip the edge of the table hard to steady myself. I closed my eyes briefly to make the room stop spinning.

When I opened them, Fortun's somber face caught my eye. "What is it?" I asked him.

He glanced away, then back at me. "My lady," he said quietly. "You taught me to watch, to listen, for certain things. And there was one thing I could not help but notice." He cleared his throat. "They all told the exact same story."

"They all saw the same damn thing, man!" Ti-Philippe exclaimed, thumping him on the shoulder. "What do you expect?"

"Look." Fortun ignored him to lean over the map of Troyes-le-Mont, still laid out on the table. "Here, here and here . . ." he pointed to positions marked on the ground and second floor, ". . . here and here, these are the stations of the guardsmen we spoke to among the Unforgiven. All of them saw a half-dozen folk that night — including Persia Shahrizai in the company of a Cassiline Brother. Look at the routes, my lady. If they're telling the truth, it's impossible that these guardsmen of the Little Court wouldn't have seen the same."

"Mayhap they lied," I suggested. "We cannot always know."

Fortun frowned. "The Queen had everyone questioned, including the guard, at length. If two-thirds of the guards on duty saw naught but Barquiel L'Envers and Persia Shahrizai, why did they not come forward then? It would have been suspicious." He sighed and rumpled his hair. "Someone is lying, yes. But I think it is these guardsmen, and not well. They have been poorly coached. I asked them why they took posts in La Serenissima. You heard Raimond; they all gave the same answer. And," he added softly, "they were all sent by the same man."

My blood ran cold in my veins, and my lips felt stiff as I forced myself to speak. "What are you suggesting?"

"My lady." Fortun folded his hands on the table, his face grave. "Ghislain de Somerville gave the guardsmen of Troyes-le-Mont leave to join the Unforgiven, and those who returned reported to his father Percy. And Lord Percy made sure, very sure, that those men were sent even farther away than Camlach, all the way to La Serenissima. It is passing strange, I think, that he should send Prince Benedicte reinforcements consisting wholly of the missing guardsmen of Troyes-le-Mont. As it is passing strange all of them should volunteer."

The others had fallen silent. We were all silent. I wanted, very much, to dismiss Fortun's conjecture. These displaced guardsmen of the Little Court had given me the answer I had sought for so long, laying it into my hands. I did not like Barquiel L'Envers; had never, ever trusted him. Nor had my lord Delaunay, who had trained me.

As I had trained Fortun, the best of my chevaliers, who had been there and listened with a critical ear, at my own behest. And if I had any faith in my own training, I could not afford to discount his analysis.

"Phanuel Buonard," I said. "He is still here, if the guardsmen spoke true. On the glassblowers' isle. We need to question him." And I did not need Fortun to say, remembering all too well on my own, that it was not the veterans of Troyes-le-Mont who had volunteered this information. They had played dumb, to a man, regarding the fate of their own comrade-in-arms. It was the long-term appointees to the Little Court who'd offered the knowledge.

"I'll see what I might learn," Fortun said quietly.

I slept ill that night and dreamed, for the first time since my visit to Gentian House. I dreamed of the first time I'd met Percy de Somerville, when the Alban delegation had visited the court of Terre d'Ange. Delaunay had counted him an ally, always, but he'd sent Alcuin to his bed to seal the alliance. Not a true friend, I thought, or Delaunay would not have felt the need. And Alcuin had gone, with never a protest, never letting it show how much he detested Naamah's Service. Percy de Somerville, with whom Delaunay had fought at the Battle of Three Princes; he and dead Prince Rolande, and Benedicte de la Courcel. In my dream, I remembered his upright bearing, his handsome, aging gentleman-farmer's features, white teeth smiling and the smell of apples in the air, heavy and cloying.

I woke gagging, breathed in the night air of La Serenissima, dank and foetid with canal water, and went back to sleep.

In the morning I found waiting a summons to sing for the Doge.

THIRTY-EIGHT

THE DOGE'S private quarters were as hot and cloistered as the Room of the Shield in which he held his formal audiences. Braziers burned in every room, and the windows were hung with dense velvet drapery that kept out sunlight and air.

For all that, Cesare Stregazza huddled in his robes of state, a woolen wrap edged in gold fringe thrown over his shoulders. Servants in Stregazzan livery came and went, bringing sweets, mulled wine with spices, the small lap-harp I requested, charcoal for the braziers, fresh candles, a pitcher of water drawn cool from the well, and their faces gleamed with sweat in the stifling quarters. Indeed, they made little effort to hide their discomfort and banged objects around with ill grace. A D'Angeline would have died of shame, to provide such poor service to a sovereign.

I did my best to conceal my embarrassment, and played sweetly on the harp, singing a couple of familiar country lays. It is not a great gift of mine, but my voice holds true and no one leaves the Court of Night-Blooming Flowers without learning to sing and play with some measure of skill. The Doge listened, his hands clasped together beneath his woolen wrap, and the hooded old eyes in that quivering face watched his ill-mannered servants with a dark, ironic gleam.

Me, he praised, and requested that I continue. I sang a haunting Alban air that I had learned from Drustan mab Necthana's sisters, alternating weaving threads of soprano and contralto as best I could. Truly, it called for a man's tenor in the mix, but I reckoned no one in La Serenissima would notice. Emboldened, I followed it with a humorous D'Angeline tune usually sung in rounds during a game of *kottabos*, about a wager between a courtesan and three suitors. The Doge laughed aloud as I sang the different roles, and I marked how his trembling diminished as he relaxed. Even the servants ceased their rude blundering about to listen, smiling at the sense of it though they did not know the words, and when they resumed their chores, it was with a greater measure of care.

When I had done, I paused for a sip of water.

Cesare Stregazza leaned back, watching my face. "Leave us, please," he said to the servants. When they had gone, he turned back to me. "Sing me the song that lulled the Master of the Straits, little Contessa."

I glanced up, briefly surprised. The Doge knew more of me than I had known. I bowed my head in acquiescence, took up the harp once more, and sang. It is a hearth-song of the Skaldi, a song such as their women sing, and I learned it among them, during that long, cold winter I spent as a slave in Gunter's steading. There are Skaldic war-songs the world has heard, of battle and glory and blood and iron. This was a gentler, homelier tune, about the sorrow of the women waiting by the hearth-side and the death of a young warrior-husband, of mourning come too soon and children unborn while the snow falls unending and the wolf howls outside the door.

I had not sung it since the day we first crossed the Straits, although I had written down the words for Thelesis de Mornay. I laid the harp aside when I finished.

"Brava," Cesare Stregazza said softly. "Well done, my lady." He lifted his cup of mulled wine and sipped it, and his hand scarce trembled at all. "Five songs, sung in three tongues; three lands you have travelled, and Caerdicca Unitas a fourth. Ysandre de la Courcel had scarce warmed her precarious throne when she chose you to send to Alba, and Marco's spies would have it that she's cast you out for girlish spite?"

"My lord Doge," I said deferentially. "Her majesty did not . . . cast me out. 'Tis a small misunderstanding, no more."

His wrinkled lips curved in a wry smile. "Oh, aye, is it? My son is a canny man, but he's never sat a throne of state. You are the best kind of weapon there is, Phèdre nó Delaunay; the kind that appears but a charming adornment. No sitting monarch with a measure of sense would leave you lying about for some enemy's hand to pick up, no, and it is my impression that Ysandre de la Courcel has a great deal of sense."

I raised my eyebrows. "My lord does me too much credit."

"Then give me some, Contessa," he snapped. "I've not held this throne by being an idiot, and I'll not hold it much longer if I can't use the tools that come to hand." Almost as if in response, the wine-cup he yet held began to tremble fiercely, hot liquid spilling over the rim. I rose with alacrity to take it from him and set it gently on the marble-topped side table. "You see, even my body betrays me, making bad puns at my dignity's expense," Cesare said dryly, clasping his aged hands together once more. "But I shall at least have the opportunity to test the accuracy of my measurement of Ysandre de la Courcel. Today I learned that your Queen has agreed to make the *progressus regalis* come autumn. And if my enemies have their way, she will be in La Serenissima in time to observe the election of a new Doge, that mutual pledges may be exchanged."

There was a great deal of information in those words. I sat back down on the hassock where I had been playing, and took too long thinking how best to respond.

"Ah, yes, indeed," he said, eyeing me. "What to say? We must gamble here, you and I. I have only one option open to me, and I have chosen it. I have chosen to believe that Ysandre de la Courcel has no part in this conspiracy against me, and thus is my only likely ally." The Doge shrugged his hunched shoulders. "And I have chosen to believe that you are the Queen's woman, and loyal. If I am wrong, in the name of your Blessed Elua, walk out the door now and tell my enemies I am wise to them, little Contessa, and let us make an end to it."

"And have you no spies yet loyal, to follow me and betray the conspirators if I did?" I inquired, provoking a wily smile. "My lord, if you gave me too much credit before, you give me too little now." I shook my head. "Why are you sure there is a conspiracy?"

"Child, there is always a conspiracy," Cesare said irritably, twisting the great gold signet ring on his right hand. "Do you see that?" I had seen it before, felt its impress against my cheek. The Crown of Asherat. I gazed at it again and nodded. "While he rules La Serenissima," he continued, "the Doge is called the Beloved of Asherat-of-the-Sea. This, this, all of this . . ." he gestured at his scarlet cap, his robes, the trappings of the room, ". . . these are the symbols of state. But this . . ." he held up his trembling hand, the gleaming band of gold, ". . . this is the symbol of that wedding. And none but the bridegroom knows what it means to wear it."

I looked from the ring to his face, questioning.

"Come now, little D'Angeline, with celestial blood in your veins and a god's mark on you," he chided me. "Do you not know better? The sacred marriage is consummated in death. The immortal bride does not set her mortal beloved free to live a few more doddering years. And yet, that is exactly what Her priestess told me. Either I have lived my life a lie, or someone has bribed the Oracle."

This time, he misgauged my silence; I was not pondering my reply, but remembering. It was Delaunay's fault, who trained me too well. My life would be simpler had he not taught me such things, that I recalled immediately the dark room in the Temple and old Bianca's querulous voice, the smell of beeswax and pomegranates. *Well, and why not, I've given counsel to a thousand and a thousand before, and never missed a day, except the one I had the grippe, when His Grace sought advice.* "My lord," I said soberly, meeting his eyes. "I believe you are right."

"Of course I am!" The Doge was snappish again, but I knew well enough to ignore it. "I'm right about all of it, aren't I?"

"Mayhap." I chose my words carefully. "I know her majesty well enough to know that Ysandre de la Courcel would have no part in plotting against a sitting monarch, and you will not err in trusting her word. Whether or not she will serve as your ally . . ." I shrugged. "My lord, why not make peace with Prince Benedicte? You place my Queen in an awkward position, if you do not. He is her great-uncle, and stands yet next in line to the throne until she gets an heir of her own. Your son Ricciardo thinks he would listen to reason, did you but approach him."

"Ricciardo." Cesare Stregazza scowled. "He thinks to set himself at Benedicte's ear, and win his support for his own bid. With Sestieri Scholae and Angelus alike supporting him, he might even do it, the serpent. But he dare not approach Benedicte without my blessing, lest I cut him off at the knees – or Marco. He could do it, if he could make that wife of his hear reason. He might do it yet, and claim my throne in the bargain. No." He shook his head. "There is no one I dare trust, little Contessa, to win Prince Benedicte's support for *my* sake. I sent for him; he ignored my summons. If I approach him myself, I lose all credibility. If I threaten him with violence, I declare against House Courcel and risk severing ties with Terre d'Ange itself. With the support of Alba and Aragon, Terre d'Ange could close the west to Serenissiman trade. No. But your Queen, she can forge a peace. And with her support and Prince Benedicte's, I have leverage to declare the elections null and expose treachery in the very Temple of Asherat. Without it . . ." He shrugged. "I step down, or die."

"And you think I can persuade the Queen to agree to this," I said.

"Yes." The Doge folded his hands in his lap and gave his canny smile. "I think you can. And I think you might. Because it involves blasphemy, does it not? And Asherat-of-the-Sea, in her wisdom and mercy, has seen fit to make this known to you, a god's chosen. You gave your promise to sing for me, Phèdre nó Delaunay de Montrève. I have named my song. Will you sing it?"

"I might," I said evenly. "What do you offer me, my lord?"

His smile broadened. "What does every good singer require? My silence. Whatever you pursue on your Queen's behalf, I leave you free to follow it. Until I know of a surety who plots against me, I shall remain a doddering old fool, with occasional moments of clarity. Let my children and grandchildren see you a charming adornment; I will not reveal you a weapon."

I regarded him thoughtfully. "Someone in your Palace gave shelter to the Lady Melisande Shahrizai, my lord. Someone with access to your wife's astrologer, who, by the way, took his own life rather than reveal what he knew. If you had that knowledge, we might have a bargain."

"If I had that knowledge, I'd use it." The Doge returned my regard with a hooded stare. "Rudely though he asked, I have given the Queen's representative Benedicte de la Courcel every support in uncovering D'Angeline traitors. It is not my fault he failed. All I ask is your Queen's support in my effort to do the same among my folk — within my walls, and not hers. Do I have your pledge?"

"Yes, my lord." I could not see that he had left me an out. "I will report honestly to my Queen what I know, and represent your request fairly. No more can I do."

"No more do I ask," he said equably. Nodding, Cesare Stregazza began to work at the clasp on a great collar of pearls he wore, that overlay the neckline of his crimson robes. His trembling fingers failed him and he made to ring

a bell to summon his servants, then paused, thinking better
of it. "Here, child, help me with this."

I rose obediently and went to his side, undoing the
clasp easily; it is a portion of the training one undergoes
as a Servant of Naamah, removing all items of clothing
and jewelry with grace. Strung on gold wire, the pearls
slithered over my hand in a broad, sinuous band, and I
proffered them to the Doge.

"No." He shook his head, fine wisps of hair flying
below his crimson cap. "That is for you, little Contessa. A
patron's gift, is it not? See, I know something of the customs of your people. Say that your singing has pleased me,
and I would honor your Naamah. Mayhap she will look
kindly on the Beloved of Asherat-of-the-Sea." He raised
one shaking hand to caress my face. "I might honor her
differently, were I a younger man. Then again, perhaps
it is well. Asherat is a jealous goddess, and I think you a
dangerous obsession for any mortal man."

"My lord is too kind," I said a trifle wryly; I daresay the
truth of his words cut close. "Thank you."

So it was that I came to walk out of the Doge's Palace
wearing a royal ransom in pearls clasped about my neck,
and heard for the first time in that place murmuring speculation in my wake that did not die after a single comment.
It made me uncomfortable in La Serenissima as it never did
at home in Terre d'Ange.

Which is why, instead of going directly back to my
rented lodgings, I did something instead that may or may
not have been foolish, though it had no bearing on our
quest. Fortun had accompanied me that day, and I bid him
order the boatman to take us to the courtesan's quarter in
La Serenissima.

The man stared at Fortun and then at me, and questioned Fortun once, uncertain he had understood his D'Angeline-accented Caerdicci. Joscelin would never have let me do it in the first place, and Remy or Ti-Philippe would have made a bawdy jest of it. Fortun merely persisted, for which I was grateful.

Shaking his head, the boatman took us a little way down the Great Canal, then turned off into the lesser waterways. Gradually, the houses grew smaller and meaner, poor wooden constructions. If my sense of direction was any good, we were not far from where Magister Acco had lodged. Presently we glided beneath a rickety footbridge and came to a quarter where the doors of the houses were painted a bright red, and there were a good many moorings with gondoli and even a gilded bissone tied at dock.

Women in cheaply dyed attire leaned languidly on the balconies above us, calling lewdly to Fortun, promising him such pleasures as his highborn lady – which I presumed was myself – would never deliver. Several of them, noting his D'Angeline features, offered to service him for free, and one of their number, teetering on high pattens along the muddy walk bordering the canal, leered and flipped her skirts up at him, exposing herself. From within the narrow houses, we heard the sounds of shouting, laughter and drunken revelry. I thought of the ordered elegance and pride of the Thirteen Houses of the Night Court, and could have wept.

"Enough, my lady?" Fortun asked me; he looked rather ill himself. The Doge had guessed well when he guessed that the subornation of the Oracle of Asherat would perturb me. Little could he have known how much more blasphemous this spectacle would appear to D'Angeline eyes. I wondered that Prince Benedicte could have stood it as long as he did, and understood better why he secluded himself in the Little Court.

"Enough," I said firmly. Rolling his eyes, the boatman stuck his long-handled oar into the waters of the canal and turned the gondola. Like the royal scions of Elua, I fled back to the sanctuary of the familiar.

At our rented home, we found the grinning team of Ti-Philippe and Remy, who had spent the day scouting out news of the errant Phanuel Buonard, the simple Namarrese soldier on whom, it seemed, an entire conspiracy devolved. Between my visit to the Doge and the courtesans' quarter, I wanted nothing more than to soak in a long bath, but curiosity compelled me to hear out their news.

"We found him," Ti-Philippe said with satisfaction. "Took a whole day fishing on the lagoon and bribing other fishermen to talk with cheap brandy, my lady, but we landed the bastard, begging your pardon! He's wed into the Pidari, a family of glassblowers – "

"Who," Remy interrupted him, "have a cousin with no knack for the trade, that they reckoned better off casting nets than breaking bottlenecks. And when we told *him* we served a great lady who might be minded to commission an entire leaded-glass window for the Queen of Terre d'Ange herself if the Pidari were willing to show her their studios, why, he fell all over himself to make the introduction!"

Their enthusiasm was contagious, and I could not but laugh. "Well," I said, when I'd regained control of myself. "Her majesty is going to be very surprised to learn what she's committed to today. Can he take us tomorrow?"

Remy shook his head. "He's got to get their consent.

Very tight, these glassblowers; trade secrets and all. But he'll take us first thing the day after."

It was at that moment that Joscelin, a day and a half absent, chose to make his return. He stood blinking in the slanting late-afternoon sunlight of the salon, gazing around at the four of us, the maps still spread on the dining table. "What is it?" he asked, frowning. "Have you learned something?"

"You might say that," I said.

Thirty-nine

IT TOOK some time to explain the last two days' events to Joscelin, though he was quick to grasp their meaning, gazing thoughtfully at Fortun's maps and the markings thereon.

When I was done, our eyes met in that old, familiar silence.

"Percy de Somerville," he said softly.

"He sent them all to La Serenissima." I twined a lock of my hair, still damp from my bath – I'd made him wait that long to hear the news, at least – about my fingers. "But why?"

"L'Envers is clever enough to set him up," Joscelin said reluctantly. "If anyone is."

"By pinning suspicion on himself?" I shook my head. "It's a long reach."

"I know." Joscelin traced the path of a corridor on the map, not meeting my eyes. "And Ghislain? We put our lives in his hands. We put *Drustan's* life in his hands."

"I know." I sighed. "I know, I know! And Ysandre put the life of the entire realm in Percy de Somerville's hands, and he did not fail her. And yet . . . oh, Joscelin, I don't know. If I could make sense of it, it would be easier to believe. Something's missing. The pieces don't fit."

"Yes. Still." He looked soberly at me. "We need to go to Benedicte with this, Phèdre. You've done enough. He needs to know. And Ysandre. Whichever it is, whysoever they did it . . . if she's planning on making the *progressus*, she'll be leaving the nation. And unless she's given reason not to, she'll leave Barquiel L'Envers as her regent and Percy de Somerville in command of the Royal Army. Either way . . ."

"I know." I propped my chin on folded hands. "Let me talk to this Phanuel Buonard. He's the last link. If we can shed more light on this . . . This is big, Joscelin. I don't dare go to Prince Benedicte unless I'm as sure as I can be. Not with this kind of supposition."

After a moment, he gave a reluctant nod. "Buonard, and then straight to the Little Court. Whatever he tells us, even if 'tis naught. Agreed?"

"Agreed." The sound of splashing and laughter in the canal outside caught my ear, and I glanced toward the window. Joscelin rose swiftly and went to the balcony, where his appearance was greeted with jeering shouts from below.

He returned, expressionless, holding back the curtains. "Callers for you, my lady."

Twisting my damp hair into a cable over one shoulder, I passed him to enter onto the balcony and gaze down. The Immortali's bissone rocked on the canal below as Severio stood unsteadily, fellow clubsmen leaning on their oars and shouting encouragement. Water rippled and their torches cast wavering reflections across it. In the prow, gilded Asherat's slender arms tilted to and fro with the rocking of the boat, as if the goddess reached to dip her hands in the Great Canal.

"Phèdre, Phèdre, Phèdre!" Severio cried drunkenly. "You made me a promise, and four days have ignored me! Now my heart is like to break! Say you will come tomorrow for the War of the Flowers, or I swear, I will throw myself in the canal this minute and end it all!"

His voice echoed across the water, bouncing off the elegant houses. Inside windows all along the canal, I saw lamps being kindled. "My lord," I called, "you will wake the whole Sestieri. If I promise to attend, will you go home quietly?"

"For a kiss, I will!" Severio made to take a step forward and the bissone pitched wildly; I daresay he would have gone headlong into the water if a few of the Immortali hadn't caught onto the dagged hem of his doublet, dragging him back and laughing uproariously. "Phèdre, a man's heart and loins could starve on the crumbs you throw me here, where you spread a feast in Terre d'Ange! Pray, one kiss, and I'll be gone till the morrow, I swear it!"

The curtains stirred behind me and I turned to see Joscelin leaning in the shadows of the balcony door. "Do you want me to get rid of them?"

"No," I murmured. Severio and his comrades had begun to sing, loudly and off-key. On another balcony, someone shouted for them to be quiet, and I heard the unmistakable splash of a chamber pot being emptied in their direction, and threats and protests from the Immortali. Even in dim light, I could see the disgust in Joscelin eyes. "He's the best cover I have, Joscelin, and a Doge's grandson. Don't make trouble. All I need is one more day." Wordless, he went inside, and I turned back to the balcony.

"Phèdre, Phèdre, come down!" Severio called, waving his arms. This time, a chorus of shouts along the canal begged him to be silent.

I leaned over the railing. "My lord, you have my word. Now go home, lest I take it back." With that, I stepped back inside, closing the balcony doors firmly and drawing the curtains closed. The shouting lasted a few minutes longer, then dwindled into silence. I looked for Joscelin, but he was gone.

There was no reason for me to break my word on the morrow and naught to be done before we could meet with the family of Phanuel Buonard on the glassblower's isle, so I took part in the War of the Flowers – and in truth, it proved one of the more charming Serenissiman customs I witnessed. 'Tis a mock battle betwixt the sons and daughters of the Hundred Worthy Families, held in a small fortified palace that perches on one of the lesser isles, across a broad waterway from the Temple of Baal-Jupiter.

It meant I was perforce confined to the fortress with the other young women, but for once an atmosphere of such gaiety prevailed that not even I could find the company dull. We were ferried across the way to find that bushels of flowers – roses, geraniums, gladioli, love-in-a-mist, orchids and violets – provisioned the fortress, as well as eggs blown hollow and filled with scraps of bright confetti or colored flour. These, it seemed, were our armaments.

At Baal-Jupiter's temple, the young men were given the priests' blessing, and set forth in a vast armada of gondoli to storm the fortress. Like the truce-parties, all enmity was set aside; this was a courting ritual, one of the highlights of the summer. We leaned from the tower windows and watched them come, oars flashing in the sunlight, swift prows cutting the water.

When they arrived, shouting with laughter and high spirits, the gondoli swarmed the base of the tower like a shoal of dark fish and the young men in their doublets and striped hose made a riot of color within them. We leaned from the windows and pelted them with flowers, until the air was filled with a petal-storm. They returned our salvos in kind, tossing nosegays and sweets, sachets and trinkets, begging us to open the sea gate or lower a rope. Severio was there, catching my eye and pleading far more winsomely than he had last night, but it was the daughter of a member of the Consiglio Maggiore who caught a pomander and weakened first, throwing out a rope ladder such as had been provided us, tied with gay ribbons.

At that, the game shifted, and the young men in their gondoli vied for position, that they might make the daring leap to catch the rope ladder. Most fell instead, splashing into the lagoon, to be hauled out by their fellows, and any who gained the ladder became the target of the flour and confetti eggs. The Immortali had allowed Remy and Ti-Philippe to crew with them, and it was their efforts that brought Benito Dandi's gondola in reach of the ladder. Adept sailors, they grinned and held the ladder for him. Despite our best efforts – Giulia Latrigan threw an egg that burst in a profusion of blue flour and coated half his head – Benito gained the tower and claimed a kiss from the first woman he caught, which I made certain was not me.

Below, the sons of the Hundred Worthy Families – and my two chevaliers – cheered, and Benito signaled his victory from the window, before going below to open the sea gate.

Afterward, the servants and the chaperones joined us, and there was a great feast with much wine served in the courtyard of the fortress. When the dancing began, I took care to keep an eye on Remy and Ti-Philippe, who met with much admiration from the Serenissiman maidens. I did not wholly trust either of them not to find it a fine lark to win with D'Angeline charm what every unwed Serenissiman woman was supposed to retain; the Hundred Worthy Families place an absurd value on virginity. Happily, the chaperones had the same thought, and kept my chevaliers in line.

"There will be matches aplenty made today," Severio observed, standing at my side. "Phèdre, if I apologize for my behavior last night, do you think you might give an answer to my proposal?"

I raised my eyebrows at him. "How can I answer, when I've not heard your apology?"

He grinned at me and went down on one knee. "My lady Phèdre nó Delaunay de Montrève, I apologize for my appallingly rude behavior. Come here," he added, rising and taking my hand. "I want to show you something."

We left the courtyard by a side gate, and Severio led me through a small garden where a flowering hawthorn bloomed on a rise. Atop the hill, we could see over the fortress wall and across the water, where the Temple of Baal-Jupiter and its great statue stood. The sun was low, and its slanting rays picked out the thunderbolt in the striding god's hand, setting it ablaze with gold.

"It's beautiful," I said, although it gave me a chill,

knowing what I did of the blasphemy at the heart of La Serenissima.

"Not half as beautiful as you." Severio gripped my arms, a little too hard. The lowering sun was behind him, and his face in shadow. "Phèdre, you're driving me mad. Will you marry me or no?"

I could have put him off longer, I think, if I'd not been so distracted with the events of the last few days; I'd done a poor job of it and given him this opening. "Prince Severio," I said gently, seeking out his shadowed gaze. "Almost, you convince me."

"Almost," he murmured. "Almost." His hands flexed, fingers digging into my arms. "I am a soft fool for stopping at almost, and wooing with tenderness what is won by force!" His voice grated with harsh desire, and he pulled me hard against him, his mouth seeking mine.

"My lord!" I jerked my head away, glaring at him. Kushiel's gift, Kushiel's curse; I could feel my body's willingness to submit. So could he. It had been a long time, and I was no Cassiline, made to endure celibacy. Severio had broken my drought before; why not now? But I remembered the courtesan's quarter and thought, there is no honor in this in La Serenissima. Naamah has turned her face away from this place, and Kushiel does not bid it, nor Elua compel. When I spoke again, my voice was firmer than I would have thought possible. "My lord, no."

Severio Stregazza was one-quarter D'Angeline. It took a while, but it was enough. He dropped his hands and looked coldly at me. "As my lady wills. My men will see you home."

And with that, he left me in the garden, walking swiftly back to the festivities in the courtyard, where any one of a score of women would gladly accept the proposal of the grandson of the Doge, little knowing what manner of violent pleasure awaited them in the marriage bed. I, who knew it all too well, was left alone and rueful, aching with a desire that had no place in the tight-bound strictures of Serenissiman nobility.

If, if, if. If I had managed Severio better — and I should have — matters would never have come to a head between us that night. If they hadn't, I'd never have done what I did later. I returned to the courtyard, where there was much rejoicing among the daughters of the Hundred Worthy Families to see that Severio Stregazza had parted with his D'Angeline infatuation. It made me an open target for the Hundred Worthy sons, and I saw a gleam in the eyes of the Immortali, who knew what I was and had kept the secret for Severio's sake. I drank two glasses of wine rather too fast, and did not trust myself. Finding Remy, I caught his arm. "Home," I murmured. "And don't leave my side until we get there."

To his credit, he didn't.

Twilight was falling over La Serenissima when we reached our lodgings, tinting the city in violet and blue. My heart ached for the day's lost beauty and Severio's bitterness, for the pieces of my life that ever seemed to slip through my fingers. My soul shuddered at the dark day's work that lay ahead. I thanked my chevaliers and bid them good evening, retiring to my bedchamber, where I left the lamp burning and stood on the balcony, gazing into the night, until a light knock sounded at my door.

It was Joscelin, a questioning look on his face. "Phèdre? Are you all right? Remy was worried about you."

He must have been, I thought, to send Joscelin. "I'm fine. Come in." I closed the door behind him, shrugging and wrapping my arms about myself. "It's nothing. Nerves, mayhap. It was a long day."

"Severio?" Joscelin raised his eyebrows.

"It's done." I laughed wearily. "I know what you thought of him, but he wasn't so bad, truly. There's merit in him. And you know, Joscelin, sometimes it was rather pleasant to be courted for my own sake instead of for an assignation, to have someone want to spend his life with me because of what I am, and not in spite of it. No matter," I added, "what his father might have decreed in the end."

Joscelin stood silent, having only heard the first part of my words. "That's not fair," he said softly. "It's what I am as much as what you are. The problem has ever lain between the two. Phèdre . . ." He took a step toward me, one hand touching my hair; I turned to him, lifting up my face.

If, if, if. If Remy hadn't sent him . . .

Joscelin was human; not even Cassilines are made of stone. His hand slid through my hair and I felt the shudder that went through him as his fingers brushed the nape of my neck. "Phèdre, no," he murmured against my lips as I kissed him, but it was he who had lowered his head to mine. Cassiel's Servant, I should have let him go; but I was Naamah's, and wound my arms about his neck instead, kissing him. I think he would have pushed me away, if his hands hadn't betrayed him, coming hard around my waist. "Don't," he whispered into my hair.

I did.

It was ungentle, for the first time – the only time – between us. Wracked between despair and desire, Joscelin was rougher than was his wont. And I could not hide the pleasure it brought me, stifling my cries against the sculpted curve of his shoulder. It was over too soon, and too late to undo. There is a madness in love. I watched him go, gathering his clothes, averting his gaze to hide the self-loathing in his eyes. Naked by moonlight, he was beautiful, muscles gliding in a subtle shadow play beneath his pale skin, fair hair shimmering. I had to close my eyes against it and hear the rustle of him dressing.

When I opened them, I didn't mince words. "You're leaving."

"Yes." Neither did he; we never had, the two of us.

"Will you come back?"

"I don't know," Joscelin said bluntly. "Phèdre, you don't need me. This isn't Skaldia. Any one of your chevaliers can serve you better here than I have, and has. They protect you well enough. I was wrong about them. If you've not found what you sought, still, you found enough. It will be in Benedicte's hands tomorrow, and better for it. You can go home and be the toast of the City once more."

"And your vow?" I made myself ask it.

Joscelin shrugged. "I broke all my vows but one for you, my lady," he said softly. "Let us say it is you yourself who have shattered this last."

There is such a thing as a grief too immense for tears; this was almost one such. Almost. I watched him go dry-eyed, and heard the click of my bedchamber door behind him, the louder thud of the front entrance door shutting, and the sleepy murmur of a servant-lad as he roused to bar the door on his exit. Only then did his absence strike me like a blow, a terrible emptiness. So many times, like the tide, he had withdrawn only to return. This time, I felt only absence, and a sucking despair. I wept enough tears to fill a void, and though I never thought I would, fell asleep at last in the whiteness of pure exhaustion on my soaked and bitter pillow.

FORTY

"WHERE'S JOSCELIN?" It was Ti-Philippe, most blithe and careless of the three, who asked; Fortun had taken one look at my reddened eyes and remained wisely silent, and Remy, who had sent Joscelin to me, avoided my gaze.

"Gone," I said shortly. "And not likely to return." I set down the heel of jam-smeared bread I'd been toying with – I had no appetite – and turned to Fortun. "You have the map?"

"Yes, my lady." He indicated the cylindrical leather case at his side. "We are all ready," he added quietly, "and the boat is waiting. Whenever you're ready."

"Let's go." I rose abruptly from the breakfast table, leaving them scrambling in my wake. My maid Leonora stared after us, shaking her head, no doubt wondering at the strangeness of D'Angeline ways. Well, if my behavior was odd this day, she'd put it down to the falling-out with Severio. If she hadn't heard it already, she would soon enough.

The fisherman-cousin of the Pidari family, whose

name was Fiorello, was awaiting us anxiously in a little
skiff with a single set of oars and a jerry-rigged sail. He
spread burlap sacking on the seat for me as I embarked,
and set to at the oars nearly the instant we were all
aboard. Any other day, I might have laughed at the way
Phèdre's Boys fell over each other at the speed of his
departure. Any other day, I might have rejoiced as we
emerged from the canal and hoisted the modest sail to scud
across the lagoon.

Well and so, I thought, staring at the green wavelets.
Today I seek audience with a Prince of the Blood to lay
forth my suspicions of one of the foremost peers of the
realm. Mayhap it is fitting that my mood matches this day's
deeds.

Isla Vitrari is one of the largest to lie within the shelter
of the vast lagoon, and 'tis a pleasant isle. Its harbor has
a deep draw, for the merchanters dock here, carrying
glassware for trade. Fiorello Pidari cast a line to a couple of
lads ashore, jesting with them; clearly, he was known here.
The harbormaster gave him a nod and a wave as we
disembarked.

We followed our guide along a well-trodden footpath,
past studios belching smoke from the glass furnaces and
jealously guarded by young apprentices. It was Prince
Benedicte who suggested the glassworks be moved to the
island some fifteen years past, Severio once told me.
Before, they had been quartered within La Serenissima
proper, and many fires had resulted. Small wonder, I
thought, glancing within a doorway open to catch the
breeze, seeing the red glow of a furnace within and a
brawny Serenissiman craftsman at his trade. He wore a
leathern apron and his lips were wrapped round the end of

a hollow rod, his cheeks puffed out like a bellows. What he wrought, I could not say.

It was not until we drew near to the Studio Pidari that our guide grew nervous.

"No smoke," he muttered as we approached the low building. "Why isn't the furnace going? The furnace should be going."

We found out soon enough.

Tall and bald as an egg was the man who emerged from the studio, and he wiped his hands absentmindedly on the front of his jerkin, as if accustomed to wearing an apron. "Fiorello," he said sorrowfully, extending his hands to our guide. "Ah, Fiorello!" And catching sight of the rest of us, his expression changed. "You! You people have done enough," he said grimly, pointing back down the trail. "Be gone from here! We want no more of your kind!"

It was enough to stop me in my tracks and drive the grief clean out of my head. Fiorello stared uncomprehendingly and my chevaliers exchanged glances; I stepped forward.

"Master Glassblower," I said gently. "I am Phèdre nó Delaunay de Montrève of Terre d'Ange. I had an appointment to discuss a commission for my Queen. I am sorry if we have come at an ill time."

"Oh, that, aye," he said roughly. "Beg pardon, my lady, only we've had a death in the family. Ruffians, most like, or those damned Vicenti, thinking to prey on the weakest link to get us to give up the formula for our greens! Like as not it's my daughter's folly, to think her lad's mates would take vengeance on him."

Weakest link, daughter's folly, lad's mates. My heart

sank. "Your son-in-law?" I asked aloud, knowing already that it was true.

"Attacked on his way home from the harbor tavern." Master Pidari's gaze turned suspicious. "Told her she was mad, wedding one such. What do you know of him?"

"I knew him, signore." It was Ti-Philippe who stepped forward, blue eyes wide and earnest. "Though I was a member of her majesty's navy and he of her guard, we fought together on the same battlefield and drank a toast, afterward, to earth and sea. May we extend our condolences to his widow?"

"Reckon so," he said grudgingly, and turned, shouting into the studio. "Serena!"

Named for the city of her birth, there was no serenity to Phanuel Buonard's widow that day; she emerged white-faced and trembling, and I knew at once I was in the presence of a grief that dwarfed my own. A grief, I thought with horror, of which I was the likely author.

"What do you want?" Serena's voice shook. "Are you guardsmen? What do you want?"

"Guardsmen, no." Fortun spoke gently, bowing to her. "Sailors once, now in the service of my lady Phèdre nó Delaunay de Montrève. We came for trade, but stay to grieve, signora. Chevalier Philippe, he knew your husband, and spoke him well."

Her lips moved soundlessly and her eyes searched all our faces, lingering longest on mine, taking in the mark of Kushiel's Dart with a kind of awe. "You," she said wonderingly. "Phanuel spoke of you. You brought the Picti, the Painted Folk, when he fought the Skaldi. Men carried your banner. They . . . they made up songs about it. You."

"Yes," I said softly. "These men. Signora, please accept our deepest sympathy."

"Why would they do it?" Her dark, stricken eyes pleaded for an answer. "His own brethren among the guard! Why? He was afraid, he would never tell me."

Behind her, Master Pidari shook his bald head dolefully and went inside. I watched him go, thinking. "Signora," I said to her. "If it was D'Angelines who did this, I will look into it myself, I promise you. But why do you think so? Your father does not."

She gave a despairing laugh that was part gulping sob. "My father! He thinks because Phanuel has a pretty face, he is girlish and weak. But he was a soldier, my lady. Ruffians could not have defeated him so easily, nor the bully-boys of the Vicenti. It was soldiers killed him, with steel." Serena Buonard pointed to her heart. "Right here, a blade." A fierceness lit her eyes. "I will ask along the harbor, and see if someone was not bribed to let D'Angeline guardsmen ashore!"

I turned to Remy, who nodded before I even spoke. "Remy. Take Fiorello, and go. If they demand payment to speak, do it. I'll reimburse the cost."

"Thank you, my lady, thank you!" Serena clutched my hands gratefully. I felt sick. "My father thinks I am mad, but I know I am not. Why? Why would they do this?"

"Signora." I fought down my rising gorge. "Why did your husband accept a post in La Serenissima?"

"He said his commander offered him money, much money," she whispered, dropping my hands. "Money to go far away. But there was something he wanted to forget, and the Little Court was not far enough for that. So he ran to me." She lifted her chin defiantly; she was pretty, beneath her grief, in a Serenissiman fashion. "He thought Isla Vitrari was far enough," she added sadly. "But it was not."

"No," I murmured. "Signora, your husband was the first to discover a terrible deed, at the fortress of Troyes-le-Mont where the last battle against the Skaldi was fought, and I think mayhap that memory is what he fled. Did he ever speak of it to you?"

She nodded, looking into the distance. "Yes." Her voice was a faint thread of sound. "He told me, once. He thought . . . he thought the man was sleeping and jested with him, as guards will do. And then he saw blood on his tunic, and his eyes open and unmoving." Serena Buonard shook her head. "No more than that. Only dawn breaking grey in the east, and the scent of apples ripening on the morning breeze."

"Apples." I breathed the word, my heart cold in my breast. Troyes-le-Mont stood on a plain near the foothills of Camlach, scourged by the Skaldi for ten leagues in every direction.

There were no apples ripening in Troyes-le-Mont, that summer or ever.

What happened after that blurs in my memory, between the horror and guilt. I promised, extravagantly, to see justice brought to the killers of Phanuel Buonard. Pale and shocked, Fortun and Ti-Philippe seconded me. I daresay none of us believed it, before. I fumbled for my purse, untying it from my girdle and giving it whole into Serena's hands. It was heavy with gold solidi, and even through her grief, her eyes widened at it. I made promises to return at a better time regarding my Queen's commission.

All of that done, we departed, discarding solemnity for

haste the instant we were out of sight. In the harbor, Remy met us, grim-faced. Serena Buonard was right. D'Angeline guardsmen had landed last night, bribing the harbormaster's second assistant.

"They should have hidden their tracks better," I said quietly. "Fiorello, take us back."

He did, with all haste, looking rather ill himself. I had to beg coin of Fortun to pay him, having given all of mine to Serena. We paused at our rented house only long enough to don suitable court attire and because, although I did not say it, I was hoping against hope that Joscelin had returned.

He hadn't.

"My lady," Leonora said reverently, bringing me a missive on a salver. "This came while you were gone."

An apology from Severio, mayhap; I glanced at it dismissively, and saw the seal. It was the swan of House Courcel. I cracked the seal and opened the thick vellum, reading.

Better and better; Madame d'Arbos had been as good as her word. It was an invitation to an audience with Prince Benedicte and his wife, for that very afternoon. I murmured a prayer of thanks to Blessed Elua for making my way easier.

The hardest thing was what I asked my chevaliers, gathering them around. "Prince Benedicte has granted me an audience," I said, raising the letter. "Our work is half done for us. And I would fain have you all at my side, for you have earned it, and 'tis a dire thing we do. But . . ." I hesitated ". . . if any one of you is willing to stay, I would be grateful for it. If . . . if Joscelin were to return, he should know of this."

They glanced at each other, all three. I saw Fortun, steady as ever, willing to assume the burden; Remy, ridden with guilt for having sent him to me, opened his mouth. But it was Ti-Philippe who stepped forward first.

"I'll stay, my lady," he said solidly, meeting my eyes. "I'm no good for this business, after all. Better lying and gambling than telling hard truths, and better for drinking and brawling than making a leg to royalty. I'll stay, and dun Sir Cassiline's hide for abandoning you if he comes back."

"Thank you," I whispered, taking his face in both hands and planting a kiss on him. "Thank you, Philippe!"

" 'Tis naught," he muttered, blushing. "When we go after the guardsmen what did for poor Phanuel, then I want in, my lady!"

"And you shall have it," I promised. I smoothed my gown with both hands, making certain it lay properly; the apricot silk with gold brocade I had worn my first day in La Serenissima, accented now by the great collar of the Doge's pearls. "Shall we go?"

"After you, my lady." Fortun swept a bow, grave and ceremonial.

I drew a deep breath, and we set out for the Little Court to denounce a peer of the realm.

Few things I have done in my life — climbing the rafters in Waldemar Selig's steading to spy on his war plans, facing the Master of the Straits, crossing the Skaldi camp by night — have filled me with as much fear. I clung to Serena Buonard's grief as we journeyed by gondola along the Great Canal, to my faith in Fortun's analysis of the guardsmen's testimony, to the memory of a dream, of Percy de Somerville's smiling face and the cloying smell of apples. If I am wrong, I thought, Blessed Elua forgive me, but if I do not speak now, others may die.

At the gates of the Little Court, I showed my letter, keeping my countenance serene. I had alerted men of the guard once; I would not do it twice. Let Benedicte handle it, once he knew. We were admitted forthwith, and ushered into an antechamber — and there we waited. Fortun fingered the leather casing that held our maps, if the proof of our investigation should be desired. Remy gave me a quick, nervous smile. I went over the words of my presentation in my head, over and over, and did my best to repress a desperate wish that Joscelin were at my side.

If, if, if.

"Comtesse Phèdre nó Delaunay de Montrève," a steward announced, opening the doors onto the throne room.

I rose, Remy and Fortun falling in behind me, and made my entrance. It was an elegantly proportioned room, not too ostentatious, but with all the touches of D'Angeline nicety. There were joint thrones, side-by-side, one slightly smaller; it would have been appropriate, for a D'Angeline noble wedding into the cream of Serenissiman peerage. Prince Benedicte sat on his, the larger throne, with the upright carriage of one who had been a soldier. Quintilius Rousse had told me as much. He had the Courcel mien, his face lined with age, but noble still, once dark hair gone iron-grey. I had seen his brother King Ganelon before he died; I'd have put Benedicte at younger than his sixty-odd years.

"Phèdre nó Delaunay de Montrève," he said, greeting me in a rich voice. "Well met."

His D'Angeline bride stood with her back to us, handing off their infant son to a nursemaid; a charming touch, I thought. She turned to take her seat on the lesser throne, and the silver netting of Asherat's Veil flashed, clear glass beads refracting the light.

"Your Highnesses." I made a deep curtsy, and held it. Behind me, I heard my chevaliers bend their knees. I spoke without rising, glancing up under my lashes. "Your highness, Prince Benedicte, I have dire news to report. There is a treason within the very heart of Terre d'Ange, that has born seeds even within your own guard."

"Yes," Benedicte said gravely, looking down at me. "I know."

I had opened my mouth to continue; I had not expected his reply and was left on an indrawn breath. With one graceful gesture, his bride drew back the Veil of Asherat, baring her face to smile at me.

What you seek you will find in the last place you look . . .

"Hello, Phèdre," said Melisande.

FORTY-ONE

I STOOD as frozen and dumb as if the earth had dropped beneath my feet.

And I understood, too late.

I had been played from the very beginning.

On his throne, Prince Benedicte shifted, nodding toward the back of the room. Only then did I hear the sound of the door being barred, the footsteps of guards and the sliding rasp of weapons drawn; only then did I hear the soft, shocked breathing of my chevaliers behind me.

And on Melisande's beautiful face, a trace of pity.

It broke my paralysis. I spun to face Remy and Fortun, one word bursting sharply from my lips: "*Run!*"

If, if, if. If Joscelin had been with us, they might have done it, might have broken free. There were only ten guardsmen; L'Agnacites, members of the garrison of Troyes-le-Mont, their loyalty bought and paid for. He was a Cassiline, trained to fighting in close quarters, and seasoned in too many battles. They might have done it.

Or Joscelin might have died with them. I will never know.

They fought well, my chevaliers. What would have happened if they had gained the door, I cannot say. They might have escaped the Little Court alive. I like to think so. They had surprise on their side, and quick-thinking agility. But I had signed their death warrants when I brought them with me into the presence of Prince Benedicte's new bride, and I had seen it writ in her expression, his nod.

I made myself watch it. I was responsible.

My steady Fortun, who had learned my lessons all too well. He went straight for the door, using the strength of his broad shoulders to push his way through, wounded thrice over before he got close. Remy wrested a sword from one of the guards and held them off for a moment, cursing like the sailor he was. Remy, who had first raised the standard of Phèdre's Boys, that dart-crossed circle of scarlet, on the road to Dobria.

I watched him die, born down by sheer numbers. He had sung marching-chants on the road, the ones I despaired of quelling. He had sung along the canals of La Serenissima in my service. The treacherous steel of Prince Benedicte's guardsmen silenced him for good.

They took Fortun from behind, a dagger low to the kidneys. His outstretched hand left a long smear of blood on the gilded woodwork of the throne room door. He still had the map of Troyes-le-Mont slung across his back in its carrying case, a fool's scabbard. I saw his mouth form a circle of pain as he fell slowly to his knees; they had to stab him again, to the heart. Then his face went peaceful, and the light died in his eyes as he slumped to the marble floor.

Fortun, who had chosen to serve me long before the

others, for carrying water to the wounded and dying on the battlefield of Bryn Gorrydum, for the stunned look on my face when I took Quintilius Rousse's sword and dubbed him chevalier.

He had a good-luck name, Fortun did.

Now I knew the emptiness of perfect and utter despair.

All sounds of fighting had ceased, replaced by the mundane clatter of the guards assessing their wounds and laying out the bodies for disposal, muttering of arrangements and cover stories. No joy in it; at least they did not relish their work. One straightened, gazing in my direction, nudging his fellow and fumbling for a pair of manacles hanging at his belt. I turned back to my sovereign lords, the Prince of the Blood and his deadly bride, seated side by side like a pair of Menekhetan effigies on their thrones.

I didn't bother with him; only her.

"Why not just kill me?" I asked simply.

Melisande shook her head slowly, a look of gentle sorrow on her immaculately lovely face. "I can't," she said, almost kindly. "It isn't just the waste, my dear, of something irreplaceable. The punishment for causing the death of Kushiel's chosen is a thousand years of torment." She paused, reflective. "So they say in Kusheth, for the other scions of Elua and his Companions. For one of Kushiel's line, ten thousand years."

With a murmured apology, the guard with the manacles approached me. I put out my arms unasked, feeling cuffs of cold steel lock about my wrists. "And for treason?"

"Elua cared naught for mortal politics, nor did Kushiel." Melisande shook her head, the wealth of her blue-black hair caught modestly in a silver mesh caul. "We played a game, Phèdre," she said softly. "You lost."

"You set me up," I whispered in answer. "From the very beginning."

"Not really." She smiled. "You got too close. If you'd not played so well . . ." she nodded to my fallen chevaliers, bodies neatly wrapped in cloaks, " . . . they might have lived."

There were tears in my eyes; I blinked them away absently, half-forgetting what they meant, and turned to Prince Benedicte. The chain betwixt my manacled wrists hung slack against the brocaded apricot silk of my gown. "My lord, *why?*"

"Elua's bloodline was not meant to be sold for political gain," Benedicte said calmly. "Not to La Serenissima, as my brother Ganelon condemned me. And not to Alba, as my grandniece Ysandre has sold herself. No." He looked sternly at me. "Terre d'Ange requires an heir of pure D'Angeline blood. I have done only what is necessary."

I would have laughed, if I could have stopped weeping. "With the woman who would have given us to the Skaldi?" I asked, gasping. "My lord, could you not have chosen wiser?"

"With the woman," Prince Benedicte replied shortly, "who could give the Royal Army into my hand." He rose from his throne, averting his gaze from my slain chevaliers, and gave a crisp nod to Melisande. "It is done, as you wished. I leave her to you."

He left the throne room through a rear entrance, two of his guard falling in behind him. I gazed at Melisande. "You gave him Percy de Somerville. How?"

"Ah, well." Her expression was unreadable. "Lord Percy had the same sentiments, you see. He was willing to lend the army's support to Baudoin de Trevalion's bid for the throne. Unfortunately, he was rash enough to say as much in writing to Lyonette de Trevalion, the Lioness of Azzalle. It seems he was passing fond of her, Percy was."

"And you have the letter." I nodded; it all made sense, now. Lyonette de Trevalion's secrets had not all died with her, nor been buried in the folio of her trial in the Royal Archives; the folio in which so many peers of the realm showed interest.

"Yes," Melisande said thoughtfully. "I thought it might be useful."

There wasn't much else to say. I gestured with my manacled hands. "And what am I charged with?" I inquired. "Officially?"

"Officially?" Melisande raised her graceful brows. "There will be no official inquiry, I think. Your falling-out with Severio Stregazza was duly noted; no one will question your disappearance from La Serenissima. But should it be necessary to comment, there is the small matter of your efforts to betray D'Angeline trade status with Alba. And you poisoned the former astrologer to the Doge, Phèdre. One Magister Acco, I believe. There were witnesses, should anyone inquire. A pity your men resisted questioning. Doubtless the others will do the same when we find them. Even your Cassiline." Restoring her veil, she clapped her hands together, summoning the remaining guards. "We are done here. Take her to La Dolorosa."

And they did. Oh, they did.

I went obediently, stumbling and numb. It is a long journey. They placed a hood of rough-spun material over my head and took me by ship the full length of the broad lagoon, making landfall at the far southern end. Once we were on dry land, they plucked the hood from my head; I did not care either way, having welcomed the oblivion of darkness.

Here the mainland had been left untended and wild. There were servants with horses waiting; Benedicte's guards helped me to mount, avoiding my eyes. Someone else led my gelding as we wended along the coastline, a narrow and forested trail.

Melisande, I thought, over and over again. Melisande. Prince Benedicte's bride.

Through the trees, I glimpsed it: The black isle. It reared up, craggy and defiant in the gloaming, separated from the shore by an expanse of churning water. Between La Dolorosa and the mainland, only the swaying bridge, a vast length of crude planks and rope, hung suspended in midair.

There was a watchtower on the mainland, sparsely manned. My guards were halted and questioned; there was a sign, a countersign. They gave it in assured tones, and I saw from the uppermost window of the watchtower a cunningly wrought signal of torches and a mirror, flashing approval to the island. From the hulking mass of the fortress, looming atop the seaside cliff, flashed an answering response, cutting through the falling dusk.

We dismounted, and two of the guards took my arms, leading me onto the bridge. I went unprotesting.

I daresay it would have terrified me, had I not been beyond the reach of fear. With the full use of their arms my guards held me lightly, clinging to the hempen guidelines with their outer hands. I walked between them, manacled and untouchable, while open air gaped between the swaying planks and far, far below, the angry sea boiled and surged. Let it have me, I thought, what did I care? I had failed. My lord Delaunay had seen fit to train us with a tumbler's skills — I have used them, once or twice in my lifetime. Let is not be said that I shamed him in the end, at least. I walked steady and graceful on that dreadful bridge, going toward my doom as if it were my final patron.

Some fifteen paces from the far end of the bridge, a pair of sentries carrying hand-axes barred the way to challenge us, blades poised over the ropes that anchored the bridge to pilings. I understood, then, why La Dolorosa need be but lightly garrisoned. Two strokes of their axes, and the bridge would be severed, sending us plunging into the roiling waters and the jagged rocks below. A sign, another countersign, different this time; my guards gave it in gasping voices and the sentries stepped aside.

It had grown dark as we crossed the bridge. One of the sentries fetched a torch from the guard hut beside the bridge and led us up the steep, rocky path to the fortress. Waves boomed and roared as they struck the rocks at the base of the isle, receding with a sound like a moan. I thought I felt the very stone beneath my feet shiver.

The walls of the fortress were thick blocks of granite, windowless save for the towers. Inside, the sound of the angry sea was muffled. I stood in an unadorned room, attended by my guards while the warden was fetched, and stared blankly at the walls, wondering where the rock had been quarried and how they'd gotten it onto the isle. It is strange, what grief does to one's mind.

The warden appeared with a pair of prison guards in tow, wiping his mouth; they'd fetched him from the dinner table. He was Serenissiman, in his late forties, with a grim face. He startled a little at seeing me, recovering quickly. "This is the one?"

"It is," one of my guards affirmed. Lifting a cord from about his neck, he produced a key and unlocked the manacles clamped about my wrists, careful not to meet my gaze.

"Garment," the warden said briefly. The slighter of the two prison guards darted forward grinning, shoving a bundle of grey wool into my unprotesting arms. He was cock-eyed, rapid gaze sliding this way and that, and I wondered if he had all his wits. "Put it on," the warden said to me. "Everything else, you leave."

I stood for a moment, puzzled. The warden waited implacably.

He meant now.

Well, I thought, I am D'Angeline, and Naamah's Servant. They will do as they will to me in this place, but I will not cringe with shame for their satisfaction. I unclasped the Doge's great collar of pearls from about my neck, handing it coolly to the warden, then turned to the wall and began undoing the buttons of my gown. I stepped out of my court slippers and slid the gown from my shoulders. It slipped to the floor to pool around my ankles, folds of apricot silk stiff with gold brocade, leaving me bare.

"Elua!" one of Benedicte's guards muttered, swallowing audibly.

Ignoring him, I unfolded the grey woolen dress and drew it over my head, only then turning to face them. With great care, I removed the gold filigree earrings I wore and unfastened the net of gold mesh from my hair.

"Here." I placed them in the warden's hand. "That is everything."

"Good." He nodded curtly to the prison guards. "Take her to her cell."

FORTY-TWO

MY CELL was a stony chamber only seven paces square.

It held a pallet of straw ticking, a low wooden stool and two buckets; one containing water and one empty, serving as a chamber pot. The door, set in a shallow egress, was brass-bound oak. There was a narrow window high on the opposite wall, barred with iron.

I thought it a kindness at first.

The dungeon of La Dolorosa lies below the fortress, a scant dozen prison cells. We passed along a corridor, and I felt the vast weight of the fortress pressing on me from above, a tremendous sense of mass and confinement. Faint sounds were audible through some few of the oaken doors; scratching and weeping, and from one, a rhythmic, ceaseless wailing. I tried not to think about why. All the cells were aligned along the cliff side of the fortress and those narrow windows, set an inch or two above ground level, looked out onto the grieving sea.

Each one has a window; I know that, now. Air and light, I thought, catching a glimpse by lantern when the prison guards brought me. Then they left, taking the lantern and locking the heavy door, leaving me in un-relieved blackness.

And I heard the sound.

It was the one I'd heard outside, the crashing sea, the sucking moan as the waves withdrew, over and over again, relentless. And in the swirling winds, a remorseless wail of sorrow. Outside, it was formidable.

Inside, it was maddening. I knew, then, why there were no windows in the fortress save those necessary for defense. La Dolorosa, the isle of sorrows, wrought by Asherat's grief for her slain son. I knew why the sailors whistled, passing it. I knew why the prisoners wept and wailed, hearing it endlessly, day in and out.

Mortals are not meant to bear the mourning of deities.

Sight-blinded and sea-deafened, I knelt on the flagstone floor of my cell and groped my way toward the pallet. The woolen dress, too long, dragged behind me. Gaining the pallet, I curled into a ball, pressing my hands over my ears.

There I lay until the grey light of dawn seeped through the narrow window to find me, shuddering and sleepless.

So began the pattern of my time in La Dolorosa. By day, the sound was easier to bear. I could stand tiptoe on the wooden stool, clutching the bars and peering out the window to see that 'twas the sea, only the sea and wind that crashed and moaned so dolefully. By night, it took on the awful tone of endless, immortal grief that seemed to vibrate the very stone, penetrating my bones, forcing me to cover my ears and whimper until morning came.

Twice a day, a guard brought food, varying in quality and quantity alike. Sometimes it was nothing more than cold porridge or a mess of lentils; sometimes bread and hard sausage, and sometimes fish broth or a slab of mutton. Once, a plate of stewed greens. At first I did not eat, having resolved to die before I went mad in that place. If I could do naught else, at least I could do that much, laying my death at Melisande's feet.

It gave me a certain grim satisfaction to contemplate as I grew weaker. Kushiel had made a poor choice of me, but his dart would have one last cast against this too-gifted scion of his line. Melisande might sit the throne of Terre d'Ange after all, but she would live out her days in fear of their end. No passage for her to the true Terre d'Ange-that-lies-beyond, land of Elua and his Companions, but ten thousand years of torment, if Kusheline lore held true.

So I thought, until the warden came to my cell.

He brought with him the largest of the prison guards, a hulking Serenissiman who was simple-minded and obedient – Tito, he was called. They came inside, closing the door behind them. Tito carried a steaming bowl and I could smell fish broth above the noisome odor of the too-seldom-emptied chamber pot.

"Tito," the warden said flatly. "Hold her and clamp her nose."

With a look that might have been sympathetic on his broad, homely face, the giant set down his bowl and knelt beside my pallet, from which I was too weak to rise. The warden dragged the stool over and sat down as Tito placed one massive hand on my chest and pinned me. With the other hand, he pinched my nostrils closed.

It went as one might expect, although I daresay I fought it harder than they anticipated. In the end, it was my body that betrayed me, gasping for air when I willed only death. The warden forced a tin ladle between my teeth, pouring broth into my mouth. Choking on it, I swallowed some, inhaling a good deal as well. Tito eased me to a sitting position as I coughed and gagged, a red haze swimming before my eyes and the blood beating in my ears so hard it drowned out the eternal wail of Asherat's sea, beating dire and hard, buffeting me like bronze-edged wings.

Well and so, I thought, hopelessly. It seems I am to live.

"My orders are to keep you alive." The warden's tone was as grey and obdurate as the fortress walls. He was well chosen for his job. "This will be done as many times as is needful, for as many days. Will you eat?"

"Yes," I said faintly.

The warden handed the bowl and ladle to Tito and departed. Cradling the bowl in one arm, the giant shifted me as carefully as a child with a new doll so I might sit propped against the wall. I coughed, my lungs burning from the broth I'd inhaled. He waited patiently until I was done, then held out the bowl in both hands.

It was the only kindness anyone had done me. "Thank you," I said gently, taking the bowl from him. In slow, painful sips, I drank the remainder of the broth, giving back the empty bowl when I had finished.

I was young, and Kushiel's chosen; I regained strength quickly. As death receded from my grasp and the profound shock of horror and betrayal lessened, my wits began to function once more and I came slowly to acknowledge my situation.

If Tito was the best of the guards, despite his fearsome appearance, Malvio and Fabron were the worst. Malvio was the cock-eyed guard I had seen on my arrival, and he spoke seldom, but grinned all the while, his slippery gaze wandering all over me when it was his turn to bring food, waiting to ensure I ate. At first, he did nothing save look. On his third visit, he reached inside his breeches, fondling himself and grinning. And on the next, he loosened the drawstring of his breeches, drawing out his erect phallus, dark and engorged with blood, and showing it to me. I looked away as he stroked himself to a climax, knowing he was grinning. When he was done, he tucked himself away, waiting calmly for me to eat and hand him my empty plate.

And I did, fearing if the warden came again, it would be Malvio he brought.

Fabron, by contrast, spoke volumes, moving close enough so I could smell his breath as he told me in lewd detail exactly what and where and how he would do to me the many things that he thought about doing to me. While he was not particularly inventive, he never tired of describing the acts in which he would engage me.

"What would it be worth to you?" I asked him once, tilting my head back to gaze at him. "My freedom? For that, I would do all you ask, and more."

At that, he blustered, then turned pale and fled, grabbing my half-eaten supper tray.

If I were a heroine in a romantic epic, no doubt, it would have been different; I'd have lured him with flirtation and subtle half-promises, duping him into aiding me in escaping. Alas, in reality, not even lowly prison guards are stupid enough to risk certain discovery for the promise of lascivious pleasure. In truth, there was nothing alluring about my plight. It was high summer and the heat was oppressive, rendering the stench of an unemptied chamber pot nigh unbearable. The coarse woolen dress itched like fury and grew rank with sweat, dragging hem and trailing sleeves growing frayed and filthy. I took it off when I dared, scrambling to don it when I heard a key turn in the lock.

It stank, I stank and my cell stank. Nights brought utter blackness and reduced the world to the crash and moan of Asherat's awful grief. Days brought tedium and misery that made madness seem almost welcome.

Such was my existence.

It was some weeks later when Tito entered my cell with arms laden. I watched curiously as he set down a brimming bucket of fresh water and a bundle of cloth. Reaching into his pockets, he drew forth two hard-boiled eggs and an apple, a rare feast. "Eat," he said, handing them to me, and then, procuring somewhat from another pocket, "Wash."

It was a worn ball of soap, smelling harshly of lye, and I daresay I have never accepted a patron-gift with as much grateful reverence as I did that lint-stippled ball. Tito averted his head and picked up my chamber bucket with one hand, holding it carefully away from him as he left my cell.

Ignoring the food, I stripped off my loathsome dress and knelt on the floor before the bucket of water. The soap was gritty and produced little lather. It stung as I scrubbed myself assiduously. It felt wonderful. I washed even my hair when I had scrubbed every inch of skin, bending over the bucket to dunk my entire head. The water was none too clean by then, but I didn't care; 'twas cleaner than I. When I had done, I investigated the cloth bundle and found it was a clean dress, of the same crude-spun grey wool.

Tito returned with the chamber bucket well scoured, and another smaller bucket of fresh drinking water. I sat curled on my pallet and finished my apple, reveling in the luxury of being clean for the first time in weeks.

"Thank you," I said as he gathered up the discarded dress, the scrap of soap, the eggshells. "For all of this." To my surprise, he gave me a look of grave misgiving, shaking his massive head and departing.

It wasn't long until I learned why.

Wearing my clean dress, I was standing on the stool at the window, working one hand through the iron bars to toss crumbs from a heel of bread I'd saved to the gulls that skirled around the isle. All it took was one to discover it for half a dozen to descend, squalling and fighting with raucous cries on the ground outside my window, fierce beaks stabbing. It was somewhat unnerving, viewed at eye level, but it relieved my tedium and their squabbling drowned out the sound of the sea.

It also hid the sound of my door unlocking.

"Phèdre, what on earth are you doing?"

It was Melisande's voice, rich and amused, sounding for all the world as though she'd encountered me in the City or at court, and not imprisoned half-underground in a forsaken dungeon by her own decree. My heart gave a jolt. Pulse racing, I turned slowly to face her.

In the dim grey light of my cell, Melisande shone like a jewel. No veil concealed her features, her flawless ivory skin, generous mouth and her eyes, her eyes that were the deep blue of sapphires. Her hair hung loose as I remembered it, rippling in blue-black waves. Her beauty was dizzying.

"Feeding the gulls," I replied foolishly.

Melisande smiled. "And will you make one your especial pet, and train him to carry messages, warning Ysandre and saving the nation?"

I stayed where I was, standing on my stool, back to the window. Whether it looked ridiculous or no, it gave me the advantage of height and kept me as far from her as possible. "You have won," I said in an even tone. "Do me the courtesy of not mocking me further, my lady. What do you want?"

"To see you," Melisande said calmly. "To offer you a choice. You have seen, I think, what your future holds; squalor, boredom and madness. And that is the least of it. While I remain in La Serenissima, you are protected, Phèdre. The warden is ordered to see you come to no harm and his guards do not molest you. When I am gone . . ." she shrugged, " . . . it will be worse."

I thought of Malvio's darting eyes and felt sick. "When you are gone," I echoed, repressing my rising gorge. "And when will that be? Autumn, mayhap, when Ysandre leaves the royal army in the hands of Percy de Somerville and makes the *progressus*, riding into a Serenissiman trap?" Melisande didn't answer, and I laughed hollowly. "You were condemned as a traitor, my lady. Do you think the D'Angeline people will forget so easily?"

"People believe what they are told." Her expression remained serene. " 'Twas your word condemned me. Already, Ysandre has disavowed you, through your own cleverness. If you are found traitor as well for conspiring against D'Angeline trade interests, few will doubt it when they are told you lied."

"I didn't conspire against D'Angeline trade interests."

"No?" Melisande raised her brows. "But Marco Stregazza will swear you did."

"Ah." I glanced out the window at the churning grey sea beyond the cliff's verge. "And did he suborn the corruption of Asherat's Oracle as well? I have endured her grief for many days now. I would not like to face her wrath."

"No." Her tone was complacent. "He wouldn't have dared; that was Marie-Celeste's idea. I am not fool enough to mock Asherat-of-the-Sea. Her temple gave me sanctuary, and I am grateful for it. If her means suit my ends, so much the better, but I do not risk blasphemy. No D'Angeline would, nor true Serenissiman. Marie-Celeste straddles two worlds, and fears answering to the gods of neither," she added. "You do not sound surprised."

"I have had some time to think, my lady," I said dryly, looking back at her. "What choice is this you offer?"

"For now, your choice of prisons. This one . . ." Melisande gestured at the stone walls, the straw pallet and empty bucket, ". . . or mine." The words hung in the air between us, and she smiled slightly. "You would make a good traitor, Phèdre. But you would make an exquisite penitent on my behalf."

I stood balanced on my stool, curiously light-headed. "And what do you propose to do, my lady?" I asked, hearing my own voice strange and unfamiliar, as blithe as hers had been when she teased me about the gulls. "Break me to your will like a fractious colt?"

Melisande smiled gently. "Yes."

I swallowed and looked away.

Too close and too small, this cell of mine, to contain the both of us. The vast wide world was too small. It is a weakness, Kushiel's Dart. The scarlet mote that marked my eye was but a manifestation of the true flaw within, the wound that penetrated to the marrow of my soul. What Melisande offered; Elua, the promise was sweet to me! To struggle no more against my very nature but surrender to it wholeheartedly, offering it up with both hands to the one person, the only person, who had always, always known the true essence of what I was.

As I knew hers.

Melisande wanted something of me.

Heart and mind raced alike, as I stood trembling before her. My hand rose unthinking to seek out the bare hollow at my throat where her diamond had hung for so long, the leash she had set upon me to see how far I would run. "Joscelin," I whispered. "You can't find him."

Her eyelids flickered, ever so slightly.

I laughed aloud, having nothing to lose. "And Ti-Philippe? Don't tell me! What makes you think I would know where to find them, my lady? Joscelin Verreuil left me, for committing the dire crime of seducing him. If Philippe evaded your guardsmen . . . how can I guess? Marco's men would do better than I, if Benedicte can't find him."

"He jumped into the canal, actually." Melisande's voice was surprisingly even. "From the balcony. It seems Rousse's sailor-lads swim like fish. Marco is of the mind that he's dying of the ague, if he yet lives. The canals are known for pestilence. La Serenissima is well-cordoned, they'll not leave it by water or land, nor send word either. Even if they did, they know too little to undo our plans. Still, too little is too much. But we will speak more of this later." She came close, too close, smiling, and reached up to lay one hand against my cheek. "Think on my offer."

Her touch was cool, and yet it burned me like fire. I closed my eyes, shaking like a leaf in a storm. I could smell her scent, a faint musk overlaid with spices. I wanted to fall to my knees, wanted to turn my head, taking her fingers into my mouth.

I didn't.

"Think on it," Melisande repeated, withdrawing her touch. "I'll be back."

FORTY-THREE

AN OFFER.
A dangerous offer.

After Melisande had left, I sat huddled on my pallet, arms wrapped around my knees, thinking. It had been different, before. There is a certain calmness in despair. Now even that luxury had been torn away from me.

I had to think.

Joscelin and Ti-Philippe, alive! They were in the Yeshuite quarter, I was sure of it. It was the one place neither Benedicte nor the Stregazza would think to look; it was the first place Joscelin would have gone. And if Ti-Philippe had escaped, if he was clever and able enough, it was where he would look. I gave thanks to Elua, now, that my chevaliers had been suspicious enough to follow Joscelin during his disappearances.

They knew enough, the two of them, to lay charges against Percy de Somerville – although they had no proof. It was what they didn't know that could kill them. Prince Benedicte . . . Benedicte and Melisande. Still, I thought,

Ti-Philippe was smart enough to run, when he saw Benedicte's guards.

Percy de Somerville's guards, whom we all thought Prince Benedicte took into his service all unwitting.

He knew Remy, Fortun and I left for the Little Court, never to be seen again.

But he would not know why, and a great many "accidents" could have befallen us between home and palace. I mulled the problem over and over in my mind, and came inevitably to the same conclusion. The scope of it was simply too vast, too hard to encompass. Neither Ti-Philippe nor Joscelin would guess Benedicte's treason.

What you seek you will find in the last place you look . . .

I hadn't thought it; nor would they. The best I could hope for was that my disappearance and the traitorous guardsmen would make them wary, wary enough to avoid the Little Court and go straight to Ysandre.

If they lived. If Ti-Philippe wasn't lying on a cot somewhere sweating out his last ounce of life with some dreadful canal-bred pestilence. If Joscelin wasn't halfway to the northern steppes, chasing some arcane Yeshuite prophecy.

And if they could reach the Queen, which Melisande, who brooked few illusions, believed impossible.

If, if, if.

It is a dire thing, to hope against hope.

I did not doubt the veracity of Melisande's claims. It is a truism; history is written by the victors. With the solid support of Duc Percy de Somerville and Prince Benedicte de la Courcel behind her, her reputation would be restored, nearly spotless. There would be protest from a few, silenced swiftly. A few might rebel; not many, I thought. I had not forgotten the murmurs among the nobility when Drustan mab Necthana rode into the City of Elua.

Many, too many, would be glad to be shed of a Pictish Prince-Consort, whose bloodline would taint the heirs of House Courcel. None of that for Benedicte, still Ysandre's heir. No, his Serenissiman-born children would inherit here. For Terre d'Ange, a true-born son, gotten on his D'Angeline wife.

Melisande's son.

And as for Ysandre de la Courcel, I thought, she would become a tragic footnote in D'Angeline history. Slain, no doubt, during some Serenissiman intrigue gone deadly awry. What Melisande had planned, I did not know, but I could guess well enough that no trace of it led back to her, nor to Benedicte.

Who would stand against her, then, with Benedicte at her side?

There was Quintilius Rousse — and him, I could not guess. Would he swallow it or no? He would never believe me a traitor, I thought, nor Melisande innocent. And yet, he knew Benedicte of old, and Percy de Somerville, too. What could the Royal Admiral do, if the army held the land? Little enough, it might be; especially if the Serenissiman navy stood in support of Benedicte's claim. And if Marco Stregazza were elected Doge, I'd no doubt that would follow. Quintilius Rousse was canny and a survivor. He might back Benedicte's claim, if he felt he had no other choice.

There was Barquiel L'Envers.

And he, I thought ruefully, was the key. The Duc L'Envers, whom I had thought my enemy. He was the reason Benedicte dared not act without the support of the

Royal Army. As Ysandre's maternal uncle, he stood the nearest challenger to the throne, with ties by marriage to Aragonia, to Alba, to Khebbel-im-Akkad. All of whom might rally to L'Envers' cause if there was a whiff of suspicion concerning Ysandre's death. Drustan would, I was sure of it; nor had I forgotten the company of Aragonian spearmen which had fought beside us against the Skaldi, and the deadly Akkadian cavalry.

They would need to act quickly, Benedicte, Melisande and de Somerville, to secure the throne and dispose of Barquiel L'Envers.

I am a fool, I thought, to have believed so easily. All is not lost until the game is played out in full, and it is not, not yet. It is a bitter hand Melisande has dealt me, but there are some cards still unplayed.

So I mused and thought, until the light began to fail in my stifling chamber and one of the guards brought my evening meal. Constantin, he was called, silent and grey. As the prison guards went, I liked him well enough, for he troubled me not.

"Constantin," I said to him when I returned my empty tray. "Will you carry a message to the warden for me?"

He shifted the tray in his arms and looked stolidly at me. "I will carry it. I do not promise he will hear."

"I understand," I said gravely. "Pray tell him I seek an audience with him."

"I will do that."

No more did he say, and with that, I had to be content. Falling night leached the last of the light from my cell. I sat on my pallet and watched the afterglow fade through my narrow window, blue twilight turning to grey and thence to star-pricked black. As vision failed, the endless moan of

Asherat's grief filled my senses. Awake, I listened, picking out the sounds of my prison mates amid the cacophony. I had named them all, in the endless nights. The Wailer, whose ululating cries rose and fell without ceasing. The Scratcher, who made sounds like a small animal trying to tunnel through solid rock. The Snarler, who had wits left to curse his fate. The Banger . . . I did not like to think what the Banger did, producing dull muffled thuds that punctuated the howling night. There were others, mayhap seven or eight. It was hard to tell, even to my trained ear. I was not sure but that the Pleader and the Screamer were not the same person. I never heard them at the same time, but I was not certain if it were one prisoner alternating between begging despair and wild rage, or merely the orchestrations of madness.

When I am gone . . . it will be worse.

It would get worse. It would get a great deal worse. I did not yet cry out in the night, but only woke whimpering from a fitful sleep. When my dreams were full of naught but Malvio's slippery, grinning gaze, Fabron's lewd whisper in my ear . . . ah, Elua!

It would get much, much worse.

If Joscelin and Ti-Philippe lived, if they stood a chance, it would be worth it.

Because I did not think I could withstand Melisande for very long.

If.

I fell asleep at last, exhausted by the torments of my mind. Morning came and wore on late; at length, a guard came with food. It was Tito, his gaze sympathetic in his broad, homely face. I asked him if the warden would see me today, and he shrugged, shaking his head. He did not know. I thanked him anyway, and ate my morning meal. A slab of cold porridge, but drizzled with honey. Tito watched hulking to see if I liked it.

"From you?" I asked.

He nodded and beamed like a child. "The beekeepers' tribute came. I had a piece this big." With massive hands held apart, he indicated the size of the honeycomb. "I saved some for you."

Despite it all, I smiled. "Thank you, Tito. It's very good."

There is no rock on which the mortal soul may founder but that contains some frail tendril of human kindness struggling to grow; this much I have found to be true. Is it a weakness in me that I sought ever to reward it? I cannot say, only that I would do the same, though Tito's simple-minded fondness proved blessing and curse alike, in the end. So I think now; then, I merely watched him carefully swipe the last telltale traces of honey from the platter and suck his fingers, at once grateful and sorrowing that this was what kindness had come to in my life.

The warden did not come that day, nor the next. I paced my stifling cell, sweating and irritable. Each time I heard a key in the lock, my heart raced with fear that it would be Melisande, come for my reply. Fear and dread bound in an awful knot of complex desire that left my mouth dry and my pulse pounding in my veins.

On the third day, the warden came.

I heard the key, this time, too soon to be a guard come with the evening meal. Quickly, with trembling fingers, I bound my hair at my nape with the loose knot we called lover's-haste in the Night Court, that will stay without pins or a caul. Gathering myself into a semblance of dignity, I stood to receive my guest, smoothing the grey dress.

When the warden entered, accompanied by Fabron, I inclined my head, according him the greeting among equals we use at court. He made no response, but only said in his colorless voice, "You asked to see me."

"Yes, my lord warden." I took a breath; I had not expected him to soften. "My lord, I wish to beg of you a boon. I wish to send a letter, no more." I paused, and he said naught. "I will not insult you by protesting my innocence, my lord," I continued. "I daresay you hear it often enough, and 'tis not your place to judge, but only to enforce. I ask only the chance to notify my Queen of my fate. As she is my sovereign, she has the right to know; no less would we accord to any foreign national in Terre d'Ange. And you may believe me," I added, "when I tell you that Ysandre de la Courcel would pay dearly for this knowledge." His expression did not change. I took a step forward. "Aught you might ask, my lord," I said steadily. "I will set it in writing, and bind her by the sacred words of House L'Envers, her mother's line, that not even the Queen herself may refuse."

And I could, too, for I now knew that Nicola L'Envers y Aragon had not played me false, but given a weapon of great power into my hands. She was right, Barquiel L'Envers and I had been stupidly blinded by our suspicions, and the throne would be lost because of it. Like squabbling children in a barn, we had ignored the open door through which the wolf might saunter.

It doesn't matter what you believe. Just remember it.
I did.

The warden stirred. Over his left shoulder, Fabron

mouthed something obscene at me, miming a wet-lipped kiss. I ignored him, concentrating on the warden.

Who said, flatly, "No."

I stared, uncomprehending, and waited for more while my heart sunk like a stone in my breast. When it was not forthcoming, I fought the ludicrous urge to laugh and said instead, "My lord, may I ask why?"

His words were measured out like the slow drip of water falling in a cave. "This is La Dolorosa and I am its warden. No more and no less. Asherat has sent you, and I will ward you until she claims you."

"Asherat!" The word burst from my lips. "My lord, Asherat's very Oracle has been subverted in the conspiracy that sent me here! Ask, if you do not believe, ask in the great temple in the Square, and see if Her prophet's place was not usurped for a day! Ask the Doge himself, the Beloved of Asherat, how Her priestesses have dealt with him! I tell you, thrones hang upon this letter, and the very sanctity of your beliefs!"

I was raving; I knew I was raving. And worse, I could not seem to stop. As the torrent of my voice continued, I saw the warden nod once to Fabron, who came forward to grip my arms, driving me backward. He maneuvered his body close to mine, licking his lips.

It was not easy, but I regained control of myself and shook him off. Melisande's bond of protection held; he let go of me ostentatiously, raising both hands in the air.

"Elua grant you may regret this, my lord," I said quietly to the warden.

"You may pray so, if you wish." No more than that did he say, but opened the door to my cell, beckoning Fabron ahead of him and exiting after. The door closed and locked, leaving me alone once more.

One hope, gone.

It left only Joscelin and Ti-Philippe . . . or Melisande.

I did not much like my chances either way.

FORTY-FOUR

MELISANDE DID not come without warning.

I knew, the next time a guard brought a wash bucket and soap, what it meant. I took no pleasure in it this time, only a certain bitter amusement. It would not do for the Princess-Consort of Benedicte de la Courcel to find me unwashed and unkempt in a foul and reeking cell, of course. No, Melisande would order me bathed, like some battle-chieftain with a choice captive of war.

I did it, though I was tempted to defiance. But having already been forcibly fed, I had no wish to repeat the experience with a scrubbing, and something in the guard's expression — he was a new one, whose name I did not know — suggested that it was likely. When I had done, I donned the clean dress he'd brought and sat cross-legged on my pallet to wait.

I did not have overlong.

This time, I did not flinch, nor retreat. I remained as I was, while Melisande's presence filled the cell like a candleflame or a song. I was proud of that small act of will. If she had brought me low, well then, that was the territory

I would claim for my own. Let her stoop, if she wished to reach me.

So I thought; being Melisande, of course, she did not, but merely looked down at me, gauging to a nicety what I did, and why. A faint smile hovered at the corner of her mouth. I had no tricks she did not know. What my lord Delaunay had taught me, he taught her, too, long ago. And in turn, she taught him to use people.

As he had used me.

"Have you decided?" Melisande inquired.

I tilted my head back against the stone walls of my cell. "What would you do with me?"

Another might have mistaken my meaning; Melisande didn't. "There is a dungeon in the Little Court. You would be held there until . . . matters in La Serenissima were resolved. Or mayhap longer. It depends on you." She glanced mildly around my cell. "It is a good deal more pleasant than this, being built for the enjoyment of Kusheline guests. Light, you will have, and comforts; decent clothing, food, a proper bath. Texts, if you wish; the library is good. Is it less secure for it, you wonder? No." She shook her head. "Not by much."

"By some."

"Yes," Melisande said thoughtfully. "Some."

"There is the chance that I might play you false and win your trust."

"Yes." A glimmer of amusement lit her glorious eyes. "There is that, too. Although I daresay if you thought it likely, you'd not say it aloud."

Since it was true, I didn't bother to answer, asking instead, "Why risk it at all? All that you have striven for lies within your reach. Is it worth jeopardizing, no matter how slight the risk, merely to toy with me? I don't believe it, my lady, and I mistrust this offer of yours."

"Do you?" Melisande walked to gaze through the barred window at the distant horizon, filtered daylight rendering her lovely features serene. "The game of thrones is a mortal one, my dear. Even if this gambit were to fail – and it will not – still, I have secured my endgame. My son, who is innocent in all things, stands third in line to the throne, the only scion of Courcel lineage untouched by treachery. No other member of House Shahrizai has achieved so much. But you . . ." Turning, she smiled at me. "Kushiel has chosen you, Phèdre, and marked you as his own. To toy with you is to play a god's game."

I shuddered. "You are mad," I said faintly.

"No." Melisande shook her head again. "Only ambitious. I will ask again: Have you decided?"

The crash and wail of the mourning sea filled the silence that stretched between us. It would drive me mad, in time; it had already begun. I knew it, the day I raved at the warden's refusal. But at least that madness would claim only me, and I would remain true to myself to the end. Melisande's way . . . that was another matter. If I gambled and lost, I betrayed a great deal more.

Torn between terror and longing, I gave a despairing laugh. "My lady, I am destroyed either way. Will you make me choose?"

"Destroyed?" She raised her eyebrows. "You do me an injustice, I think."

"No," I said. "There is Ti-Philippe. And Joscelin."

"You really do love him," Melisande said curiously. I looked away, heard her laugh. "Cassiel's servant. A fitting torment, for Kushiel's chosen, and Naamah's . . . did he truly flee your charms?"

"Yes," I whispered.

"Ah, but you can guess where he fled. Phèdre." Her voice turned my head. There was pity and inexorable cruelty in her gaze. "Either way, he is gone. What does it merit, this blind and unthinking loyalty?" she asked gently. "To your Cassiline, who left you; to Ysandre de la Courcel, who used you at her need. It is all the same to Elua and his Companions, who sits the throne of Terre d'Ange. Tell me, do you believe I would make so poor a sovereign?"

"No," I murmured, surprising us both with the truth. "What you do, my lady, you make a habit of doing very well. I do not doubt that once you had the throne, you would rule with strength and cunning. But I cannot countenance the means."

"Phèdre." My name, only; Melisande spoke it as if to place a finger on my soul, soft and commanding. "Come here." She crossed to stand before me, extending her hand, and I took it unthinking, rising obediently with instincts bred into my very fiber, trained into me since I was four years old. With nothing but the force of her will and the deadly allure of her beauty, Melisande held me captive and trembling before her, cupping my face in both hands. "Why do you struggle against your own desire? Blessed Elua himself bid us, love as thou wilt."

If there had been somewhere to flee, I would have. If I could have fought her, I would have. There wasn't, and I couldn't. I couldn't even answer. Her scent made my head spin.

I stood, stock-still and obedient, my heart beating too quick, too rapid.

So close, so beautiful.

So dangerous.

Melisande lowered her head and kissed me.

The shock of it went through me like a spear; I think I gasped. A flaw, a weakness; Kushiel's Dart, piercing me to the very marrow. And in the aftermath of shock came desire, a vast drowning wave of it that swept away my will like a twig in a flood, swept away everything in its course. Yearning, ah, Elua! This had been coming between us for a long time, and it was sweet, far sweeter even than I remembered. Anchored by Melisande's hands, I swayed, dissolving under lips and tongue, craving more and more. It turned my bones to molten fire, my flesh shaping itself to the form of her desire. My breasts ached with longing, a rising tide surging in my blood, my loins aching, body seeking to mold itself to hers. All that she asked, I gave. All that I was, all I was meant to be, I became under her kiss.

It felt like coming home.

Melisande knew; how could she not? Struggling to breathe, I clung to her, hands clutching her shoulders. I did not even remember raising my arms. A faint, triumphant smile curved her lips as she released me.

I took a deep, shaking breath and stepped back . . . one step, two, her smile turning quizzical . . . and jerked my head backward with all my might, slamming it hard against the stone wall of my cell.

It was a hot, splitting pain that told me I had erred, catching not the flat wall, but the edge of the corner where the door recessed. It beat against the confines of my skull like Kushiel's bronze wings, a throbbing agony that drove a haze of red across my vision, beating and beating, driving out Melisande's allure.

I laughed as I slid helplessly to the floor, seeing the shock dawn across her lovely face.

"Phèdre!"

It was only the second time I had heard it, her melodious voice unstrung with astonishment. Wet warmth made its way down the back of my neck, trickling forward to pool in the hollow of my throat, a scarlet rivulet. Truly, I had cracked my skull.

"What in the seven hells are you thinking?" Melisande muttered urgently, eyes intent and fearful as she knelt by my side, pressing a wadded kerchief to the back of my head. Dizzy and pain-battered, I righted myself to look at her. "I swear, Phèdre, you're ten thousand years of torment to me living!"

Melisande's face and my cell reeled in my sight, swamped by agony. She cared, she really did care about me, and I could not stop laughing at it, having found my own useless triumph in the dazed madness of pain. For all that Kushiel's red haze veiled my eyes, for all the ache in my head, my thoughts were clear. The balance of power had shifted, rendering us, for once, equals. A frown of concentration creased that flawless brow as Melisande sought to staunch the flow of blood.

"Hold this," she said shortly, pressing my limp fingers about the blood-soaked kerchief. I obeyed, watching her go to the door, knocking sharply for the guard. "Fetch a chirurgeon," she ordered him in crisp Caerdicci. "Or the nearest thing you have in this place."

He must have gone quickly; I could hear his footsteps

receding down the hall. Melisande eyed me silently, drawing a dipperful of water from my drinking bucket and using it to rinse my blood from her hands, carefully and thoroughly. I sat with my back to the wall, pressing her kerchief against my head. Already my hair was matted with blood.

"You'll have to move fast," I said presently, as if I were not sitting bleeding on the floor of my cell. "Barquiel L'Envers is no fool, and he has his suspicions. He'll retain the throne as regent the instant he hears the news, and demand a full investigation before he cedes it."

"Four couriers on fast horses will depart La Serenissima the instant the bell tower in the Great Square tolls Ysandre's death," Melisande said coolly. "With fresh horses waiting on relay all the way to the City of Elua. Percy de Somerville will take the City before Duc Barquiel hears the news."

"And he named a conspirator, I suppose." I shifted on the flagstone, sending a wave of fresh agony pounding in my head. "How is Ysandre to die?"

"You know enough." A key in the door; Melisande stood back to admit the warden and a guard. He looked expressionlessly at her and came over to examine me, drawing my head forward and parting the blood-damp locks. I felt his fingers probing my wound.

"A gash to the scalp," he pronounced, rising and wiping his hands on a towel. "It is not serious. Head wounds bleed. It is not so deep that it must be stitched. Already, it begins to clot." The warden turned his flat stare on the guard. "Let her rest undisturbed for a day. Principessa." He inclined his head briefly to Melisande. "Is there aught else?"

"No." Her tone was unreadable. "Give me a few more moments with the prisoner."

He nodded again. "Knock when you are ready."

Melisande gazed at the door as it closed behind them. "The tradition holds that a member of his family has served as warden of La Dolorosa since Asherat-of-the-Sea first grieved," she remarked. "They first guarded the body of Eshmun, after Baal-Jupiter slew him. So they say. And they say he is incorruptible, having been appointed by the goddess." She looked at me. "But you already learned that."

I shrugged. "Would you expect me not to try?"

"Hardly." She glanced around the barren cell. " 'Tis a dire reward for his ancestor's service. It seems to me a dubious honor, to win a god's favor."

"Yes, my lady," I said wryly. "I appreciate the irony. But Asherat-of-the-Sea did not make this place a prison. 'Twas mortal cruelty did that, and mortal forgetfulness that warped the warden's purpose, over the long centuries."

"Mayhap. They are not like us, who cannot forget." Melisande made a simple, graceful gesture. I met her gaze without speaking. "Two years ago . . ." she nodded toward the wall, ". . . you would not have done that."

What did she expect, she who had sold me into slavery among the Skaldi? I had fought hard for my survival, and won greater hardships for my pains. It was true, Ysandre had used me at need, sending me into danger as great as that I'd left behind. But I had gone consenting, then. I had faced death, more than once. I walked into death's open arms on the battlefield of Troyes-le-Mont, and I went knowing what I did. I had lost comrades and loved ones, and grieved. I was not what I had been, when Melisande first had me. These things I thought, sitting on the flagstones of my cell and gazing up at her impossibly beautiful face.

"I was a child then, my lady," I said softly. "My price is higher now."

For once, I did not fear her; I was safe in Kushiel's dreadful shadow, and the sick, throbbing ache in my head protected me still. Melisande simply nodded, accepting my reply. "I will give you a day," she said. "On the morning after tomorrow, two of Benedicte's guards will come for your answer. They will speak to you in person. If your answer is yes, you will leave with them. If it is no . . ." She shrugged. "You stay. Forever. I will not ask again."

"I understand."

"Good." Melisande turned to knock at the door, then turned back. "You were unwise to play this hand so quickly, Phèdre. I will be more careful in the future."

"I play the hand you dealt me, my lady," I replied.

"Do you?" She looked curiously at me. "I wonder, sometimes."

To that, I had no answer. Melisande gazed at me a moment longer, then knocked on the heavy door for exit. Once more the key snicked in the lock, the hinges creaked open. I watched her go, taking every ounce of color and beauty with her.

Only her scent remained.

I opened my hand, revealing her wadded, blood-soaked kerchief, folds already beginning to stiffen until I smoothed it open. It was fine cambric, trimmed with lacework, with the swan of House Courcel embroidered small

in one corner. A suitable lover's token, as matters stood
between us.

One day.

And then I had to choose.

FORTY-FIVE

İ THOUGHT a good deal about Hyacinthe that day.

It was ironic, in a situation laden with bitter ironies. I had chosen this very fate when I had fathomed the riddle of the Master of the Straits; not merely a lifetime, but an eternity, bound to a lonely isle. I would not have faced the madness of Asherat's grief, of course, but I daresay centuries of tedium would have served much the same.

Hyacinthe had used the *dromonde* to read the past, and stolen my doom.

And now I faced it once more.

How had he stood it, I wondered. How did he fare now? The Master of the Straits had warned it would be a long apprenticeship. Ten years? Fifty? A century? I had sworn to do all I could to free him. Instead, I was imprisoned, and all my efforts had done was guide Joscelin to the Yeshuites so I might lose him. Now, I peered out the narrow window at the maddening sea, and wondered if there was any way Hyacinthe might free me. I had wondered, idly, aboard the ship from Marsilikos, how far the domain of the Master of the Straits extended.

Would that I'd come to some other conclusion. But his reach had never gone more than a few leagues beyond the Straits, and I was far, very far, from there.

And very, very alone.

I bowed my aching head against the lip of the window. Melisande was right, I'd been a fool to reveal the lengths to which I would go to defy her. All it had got me was a sore head and the fleeting satisfaction of seeing her surprised. It was an idiot's ploy, and not one I'd care to use often. And yet . . . I had needed to know, for my own sake. I *could* defy her, if I summoned the will for it.

Although it took a split skull to break the spell of one kiss.

And Melisande was capable of much, much more than that.

I knew; I remembered. I remembered altogether too well. An *anguissette* is a rare instrument; most of my patrons lacked the art to sound all my strings. Pain and pleasure, yes, of course, but there are others, too. Cruelty, humiliation, dominance . . . and compassion and kindness. It took all of these, to make truly exquisite music. That was the part so few understood.

Affection.

It was my bane with Melisande, always the potential key to my undoing. No matter how much I hated her — and I hated her a great deal in a great many ways — there was a part of me that did not, nor ever would. Waldemar Selig had been a formidable foe with the advantage of owning me outright, but no matter how many times he mastered me, nor how many ways, I never risked losing myself in him. I had not been at least a little bit in love with him.

Still and all, now I knew; that sword cut two ways.

Melisande cared enough for me to make her vulnerable, at least a bit. Even so had Kushiel cared for the damned in his charge, when he was still the Punisher of God; he loved them so well they received pain as balm and begged not to leave him. So too it made Kushiel vulnerable, for the One God was displeased with him and would have cast him down. But he followed Blessed Elua, who said, *love as thou wilt.* I wondered if he feared, mighty Kushiel, this scion of his who burned so brightly. Elua and his Companions did not quarrel among themselves; not for them the jealousy of other gods. No, but each claimed his or her province in Terre d'Ange, and held it solely. Each save Blessed Elua, who ruled without ruling, wandered and loved, and Cassiel, who stood at his side and cared only for Elua.

The others — Kushiel, Azza, Shemhazai, Naamah, Eisheth and Camael — were they jealous of their immortal thrones, in the Terre d'Ange-that-lies-beyond? It might be so. It was so, among other gods, other places. Standing at the heart of Asherat's grief, I knew that much to be true. Mortals conquer and slay; gods rise and fall. The games we play out on the board of earth echo across the vault of heaven.

Melisande knew it.

I bore the mark of Kushiel's Dart.

My thoughts chased each other around and round. I tried to pray; to Kushiel, to Naamah, who were my immortal patrons; to Blessed Elua, who is lord of us all. But the pounding rage of Asherat's grief scattered my thoughts, driving away the solace of prayer.

If I were not chosen for somewhat, I would be dead now, as surely as Remy and Fortun. But what? To thwart

Melisande by choosing no, denying her the chance to break Kushiel's Dart? Or to face her, and dare win a greater stake?

She would be cautious; she would be very, very cautious. My chances of defeating her plans were nearly non-existent.

Nearly.

And the deeper game she played? I didn't know. By the end of my day of grace, I was no wiser. I stared out the window, brooding, while the rays of the setting sun bloodied the waters. I wished that Hyacinthe were here with me now, to speak the *dromonde* for me. Not that he would; he never would, for me. Out of fear, at first. His mother foretold that I would rue the day I learned the answer I sought, the riddle of Delaunay. She was right, for 'twas the day he died. Afterward, Hyacinthe said he could not see, for the path of my life held too many crossroads. Truly, I stood at a dire one now. Still, I wished he were with me. My one true friend, I used to call him. Even Joscelin, bound by his vow, had not proved so true.

Only love had bound Hyacinthe and me.

And he would be lost, too, if I told Melisande no. However slim the hope that I might find a way to break his *geis*, it would die with me here in La Dolorosa. If I said yes . . . texts, if you wish, Melisande had said. I could continue. And there was nothing, *nothing* she could do to Hyacinthe, which gave me a certain grim satisfaction.

But there was Ti-Philippe . . . and Joscelin.

My Cassiline, who left me. I hated him for that; hated and despaired, for it may have been the one thing that would save his life. But it had left me bereft, well and truly alone. I had been stronger with him at my side, my Perfect

Companion. He lent me the courage and strength to cross the Skaldic wilderness in winter, and when Ysandre bid me go to Alba, he left the Cassiline Brotherhood itself to go at my side.

And then he left me.

The light on the water faded to mauve, and Tito came with my evening meal, looking with worriment at my face, my bloodstained dress, and coaxing me to eat before the light went altogether. I did, finally, if only to ease his distress. If I chose no, if I stayed, his hulking kindness would be the only spark in my life. I wondered, would it continue? If Melisande's ban was lifted and the warden freed his men to use me as their plaything, would Tito be among them? Simple and kind, yes, but a man, confined to this rock. I imagined Malvio showing him what to do, grinning all the while, and shuddered.

The worst of it . . . I did not like to think.

I thanked Tito as he took my tray, closing the door behind him. It was hard to make out shapes by now. I fumbled my way to my drinking bucket, rationing the water I consumed to save a little for washing my face. The hair at the back of my head was stiff with matted blood, but I didn't have enough water to cleanse it. I dampened my fingers enough to part it, touching the wound gingerly. It had clotted over cleanly, I thought, beginning to heal. More of Kushiel's questionable mercy, keeping me hale to endure fresh torments.

With the encroachment of night came a fitful wind and scudding clouds, obliterating the stars. Awake, I stood clinging to the bars of my window, facing unrelieved blackness and feeling the warm breeze on my skin. Asherat's grief moaned in the wind and surging sea. I separated the threads of sound from my various cell mates, finding a new voice among them, or mayhap only a new phase of madness. This was a deep cry on a rising tenor that reached a certain pitch and broke off in a throaty gurgle; the Howler, I named him. I listened for the others, counting, and did not hear the Screamer, although the Pleader's voice was among them, an endless litany of begging.

Well, I thought, mayhap they were different all along, and the Screamer has become the Howler. It could be that this Howler was a new prisoner, but I listened further and decided no, that the sounds were too far gone from human. An old cell mate with a new voice, then. A new phase of madness.

I made my way back to my pallet by touch, wondering, what voice will I have when first I break? A Ranter, mayhap. I liked to think I would retain intelligible language, at least for a good while. Longer than most, likely. It would take a long time, for Kushiel's chosen to forget entirely what it meant to be human. *They are not like us, who cannot forget.*

Mayhap I never would, until I died.

I do not think I lack for courage, although admittedly, it is my own kind. I am no warrior, to face naked steel on the battlefield, but it is true, what I considered earlier; I have faced dire fates before. If I feared, if I prayed and pleaded it might be otherwise, still, I went. Into the Skaldic winter, into the teeth of the Straits, into the hands of Waldemar Selig. I was not a coward.

But this fate I could not face.

So be it, I thought, sitting alone in blackness. I cannot do this thing. Blessed Elua have mercy on me, but I would rather be Melisande's creature than a broken thing in a cell. At least it gave me a chance, a fragile, deadly chance, but a chance all the same. Here, I had none.

I had chosen.

My decision made, I felt somehow calmer, and at last was able to pray. I prayed for a long time, to Elua and his Companions, all of them, to protect and guide me, and above all, to give me strength not to betray my own companions. And if there was some chance, any chance, that Ti-Philippe and Joscelin lived, that they might yet act against Melisande and Benedicte, let my lips remain sealed. She would be cautious, but she would press; it made her uneasy, to know they had evaded her. Well and good, then let me serve as living distraction, no matter what the cost, no matter what she might do. Let my pain atone for the deaths I had caused.

Let me keep silent. Let me be the sacrifice.

It was better than this.

When I was done, I felt at peace for the first time since I had beheld Melisande, and despite the maddening wail of Asherat's grief, despite the cries and howls of the other prisoners riding the night winds, I laid my head down on my pallet and slept soundly.

It was the sound of shouting that awakened me.

I came awake in an instant, heart pounding, gathering myself to crouch on my pallet. No wind or sea, this, nor prisoner's madness; no. The sound echoed in my memory, recalling others like it. Men, shouting; reports and urgent orders. I'd heard it last in Southfort, among the Unforgiven, when Captain Tarren d'Eltoine sent riders north to seek out the guardsmen of Troyes-le-Mont. It was the sound of a garrison, only a garrison roused. A torch flame streaked the darkness outside my narrow window, a voice called out in Caerdicci.

And through the heavy door of my cell, I heard quick footsteps in the corridor, the sound of keys jangling, doors opened and slammed.

They were checking on the prisoners.

La Dolorosa was under attack.

I'd scarce had time to think it when my own door was thrown open, and the sudden glare of lamplight made me wince. I shielded my eyes with one hand, making out the silhouetted figure of the guard even as he went to close the door, satisfied that I was safely contained.

"Fabron, please!" My voice outstripped my thoughts, pleading. He hesitated, and I rose from my pallet in one graceful motion, using all the art of the Night Court. "Please, won't you tell me what's happening?" I begged him, turning out both hands. "I heard shouting, and it frightened me!"

He hesitated, then jeered. "Yah, D'Angeline, too good to look at me, until you're scared, huh? You think I'll protect you, when I amn't even allowed to touch you?"

"Please." I didn't have to feign a tremor in my voice. "If you'll only tell me, I'll . . . I'll let you, I swear it. I won't say a word."

Fear and obedience were strongly ingrained in him; even then, he paused before taking two swift steps into my cell, closing the door and setting down the lantern. Lit from below, his face was eerily shadowed. "Let me see, then," Fabron said hoarsely. "Make it fast."

Holding his gaze, I slid the overlarge woolen gown from my left shoulder. The neckline dipped low, laying

bare one breast. He made a guttural sound and stepped forward, reaching for me.

It is not in my nature to be violent. I have killed one
man, in self-defense, and I begged him not to force my
hand. Harald the Beardless, he was called; a thane in
Gunter's steading. He was kind to me, and gave me his
cloak. But he rode out after me, for the honor of his
steading, and would have slain Joscelin and dragged me
back to Selig.

One does what one must.

What I did to Fabron, any child of seven or more in
the Night Court knows to do, from listening to the adepts'
gossip. To be sure, it would have carried a severe punishment, but we knew of it all the same. As his fingers brushed
my skin, I brought one knee up hard and fast, squarely
betwixt his legs. I daresay the years of dance and tumbling
helped; it was a solid hit, and hard. It made a dreadful
sound, Fabron made a dreadful sound, high-pitched,
doubling over and clamping his hands over his groin. I
couldn't afford guilt or pity; I whirled, still without thinking, and snatched up the wooden stool, bringing it up in a
sharp arc to connect with his bent head.

It caught him across the temple with a dull thud, and he
fell over. Unmoving, he lay on the floor of my cell.
Breathing hard, I dropped the stool and dragged my gown
back up to cover myself, then stood listening.

In the distance, a confused shouting continued. I went
to the door, pressing my ear to the heavy wood. In the
corridor, nothing.

Returning to Fabron's unconscious form, I fumbled
beneath him and found the ring of keys on his belt. There
was a bruise already visible on his temple, but his breathing

was steady. I took the keys and the lantern. It took me several tries to find the right key for my cell; then I did, and the door opened onto the dark corridor.

I emerged, carefully locking the door behind me, and Fabron inside.

The corridor was silent and empty, the lantern casting wild shadows on the stone walls as it trembled in my unsteady hand.

Twelve doors of brass-bound oak, all locked in a row.

I couldn't leave them.

Mine was third from the end. I went to the first, desperately trying key after key, until it opened . . . to find it empty. I tried the next, wasting precious seconds, only to find the same result, an empty cell, eight paces by eight, not even a pallet to relieve it. I moved past my own door — no sound yet, Fabron still unconscious — and tried the fourth door.

Empty.

Cursing softly under my breath, I fought with the jangling iron ring, seeking the key for the fifth door. At last I found it; it fit, the door opened.

I knew from the stench that this one was inhabited.

What I saw in that cell, I do not like to remember. A man's figure or somewhat like it, crouching at the wall beneath his window, scrabbling at the stones with long, curved nails. He turned toward the light with a whimper, throwing up one forearm to shield his eyes, showing his teeth in a grimace. His hair was greying, snarled and matted with long years' neglect. I took a step back from the doorway, holding the lantern high to illuminate my face and show I was no guard.

"You are free," I said softly in Caerdicci. "Although I

do not know for how long. Someone attacks the fortress. Stay if you wish, or go if you will risk it. You are free to choose."

He lowered his arm and peered at me, blinking. His mouth worked, but no human sound emerged. "Wh . . . wh . . . wh . . .?"

"I don't know," I said. Whatever he sought to ask, I had no answer. "All I can offer is a chance. Take it or not, and Blessed Elua keep you."

Swallowing hard against the horror of it, I hurried to the next cell and the next, fear and bile rising in my throat. I set them all free that night, my prison mates, Asherat's captive mourners. Nearly every cell was as bad as the first. Some I knew by sight. The Banger stood before his window, pounding his bruise-blackened forehead against the bars – that was the sound I'd heard for nights on end. The Pleader had been there the shortest time, next to me. He stood upright, blinking wide-eyed at the light. A youngish man, not thirty years old; his hair had grown only to his shoulders. "Please?" he asked tentatively. "I swear, 'twas not my dagger, I swear it, my lord! Only let me go, and I'll prove it, I'll bring you the man who did it. Please, my lord? Please?"

"You are free to choose," I murmured, sick, repeating my litany. Six times I had said it already; eight times before I was done. All along the corridor, the brass-bound cell doors stood open and ajar, dark, gaping mouths emitting the reek of ordure and foulness and the rhythmic surge of grieving sea, pierced with distant shouting. Somewhere, above, I could hear the sound of running steps.

But the corridor stood empty, save for me; and quiet. All their voices had fallen silent.

I could not force them to go, could not force them to choose, when I knew not what transpired. I had done all I could. Bending at the waist, I set down my lantern at the head of the corridor, leaving it to illume the empty walls. Let them have that much, at least, I thought.

It was safer for me to move in darkness, even if I knew not where I went. It had been a long time, since I'd employed the physical arts of covertcy in which Delaunay had trained me, but I had not forgotten. A body in shadow stands less chance of being seen. Watchers in light are blinded by light; always, always, stay to the shadows.

Wrapping Fabron's keys in a fold of my gown to stifle their jangling, I made my way to the foot of the stairs that led away from the dungeon.

FORTY-SIX

FOR SEVERAL long moments I crouched and listened at the head of the stairs. There were voices somewhere on the far side of the door, faint with distance. I tried to remember the layout of the fortress from my single glimpse of it. I would have failed miserably had Delaunay been quizzing me on it; numb with shock and wanting only to die, I'd paid scant attention. Still, I did not remember any guard set on the door itself.

I had to take a chance. I tried the handle, and found it locked.

Well and good, there must be a key on Fabron's ring. I unfolded them from my gown and sorted through them by touch in the dim light cast by the lantern in the corridor behind me. There were three that were larger than the others, and one smaller. I tried one of the larger, then a second, and that one unlocked the door. Muffling the keys once more, I worked the latch and opened the door a crack, peering through the gap.

There was not much to see, and little light in which to see it. An empty wardroom, it seemed, with a bench along the section of wall visible through the cracked door and an unused charcoal brazier. I daresay the cells grew cold and dank in the winter; the room must serve as a place for guards to warm their hands between trips below. The voices I heard came from well beyond the wardroom.

Nothing else for it, I thought, and slipped cautiously through the doorway, leaving the door an inch ajar behind me. Strange, to hear the endless roar of the sea muted at last.

Beyond the wardroom lay what would have been the great hall in any other fortress this size. Only a few torches lit it, and those guttered low. I gazed cautiously around the corner of the arched entryway. A fireplace at one end, cold and bleak, and a long table; only a few chairs. There were hallways at either end. From the entrance at the far right came lamplight and the sound of voices.

The other was dark, but it was from thence that I heard running footsteps. I drew back into the shadows as a hurried guard emerged, boot heels echoing across the hall. The faint light gleamed on his steel helmet and corselet, and he carried a short spear in one hand.

Lack of knowledge is deadly. I left the wardroom and followed him, keeping to the shadows. Even if I had not known how to move silently, my bare feet made no sound on the cool flagstones.

The hallway branched, a broader corridor leading to the left, a narrower one lying ahead. Light spilled out of a room to the right on the narrow way, and that was where the voices came from. Feeling dreadfully exposed, I crept near enough to hear.

". . . no answer from the watchtower, warden sir!" the

guard I'd followed was reporting, an urgent strain in his voice. "We gave the signal three times, sir, as ordered!"

The warden's voice, flat and implacable. "And on the island?"

A deep breath. "Nothing visible, sir. It's too dark to make out the ground, even."

There was a pause before the warden spoke again. "Continue combing the island. Double the number of torches; there aren't many places an intruder can hide. Gitto, leave four men to hold the bridge on this end, and take four across and secure the watchtower. Signal when you hold it. Balbo, on post in the tower, and alert me the moment they do." Silence, and then his voice rose a notch. "What are you waiting for? Go!"

I hadn't waited for his order; by the time he gave it, I was retreating stealthily to the corner. Ducking around into the wider corridor, I hitched up the trailing skirts of my filthy dress and ran, fear lending wings to my bare heels.

And I saw, ahead of me, the torch-cast shadow of a figure emerging from another side corridor.

There was a small alcove holding a statue of Eshmun on a black marble plinth; a smiling youth crowned with a grain wreath. I had no other choice. Whispering a plea for forgiveness to the slain deity, I slipped into the alcove, huddling crouched in the shadow of his plinth.

Jogging footsteps sounded in the hall, a rattle of sticks. I dared not look, keeping my head down lest my face catch the light. Spears, I thought, or torches; somewhat from a storeroom. Intent on his errand, the guard passed me by unseeing, and I heard the even pace of his steps fade down the corridor.

I could not go back that way. What lay ahead? Storerooms and what else? Willing my pounding heart to steady, I concentrated my attention, straining my ears. Fool that I am, I nearly forgot my own advice and ignored my other senses. Fixed on listening for danger, I muttered a silent curse against the distractingly sharp odor of fresh-cut onion coming from somewhere beyond me.

Onion. The kitchen. I had learned from Tito that the guards took turns at cooking duty, for better or worse. The garrison fed itself with foodstuffs provided as tribute by the mainlanders; the prisoners ate their leftovers.

If there was one place on the island that would be deserted that night, it was the kitchen.

Now I did listen, and found the corridor quiet. Offering silent thanks to Eshmun for his protection, I rose to my feet and slid out from behind his statue. Keeping to the shadows as best I could, I made my way swiftly down the hall, following the scent of onions.

The kitchen was not far, located to the left at the end of the corridor. It was vast and dark, lit only by the glowing embers of the oven, the door of which stood ajar. A small stack of kindling and cordwood lay on the floor beside it, abandoned. A mound of coarse-chopped onion sat on the counter, and a string of sausages, not enough for garrison and prisoners alike. A meal, I guessed, for the guards coming off the first night shift of serving sentry duty at the bridge.

Only someone had crossed the bridge, or they would not be searching the island.

I don't think, then, I even dared to hope. Whatever it was, whoever, however — I had walked the bridge to La Dolorosa, swaying above the killing sea, while the sentries waited at the end, hand-axes poised above the hempen ropes. I could not imagine anyone crossing it in stealth. Partway, mayhap; even half or better, but there was no way to cross the whole of it unseen. So I did not dare hope or even plan, only sought, like a trapped creature, any avenue of escape.

By the dull glow of the embers, I explored the kitchen. It reeked of fresh onion and the stale odors of a thousand bygone meals. There were kettles and pots, a set of knives, and a stack of the trays used to bring food to the prisoners. Nothing more. Beyond a low archway lay the pantry. Here no light penetrated, and I was forced to explore blindly. Rashers of salt-cured bacon hung from the ceiling, easy to detect by smell. There were sacks of grain stacked along the walls, lentils and coarse-ground flour. I found baskets of aubergines, smooth-skinned and firm to the touch, and another of ripe gourds. They did not eat so poorly, the garrison of La Dolorosa, although from the leftover fare I'd been served, I could not give much credit to their culinary skill.

Well and good, I was surrounded by food. What of it? I was safe, and as trapped as before. Since there was nothing else to do but backtrack and face the guards, I knotted Fabron's keys in a fold of my dress and began to make my way around the perimeter of the pantry, avoiding piles of provender, feeling along the cool stone walls with both hands.

It was out of a futile sense of obligation I did it, and no real thought of finding aught to serve my need. Which is why, when my hands encountered rough wood instead of stone, I stood stock-still in disbelief.

I swear I stood a full minute that way before I moved,

feeling with cautious fingertips the arched shape of a window covered with heavy wooden shutters, brass-bound and sealed with an iron bar and padlock. A service window, I thought, to the outside. This was where goods were delivered to the pantry.

It was big enough to admit a sack of grain. I could fit through it.

My fingers trembled as I undid the knotted fold of my dress and removed Fabron's keys, fumbling for the small one. It had to be! My lips moving in silent prayer, I fitted the key into the padlock. It took me three tries, my hand shook so.

But it fit.

With a faint click, the padlock opened. I removed it carefully and stooped to lay it on the floor. With agonizing slowness, I drew back the bar and then pressed my ear to the wooden shutters, listening.

On the far side, I could hear the pounding sea, and naught else. No way to know but to try it. How much worse could it be, if they caught me?

A great deal. I knew that already. But that would happen anyway. Swallowing my fear, I drew open the shutters.

Night air blew in and the wail of Asherat's grief filled my ears. In the darkness that lay beyond, I saw the bright sparks of torches moving here and there across the island, working in pairs. Too far away to see, I thought. A torch casts a pool of light some fifteen feet in diameter, mayhap; no further. Beyond the circle of light, the bearer is sightless. The night skies were clouded, no moon or stars to betray me. Even if they were looking — and they were not, they were seeking an intruder, not watching the fortress — they would not see.

All of this I knew to be true. Still, it was a terrifying thing, to clamber out the window, rendering myself vulnerable, dropping, exposed, to the stony path below. For a moment, I merely crouched at the foot of the fortress wall, breathing hard.

I could not stay. Above me, the service window gaped open, a breach waiting to be discovered. I gathered my wits, assessing my position. I was on the inland side of the fortress, furthest from the cliffs. To my left lay the rear of the fortress; to my right, the front, and the steep, rocky path to the bridge.

It was in that direction that the most torches were concentrated, and periodic faint shouts were audible over the sea. I listened hard for the clash of arms, and heard naught. Well, I thought, if I cannot go that way, I must go around the other, and pray for an opening. Whatever has passed, they have not found the intruder. Someone had taken the watchtower on the mainland, that much I knew; whether or not the warden's men had reclaimed it, I did not know. If they had not . . . there was a chance.

I had to gain the bridge. There was nothing else for it.

When we were children, Delaunay would set up courses for Alcuin and me, mazes that we must negotiate blindfolded, until we could move silently and swiftly in the dark. I dreamed then of exploring the quarters of some wealthy patron while they slept, searching out Elua-knows-what dire secrets. I never used those skills, then, but I used them now, making my way around the base of the looming fortress.

How long it took, I could not say. It seemed forever, although I daresay it was no longer than it took to heat water for the bath. Once a pair of guards passed close by me, forcing me to retreat noiselessly beyond the doubled circles of torchlight they cast. The volcanic rock of the island had sharp, jagged edges that bit painfully into the bare soles of my feet, but I bit my lip and kept silent, letting the pain sharpen my focus.

Sometimes it is an advantage to be an *anguissette*.

The guards were nervous, I could hear it in their low voices. ". . . grandfather saw it, and never spoke another word," one of them was muttering. "If you ask me, nothing *human* could cross that sodding bridge without being seen."

"Pascal saw it," the other said shortly. "It ran off before it finished him, and he was still alive when Gitto found him. He died trying to say what he saw. It didn't come *over* the bridge, it crawled *under* it."

"Yar, like a giant sodding spider!" the first retorted. "I tell you, whatever we're looking for, it's not human. No man could do that."

As I crouched in the dark, scarce daring to breathe while they moved out of range, I tried to imagine it — crawling *beneath* that deadly bridge, clinging to the underside, fingers and toes wedged between the knot-joined planks, moving one torturous plank at a time, suspended upside down in the howling winds, above the raging cauldron of sea and rocks . . . who would even dream of attempting such a thing?

I knew only one.

Joscelin.

Don't dare to hope, I told myself, watching the torches recede; don't even think it! It was too much, too impossible. How could he have even found out where I was? It must be something else, some political coup, enemies of Marco Stregazza launching an attack on one of his strongholds. Who knew what intrigues lay behind the other prisoners of La Dolorosa? It must be, and I dared not dream otherwise.

And yet I could not help myself. Hope, faint and tremulous, stirred in my heart. It strengthened my resolve and lent me new courage as I picked a path around the benighted fortress to gain the cliffside. There, at ground level, were the narrow, barred windows of the prison cells, peering out across the stony cliff toward the sea. A faint light emanated from them, but no sound. I knelt beside the first and looked inside.

It was empty. They were all empty, even mine, which I knew by the guano on the ground outside the window where I'd fed the seagulls. The light came from the corridor beyond the open cell doors, where I'd left the lantern. I stood up and moved away from the cell windows, into the deeper shadow of the fortress wall.

Asherat's wind was stronger here, moaning in my ears. The cliffside was deserted for now; there was nowhere to hide between the fortress and the cliff. I could feel the rock tremble under my bare feet from the impact of the waves. So Fabron was free, and they knew I had escaped.

Where were the other prisoners?

I stood still, straining my ears against the roaring wind. There, yes; toward the front, I could hear faint wind-whipped cries and the clash of arms. Slipping quickly past the low windows, I made my way forward.

I'd not gotten far before the battle came to me.

At whatever point the prisoners of La Dolorosa emerged, it is a safe bet that they caught the garrison in disarray. No one who served in that place but was wraith-haunted in the first place; it must have shocked them, this outpouring of eight gaunt, wild-haired apparitions, roused to a furor of madness that knew no fear.

It was a melee that spilled around the corner, full of confusion and panic. At least half the prisoners were armed, with short spears wrested from the first guards they'd encountered. I daresay the full garrison of La Dolorosa was no more than thirty or forty men at best, and only a handful had been left to ward the fortress proper.

Others had been sent to comb the island, and it was they who came at a run, torches streaming, illuminating the incredible scene. Knots of violence surrounded the prisoners, who fought with bared teeth and stolen weapons when they had them; bare hands and demented fury when they did not, giving ground slowly. For all their superior numbers and armor, 'twas no easy task for the guards, encumbered with torches as they were; and darkness favored the prisoners with their night-accustomed eyes.

Still, it could not last. As more and more guards came, the prisoners retreated further. Tito's massive figure appeared, crashing into the melee. Eschewing his spear, he carried a torch the size of a beam, swinging it in mighty arcs, trailing flames and roaring so loudly I could hear it above the wind. I should run, I knew; retrace my steps around the fortress, dare the other side and see if the bridge was perchance unguarded.

Indeed, one of the prisoners wielded a hand-axe, mayhap wrested from the sentries. It was the Pleader, whom I knew by his shoulder-length hair. He was not pleading now, but grimacing, chopping wildly at the pair of guards who forced him back, step by step, toward the edge of the cliff.

I couldn't run. I had freed them; I had led them to this end. As with Remy and Fortun, I could not look away. I watched through my tears as the Pleader swung his axe, panting, unable to get beyond the reach of the guards' spears.

And saw, by wavering torchlight, a hand reach over the edge of the cliff behind him.

It was hard to make out the figure that followed, heaving itself up and rolling, dark-clad and hooded, coming up into a fighter's crouch. It didn't matter. I knew. Before the twin blades of steel flashed up before him, before he spun, taking out one guard with deadly grace, before the second grasped ineffectually at him, succeeding only in tearing the hood loose to reveal wheat-blond hair shining in the flickering light; I knew.

Something in my heart gave way; a wall of despair and loneliness built long ago, on a rainy night in Montrève, when he came in from the garden. And in its place came joy and relief, and – ah, Elua! – love.

Caught between laughter and tears, I stepped away from the shadow of the fortress, into the torchlight that washed the stony ground. He dispatched the second guard, shoving the gaping Pleader toward the steep path to the bridge. In the melee between us, guards began to turn, realizing they faced a new menace from behind.

As he made his sweeping Cassiline bow, I cried out his name with all my strength, pitching my voice to carry as best I could above the wind and sea.

"Joscelin!"

Whether he heard me or not, I never knew; but he

saw me as he straightened. Across the distance, two-score guards and prisoners fighting between us, our eyes met.

That was when I felt the point of a spear press into my spine.

FORTY-SEVEN

"DON'T MOVE, lady," a voice whispered in Caerdicci at my ear.

It was no voice I knew.

I stood rooted and felt my arm taken, spinning me roughly; Malvio, who never spoke. He grinned at me, and his slippery gaze looked quite mad. With a shortened grip on his spear, he circled around me, placing himself between me and rescue. I moved cautiously, turning to face him. I could hear the sounds of battle still, but they seemed suddenly very far away.

My world had shrunk to the two of us.

"Go," Malvio said, seldom-used voice sounding almost friendly. He jabbed the spear toward me, and I retreated a step. He continued to grin. "Go."

I took another step backward.

There was nothing behind me but twenty yards of rocky ground and the cliff's edge. I knew, it had been my view for endless days. And beyond the cliff — nothing. It was the farthest point, overhanging the angry sea.

"Go." Malvio jabbed the spear again, cheerfully. I

stood without moving and he did it again, hard enough to pierce the coarse wool of my dress and prick the flesh beneath. "Go!"

I took another step, sharp-edged rock beneath my bare feet. Over Malvio's shoulder, I could see the melee broadening, Joscelin penned behind a thicket of spears, dodging and twisting. It might have been different, if he'd had his sword; it would have lessened the difference in reach. But no, he had crawled the underside of the hanging bridge. The weight of his sword would have been too great.

He had come to rescue me with nothing but his daggers. And he could do it, too, given time and aided by chaos.

The prisoners were providing the chaos. I needed to buy time.

"Whatever you want," I said steadily to Malvio, "I will do."

It gave him pause. Then he shook his head, grinning, and gave me another jab. I took another step. "No," he said. "It's too late. You belong to Asherat now."

Behind me the sea-surge was growing louder, and I could feel a change in the way the ground shuddered beneath my naked soles. A deeper tremor, a hollow vibration. We were on the overhang. How far to the edge? Twenty feet? Ten? The wind battered me, whipping my already-matted hair into worse tangles, flattening my dress against my legs.

It was getting darker, further away from the torchlit battle. I could scarce make out his face. "Malvio," I said. "Do not do this thing. I swear to you, it is not the will of Asherat. Her followers have betrayed her, who put me here."

"You were put here to die," he said agreeably, jabbing.

"No." I took a quick step backward, then darted sideways, seeking to get around him. But he was quick, for a Caerdicci, and he had a spear. He brought it sweeping about to bar my way, maneuvering behind it. A distant flicker of torchlight slid across his grinning face, his off-kilter gaze.

"Go," he said, jabbing.

I went, as slowly as I dared. Beyond us, I saw that the numbers of the guards had thinned, but they were organized now, and an armored figure with a full-length shield paced the outskirts, shouting inaudible orders.

The warden, I thought. He had formed the remaining guards in two lines, back to back; one held the prisoners at bay, and the other, Joscelin. Two men stood back from the fighting, holding torches aloft – one was hulking Tito. I saw the warden flash his shield at the tower, and movement in a darkened window. An archer, armed with a crossbow.

La Dolorosa would have been easier to defend with proper ramparts and arrow-slits, *muertrieres* such as Troyes-le-Mont had sported. But they would all have been mad as Malvio if they'd manned it thusly, listening to the winds hour upon hour. It was bad enough for the sentries at the bridge. I took another step backward, watching the bowman.

It was too dark to see and too far; I couldn't see when he began shooting, slow pauses between reloading. One of the prisoners staggered, grey hair swirling, and then two broke away, and the line of guards holding them at bay began to crumble as the prisoners retreated out of bowshot.

"Go," Malvio repeated for what seemed like the hundredth time.

I took a step and stopped. The wind tugged at me and the sea boomed and wailed, almost beneath my very feet, from the sound of it. I was almost on the edge. And this was the overhang, a deep curve bitten out beneath it. I knew, I'd seen it aboard the *Darielle* on that fateful trip, while the sailors whistled past the black isle. I would find no ledge here such as Joscelin had done, to crouch concealed beyond the lip of the cliff.

No rocks below, only sea. It was small consolation.

I was not ready to die.

Malvio jabbed the spear at me. In the darkness, I stood unmoving. He jabbed again, and this time I caught the haft with both hands, below where the lashings bound the spearhead, wrenching it hard, up and away from me. It took him by surprise; I daresay he hadn't expected it. Face-to-face atop the high cliff, we struggled, two pairs of hands locked tight on the spear.

My grip on the smooth-worn wood was slipping. Grinning wildly, Malvio twisted the spear, using his superior height and strength to lever it out of my hands. He would have it, in another few seconds. Knowing myself lost, I cried out desperately in the direction of the battle. "Joscelin! It's Benedicte, Benedicte and Melisande! Benedicte is the traitor!"

We were too near the edge, too near the booming sea. Even I could hear my own words were lost, torn from my lips by the keening wind. Malvio rotated the spear further and jerked. I made one last, frantic grab, nails scraping the leather thongs; and then he had it, bringing the butt end up in a sweeping arc, slamming into my chin.

My jaw closed with an audible click and a burst of pain filled my head. I wasn't aware I'd fallen until I felt the sharp rocks beneath my palms. On hands and knees, I blinked against the starburst of pain, trading it for Kushiel's red haze. Bright, so bright! Streaks like flame blurred my vision, and through the dank locks of hair hanging over my eyes, I saw Malvio, still grinning, step forward, raising the spear point-downward, positioning himself over my fallen form.

"No!"

A deep Caerdicci voice, bellowing rage; not Joscelin, no. Another fiery streak etched the night and a thud sounded, wood on flesh. Malvio staggered away from me in a shower of red sparks. The spear fell, clattering harmlessly off my back and onto the stones.

It was my guard Tito.

I pushed myself to my feet in time to see my rescuer's second blow as Tito swung the beam-sized torch at the retreating Malvio. It struck him on the side of the head, with another flurry of sparks and a crunching sound there was no mistaking. Malvio dropped like a stone, and did not move. Unlike Fabron, he would not rise again.

Tito turned back toward me, a profound look of sorrow on his simple, homely face.

"Tito," I whispered as he took one step toward me, staring past him with horror at the descending pursuit. "Ah, no!"

It was the prisoners, wild and maddened, who surged after him, who brought the battle to the cliff. I have never known, to this day, why they did it; whether they pursued him as a hated guard or whether they did it out of some demented gratitude, thinking he threatened me, who had freed them. With spears and axe, they brought him to bay and he stood his ground like a colossus, roaring, carving a half-circle of space before him with great swings of his blazing torch.

"Stop it!" I shouted frantically, trapped behind him. "Let him be!"

To no avail. And then the now-disorganized mob of the guard fell upon them from behind, the warden running beside them, wading into the mix and shoving with his shield, cursing and giving orders no one heeded, and to the rear of it all, Joscelin, half-forgotten, who had acquired a spear which he wielded like a quarterstaff, with eye-blurring speed, forging an alley up the middle.

Close, so close.

I saw one prisoner fall, stabbed from behind. I saw another whirl away screaming, ragged garments aflame, rolling on the ground and beating at himself. I saw Joscelin, grim-faced, stun one guard with a blow to the helmet, reversing the spear and slicing the man's un-protected throat, never stopping, but moving still, plunging onward.

It was all very much like a dream.

And then I saw the warden, calm and implacable, draw one of the guards out of the melee, moving to the right of my giant defender, and pointing.

At me.

I saw the guard, faceless in the shadow of his helmet, draw back his short spear and cock his arm to throw, the point aimed straight and sure for my heart. And I knew I was trapped, with nowhere to go. Behind me, naught but the crumbling edge of the cliff. Around me, naught but the sorrowing wind. Joscelin's face, turning, seeing too late, a cry of despair shaping his lips. Between us, Tito, massive in the torch-cast shadows, turning slow and ponderous as a mountain.

The guard, his arm cocked; the warden, speaking one word.

A spear aimed at my heart.

He threw.

'Tis passing strange, how such moments are etched indelibly in memory. Even now, if I close my eyes and listen to the ocean pound the shore, I can see it unfold in agonizing slowness. Joscelin, moving too slow, too late, though guards fell away from him like wind-blown chaff. The concentration of the spear-thrower, weight shifting onto his forward foot as he threw, the graceful arc of his casting arm and his open hand as he made his release, fingers outspread. The hard, flat line of the thrown spear, headed for my heart.

And Tito, lunging to place himself in its path, swinging his torch like a club.

I cried out, strove to grasp him by one massive arm, dragging him out of the way; too late. Seeking to bat the spear from its flight, he missed. The spear struck him full-force, piercing the gap in his armor below the arm hole. A vast gap, on so large a man. It was the impact that staggered him, sent him crashing into me, bearing us both backward to the verge of the cliff, the burning torch still clutched in his loosening hand.

It was his dying weight that bore me over the edge.

I fell.

Through wind and howling darkness, I fell unendingly

toward the cauldron of the sea, and above me in the night, I saw the torch, plunging after me like a shooting star.

Until I hit, and saw no more.

FORTY-EIGHT

IT CAME as a shock that I was still alive.

The blow of landing had driven all the air from my lungs. I could feel naught of my limbs, and knew neither up nor down; all was blackness, and only the sensation of air on my face told me I had surfaced.

Alive.

My chest heaved futilely as I struggled to draw breath, and waves churned all about me. One broke over my head, driving me downward. I felt water fill my mouth, and knew I should cease my efforts to breathe; yet I could not. A great pressure, and somewhere, distantly, a sharp pain. Were my eyes open or closed? I could not tell.

There had been air; air! I willed my legs to move, uncertain whether or not they obeyed, uncertain whether I drove myself upward or deeper down. All was turmoil, and the sea roared in my ears.

I thought myself drowned, and then I felt it again; air, upon my face, laced with salt-stinging spray. And the stricture about my chest gave way, and I drew in a raw, gasping breath. As much as it burned, it was sweet. I flailed my arms, feeling the water's resistance, thinking, for a second, I would survive.

And then the sea mocked my folly, surging over my head, the indrawn susurrus of breakers at the foot of La Dolorosa drawing me down, down. Every which way waves broke and withdrew against the jagged rocks of the black isle, forming a maelstrom. 'Twas better to have thought myself dead; alive, and knowing it, I fought desperately against the churning waters. The immersed folds of my woolen prison dress twined my limbs like a shroud, heavy with water, dragging at me like a sea anchor.

So do they bury the dead, in the deeps.

A breath; one breath. My lungs ached to expel it, to suck in another. I clenched my teeth against the urge, feeling the pressure of the sea. Underwater. A simple desire, to breathe. One does it a thousand times an hour, never thinking. There is life, not death, in breathing.

But it is death underwater.

My chest began to jerk involuntarily with the effort of holding in air. I splayed out my hands, reaching, finding nothing, beating futilely, legs kicking. The roiling water pulled mercilessly at me, tugging me this way and that, ever deeper. The raging sound of the sea was dreadful, here in the pounding, elemental heart of Asherat's grief. At a distance, it could madden. Here, in the heart, it would kill.

They knew, the ancient Hellenes, that to behold certain things was death.

This was one of them.

I sank, deeper and deeper, wound in my swirling woolen shroud. And below the raging waves, below the howling anger, I found the still, silent core of grief. Here, in the blackest depths, all was nothing. Only unbearable pressure, and the quiet certainty of death. I could bear no longer the aching in my lungs and released my last, precious breath, hearing it trail away from me in a series of bubbles, one last offense wrought by mortal flesh against the sacred depths of Eshmun's cenotaph, marker for a slain deity, a beloved son.

All the life remaining in my body could be measured in a span of failing heartbeats. I yearned for air as I had yearned for naught else in my life; not Delaunay's approval, nor Hyacinthe's company, nor Ysandre's regard, nor Joscelin's love, no, not even Melisande's kiss. My body burned for it, chest heaving, muscles quivering. In a second, ten seconds, I would give in to it. I would open my mouth and inhale deeply; not air, but rushing water, filling my lungs. It would be the end, the final weight, never to rise again.

Elua, I prayed in the final seconds remaining to me, Blessed Elua, forgive me, for I have failed you and all those you love! Naamah, take pity on me, for I have served you well and true. Ah, Kushiel, harshest of masters, have mercy on your chosen. All you have asked me, I have done; forgive me that it was not enough.

My prayers fell unanswered. Not even the cruel beating of Kushiel's bronze-winged presence sounded in my ears, but only the thready pulse of my failing heart, blood beating in my ears, bidding a faint farewell. I was far away, too far from the land of my birth, for the gods of Terre d'Ange to hear, too far.

I knew true terror then, open eyes bleeding salt tears into an ocean of grief. To die, alone and forsaken! It is the worst fate a D'Angeline can face. I had come to the

scantest raw end of my courage, and like a child, reached
for the only solace I could, releasing will and volition to
place my fate in another's hands.

Asherat, I prayed silently, mouth shaping the words
against the pressing waters, Asherat-of-the-Sea, forgive
me. For the death of your son Eshmun, I am sorry; I have
heard your grief and shared it. Only spare my life, and I
swear to you, I will do you honor; on the name of Blessed
Elua, your bastard-gotten son, I vow I will return to La
Serenissima and cleanse your temple of those who turn
your worship to their own ends.

I, Phèdre nó Delaunay, swear it.

I swear it.

Was there an answer? I cannot say in certainty, not
being bred to the worship of Asherat-of-the-Sea. I was
faint and delirious, stunned by the fall and bereft of air, but
this much I know to be true. As the last vestiges of control
gave way in my beleaguered body, my mouth opening and
closing helplessly against an influx of seawater, seeping
past my choking throat into my lungs, I heard something;
a sound, a movement. A deep, steady thrumming filled the
waters, the sound of a strong current, bent around the
rocks of La Dolorosa.

A current, a strong current.

*The currents around La Dolorosa are strong and uncer-
tain . . .*

So the Captain of the *Darielle* had said; so it was. Deep,
deep beneath the surface of the waves, a powerful current
flowed, and it clasped me like a pair of arms, drawing me
away from the isle.

Away, and up.

My head broke the surface of the water and I drew in

one ragged, whooping gasp of air, expelled it choking, flailing my arms, not realizing in my frantic efforts that the sea in which I had surfaced was calm, calm and still, save for the smooth, steady pull of the current. 'Twas all I could do to breathe, coughing up seawater and feeling it trickle, bitter and warm, down my chin. My lungs burned, my stomach burned, and somewhere in the vicinity of my ribs, a sharp pain reestablished itself. I churned my legs, struggling to keep myself afloat, and realized I truly was alive, alive and breathing.

A solid object bumped at my arm, making me start and thrash at the water, and my reaching fingers encountered wood, sea-sodden and slimy to the touch, but solid and floating, a great beam-sized length of it, one end sticky with pitch.

Tito's torch, caught in the same current.

"Thank you," I whispered hoarsely, my throat raw with pain. I clung to the torch, wrapping both arms around it, desperate as any shipwrecked sailor clinging to a broken spar. It dipped, but floated still, bearing my weight enough to keep my head above water. "Thank you."

Only then did I think to look about me, gazing over the waters to see where I was. When I saw, I gasped.

Asherat's current was no jest. Without rocks or shore to provide resistance, it flowed like a silent river, swift and sure, charting an invisible course across the sea. La Dolorosa lay well behind me, a black, jagged form marked by tiny pinpricks of flame.

One was moving lower than the others, scrambling down the crags toward the base.

Joscelin, I thought in agony as the current bore me away, sweeping me further out to sea. Oh, Joscelin!

Though it was in vain, I cried out, shouting over the bobbing waves until my ragged voice failed and the pain in my ribs rendered it hard to draw breath. No one could have heard at that distance, over the pounding surge at the base of La Dolorosa. It didn't matter. When I could do no more, I laid my cheek on my arms, still wrapped about the torch, and wept with exhaustion, drifting on the relentless current.

I lived through that night, and Blessed Elua grant I never pass another like it. I daresay in any other season, I would have died of exposure, but it was late summer yet and the sea was mild. In the final hour before dawn, the temperature of the air dropped and I shivered violently. My head ached, my jaw ached and sharp pains shot through my midsection; I cannot even begin to describe the pain in my arms, locked about the floating log of Tito's torch. With a truly heroic effort, I managed to drag my sodden skirts to my waist and wind a length of woolen fabric about the torch, securing me to it.

There were things moving in the deep. I heard them and sensed them — twice, something large brushed against my bare legs, making me shudder with fear and revulsion. Asherat-of-the-Sea, I prayed, you have spared me; let your creatures treat me gently!

Whether 'twas Asherat's mercy or some other protection, no harm came to me from the denizens of the sea. And although I thought that night would never end, in time it did. I had not known, until the sky began to turn grey in the east, which way the current bore me. In the utter blackness of clouded night, I'd harbored some faint hope that it had bent to carry me alongshore, mayhap in sight of land. But the scrap of pale orange rising on the far horizon told me otherwise; it had borne me out to sea.

I remembered the captain's tale of the merchant who had drowned off La Dolorosa and washed ashore on the Illyrian coast, and knew fresh fear. Cloud-hidden and ghostly, the sun crept slowly above the horizon. Mist hovered over the sea, where the air was still cooler than the water. But the sun would rise, I thought, and warm the air, enough to burn off the mist, whether the clouds cleared or not.

And it would grow hot.

Clinging to my makeshift float, I licked my dry, salty lips. Beset with the terrors of drowning or being devoured by some monster of the deep, wracked with the pain of my injuries, I'd not given thought to thirst.

But once I had thought it . . .

My tongue felt swollen, my throat and lungs raw with the seawater I'd breathed. I'd feared the blind horrors of night, but it was day that was more likely to kill me. One can go a long while without food; I knew, I'd done it. Not water. And I had none.

I didn't pray, then, when the full, deadly irony of it struck me. I had been deceived, betrayed and imprisoned; I had escaped death too many times, and left too many dead behind me. To think, over and over again, so this is how it ends — it was too much.

I laughed, I think, or made some noise that was meant to be laughter. A harsh sound, like the calling of crows. I didn't know I was making it until I strained to catch another sound, faint and distant, that carried over the water, and found myself wishing irritably for the ratcheting noise to cease. It did, when I realized it was me.

And in the silence that followed, I heard another sound, faint but drawing nearer; a steady rush of water moving along a wooden hull, the rustle and snap of sails catching the breeze.

From my vantage point a scant foot above the waves, the nearest ship emerged from the mists like a great bird, skimming low over the sea. One, two, three . . . there were six of them in all, canted sails bellied full of wind like white wings, oars locked and untouched.

Heaving myself as far as I could above the surface of the water, struggling against the knotted fabric that tied me to the log, I pried one rigid arm loose and waved it in the air, shouting. "Here! Here! Name of Elua, help me!"

My voice scarce sounded human, and the effort of raising it threatened to tear my swollen throat. Two of the ships passed, disappearing swiftly in the lingering mists, and I bobbed futilely in the water. For a moment, I was sure they had not heard, had not seen, thought me as much an apparition as they seemed. Tears stung my eyes, and I thought stupidly, there is more of my body's moisture gone, well and good, I will die that much the faster if I weep.

And then a voice shouted an order in no language I knew, and one of the ships heeled, spinning quicker than I would have thought possible. The triangular sail luffed loose against the mast, spilling wind, then, with coordinating shouts, a rope snapped tight and the prow swung my way. Another order, crisp and commanding, and out came the oars.

In the middle of the ocean, I clung to Tito's torch and trod water, gazing up at the ship as it came alongside me. The rowers rested on their oars, faces peering over the side in amazement. *"Sa ёshta?"* one exclaimed, making a super-stitious gesture. *"Nё* Vila!"

Another man appeared behind them, leaning forward to look down at me; and a fiercer figure, I have seldom seen. His long, black hair was caught back in a topknot, and long, drooping mustaches framed his white grin, which revealed one missing tooth on the upper left side.

"Djo," he said decisively. *"Ёshta D'Angeline."*

And with that, he threw me a rope.

FORTY-NINE

IN THE space of a few heartbeats, my unexpected rescuers had me aboard the ship, hauling in the rope I grasped and unceremoniously heaving me on deck. Unsteady and nerveless, I could do no more than kneel in a shuddering heap, dripping saltwater onto the planking.

The crew muttered in their unfamiliar tongue, while their topknotted captain — so I guessed him to be — ignored me, shouting out another series of commands. They obeyed with alacrity, springing into action. Once more, the sail flapped loose from the long yard and the vessel lurched, spinning. My stomach clenched at the suddenness of it. The oarsmen set to with a good dozen strokes, then the ropes were tightened and the sail swelled taut. They put up their oars and locked them.

In the prow, a shirtless youth leaned over the water and waved a crimson pennant, gesturing to the other five ships that idled at close range, sails slack. One by one, with remarkable coordination, they followed our lead.

And then we were off, following an eastward course over the misty sea.

With difficulty, I raised my head to assess my situation. There were some fifteen men aboard the ship, ranging in age from the flag-waving youth, whom I guessed to be no more than fourteen years old, to a hardy-looking grey-beard. Most were as dark as the captain, although here and there a rufous hue prevailed.

Each one, even the lad, wore a short sword at his hip, and there were round bucklers pegged neatly under the oarlocks, though it was far too small for a warship. In the open hold, I could see crates and chests neatly stowed, lashed down with canvas. It could be a small, well-guarded cargo ship, I thought. Still kneeling, I gazed at the top of the mainmast, bobbing gently against the brightening sky. Where a cargo vessel's colors would have flown, it was barren of aught but sail and line.

All of which meant my rescuers were very likely pirates.

His company safely underway, the Captain picked his way across the deck back to me, squatting down before me while a half-dozen of his men crowded behind. Shivering, I drew myself up to the formal *abeyante* kneeling position of the Night Court.

"Kur të vend?" he asked, frowning and thumbing the narrow strip of beard that adorned his chin. *"Sa të atje?"*

"I'm sorry," I said humbly, "I don't understand. You said . . . you said D'Angeline, my lord; yes, I am D'Angeline. You do not speak it?"

"D'Angeline." He turned his head and spit contemptuously over the side of the ship. Two sailors nearby muttered, crossing their fingers and knocking their brows, another curious gesture. "D'Angeline, *djo*," he said, adding carelessly, "Caerdicc'."

It took me a moment to realize his meaning, so rattled were my thoughts. Even then, I had to fumble for words not in my mother tongue. "Caerdicci," I said, echoing him, hoping I'd understood aright. "You speak Caerdicci?"

"Yes, of course I speak it, I." He stood up, folded his arms and shot me an imperious look. "You think I am an unlettered peasant, eh? I am noble-born in Epidauro, I!"

I sat back on my heels, putting the pieces together. "You're Illyrian."

"Illyrian, yes." He grinned unexpectedly and bowed. "From Epidauro."

Of the nations of Europa, I knew little of Illyria save that it had ever occupied a precarious position, torn between the conquests of Hellas and Tiberium, La Serenissima and Ephesium, and vulnerable to invasion from the great northeastern mainland. Like Terre d'Ange before the coming of Elua, it bent in the winds, surviving as best it could. All but the stronghold city of Epidauro; that held out a measure of independence.

So much I knew, and no more. It seems odd, now.

"Well met, my lord, and my thanks to you," I said courteously – if thickly – inclining my head. "Believe me, your rescue this day will earn great gratitude from Queen Ysandre de la Courcel. I am the Comtesse Phèdre nó Delaunay de Montrève, of Terre d'Ange."

"Yes, great . . . gratitude." He smiled and nodded, following my pronunciation carefully in his less-than-fluent Caerdicci. "I am Kazan Atrabiades, I. I am honor to have you as my . . ." Turning his head, he called out to one of the greybeards, querying him in Illyrian. The man replied respectfully, providing the Caerdicci word for which the captain searched. He had been trained as a scholar, I guessed upon hearing his formal accent. As it happened, I was right, though I gave it little thought at the time, for my blood chilled to hear the word he pronounced. ". . . my hostage," Kazan Atrabiades finished with pleasure, turning back to me.

At that point, I fainted.

It was not, I daresay, so much the shock of his words as it was the cumulative effect of the trauma I'd undergone. Nonetheless, whatever the cause, 'twas a full faint such as I have seldom known; and then only with a few choice patrons. The sky reeled in my sight, taut lines and white sails spinning, and then I saw the wooden planking of the deck rushing up to meet me.

When I opened my eyes, I was beneath a canvas awning, shielded from the still-rising sun. A neatly-stitched bag containing scraps for repairing sails rested beneath my head, forming a bolster against the wall of the forecastle, where I'd been placed out of the way.

"You are awake, good. Here."

The voice spoke Caerdicci; the greybeard's voice, which had answered Atrabiades. A brawny hand, wrinkled and weather-tanned, thrust a waterskin under my nose.

I took it gratefully, feeling water slosh under both hands as I raised the spout to my mouth and squeezed. Water, warm and stale, gushed into my mouth. It tasted better than the deepest well, the coldest spring. For a moment, I merely held it in my mouth, swishing it around, feeling moisture return to my salt-ravaged tissues. Then I swallowed cautiously, in small increments.

"A little more," he said. "Not too much."

I made myself obey, reluctantly; although it felt as though I could down gallons without being quenched, I knew full well it would sicken me. When I had done, he helped me lower the waterskin. "Thank you," I said, struggling to sit and turning my head to get a better look at his face. "You have saved my life, I think. May I have your name, my lord?"

"Glaukos, I am called." Laugh lines crinkled the brown skin about his grey eyes. "And no one has called me lord in all my days. Slave, aye, and brigand; lord, never. Only Kazan Atrabiades commands here, and he holds no title, nor ever will. But you, I think, are noble-born, my lady, is it not so?"

"I am Comtesse de Montrève," I said, temporizing slightly. Toward the stern, Atrabiades conferred with the sailor manning the rudder-bar, studiously avoiding gazing in my direction. "The title is an inherited one, and the right to bear it bequeathed me by Her Majesty Ysandre de la Courcel, Queen of Terre d'Ange. Glaukos, it is very urgent that I speak with Her Majesty. How does Lord Atrabiades treat with hostages?"

"Ah, now, don't fret." He settled himself comfortably on the deck. "He's never fished one out of the sea, nor had one half so beautiful, but he'll honor the conventions, Kazan will. You have someone who'll stand you ransom?"

"Yes, of course." It was on the tip of my tongue to say that Ysandre would throw open the Royal Treasury for the news I bore, but mercifully, the habit of discretion made me pause. "I will write him a letter of surety myself, for my factor in La Serenissima."

Glaukos chuckled. "Where they're like to have his head if he sets foot on land? Nay, my lady, don't think it. Kazan Atrabiades will not go to La Serenissima. Give him silver in hand, and he'll set you free as a bird."

"It's very urgent," I repeated politely.

"No doubt." Amiable, he passed the waterskin back to me. "Have another swallow. You've a voice on you like a split reed. No wonder the men thought you were one of the *Vili*."

I drank a little more, feeling life return to my limbs with each gulp. "What are the *Vili*?"

"Spirits," Glaukos said affably. "Spirits of the dead, that appear in the form of beautiful maidens. If a man do look at a *Vila*, his heart sickens with love, and he will neither eat nor drink, until he dies. I nearly believed it myself, my lady Phèdre, and I have seen D'Angelines before. That spot of red, in your eye; is it an injury? It's passing . . . haunting."

"No." I lowered the waterskin, wincing at the pain that tugged at my midsection. "Not exactly. Where do you come from, Glaukos? Not Illyria, I think."

"Ah, now, that's a long story." He took up the skin and squirted water into his mouth. "I was slave-born in Tiberium; my mother was Hellene, a slave herself, and mistress to a powerful man. I was gently reared, I was, and bought by a wealthy member of the Comitia to stand tutor to his children . . . tell me, does it hurt when you breathe?"

"Yes," I said absently, thinking. How long had I been in La Dolorosa? Weeks, I knew; was it months? I'd not kept a count, throughout those first long days. 'Twas summer yet, but growing later. If Ysandre had not departed already to begin the *progressus*, she would have done so by the time a messenger could reach the City of Elua. No, I thought; Marsilikos is a better wager. Surely Roxanne de Mereliot would pay whatever ransom Atrabiades might ask – and Quintilius Rousse would be there, too. 'Twould be well done, if I could enlist the Admiral's aid. Whatever the nature of Melisande's plan, even Marco Stregazza would think twice about acting if the D'Angeline fleet stood off the coast of Caerdicca Unitas. "Glaukos, I need to speak with Lord Atrabiades."

"You've broken a rib, is what it is; maybe two." He felt at my rib cage with surprising gentleness. "Don't worry, I mean you no harm. My mother was a physician's daughter, before she was sold. They fell on hard times, you see; a bad settlement in a lawsuit. Never go against a Tiberian magistrate, I tell you, but never mind that. No doubt Kazan will hear you out once we're safe at harbor. There's a little matter of pursuit, you see. 'You take care of the girl until we make landfall, Glaukos,' he said to me. 'You speak her tongue, you know how to patch folks up.' So never fear, I'll keep my word."

"Ouch!" I flinched away from his prodding fingers. "Glaukos, thank you, but my ribs can wait; my ransom cannot. Will you call Lord Atrabiades for me?"

He sat back and regarded me calmly. "Well, now, he'll not thank you for calling him lord, nor will he turn course for a D'Angeline noblewoman fished out of the sea, no matter how fair her face. And if you ask, he'll only have to refuse and storm and shout a bit, show you the back of his hand to let his men know you're no *Vila* to sicken his heart and make him weak. So no, I'll not summon him for you."

"Never mind," I said, struggling to my feet. "I'll speak to him myself."

Glaukos sucked in his breath and shook his head, watching me go. I made my way toward the stern on unsteady feet, clutching at the rigging as the ship pitched. Sailors moved out of my way, looking askance. Catching sight of me, Kazan Atrabiades stood with one foot braced on the raised edge of the hold, arm propped casually on his knee, watching my progress with narrowed eyes.

Later, I realized what a sight I must have been, with the wind whipping my sea-tangled hair and the ragged grey dress about me, baring vivid red-and-black glimpses of the intricate marque rising betwixt my shoulder blades to my nape; at the time, I gave little enough thought to my appearance. Small wonder the superstitious among them questioned my mortality. But Kazan, I could see, knew better.

"What is it you want, you?" he asked as I approached him, raising his brows. "I ordered Glaukos to tend you; it is enough, yes?"

"My lord." I made him a wobbly curtsy. "You wish to ransom me, I understand. Do you but set sail posthaste for Marsilikos, and the Duchese Roxanne de Mereliot, who is Lady of Marsilikos, will pay in gold; a prince's ransom, I swear it."

"No," he said lazily, looking away. "Go back to Glaukos."

"My lord Atrabiades," I implored, placing a hand on his arm. "Please, it is very important that I carry word to my Queen, and I have no time to lose. I promise you, in Blessed Elua's name, she will grant you clemency for claiming me hostage."

"You listen, D'Angeline!" His hand clamped onto my wrist with startling speed, and his black eyes gleamed with anger. "I do not know, I, why you were in the middle of the sea, but I have saved your life, yes. Your country, you stand by and watch, when Serenissima takes Illyria for her vassal. We ask for aid, yes, but you, you make marriages and treaties with Serenissima." Atrabiades spat again with eloquent contempt. "Now you mock me with fine language, you stand before me in rags and claim a noble title, you ask me to make haste to help your country, yes? To make a journey without provision, when there are Serenissiman warships chasing?" He released my wrist so abruptly I staggered. "I will ask for ransom, I, in *my* time, in *my* way." Raising his voice, he roared at me. "Now go back to Glaukos!"

"Yes, my lord," I whispered, making my trembling retreat.

So much for that idea.

"I told you as much," Glaukos said comfortably upon my return. "Do you stick your head in a lion's mouth, don't be surprised if he bites it off. Well, then, my lady, will you take a deep breath, and permit me to listen to your chest? I have a concern about these ribs of yours."

"You may as well," I muttered, ignoring the ogling stares of Illyrian sailors as Glaukos pressed his grizzled head to my breast. He managed it deferentially; no mean feat, on a ship full of pirates. It lent credence to his tale of servitude.

"Your lungs sound clear," he said, pleased. "It is not a stabbing pain when you inhale?"

"No. Glaukos, is it true that we refused aid to Illyria?" I asked him, adding, "Terre d'Ange, I mean."

"True enough. Lift your arms, I'm going to bind your ribs. 'Twill manage the pain a bit, and keep you from doing further harm while they heal. I've a lass I've trained will do it proper when we make landfall." Concentrating, he wound a length of clean, rough-spun cotton about my rib cage, over my clammy dress. " 'Twas some forty years ago, if I remember aright. The Ban of Illyria begged King Ganelon of Terre d'Ange for an alliance, but the King gauged La Serenissima the greater power, and forged alliance with them, marrying off his brother to the family of the Doge. How's that?"

I took an experimental breath. "Better, thank you. I never heard anything of it. My lor . . . Kazan seems bitter."

"Ah, well now, I doubt most D'Angelines even knew, save the King and his councilors. Illyrians, though; 'tis another matter. One never forgets those who refuse aid in one's time of need. D'Angelines may not be enemies, but you're no friends, mind. And Kazan . . . ah, well, 'tis a long story, that." He wound the extraneous bandage into a ball and placed it in a satchel at his feet. "Surely you know Terre d'Ange is the envy of a great many nations, my lady. To see so many gifts bestowed so profusely on a single people; it rouses covetousness and anger."

"What we have, we have fought to keep," I said, remembering all too well Waldemar Selig's desire to make my land his own. "Glaukos, how did you go from being a Tiberian slave to an Illyrian pirate?"

"I was sold," he said simply, placing a pinch of herbs in a leathern cup. "When my master's children were grown, he'd no need of a tutor, and sold me to another wealthy citizen, who'd need of a trained clerk. He was travelling with his household on a matter of trade, aboard a merchanter bound for La Serenissima, when we were attacked."

"And Kazan Atrabiades took you prisoner?" I surmised sourly.

Glaukos laughed, pouring water into the cup and swirling it. "Not hardly, my lady. He gave me the choice of fighting for my master and dying, or joining him a free man. Ah, now, I'd lived my whole life in slavery, hadn't I? I thought I'd spend the last years of it a free brigand. Kazan's always found a use for me, and I've never had cause to regret it. Here, drink this," he finished, handing the cup to me.

"What is it?" I took it and sniffed, looking questioningly at him.

" 'Tis but valerian, to aid the pain and let you sleep," he said gently. "Your body requires rest, to heal itself. Do you not see, there, how your hand shakes?" He spoke true; I noted with surprise how the leathern cup trembled in my grip, the tincture sloshing. "Indeed, you bear it better than a soldier, but you have suffered a trauma this night past, and the telling of it must wait. Drink, and I will ward you." He smiled at me, and his eyes were kind. "No harm will come to you, I promise it."

Foolhardy or no, I had little choice. I believed him, and drank. Soon weariness overcame me, and I slept, and knew no more.

FIFTY

MY DREAMS were fitful and vivid, filled with disturbing images; darkness streaked with flame, and the violent clash of metal on metal. Always, I was unable to move, bound and restrained, while Melisande's voice whispered like honey in my ear, bidding me to give my *signale*, and beyond, somewhere, other voices pleaded in torment for me to do it, to give it and release them. Fortun, I heard, and Remy; once it was Joscelin, and his face swam in my gaze, blue eyes wide with agony.

It is a dream, I thought, in my drugged, restless sleep. A dream, and no more, Blessed Elua forgive me!

'Tis no wonder, then, that I woke not knowing where I was, nor whether I was awake or dreaming. The rocking motion of the ship was as lulling as sleep, and the strangeness of Illyrian voices around me as incomprehensible as words spoken in a dream. The sun was lowering through clouds behind us, and the sky to the west was shot with fire.

And there, coiled atop the mizzenmast toward the stern of the ship, a moving shadow.

I lay curled against the outer wall of the forecastle,

staring up at it from beneath the canvas awning. A trick of the light . . . no. It moved, sinuous and serpent-bodied, spreading veined wings against the darkling sky; a wedge-shaped head lifted, with glittering eyes the color of old blood. Its mouth opened in a silent hiss, and a three-tined tongue emerged, flickering.

I am not ashamed to admit that I let loose a shout of pure terror.

It sent the entire ship into an uproar, sailors running hither and thither, fearing that the Serenissiman navy was upon them. Glaukos hurried to my side, pale with fright. "My lady, my lady!" he cried in breathless Caerdicci. "What is it?"

Only Kazan Atrabiades had not moved, bestriding the deck with feet planted wide, his dark eyes watching me across the length of the ship.

I looked again at the mizzenmast, and saw only the bobbing tip of the mast, the fluttering sail washed in the red light of the setting sun, a loose rope dangling from the yard. "Forgive me," I murmured to Glaukos, passing my hands over my face. "I awoke from a dream and thought I saw . . . something."

He turned to the nearest sailor and said something soothing in Illyrian; the sailor relaxed, laughed, and passed it on to a comrade. I heard Glaukos' words passed from mouth to mouth, and presently one of the other ships drew in shouting distance alongside us, and the tale of the D'Angeline hostage's hysteria was bantered back and forth across the waves.

I noted that Kazan Atrabiades smiled grimly, and did not laugh.

"I made the dose too strong," Glaukos said

apologetically. "My apologies, my lady; I'm used to dosing full-grown men, you see. Ah, well, you're awake now, and no harm done. We'll be coming soon to harbor, after moonrise . . . will you eat? 'Twill do you good, and we've food to spare; lamb and rice wrapped in grape leaves, if it's not gone off."

"Yes," I said, watching Atrabiades. "Thank you, that's very kind. And water, if I may."

Glaukos brought the food and I ate while he fussed over me like a nursemaid. The setting sun dowsed its flames in the west, leaving ruddy streaks to fade across the horizon. As darkness fell, our pace slackened not a whit; these Illyrians navigated by stars where visible, by touch and feel — mayhap even smell — where not. In the prow of each swift ship crouched an agile sailor with a lantern, cunningly wrought, that provided a bright spark of light by which they remained in communication.

Later, I would learn, there was no pirate more feared along the Serenissiman coast than Kazan Atrabiades the Illyrian, for his seamanship, and the speed and maneuverability of his vessels, were legendary. He fought with ferocity and ruthlessness, and his men were trained to a precision a Camaeline drill team would have envied. He struck swiftly and fled swifter, and no one had ever caught him; in part because he sailed like a demon and in part due to the island-riddled coastline of Illyria, that boasted a dozen or more secret harbors. In eight years of pirating, he had lost only three ships.

All of that and more I would discover to be true; then, I merely wondered distantly at the skill of the Illyrians and huddled drowsily against the forecastle, a worn blanket from Glaukos' stores over my shoulders to ward off any chill. My ordeal and the remnants of the drug had left me weary and drained, my mind as empty as a sounding drum, containing only the hollow echoes of the fearful visions I'd seen. Tomorrow, I told myself. Tomorrow, in the light of day, I will think anew, and find some way out of this predicament.

I was dozing when the footsteps woke me, a deliberate tread unlike Glaukos' soft-footed approach, and I opened my eyes as Kazan Atrabiades hunkered down on his booted heels beside me, back braced against the forecastle. The moon had risen, and I could make him out by its faint light. It gentled his fierce features, picking out a tear-shaped pearl eardrop that dangled from his left lobe, casting a silver sheen on his topknotted black hair that was as coarse and thick as a mountain pony's.

All about us, the ship was quiet; four or five men manned the lines and rudder-bar, speaking in murmurs, while the rest caught naps where they might. The breeze was light, and our progress slow but steady, wavelets lapping along the hull. I sat silently, waiting for Atrabiades to speak.

Presently, he did.

"You cried out, you," he said without looking at me, his low voice blending in with the sounds of the night-bound ship. "When you awaked at sunset time. What did you see?"

I hesitated, then told the truth. "A creature, my lord; or so I thought. Like unto a serpent, but winged, coiled in the mizzen. It raised its head and hissed at me."

"Yes." Atrabiades exhaled sharply. "With a tongue, like . . ." He scowled, searching for the word in Caerdicci, failed to find it and thrust out three fingers, forked like a trident. "Like so?"

"Yes!" I sat upright, wide-eyed and wide-awake. "That's it, exactly!"

He nodded, mouth twisting wryly in the frame of his mustaches. "You do not need fear it, D'Angeline. This is what I come to tell you. The *kríavbhog*, it waits only for me. I am blood-cursed, I, Kazan Atrabiades. It will not harm you."

I rubbed my hands over my eyes, as if to erase the sight. "But my lord, I saw it."

"Yes." Atrabiades turned to look at me then, eyes glinting by moonlight. He wore a pearl eardrop in his right lobe, too; this one black, with a faint, iridescent glimmer. "You bear . . . markings." He touched my blanket-shrouded shoulders, where my marque lay hidden. "I saw, today. I know what it means, I." I regarded him mutely; he responded with a fierce grin. "You think I am a, a barbarian, eh, who knows nothing of your fine ways? I was a warrior always, I, but my brother, he was a scholar, he studied in Tiberium. Daroslav, he knew D'Angelines there, they told him, ah!" He drew in his breath and clicked his tongue. "Men and women, sworn to your goddess of whores, eh, marked for pleasure. He swore to have one for his own, one day. I know what you are, I. The *kríavbhog*, it shows itself to make warning to your goddess, no more."

"Naamah," I said automatically. "I am a Servant of Naamah, my lord, and believe me, she takes no interest in your blood-curse."

"Maybe." He shrugged. "Maybe not. I find you floating in the sea like so, what am I to think, I? Do not tamper with the fate of Kazan Atrabiades, the *kríavbhog* warns. Your Naamah of the bedroom pleasures, she will be sorrowful."

I gave a hollow laugh, passing my hands through my salt-tangled hair. "My lord Atrabiades, I am Naamah's Servant and Kushiel's Chosen, which I think is betimes a curse to put your own to shame. I owe fealty to Asherat-of-the-Sea, who saved my life, and I am bound to cleanse her worship in La Serenissima by my own oath. I bear an ill-luck name, and of those who have aided me, more lie dead or ruined than live. I would caution you and your *kríavbhog*, whatsoever it may be, to steer as clear of my fate as you warn me of yours. And you might do that, my lord, by sailing to Marsilikos at all haste and claiming your ransom."

"Do not name me 'lord.' " He ignored the rest. "I am Kazan Atrabiades, I. And I do not sail at your bidding."

As I opened my mouth to retort, the sailor in the prow gave a soft cry, pointing over the horizon to where a light glimmered. In the clear night, I could make out a low landmass. Atrabiades rose with leisurely haste, giving commands as the ship stirred to life.

I stayed where I was. He paused before he left, staring down at me. "I will claim your ransom, D'Angeline, do not fear. But know this. If he lived, I would give you to my brother Daroslav, eh, my little brother the scholar, who never got to keep his vow."

Whether or not 'twas meant as a warning, I took it as such, gazing up at his shadowed face. "What happened to him?"

"I killed him, I," Kazan Atrabiades replied curtly.

And with that, he strode toward the stern of the ship, leaving me to ponder his words.

If I had thought that our journey was done when we made landfall, I was mistaken. By moon and starlight, aided by the lamphouse at the outermost point, our six ghostly ships sailed into the harbor of a small town whose name I never knew, on the isle of Gavrilos, which is famed for its olive oil. There we dropped anchor, and a delegation of townsmen came out to meet the pirates on the wharf, bleary-eyed by torchlight, but full of good spirits and jest.

Some manner of trade, it seemed, was taking place. Too alert for sleep, I stood watching on the deck while Kazan's sailors ducked in and out of the hold, carrying out goods for the townsfolk's consideration. Salt and spices were met with cries of excitement; silks and fine linens with shrugs, although, here and there, I saw men fingering the fabrics with guilty pleasure.

To my surprise, Kazan was treated with respect and admiration. I did not know, then, the degree to which trade had been suppressed on the Illyrian coast, nor the heavy tariffs imposed on imports. His goods were stolen, true, but among his countrymen, Kazan Atrabiades bought and traded at a fair price. If he made a profit at it, so be it; 'twas at the expense of La Serenissima, and the Illyrians admired him for it.

At the time, I could only gauge this by their demeanor and attitudes, grateful that Delaunay's training allowed me that much. All around me was the give and take of conversation, a hushed midnight banter, full of barter and exchange. I understood not a word of it, and it was maddening.

No few of them cast glances my way, and I saw their hands move surreptitiously in gestures to avert evil. I daresay I looked unearthly enough, a bedraggled D'Angeline apparition in trailing grey, oddly corseted in bandages.

Kazan Atrabiades took little heed, ignoring my presence, busy with matters of trade.

I was relieved when the deal was concluded and Glaukos reappeared at my side, tutting with concern and ordering me off my feet. He sat companionably with me while Kazan's men loaded massive jars of oil into the hold, lashing them in place with ropes.

" 'Tis sleeping you should be, my lady," he said to me. "We'll be off again at first light, and no more than three hours' journey to port."

"Another trade venture?" I asked wearily. I was bone-tired, sick of the sea, and my skin itched fiercely from a fine coating of salt.

"Ah, now, next stop's the last, and glad enough I'll be to see home. You'll feel better in a proper berth, you'll see." Glaukos peered at my face, turning my chin in his hand. "Though you're healing up well enough, I reckon. Unless the moonlight plays tricks on me, that nasty bruise on your jaw's well-nigh faded, my lady. You were ill-treat-ed, were you?"

"Yes." I answered absentmindedly. "As you say, 'tis a long story. Glaukos, why did Kazan Atrabiades kill his brother?"

He made a hushing sound, glancing quickly about, although there was no one to hear but the sailors, who spoke no Caerdicci. Kazan remained ashore, drinking toasts and laughing with the villagers. "We should not speak of this aloud. Who told you that?"

"He did," I said reasonably. "Who else? That thing I saw on the mast, 'twas no figment of my dreaming. He called it somewhat, a, a *kríavbhog*. He said it had to do with a blood-curse."

"Aye." Glaukos sighed. "These Illyrians, they are superstitious, and no mistake. What wasn't bred into them since the mountains were young, the Chowati brought when they invaded and mingled their blood and their ways with the Illyrians. Five hundred years later, they hear *Vili* singing in every breeze, *maredonoi* in the waves; every kitchen hearth must have its *ushkova*, and every home its *domuvic* to be coaxed and bribed. In the fields, they hide eggs for the *pölvu*. In the forests, they turn their clothes backward so the *leskii* won't find them. Kazan, he's better than most. He fears only the *kríavbhog* and mocks the rest."

"He is right to fear," I murmured, "if what I saw was real."

"Who can say?" Raising his hands, Glaukos shrugged. "His mother cursed him, by the blood he shed himself. Kazan believes if he ever returns to Epidauro, the *kríavbhog* will take him, for such were the words of her curse. Other than that, he thinks himself invulnerable. Because he believes it, his men believe it too, and follow him unquestioning."

"And you?" I searched his face in the faint light. "Do you believe it?"

He smiled into his beard. "I am old, my lady, and trained too well to the rationalism of Tiberium, city of my birth. I believe what I see. Ah, now, I've gone and said too much. If you want to know more of it, ask Kazan yourself, and don't blame me if he snarls. Though if you've any sense, you'll heed my advice and sleep."

In the end, since there was nothing else for it, I did, waking only when we headed out to sea once more, oars dipping in long, swift strokes until we were far enough out to hoist the mainsail and catch a bellyful of wind.

Dawn broke fair, pale violet sky giving way to orange, and the Illyrians sang as they sailed. With the relative safety of the coast on their side, holds full of goods and homeward bound, they were in high spirits. Glaukos had spoken true; 'twas still high morning when we came upon a small archipelago of islands. Six or eight, I made out at a distance, though only a few of them looked inhabited.

Our fleet made for one of the smaller islands, steep-cliffed, by the look of it, crowned with a pine-forested range of hills. I felt my breath catch in my throat as we navigated the sheer coast, uncomfortably reminded of La Dolorosa's crags. There was no sign of human life, no harbor or bay, and I wondered what Atrabiades was about. From any approach, I saw no means of access.

So I thought, until we rounded a sharp outcropping and Kazan Atrabiades shouted out a command. The sail cut loose, yard swinging abruptly as we heeled with that stomach-lurching swiftness. Then I saw, before us, a narrow inlet hidden in the shadows of the overhanging cliffs. The Illyrians trimmed the sails close and went to oars, jesting good-naturedly, and as the lead ship, we glided into the cool shade.

Cliff walls, high and grey, rose on either side of us to form a towering corridor. The water lapped softly at the sides of the ship, nearly black in the absence of sunlight. The splashing of the oars echoed oddly. So we proceeded, for several long minutes, hearing the sounds of the other ships following.

And then the cliffs fell away, and the vista opened onto a perfect natural harbor, a sandy bay sheltered on all sides. The sun shone bright overhead in a clear blue sky, and the water glittered aquamarine beneath it, dotted here and

there with fishing boats. Along the half-moon of the shore,
I saw a charming village. A low terrace rose on the hill
behind it, invisible from the sea, planted with grapevines;
further to the right, below the pine forests, I could
make out white specks that were surely grazing sheep on
the hillside.

"The isle of Dobrek," Glaukos said, standing beside
me. "Home."

"It's so . . ." I could hear the bewilderment in my
voice, " . . . *pretty!*"

He chuckled. "Ah now, did I not tell you I had no
regrets?"

FÍFTY-ONE

ACROSS THE bay, the wind picked up once more, a merry breeze that sent our six ships scudding across the water like seabirds. We were spotted ashore, and it seemed the village entire turned out to meet us.

At some twenty yards out, the sailors launched into a flurry of action, taking down the sails and lashing them to the yard with swift, coordinated gestures. Others took to oars, checking our incoming speed and maneuvering the vessels skillfully alongside the waiting docks. The heavily laden craft wallowed a bit, but flat-bottomed as they were, they had a shallow draw and managed the docking without scraping the sandy bay.

Throughout it all, Kazan Atrabiades stood in the prow of the lead ship, legs braced, arms upraised in a sign of victory. And the folk ashore cheered him mightily, men and women alike.

It was a hero's homecoming, and no mistaking it. Kazan leapt ashore once the first line was lashed to the pilings, greeted with hearty embraces by the men and doting smiles or squeals of admiration by the women. 'Twas a grand reunion all around, as the other sailors were welcomed home by family and friends; even Glaukos moved spryly to disembark, greeting a sturdy young woman less than half his age with resounding kisses on both cheeks, making her blush prettily and clasp his hands.

Amidst it all, I stood on the ship, forgotten.

It did not last long. I saw the first glance, heard the first voice fall silent, a silence that spread like a ripple from a dropped stone, rings of soft murmurs following in its wake. "*Ështa në* Vila!" I heard more than once, knowing now what it meant; now, it merely made me glance uneasily at the mizzenmast, sail furled harmlessly. If the *kríavbhog* was there, it did not show itself.

"*Djo djo,*" Kazan Atrabiades said soothingly, holding up one hand for silence. Once they were listening, he pointed to me and spoke at length in Illyrian.

I could see from the way the tension left their expressions that he was explaining I was no *Vila*, but a mortal hostage, reassuring them. Nonetheless, my inability to comprehend a word he spoke filled me with mingled fear and frustration. When I cast an imploring look in Glaukos' direction, he hurried to the dockside. "Ah, now, don't fear, my lady!" he exclaimed. "Kazan, he's telling them you're D'Angeline, that's all, and to be treated as an honored guest during your stay here. Didn't I promise you he'd honor the conventions?"

"You did," I said, taking little comfort in it. Kazan Atrabiades' words were all too fresh in my mind. *If he lived, I would give you to my brother.* I did not care overmuch to trust to the honor of a fratricide, no matter how much his people admired him. Better a hostage than a slave, but it came down to much the same. In the end, I was what I had been all too often for the duration of my short life: valuable goods.

Whatever Kazan said, they seemed to accept it, reluctantly setting aside their curiosity to go about their business, unloading the ships and implementing a complicated system of distribution. Glaukos led me over to where Kazan was directing the operations.

"My lord," I said, taking a deep breath, forgetting once more not to address him thusly, "if I might speak to you—"

"Sa të djambo!" he snapped at me, and I did not need a translator to know I'd been told to keep quiet in the rudest possible terms. I closed my mouth sharply, and Kazan Atrabiades turned to Glaukos, giving him instructions in a string of rapid Illyrian. Glaukos replied in the same tongue, explaining somewhat and pointing to my bandaged midsection. The exchange continued for some time, growing heated. In the end, Kazan shrugged and turned away, dismissing us.

"You're to come with me, for now, my lady," Glaukos informed me. His weathered face was flushed. "Come, my little Zilje will see to those wrappings and draw you a bath." His young wife – for I learned later she was such – came forward with a half-curtsy, coloring to the roots of her red-blond hair.

"Thank you," I said, with as much warmth as I could muster. "Glaukos, how do I say 'thank you' in Illyrian?" I repeated it when he told me, smiling at her. *"Falemir dít,* Zilje."

And with that, Glaukos lent me his arm, and with his young wife fluttering anxiously at his side, aided me in my slow, painful process across the hot sands toward his lodgings.

All told, I was three days in the house of Glaukos, recuperating.

Young and resilient though I was, my ordeal had taken a greater toll than I cared to reckon. Each day I rose, insistent, by mid-morning; by mid-afternoon, I was limp with exhaustion and my ribs ached dully. Zilje scolded me in Illyrian, regarding me with a certain proprietary awe, as if I were a willful and exotic pet her husband had brought back from his seafaring, while her younger sister Krísta, who dwelt with them, stared at me wide-eyed.

There was a great deal of traffic by the women of Dobrek to the physician's house in those three days. I daresay the village had never seen so many toothaches at once. Glaukos, for his part, ignored it; I smiled and nodded, trapped by my own weakness. Zilje dispensed cloves to chew for the pain, and gossiped eagerly with the visitors.

It nearly drove me mad, being unable to understand. I have always been good with languages, and thanks to Delaunay's insistence, I mastered the trick of learning them early. I may have been a slave in Skaldia, but at least I always knew what was being said in my presence. Here, it was different. I speak D'Angeline, Caerdicci, Skaldic and Cruithne with a considerable degree of fluency; I do passing well at Habiru and Hellene, and can make myself understood among Tsingani.

Illyrian, it seemed, was unrelated to any of these.

Since I had naught else to do save heal, I set myself with grim determination to mastering what I might of the Illyrian language. My task was complicated by the fact that Glaukos was often absent or unavailable, and Zilje and I shared no tongue in common. Still, I garnered some small stock of phrases, and was able by the end of my stay to say "please" and "thank you," along with a few simple courtesies. From these, I was able to extract a glimmering of the syntax of Illyrian. It was a beginning.

As to Glaukos' whereabouts, I learned that he served as bookkeeper to Kazan Atrabiades as well as physician, and had been busy cataloguing the inventory and distribution of their latest plunder, entrusting Zilje to see to the day-to-day needs of the villagers. There was genuine affection between the ex-slave and his young wife. I confess, it had been my first thought that she had been given him as reward for good service, but in this I was mistaken. He regarded her fondly, and she him; and so she should, for he had a kinder heart than many who served Kazan. Her sister Krísta treated him as an indulgent uncle, which seemed to suit all three.

On the second day, a fine gift of fabric arrived from Kazan – a silk damask of deepest rose, woven with a trefoil pattern. I ran a fold of it through my fingers, bewildered, and gazed questioningly at Glaukos.

"Ah now, my lady, you should be attired according to your station, shouldn't you?" he said, avoiding my eyes. "I told you he'd do right by you, after all. Old Noní is coming this afternoon. Six fine needles, he promised her, if she'd stitch up something suitable."

I tried to give the fabric to Zilje and her sister, to no avail. What Kazan Atrabiades willed would be done. Old Noní came in turn, a hunchbacked crone with a grim look to her, who muttered and prodded and measured me with a string, returning a scant day later with a garment that startled me in its elegant simplicity, gathered below the breasts and hanging straight to the floor. The design came from an ancient Illyrian poem about a tragic heroine; I wished I'd had a translation, to give to Favrielle nó Eglantine. It would have interested her. At least it left considerable remnants of fabric, which I gave to Zilje and Krísta, much to their delight.

What they made of it, I never learned, for by the end of my third day of convalescence, I was hale enough to have regained my impatience – and for all of his reluctance, Glaukos could not deny that I'd made a remarkable recovery. He acceded to my demands and sent word to Kazan Atrabiades.

So it was that the pirate captain ordered me sent to him, attired in stolen finery after the style of a long-dead epic heroine.

Unlike the weathered pine buildings in the village, Kazan's house was built of stone; blocks of creamy marble quarried on a nearby isle and brought by water to Dobrek. It lay a short walk from the village proper on a rocky escarpment on the bay, gazing out at the sea. A stand of cypresses provided a charming screen, and there were colorful, late-blooming vines I could not name sending tendrils up the marble walls. The house itself was low and meandering, and large enough to be a nobleman's estate. At any given time, it housed not only Kazan, but a small staff and three or four of his men who had quarters of their own. There was a stable, too, with two horses in it; the only ones on the isle. For everything else, they used donkeys.

Kazan was waiting for us on the terrace overlooking the sea when we arrived, flanked by two of his men. His black, topknotted mane was glossy with recent brushing and he wore loose trousers tucked into boots, and over his shirt, a close-fitting vest decorated with Illyrian embroidery. The strip of beard on his chin was fresh-shaven, and even the points of his mustache had been waxed to sharp perfection.

"Lady Phèdre," he announced, bowing, mangling my name only a little. "I welcome you to my house, I! You are my honored guest on Dobrek, eh?"

His men followed suit, staring at me and elbowing each other. Since there was nothing else for it, I curtsied. "*Mirë daj*, Kazan Atrabiades. *Falemir dít*; I thank you for your hospitality."

He started at my greeting him in Illyrian, gazing at me open-mouthed. It showed the gap of his missing molar and rather ruined the overall effect of his appearance. He must have realized it, for he closed his mouth and said hastily, "You did not say you spoke Illyrian, you!"

"I don't, my lor – Kazan." The habit was not easily broken. "Only these few words, which I have learned in your tongue, that my pleas may fall more gently on your ears."

He frowned. "You are like a dog with a bone, eh, worrying at it always! We will speak of this ransom in time, when *I* say. Now you are my guest, and Glaukos, he say you must rest still. So you will go, and do this." Turning away from me, Kazan raised his voice. "Marjopí!"

A vast figure moved out of the shadow of the house's small arcade into the bright sun of the terrace; a woman, massive arms folded across her solid bosom. She was of middle years or older, though her hair, bound atop her head, was a black untouched by grey. Hard black eyes in a doughy face regarded me without favor.

"Marjopí, she has been with me since I was a sucking

babe, I. She will take care of you, eh? Marjopí! *Të lesh gezuan, eh?*" he added, calling to her.

Marjopí — for that was her name — unleashed a stream of Illyrian invective at him, to which he retorted in the same. His lieutenants grinned unabashedly, and Glaukos shifted uncomfortably at my side.

"What is it?" I asked him.

"She thinks you're bad luck," he muttered. "The Illyrians; I told you, they're superstitious. Ah, now, she wouldn't be the first to claim D'Angeline beauty unnatural, but the spot in your eye, now, well, it seems the *kríavbhog* is a red-eyed beastie. It's something to do with that, I gather."

"Mayhap she has the right of it," I answered dourly. Of a surety, the creature I'd seen — or thought I'd seen — had an incarnadine gaze, and I harbored no illusions but that I'd feel the prick of Kushiel's Dart soon enough.

Whatever the cause of the argument, Kazan's will prevailed, and Marjopí conceded defeat with a sniff, nodding at me and jerking her head sharply toward the interior of the house. Given little choice in the matter, I made my thanks to Glaukos and followed her.

Inside, the house was cool, well shaded by its cypress screen. The furnishings were quite fine, albeit mismatched; dark woods and ashen, inlay and scrollwork, Akkadian carpets with Hellene vases. I followed Marjopí to my chamber, which was quite small and barren, holding only a small clothing-press and a narrow bed over which a rich coverlet trimmed with marten had been arrayed. It had a window, which looked out toward the hills, and the shutters had been opened to let the room air.

There Marjopí left me, and there I sat, perched on the narrow bed.

It took no longer than it takes to core and eat an apple for me to grow bored. There are those who are able to endure enforced idleness with grace, spending their time in useful contemplation. Joscelin, who could maintain his Cassiline vigils for hours on end, was one such; save for a patron's whim or at need in the arts of covertcy, I was not. In La Dolorosa, I endured it because I had no choice. Here, it was different.

I gazed out the window, where the honey-colored sunlight warmed the distant pines, releasing their resinous fragrance into the air. I gazed at my feet, clad in unlovely sandals Glaukos had gotten from Dobrek's cobbler. I got up and opened the clothing-press, which was empty except for a cloak of fine-combed, dark-blue wool, bordered with a white pattern.

Well and so, I thought, if Kazan Atrabiades did not want me to leave, then he would have left a guard on me or ordered the door locked. Since it stood open, it must be that I was free to wander. After all, if I had it in mind to escape, where would I go? Dobrek was an island, secluded and secure. I was imprisoned by water as surely as walls.

The house stood quiet and empty in the morning hours; in these parts, people labored until the unbearable heat of midday drove them to rest, resuming in the early evening hours. There was, alas, no library, though I hadn't really expected to find one. Kazan Atrabiades was no Waldemar Selig to grasp with both hands generations of recorded thought as a tool to shape his destiny. No, it was Kazan's slain brother who had been the scholar. Clearly, my pirate lord wanted no reminders of that pursuit. I did find one room that surprised me into pausing outside the door when I heard a sound within. Inside was an old-fashioned vertical loom, at which sat Marjopí, her back to the door, weaving. She was humming as she wove, plying the shuttle with a speed and dexterity that belied her bulk.

As I had no wish to catch her attention or disturb her pleasant mood, I slipped quietly past the door to continue my exploration. Kazan's room I recognized without difficulty. It held an enormous bed with a carved, gilt-trimmed headboard depicting a frieze of hunting dogs. Items of clothing were strewn carelessly across the bed, and a pair of well-worn boots leaned against each other on the floor beside it. By contrast, his arms were hung neatly on a stand in the corner. The short sword in its tooled-leather scabbard, I knew by sight; I did not recognize the corselet and helm with its crisp scarlet plume, the full-length shield painted with a bird of prey clutching a leafy branch in its talons, black on red.

These were not the arms of a common soldier, and by the care he took with them, I guessed they were his own, and not stolen plunder, like so much else in the house. Well, I thought, he said he was nobleborn; mayhap it was true. I glanced around the rest of the room, seeking to learn what I might about my erstwhile rescuer and captor.

On a table by the bedside sat a pomander of silver filigree, unmistakably D'Angeline in workmanship. It was wrought to resemble a twining ball of grapevines, rounded bunches of grapes showing in rounded relief. It opened with a cunning twist, holding a lump of camphor, aromatic as the sun-warmed pines. So, I thought, Kazan Atrabiades has a liking for beautiful and pleasant things. Well, that was good for me; and bad, though no worse than I expected. If he takes a care with them, so much the better.

The only other item of note in the room was a rather battered cabinet of dark cypress wood, inlaid with ivory in a pattern of moons and crescents. The ivory was yellow with age, cracked in places, and the wood bore old scratches long since worn dark with handling. I daresay it had been a fine piece, once, but it seemed an odd item for plunder. I opened the doors onto the lower shelves, which held only clothing. At the top were two small drawers.

One held some parchments, written in Illyrian, and a gold signet ring. Tilting it toward the window and peering at the seal, I made out a device of three bees and a faint inscription. I replaced it carefully and opened the other drawer.

What I had expected to find, I cannot say, but surely not a child's toy. Still, so it was; a wooden soldier and horse, neither much larger than my hand. The soldier's limbs were jointed, so he could sit astride or pace forward and back, and raise his sword and shield. Worn traces of red and black paint were visible on the wood.

I was still holding it and frowning when I heard Kazan's footsteps.

There was nowhere to go, and I could do naught but put the best face on it I could as he came through the door. Careless, to let myself be caught thusly, I was thinking; Delaunay would have lectured me.

Kazan Atrabiades took one look at me and grew still with anger. "Put that down."

FÌFTY-TWO

THERE ARE things we all hold dear; privacies that brook no transgression. I did not need to be told that, for Kazan, this was one such. 'Twas in his face and in his voice, a cold rage more terrible than his shouting. I replaced the toy quietly, closing the drawer.

"I am sorry," I said simply, meeting his eyes. "I meant no harm."

He drew a deep breath and released it in harsh words. "You should not be here, you! I told Marjopí to take care of you! You listen to her, eh, and heed!"

One knows, with patrons, what path their violence will take, and why. And I knew, once he shouted, that the true source of his anger lay far from me. My actions had but kindled it.

"She showed me a room, and left me. Forgive me, but I am unaccustomed to idleness." I added humbly, "I wanted only to know who you are, my lord."

"I will tell you, I, what you need to know, and you will enter this room at my command, eh? You see too much." Gritting his teeth, he caught me by the arm and pulled me after him, out of the room. "If you have a tedium, you speak to Marjopí, and she will give you woman's work to do, eh, to weave or spin, or make the embroidery!" He ushered me to the large inner salon, where Hellene-style couches mixed with rigidly upright Caerdicci chairs. Marjopí had left off her weaving, and hovered in the hall behind us. Kazan still had my arm in his grip and stood close, glaring at me. I could feel my pulse beating beneath the tight grasp of his fingers and feel the heat of his body, mingled with a strange, acrid tang.

Ah, Kushiel, I thought, have mercy on your chosen! Is it not enough that I suffer this? Must I bear humiliation as well? What showed on my face, I cannot say, but Kazan saw somewhat; his grip loosened, and his eyes reflected a measure of puzzlement and awe.

"I cannot do these things," I said aloud. "I was taught other skills."

"Whore's work," he said contemptuously, but conviction was not in it.

"Naamah's work, yes," I replied. "But the Queen employs me as a translator. It is the study of language and politics in which I have been engaged, and not spinning and weaving. My lord, if you order me confined to women's quarters, then so be it; yet I thought you welcomed me as your guest, and not your prisoner."

He tucked his chin into his chest and fingered his mustaches, thinking. "We honor . . . hostages . . . in Illyria," he said slowly. "They are treated as their rank calls, eh, unless those who pay ransom break faith. You are not a prisoner, you. I come to say, you will eat with me tonight, and I will hear your words. But you must not go where it is not permitted, eh?"

"Yes, my lord. Where, then, am I forbidden to go?"

A look of disgust crossed his face. "Already, you see too much; go where you like, you. I will set you a guide." With that, he stalked from the room muttering; I heard Glaukos' name, and the word for "rest," which I had heard often enough to recognize. I waited under the dourly watchful eye of Marjopí until Kazan returned with a young man in tow. "Lukin, he will show you what you wish," he said shortly, exiting again. Marjopí threw up her hands and returned to her weaving.

Thus did I acquire an escort on Dobrek, a good-natured youth of no more than sixteen. He had black hair which he wore in a topknot in emulation of Kazan Atrabiades, and a grin that stretched ear to ear at his assignment; here was one who had decided I was no *Vila* bent on stealing his heart — or at least he reckoned it worth the risk. Although we shared no common tongue, we had youth in common, and Lukin was open and cheerful, eager to communicate where Zilje and her sister had turned shy or reticent. For everything we saw, everything I touched, I made him tell me the word in Illyrian. To this day, there are plants I can name only in that tongue, and fish and birds, too.

It was Lukin who showed me the stable, pointing with pride to Kazan's two horses. I watched his eyes shine with delight as a battlescarred old gelding nibbled from his palm, and was reminded with a pang of Hyacinthe. Not as I had left him, brave and lonely, but as he had been at Lukin's age, merry and daring with a knack for horses.

Beyond the stables, a group of men were gathered around a stone furnace, bare-chested and sweating in the late-morning sun. I pointed inquiringly, and Lukin led me

over to see. There was a great bustle, and Kazan was
supervising the operation, ordering the fire fed and the
bellows worked while two men in leather aprons tended
the crucible. The acrid odor I'd smelled earlier was molten
metal.

"What are they doing?" I asked Lukin. He went over
to fish a silver coin out of a coffer, showing it to me, and
pointing to a mold where silver ingots were cooling on the
ground. I stared in perplexity as he turned the coin, showing me both sides and offering a helpless explanation in
Illyrian. Although the coin was worn and the workmanship
crude, I could make out a man's face in profile on one side,
and on the other, the device I'd seen on Kazan's shield, a
bird of prey clutching a branch.

At length I shrugged, and Lukin returned the coin.

"You want to know why we melt good coin, eh?" It
was Kazan Atrabiades himself, who'd come to glower at
me. He'd laid his good clothes aside and was bare-chested
as the others. "The Serenissimans – " he turned his head
and spat reflexively, " – they make a law against Illyrian
coin that shows the face of the Ban or his arms, old or new,
living or dead. Only in Epidauro is it safe, and not there
any more, maybe. Any man who trades in Illyrian coin, he
have his money taken, and Serenissiman officials, they do
not pay. They put him in prison if he makes complaint. So
people are scared, eh, and poor even though they have
coin. We take in trade, we, and melt it."

I thought how simple a means it was to oppress a
vassal nation. And I thought of Kazan's arms, hung with
pride and care in his room, and the device they bore. "You
served in his guard," I said. "The Ban of Illyria."

His scowl deepened. "It is not your concern, you, what

I did," he said, and turned to Lukin, issuing an order in Illyrian. My escort nodded, and indicated to me that we should leave. By that time, I was glad enough to do so, for my ribs had begun to ache. The sun stood high overhead, and its heat coupled with the blast from the furnace made my head swim. When I looked at Kazan Atrabiades, I saw strange, twining shadows about him. Only sunstroke, I told myself; but I remembered the *kríavbhog*, and was uneasy.

In the house, Marjopí took one look at me and shook her head in disgust, giving Lukin a bucket and a sharp command. He grinned at her and trotted off good-naturedly, while she gave me an ungentle push toward the room I'd been given. I lay down on the bed, and a few moments later, Marjopí came in with a basin of cool water and a linen towel. She dipped the towel and wrung it, laying it on my brow, shook her head once more, and left me.

I slept clean through until supper, waking when a servant lass I'd not seen before came creeping in to awaken me in the twilight. She pointed to the door, saying only, "Kazan." It was enough. I rose and smoothed my crumpled dress, washing myself with the tepid water remaining in the basin, then went to meet him.

The terrace had been prepared for dining, and I own it was a pleasing sight. A table was set below the arbor, where bunches of grapes hung, still green, but swelling. Stands with fretted lamps were set about, casting a gentle glow, and the sea murmured gently. Kazan stood as I emerged onto the terrace, and his eyes drank in the sight of me.

"Phèdre," he said, forgetting his earlier anger. "Sit." I took a seat opposite him, and he sat too, smiling and pouring me wine from a clay pitcher. "What do you think, eh?"

he asked, waving his hand around the terrace. "Does your land have such beauty?"

"Not like this." I drew a deep breath. "My lord Kazan, you said you meant to hear me out. May I speak?"

"No." His quick scowl darkened his features. "First we will eat, you and I. Such talk is for after, yes? That is how we do it in *civilized* countries."

"I – " I paused. "Yes, of course. Forgive my rudeness."

We dined on fish fresh-caught and poached in a wine sauce, a dish of greens and fennel, and bread dipped in oil, and I confess, my appetite was sharper than I had reckoned. When we had done, Kazan gestured for the servant lass to clear the plates. He poured more wine – a pale wine, with a faint taste of resin from the pine casks in which they store it – and regarded me.

"Now," he said, "you may speak of these matters, you."

I nodded. "Thank you, Kazan. What I said to you before, on the ship, is true. It is a matter of great urgency to my country that I am restored to it swiftly. This is my desire, and of no import to you; this I recognize. But it is also true that my friends and kinsmen will pay handsomely for my swift return, and you stand to earn the gratitude of the Queen of Terre d'Ange." I had no kin to speak of, but he need not know it.

Kazan toyed with his wine-cup and looked shrewdly at me. "Why? I find you in rags in the middle of the sea, eh, and you ask me to believe this? Glaukos says it is true, that you are who you say; I know he is right, I, because he is not wrong about such things. Who, yes, but why is another question, yes?"

I had thought about it; I knew he would ask. I would have, if I were him. "The Queen has enemies," I said simply. "I know who they are, and where. If I do not warn her of their plans, she will be in danger."

"Enemies, ah!" He rubbed his chin. "In Serenissima, eh? You tell Glaukos you have money there, you, but you do not say to go to the D'Angeline Prince there, no. When he says I will not go to Serenissima, you say Marsilikos, that is so much farther."

"If you will go to La Serenissima," I said without a tremor, "we will have done with it swiftest of all. I am my Queen's servant and Prince Benedicte does not know me to pay a ransom, but I have money on account with a factor there. I sold lead at a good profit. Name your price, and I will match it if I may."

"Ah, no." He shook his head. "Glaukos, he spoke true. I will not go there, I, nor send any man loyal to me. Maybe you set a trap, eh? Serenissima will pay a good price for the head of Kazan Atrabiades, more than any ransom."

"So." I spread my hands on the table. "Then Marsilikos is closest, where her grace Roxanne de Mereliot is my hearth-friend, and will honor my letter. I will swear to you, by any oath you wish, that no harm will come to you or your men and there is only profit in it for you."

Kazan regarded me, black eyes glinting in the lamp-light. "This we say in Illyria: May the *kríavbhog* swallow my soul if I lie. You have seen it, you. Do you swear this?"

I thought of the thing I had seen, coiled and hissing in the mast. I thought of the shadows twining around Kazan Atrabiades, and shuddered. "Yes," I said hoarsely. "I swear it. The ransom paid, and no harm to you or your men. May the *kríavbhog* swallow my soul if I lie."

"Good." He drained his wine-cup and refilled it. "Why did you fall off a cliff, you?"

I'd thought we were done; I closed my eyes wearily. "It was an accident, my lord. Kazan. It happened in a riot, when some prisoners escaped."

"I think there are many . . . riots . . . where you are, you," he said wryly. "You say you are translator for the Queen, eh, but I think maybe there is another word, and that is spy."

I opened my eyes and returned his regard. "Will you send to Marsilikos or no?"

"I will send, I." He scratched his chin thoughtfully. "What are you worth, eh? Only to make the journey, for the men I will send, the time and the crossing, it is costing me a hundred silver denari. More than that, eh?"

Fury kindled in me, a slow-burning anger at Kazan, at the injuries and indignities I'd endured, at the horrible toll my fate had exacted. "Severio Stregazza, grandson of the Doge of La Serenissima, once paid twenty thousand gold ducats for a single night with me," I said in bitter precision. "Yes, my lord pirate, I am worth more than a hundred denari."

"Glaukos is right, it must be true who you say," Kazan retorted, grinning and showing the gap in his teeth. "Or you would not be so angry, eh? So, good. I will ask for thirty thousand gold, I. You are rich, to have so much! I am not so greedy, and more is to tempt the gods, yes? If they pay, then I believe everything you say."

"They will pay," I murmured. "You may believe it."

"We will see, we," he said off-handedly. "You want me to send swiftly, yes? To me it is no matter, now or in the spring. It is you who asks for speed. What is it worth to you, eh, that I send now?"

I had no illusions about his query. "Does it matter?" I asked, gazing at him in the lamplight. "All I have, you are capable of taking, whether I offer it or no. You said if he lived, you would give me to your brother. What sop does your conscience require now, my lord, that you must force my acquiescence and put a good face on rape?"

His face hardened. "Do not speak of my brother to me," he said shortly, rising and walking some distance away to stare at the dark bay. "I would give your life, yes, and your Queen's too, to have Daroslav alive again. That is what you are worth to me, you. No more." He turned around, expressionless. "I have treated you as a guest, eh. Other men, they would not ask. I ask, I; I offer fair trade."

I thought of the weeks and months I had spent in my vain pursuit, and all those who advised me against it. I thought of Fortun and Remy, who had died because of it, and Ti-Philippe, not knowing if he lived or died. I thought of Joscelin, whom I had judged so unfairly, fighting single-handed against the garrison of La Dolorosa to free me. Did he live yet? I thought so; he had well-nigh prevailed, and that Cassiline was too stubborn to die. I had seen the torch moving on the crags at the isle's base, where only he would be reckless enough to clamber.

I thought of Ysandre de la Courcel, who had once trusted me enough to stake her throne on my bare words, who had asked me not to do this thing; of Quintilius Rousse, who had begged me to accept an escort.

And I thought of Melisande's triumphant smile.

Whatever was necessary, I would do.

"Fair trade," I said evenly. "So be it. Do you send your

swiftest ship on the morrow, I will come willing to your bed, my lord pirate."

Across the terrace, Kazan Atrabiades inclined his head. "Then we have a bargain, yes? I will send Glaukos in the morning, with paper and ink, so you may write this letter." He paused, then added roughly, "I do not ask now, eh? Glaukos, he says you are injured still, and must have time to rest and heal. I am not a barbarian, to ask this of a woman."

'Twas something, at least.

FÍFTY-THREE

WHETHER Í doubted his honor or no, in this, Kazan
Atrabiades kept his word. He rose early, and had made
arrangements for the ship's crew by the time I'd broken my
fast.

The men were in high spirits over the adventure.
Kazan chose a man by the name of Nikanor to oversee the
mission; his longtime second-in-command. He was quick
and restless, with a reputation for making good decisions in
battle, and getting itchy feet on dry land. Well and so; I had
no say in the matter. Nikanor had eleven men on his crew.
Of these, ten would go. For the last, Kazan ordered a sub-
stitution, an elderly fellow named Gorian. He mended
nets, now, but in his youth, he had travelled, and learned to
speak Hellene in those lands. In a pinch, he would do as
translator. Marsilikos was a major port; there was always
someone to be found who spoke Hellene. I'd no doubt that
the Lady of Marsilikos did.

I was glad Glaukos was not to go, though 'twas
naught to do with me; Kazan had too much use for him
here. He came to the house as promised, bearing several

sheets of crudely pressed paper, a fresh quill and a bottle of ink.

Since there was no suitable desk, I knelt at a table, thinking over my words and writing swiftly – in Caerdicci and not D'Angeline, that Glaukos and Kazan might scan my words for any hint of subterfuge. " 'To Roxanne, Duchese de Mereliot and Lady of Marsilikos,' " I wrote, " 'greetings from Phèdre nó Delaunay, Comtesse de Montrève. Blessed Elua grant that this letter finds you in the best of health. I write to you from the keeping of Kazan Atrabiades of Illyria, to whom I owe a debt of ransom. I am well and hale, and commend him in all ways for tendering the courtesies due my station. This letter he bears at my request, and in exchange for its swift delivery, I have promised clemency for him and all his men. I pray you treat them gently, for if you do not, I shall be forsworn and my immortal soul forfeit. Your Grace, by the friendship you bear for me and our mutual service undertaken on behalf of Her Majesty, Queen Ysandre de la Courcel, I beg of you the boon of rendering payment of a ransom of thirty thousand gold ducats to Kazan Atrabiades: half to be paid unto the bearer of this letter, one Captain Nikanor, and half to be paid to Kazan Atrabiades after he has guaranteed my safe-conduct to a place of exchange, to be divulged by Captain Nikanor. For surety of this loan, I pray you seek out my uncle Quintilius, whom you know, and remind him of the aid he pledged to send me in La Serenissima ere I journeyed. I am grateful, for there was no loan of assistance to be had in that city. Pray convey to him my apologies that I needs must ask him to give it to the fullest extent, and please be assured that I will render remuneration in full. My undying thanks to you, my lady, and Elua's blessing upon you and your house.' "

Once done, I signed my name and sprinkled sand to dry the ink. Kazan held the letter at arm's length and pondered it, frowning, until Glaukos took it and read it aloud. Kazan could read Caerdicci, but he was long-sighted and my D'Angeline script was hard for him to make out.

"This uncle of yours, he is rich, he?" he asked when Glaukos had finished.

"He has ships," I said. "Enough to stand surety for the loan. And he will verify the authenticity of the letter, for only he and I know of his offer to send aid."

"Good." He nodded his head briskly. "It is well thought, eh?" He said something to Nikanor in Illyrian, then grinned and clapped my shoulder. "Three weeks, no less! You will see, you, how a true sailor flies!"

The men laughed and made comments I could not understand; for once, I could have cared less. No one had recognized my "uncle" as the Royal Admiral of Terre d'Ange. I daresay any D'Angeline would have done so, for Quintilius is a Caerdicci name, and unusual among us. But it is common in Caerdicca Unitas, and raised no brows among the Illyrians.

He will know, I thought, sealing the letter with wax and blowing on it. He will remember; he must! He had promised me: *If you've need of aid, Phèdre nó Delaunay, know this. Do you but send word to the Lady of Marsilikos or myself, I will come. I will come with ships; and I will come in force.* I only hoped he would understand from my words that 'twas La Serenissima I meant him to assail, and not the Illyrians. Well and so; I had written as plainly as I dared, under the circumstances. The wax having cooled, I slid the letter into an oilskin pouch and gave it to Nikanor, who accepted it with great ceremony, tying it to his belt.

It was not yet noon when the ship set sail. I went, because I could not bear not to see it, and because it was a grand occasion in the village of Dobrek. An old priest hobbled down to the harbor, offering prayers in Illyrian, libations of wine and — to my squeamish dismay — a rooster. Bindhus, they prayed to, who is Lord of the Seas, and Yarovit, who is their Sacred Warrior; I had not known, until then, that the Illyrians had aught but nature-spirits and ghosts and curse-creatures in their pantheon, but they do.

Kazan Atrabiades gave the call to hoist anchor from the shore and Nikanor echoed it aboard the ship, drawing his sword and raising it to flash in the bright sunlight. The sailors set to at the oars, and the ship moved slowly away from the harbor; once in the middle of the bay, they scrambled to raise sail. It luffed and flapped and bellied full, and then they had caught it, angling steadily toward the hidden egress.

And there, I thought, standing on the sun-warmed sands and watching the vessel dwindle in the distance, goes the hope of an entire nation, in the hands of a pack of unlettered Illyrian pirates intent only on booty.

Still and all, 'twas done, and I could do no more. For the first time in days — weeks, mayhap months — the terrible burden of urgency was lifted, leaving me weak with relief. Now, when no one threatened me, I found myself shaking. Tears blurred my vision and I fought to keep from blinking, staring out at Nikanor's receding sails.

"Ah, now, don't fear, my lady," Glaukos said kindly, seeing my distress. "They're good men to a lad, they'll be back before you know it, and 'twill all be resolved, you'll see." He patted my hand awkwardly, and I shook my head, wordless, tears streaming down my face. "Ah, now, now, don't cry, child . . . do you want me to take you back to Kazan's house, eh?"

"Yes, please," I whispered; I dared trust my voice no further.

Elua be thanked, he did just that – for once started, my tears flowed unceasing. All that time in La Dolorosa, I had not wept. From the moment Benedicte had ordered the deaths of Remy and Fortun, despair had turned my heart to stone. Not until I saw Joscelin had the stone cracked and I begun to feel. But hope had been snatched away too soon, and despair returned as my familiar companion.

And now hope, frail hope, undid me again, and hard on its heels came the great, rushing wave of grief I'd walled out for so long. Glaukos got me somehow to Kazan's house; I could scarce see by then, putting one foot before the other. I heard his voice murmuring to Marjopí as I lay on my bed, curled in a ball and wracked with silent, shuddering sobs.

It is enough, I think, to say that I lived it all over again that day, the terrible, endless moment in Benedicte's hall, where I watched my chevaliers cut down out of hand, overwhelmed and brutally slain before my eyes. Remy, cursing, holding them all at bay for a few seconds, then going down like a hunted stag. And Fortun, coming so close, his reaching hand leaving a bloody trail on the door. All this and more, every minute of every day I spent in the confines of La Dolorosa; the poor, awful madmen, and ah, Elua! Dumb, kind Tito, who brought me honey, and died protecting me, so nearly taking me with him.

And the look, the dreadful look on Joscelin's face . . .

Truly, I have an ill-luck name.

Grief heals, they say in Eisheth; unshed tears fester like a canker in the soul. Whether or not it is true, I do not know. I wept until I could weep no more, and then slept as long and as hard as I had that first night in Glaukos' house.

Thus began the long, slow days of waiting, wherein I learned sympathy for sailors' wives, who spend their days scanning the horizon for sight of a sail, betokening the safe return of their loved ones. Glaukos came each day to the house, and we sat in the cypress shade, eating salted melon while he taught me to speak Illyrian. It had taken him nearly three years to learn it, but he'd had no formal structure of teaching, only such skills as he could glean in conversation with Kazan. I made him teach me as I had learned to study language, establishing basic rules of grammar and working outward.

Sometimes Lukin would join us, and others of Kazan's men, the young ones, lounging in the cool shade and listening, interjecting to teach me jests and use-words such as made Glaukos blush. I daresay they picked up some few words of Caerdicci along the way . . . in truth, mostly they came to look at me. I came to know them that way; Epafras the romantic, who sighed and cast puppy-eyes; shy Oltukh, who swam like a fish and brought me offerings of shells strung on leather thongs; Stajeo and Tormos, who were brothers and endlessly competitive; Volos, whom everyone said could talk to birds; and Ushak, whose ears stuck out like jug handles.

None of them would have dared lay a hand on me, for whatever the status of hostages on Dobrek, of a surety, I was marked as Kazan's — and that, they respected. For his part, Kazan Atrabiades tolerated it better than I would have reckoned, keeping a wry eye on his lads and setting one of the older, more sober men to chivy them back to work as needed, performing the myriad tasks it seemed a life of piracy entailed. There were sails to be mended and rigging restored. Pitch was rendered into tar, and each ship sealed anew.

There were trade excursions, too, to outlying islands in the archipelago. Kazan went on one such a few days after Nikanor's ship had sailed, and was gone overnight, returning in good spirits after unloading his booty at a profit. He had left me well enough alone before his journey, heeding his promise to put off his claim while I continued to heal. But I saw upon his return that it had been much on his mind, and his gaze followed me hungrily.

In the morning, he oversaw the distribution of the grain he had bought in trade. All of it was done in barter on the island, the villagers trading for wine and wool and the like. Afterward, I had my daily lesson with Glaukos, and then, when the worst heat of the day had passed, Kazan approached me.

"You come with me, you," he said. "There is a thing I would show to you. Do you know to ride a horse, eh? It is said that noble-born are taught in your country, yes?"

"Noble-born or no, I can ride," I said, rising.

They'd gotten the horses ready, and young Epafras cast adoring looks at me, holding the head of the quiet mare as I mounted. Kazan swung astride his old gelding with careless ease, and I could see by the way it responded to his touch that he'd ridden it long and well; probably, I guessed, in battle. I'd noted before that it was scarred like a cavalry mount, glancing blows on the chest and flanks.

"Come," was all he said.

We rode to the foothills, where the pine forest began and a rutted logging trail cut into the deep green shade, pocked by donkeys' hooves and the deep traces of the logs they dragged to the village. The air was cooler and fragrant, and I breathed deeply of it as we made the ascent. The farther we went, the larger the trees. This was old forest, where the Illyrians say the *Leskii* abide. They are the green-eyed protectors of the forest, covered in black fur, with cloven hooves; anyone who takes a tree without asking permission of the *Leskii* first may be doomed to wander the forest until he dies and his flesh nourishes the earth.

I could nearly believe it myself, once the logging trail ended and we turned onto a narrower route, a worn footpath marked by blazes on the trees. It was steep going and we rode single file; I found myself looking around at the crowded trunks, half-expecting to find a pair of green eyes peering back. Kazan was impervious; Glaukos had spoken truly, he feared naught but his own especial demon.

It took an hour's time, but we reached the summit of the island without seeing a *Leska*. Here, the trees thinned, giving way to barren stone – and a spectacular view of the archipelago. I confess, I gasped in awe to see it, spreading away from me in all directions. In the late-afternoon sun, the distant sea shone like hammered gold, other islands lying dark and hazy on the horizon. Behind us I could see the harbor of Dobrek clearly, shaped like a crab's claw.

A simple watchman's hut stood atop the summit, and a great pyre of wood some distance from it in a circle of well-cleared ground. A pair of Kazan's men came out to meet us, saluting and grinning. He greeted them in Illyrian, which I more than half understood. I sat patting my mare's sweat-darkened neck and wondering why he had brought me when Kazan pointed to the west and said, "There."

There was the vague outline of a low island — Halijar, it was called — a bit to the left, and beyond, only the sea, and a broad, shining path laid on it by the sun. "My lord?" I asked politely.

"Is in that way Marsilikos lies, eh?" he said, glancing sidelong at me. "I am thinking you would want to see it, you. When Nikanor comes, we will see his sails, eh, and a runner will come to tell of it. So you see, and you will know, you, when he comes."

It was an unexpected kindness, and it touched me; tears pricked my eyes and the bright vista swam blurrily. "Thank you," I said, meaning it.

"Yes. You are welcome, you." Kazan sat at his ease in the saddle, reins loose, hands crossed on the pommel, and looked steadily at me. "I am thinking too, that you are well now, eh? And we have a bargain."

I took a deep breath, without so much as a twinge from my ribs, and let it out slowly. "I am, my lord, and we do. Let it be kept."

Kazan inclined his head. "Tonight, yes?" he said, then added, grinning, "Or earlier, if we ride fast, eh!"

I laughed despite myself.

FIFTY-FOUR

FOR ALL his jesting, Kazan did not hasten our return, but held his eagerness in check and rode at a measured pace. Dusk was falling by the time we reached the house and turned the horses over to the care of Lukin and Oltukh, and I saw that the terrace had been made ready for dining.

Well and so, I thought, he wants this to be properly done. "As it please you," I said to him, plucking at my skirts, "I would bathe, and change into somewhat smelling less of horse, my lord. So it would be done in Terre d'Ange."

"I guessed that, I," he said, amused. "D'Angelines, you are always bathing, eh? Go."

I went, and found that in my room, the rose-damask gown had been laid out fresh, pressed with hot irons. In the bathing room were clean linen towels, and a small flask of scented oil. It amused me that Kazan had prepared so well for this, and made me like him a little better.

'Twas nonetheless true that he had forced me into this bargain, and that I did not forgive. Still, I had made it, and so doing, given consent. And as I was Naamah's Servant, so was I bound by it. I thought on that, smoothing fragrant oil into my skin in the steam-wreathed room. Naamah herself had made bargains for less.

Mayhap there were other ways she could have achieved the same end, but such was her gift, and such she gave. Well, I thought, combing out my hair in my bedchamber; if I am truly her Servant, it is much the same. Let it be done, then, and the bargain kept freely. My lady Naamah, pray you see that Kazan Atrabiades keeps his as well as I do. I am in your hand, and must trust to your mercy.

I asked Marjopí in faltering Illyrian if she had a mirror I might borrow, but she merely looked at me askance and made a sign against evil, disgruntled by the night's proceedings. I knew full well the Illyrians had no proscriptions against mirrors, for Glaukos' wife Zilje had a bronze-handled one she used. No mirror, no cosmetics, nor adornments, nor hairpins; still, I made the best of it, donning a long, shimmering necklace of shells given me by Oltukh and twining my hair into a lover's-haste knot at the nape of my neck.

It would have to do.

And it did well enough, I daresay, for when I walked onto the terrace, Kazan did not rise, but merely sat and stared, open-mouthed. There is a feeling one comes to know, in the Service of Naamah; when one entrusts oneself wholly to Naamah, her grace enfolds one like a cloak. So said Cecilie Laveau-Perrin, who taught me in the arts, and she should know, who was the pride of Cereus House. I have found it to be true.

"You," Kazan said hoarsely, rising to his feet and bowing. "You are enough to make the gods jealous, you."

There is something else that comes of placing oneself in Naamah's hand, and that is desire. It would have happened with me anyway, but it comes sooner with Naamah's surrender than when pressed to it by Kushiel's Dart. I gazed at Kazan Atrabiades, and felt my blood quicken in my veins.

He was not ill-made, Kazan, although I had been reluctant to concede it. In truth, his fierce good looks were much sought after by the young women of Dobrek. And he was vain, after a fashion; if the Illyrian style of pointed mustaches and narrow beard were not to my taste, I had to admit he maintained his with care. He'd even paid a visit to the bathing room himself, and his black hair gleamed with brushing.

When all was said and done, he did cut a rather dashing figure.

It was a balmy and beautiful night, with bright stars emerging in the canopy of black overhead. The sea murmured and sighed as we dined on chicken roasted with rosemary and stuffed with goat cheese, accompanied by a salad of lentils and parsley — and wine, a good deal of wine. It was a red wine, new and a little harsh on the tongue, but I drank it recklessly and it made the lamps burn brighter. Kazan had two cups to my every one, and his gaze never left me. When his speech grew thicker, it was with desire, and not wine.

A cord may only be drawn so taut before it snaps; so with him. The servant lass had not yet cleared the dinner things when Kazan pushed back his chair and stood, extending his hand to me. "Come here, you," he said in his hoarse whisper.

Naamah's Servant, I went.

His hands closed hard about my waist and his mouth came down on mine; his tongue parted my lips, and he kissed me as a starving man eats. Urgency went through me like a bolt, and I wound my arms about his neck, his long hair sliding over my bare skin, kissing him back. He groaned aloud in my mouth, hands sliding lower to cup my buttocks, kneading my flesh and drawing me hard against him. Crockery slid off the table and smashed as he leaned me back against the edge of it, bracing his thighs against mine. I put my head back as his hands rose to fondle my breasts, nipples rising taut in response beneath the fabric of my dress. He moved his mouth over my neck and throat as if to devour me whole, tearing away my necklace of shells with one sharp jerk.

Never mind, I thought foolishly, Oltukh will make me another. I was ready for Kazan to take me then and there; Elua knows, more than ready. It was he who reined himself in, raising his head and breathing hard.

"It is not right, here," he said harshly. "Inside!"

Inside, outside; it mattered naught to me. Grasping my hand hard enough to hurt, Kazan strode into the house, dragging me stumbling after him. I caught a brief glimpse of Marjopí's face as we passed, too astonished to be disapproving. Moving like the wind, Kazan hauled me into his bedchamber and slammed the door shut behind him.

"Here," he said, reaching for me.

"Wait," I whispered; I had regained a measure of composure and guided him to the bed. The room was dimly lit by a single clay lamp. He sat staring avidly at me as I stood before him and loosed the ties that bound my dress, letting it slide from my shoulders. Stepping neatly out of it, I knelt before him to remove his leather boots.

Undressing is the first of the arts of the bedchamber proper that one learns and it is one of the hardest to execute with grace, being fraught with awkwardness in a way that lovemaking is not. I did not practice it often, as an *anguissette*; still, I knew what I was about. When I had done with his boots, I rose to remove his shirt. There is a trick to it, sliding one's hands under the hem that they may glide over the flesh as the shirt is raised. I could feel his chest rise and fall with his swift breathing.

When I unlaced his breeches, fingertips skimming the rigid phallus trapped beneath, he made an inarticulate sound. Still, he managed to stand. I drew his breeches down slowly, dragging my nails lightly over the skin of his hips and legs as I sank to my knees.

And that is as far as I got with D'Angeline subtleties and Kazan Atrabiades, who was shuddering all over like a fly-stung horse. In a trice, he had me on the great bed with its gilded headboard, and his face hovered over mine, flushed with triumph and desire as he forced my legs over his shoulders. With a great groan of relief, he sheathed himself in me to the hilt.

It had been a long time; a very long time, as I reckoned such things.

I daresay he took rather longer at it than I had expected. For all his impatience, Kazan knew the value of self-control, and he was no green lad to spend himself in one furious spurt. Conquest was his trade, and he plied it with women as well as enemies. Once inside me, he moved in long, steady thrusts, increasing his pace until it brought me to the brink of pleasure and beyond, then slowing until I whimpered with frustration and dug my nails into his back, pleading in D'Angeline. Only when I had been well and truly plundered did he take his own pleasure, his expression turning far-off and distant as the critical moment came.

Afterward he slept, as deep and sound as a man who has achieved his goal after long, hard labor. Since he had not told me to go, I stayed beside him, and lay awake thinking long after the lamp had sputtered into darkness, remembering the *kríavbhog* and wondering. In time my eyes grew heavy, and I, too, slept.

When I awoke, the sun was well above the horizon and Kazan was gone.

Marjopí gave me a breakfast of dates and honey with fresh bread to sop in it, giving me the evil eye and muttering in Illyrian. I ate in the bright, sun-lit kitchen, with several house cats twining around the legs of the table, and listened to her until I could endure it no more.

"I understand, a little," I said in Illyrian. "I do not mean harm to Kazan. When Nikanor comes, I will go."

She gave me the same look she had when I'd asked for a mirror; as if I were one of her cats that had suddenly opened its mouth and talked. "Oh, you are not bad in yourself, I know this," she said grudgingly. "But better you go now than later, before you steal his heart." She pointed to my left eye, marked by Kushiel's Dart. "It is bad luck, this says, and when blood-curse crosses blood-curse, someone will die."

Or somewhat similar; I was guessing, a little bit, but I understood the sense of it. "He will not let me, until the money comes. Marjopí, why is Kazan . . . " I stumbled over the word ". . . blood-cursed? Because he killed his brother? Why?"

But she would not answer, and only turned away muttering again, too low to make out.

Thus was the pattern of my days and nights of waiting established. I have no words to describe my relationship with Kazan Atrabiades during that time for, in many ways, 'twas stranger than any I have known. By day, it pleased him to think himself my host, and not my captor; sometimes he played the role so well I daresay he forgot it himself, although I never did. By night, it was different, and sometimes I did forget that I was in his bed because I was a hostage, and not a Servant of Naamah.

And sometimes he was nearly like a friend, which was strangest of all.

Those were times when he was light of heart, and wanted to spin out the night with talk and love-play. It came to be a running jest among his men, to number the reasons why Kazan Atrabiades was short of sleep. "Kazan had fleas in his bed last night and could not sleep for itching," one would say to the others with a straight face. "Do not trouble him today." And the next day, another; "An owl kept Kazan awake all night; beware his temper!" And Glaukos would color, knowing I understood.

Other times, he was moody and withdrawn, and those were the times when the crawling shadows in the corners of his room made me uneasy. It was not until I awoke one night to find him standing in a square of moonlight, holding the wooden soldier, that he spoke of it.

"Kazan," I said gently, sitting up in bed. "What is it?"

For a moment, he said nothing, then answered roughly. "No matter, eh? I dreamed, I. It is nothing. Go to sleep, you."

I watched him put the child's toy carefully back in the drawer and close it; I'd not gone near it since the first time. "There is truth in dreams, sometimes. It was a dream that sent me to La Serenissima. Do you speak of it, my lord, mayhap I can help — "

"I dream of my brother when he was a boy." Kazan interrupted me, his voice grim. "He comes to me covered in blood, eh, and asks why I killed him!"

I caught my breath, and waited; he glared at me across the moonlit room. For the space of three heartbeats I waited, and finally asked it, quietly. "Why did you?"

For a short eternity, he only glared, and then the anger went out of him with a shuddering sigh and he sat on the edge of the bed, burying his face in his hands. I could barely make out the muffled words. "It was an accident."

Naamah's arts are not only for love, although ignorant people think so. I drew the story out of him that night like a thorn, piecing it together. The Atrabiades line was an old one and noble in Illyria; his father had been a captain in the Ban's Guard, with estates in Epidauro. A gently-bred wife, he had, and two sons; Kazan the warrior, his father's pride, and Daroslav the scholar, his mother's favorite. When he died in a skirmish, Kazan resigned his commission in the Epidauran navy to follow in his father's footsteps and join the Guard.

All of this was some ten years ago, and he but twenty-two or three years of age, a fierce, bright young warrior, rising quickly in rank until he had a unit of his own to command. It was the time of Cesare Stregazza's last great effort as the Doge of La Serenissima to subdue Illyria entirely and place a regent in Epidauro to rule it.

And it was a time when Kazan's brother Daroslav was home on leave from his studies at the University of Tiberium, much against his mother's wishes.

"He begged and begged, he," Kazan told me, staring

open-eyed at his memories. "He had been studying the great battles, eh, the great generals. Always, he wanted to be like me, you know? To carry a sword, and be a soldier, to fight for Illyria like our father. Since he was a boy, he has this wish, to be something from the tales he studies. And our mother is so proud, she, to have a scholar-son; a great statesman, eh, this is what she sees for Daroslav, not to die on the end of a spear, like his father, like his brother will, she thinks."

I poured him water from the pitcher on the bedstand; he drank it at a gulp and told me the rest: How the Ban's Guard had ridden down a Serenissiman contingent in the foothills, and learned of an assault to be launched on the armory in Epidauro in two days' time; how they had planned to conceal themselves within, ambushing their attackers. And how Kazan had relented, and told Daroslav of their plan, that he might observe it from a safe distance.

It had not been enough for Daroslav Atrabiades, who had drawn on the cunning of the great generals he had studied to conceive a brilliant rear-guard attack. Armed with his elder brother's second-best sword, he rallied a handful of young men disgruntled at having no post in the Ban's Guard. When the trap was sprung, they fell on the Serenissiman rear.

By all accounts, Daroslav fought very well indeed, wresting a Serenissiman helmet and a full-body shield with the Stregazza arms from the first man he killed. Thus armored, he broke through the Serenissiman line and burst into the arsenal in the flush of first triumph, racing to take his place fighting at his vaunted brother's side.

"He opened his arms, he," Kazan said. "He opened his guard, and said my name, eh? And I saw only the helmet and the shield, I, the arms of Serenissima. I stabbed him in the heart."

I had thought . . . I don't know what I had thought. Something else — a quarrel, a woman, something. Kazan was hot-tempered; 'twas easy to cast him as the villain. Not this awful, tragic dupe of fate. "I am sorry," I said at length. "Truly, my lord, I am."

He stirred; I nearly think he'd forgotten me, telling it. "No matter," he said, his voice hardening. "It is done, and I am blood-cursed, I, with my mother's bitter words to make it stick, eh? So she spoke them, when we carried him home, and I followed the bier, I, with Daroslav's blood on my hands. No more to have a home, no more to go to Epidauro, or the *kríavbhog* will swallow my soul. Always it waits and watches, yes, but it will not have me yet!" And he stared fiercely into the darkness in the corners of the room, as if daring it to defy him.

Well and so; that was the story of Kazan Atrabiades, who slew the brother he loved. I got him to sleep in time, and the ghost of Daroslav troubled him no more that night, nor in the nights that followed.

FIFTY-FIVE

A LIGHT rain was falling the day that Nikanor's ship returned.

I was sitting on a bench in the arcade with Glaukos, enjoying the coolness in the air and practicing my Illyrian when the runner came from the summit, panting and barefoot. Someone ran to fetch him a dipperful of water and someone else ran to get Kazan.

By the time the ship had entered the harbor, we had all assembled on the beach to greet it. Though I kept my features composed, my heart was beating like a drum. There wasn't much of a breeze, and it seemed to take forever for the ship to cross the quiet bay. I dashed the rain from my eyes repeatedly and struggled to conceal my impatience.

At twenty yards out, I realized something was amiss; Nikanor's crew was undermanned. Twelve had gone forth, but I counted no more than six on deck. Kazan saw it too. I noted his thoughtful frown before he drew his sword and hailed the ship. The gathered crowd murmured. They could count, and they had sons and brothers and husbands aboard that vessel.

Nikanor returned Kazan's hail with a shout, drawing his own sword in salute as the oarsmen put up and the ship glided alongside the dock. Some few of Kazan's men ran out to meet it, leaping agilely aboard to aid in furling the sails while the rowers rested on their oars.

"Wait here," Kazan told me, striding toward the dock.

I waited in agony as he conferred with Nikanor, trying to read their conversation in their expressions and gestures. Kazan was frowning, but he was not in a rage; Nikanor explaining. While they talked, men disappeared into the hold, reemerging with heavily laden coffers, which they bore onto the beach under Kazan's scowl. Everyone crowded round, straining to see or hear, and I felt jostled and anxious.

Presently Kazan and Nikanor disembarked, and Kazan addressed the villagers, sparing a brief glance in my direction. "The D'Angelines will meet our terms," he announced in Illyrian – I understood it passing well by now, though I spoke it poorly, "but they have claimed six men as surety for our bargain, until it be finished. As surety for their good faith, they send this." And he ordered the locks struck on the coffers.

Gold coins gleamed in the dismal light, fresh-minted D'Angeline ducats, stamped with Ysandre's elegant profile on one side, and on the other, the lily and seven stars of Blessed Elua and his Companions. A full half my ransom – fifteen thousand in gold, all at once.

A soft sigh arose from the villagers; I daresay none of them had seen so much gold in one place before. Kazan grinned wolfishly. He'd won them over with it, and he knew it. "And our lads home safe and as much again in gold when the Lady Phèdre is restored to her people!" he shouted, rousing a cheer. Some of those crowded nearest even pressed my hand in thanks, as if I'd willingly chosen to provide them a fortune in ransom.

After this, Kazan gave swift orders for the conveyance of the ransom into safe storage, and the arrival party began to disperse. I caught at Nikanor's arm as he made to pass me.

"Please, my lord Captain," I said to him in halting Illyrian. "Does my lady of Marsilikos send word for me?"

Nikanor's eyes flickered and he drew himself up wearily. "She says . . . yes, she sends word. No token, for fear we would be captured. She says to tell you, your uncle received your message, and he sends the aid of which you spoke. Also that she will keep your vow, do we play her fair, and Kazan's men will be restored to us." He made me a brief bow, and I saw that lines of exhaustion and bitterness were etched into his features. "It is enough, I hope."

"Yes," I said, releasing his arm. "Thank you, my lord Captain. It is enough."

It was; it had to be. It was all I had hoped . . . and yet. It was less.

They conferred that night in private, Kazan and Nikanor and his men, and their talk ran late into the small hours. A keg of wine was breached, and I lay awake in my narrow guest-bed for the first time since Kazan had taken me to the summit of the isle, listening to their voices carried on the night breezes as, toward the end, they got roaring drunk and sang Illyrian war-songs. I knew something of Kazan Atrabiades now, and knew that he meant to have his men back, hale and whole, come what might. I could not blame her, but 'twas a risky thing, this choice of Roxanne de Mereliot's, to keep his men hostage against my return. I'd sooner she had taken his bargain on faith.

Still, without them, she had no surety; fifteen thousand ducats was a mighty sum, and Kazan would be no fool if he took the half and slew me out of hand. It was wisely done. So I told myself and prayed it was true, falling asleep to the distant sound of war-songs.

On the morrow, Kazan was brusque and distant, keeping me out of the way while he closeted himself with his captains and discussed strategy. I found Lukin inspecting javelins in the armory and pestered him for information, grateful that my studies in Illyrian had progressed to a point where I might do so.

"He's right angry, my lady," Lukin said, shrugging apologetically. "Though likely he would have done the same thing himself. Still, it put them at risk, to sail such a distance in a half-manned ship. But 'tis no fault of yours, and Kazan knows it, I think."

"Where is the . . . trade . . . to take place?" I asked him.

"Off the southern Caerdicci coast, there's a little isle, near Baro; small traders put in to take on fresh water, sometimes, but there's naught of value that the Serenissimans would garrison it, and Baro has no navy. The D'Angeline ship should be on its way already, slow as it is." He grinned at the latter; Illyrians have no respect for anyone else's seamanship.

"We trade on land?"

Lukin shook his head. "Nay, we'll anchor at sea, and come alongside her. We're mobile at sea, my lady, more so than any war-galley or merchanter. Kazan's not like to give up that advantage. Nor will he give you over until his men are safe."

In another corner of the armory, two men were tallying barrels of pitch and stripping rags. Kazan Atrabiades was taking every precaution, I thought. "He will, though, yes? Give me over?"

"Of course!" Lukin jerked his head up, as though I'd stung his honor. "If your people do not break faith," he added grimly.

"They will not," I said quietly, taking my leave.

We were four days making preparations for this journey, and I was right, Kazan was indeed preparing for the worst. For three days in a row he drilled his men mercilessly, at close fighting with short sword and buckler, and at javelins and archery with straw-stuffed targets under the blazing sun, until they sweated buckets and cursed his name. I could believe, then, that he had commanded a unit in the Ban's Guard. I do not know much of soldiering, but I have seen some little bit of it, and from what I saw, his men were well-trained; better than one would expect of lawless brigands.

Me, he ignored during this time, and while I was glad enough of the reprieve, it made me uneasy. I knew his mind and his temper well enough by then; I misliked this brooding discourtesy.

Still, the days passed, though they crawled in my eyes, and in time Kazan bade me to gather my things and make ready to sail on the morrow. I thought he had done with me by then, but I was wrong; he had me that last night, summoning me once more to lie in his great bed with the gilded headboard. I went, praying to Naamah to have a care for her Servant, who kept the honor of her bargain so well. He was fierce with me that night — he had learned how well I responded to that, although I do not think he ever fully reckoned why — but his face as he labored above me was closed and distant. What visions Kazan Atrabiades saw behind that fixed gaze, I do not know; his brother, mayhap, or his captive men wearing his brother's face.

What he asked, I gave; I cannot help it.

And on the morrow, we sailed.

Once again, we assembled on the beach, and the old priest gave the blessing. We sailed at dawn, and I stood shivering a little in the rose-damask gown, a woolen cloak over my shoulders. All six ships would set forth on this venture. Marjopí was there, and fell wailing on Kazan's neck; he bore it better than I would have reckoned, until she began to berate the priest on his behalf. To me, she nodded a stoic farewell, and I daresay she was glad enough to see the last of me.

Glaukos would sail on our ship, and he was there, cheerful and smiling; his young wife had come too, and her sister. They bade me shy farewells, thanking me once more for the meager gift of fabric I had given, awestricken by the language I had acquired. I met their parents, who were a shepherd and wife, tongue-tied and staring, murmuring about *Vili* and thinking I did not understand.

At last it was done, and Volos, the boy who could talk to birds, handed me aboard Kazan's ship. I breathed deep of the scent of sunwarmed pine boards. Kazan gave the command to hoist anchor and it was done; the oars dipped and splashed in the morning light, and our prow turned, nosing outward.

Green water sluiced along the sides of the vessel and a brisk breeze plucked at our furled sails; Kazan gave the command, and his men leapt to obey, scrambling along the yard to unlash the sails. One, three, six ships a-sail . . . we were off, darting across the sunlit bay toward the narrow passage, and the charming village of Dobrek falling away behind us.

It was a different thing, this journey, from my first sojourn as Kazan Atrabiades' hostage. I had expected similar treatment, reckoning to stake out a place on deck and keep myself out of the way, but he accorded me instead the small cabin within the forecastle for my quarters. There he left me well enough alone, and I reckoned his anger at D'Angelines in general and the Lady of Marsilikos in particular had spilled over onto me. I understood much more of the Illyrian tongue by this time and Kazan's men did small kindnesses for me when his eye was not on them, but there was grim purposefulness to this journey, as opposed to the light-hearted, victorious spirit of the former.

For three days, we wended south down the Illyrian coast and the weather held fair. The long, shining summer was giving way at last to fall, but the seasons change late there and the days remained warm. I judged the time of year by the length of days, and wondered where Ysandre was now, making her *progressus*. Not far, I thought; she would likely have set forth by sail to Ditus, at the tip of Caerdicca Unitas, and would travel by land up the western coast before crossing inland to La Serenissima, seeing how the northern city-states held against the Skaldic border. Quintilius Rousse would have ample time to intervene. If he were canny — and I knew him for no fool — he would send word to Ysandre. With the D'Angeline fleet prepared to move by sea against La Serenissima, surely the city-states of Caerdicca Unitas would mobilize on land. Ysandre would arrive in La Serenissima with an army of allies at her back.

Percy de Somerville was the only danger. I'd not been able to think of a way to warn the Lord Admiral against him. Still, Rousse was unlikely to recruit the Royal Commander in this venture. No, I thought, he will send word to de Somerville, but only to alert him. Else, it would leave Terre d'Ange undefended, with the fleet away. Well and so, Percy de Somerville is no fool either. He will bow with the winds, and look to save his own hide. And if Ghislain is with him . . . Ghislain's troops and estates lie in Azzalle, he has Alba to contend with, and dares not risk the wrath of Drustan mab Necthana. And Barquiel L'Envers rules yet as regent in Ysandre's name, and commands forces of his own.

It would fall out well enough, I thought, and we had surprise on our side yet, for all that I'd lost weeks as Kazan's hostage. I would be safely returned to give word of de Somerville's treachery ere he could act on it; the web of those loyal to Ysandre would hold long enough for that.

So did I muse, and pass the time aboard the ship, while sun-gilded isles slid past us along the coastline. Glaukos called me aside one day, pointing to the distant east, where a causeway from the mainland rolled out to meet a mighty walled city on the sea.

"Epidauro," he murmured, as if fearful Kazan would hear. I saw many bright-sailed ships gathered in the harbor there, tiny flecks of color against the granite walls. We had given the city a wide berth. Even so, men muttered and made signs against evil, while Kazan stared straight ahead, his jaw clenched with anger.

It was on the following day that we turned west and into the open sea.

A steady breeze blew at our backs, and the ships leapt forward like winged creatures, plunging buoyantly over the deep-blue waves. Seldom were the decks level for long, and I gave thanks to Blessed Elua that I had a strong stomach for sailing. Joscelin would have been green-faced and wretched; it is the only time I was glad he was not with me, though the thought of him made me smile. It was a little frightening, but mostly exhilarating. Even Kazan's mood lightened somewhat, although he would not look at me.

Two days we took making the crossing, and at dawn on the third, he turned back to the grim business at hand, issuing curt orders which were passed by flag-signals from ship to ship. Arms were brought forth from the hold, wrapped in oilcloth against the dampness; swords were honed and bowstrings waxed and plucked, bucklers hefted to test their balance on the swaying decks, javelins sighted down their lengths, ropes snapped on grappling hooks to measure their strength.

By noon we saw the island, a grey hummock rising out of the sea, a patch of green scrub showing faintly where the harbor lay, and the freshwater spring by which sailors knew it. Some leagues beyond it, the Caerdicci coast was a dim haze on the horizon.

And there before it, at deep-sea anchor, rode a single galley. Her sails were lowered against the wind, but there, atop the center mast, flew a familiar pennant – the silver

swan of House Courcel. Tears stung my eyes to look upon
it, and my heart soared within my breast.

We dropped sail some distance away, Kazan signaling
the other ships to fan out in an encircling crescent,
bringing the larger craft to bay. Six sailors on each
vessel went to oars, using them cunningly to maintain
position on the rocking waves. Two scrambled atop the
forecastle of each, training arrows on the D'Angeline
galley. No sign came from the galley, although I could
see people aboard watching, and sunlight glinting off
armor.

When he was satisfied that his men were in position,
Kazan stepped up to the prow and cupped his hands about
his mouth, hailing the galley in Caerdicci.

"No trade until my men are returned!" he shouted. "I
will see them safe first, eh? You put them in a skiff, you,
and send them out to us!"

The figures aboard the galley moved, conferring, and
then a single figure came forward to reply. His words carried faintly over the water, spoken in D'Angeline-accented
Caerdicci. "Show us the Comtesse!"

Glaukos took my arm, leading me the length of the
ship to stand beside Kazan. Whatever they saw at that
distance, it was enough to satisfy them, for presently a
small skiff was lowered into the water and eight men
clambered down a rope ladder into it. Kazan pointed
toward the other ships. For long, agonizing moments we
waited as the skiff was rowed out to meet the Illyrian
vessels, three ships taking aboard two men. With each
careful exchange, the flag-bearer signaled victory to
Kazan. At last it was done, and the two rowers rested their
oars, looking back at the galley for orders.

"Now send the gold, you," Kazan called to the galley, "and I will send the girl!"

Another conference aboard the galley, and the spokesman's reply. "We have given our surety, pirate! Send the Comtesse first and we will send the gold."

It needed only one look at Kazan's face to know he would refuse. I put my hand on his arm, pleading. "My lord, please! I've given you my word, I've sworn my very soul on it. Her Grace's men will not break faith with it, I promise you!"

"Be silent!" Blood darkened his face as he glared at me. "You do not know what you speak of, you! No one treats fairly with pirates, eh? No trade without the gold." Cupping his hands once more, he shouted it to the galley. "No trade without the gold!"

Gulls wheeled overhead, giving their raucous calls during the long pause. I waited it out with my heart in my throat until the spokesman answered. "If you will not send her, then bring her and take the gold yourself! It is our best offer."

Kazan nodded grimly; he had expected no less. "They are ready?" he asked his second officer, a man named Pekhlo.

Pekhlo spoke to the flag-bearer, and a ripple of signals ran from ship to ship. "All are ready, Kazan."

"Then we will do this." Kazan raised his voice. "Go!"

It happened quickly, so quickly it near bewildered me; I never doubted, after this, their deadly skill as pirates. I daresay dozens of merchanters have felt the same astonishment, being set on by Kazan Atrabiades. The oarsmen set the water churning to white foam, and the ship crossed the distance in a trice, swinging alongside the galley — on the far side, another ship followed suit, while the others drew in easy range of a bow. Grappling hooks soared through the air, thunking deep into the wood of the galley's rails; someone leapt to grab the dangling ladder, and in less space than it takes to tell it, a full dozen Illyrian pirates had swarmed onto the galley.

Beneath the galley's shadow, I could see nothing, heard only scuffling, curses and a brief clash of arms, then muttering stillness. I gazed at Kazan, who looked grimly back at me.

"Very well, pirate," came the voice of the D'Angeline spokesman, sounding distinctly annoyed. "Send up the Comtesse, and take your Elua-cursed gold! We've shown you no reason to break faith, and your men are outnumbered here."

The rope ladder was dangling near at hand, the oarsmen holding the bobbing ship steady. Kazan drew his sword and pointed it at me. "Go," he said softly. "I will follow behind you."

I stared uncomprehending at the point of his sword. "My lord?"

"Go!" he roared.

I went, with Kazan close on my heels, buckler dangling at his back.

It was the D'Angeline spokesman who helped me over the rails, and he gave me no greeting, stepping away quickly as though he were reluctant to touch me. Kazan came up behind me, his free hand closing hard on my elbow. I saw why, then.

On the deck of the galley, a dozen Illyrians held two-score armed soldiers at an uneasy standoff, their slighter numbers backed by those watching on the other four ships, weapons trained on the galley.

The only D'Angeline things in sight were the spokesman, the Courcel pennant and me.

It was a Serenissiman galley.

Fifty-six

I WHIRLED so fast I broke Kazan's grip, hissing at him, "You betrayed me!"

His face was shuttered. "No. There was a blockade, at the Caerdicci point. Nikanor never got through it, eh? They caught him, and found the letter." For a fleeting moment, something altered in his expression. "I am sorry, yes. But they had my men, Phèdre. What was I to do, I?" And then his voice hardened again, and he wrenched me around, pushing me forward. "Here is what you want," he said curtly. "Take her."

I stumbled, fetching up before a stocky Serenissiman in a Captain's helmet, a badge on his doublet worked with the familiar tower-and-carrack insignia of the Stregazza family.

"This is the one?" he asked aloud, glancing at Kazan. Without waiting for a reply, he took my chin between finger and thumb, wrenching my face up toward him and scanning it. "A scarlet mote, by the Spear! And the markings?" Turning me, he gathered up my hair in both hands, peering at the nape of my neck where the finial of my marque was visible. "Sure enough. A damned waste of beauty." He released me, nodding casually to two of his men. "Kill her."

My blood turned to ice and I stood frozen to the spot. Several paces away, Kazan's mouth opened in shock. His men, who had not understood the Caerdicci, shifted restlessly and looked to him for guidance.

"Captain!" It was the D'Angeline spokesman, sounding as startled as Kazan looked. "I have orders to bring her to Prince Benedicte!"

"Yes," the Captain said mildly. "And I have orders from my lord Marco Stregazza to make certain you do no such thing. This woman is a spy and an escaped criminal, and if your doddering princeling has some idiotic fear of D'Angeline curses for shedding her blood, be assured that Lord Marco does not. She dies here, guardsman, and let your Prince take it up with Lord Marco. For the good of the Serene Republic, I have my orders."

"Kazan," I breathed; I had begun shaking. He stared at me, still dumbstruck. "Will you let them do this thing?"

He made no reply.

"Ah, right," the Captain said thoughtfully. "Your gold, pirate." He drew his sword, pointing at a pair of coffers sitting on deck. "Take it and begone, then, with our thanks. Though if I were you . . ." He glanced meaningfully toward the distant island, where two war-galleys were easing into view around the curve of coast, single-masted biremes propelled by a double bank of oars. "I would go with haste, for our bargain ends the instant you take it. The girl's life is worth more than yours to the Serene Republic . . . but not by much."

"Kazan!" I cried.

His head bowed as he averted his face. "Rachlav, Zaiko . . . take the gold."

I stood in disbelief as the Illyrians moved to obey him, two men each on a coffer, under the watchful eyes of the Serenissimans. The others warded them, forming a line on either side of the galley as the coffers were handed down into the Illyrian vessels.

"Good enough." The Captain was pleased. "If you move fast enough, you may even escape, sea-wolf, though Asherat grant you fail. You . . ." he snapped his fingers at one of his men, ". . . and you. Do it now. It is to be done on the instant, Lord Marco says."

They moved swiftly, doubtless hand-picked for discipline and loyalty. I struggled briefly, to no avail, and was forced to kneel on the deck. I heard a voice cry out a protest in Illyrian, quickly stifled; Lukin, I thought. And then a hand tangled roughly in my hair, dragging my head back to bare my throat for the sword. It was all happening so fast, I scarce had time to feel the terror of it until I saw a Serenissiman soldier move in front of me, drawing his sword back for the swing.

I understood then that I was going to die.

It is fixed in my mind, that moment; sunlight glinting off the edge of the blade, the Captain's impassive face behind my executioner, even the feel of the sun-warmed planks beneath my knees. And Kazan's wordless shout, building full of rage and fury until it seemed it would crack the very sky.

I never saw the blow that separated my would-be executioner's head from his shoulders, only his body crumpling at my knees, blood pooling about his truncated neck. My gorge rose and I suppressed a wave of sickness, scrambling away from the soldier who'd held me. By the time I gained my feet, chaos reigned on the deck of the galley – and in the center of it all was Kazan Atrabiades, wielding his sword like a man possessed.

Outnumbered, the Illyrians fought to secure their retreat, aided by a volley of javelins and fire-arrows from the outlying ships. Set aflame, the pitch-soaked rags wrapped about the arrows set a dozen small fires on deck, adding to the confusion. Kazan and the Serenissiman Captain alike were roaring orders, half-heeded by skirmishing soldiers and pirates. And then I saw no more as one of the latter grabbed me about the waist, hauling me over the railing and handing me down into the waiting arms of Glaukos, waiting anxious-eyed in the ship below.

How long it lasted, I could not say – hours, it seemed, though I daresay not more than a span of heartbeats had passed before the rest followed, of those that might, and Kazan himself came over the railing. Our ship wallowed under their staggering weight, archers atop the forecastle grimly firing arrow after arrow at the galley to cover their retreat.

"Fly!" Kazan shouted at the oarsmen, flushed with fury. *"Fly!"*

And fly we did, oars churning at ragged speed while others dropped their arms where they stood, racing to hoist the sails. In the prow, the flag-bearer signaled frantically to the other ships, urging them to flight.

There would be no pursuit from the galley; Kazan's pirates had done their job well. Even in bright daylight, I could see the flames that licked at the mainsail. Small figures raced around the deck, forming a bucket brigade to keep the vessel from going up entire.

But there were the others, those hidden by the isle, and they moved swiftly, looming out of the distance. The wind that had blown steady at our backs all the way from Illyria worked against us now. Gone was the elegant, concerted flight of before; now, all six ships scattered wildly, working against a strong headwind. Three men lay wounded on the deck, groaning. I made a count; two had never returned. Glaukos worked steadily, satchel open beside him, endeavoring to bind the worst of their wounds. I went to aid him, and he glanced briefly up at me.

"I didn't know, my lady," he said. "I swear it."

"I believe you." I did; there was naught else I could say, and no more time for speech. We worked quickly together, doing the best we could for them, and I thanked Blessed Elua that I had learned somewhat of field medicine after the terrible battle of Troyes-le-Mont. And all the while, the Serenissiman war-galleys bore down upon us.

They caught the sixth ship, the straggler, when we were scarcely three hundred yards away. I knew from the resonant, thumping sound that carried over the waves that the war-galleys had ballistae mounted on their forecastles. It was an unlucky shot that did them in, a springloaded bolt that split the yard and brought down their sails. We could not help but watch as the smaller craft wallowed in the water, helpless and waiting. Serenissimans swarmed the vessel, for it had one of the coffers of gold. It went quickly, at least.

Lukin was on that ship, I thought, remembering hearing his voice. The one that boarded the far side of the galley; it had been the slowest to make its escape. I would have wept, if I'd had any tears to spare.

So began our flight, that even in memory seems endless. Like hares coursed by hounds, we fled the Serenissiman war-galleys across the great, roiling sea, day and night, tacking and doubling without surcease. Against the speed and agility of the Illyrian vessels was pitted the remorseless beat of the great war-galleys, that cared naught for the wind and had manpower to spare. I learned, later, how many men Marco Stregazza contributed to that enterprise; it numbered well into the hundreds. Betimes they drew near, and the ballistae thumped; then, bolts split the air, sending up great geysers of water all around us. One such pierced our mizzen sail, and Kazan shouted commands, unfaltering, ordering the sail stripped and the storm-sail raised. How they managed it in those surging waves, I do not know, but they did.

I did my best to give aid as I might, bringing food and water to those in need. By the second day, all were hollow-eyed from exhaustion and lack of sleep – and still the galleys pursued us. It was on that day that another ship was lost, floundering as it cut too close to the wind. It came nigh to overturning and took on water, too much water. Once again, we could do naught but watch from a distance as they righted themselves slowly and wallowed, sunk halfway to their railings, waiting for death as one of the biremes drew nigh.

Four ships left, running for our lives.

And when darkness fell, Kazan's second officer began to argue with him.

"They'll follow us to our cursed *graves*, Kazan! What will you do, lead them straight into Dobrek harbor and let them have us all? I'm telling you, it's the only way!"

And Kazan, grim-faced. "No. We will lose them in the night."

Pekhlo swore at him with a sailor's eloquence. "You said that last night, and here they are still, on our trail like a hunting pack! Will you condemn us all for your mother's grief, Kazan? I'm telling you, we're leading death on a string here, and Epidauro's got the only forces will halt them! How many will die, if we let them run us aground elsewhere?"

"And will you ask the Ban to challenge the Doge's son on our behalf?" Kazan reminded him. "He won't; he'd be a fool if he did. We're pirates, Pekhlo! Stregazza has the right of it!"

"Not in this," his second officer said stubbornly. "He'd see us given a fair trial, he would, and we've kept our bargain; it was the Stregazza who broke it. I'm willing to die for you, Kazan, but not for your damned blood-curse, no!"

"My lord." By the dim light of the storm-lanterns, I had groped my way to the forecastle, where they quarrelled. "My lord, does the Ban of Illyria swear me his protection, he may claim aid of the throne of Terre d'Ange. I promise you it is so."

Kazan looked at me with haunted eyes. "Do you say so, my lady?" he asked in Illyrian. "Well, I have disregarded you often enough, when you tried to tell me as much. Still, it seems the Serenissimans are willing to kill or die to have you, when I reckoned they had no greater enemy than I." He sighed. "So be it. If they are with us come dawn, we make for Epidauro."

The command went out, relayed by lantern from ship to ship. I heard ragged cheering burst forth, faint across the water. Pekhlo went eagerly to consult with the sailors manning the rudders. Left alone, Kazan Atrabiades closed his eyes.

"My lord," I said to him in his own tongue. "I owe you my life."

"Yes." His eyes remained shut. "I did not think they would kill you, Phèdre nó Delaunay. They told Nikanor that the D'Angeline Prince would pay your ransom, if we delivered you. I thought it would be well enough. You said you would have gone to him, only he did not know you."

I swallowed hard, remembering. "It was not true, my lord. Prince Benedicte is a traitor, in league with Marco Stregazza. I knew this. I let you think otherwise. And I am deeply sorry for it. If I hadn't, the . . . the others might yet live, those who died."

"No." Kazan opened his eyes. "Serenissima laid a trap for us, thinking to have us both, although they wanted you the more. It would have happened anyway." He gave me a weary smile. "You told me it was an accident, that you fell into the sea."

"It was," I said.

"Escaping prisoners, near the sea." He gazed up at the night sky, scudding clouds veiling the stars. "I did not think, when you told me. I thought, then, a riot in the harbor, maybe, such as may sweep bystanders into its path. But I think you were one of the prisoners, yes? There is only one Serenissiman prison I know on the sea, where the currents run strange and deadly. It is a place all sailors know, a place to avoid." He glanced back at me. "No one has ever escaped from the black isle. Who are you, to do such a thing?"

"I had help, my lord." There was no point in denying it. "A rescuer."

Kazan stirred. "Then there is a force in Serenissima, loyal to you?"

"No." I shook my head. "It was my companion, Joscelin."

He looked at me without speaking for a moment. "One man?" he asked eventually. "One man assailed the black isle on your behalf?" I nodded. Kazan gave a short laugh. "Then he is mad, I think, or too much in love with you."

"No." I rubbed my eyes, itching with tiredness. "I don't know. A little of both, maybe."

"You look different when you speak of him."

I made no reply. There was too much to say, and too little, and the thought of Joscelin was more than I could bear. In the absence of words, beyond the sound of waves and creaking rigging, came the distant sound of a drumbeat, steady and relentless.

Somewhere behind us across the dark seas, the Serenissiman war-galleys pursued, chasing our faint, flitting lights. Kazan gazed across the waters. "So it will be Epidauro, then," he said softly. "Just know . . ." He switched to Caerdicci, the language we had always shared between us. ". . . I didn't think they would kill you, eh? Remember me kindly, you." He touched my hair, and gave me a faint smile. "Marjopí was right, yes? Bad luck, after all. But I will think of you, when I die. It would please Daroslav, that I knew one such as you, before the end."

For that, too, I had no words; I watched him go, consulting with his men, lending a word here or there, giving them hope.

A roiling dawn broke in the east, purple clouds shot through with ragged streaks of orange, beating the waves into bronze. The winds picked up, errant and fitful, gusts from the north driving us sideways and setting peaks of white foam atop the wave crests. Our pursuers were behind us still, and if they began at last to flag, so too did our progress slow.

A half a league behind us, no more, did they follow. If the winds had favored us, we might have done it; Kazan's ships could have scattered in one of the many archipelagos, disappearing in minutes. It had ever been their plan for evading pursuit, and a successful one; but the pursuit had never been so well-planned, so dogged. In the past, Kazan Atrabiades had struck as an opportunist. This time, the opportunity had been Marco Stregazza's, and he had taken it to its fullest.

We made for Epidauro.

Kazan spoke briefly to his crew. "You know what we face, all of you, behind and before. Let my mother's curse claim me then; 'tis long enough overdue. If the Ban may profit from it, 'tis worthwhile in the end. Pekhlo, tell Nikanor I bequeath command to him when I am dead. I ask only that he leave the house to Marjopí, and see that she is given a proper loom, an upright loom like the D'Angelines use." He raised his voice, shouting the order. "All sails out for Epidauro!"

They did not cheer, then, but merely obeyed. I made my way to Glaukos' side, to see if I could be of assistance to him. He was working in the dark hold, where the injured had been secured, and his normally cheerful face was set and lined.

"All the gods be thanked," he muttered, "that he's set aside his damned superstition long enough to save our hides. Did you talk him into it, my lady?"

"A little." I caught his satchel as it threatened to overturn as the ship lurched sharply. "He thinks he's going to die, Glaukos."

"I know." He steadied himself against the inner wall of the ship, then bent over to check a dressing, sniffing to see if the wound had gone bad. The sailor, half-conscious, murmured in pain.

"Do you believe it?"

"Ah, now . . ." Glaukos glanced at me. "I don't know, my lady. Do you ask me do I think the *kríavbhog* will take him, well, no, I think no such thing. 'Tis Illyrian superstition, that, and naught else; tales to frighten children. But when a man sets himself to die, I have seen it, how his spirit may go out like a blown candle flame. Kazan, he's more life in him than any ten men. But still . . . I don't know."

At that, the ship heeled sharply again, rendering talk a wasted effort. I helped him as best I could, and when I could do no more, I went back above deck. The morning's clouds had thickened, and rain squalls threatened here and there, moving across the surface of the sea as if of their own volition. The Serenissiman galleys had drawn closer.

And ahead of us lay Epidauro.

FİFTY-SEVEN

THE CİTY of Epidauro has stood for a long time, as Illyrians reckon history; always it has been populated, although it was the Tiberians who build the first fortifications there. Once an island, it is linked to the mainland by the causeway, and defended on three sides by water and sturdy walls all around.

We bore down upon it like so many leaves driven hither and thither before the wind, Kazan's sailors scrambling frantically with each new tack. And all the while behind us came the relentless drumbeat, the banked oars of the Serenissiman war-galleys churning double lines of foam.

There can be no doubt that our approach was spotted by the harbor ward-towers, for the response was swift. At such a distance that they resembled child's toys, we saw them; ships of the Illyrian navy, mustering in the harbor, their square sails dyed scarlet with the black insignia of the Ban's bird of prey on them.

Let them take us into custody, I thought; it matters naught, so long as we do not die at the hands of the

Serenissimans. If this Ban of Illyria has half a wit to his name, he will hear me out and accept the promise of Ysandre's favor. I will plead clemency for Kazan and his men on behalf of Terre d'Ange; whatever they have done in the past, La Serenissima has no claim in this matter. Let the Serenissimans blockade the Caerdicci point as they will, there are other routes, though they may take longer. They cannot cover the whole of the Caerdicci coast. Surely, we may find a way to win through, and if I cannot reach Marsilikos, still I may intercept Ysandre in her *progressus*.

So I told myself, and fed the guttering spark of hope that remained to me, while the sullen sky muttered with thunder and the walls of Epidauro grew nearer.

The men grew heartened at the sight of the massing Illyrian naval force, offering cries of thanks and praise in voices that cracked with weariness. One of the ships caught a rare good gust of wind, coursing ahead with its triangular sail at a stiff angle; Nikanor's ship, I thought, and someone cheered as they surged into the forefront. Behind us, the war-galleys faltered, commanders questioning the wisdom of pursuing their quarry into the arms of the sole undefeated seat of a vassal nation.

And in the prow of the ship stood Kazan Atrabiades, his face ghost-white.

My skin prickled all over with awful presentiment.

I had managed to forget, until then, the full truth of the waking vision I had seen aboard this ship; attributed it to fear and shadows, cast by a half-dreaming mind tainted by remembered blood-guilt. What had happened to Kazan's brother was a dreadful thing, and reason enough for nightmares. They had ceased, since I'd drawn the story out of him. And as for what I had seen myself, I had been more than half delirious, plucked from the sea after an ordeal that would have driven many a warrior to madness.

But I knew better.

Blessed Elua, I prayed, salt-spray stinging my eyes to tears, spare him! Please, please, let us come safe to land. Naamah, have a care for your Servant, who has served you well and faithfully! If he is a patron, let it be said he has not stinted the offering; men died that he might save my life. My lord Kushiel, ah! You have set your hand upon me and cast me forth; if you would not see me perish now, then offer me your protection. And I prayed, too, to Asherat-of-the-Sea, to whom I owed a debt of honor; my lady, if you would see it kept, bear this ship upon your bosom, and do not let it fail!

Though the clouds gathered overhead and spat rain upon us, though lightning flickered in the sky's dark underbelly, I felt my prayers heard, a waiting presence enfolded around me. *Thus it may be*, a voice spoke in my heart. *But he is not ours.*

Rain beat down in sheets, and the sailors cursed, grappling with lines whipping slick and wind-torn. A flash of lightning brightened the skies, and I saw all three of the other ships leaping ahead of us now, gaining entrance to the harbor, sails stark white against the leaden grey. And in the dark eye-blinding aftermath, a hoarse cry.

I did not see it until the lightning flashed again: Kazan, still standing, enwrapped in the coils of the *kríavbhog*. From ankles to chest its serpentine tail entwined him; its sinuous neck rose above his head, veined wings outspread and beating at the glowering air. Eyes glittered like rubies in its wedge-shaped head and the mouth opened in a hiss, tripleforked tongue flickering at his face. He fought hopelessly against it, sword-arm still free, making no dent in those preternatural scales.

What the others saw that day, I do not know; it is not a thing of which they will speak. I know what I saw. It is enough.

The northerly gusts of wind that had plagued us all day struck once more, slamming a rain-driven fist into the side of the ship. The sailors shouted with helpless rage and fought the pitching waves, fought the wind, fought the lines.

And Kazan Atrabiades fought the *kríavbhog*.

It was too much, too vast and strong, growing larger with each inch we struggled forward toward the harbor of Epidauro. I did not know, until I heard the rattle in my throat, that I was sobbing. Its head reared over him, blotting out the rain, a hinged jaw lowering and extending.

May the kríavbhog *swallow my soul if I lie . . .*

Half-blinded by tears and lashing rain, I struggled across the pitching deck to the stern of the ship; an oar broken loose of its lock nearly knocked me overboard, before I made it. I clung to the mizzenmast, sodden hair plastered across my cheek by the wind, scarce able to hear my own voice shouting above the din. "Turn back, name of Elua, turn back! Can't you see it's killing him!" In the sudden glare of lightning, I saw the steersman staring at me open-mouthed, eyes showing the whites all around, and I realized I'd been shouting in D'Angeline. Groping for the Illyrian words, I drew a deep breath and loosed it with all my might. *"Turn back!"*

A sharp, double-clap of thunder echoed my words. With terror writ on his face, the steersman yanked hard on the rudder-bar, and the ship heeled, her prow swinging to the south and her sail coming around with a vengeance. Men cried out, staggering, grabbing for support; two I saw were lost, thrown overboard at the sharp turn. I had time only to spare a fleeting prayer that they might yet swim to safe harbor, and then the northerly wind bore down upon us and our sails snapped taut and we were running, running before the wind.

I sank to my knees at the base of the mizzenmast and wept.

Would we have reached Epidauro that day if I had not spoken? I cannot say. I chose in the space of a heartbeat, and once the decision was made and the deed done, it could not be undone. And yet, if I had it to make again, I would choose the same, though the throne of Terre d'Ange hung in the balance. Too many have died, who aided me. In that terrible, storm-ridden moment, I could not knowingly choose to condemn Kazan Atrabiades to his death. I never understood, until then, how Joscelin could have chosen to remain at my side in Skaldia, when he had a chance to escape and warn the nation of Selig's plan. I understand it better now.

So it was that we fled before the storm, and that journey is grim beyond telling. I did not think any mere force of nature could be more dire than the wrath of the Master of the Straits. I was wrong. That craft and crew survived is a testament to the skill of the Illyrian sailors; never again will I smile to hear one boast of his seamanship. Night and day, the wind howled at our backs, harrowing us ever southward. More than once, I thought our ship would surely crack in two as it plunged into a trough; more than once, I thought we would capsize when a towering wall of green water broke like thunder over the ship, setting the decks awash. Half our stores were spoiled by salt water, and one precious cask of fresh water was cracked and leaking. Glaukos could do naught for the wounded but pray.

As for Kazan, he was like a man caught in a waking dream, open-eyed and insensible. It was all I could do to keep him in the forecastle out of the way, while his sailors fought for our survival. He would look at me when I spoke to him with no sign of understanding.

There was no question of pursuit by the Serenissiman war-galleys. Even if they had had the will to follow, they could not have; no oarsmen could have outlasted that gale. Sodden and bone-weary, I could do naught but wonder and pray, hoping that they had turned back rather than risk confrontation with the whole of the Epidauran navy.

Pekhlo, Kazan's second-in-command aboard the ship, was one of the men I'd seen thrown overboard when we fled. With Kazan useless, it was Tormos who took command, and he found steel in his soul on that fateful day, for as grim as it got, he never faltered. It was his decision to ride out the crest of the storm, although I daresay if he'd known how long it would last or how far it would drive us, he might have tried to make landfall. But once we had turned, we never had a chance; the winds chivvied us away from the coastline and into the raging seas. Three times he sought to make for land; three times, the storm blew us back.

How long did it last? Six days, mayhap seven. I lost count. Of our position on the face of the earth, I had no notion. I am no navigator, to reckon my place by the stars; even if I were, there were no stars to be seen during that terrible flight. Only waves and more waves, and the vast, wrath-filled skies, until at last the storm blew itself out and subsided into meekness, leaving us dazed and exhausted, clinging to our half-crippled ship floating on the bosom of a gentle sea.

It was bright morning when it happened, the sun dazzling silver on the water. I made my way to Tormos' side with exaggerated caution, unused to the bobbing steadiness of our craft. He looked at me with red-rimmed eyes, weary beyond words.

"Tormos," I said. My voice cracked on his name; I had lost it shouting above the pounding sea. I cleared my throat, addressing him in Illyrian. "Where are we, do you know?"

He merely looked dully at me and shook his head.

All around us, the sea sparkled in the sunlight. Dark blue, the water was, and deep. On deck, sailors moved slowly, straightening limbs cramped by long resistance to the storm. Glaukos' head and shoulders appeared in the opening of the hold as he hoisted our last cask of fresh water on deck. It seemed pitiably small. I felt light-headed, and could not remember when last I'd eaten.

"Look!"

It was Oltukh who shouted, pointing; Oltukh, who had made me necklaces of shells. We all looked and saw where he pointed, a pod of dolphins breaching the surface of the waves, sleek and grey, wearing their perpetual smiles. One spouted very near the ship, blowing a plume of spray into the air.

Asherat-of-the-Sea, I thought, loved dolphins.

"There." Glaukos' voice, for once quavering with age. He leaned over the railings, staring past the merry dolphins. "There, there! Don't you see it? Land!" His hand

rose, trembling; I realized then that he had spoken in
Hellene, reverting to the milk-tongue of his infancy, that
his slave-mother had taught him. "Land!" he cried, pointing. "Land!"

Tormos frowned, shoving sailors out of his way. He
had understood the urgency, if not the words. We all
jostled for position then, gazing across the waters while our
torn sails flapped mildly in the calm breeze.

There, on the horizon, lay a smudge of darkness.

Land.

We cheered, and we wept, and we set our sails for land.
The rudderbar had snapped and the rudder itself split in
two under the dreadful force we had endured; still, we
limped over the surface of the water, and the island before
us loomed larger and larger. No Dobrek, this isle; no, it
was vaster, its size deceptively diminished by distance. The
nearer we got, the larger it grew, and what had seemed hills
at its center became mountains, forest-shrouded and gilded
in the bright sunlight.

I saw Glaukos' face, the moment he recognized it. He
drew a sharp breath, and awe came over his features. He was
Tiberian by rearing and Illyrian by choice, but his blood
was Hellene, and what he knew, he had learnt at his
mother's knee.

"It is Kriti," he said reverently. "We have come to
Kriti."

I measured our course in my head and thought, it may
be so. Pure south had we been driven, down the coast of
Illyria, of mainland Hellas. Had we truly come so far, that
we had reached the isle of the House of Minos? I remembered Delaunay's study, maps spread on the table, awash in
late afternoon sunlight. In truth, mayhap we had.

At Tormos' command, we followed the dolphins, and no one questioned it for superstition. Kazan came forth from the forecastle and watched with childlike interest, his face disturbingly blank. I took his arm, and steered him to a place of safety along the railing; he went unprotesting.

We drew near enough to make out the shape of the isle, measuring some thirty-odd leagues from tip to tip. The sides were sheer and rocky but, here and there, sandy beaches beckoned. A flock of gulls skirled above us, giving out their harsh cries; young Volos, triumphantly alive, lifted his head and gave back their raucous cries. The gulls veered landward, heading for the smallest of bays, a crescent of white sand cradled betwixt horns of stone. Half-laughing and half-weeping, Tormos ordered the ship to follow.

Deep-blue water gave way to sapphire, and our breeze died entirely. Undeterred, Tormos ordered the Illyrians to oars, and they pulled to a ragged beat as he stamped out the rhythm. Faltering yet game, ragged sails flapping emptily, we slid through the waters, until they grew shallower and turned to aquamarine.

We had entered the horns of the harbor.

Light-headed as I was, it took me a moment to realize that the sound I heard was mightier than the oarsmen's beat, echoing across the water. There is no mistaking that beat, once one hears it. It is measured to the pace of the mortal heart and it is measured out in bronze, eldest tool of the earth that ever humankind shaped to serve its need. I did not see, until we were well and truly betwixt them, the caves that riddled the horns of the harbor, layer upon stony layer, rising above us.

Then I did, and knew it was from thence that the sound

of beating gongs came, and my hair rose at the nape of my neck as we glided below the caves. This was no ordinary port. We had crossed the threshold of a sacred place.

So did we enter the harbor of the Temenos.

FIFTY-EIGHT

THERE WERE children on the beach; I had not expected that.

They greeted our arrival with eager cries, swooping like gulls over the gritty white sands as our ship ran aground in shallow water. Bemused, Tormos cast a line ashore, and a full dozen eager hands grasped it, children setting their backs to it with a will, hauling our vessel nearer to shore. It was a lucky thing the Illyrian ships had such a shallow draught, that we were able to disembark and splash our way ashore. Kazan came without assistance, and it seemed to me that there was an alertness in his face for the first time since Epidauro.

The sound of bronze gongs had ceased, and left in its wake a profound silence.

Salt-stained and aching and unsteady on my legs, I waited with the others, standing on the beach and gazing at steps carved into the living rock, easing down toward the sea.

'Twould be a party of guards would meet us, I thought; one expects such a thing, landing uninvited in a foreign harbor. Instead, there came a single man, unarmed, escorted by a retinue of seven youths and seven maidens. He was of middle years, dark and bearded, with a diadem of ribbons bound around his curly hair, wearing rich robes encrusted two hand-spans deep with embroidery. One of the youths held a parasol above his head, and tasseled pearls hung from its spokes, glimmering in the sun.

"Welcome, strangers," he said in a sonorous voice, giving us greeting in Hellene. "I am Oeneus Asterius, Hierophant of the Temenos. You have passed by the wide harbors and the company of men to enter here. Mother Dia grant you welcome. Who is it among you that comes to be cleansed?"

I daresay we gaped foolishly enough; of our number, only Glaukos and I understood his Hellene speech, and neither of us knew what he meant by it.

Thus it was doubly startling when Kazan stepped forward, clear-eyed and willful.

"I am Kazan Atrabiades of Epidauro," he announced in Illyrian. "I come bearing blood-guilt for the death of my brother."

The Hierophant gazed at him with deepset eyes and nodded, then turned to one of the maidens. "Iole, fetch Mezentius, who speaks the Illyrian tongue."

I glanced at Glaukos, who opened and closed his mouth helplessly, shocked speechless. "My lord Hierophant," I said in Hellene, pushing my damp, salt-stiffened hair back from my face and wracking my brain for the proper words. "I speak Illyrian, a little. So does this man, Glaukos of Tiberium," I added, nodding at him. "And my lord Atrabiades speaks Caerdicci, as well. We have had a dire journey, my lord, and it is a tale long in the telling. If you will offer us your hospitality, we can recompense you in gold."

'Twas true, too, for ragged though we were, we had in our hold half the remaining ransom; seven thousand five hundred D'Angeline ducats in gold. The Hierophant looked at me with his unblinking gaze, the way a hawk will, or a wolf, then turned to Kazan and addressed him in Caerdicci. His words came a bit more haltingly, but no less resonant. "You understand, then, where you have come?"

"Yes, son of Minos." Kazan bowed his head. "I understand, I."

Glaukos was translating for the rest of the crew, recovered enough to accomplish that much. I stared at Kazan, and something stirred in my memory; I heard again Thelesis de Mornay's voice. *The Hellenes claim the descendants of the House of Minos have the ability to cleanse a man of a blood-curse; it is a gift of Zagreus.* "Kazan," I said softly. "Are you certain?" For I remembered too what she had said afterward. *I have heard, too, that few mortals can bear the process at less than the cost of their wits.*

"Yes, Phèdre." He spoke calmly, a thinking presence restored to his features. "I am certain, I."

"Phaedra." The Hierophant drew out the word, tasting it in his mouth. "Ah. You bear . . ."

". . . an ill-luck name," I finished for him wearily. "Yes, my lord, I know the history of your house, and the origins of my namesake. Well and so, Kazan Atrabiades has come for atonement; the rest of us are parched and hungry and tired to the bone, and there are wounded aboard the ship. Will you offer us your hospitality or no?"

A glimmer of amusement lit his dark eyes. "You are impatient, little one, but you may find a deeper truth beneath the tale you think you know. Come, and I will escort you to the Palace of the Temenos, where you may find rest and refreshment. It is my thought that the Kore will want to meet with you in addition to this supplicant, for the Children of Elua come seldom to this isle, and you bear a name of some significance. Perhaps there is more to you than meets the eye, although it is hard to say just now, bedraggled as you are."

My blood scalded my cheeks, and I bit my tongue on a tart reply. There was a hasty conference among the sailors as to what to do regarding the ship, and the Hierophant dispatched the maiden Iole with instructions to bring the Illyrian-speaking Mezentius and a handful of fisherfolk from the village to aid in removing the injured men and hauling our damaged vessel ashore. I left Tormos and Glaukos in charge, with assurances that they would be lodged in the initiates' quarters and well tended to. For all his regained lucidity, Kazan showed no interest in the fate of his ship and crew.

It was a short walk to the Palace. The Hierophant proceeded at a stately pace, flanked by his initiates. Naked and near-naked children scampered around us, making a game of it; no one seemed to mind. Struggling against exhaustion and sea-wobbly legs, I made my way to the Hierophant's side, working around the youth holding his parasol, who smiled at me. Like the others, he wore a robe of unadorned white linen, so finespun it was nearly transparent.

"My lord Hierophant," I began. "If it please you, my full name is Phèdre nó Delaunay, Comtesse de Montrève, and I am on an errand of much urgency for her majesty Ysandre de la Courcel, Queen of Terre d'Ange. I fear that the storm which brought us here has set me much out of my way, and I must needs petition you for aid in addition to your hospitality; or if not you, my lord, then whomsoever you deem proper. Will you grant me audience, or offer me a letter of introduction to the appropriate party? I promise you, her majesty will render your aid well worthwhile."

In the soft shade of his parasol, he looked mildly at me. "You have come to the Temenos, little one. You have passed by the wide harbors and the company of men."

"Yes, but . . ."

"Phèdre." It was Kazan who had spoken. "We have come here because it is needful, eh? What is to be given will be shown."

Despairing, I gave up. The youth with the parasol glanced at me sidelong, still smiling.

So we came to the Palace of the Temenos, low and splendid by the sea, at the base of the inland mountains. It is one of the oldest palaces on the island, and one of the smallest, for all its brightly-colored splendor. A village nestled at its foot, tiny whitewashed buildings gleaming in the sun; it was thence that our escort of children ran, laughing and shouting.

The Palace itself was wholly unguarded, which seemed strange to me, for I had not yet taken the measure of the place. We passed beneath a broad gate with a crescent of horns mounted above it, and entered the Palace proper. 'Twas a different world within; winding arcades of the squat columns the Kritians dearly love, their rounded, tapering figures painted bright red and blue, with gilded capitals.

In one such, the Hierophant halted, raising his hand and addressing Kazan with great solemnity in Caerdicci. "You understand, now, that you must be secluded before undergoing the *thetalos*, and take neither food nor drink?"

Kazan nodded firmly. "It is understood, yes."

"Well and good. Proclus will tend to you, until it is time for your dedication." He waited until the initiate had led Kazan away, then turned to me. "For your part, little one, there are no such proscriptions. Euralyke will show you to a chamber, where you may rest, and refreshments will be brought to you. Perhaps a bath would be welcome, as well?"

I heard a trace of amusement return to his voice, and it stung me. I thought of all I had endured to reach this place alive, and drew myself up despite the dizziness of hunger and exhaustion. "Yes, my lord," I replied coolly. "A bath would be welcome, indeed. And when I have done, if you will not grant me audience, I will seek someone who will."

"No offense is intended, young Phaedra. If it is political asylum you sought, you would have gone to Kommos harbor, and not the Temenos. But it is here you have come. Your companion has a need that compels, and you . . ." The Hierophant smiled. "I shall speak to the Kore of you, and we shall see."

With that, I had to be content for the moment; and in truth, I was sufficiently weary that I made no further protest. The maiden Euralyke, grave and smiling, showed me to a pleasant chamber, with frescoes of birds adorning the walls. There was a bathing room adjacent, with a tub of painted earthenware, and servants brought hot water in jugs to fill it. While I bathed, they laid out fresh clothing for me, a dress of white linen and a blue mantle, plain but fine. I sat afterward and combed out my hair, enjoying the feel of clean fabric against my skin. Food came as promised, fresh bread and sharp goat's cheese, and a lamb dish that tasted faintly of cinnamon. I ate everything, feeling the world grow more solid around me, and washed it down with cool water and a good red wine.

It was my intention to pursue the matter of an audience immediately after eating, but when I had done, a great wave of tiredness overcame me. However long it had been that we had fled the storm, we had none of us slept much for days on end, save for brief naps snatched here and there, between buffets. I will close my eyes only for a moment, I told myself, stretching out on the bed; only for a moment, and then I will seek out this Kore, whomever she may be.

I was still thinking it as I fell down the deep, dark well of sleep.

Lengthening shadows woke me, creeping across the frescoed walls; I awoke disheveled and confused, uncertain where I was. I had slept the better part of the day. Remembering, I rose and stretched my sleep-stiffened limbs, smoothing out my wrinkled garments. Scarce had I done when the door to my chamber opened to admit the Hierophant, accompanied by two initiates.

"The Kore will see you."

Trying not to yawn, I went with him down another set of corridors, bright colors mellowed by the slanting light that came in at the windows. The Hierophant's expression was unchanging, but the initiates stole glances at me out of the corners of their eyes; I do not think they had ever seen a D'Angeline before.

We entered a large chamber, painted all around with a processional of youths and maidens alike bearing libational vessels — and at the far end stood a throne, in which a woman sat awaiting us. With a small shock, I came to full alertness.

It is no easy thing, to describe the Kore of the Temenos, nor my reaction to her. A woman, yes, with fair skin and hair the hue of bronze, though her eyes were as dark as the Hierophant's, heavy-lidded and lustrous. She wore a blue gown wrought with gold stars, and a great collar of ivory plaques set in gold, and over it all, a saffron mantle. Although her skin was smooth and her breasts firm, I guessed her age at some forty years. A woman, and yet — a shudder ran through me as I gazed upon her, and I felt such a jumble of thoughts and emotions I could scarce name them all. Awe and fear — and desire, sudden and unbidden. I thought of the great statue of Asherat in her temple of La Serenissima, and the blind priestess Bianca, reaching her crabbed hand to touch me. I thought of the Great Temple of Naamah and saw her face before me, transcendent and generous.

I thought of Melisande, too.

And I thought of something I had not remembered in years; my mother's face the last time I saw her, in the courtyard of Cereus House, the day she sold me into servitude.

All of these and more flickered through my mind too swiftly to number before the Kore spoke, her clear voice stilling the whirlwind inside me. "Phèdre nó Delaunay," she said, giving my name the proper D'Angeline inflection. "Be welcome."

I sank down to kneel *abeyante*, the marble floor cool beneath my knees. "My lady."

"Come, that will never do. Let me see you, Elua's child." Leaning forward, she lifted my chin with two fingers and gazed at my face. I saw her take in my scarlet-moted eye, and mayhap somewhat more, for her brows raised. "Oh, Oeneus! This one, you should have brought sooner. There is a bright shadow about you, child. Know you that a god has set his hand upon you?"

"Yes, my lady." I was content to look at her. "It is Kushiel's Dart that marks me; Kushiel, who was once the Punisher of the One God, the Yeshuite's Adonai. But I am dedicated also to the Service of Naamah, who is the Mistress of Pleasures. And as I am D'Angeline, I owe homage to Blessed Elua, who is the Protector of us all."

"Thrice-marked, and more," she mused, releasing me, "for there is somewhat else besides."

"Yes, my lady Kore." I settled back to sit on my heels, liking the mild discomfort of the hard marble. It had been a long time since I had been able to make obeisance to anyone with unadulterated pleasure; I led a strange life, for an *anguissette*. "I have made a promise to Asherat-of-the-Sea, as well."

"So." She smiled, faint lines crinkling at the corners of her eyes. "And yet you have come to the Temenos asking only political aid, Oeneus tells me. How is this, then?"

Drawing a deep breath, I spun out the story for her, telling it in its entirety, from my reasons for going to La Serenissima to Kazan's struggle with the *kríavbhog* and our fearful, storm-lashed flight to Kriti. She listened without comment, while shadows darkened the corners of the throne room and white-clad initiates moved softly around lighting the wall sconces. Oeneus Asterius the Hierophant stood beside her, watching and listening too. It did not occur to me to lie or withhold the truth, for I understood at last that this was a holy place I had come to and they were priest and priestess alike, although she outshone him as the sun does the moon.

There was a little silence when I had finished, and they exchanged glances. I saw then that they shared common blood, for all that their coloring differed. Well, and they are Hellene all, but there is mainland Achaian blood in the House of Minos, and has been since the time of my namesake. I shuddered again, and made myself address her.

"Will you aid me, daughter of Minos?"

Her gaze returned to me, deep with compassion. "My power lies elsewhere, Phèdre nó Delaunay; such aid is not mine to give. Since the redemption of the great betrayal, the House of Minos has accepted such a gift from Zagreus as renders the isle of Kriti in the world, but not wholly of it, as you understand politics. It is my thought that Mother Dia has guided you here for the healing of your companion, for he is the one who is appointed to aid you in this matter, and his country in need of the friendship of Terre d'Ange. If he survives the *thetalos*, this I think he will do. But . . ." she raised one finger, seeing me open my mouth to protest, ". . . this much, I may do. We will give you aid, for the repair of his ship. We will tend to your wounded. And I will see you granted audience with the Archon of Phaistos, that lies on the plains beyond the Temenos. Kriti will not sail to war on your behalf, no, but I think perhaps he will grant you one ship to serve as courier."

I bowed my head. It would be enough; it had to. "You are kind, my lady Kore."

"You may call me Pasiphae," she said, and smiled once more.

FIFTY-NINE

IT SEEMED that my audience with the Archon of
Phaistos would not be granted until Kazan had undergone
the cleansing ceremony of the *thetalos*. In truth, I was not
sorry for it, for I was in two minds about what I should
request of him.

A great deal rode on Kazan's survival, and I could get
no clear answers concerning the nature of this ritual. I had
not known, until then, how fond I had grown of him, and
it fretted me deeply.

"He was your captor," Pasiphae said curiously;
although she would not divulge the details of their mysteries to me, she had taken me much into her confidence,
for she regarded my presence in the Temenos as a mystery
unto itself. "He betrayed you to your enemies. How is it,
then, that you care for him?"

I frowned, not sure how to frame my reply. "My lady,
what you say is true. But the blood-curse that made him a
pirate was a tragedy not of his making, as are the politics
that made him resent my country. He treated me fairly,
within his own constraints, and did not mean to betray me.

When it came to it, he risked his life to save mine." I shrugged helplessly. "Yes, my lady, if you are asking it; I care for him. And I am D'Angeline, and bound to the precept of Blessed Elua. I do not forgive him, for what he did. But to deny my own feeling . . .'twould be a violation of Elua's sacred trust."

"Elua." She examined a painted kylix, shaking her head. An initiate moved quickly to lift the wine-jug, refilling her cup. We sat on the gracious terrace of the Palace, overlooking the sea. "Many gods have there been, for Mother Dia has many sons; they wear as many guises as she wears faces. But never has there been one such as Elua, who got himself a whole people and slipped the chains of rebirth. What shall Earth's eldest children make of her youngest, Phèdre? I cannot say whither you are bound."

I made her no answer, for I had none, but looked instead at the horns of consecration atop the Palace, rearing upward to gore the sky. The folk of the Cullach Gorrym, the Black Boar, had claimed too to be Earth's eldest children. Who was to say? Mayhap they were one and the same, when one came to it. There are truths and truths. "My lady, I have always been told I bore an ill-luck name, but Oeneus Asterius the Hierophant suggested to me that I did not know the truth of that tale, and you yourself bear an equally ill-starred name, for Pasiphae was mother to the Minotaur, do I not mistake my history. Is it not so?"

"It is so, and it is not so." Pasiphae reflected, and answered me at length. "Always, there has been a conflict between earth and sky, old and new. Mother Dia endures, but her sons, ah! Ever do they seek to cut the cord that binds them to Her, and yet ever do they fear begetting their own successors. It was Ariadne the Most Holy who betrayed her Mother's son, giving him unto the blade of Theseus the Achaian. And as my namesake Pasiphae prayed for the means to redeem this tragedy and the loss of her child, Zagreus did answer, who is called Iacchos by the Achaians, and bears the gifts of insight and madness. Himself, he claimed Ariadne, whose fate you know — and 'twas your namesake, Phaedra, who took revenge on the supplanter, Theseus the Achaian, offering herself as sacrifice that the supplanter's son might be slain by his own father's curse, bringing the circle to close in Mother Dia's lap. Thus do we honor her memory, and thus did Zagreus grant us this gift, that we might be cleansed of the evil we had done. The Achaians tell the tale otherwise, and their poets are the ones the world has heeded, but here at the heart of the world, we hold to the ancient truths." She tilted her head at me. "Do you understand, now?"

"No," I said softly. "A little better, mayhap. I don't understand this business of jealous gods slaying one another and fearing their own offspring. It is not so, with Blessed Elua and his Companions."

"No?" Pasiphae smiled gently. "And yet, from what you tell me, I think your Kushiel the Punisher has gotten a scion he fears."

I remembered Melisande's words, and shuddered. *Kushiel has chosen you, Phèdre, and marked you as his own. To toy with you is to play a god's game.* "Mayhap," I murmured. "But I am only mortal, my lady, and I am trying to save the throne of my Queen, to whom I have sworn loyalty, and I would like also to save the life of my friend, whose men died in the effort of rescuing me. Let the gods claim what they will; my allegiance lies with those I have known and loved. And do you speak against it, I will say, Blessed Elua preached the same."

"That," said Pasiphae, "is what makes him so interesting." Rising, she walked to the edge of the terrace, where the fisherfolk below could see her and stretch out their hands, beseeching her blessing. She gave it freely, opening her arms to them, and the lowering sun limned her in light. I had gotten over the shock of our first meeting, but still her presence filled me with awe. It is a different world, Kriti. The setting sun laid a burning path on the water, and I saw in the caverns that riddled the harbor walls a flicker of white robes, betokening the presence of initiates. It was they who had sounded the gongs upon our arrival.

So I had learned, although I may say too that those caverns are ancient, beyond even the remembering of the House of Minos. They have been used as dwelling places since first man struck two flints together, crying out in awe at the blue spark that resulted. But it is a sacred business, this, and best not spoken.

The lower rim of the sun's disk sank below the horizon and Pasiphae lowered her arms, turning back to me. "Your Elua does as he wills," she said gently. "But this is my place, and this is my gift. Tomorrow Kazan Atrabiades will undergo the *thetalos*, and if Mother Dia wills it, he will survive. I grant you leave to attend the ceremony, if you will it. Do you so choose?"

I shivered in my skin, and knew her words for truth. "Yes, Pasiphae. I will attend."

On the following day, I did not see her at all, nor Kazan, whom I had not seen since he had been secluded. I went instead to the harbor of the Temenos, and spoke with Tormos and Glaukos, who were overseeing the repairs to our damaged vessel. That, at least, was well done; the Kritians are great sailors, after all, and the island is rich in oak and cypress. I was happy to see that they were well-rested and of reasonably good cheer; and, too, they had seen to the security of our coffer of gold. And I confess, I was glad too of the Illyrians' company and their simple jests, taking comfort in what had become familiar to me.

They believed to a man that Kazan would overcome the challenge of the *thetalos* and return to them as he had been before, a fierce and cunning leader who would inflict great damage on their enemies and escape unscathed. Indeed, they had begun to spin their own myths out of the events that had befallen us, endlessly enumerating the ways in which Kazan would take his vengeance on the treacherous Serenissimans.

I smiled and jested with them, and prayed that they had the right of it, for Kazan's sake and my own. For vengeance I cared naught, but somewhere in Caerdicca Unitas, Ysandre's *progressus* continued on its steady, unwitting course toward a deadly trap, while in Terre d'Ange, Percy de Somerville awaited word to seize the City of Elua. This long waiting was a torment.

When the sun began to set, I returned to the Palace, where preparations were beginning for the ritual. Make no mistake of it; I had no place in these rituals, save as an onlooker, and that by the grace of the Kore, my lady Pasiphae. Still, they suffered my presence, and as my lips were not sealed by oath, I may relate what I saw of the ceremony – and what I saw afterward, although that is another matter. It began outside the Palace, at the base of the mountain, with three tiers of initiates providing the music, chorus and dance. Torches lit the procession and the dancers wheeled in circles, this way and that, their mingled voices providing the harmonies. They had put off their robes for this and wore only kilts of white linen, cinched at the waist with rolled leather belts, and their dark skin gleamed in the torchlight, freshly oiled. At the center of it all stood Kazan Atrabiades, swaying on his feet, and his face was like a stranger's to me. Neither food nor drink had he taken since we had made landfall; two full days. He looked gaunt and parched, and his eyes burned in their sockets.

This is his choice, I reminded myself, remembering the *kríavbhog*; if he has a chance to be free of it, 'tis not my place to gainsay it. Still, I feared for him.

There came then a great clash of bronze cymbals, and two torches were lit, great pitch-soaked logs stood on end. I could not help but remember La Dolorosa and my fall from the cliffs, Tito's massive torch spinning through the dark night above me; but betwixt them stood the Kore, and her presence drove out aught else.

The Maiden, it means, her title; and I daresay 'twas no more than that, for I had already gauged by the thickening of her waist that she had born children. No matter, for she was well and truly what she claimed by right of that title, the handmaiden of Mother Dia. She wore the ancient regalia for that rite, the flounced skirts sewn with ivory plaques, and the bodice that bared her breasts, nipples darkened with henna. A gold diadem was set atop her head, and her hair had been crimped with hot irons, falling in spiraling curls over her shoulders.

Although there were men and women alike among the initiates, here the Kore was attended only by priestesses. On Kriti, as in too many other places, the rule of law is given unto the province of men, but at the heart of matters, it is women who hold authority. So it was that while the Hierarch saw to the daily governance of the Temenos and oversaw the initiates in the ways of the mysteries, it was the Kore who sanctified them.

Flutes skirled and fell silent, and the revolving dancers came to a halt. The Kore spoke, then, and some trick of the acoustics of that place made her clear-spoken words resonate in every ear. "What do you seek, supplicant?"

Wavering but upright, Kazan made his reply, his tongue thick with thirst and garbling the memorized Hellene speech. "I seek to be cleansed of blood-guilt for the death of my brother."

"What do you offer in sacrifice?" Her words were measured out like pearls on a string.

"I offer my name, and my memory." Swaying, Kazan caught himself, and continued in a firmer voice. "I offer whatever you will take."

A pause, and then she spoke again. "It is enough."

Ah, Elua! I thought, as the Kore's priestesses brought forth water and grain, scarce enough to moisten his mouth to swallow. 'Tis monstrous unfair, that a man should be so beleaguered for a terrible accident. Kazan Atrabiades had not *meant* to slay his brother. And yet I had seen for myself how the curse had come home to him, fair or no. It was his right, to seek expiation, and not my place to protest the means of it. And who was I, to judge such a thing? I had sought atonement betimes myself, at the hands of Kushiel's priests; indeed, the Unforgiven of Camlach reckoned me the instrument of the same.

Still, it was something I understood, to purge one's memories in pain. It was somewhat else altogether, to offer the memories themselves on the altar of atonement. Mayhap the prospect would not have unnerved me so, had I not spent time in La Dolorosa, but I had seen madness at close hand there and come to reckon it a boon companion, and the thought of risking it voluntarily filled my heart with terror.

The Kore made a sign, and the drums started, and flutes and cymbals, while the Hierophant stepped forth to point the way to a path up the mountain. Initiates bearing torches moved ahead in pairs, pausing at stations along the path to light the way for the procession that followed. So we made our way up the mountain, a steep path and narrow, while the lights of the Palace dwindled below us.

Kazan walked alone, with priestesses before and behind him. More than once, he stumbled, but no aid was given him. Trailing at the rear, I struggled to see and yearned to help him, guessing without being told that it was forbidden. I was not sure he would make it, for the path was treacherous, but he did.

Some distance from the summit, we reached our goal; a cavern, dark-mouthed and vast, larger than those that I had seen lining the harbor walls. There was a little plateau before it, and it was there that the Kore halted. Torchlight cast weird, twisting shadows on the threshold of the cavern, but it was deep, and the rear of it remained dark and impenetrable.

With trembling fingers, Kazan divested himself of clothing until he stood mother-naked before the Kore, and she purified him with water and anointed his brow with oil. He knelt, and she cut a lock of his hair with a sharp little knife, tying a red thread around it and setting it on a tray, offering an invocation for his safety. Then she placed around his neck a single cowry shell on a leather thong, to dedicate him to Mother Dia.

It went on for some time, and I found myself blinking with weariness, half-hypnotized by the torchlight and the whispering music that seemed to come from the very mountain, for the initiates had scattered across the face of the rocks. At length, the Kore offered a final libation of wine and took a step back from the cavern.

"It is commenced," she said softly, her words pitched to echo in the cavern's mouth. "Go forth, Kazan Atrabiades, and seek to be free of it."

From where I stood, I saw Kazan hesitate, then square his shoulders.

He entered the cavern, and I saw him no more.

Sixty

It is a long vigil the Kritians maintain during the *thetalos*.

For a considerable time, I stood with the others, waiting and watching, but I was leg-weary from the climb, and my body ached still in every part from the pounding it had endured aboard our storm-tossed ship. At length I gave up, and sat down in the hollow of a boulder, still warm from the day's sun. One can find comfort anywhere, when one is tired enough. The Kritians stood unfaltering, the Kore and her priestess on one side of the cavern's mouth, the Hierophant on the other, and agile initiates perching on crags like goats on a mountainside.

The music was muted to a thrumming murmur. The torches burned lower, sparking and crackling softly. Every now and then came the whispering sound of someone shifting — they were human, after all — but otherwise, nothing moved save the stars overhead and no other sound was heard.

Truly, I did my best to remain awake; it never occurred to me that I would fail. I was fraught with worry on Kazan's behalf and plagued as well by a thousand other concerns. I went over in my mind the speech I would make to the Archon of Phaistos, searching for the right words to present my plea. My rhetorical training was in Caerdicci, not Hellene, and I wanted to be as polished as I might when I entered "the wide harbor and the company of men," as the Hierophant said. They are ancient in the craft of statesmanship, Hellenes, and Kritians most ancient of all.

I polished my speech in my mind until it shone, and fell asleep in the process.

How long I slept, I cannot say. I awoke, once, and heard nothing but the thrumming music, the distant buzz of cicadas. It reminded me of being a child in Delaunay's household, and waking in my bed to hear the murmur of conversation coming from the faraway courtyard when he entertained into the small hours of the night. Taking comfort in the memory, I wrapped my mantle around me against the night chill and slid back into sleep.

It was the sound of my own blood beating that awoke me, a rustling sound, but near, not far; a soft, insistent tide that beat in my ears.

I knew that sound.

I opened my eyes to see the mountainside awash in a red haze, motionless Kritians, torches and all. With a sure sense of dread, I waited, but it was not Kushiel's voice that spoke.

Instead there came a cry, a great, wordless cry of horror, emanating from the mouth of the cavern. A ripple ran through the Kritians, and somewhere above me, an initiate drew in her breath sharply. Then the Kore raised one hand in a gesture of forbidding, and they fell still. The cry sounded again, ragged with terror; and again, and again.

Blessed Elua, I thought, is there to be no end to it! Tears stung my eyes, and I bit my lip to keep silent. I had heard cries like this before, in the endless nights of La Dolorosa, where the grieving sea-surge stripped away prisoners' sanity bit by bit. And I had seen, too, the results of that torment, the pitiable, half-human wretches I had released from confinement.

I could not live through it again.

Moving silently, I wrapped my dark mantle more tightly around me, drawing a fold over my head to shadow my face. I had been sorry to be at the end of the procession as we mounted the trail, but now I welcomed the luck that had placed me on the very outskirts of those gathered, for it enabled me to slip back into the darkness and circle around the watchers' perimeter.

It was not so easy as it sounds, for I needs must move silently in complete darkness, over treacherous and unfamiliar terrain. With grim determination, I timed my movements in accordance with Kazan's hoarse cries, working my way toward the mouth of the cavern. All the while, I wrestled with my conscience over the fitness of my actions. I trusted Pasiphae instinctively, and knew beyond a shadow of a doubt that there was power in this place, and she was rightfully invested in that power in her role as the Kore. But even so, there had been power in La Dolorosa, the awful power of Asherat's immortal grief, and it was human error that made it a place of horror.

The Kritians tell a different tale of my namesake's end; who is to say which is true?

For what had Kushiel compelled me if not for this?

I had no answers, save the one I had given Pasiphae earlier; I was D'Angeline, and could only follow the

allegiance of my mortal heart. My actions had brought
Kazan to this place. I could not bear to stand idly by and
listen while it drove him mad.

There was a narrow gap that led to the left-hand side of
the cavern's mouth. The Hierophant stood before it, some
five paces forward. From the darkness outside the uneven
ring of torchlight, I sat on my heels and surveyed my
course. If I could get there, I could pass behind him easily
enough, but there were two initiates between us, and no
safe way of passing them.

Kushiel, I prayed silently, I have gone where you bid
me, and never refused you. If it is truly your will that I do
this thing, lend me your aid.

No answer but silence; and then Kazan cried out again,
naked fear in his voice. A sudden breeze sprang up from
the sea, and the nearest initiate's torch guttered out. The
other picked his way cautiously to his side, and they turned
their backs for a moment, huddling against the wind to
ignite the extinguished torch.

Well, I thought; that's clear enough.

I slipped like a shadow past the initiates, behind the
Hierophant's unmoving figure, and into the mouth of the
cavern beyond the range of torchlight.

It was black inside the cavern, lightless, impenetrable
black, and once inside, I realized it was deeper than I had
guessed. Kazan gave another fearful cry, the sound coming
from beyond and a bit below, for the cavern floor slanted.
I put out both hands before me and moved blindly toward
the sound. I could hear his breathing, now, hoarse and
ragged, stirring echoes in the blackness.

Was it too late, even now? It might as well be, I
thought, despairing. How many others lay slain or

destroyed in my wake? An ill-luck name, I had told myself, with all the self-deceiving guile of a child. It was not so. I had set myself willfully on this course from the day Melisande Shahrizai's parcel arrived; I had taken her gambit, knowing it for a fool's move. Wiser heads had sought to dissuade me, from Thelesis de Mornay and Ysandre de la Courcel to Quintilius Rousse; yes, and Joscelin too.

And I would have none of it, heeding none of them, dragging Joscelin and my poor, dear chevaliers to their doom. Nicola, Nicola L'Envers y Aragon, had tried to show me my arrogant mistrust for the folly that it was, and I had been too proud to hear her, so pleased with my own cleverness, so certain that I was master of my game.

So clever had I been on Dobrek, concealing the truth of my situation from Kazan, concealing its weaknesses; oh, clever indeed, Phèdre! So clever that it led him to give me all unwitting to my enemies. What was the cost of death for that rescue, that I might live? One ship? Both of them? How many men had died aboard the Serenissiman vessel? And now Kazan lay screaming out his wits in torment at the back of a cave, thanks to my cleverness.

I fixed onto that thought and held it, forcing myself to take another step in his direction, and another, dimly aware in some part of my mind that there was somewhat unnatural in this flood of guilt that paralyzed me.

But it was true, it was all true.

And Kazan was the least of it. Oh, yes, I had gone reckless and heedless into danger, and I had taken my best beloved with me. Remy and Fortun, slain in cold blood, for the foolish sin of loyalty to one such as me. Ti-Philippe, who might be alive or dead, and Joscelin; ah, Elua, Joscelin! How many times over had I wronged him, how many cruelties had I subjected him to, straining the loyalties of his last remaining vow until either it broke or he did.

Worst of all, I'd taken pleasure in it. I'd driven him to lash out in cruel words, and I had taken an *anguissette's* terrible pleasure in the pain it provoked; the pain of a wounded heart, deeper and more exquisite than any torment of the flesh.

And if I thought I'd known pain then, it was naught to this.

I saw my flaws and follies revealed in all their hideous vanity, and the awful cost in mortal lives and pain that had resulted. I knew my soul laid bare and scourged on a rack built of my own deeds. Names and faces, too many to count, for it was not only in this venture, but nigh everything I'd done since I had no title to my name but that of Delaunay's *anguissette*. His man-at-arms Guy, foully murdered, a murder that might have been prevented had I not kept silent about Alcuin's plans. Alcuin, Alcuin and my lord Delaunay . . . I choked on the memory, remembering them in a welter of gore, and how I had concealed my slip of the tongue that revealed the depth of Melisande's knowledge; it might have saved them, had I not been too cowardly to speak, it might have given Delaunay the key to evade a deep-laid plot.

It went on, unending, and I struggled against the tide of it while Kazan's cries rang in my ears. I understood, now, why he screamed. In a sea of anguish, I made my way to the back of the cavern, until I heard his raw breathing and fell to my knees, feeling blindly.

He was there, lying on the cavern floor, his skin cool to the touch, but alive. "Kazan," I whispered, shaking his shoulder. "Kazan, it is not worth the price of madness. Kazan, come with me!"

He moved, one hand groping, feeling along my arm to take my hand and grip it hard, and then the pain of remembered guilt struck again and his grip bore down on mine, until I could feel the bones in my hand grinding, and I was remembering, remembering

. . . how I had led Joscelin to murder the thane Trygve, strangling him to win our freedom, letting Joscelin take that darkness on his soul; how I had stabbed Harald the Beardless, killing him with my own hands, and others, so many others! I had done it, I had done it all. I whispered a hoarse, futile plea for forgiveness, remembering. All the dead of the Dalriada, whom I beguiled into war; Eamonn mac Connor, his bright hair against the blood-soaked battlefield. Hyacinthe, ah, Elua, Hyacinthe! Not dead, but a worse fate; I wept in the darkness. Magister Acco, whom I drove to take his own life, and poor Tito of La Dolorosa, whose kindness I had cultivated to my own ends.

It was my fault, all mine.

I have known pain — Elua knows, I have known pain. It is my gift and my art to endure it, and even I have known pain beyond bearing, under Waldemar Selig's knife on the fields of Troyes-le-Mont.

This was worse.

After a time, I was no longer aware of specific incidences of blood-guilt, but only the vast, featureless agony of it. It bore me up and carried me down all at once, and I felt the surge of it in my very bones. A scream gathered at the back of my throat and I locked my jaws on it, thinking, I will not scream, I will not scream, until I was not sure whether I thought it or said it, whether I screamed or not.

I saw red in the blackness of the cavern, and Kushiel's face before me, stern and bronze, lips shaping words I could not understand; I thought, if only I could, all would be redeemed, but I could not concentrate for the vastness of my sins. And then it came to me that if only I gave my *signale*, all of this will end, and I heard Melisande's voice telling me as much, rich as honey, coming from somewhere beyond the pain . . .

    . . . and thought with my last gasp of consciousness, *no!*

Sixty-one

THERE WERE voices speaking somewhere.

It seemed I had to come back from a very long distance to make sense of them, to derive words and sentences from the meaningless sounds assailing my ears. I could not understand why it seemed so very difficult, but it did, for even when I recognized the sounds as speech, I could not make out what they said, although they seemed very close at hand. Ah, I thought, pleased at the discovery, it is because they are speaking Hellene, and it seemed to me that I knew that tongue. I fumbled for it with difficulty, and thought perhaps if I opened my eyes, it would be easier to think. I tried to do so, but it was hard, for my lashes were glued shut with sticky matter.

". . . move her or tend her here?"

Yes, I thought, I know that voice; that is the Hierophant of the Temenos. I am on the island of Kriti in the place called Temenos, and I have profaned their mystery.

"Hush. She is waking."

I knew that voice, too. It belonged to Pasiphae

Asterius, daughter of the House of Minos, who is called the Kore.

"Here." There was a sound of someone moving, the faint slosh of water, and then I felt my eyes gently bathed with a damp cloth. I opened them, and saw the Kore kneeling beside me, frowning gravely, still clad in her ritual regalia. "Can you speak, Phèdre?"

I wasn't sure. I opened my mouth and tried it. "Yes, my lady."

A war whoop sounded somewhere behind her; loud enough to split the cavern roof, I thought, and surely loud enough to split my skull. And then I was scooped up from the floor where I lay into a vertiginous, bone-rattling embrace by a grinning Kazan Atrabiades.

"Kazan! Put her down!"

He did; if he did not know Hellene, he knew what the Kore meant. I wavered unsteadily on my feet, clinging to his sleeve. He was still grinning, and his face was as joyous as a lad's. I moved my head slightly, tested my limbs to see if they yet worked. It seemed they did. The Kore and the Hierophant and a handful of initiates all stood within the sunlit cavern, staring at me with incomprehension in their dark Kritian eyes.

"You are . . . well?" Pasiphae asked cautiously.

I moved my tongue around in my mouth and swallowed. It seemed that worked, too. "I am . . . alive, my lady."

The scions of Minos exchanged a glance, and the Hierophant spread his hands, relinquishing judgement. Pasiphae shook her head, still frowning. "No one has ever undergone the *thetalos* undedicated and lived to tell of it. I cannot bestow the rites of absolution upon you, Phèdre, but Mother Dia has spared you, and where She shows mercy, we can but follow. If you are able to walk, we will return to the Palace and speak of this later."

"I understand."

I made the return journey unaided, although the procession had to stop many times so I could rest. By light of day, the Kritians — even Pasiphae — looked worn from the ordeal of the ritual; among the initiates, flutes and drums dangled loosely from their hands. They looked at me often, uncertainty in their dark eyes. Only Kazan was exultant with energy and high spirits. Whatever had transpired in the cavern, he had come out of it changed.

In the Palace, I was shown to my former chamber and given fish broth and mulled wine to drink. One of the elder initiates remained at my side, and Kazan hovered in the room until she made to chase him away.

"She wants you to leave, Kazan," I informed him; through layers of exhaustion, I was aware of being amused. "I'm supposed to rest. Go speak to Tormos and the others; they're waiting to hear news of you."

"I am in your debt, now." He sat on the edge of my bed and looked serious, speaking in Illyrian. "I would not have survived it without you, Phèdre. When I would not leave, you held onto my hand and spoke to me, telling me you would not leave me, that you would stay and we would endure it together and live to greet the day."

"I did?" I stared wearily at him; I had no recollection of having said such things.

"You did." Unexpectedly, he grinned again, showing the gap in his teeth. "And I followed the thread of your voice like Theseú in the labyrinth! Only . . ." he sobered,

". . . only the Kore opened the door for me at the end, and you were left in darkness. Why, I do not know."

"I do," I said softly. "Kazan, I was trespassing there."

"Maybe." He thought about it and shuddered. "Still, I would have died."

"You didn't. And I didn't. Now go and talk to your men." I closed my eyes and leaned my head back on the pillows. Through the veils of approaching sleep, I could hear Kazan threatening the initiate with vile consequences if any harm came to me, and her indignant insistence that he leave. Neither one understood a word the other was saying, which would have made me smile, if I could, but I was too far away, and presently I heard no more.

All that day and through the night I slept, waking to the light of a new day. The world seemed bright in my eyes, new-washed and clean, all the colors more vivid than I remembered them. Though I was as weak still as a day-old kitten, I felt peaceful and calm. Not long after I had broken my fast, a second initiate came — for I had been watched and tended in shifts while I slept — bearing a summons to see the Kore.

New clothing had been laid out for me, rather finer than before; a gown of saffron with a crimson mantle. I took my care with dressing, settling the mantle about my shoulders, and went to answer Pasiphae's summons.

She received me in the throne room, waving me to a stool when I would have knelt. "Sit." Once I had done so, she regarded me for a moment without speaking. "I do not know what to make of you, Phèdre nó Delaunay. I have consulted the records, and they do not speak of such a thing, that one should profane the mystery of the *thetalos* and emerge intact. No auguries speak; the house snakes

take their milk and bask content; Mother Dia is not w̶
and Zagreus is silent. And yet I think you have not escape̶
unscathed."

"No," I said. "I would not say so."

"Tell me what transpired."

I told her willingly enough, speaking from the small, still core at my center. When I had done, she nodded gravely. "Yes. That is the nature of it, to confront the worst of one's inner self unveiled. It grieves me that I cannot absolve you of these things, and yet . . ." She shook her head. "The gods keep their silence. It may not be. What you have seen, you carry with you."

"I know," I said softly. "I understand, my lady; truly, I do."

Pasiphae looked at me with compassion. "Understand this, then. It is the darkest truth that is revealed in the cavern of the *thetalos*; the truths we seek to hide from ourselves. That does not mean it is the whole truth, Phèdre."

"No." I considered my answer. "I know that, too. My lady, I saw things in that cavern I would undo, if I could; acts of pride and selfishness I shudder to think on. But others . . . who can say? Many have died for my choices; many have not. The Goddess looks out from the past and counts the dead, but she does not number our living."

"Oh . . ." Pasiphae's lips curved in a faint smile, ". . . she does, you may be sure of it. But that tally is never given to us to know. Still and all, it is clear to me that some god's hand is on you in this matter, and I will not intervene, nor gainsay what is done. When you are able to travel, I will give you the aid I promised – a letter of conduct to the Archon of Phaistos, and conveyance to the city. It is only an hour's ride."

"To the wide harbor and the company of men," I mused aloud. "Thank you, my lady Kore."

"It is nothing." Her thoughtful gaze rested on me. "Kazan Atrabiades has made a dedication-offering of gold, as is fitting, and Oeneus has seen to it that his ship has been rendered seaworthy. But you . . . you have brought a mystery for me to ponder, and that is worth more than gold. I am grateful for it, Phèdre nó Delaunay. It does not always come to pass during the lifetime of those who serve as the Kore of the Temenos. I hope that you have found here what you sought."

I shifted on my stool. "My lady, if it allows me to return from whence I came and prevent my Queen from being slain out of hand, then yes, I have. Is it possible that we might leave for Phaistos on the morrow?"

It startled her, enough so that an ordinary mortal woman looked out from her deep priestess' eyes. "*Tomorrow?* You would ride so soon, after what you have endured?"

"Time is a luxury I do not have." I rolled my shoulders; my body was stiff and sore, but it would serve. "For good or for ill, I am Kushiel's Chosen, my lady."

"A harsh god," she murmured, "and a strange one. Well and so, it shall be as you wish. I will speak to Oeneus, and he shall make the arrangements. Demetrios Asterius is Archon of the city; he is of the Kindred, with a keen eye for trade. You will like him, I think," she added, smiling. "He is high-spirited, but do not be fooled; he is shrewd for all his play. I will commend you to him."

"I am in your debt."

"No." Pasiphae shook her head. "As you were sent, so do I serve. These things we do, at the command of the gods. Phèdre, though I cannot grant you absolution, you may have my blessing if you will it."

"It would please me, my lady," I answered truthfully. So I knelt to her after all, and she laid her hand upon my head and gave the invocation in her clear voice. I felt the power of it echo in my bones, and knew I had brushed the very heart of a mystery in this place.

She was as good as her word, and in the morning, we were granted transport. There were ten of us, all told, for those men who were injured had recovered well enough under her care; six would sail the ship to Kommos harbor, under Tormos' command, to await Kazan's orders there. Glaukos would travel with them, to serve as translator. For the rest of us, Kazan and I and two others — Spiridon and Gavril, their names were — we would travel by oxcart to the city of Phaistos.

No farmer's wagon, this, but a splendid conveyance, the sides worked with elaborate trim and a device of wheat sheaves and twining vines which symbolized the union of Mother Dia and Zagreus, her consort-son. Even the oxen were noble beasts, with broad brows and gentle eyes, their horns tipped with gilded caps. They know a thing or two about breeding cattle, on Kriti. Our driver was slight and dark with a quick smile, though he spoke seldom.

Thus did we take our leave.

If the Temenos seemed a world unto itself, displaced from time, such was not true of the rest of the isle. We left by a narrow road winding between the low mountains, but soon gained the fertile plains of the Messara valley, where all manner of crops grow bountifully. The road widened and we met other travellers on foot and on horse- or donkey-back, and indeed, in farmer's wagons laden with produce, for it seemed it was market day in Phaistos. Our driver whistled through his teeth and nodded greetings from time to time; other travellers touched their brows in acknowledgement, and I knew without asking that they knew he served the Kore.

Kazan took it all in with a boy's wide-eyed wonder, and I am not too proud to admit that I envied him that, a little. No shadow of pain overlaid his soul; absolution had granted him a fresh-washed slate. But I was an *anguissette*, and the memory of pain was a familiar companion to me, never wholly unwelcome. I was what I was. It was enough.

And I had my own troubles to brood upon still.

When we were well clear of the Temenos, I asked him, though I feared to broach the topic. "Kazan," I said softly, below the creak of the oxcart, speaking in Caerdicci that none of our companions would overhear. I did not wish to pressure him unduly. "What will you do, now that you are free of the blood-curse? Will you return home, to Epidauro?"

"Do?" He looked at me in surprise. "Did the Kore not speak to you of this, Phèdre? If this Archon, he will grant you the aid of Kriti, eh, then it is good, and I will go, but she does not think he will send warships, he. So we will see what he does, yes, and I will do what you ask, for I have a debt to you, eh?" His expression turned sober. "It is not only that I owe you my life, you, although I do. If I had done as you asked, if I had sailed to Marsilikos and not Dobrek, eh, none of this would have happened. And if I had spoken true when Nikanor returned; then, too. I could have sent you to Epidauro, yes, though I could not go myself; the Ban could have made a mighty alliance with your country. Such things did I see, I," he added quietly, "in the cavern."

I could have laughed, or wept; for the deaths we shared in common, his visions were as true as my own. "Then if the Archon does not aid us — "

"We sail to Epidauro," Kazan finished for me, grinning once more. "And I will see to Nikanor and the others, eh, and I will ask the Ban to aid you, I, for I once stood in his favor, and only my mother's curse put me from it. And if he will not, then where you wish to go, I will take you myself, yes!

Tears stung my eyes. "Thank you," I said, and repeated it. "Thank you."

"No matter," he said, shrugging, and added in Illyrian, "We have a score to settle with the Serenissimans!"

The latter part, Spiridon and Gavril overheard and cheered, chiming in with bloodthirsty vows of revenge. So it continues, I thought ruefully; though I could not help but be glad of their support. Even after the *thetalos*, Kazan is ready to shed fresh blood. Though he remembers, he has been cleansed of it; he begins anew.

Mayhap 'twas not such an ill thing, to carry the living memory of that pain.

With such thoughts did I occupy my mind, and we came in short order to the outer walls of Phaistos. Here the outer market thronged, small-holders trading amongst themselves and those artisans and merchants from within the city who sold shoddy goods at cut-rate prices to the countryfolk. We picked our way between them, making slowly for the gates of the city.

Phaistos is situated on a gentle hill, with the Palace at the crest and the city sprawling around it and sloping down to Kommos harbor. It is a low wall that surrounds the city, although the Archon's guards were posted at the tall ceremonial gate. They wore light armor in the early autumn heat, helmets with red plumes, steel cuirasses over linen kilts that left bare their legs, with sandals and greaves. They carried short spears and ox-hide shields, although some half the squadron had left their shields leaning against the walls while they talked and jested together.

Our cart was given a cursory glance and waved into the city; some few of the guards smiled and touched their brows to our driver, and some few of them nudged each other and stared after us, pointing. I heard the buzz of speculation follow as we entered the city, but it was soon lost in the noise of the Kritian marketplace.

We had reached Phaistos, city of the wide harbor.

SIXTY-TWO ☉

PHAÏSTOS WAS a worldly city indeed, bustling with activity and markedly different from the calm of the Temenos. It is not so large as other harbor cities I had seen, Marsilikos and La Serenissima, but it lies along the trade routes and one sees folk of many nations mingled among the Kritians. There was an Ephesian ship at harbor that day, and a handful of Umaiyyati in the markets, as well as Hellenes from the mainland and a number of Caerdicci from one of the southern city-states. I kept my eyes and ears sharp for D'Angeline faces or voices, but none were forthcoming.

Most of the streets are narrow and meant only for foot traffic, although there are a few broad avenues to the marketplace, the harbor and the Palace. We plodded slowly along one such, making for the hill of the Palace; here and there, Kritians touched their brows. The oxen nodded their heads as they trudged in harness, dipped their gilt-tipped horns as if in acknowledgment.

I am city-born and bred, and it was good to be once more in a familiar atmosphere. I noted the strata of society all mingled in one place, commoners rubbing elbows with lords and ladies. A rich array of odors pervaded the air; the salt tang of the sea, perfumed oils, lamb kebabs sizzling on charcoal braziers, fresh-caught fish, sharp spices and human sweat, and occasionally a waft of distant incense.

Spiridon and Gavril stared in bewilderment, and it came to me that they had never seen a proper city before.

"There would have been Illyrian traders here too," Kazan said in a low voice. "Twenty years ago, eh. Now the Serenissimans have taken all our trade-rights, and there is a heavy fee for those who would trade directly with any but they. And yet I am called a pirate, I! They would take Kriti if they dared, yes, and all of Hellas, but Kriti has never fallen."

It is true, although Tiberium tried during the golden years of her empire. When all of mainland Hellas fell under Tiberian rule, Kriti retained its sovereign status. Although the isle no longer rules the Hellene seas, when her shores were breached, the Kritians retreated to the mountains and fought with ferocity and cunning, luring Tiberian troops to their doom. So the island was never conquered, and when the Tiberian empire crumbled, the Kritians reclaimed their shores.

We came at length to the gates of the Palace, and here the Archon's guards mounted a shrewder watch. Our driver conversed with the leader of the squadron, and I presented Pasiphae's letter. He examined the seal, sun glancing off the steel of his bowed helmet, then gave a courteous nod.

"You are welcome, by order of the Kore of the Temenos. Please dismount from the oxcart, and I will send word to the Archon."

Obeying, we waited, ushered within the gate. Our driver touched his own brow in farewell and set about turning the oxcart, making his slow way back through the city. I occupied my time in studying the Palace of Phaistos, which was far grander than that of the Temenos. It climbed the low hill in terraced layers, red-columned porticoes looking out at the city sloping down to the sea. Presently, a Palace attendant came to greet us, a distinguished Kritian of middle years, with a chain of office about his neck and a white tunic worked with embroidery at the edges. He bowed, addressing us in Hellene.

"Phèdre nó Delaunay of Terre d'Ange, Kazan Atrabiades of Epidauro, I will conduct you and your men into the presence of the Archon."

I translated briefly to Kazan and the Illyrians, and we followed the attendant across the courtyard and mounted the wide staircase, passing beneath a great alabaster archway to enter.

It is a lively place, the Palace of Phaistos. We passed fine Kritian lords and ladies, travelling on foot and in servant-borne palanquins, bound to and from the city's market; they chattered amongst themselves, laughing and gesturing. They dress for the heat in Phaistos, and I saw Spiridon and Gavril stretch their eyes to see noblewomen in linen so fine it showed the contours of the bodies beneath, nothing so modest as Illyrian attire. It made me smile.

The attendant led us to the Upper East Wing of the Palace, and paused outside a doorway. I could hear odd sounds coming from within, grunting and thudding. Kazan looked inquiringly at me and I shrugged. The attendant cleared his throat and knocked three times, then opened the door.

It led not into a room but onto a small, open-air courtyard with a sandy floor. There was a well at the rear of the yard, and it was set about on all sides with benches and date palms in massive clay pots. Kritian nobles sat on the benches, attended by servants with parasols, eating and drinking and conversing while they watched a wrestling match. Some half a dozen other wrestlers stood watching, laying odds and wagers.

We stood discreetly to one side and waited. I gazed at the seated nobles, trying to guess which one was the Archon while the match played out. The contestants were both naked and oiled, hair bound in clubs. One had the advantage of height and reach, but the smaller man was quick, slipping out of his hold time and again. The spectators oohed and aahed, exclaiming over each near throw and escape. Kazan stared, frowning in perplexity; the other two Illyrians looked uncomfortably at the scene. They will strip to swim, but not much else, and even that, not in the presence of women.

In time, the wrestlers closed in a grapple, legs braced, hands locked on each other's upper arms. I watched their feet scuffle for purchase and advantage in the deep sand as each sought to unbalance the other. The smaller man feint-ed left, seeking to hook his opponent's ankle; but he was ready for it and threw a hip-check, using the leverage of his long arms to throw the other. Down went the smaller contestant, landing with a resonant thump. The audience sighed and the winner stepped back and bowed deeply; when the loser bounded to his feet grinning, they all applauded, and I realized he was the Archon.

He came over to us as he was, mother-naked with the Seal of Minos strung on a cord about his neck, skin gleaming with oil save for a few patches of sand.

"I am Demetrios Asterius," he said cheerfully, "the Archon of Phaistos. I hear that Pasiphae has sent you to me. Has anyone ever told you that your hair shines like stars caught in a net of the night sky?"

I flushed, kneeling in the sun-warmed sand. "My lord Archon, pray accept my greeting. I am Phèdre nó Delaunay, Comtesse de Montrève, of Terre d'Ange."

"Mother Dia, I think I could guess *that!* You're enough to send the Goddess of Love running for her mirror." Setting his hands on his hips, the Archon surveyed Kazan, who bowed, eyes averted. "And you must be the Epidauran. Well, you two are an unlikely pair!"

"I am Kazan Atrabiades, I," Kazan said stiffly in Caerdicci.

The Archon raised his brows and switched languages without effort. "If that's so, you've a name for a pirate, Illyrian!"

Kazan grinned wolfishly; I daresay he was pleased to find his reputation had preceded him. "It may be, eh? But I have undergone the *thetalos*, I."

"So I am told." A shrewd look crossed Demetrios Asterius' face, and I remembered well what Pasiphae had said of him. Although he was slender and dark-complected, he had a look of her about the eyes; the deep-set eyes of the House of Minos, who call themselves the Kindred. "You have a letter, I believe?"

Still kneeling, I handed it to him. His slim fingers closed hard about my wrist instead of taking the letter, and he drew me to my feet, laughing. "You need not kneel to me, Lady Phèdre, charming though it looks. Let us see what Pasiphae has written." Plucking the letter from my hand, he gave a sharp whistle in the direction of the gathered wrestlers. One raised his head, smiling in answer, and came over to join us. He was tall and well-made, with hair the color of darkened bronze and grey eyes that held a quiet amusement. "This is Timanthes," the Archon said absently, throwing an arm over his companion's shoulders as he scanned Pasiphae's letter. "He can beat me two falls out of three, too, although he never boasts of it. Here, Timanthes, see what you make of this."

Timanthes read the letter silently, and their eyes met when he had finished. "You'll have to hear her out in a proper audience, Demetrios. This is too heavy to be decided here."

"That's what I thought." The Archon clapped his hands together, turning to address the gathered Kritians, who clustered on their benches, staring and whispering. "Thank you for coming," he called to them. "I hope you have been well entertained!" They applauded again politely, and dispersed in short order, taking their retinues of servants with them, eyeing us sidelong as they went. In the background, the other wrestlers began sluicing each other down with buckets of water drawn from the well. Demetrios Asterius touched his fingers to his lips, brows drawn in thought. "You have a ship in the harbor, yes?" he asked Kazan in Caerdicci. "I am unclear what is your stake in this matter, pirate. The law of the Temenos protects you as a supplicant, but it does not extend to matters of state if you intend harm."

Kazan looked down at him; he was a full head taller than the Archon. "What I came for, I have, son of Minos.

Now I am here to see what you will do, eh, and what you will not, I will. Do you understand, you?"

"I think so." The Archon nodded briskly. "Well and so, I will hear out this request of yours, Lady Phèdre, and your . . . consort, is he?"

"No," I said softly. "My lord Kazan Atrabiades and I are bound together by . . . mutual debts, you might say. He is not my consort."

"No?" He raised his brows again and grinned. "That's well, then. Timanthes, does her hair not shine like stars caught in night's net?" They exchanged another glance and Timanthes shook his head, smiling. "Your sister would be wroth, to hear me say such things," the Archon concluded, sounding not at all put out. "But what am I to do, hmm, when the Kore herself sends one such as this to my door? Ah, well! My dear pirate," he said to Kazan, "I suggest you find lodgings for your men in the city. I am told there are a good many inns of quality, if you have coin to pay. For your part, we will honor the dues of a suppli-cant who has undergone the *thetalos*; here, you may stay. And you, my lady." He made me a bow, the Seal of Minos banging against his bare chest as he straightened. "You, we will surely house. Timanthes, will you see it done?"

"Yes, Demetrios." Timanthes smiled at me. "It will be done."

I do not think Kazan liked the arrangements – I do not think he liked the Archon overmuch – but so it was done, and Timanthes escorted me to pleasant quarters in the West Wing of the Palace.

"The Archon will see you within the hour," he said gravely to me. "He will not keep one waiting overlong whom the Kore has sent."

"Thank you, Timanthes." I considered him. "You are very fond of him, are you not?"

One corner of his mouth rose in a smile. "Yes, my lady. I am."

I had guessed that they were lovers; rightly, it seemed. "You read the Kore's letter. Will he treat me kindly, do you think?"

Timanthes studied the beams of the ceiling. "He will hear you out in fairness, my lady. As much would he do for any supplicant, and the children of Minos heed one another's advice, most especially when it comes from the Temenos. Will he grant you aid?" He looked soberly at me. "I cannot say. If I have read aright, you have incurred the enmity of a mighty nation, and La Serenissima lies closer to Kriti than Terre d'Ange. Consider your request wisely, my lady."

"I will," I said. "Thank you."

He left me, then. I made shift to freshen myself, washing my hands and face in a basin of water set out for that purpose, and then sat and waited, thinking on what I would say. The fine speech I had polished once upon a time had gone clear out of my head in the cavern of the Temenos, shredded to bits and lost forever by what I had undergone there. Even so, I had composed it with a very different audience in mind; I did not know what to make of this Archon, who thought nothing of receiving petitioners on the wrestling floor, whose gaze hinted at an intellect his manner belied.

In the end, I resolved to tell the truth. If there was one thing I learned in the cavern of the Temenos, it was that my efforts to be clever had led only to a bad end. So it was that when I was sent for at last and received by Demetrios

Asterius in his throne room, I laid out my tale earnestly, speaking in Caerdicci for the benefit of Kazan, who stood glowering beside me.

The Archon listened thoughtfully, interrupting me only to ask for a point of clarification here or there, and his questions were sensible. In white robes of state trimmed with purple-and-gold borders, he seemed more the ruler. A finely wrought gold diadem adorned his head, though I could see his black, curling hair was still damp from bathing. Timanthes stood beside his throne, and by his fresh attire, I guessed he was of noble birth, too.

When I had done, the Archon nodded soberly. "Your dilemma is clear, my lady Phèdre, and what you say, I believe. The Kore would not have commended you to me if you did not speak the truth. What is the nature of your request?"

I drew a deep breath. "My lord Archon, my needs are twofold. I fear it is too late for me to intercept the Queen on her *progressus*. My only hope of preventing her assassination is to go to La Serenissima itself, and pray that I reach it before her. In this matter, I ask only that you lend me passage and an escort, that I might gain the city safely."

"And in the other?"

"A swift ship and a courier, my lord Archon, to bear a letter to the Lady of Marsilikos." I met his eyes. "Betrayal lies at home and abroad in this, my lord. If I fail in preventing the death of my Queen, still I may prevent the seizure of the throne."

Demetrios Asterius touched his fingertips together, glancing at Kazan. "And what is it you say, pirate? You will do what I will not?"

"I have said it," Kazan said shortly.

"So you have, and in a very succinct manner." Ignoring Kazan's muttered growl, the Archon returned his attention to me, raising his brows. "Forgive me the crassness of this question, my dear, but it is one I must needs ask. Many of the Kindred of Minos are gifted with insight, able to discern the will of the gods; I am not one such, and must rely on what small skills I have in the way of ruling. So I ask: What merit in this boon is there for Kriti?"

I was ready for the question. "If I succeed even in part, my lord, you will earn the gratitude of Terre d'Ange, and may name your own reward. Money, do you wish it, trade rights with Terre d'Ange and Alba, or the skills of D'Angeline engineers; mayhap even alliance through marriage, although that is not mine to promise."

"And if you fail entirely?" he asked, not unkindly.

I paused, and shook my head. "I can make no guarantee, my lord. Still, there is much to be gained, and little to venture."

"Fairly stated, my dear, though there is more to weigh than you may reckon." The Archon steepled his fingers once more, touching them to his lips and staring into the distance. "Please believe me when I say I understand the urgency of this situation," he said abruptly, coming to some conclusion. "But it is not a request I can grant or deny on a moment's whim. Allow me one day to consider it, and on the morrow I will have an answer for you. Is that acceptable to you?"

I glanced at Kazan, who gave a shrug. We would need a day at least to properly outfit the ship for travel, for although it had been rendered seaworthy in the Temenos, we had not been able to replace necessary items such as water casks and other stores.

"Yes, my lord Archon," I said, curtsying to him. "It is acceptable, and I am grateful for your kindness."

"Good." He smiled, his mood lightening. "Then will you do me the honor of attending a dinner party this evening as my guest? The Lady Althaia has made it known that she will be most put out if our exotic visitors are not invited." The Archon gave an amused sidelong glance at Timanthes, who shook his head silently, then added to Kazan, "You too, of course, my dear pirate. The ladies are intrigued by your ferocious scowl. It will make for an interesting evening."

Kazan's face was unreadable, his bow precise. "Thank you, Lord Archon," he said, taking care with his words, "but I have business with my ship. With your permission, I will return on the morrow."

"As you wish." Demetrios Asterius waved one hand, then cocked his head at me. "But you, I hope, will not disappoint me. We see few enough D'Angelines; it would be a pity to miss your company."

"My lord," I said, "It will be my honor."

SIXTY-THREE

AFTER THE audience, I was shown back to my guest-quarters and thence to the bathhouse, where I was drawn a sumptuous bath that would not have been out of place in the Night Court. They have servants in the Palace of Phaistos whose sole purpose is to attend the bathhouses, seeing to the temperature of the water, laying out fresh linens and such. While I luxuriated, a plain-faced young woman entered bearing a tray with a jar of sweet oil and knelt beside the tub, murmuring that the Lady Althaia had sent her personal attendant to minister to me, as she was skilled in the arts of massage.

Although I have certainly lived without it, I have never turned away luxury. So it was that I rose dripping from my bath to lie upon one of the alabaster benches, spread with a clean linen sheet. The girl kept her eyes averted as I did, but when she went to spread the oil upon my back, I heard her indrawn gasp. I had forgotten Naamah's marque, vivid black and red against my fair skin.

"Do not be alarmed," I said to her in Hellene. "It is

only the marque of Naamah, whose servant I am. You would name her a goddess, I suppose."

She shook her head, whispering something in a dialect I did not recognize, and smoothed on the oil. Whether or not her concerns had been allayed, she set about her work without further delay, and in short order, a feeling of well-being suffused my limbs. I closed my eyes, head pillowed on my arms, and let her skilled hands work the deep knots of tension from my muscles.

In this drowsing and pleasant state, I paid scant heed to the comings and goings in the bathhouse until I heard an unfamiliar voice say, "I am pleased, Lady Phaedra, that you seem to be enjoying the services of my slave Chloris."

I opened my eyes to see a Kritian noblewoman standing before me, a faint, measuring smile curving her lips. By her elaborately-coifed bronze hair and grey eyes — and her familiarity — I guessed her to be Timanthes' sister. It gave me a start, to hear her refer to my masseuse as her slave; nonetheless, I answered politely. "You are the Lady Althaia, I think. I am in your debt, my lady."

"Yes, indeed." She prowled around the bench, eyeing me. "I should have gone to the wrestling, it seems, and not the marketplace; I have missed being first informed. Timanthes didn't tell me you bore the mark of a *hetaera*."

"Timanthes," I said, "did not know. I am here as a servant of her majesty Ysandre de la Courcel, Queen of Terre d'Ange, and not Naamah, my lady. It is a D'Angeline matter."

"Is it?" Pausing in front of me, Lady Althaia looked down her nose and raised her gracefully arched brows. "Demetrios Asterius is steadfast in his regard for my brother, but he is known to have a fickle eye for women.

We have an understanding, yes, but I am not yet pledged to the son of Minos. What better way to bait a trap for the Archon of Phaistos than with a D'Angeline noblewoman who practices the *hetaerae* trade?" Her mouth turned down sourly. "I know something of your people, Lady Phaedra. You are known for the art of spell-casting in the bedchamber."

I propped my chin on one fist. "It is not my intention, my lady, to seduce the Archon."

"No?" She looked uncertain.

"No," I said firmly. "It is a matter of state. No more, and no less."

"And if he were to offer?" Althaia challenged me. "Kriti's aid, for the pleasure of your company in the bedchamber. Would you refuse?"

I considered it. The slave, Chloris, realized she was eavesdropping, lowered her head and continued to rub oil into my skin, smoothing away the myriad aches of my long ordeal. "You know the Archon, my lady Althaia," I said. "Would he?"

She looked away and murmured, "No." Her mouth quirked with a trace of the self-effacing humor I had seen in her brother. "Well, he might. But I wouldn't trust it, if he does. He's a shrewd trader, Demetrios is. He'd not offer any advantage he wouldn't give willingly otherwise. But he might try to make you think he did."

Her voice held the reluctant ring of truth, and there were none of the telltales of a lie in her demeanor. I smiled. "Then you have done me twice a kindness here, my lady. In turn I swear to you, my purpose here is naught but what I have said."

"Well, then." Althaia's manner relaxed. "Why won't

you bring your pirate to my dinner party, Lady Phaedra?"
she said playfully. "I hear he cuts a most manly figure, and
even dared rude words to the Archon himself. It would
irritate Demetrios in a most useful manner if you brought
him!"

I could feel the tension in Chloris' hands. "Kazan
Atrabiades is not mine to command, my lady," I said
quietly. "He is a pirate, yes, but he has committed no crime
against Hellas, and he is a free citizen of Illyria."

"Oh, pah!" She made a dismissive gesture. "You could
have convinced him, I am sure. You're so serious, for a
hetaera! I hope you won't be so dull at my dinner party.
Everyone is hoping for rare entertainment."

"I shall do my best to amuse, my lady," I said wryly. I
do not think I had ever been accused of being dull company before, but I took a warning from it. Kritian society
is ancient in sophistication, even among Hellenes. If I
wanted the Archon to consider my request a valid one,
I had best appear in truth a D'Angeline noblewoman, and
not a ragtag refugee in desperate straits. The fact that I felt
myself far more the latter than the former was of no
account.

"I shall count upon it," Althaia said carelessly, adding
in a rather different tone, "Chloris! Leave off your moon-
ing and be about your work. I'm sure the Lady Phaedra is
accustomed to far better service in Terre d'Ange; do not
disgrace me!"

The slave bowed her head and murmured an apology,
hands kneading my shoulder blades. I waited until Althaia
had made her exit to speak to her. "It is not true in the
slightest," I said in a gentle tone, leaning on my elbows and
turning my head to look at her. "You're very skilled,

Chloris; you could find employ in any D'Angeline house-hold."

She flushed unbecomingly, ducking her chin toward her breastbone and replying almost inaudibly. "I am not free to seek employment."

"Freeborn or captive?" I asked sympathetically.

Her chin came up and she met my eyes. "Freeborn."

There was a world of sorrow and loss in that single word, and although I never learned more of her story, I grieved for her. I have known servitude, and I have known slavery, too, and there is a difference betwixt the two. *It is one thing to observe the courtesies of rank,* Anafiel Delaunay said to me, the day he bought my marque and took me into his household, *and quite another to treat humans as chattel.* I was sold into servitude as a child; I never fully appreciated the difference until I was a slave in Gunter Arnlaugson's steading. "I am sorry," I said to Chloris, knowing the words to be inadequate.

She lowered her head again, and her mouth twisted with bitter satisfaction. "You make her nervous, *lyp-iphera,*" she muttered. "Looking like a roe deer amid cattle as you do. It's good to see." After that, fearing she had said too much, my efforts to draw her out met in failure . . . but her words came back to me when I returned to my quarters and found that the Archon had sent an array of attire for that evening's entertainment, as well as attendants to see to my robing. Well and so, I thought; if it is D'Angeline beauty he wished, I shall oblige. I chose with care among the garments presented, selecting a gown that seemed amid the height of Kritian fashion as I had observed it; sheer folds of white, draping low fore and aft.

My marque showed clearly through it, and I rouged

my nipples in the Kritian manner, but my hair I dressed in D'Angeline style, caught at the nape of my neck with a few tendrils allowed to escape. A kneeling servant presented a tray with a dozen tiny jars of cosmetics and unguents, but I partook lightly of those, only a touch of carmine for my lips and a smudge of kohl to darken my lashes. Gazing in the mirror, I saw my face clearly for the first time since La Serenissima. It seemed odd that I had not changed more to myself; thus the cant of my cheekbones, and lips shaped for pleading or kissing, thus the sweep of lashes, thus the familiar arch of brow and dark wide-set eyes with the crimson fleck vivid against the left iris. And yet there was a difference, some difference, a shadow of gravity that had not been there before.

What you have seen, you carry with you.

Well, I thought; I am D'Angeline, I will learn to carry it with grace. And shortly the Archon's servants came bowing to escort me to his side, and thence to the dinner party of the Lady Althaia.

Demetrios Asterius looked long and hard at me when I was ushered into his presence, breaking off at last with a shake of his head. "The Kritian style suits you, my dear Phèdre," he said mildly. "Would you had come here under more auspicious circumstances. Come, then, and let us enjoy ourselves while we may."

We were the last to arrive at Althaia's elegant quarters, where a dozen guests, lords and ladies both, reclined on couches in the spacious salon. They rose and bowed or curtsied when the Archon entered, and then Demetrios moved among them exchanging informal greetings, punctuated with kisses and exclamations. I was introduced to each and soon heard my name fluttering about the room, pronounced by some in D'Angeline fashion, some in Hellene. They were familiar with each other, dropping honorifics to use given names. Althaia greeted me as an old friend, kissing me on both cheeks, and then clapped her hands to order the wine poured.

It was at once pleasant and strange to be thus entertained. The conversation was witty and lively; so lively I was hard-put to follow it at times, for my Hellene was slower than theirs, and the Kritian accent a trifle strange to my ear. They spoke of light matters; love affairs, theatre, fashion. So it is at such gatherings, and more solemn conversation saved for later. Even so, it was not in my heart to banter thusly, though I concealed it well enough.

"Is it true, Phaedra," one lady asked me breathlessly, "that in Terre d'Ange, everyone has four lovers, men and women alike?"

"No, my lady." I smiled at her wide-eyed interest. "Of a surety, there are those who do; as many and more. But there are others whose pleasure is to cleave solely to one mate, and no other."

"As a *hetaera*, you must surely fall into the former category, my dear," Althaia said sweetly, reclining on the couch she shared with her brother; Timanthes bit his lip, hiding a smile. "How many lovers do you claim?"

"None." I met her disbelieving gaze and shook my head. " 'Tis not the same thing, to take a patron as a lover. For a Servant of Naamah to bestow a lover's token and privileges upon a patron is a great honor, and I have never done it."

"Never?" Demetrios raised his eyebrows. "No husband, no consort, no lover . . . that is very nearly a crime, I think!" Two lords and one lady near him added laughing agreement.

I inclined my head to him. "Ah, but my lord Archon, you never asked if I had a consort."

"I asked – "

"You asked if the *pirate* was her consort, Demetrios," Timanthes called, flushed with wine and high spirits. "Not if she had one."

"I . . . ah. Yes." He reflected. "I did. It seemed likely enough, the way he stands at your side and glares at me. So." He sighed. "Not the pirate, then."

"No, my lord." I pictured Joscelin's face, outraged at the comparison, and smiled to myself. "Not the pirate."

"Well, it would be too much, I suppose, to imagine one such as you lacked for companionship." Demetrios Asterius gave another sigh. "Althaia, you promised us entertainment, did you not?"

"Of course, Demetrios," she said smoothly, clapping her hands once more to summon dancers.

There were six of them, young men and women, and very skilled, executing a complex series of dances in the center of the ring of couches, with tiny bells at their wrists and ankles that marked out an intricate rhythm. I watched them with my mind elsewhere, thinking of Joscelin. I had no right to make any claim on him, no right to name him my consort. Once, he had held that role, but he had abjured it. I remembered his long vigil in the rain-soaked garden, the day I told him I was returning to Naamah's Service. It was true, what I had seen in the *thetalos*; I had wronged and injured him deeply.

And if I had not, he would have stood at my side in the Little Court when Melisande Shahrizai drew back her veil, and Prince Benedicte ordered the death of my companions. The tally of the living is never given to us to know.

After the dancing, the wine went around again, and then dinner was served, course upon course of Kritian delicacies. There was a good deal of seafood, which is excellent there, especially the tender squid served in a sauce of its own inky effluence, although it is unnerving to behold. After the main dishes came a mixed platter of sweet melons and sharp cheeses, which some couch-mates served to each other with their own fingers, and then a delicate ice flavored with almond milk for dessert. I could not imagine how they came by ice in that clime, but the Archon assured me that there is snow on the highest peaks of Kriti in winter, and they freeze great blocks of ice which they hoard throughout the summer in deep, cool cisterns.

When the dinner things were cleared, the slaves came around with the wine once more, and I thanked the young man who poured for me without thinking.

"It is my pleasure, *lypiphera*," he murmured, not raising his eyes.

It was the same form of address the masseuse Chloris had used, and one that was strange to me; I sensed Demetrios Asterius' head come up sharply, and felt his measured gaze. "They call you that, do they?" he asked me.

"I don't know, my lord," I said honestly; the wine-pourer had moved onward. "I heard it once before, only today. What does it mean?"

He was silent for a moment, then answered thoughtfully. "Painbearer."

"Oh." Since I did not know what else to say, I gazed into my wine-cup. It was very finely made, of a porcelain so thin it was nearly translucent, painted on the inside with a scene of Kritian ships at sail. Demetrios Asterius reached out to touch a loose tendril of my hair, running it between finger and thumb.

"Like silk to the touch," he said ruefully. "My lady Phèdre, like as not I will wed Althaia, who brings with her a vast dowry of lands stretching the coast of my demesnes, of whom I am fond, and whose brother I love well. If I wish to be named Minos' successor, and I do, it is the wise course. But I wish, I very much wish, that you had come here under more auspicious circumstances. And I very much wish that my dear cousin Pasiphae had seen fit to offer her guidance. There are deep things involved here, and my skills lie in dealing with the surface of matters."

I think I knew, then, what his answer would be.

"My lord Archon," I said softly. "If the Kore could have answered me, she would have. I did not come seeking what I have found on Kriti, whether it was destined or no. I ask only for your aid, for ships and men. It is a question for a ruler, and you must answer it thusly."

"So I must." He sighed, then summoned a grin. "On the morrow. For tonight, you are still my guest, and there is entertainment to be had!"

The center of the ring of couches being cleared and the wine-cups refilled, Althaia's slaves brought out the standing silver crater for a game of *kottabos*, balancing the *plastinx* carefully atop the spire. My throat tightened a little; I had not played at *kottabos* since my lord Delaunay had died. Although it is a Hellene game, it is popular among D'Angelines; I had played it for the first time the night Alcuin made his debut, when Delaunay won Cecilie's game and claimed an auction as his forfeit.

Six thousand ducats, Alcuin's virgin-price had brought. No one could remember such a price paid for a Servant of Naamah, not even I, raised in the Night Court. I envied him that, then, I remembered; my own, when my time came, was lower. I wouldn't have done, had I known how he truly felt about it.

Delaunay told me my asking-price would only rise with time. He was right about that too, and I would willingly trade it all, to have them both alive once more.

Such things are not given to us to choose, and so it was that I smiled and laughed and played at *kottabos*, surprising the Kritians by winning a round with a skillful toss of the lees in my wine-cup, for Delaunay taught us both to play with skill after Alcuin's auction. For my forfeit, I claimed the right to share a couch with our hostess' handsome brother, which was amusing to all and pleased Althaia, who then shared Demetrios' couch, and Demetrios watched me with his shrewd, wry gaze while Timanthes made pleasant conversation, neither of them deceived by my motives.

And thus did the evening pass, until it was time to leave.

"You have a courtier's skills, my lady," Demetrios Asterius said to me, cupping his hands about my face as we lingered outside Althaia's quarters, his servants and Timanthes waiting patiently. I stood quiet under his touch. "It is as well, I suppose." He raised his dark eyes to Timanthes'. "Will you see her back to her apartment?"

"Of course."

"Good." Demetrios sighed. "Then, Phèdre, I bid you farewell tonight as a man, since tomorrow I must be a ruler," he said, and lowering his head, kissed me. His lips were warm and soft and he kissed with the skill of long

practice. A shiver of pleasure ran through me, and
Demetrios dropped his hands, almost pushing me away.
"Go on, little pain-bearer," he said in a rough-edged voice.
"You've given me an ache I'll remember, surely enough."

"I'm sorry, my lord." My own voice came a little fast.

"Don't be. I'll remember it with pleasure." Gathering
himself, the Archon grinned. "Timanthes, escort our guest
to her quarters, but do not think on dalliance. There are
things our friendship cannot endure, and this may be one of
them."

"If it can survive my sister, it can survive anything,"
Timanthes replied, unperturbed.

Sixty-four

In the morning, Demetrios Asterius received us once more, and true to his word, he was every inch the Archon, no trace anywhere in his demeanor of yesterday's wrestler or drinking companion.

I was reunited with Kazan in the antechamber, and found myself passing glad to see him. We had been through a great deal together, he and I, enough so that he represented the comfort of the familiar. He had spent some of the ransom money on clothing and a visit to the barber, and looked rather more presentable, if no less fiercesome; his black hair gleamed in its long topknot, and his mustaches were waxed to points, the narrow strip of beard shaved with precision. "It is not for this petty king, eh," he said scornfully when I remarked on his garb. "But I will sail this day, for your people or mine, I, and for that I will not set forth in rags."

We did not have long to wait before we were summoned, and the atmosphere in the throne room was somber.

"Comtesse Phèdre nó Delaunay de Montrève of Terre

d'Ange." Demetrios acknowledged me in steady tones. "You have laid a heavy request upon us. Two boons, you have asked; one, I will grant." He touched his fingertips together. "I pray you understand, if it were a matter of sympathy only, I would willingly grant both. But to escort you to La Serenissima . . ." He shook his head. "This I will not do. Whether the Serenissimans are right or wrong in seeking your death, to defy them thusly at their own gates is an open act of hostility. And if you fail in any part, Phèdre nó Delaunay, I will have earned Kriti — and indeed, all of Hellas — a powerful enemy. Nay, not one, but two, for if I understand matters aright, if you fail, the D'Angeline throne falls to this Benedicte de la Courcel, who stands in alliance with the Stregazza. Is it not so?"

"Yes, my lord Archon," I murmured. "It is so."

"I am sorry." His dark eyes were compassionate. "You asked a courier be sent to Marsilikos, and it shall be so. Anywhere else on the face of the earth you wish to go, I will send you. But I cannot risk exposing Kriti to the united wrath of La Serenissima and Terre d'Ange, no matter what rewards the risk may pay if you succeed. To rule wisely, one must weigh all options. There is no gain here that is worth the price of failure. Can you understand this?"

"Yes." I swallowed, and bowed my head. 'Twas no more than I had expected, but disheartening nonetheless. "I understand, my lord Archon."

"If you weigh your own options, Phèdre," he said gently, "you may find it is much the same. If what you tell me is true, your chance of succeeding in La Serenissima is slim. Capture or death are likely, if not certain. You have done all that you might and more, though the hand of fate has been raised against you at every turn. Listen well, then, and heed my advice. A courier is no certain thing, my dear, and a message in a stranger's hand too easily ignored. Do not send word to Marsilikos, but go, bear word yourself, and rouse those allies you trust, secure the throne against betrayal abroad. Your Queen's life may be forfeit for it, yes, but you have the surety of the realm to gain — and your own life as well. What do you say?"

He waited, watching, and I gave no answer. At my side, Kazan stirred restlessly. "He speaks wisely, he," he muttered. "I would say the same, did you ask."

It was tempting — Elua, it was tempting! To sail not back into danger and near-certain death, but to Marsilikos and safety; home, to go home. To the calm wisdom of Roxanne de Mereliot, who would take matters into her capable hands, to the reassuring might of Quintilius Rousse, yes, even to go to Barquiel L'Envers, that clever, cunning Duc I had been so sure I could not trust . . .

. . . and condemn to death Ysandre de la Courcel, who had once trusted me enough to risk the entire nation on my bare word; not only Ysandre, but mayhap all who travelled with her in the *progressus*, all who supported her in La Serenissima . . .

Joscelin.

I pressed the heels of my hands into my eyes, thinking. Demetrios Asterius was right, there was danger in trusting to a message in a stranger's hand, almost reason to go. Almost. I lowered my hands and opened my eyes. "My lord Archon, do you swear to me that your courier will do all that is humanly possible to deliver my message to the Lady of Marsilikos?"

He paused, then nodded soberly. "That much I do

swear, my lady. By Mother Dia and the House of Minos, I swear it."

"And you . . ." I turned to Kazan, ". . . you will get me to La Serenissima, no matter what happens in Epidauro?"

Kazan's eyes gleamed. "I have said it, I; may the *kríavbhog* swallow my soul if I lie! This is the debt I owe, and I will honor it, I." He gave a broad grin. "If you did the wise thing always, I would be dead, yes?"

I turned back to face the Archon. "I thank you, my lord, for your offer, which was generous," I said softly. "And for your advice, which was well-conceived. But I believe I can send a message that will not go unheeded."

"So be it." There was a starkness to his features, and I knew he did not look to see me alive again. "Deliver unto me your letter, and I will have the ship sail at once. May your gods protect you, Phèdre nó Delaunay. They've done a poor enough job of it thus far."

I made no reply but knelt briefly to him, and we took our leave, though not before I caught a sympathetic glance from Timanthes, standing at his post beside the Archon's throne. Kazan departed for the harbor, where I was to meet him in two hours' time.

This time I spent writing my missives, and the first was the lengthiest; that was for Roxanne de Mereliot, the Lady of Marsilikos. There was no need and no purpose in concealing my intent now, and I wrote frankly of the situation in La Serenissima, of Benedicte's betrayal, of Melisande's role, of the plans of Marco Stregazza. I wrote too of the compliance of Percy de Somerville, and his role in Melisande's escape from Troyes-le-Mont, as well as the means by which she had blackmailed him, the letter regarding the ancient matter of Lyonette de Trevalion's betrayal.

And I wrote such things as might verify my identity, bidding her if she were uncertain to ask of Quintilius Rousse who it was that counted grains of sand on the beach in Kusheth, likening their numbers to the Skaldi. That I was certain he would remember, for it had been the turning point that had persuaded him to pursue Ysandre's fool's errand to Alba, and it was known only to him and me.

All of this and more I wrote, suggesting allies and courses of action, debating the allegiance of Ghislain de Somerville, who may or may not have been complicit in his father's plans. I wrote too much, no doubt, for I had been alone with these thoughts for weeks on end, and putting them to paper was almost like sharing them. At last I gauged the position of the sun and saw how much time had passed, and set myself to writing the second missive.

This one was to Duc Barquiel L'Envers.

To him, I wrote only this, my hand shaking somewhat as I set pen to paper. "Your Grace, pay heed to the words of the Duchese Roxanne de Mereliot, the Lady of Marsilikos. All that I have told her is true. By the burning river, I adjure you to hold the City of Elua against all claimants, including Duc Percy de Somerville."

It was done. I sanded my writing, tilting the page to remove the excess and blowing on the ink. It was only one city in a realm of seven provinces, but it was the City of Elua, the only place in Terre d'Ange that Blessed Elua made his own, and no one, man or woman or child, may be rightfully crowned sovereign of the realm anywhere but there. If this worked — oh, Elua, if it worked! — I owed a greater debt than words could utter to Nicola L'Envers y Aragon, who had sought in good faith to convince me that her cousin Barquiel and I threatened to tear Ysandre in twain with our mistrust of one another, who gave me the sacred password of her House as proof of her earnestness. *It doesn't matter what you believe. Just remember it.*

And Delaunay's pupil to the end, I had recorded it in memory, along with her wry smile and farewell kiss. *Do me a favor, and don't put it to the test unless you're truly in need.*

I am in need now, Nicola, I thought, sealing this second letter with a wax taper, I am well and truly in need now, and whatever bargain you ask of me, I will make. Ah, my lord Kushiel, if your blood truly runs in the veins of House L'Envers alongside Naamah's and Elua's, let him heed this plea!

It was Timanthes who came for the letters. I gave them into his keeping.

"Demetrios is truly grieved that he could not grant your request in full," he said quietly to me. "I hope that you know this."

"I do." I met his calm gaze. "He's a good ruler, isn't he?"

"He . . ." Timanthes took a deep breath. "Yes. He is."

It could have been like this, I thought, with my lord Delaunay and Rolande de la Courcel, who loved him. Delaunay would have been like this man Timanthes, with pride of place at his side, a steadfast beacon no matter whence his lord's whims turned, knowing he would always return in the end. It would have been so, if Prince Rolande had wed his first intended, Edmée de Rocaille, who loved them both and smiled upon their friendship. The Lady Althaia understands as much, and asks no more, loving her brother and lord alike. Let Demetrios Asterius wed her, then, and have his Timanthes as well; let no bitter rival come between them as Isabel L'Envers had done, setting in motion an irrevocable chain of betrayal and hatred.

Those events made Anafiel Delaunay what and who he was when I knew him, brilliant and ruthless and wise, and kind, too; Elua knows, I had reason to know it. And yet, I never knew him happy, save those few precious weeks before the end, when Alcuin won through his stern walls to offer him a measure of love — and even that, I had begrudged, with a child's jealousy.

"Love him well, then, Timanthes," I said, tears stinging my eyes. "It is a rare enough thing to find, a good ruler and a dear friend. Love him well, and let him do the same in turn, for Blessed Elua asks no more of us."

"I will," he said gravely, looking only a little startled. "I do. Lady Phaedra, Demetrios bids me ask you, are there some words you would have the courier commit to heart? I do not think the Serenissimans will dare blockade and search a Kritian ship, but if they do, 'twere best your message was engraved in memory, lest it be necessary to destroy your letter."

It was well-thought of him; I paused a moment to gather myself. "Yes. Bid him memorize this: Benedicte is a traitor, he has taken Melisande to wife. They plan to kill the Queen. Percy de Somerville is in league with them. Tell Barquiel that by the burning river, I adjure him to hold the City against them all."

He repeated it several times, until I was sure he had it letter-perfect; he was a quick study. When he had done, he took my hands in his own. "The message will be delivered, Lady Phaedra. The Kindred of Minos do not swear lightly, and that ship will sail with the Kore's blessing on it; Mother Dia herself will see it brought safe to harbor. Word has come from the Temenos only this hour past." He smiled slightly at my expression. "There are things the Kore knows untold, and of those, we do not ask."

"Pray you give her my thanks," I whispered.

Timanthes nodded. "I shall." Still holding my hands, he hesitated, searching for words and gazing past me. "There are . . . other rumors, that have come from the Temenos," he said slowly. "Servants will talk, where priests and priestesses hold their tongues, although surely this too is a thing the Kore permits. But . . . this thing they name you, *lypiphera*; they speak it with awe and hope, they who serve."

A shiver ran the length of my spine, as though a great wing had brushed me unseen. "It is not always an ill thing, to know pain," I said, meeting his eyes as his gaze returned to my face. "To remember. I have been a slave, Timanthes. It is a pain I remember. And it is poorly done, to treat humans as chattel."

He looked at me for a long time without speaking, and then looked away. "Others have argued as much; but Kriti is ancient, and we are ancient in our ways. Still, ways change, and there are new things born under the sun. You are one such, you children of Elua. I will think on what you have said, and speak of it to Demetrios."

"Thank you." Pressing his hands, I gave him a kiss of farewell. "Tell the Archon I am grateful for his aid, and keep you well." I stepped back, smiling. "Next time, I will come at a more auspicious time, I promise."

At that he laughed, and shook his head, and we parted on a note of cheer. It was naught but bravado on my part, but so will warriors make jest on the battlefield, and having said a thing, be heartened by it. So it was that I half-believed my own words and found my spirits rising as I left the Palace of Phaistos, escorted by a squadron of the Archon's guards through the city to Kommos Harbor. Though I was headed once more into certain danger, the sun shone brightly overhead, the glances of the guards and the folk in the streets were filled with covert admiration, and I left behind me at last a thing well-done.

If the Kritian ship could not win through to Marsilikos, 'twas out of my hands, whether I was aboard it or no. And if it did — well, Roxanne de Mereliot would heed my words, that much I trusted. I had not told the Archon of my past, beyond those events in La Serenissima which pertained to the situation, but the Lady of Marsilikos surely knew I of all people would send no false warning. As for Barquiel L'Envers, he would honor the password of his House or not; he did not love me so well that it would help to plead the cause in person. In truth, if the letters arrived safely, I thought, I could do no more if I were there myself.

The harbor was crowded and busy, for trade was urgent in these last fair weeks of autumn. My escort surrounded me, forcing a path along the wharf until we came to Kazan's ship. Sharp-eyed Oltukh spotted me first and gave a cry of welcome, and all of them echoed greetings, jostling for a place at the rail to aid me aboard the ship; a warm welcome, from the superstitious pirates who had once shunned me as a fearful spirit. Glaukos, who had never been aught but kind, folded me in a great embrace.

Kazan watched it all with a look of irony. "You have become a luck-piece, eh?" he said to me. "It is a thing I never dreamed, to go home to Epidauro. If you are ready, we sail, we."

The wind was blowing fresh and steady, the sea

beyond the harbor dancing with white-crested ripples; a brisk sea, but not treacherous, the kind of challenge Illyrian sailors dearly love. I felt the wind tug at my hair and smiled.

"I am ready, my lord pirate. Let's sail."

SIXTY-FIVE

IT WAS, for once, an uneventful sea journey. Although the nights were cool, the winds and the weather held fair. The repairs made to the ship in the Temenos served admirably, and it was wholly seaworthy. Kazan had made good use of his time in Phaistos and our stores were replenished; moreover, he had bartered for charts of the Hellene waters, enabling him to plot a swift course homeward.

We crossed first a vast expanse of open sea, the steep mountains of Kriti dwindling quickly to a speck behind us. From thence it was a mere day's sail to reach sight of the Hellene mainland. Mindful of our terrifying, storm-born flight southward, Kazan was careful to keep always within sight of the coast, which lay off our starboard bow.

Although our progress was steady, it was a slow business, working our way up the coast. My euphoria at the sending of the Kritian courier had faded, and my thoughts turned once more to La Serenissima, rendering me fretful and overly conscious of the passing of time. I spent fruitless hours guessing at the course of Ysandre's *progressus*, and I daresay strained even Glaukos' patience quizzing him on the length of Caerdicci roadways. He knew them well enough, having been a merchant's clerk during his slave days, but he could guess no better than I how swiftly a *progressus regalis* would travel, nor how long the D'Angeline monarch would linger in any given city.

Of a surety, though, we were well into autumn, and Ysandre's entourage would turn for home before the season's end. I slept poorly at night and took to wandering the decks, wrapped in my woolen mantle, the Kore's gift. The sailors on watch seemed glad enough of my company, and taught me Illyrian songs and jests, showing me, too, such games as they played to pass the time. I learned to throw dice on Kazan's ship and became a passing fair hand at it, for it requires a certain deftness of wrist, not unlike some of Naamah's arts.

As for those, Kazan Atrabiades never laid a hand upon me; and in truth, I am not sure what I would have done if he had. It was due in part to shipboard discipline, for Kazan was one of those leaders who would do without whatsoever his men did — and too, there was little privacy on a ship of that size. Indeed, I was acutely reminded of this each time it was necessary to relieve myself, which, I may add, is no easy chore on a ship lacking a privy. I had cause then to be grateful for Illyrian modesty.

But in greater part, Kazan's forbearance was due to what he had undergone in the *thetalos*, for he spoke candidly of it to me on the first day aboard the ship.

"What we had between us, you and I; know that I do not look for that again, to have you in that way." He shook his head, tear-shaped pearl eardrops glimmering in the dim light of the cabin. I had learned since first we met that

Illyrian sailors believe they enhance vision; even Kazan was superstitious enough to believe it. "It is a thing I saw, in the *thetalos*, I. A guest, I named you, for although I lost my birthright, I had pride, I, in what I made of Dobrek, yes." He laughed. "To shun the title of lord, and to live as one, eh? And a pirate, too, as it pleased me. I made you a bargain, you, that was no bargain. I knew you could not say no. If I had not, maybe things would have been different, eh? If we had trusted to speak truth, we, the Serenissimans would not have tricked us. So." He shrugged. "Now, I do not ask, I."

"Thank you, my lord Kazan." I smiled. "It is a lordly gesture, truly."

"Maybe I will be that again, eh? Lord Atrabiades." Kazan glanced unerringly through the cabin walls toward the north, homeward, undisguised yearning on his face. "Whatever happens, it is all worthwhile, to set foot in Epidauro." Another thought crossed his mind and he looked back at me with narrowed eyes. "Did you go with him, you?"

"Who?" I was genuinely unsure whom he meant.

"That . . ." He made to spit, then thought better of it. "That Demetrios, that Archon, with his oils and curls and his fancy-boy."

I raised my brows. "It is no concern of yours, my lord, if I did."

"Well." Kazan grinned, unabashed. "I said I would not ask, eh; I did not say I would not think about it, I!"

At that, I rolled my eyes and gave him no answer; he left the cabin laughing, well-pleased with himself. It is a thing I have noted, that men will compete with one another even when there is no prize to be gained. Mayhap women are no better, on the whole, but we are more subtle about it, and quicker to reckon the stakes.

And quicker to play men for fools.

I could not but think of Melisande, then, and in some part of me, shake my head in admiration. She had played us all for fools, men and women alike. The outrageous brilliance of her ploy fair dazzled the mind. To hide in plain sight, in the very place she dared us seek her — Elua, what nerve! Even I, who knew what she was capable of, had never dreamed such a thing.

Tell me, do you believe I would make so poor a sovereign?

It is a dangerous thing, to admire one's enemy.

I forced down my hand, that had risen to clutch at my bare throat where her diamond used to lie, and thought instead of the terrible, blood-shot darkness within the cavern of the Temenos. There I had faced the trail of death that lay behind me, those who lived no more due to the folly of my choice. But the Kore had spoken true; it was the darkest truth the *thetalos* revealed, and not the whole of it. Betimes I had chosen poorly, yes; but it was Melisande who led me to the crossroads of the worst of those choices, and the blood-guilt of it rested as squarely on her shoulders as on mine.

No wonder the Unforgiven named themselves as they did. It was proud, doomed Isidore d'Aiglemort who led them to that crossroads, yes, but who led him? Melisande.

Ah, my lady, I thought, gazing beyond the cabin walls. You have made your choices, and it is I who count the cost and bear the pain of them. But it is in good part yours, this shadow I carry, and Blessed Elua willing, I will bring it home to you, from whence it came. And then we will see how you like it.

So I looked northward too, with as much yearning and a good deal more fear than Kazan Atrabiades, and league by league, we crawled up the coast of Hellas and into Illyrian waters, the sailors shouting and cheering when we passed the lamphouse off the isle of Kérkira, that marks the beginning of Illyria proper for all seafaring sojourners. And Elua help me, I cheered with them, as if I were Illyrian myself. We had become comrades-in-arms, Kazan and his men and I, and we had faced common enemies together; the Serenissimans, the *kríavbhog*, the storm, and even the terror of the *thetalos*.

On the third day after we entered Illyrian waters, we reached Epidauro.

I had seen it twice before; 'twas very nearly a familiar sight by now, the generous harbor encompassed by solid granite walls, fortified ward-towers looming at either side of the entrance. I do not know who first sighted the city, for this time, no one gave cry, and in time, we all saw it. In the harbor, one could make out a dozen or more ships; members of the Ban's armada with the red sails, fishing vessels and traders. No Serenissiman war-galleys. The day was fine and bright, a lively nip in the wind that drove warm-blooded types like Glaukos and myself to don our woolen outerwear. It ruffled the sea into wavelets, sunlight glinting from a thousand peaks.

And it chuffed loudly in the flapping canvas when Tormos, unbidden, gave the order as second-in-command to loose the sail. He remembered — we all remembered — far too well what had happened the last time we sought to enter Epidauro.

Sailors held their posts, ropes slack, rudder-bar loosely tended, and our vessel drifted harmlessly sideways while we all gazed at Kazan Atrabiades; he looked back at us, seeing the fear writ in our faces.

"Why do you idle?" he asked in Illyrian. "Have I not set a fair course? We sail to Epidauro."

With that, he turned his back on us, crossing the length of the deck to stand in the prow, setting his face toward home.

Tormos gritted his teeth and gave the order. "As he says. To Epidauro!"

Our sails snapped taut in the wind; the ship swung around, nosing back to true. Young Volos threw back his head with a defiant shout as we began to skim over the waves, and a gull circling overhead gave it back, raucous and wild. I made my way to Kazan's side. He stood with legs braced and arms folded, and if his face was calm and purposeful, still I saw how shudders crawled over his skin.

"If it comes for me," he said out of the side of his mouth, "don't stop. Push me over the side and keep going, if the *kríavbhog* comes."

The fortressed harbor walls were rushing nearer, looming in my sight. I could make out men aboard the ships, pointing and shouting, the black bird of prey on the red sails of the Ban's vessels and sunlight glinting from the steel helms of those who manned them.

"It won't," I said, willing it to be true.

Kazan's lips moved soundlessly for a moment, his gaze fixed unwaveringly on the shore. "I pray you are right." He drew in a breath as if in pain. "Ah!"

We had entered the waters of the harbor.

The ship erupted in a mad ecstasy, the sailors roaring cheers, laughing and stomping their feet on the wooden deck, shouting out to the Ban's fleet that swiftly surrounded us. "Kazan Atrabiades! It is Kazan Atrabiades of Epidauro! Kazan! Ka-zan! Ka-zan!"

An answering shout arose and spread like wildfire, passed from mouth to mouth and ringing across the harbor, while the Ban's guardsmen beat their shields. "Hëia, Ka-zan! Hëia, hëia, Kazan! Hëia, Ka-zan!"

In the prow, Kazan Atrabiades grinned fit to split his face and raised his arms in acknowledgment.

I watched it all, wide-eyed and gaping. I had forgotten, in ancient, civilized Kriti; forgotten that Illyria was a vassal nation of an oppressive ruler, forgotten that the dubious fame that had brought Kazan's name even to the ears of the Archon of Phaistos – whence mine own, I may add, evoked only the shade of an ancient tale – rendered him renowned in his homeland.

The Illyrians welcomed him as a hero.

An escort of the Ban's armada saw us into the harbor proper, while cheers rang even from the tops of the fortress towers. Our sailors clung precariously to the rigging, hanging out over the sides of the ship to shout to other sailors, trading news and asking after their erstwhile companions; it was Tormos who kept sufficient order to see us into port, scowling and bawling commands. Kazan merely grinned and waved, beatifically, resplendently alive and home. And I . . . I was well-nigh forgotten in the uproar.

"Do not take it ill," Glaukos said, laying a comforting arm about my shoulders. "Ah, now, he'll not forget you, not him. He knows his debt, see if he doesn't. Only let him have this moment, my lady, and you'll see I've the right of it."

I shivered, unaccountably alone and fearful with my thoughts. "I hope so. A moment is all I have."

By the time we reached the wharf, a small crowd had gathered; such lads as haunt every port hoping to catch the eye of their heroes had been sent hither and thither, carrying the news of Kazan Atrabiades' return throughout the city of Epidauro. I was glad enough when we disembarked to have Glaukos' sturdy presence at my side, protecting me from the jostling throng of humanity. As a Tiberian-born Hellene, he was at least as much an outsider as I.

Nearly all those gathered were men, and the news they passed swirled above my head in a cacophony of Illyrian, nigh overwhelming my comprehension; I grasped at phrases here and there, and gathered that the other three ships had come safe to land when we fled the Serenissiman galleys, that the Serenissimans had hovered outside the harbor-waters, seeing the darkness that coalesced above Kazan's ship, and turned aside when the storm's mighty hand hurled us southward. From shore and ship, the Epidaurans had watched it all and reckoned us lost. The Ban had given asylum to all of Kazan's men, claiming no proof of transgression; all who had survived — and Pekhlo, thrown from our ship, was one — were here in Epidauro.

And of a surety, they came to greet us, summoned from cheap lodgings to spill onto the wharf, ebullient and joyous. Not until a squadron of the Ban's Guard arrived was a semblance of order restored, their scarlet-crested helms parting the crowd, clearing a space. Kazan yelled to his men, then, gathering them behind him as the squadron leader approached.

"Well, well," the leader said softly. "So Kazan Atrabiades has returned, eh?" Unexpectedly, he feinted a punch at Kazan's face; Kazan dodged it easily, grinning, and dragged him into an embrace.

"Czibor, you son of a eunuch!" he exclaimed, thumping the other's back. "I taught you to draw a sword! What is the Zim Sokali thinking, to grant a command to one such as you?"

"That you were long gone from Epidauro, like as not," Czibor laughed, returning his embrace. "By Yarovit, it's good to see you! How does this come about?"

"I have been to Kriti, and the House of Minos," Kazan said soberly.

"Ah." Czibor stepped back and eyed him. "It is true, then, what they say? There is power there to cleanse a man of a blood-curse?"

Kazan spread his arms. "You see me here before you, Czibor. It is a dire thing, but a true one."

The squadron leader nodded. "Then it is well done. The Zim Sokali will wish to hear of it. You pose him a problem, Kazan, indeed you do. Your name and your deeds are known to the Serenissimans, and they will hear of your return if this clamor is any indication." His gaze raked the gathered throng and he took in the sight of me, standing at Glaukos' side; his eyes widened. "Your men came bearing tales of a D'Angeline woman worth thirty thousand gold solidi, Kazan," he said slowly. "And there have been Serenissiman traders asking questions in the city, and an ambassador sent to the Zim Sokali, who denied all knowledge. I did not credit such stories, myself, but if such a thing may be, I think I am seeing it now."

"You are," said Kazan. "And I am thinking the Ban will wish to see her too."

"I think you are right," Czibor said wryly.

So we began to make our way to the fortress of the Ban of Illyria, whom I learned was addressed by his people as the Zim Sokali, the Falcon's Son. It is a strong city, Epidauro, wrought of stone and surrounded by thick walls. Escorted by Czibor and his men, we had not progressed far along the narrow, paved streets before a frantic clatter of hooves arose and a carriage plunged into the midst of the crowd of men and youths that travelled with us, scattering them. Even as the Ban's guardsmen began to react, the carriage door was flung open and an older woman stumbled out, her face drawn and tear-stained.

"Kazan," she wept, opening her arms to him. "Kazan!"

He took a step toward her, wonder dawning in his eyes. "Mother?"

A lump rose to my throat as I watched their reunion. Of the gifts of the *thetalos*, this, mayhap, was the most precious: Forgiveness, given and taken freely on both sides. I knew well the pain Kazan had born, the bitter guilt at his brother's death by his own unwitting hand; I had lain beside it, seen it staring wakeful and dry-eyed in the small hours of the night. Of his mother's pain, I could only begin to guess. Some little I learned in those moments, that she was a widow bereft of her beloved younger son, waking from the first madness of grief to realize her elder son was lost to her too, condemned by her own wrathful curse. When the tale of the Serenissiman war-galleys and Kazan's battle with the *kríavbhog* came to her ears, she thought him dead and wept anew, grieving thrice for the two sons born to her.

Well, I thought, if I have done naught else, this at least is done and done well.

"Lady Njësa," Czibor said gently to Kazan's mother, removing his helmet and tucking it under his arm as a gesture of respect. "I beg of you, forgive me, but my orders are to conduct your son directly unto the Ban's presence."

"Yes, of course." She smiled through her tears, grasping his arms one last time as if to assure herself of his solidity. "So tall, my son! I had forgotten how tall. Marjopí has cared well for you. Does she live, yet? Is she well? I would tell her, if I could, that I repent my harsh words."

"You will tell her yourself, Mother, for she is well and hale in Dobrek, and I will send for her myself." Disengaging himself, Kazan bent to kiss her cheek. "Only I must see the Ban first," he added softly, "and there are debts I must honor before I set matters aright in our household."

Czibor set his helm back on his head. "Come. The Zim Sokali is waiting."

Sixty-six

SOKAL FORTRESS sits at the heart of the city of Epidauro, steepwalled and massive, a structure built to be defended in a city walled for defense. Once, I daresay, it may have been a gracious haven for the Illyrian folk, with gates standing open and pennants fluttering from every peak. Now it had an air of grim defiance, proud and resolute, its walls stripped of adornment and gates bolted tight, cautiously opened at Czibor's password.

One could see, from atop the lower terrace of the fortress, why Epidauro alone had not fallen to La Serenissima. An enormous gate flanked by towers defended the narrow causeway from the mainland, and all the rest was bordered by water. Even the mighty Serenissiman navy would be hard-pressed to find a weakness assaulting Epidauro from the sea, met all around with those faceless grey walls manned by the Ban's Guard with archers, trebuchets and ballistae.

"Ah," Kazan sighed, gazing over the city. "Home!"

I did not say what was in my mind; that the charming village of Dobrek was more pleasant by far. I saw with a stranger's eyes. To Illyrians bred and born, walled Epidauro housed the soul of the land, the clenched fist raised in defiance at the oppressor. This I saw most of all reflected in Kazan's hungry gaze, but I saw it too in the faces of the others, his island-born companions who had never seen a city before Phaistos.

Well and so, I would not expect them to ache with longing for the gilded fields of Terre d'Ange, ancient olive groves and vineyards, and the lavender in bloom filling the air with fragrance. Even thinking on it made my heart contract painfully in my breast. If naught else, I knew what it was to be an exile. We shared that much.

Once inside the fortress, Kazan's men were taken into the good-natured custody of the Ban's Guard, to be fed and housed.

Only Kazan and I were conducted into the Ban's presence, and I felt nervous and ill at ease, conscious of my unwashed state and my salt-stained attire. For his part, Kazan was in confident high spirits, secure in his welcome.

The Ban received us not in state, but in his study, a generous room strewn about with official papers and petitions. A small fire burned in the hearth, dispelling the autumn chill, and two elderly hounds dozed in front of it on a threadbare rug. Czibor stood at attention until the Ban looked at him.

"Zim Sokali," he announced. "I bring you Kazan Atrabiades, once of Epidauro, and . . ." His voice trailed off helplessly; he had not bothered to learn my name.

"Phèdre nó Delaunay de Montrève of Terre d'Ange," the Ban said in a deep voice, his considering gaze resting upon me. He sat without moving in his chair by the fire. "Her name is known to me."

He spoke Caerdicci. I knelt to him, bowing my head. "My lord, I speak Illyrian, if it please you," I said humbly. "I am sorry if I have inconvenienced you."

"Yes." He spoke thoughtfully, the Ban; he was a thick-set man of some fifty years, black hair and beard still untouched by grey. His features were fleshy, and yet there was a suggestion of leanness about him, as if he were pared to the bone by a hunger that had naught to do with sustenance of the body. "Whether or not you have is yet to be known." He looked at Kazan then and gave a slow smile. "So. Pirate."

Kazan bowed and flashed an answering grin. "Zim Sokali. I return to your service."

"So you do, pirate. So you do." At that the Ban laughed, and bade us both to sit. Presently servants came bearing pots of strong tea, which they served in small silver cups, and a platter of sweets, a confection made of almond paste. When they had left, his lady wife came to give us greeting and see if there was aught else he desired. She was ten years or more younger than he, with fair hair, pale eyes and the broad, slanting cheekbones that marked her as being of Chowati blood, those invaders who had long since been assimilated into Illyria. By that alone I guessed him to be a shrewd ruler, who knew well how to unify his people.

Vasilii Kolcei, the Ban was named; his wife was called Zabèla. She kept her eyes downcast until he dismissed her with thanks, exhibiting a modesty proper to Illyrian women. And by this I guessed her a shrewd ruler's wife, for there was naught of the demure in the strong lines of her face.

Over cups of strong tea, Kazan Atrabiades laid out

the history of our acquaintance for his lord, offering an explanation of who I was and the trade he sought to make for me, of how his men came to be pursued by Serenissiman war-galleys into Epidauro's harbor, and what had befallen us when we turned aside to flee the *kríavbhog's* wrath.

"So," the Ban said heavily, looking at me. "And now Kazan Atrabiades is freed of the blood-curse, but not the blood-price the Serenissimans have laid on his head. And you, young D'Angeline, spurned by Kriti, come begging Epidauro's aid."

"For Kriti and Hellas, the gain was not worth the risk, Zim Sokali," I said, keeping my voice steady. "Can Illyria say the same?"

He stirred, causing the hounds to lift their heads and settle back with sighs. "I was a boy when the Serenissimans began taking our coast, piece by piece, and my father wrote to the King of Terre d'Ange to seek his aid in alliance. Shall I tell you how he replied?"

"No." I shook my head. "I have heard, my lord, and I am sorry for it, grievous sorry. But that was then, and this now. Will you spite the present to avenge the past?"

"It is dangerous." Vasilii Kolcei sipped his tea and stared into the fire. "The Archon of Phaistos spoke truly. Epidauro has stood against Serenissima; it cannot stand against Serenissima and Terre d'Ange both, if you fail. And where we are strong, the coast of Illyria lies weak and vulnerable, garrisoned by Serenissiman soldiers. What price will they pay for your failure, if we are named a treasonous vassal?"

"We can fight," Kazan said fiercely. "Zim Sokali, the islands are stronger than you know, stronger than the

Serenissimans reckon. What have I done for eight years, if not that?"

"You have done that, yes, and preyed upon the Serenissimans like a hawk upon a rabbit warren," the Ban said grimly, "until half of Illyria and all of Epidauro, and every merchant and galley-captain on the seas knows your name, Kazan Atrabiades. And now you come seeking . . . what? Asylum? A return to my service? It is no easy boon you ask. Epidauro crawls with Serenissiman spies; I cannot shut out the traders without violating the terms of our independence. If you had come in stealth, it would be an easier thing. I can only be grateful that the furor you aroused covered word of the lady Phèdre's arrival, for it seemed to me that the Doge's emissaries had more interest in her than in you, Atrabiades."

"Not the Doge," I said. "His son, Marco Stregazza."

Vasilii Kolcei shrugged. "It is the same. They have held elections, in Serenissima; the Consiglio Maggiore has voted. Marco Stregazza is elected Doge. He will be invested, in a week's time, and his father will step down." He gave a thin smile. "It is the will of Asherat, so they say. And your Queen will arrive in Serenissima to observe the ceremony and exchange vows of goodwill with the new Doge."

The world reeled around me, and I grasped the arms of my chair with desperate fervor, willing myself to keep focus. Marco elected Doge! And Ysandre but a week away, riding all unwitting toward certain death. All my wondering, all my uncertainty; it came to this.

I had a week's time, and no more.

Kazan, seated opposite me, had blanched, although not on my behalf; he had come home to a hero's welcome, not reckoning the cost to Epidauro. "The Serenissimans . . ." His voice was hoarse. "Czibor tried to tell me. They will hear of my return, and they will ask you for my head, Zim Sokali."

"Yes," the Ban said gravely. "They will."

Kazan stood and paced the room, gazing at the treaties and petitions scattered about every surface. The Ban watched him unmoving, and the hounds lifted their heads from their paws, following him with their eyes. "The Hierophant of the Temenos, he told me that the law of the *thetalos* is absolute, eh," Kazan said presently, smiling wryly. "What Mother Dia has forgiven, a man is held blameless of. But I think the Serenissimans will not honor the law of the *thetalos*, with Kriti lying so far from their shores. Not if you are right," he added, shooting a glance at me, "and they profane their own temples."

"They have subverted the will of Asherat-of-the-Sea," I said softly. "That much I know is true. I have sworn to cleanse her temple."

"So." Kazan shrugged, flicking a parchment with one forefinger. "Thus for the will of the gods, measured against the politics of man. Zim Sokali, I have tried to rule well over what was given into my hands, but I am a warrior first, and I cannot reckon power gained and lost on paper, nor the cost of men's lives. How soon will Serenissima come seeking me, do you think?"

One of the hounds clambered to its feet and pushed its nose in the Ban's hand; he scratched its head automatically, his thoughts elsewhere. "Not so soon as they might, with the ceremony of investiture nigh. If the D'Angeline lass speaks true . . ." he nodded at me, ". . . Marco Stregazza will not over-extend his reach until he has secured his throne. Two weeks, perhaps more."

"Then it is a simple matter, Zim Sokali." Kazan spread his hands. "I will sail to Serenissima with those of my men who are willing, and with Phèdre nó Delaunay. I am a pirate, yes? Whatever happens, you have leave to tell the Doge I defied your orders." He grinned at me, eyes gleaming. "Tell them she is a *Vila*, and bewitched me. Maybe they will believe it."

"Kazan . . ." I had seen his mother weep for joy at his return. My heart ached, at odds with the urgency of my need. "I don't know."

The Ban was shaking his head. "No," he said somberly. "Not so simple, pirate." He glanced up as his wife, Lady Zabèla, returned to the room, nodding briefly to her and continuing as she took her place standing beside his chair. "On your own, you will not gain the harbor. The Serenissimans will search your ship, as they will search every ship, and if they do not know you by sight – and maybe they do – they will surely know the woman." He favored me with a humorless smile. "A young D'Angeline woman of surpassing beauty, fair of skin with dark hair and eyes, and a spot of scarlet on the left, like unto a thorn-prick. I fear you are not easily disguised."

"Surely there is a way!" Kazan said in frustration.

"Kazan, no." My voice was shaking, but I continued. "It is not worth your life, nor the life of your men, when so many have died already. If you would aid me, give me enough of the ransom you won to let me book passage with a merchanter, and take my chances with the harbor guard. I cannot render your mother childless again so soon."

"And will the Serenissimans be more gentle when they come for me?" he asked sharply, as quick to quarrel as if on his own estate in Dobrek. "Will it be boldly done of me to place the whole of Epidauro in jeopardy?"

"The Zim Sokali can invoke the law of the *thetalos*." I glared at him, forgetting myself equally. "If Marco Stregazza wishes to quarrel with it, let him take it up with Kriti; all of Hellas will take it ill if the Kore's rule is subverted!"

"I owe you a debt — "

"Twice you have saved my life; once at sea, and once from the Serenissimans. We are at quits, Kazan, and I do not know that I can carry another death on my conscience!"

"It is not for you to say what debts I owe! I have seen, in the *thetalos* — "

"Hide her." It was a woman's quiet voice that interrupted our argument, addressing the Ban. "In the tribute ship."

Kazan and I left off our quarrel to stare foolishly at the Lady Zabèla, for it was she who had spoken. The Ban tilted his head back to look consideringly at her, fingers working in the ruff of the hound's neck; it leaned against his legs and laid its chin on his knee. "Hide her how?"

She smiled down at him. "When my many-times removed grandmother fled the steppes, she did as many Chowati, and sewed false bottoms into her saddle-packs to hide gold. It is a fitting tribute for Marco Stregazza, I think."

My heart quickened. "A tribute ship. You are sending a tribute ship to La Serenissima, my lord?"

"And young Atrabiades and his men may take their place among my tribute-bearers, with none the wiser," the Ban said to his wife, finishing her thought; a broad smile spread across his face. "It is well-thought, my dear, and a fitting gift indeed."

"Yes!" Kazan said eagerly. "And if anything goes ill, we can claim to have taken the ship by force, that there is no blame on you, Zim Sokali!"

"Kazan, no — "

Vasilii Kolcei held up one hand for silence, looking sternly at me. "It is not for you to choose, what Kazan Atrabiades does or does not do. As he is an Illyrian subject, he is under Serenissiman rule, and those laws he has broken, to the extent that neither I nor, of a surety, the children of Minos can protect him from prosecution. It is an honorable course he proposes. That you do not wish his blood on your head is commendable, D'Angeline; but you wish to save your Queen. You have put it to two rulers, and now I put it to you. Is the gain not worth the risk?"

I looked at Kazan and thought of his mother's face, old and grief-worn, streaked with tears of joy. And I thought of Terre d'Ange, my beloved gilded fields churned into bloody strife by civil war if Ysandre was slain and Benedicte de la Courcel took arms against Barquiel L'Envers to contest for the throne. I thought of a nation weakened by internal struggles, and the Skaldi massing on our borders, needing only some second Selig to see and seize the opportunity.

And Melisande Shahrizai's smile.

"Yes." I bowed my head. "Yes, my lord. It is."

In the arts of covertcy, it is death to second-guess

oneself. An action, once done, cannot be undone; a word, once spoken, cannot be taken back. For this reason, Delaunay taught Alcuin and me to think thoroughly at leisure and swiftly at need, and having once chosen, never to seek to return to the crossroads of that decision — for even if one chooses wrongly, the choice cannot be unmade. So it was with this. In truth, I needed Kazan's aid; without aid, I had no chance of succeeding. If the pain it cost was too great, well, the reckoning would come; but first, I would see it done.

Our arrival had been timely indeed, for the tribute ship was set to sail on the morrow, bearing gifts in honor of Marco Stregazza's investiture as Doge. Carpenters labored throughout the night to construct a false-bottomed trunk fit to hide me and hold the tribute; gold in plenty, as if La Serenissima had need of it, marten skins and civet, and amber from the Chowat. There were air holes drilled cunningly into the richly carved cypress wood at the base of the trunk so I could breathe.

Still, I did not relish the prospect.

The Ban and his wife gave me lodging that night, treating me kindly. Already they had begun a campaign of misinformation, at her suggestion, giving the lie to the widespread rumor of Kazan Atrabiades' return. Small traders lost at sea come home safe at last, ran the counter-rumor; and oh, yes, a young Hellene slave girl aboard the ship with them if any had heard of it, her freedom purchased dearly on distant Kriti, not a D'Angeline, no, but passing fair.

To be sure, too many people had seen it firsthand to believe the lie, but enough had not. Enough to give them grounds for denial if it came to it. *People believe what they are told*, Melisande had said. It was unnervingly true.

It was a long night and I slept poorly, although it seemed foolish when in truth I would do naught but climb aboard another infernal ship come daybreak. We would be four days at sea, and I had no intention of clambering into that trunk until I saw the cursed rocks of La Dolorosa. But it was the beginning of the end of this long game that had begun the day Melisande Shahrizai folded my *sangoire* cloak and wrapped it in a parcel. If I lost this round, there would be no other, no second cast, no last ploy. Whatever befell Terre d'Ange, Melisande would have won her game. Ysandre would be dead, and all who sought to aid her; including me, if Marco Stregazza had his way.

And if he did not . . . I would be *hers*.

I wasn't sure which was worse.

More than anything, I missed Joscelin that night. I do not think I ever fully reckoned, until then, how much he served to keep my demons at bay. For the worst of it was, despite everything, despite the manipulation and betrayal, imprisonment and abuse, near-drowning and living as a hostage, despite all the horrors of the *thetalos* and the terrible knowledge it had given me, ah, Elua, despite it all, I longed for him still. I could not help it, any more than I could erase the prick of Kushiel's Dart from my eye, and the more I struggled against it in the shuddering depths of my soul, the more I yearned in my heart for Joscelin's presence. As gloriously, splendidly, intractably single-minded as he was, loving him was like grasping a knife, a clean white blaze of pain that kept me anchored to myself.

Cassiel's dagger, with which Elua made reply to the

messengers of the One God; Cassiel's Servant, touchstone
of my dart-riven heart. Pondering such mysteries, I fell at
last into a fretful sleep and awoke at dawn to the beginning
of the endgame.

SIXTY-SEVEN

MORNING BROKE chill and misty; the tribute ship was fogwraithed in the harbor. I stood shivering on the wharf as the great trunk was loaded, and supplies for our journey. Zabèla had made me a gift of a heavy woolen cloak, dark-brown and hooded, and I set aside the Kore's blue mantle in its favor. It closed with a silver brooch, shaped like the falcon of Epidauro.

The self-same shape adorned the garb in which Kazan Atrabiades and six of his men were attired, rendered bold in black against their new crimson surcoats, which they wore over light mail. I knew all six by name; they were the young ones, the daring ones, who had come to sit at Glaukos' lessons and teach me Illyrian: Epafras, Volos, Oltukh, shy Ushak with the jug-ears, and the brothers Stajeo and Tormos, still competing. Tormos would go, for he had secured rank as Kazan's second-in-command, and his brother would not let him go alone.

Missing was Lukin, whose quick smile had reminded me of Hyacinthe; he was gone, slain by Serenissimans. I tried not to think on it. Others had come to see us off, gathering in the misty dawn. One was Glaukos, who took me into his embrace, eyes damp with tears.

"Ah, now, my lady," he whispered. "I'd go with you if I dared, but this is a young man's task. I'd only slow you down, I fear."

"I'd order Kazan to put you ashore if you even *thought* to try it, Glaukos." Remembering his many kindnesses, my own eyes teared, and I sniffled indecorously. "Go home to Dobrek, and your pretty wife, and if you think of me, say a prayer to whatever god will hear you."

He laid his hands on my shoulders. "You've shown me wonders, you have, such as even an old Tiberium slave might believe, and you've made Kazan Atrabiades a nobleman despite himself. I'll not forget you soon, child."

"Thank you." I hugged him swiftly, kissing his grizzled cheek. "Thank you for everything."

And then it was time to board the ship under the command of Pjètri Kolcei, the Ban's middle son, who would oversee the tribute mission. He was young, only a few years older than me, with the air of a seasoned warrior. After seeing us all aboard, he made a formal farewell to his parents, who sat mounted alongside the wharf amid a cordon of the Ban's Guard. Crossing the gangplank, he gave the order to cast off.

It was strange, after so long on Kazan's pirate ship, to be aboard a proper vessel with square sails, broad decks and bunks in the hold. I stood gripping the railing as the ship moved slowly away from the shore and gazed back at the harbor. The Ban and his wife sat on their horses unmoving, watching us go as the early morning sun slanted through the mist.

"Your mother did not come?" I said to Kazan, finding him beside me.

"No." He shook his head. Droplets of moisture clung to his hair like gems. "I said good-bye at our house, I. My old boyhood home, eh?" he said, answering me in Caerdicci out of habit. "She says to me, she; Kazan, come home soon, come home twice a hero."

"Blessed Elua grant it may be so," I murmured.

Once we had cleared the harbor, Pjètri Kolcei gave the order to hoist sail and we were away, moving steadily and surely across the surging blue sea. Some twenty sailors manned the ship, neat-handed and competent. The Ban's hand-picked embassy numbered twenty as well, under Pjètri's leadership; and seven of those were Kazan and his men. When we were underway, the Ban's middle son made his way across the deck to join us.

Pjètri had his father's dark complexion, but the broad, slanting cheekbones and grey-blue eyes of his mother; he wore his hair in a topknot, and had long, pointed mustaches like Kazan. I wondered if it was in emulation, or if 'twas a style set by the Ban's Guard. I never did learn which was true.

"Phèdre nó Delaunay," he said, greeting me with a sweeping bow. "Kazan Atrabiades. You come late to join this mission. I was awake into the small hours of the night, briefed by mother and father alike."

"I am grateful for your aid," I said formally. "On behalf of Terre d'Ange, I thank you."

He smiled, and there was somewhat of his father's tight shrewdness in it, and somewhat of a warrior's grin. "I have my orders. If aught goes awry, my men are to throw down their weapons," he said to Kazan, "and yours to make shift to hold them hostage, that we may claim you overcame us, by treachery and surprise. Such is the lot of a middle son, whose honor may be cast aside at need. But if all goes as planned . . ." His grin blossomed fully into a warrior's ferocity. "The Serenissimans will pay a heavy toll for the tribute they exact!"

"And the middle son rises in the eyes of the Zim Sokali!" Kazan agreed with bloodthirsty good cheer. "Yarovit's grace upon your sword, Pjètri Kolcei. Did you train under Gjergi Hamza?" he added, eyeing the afore-mentioned weapon.

I left them to compare notes on the merits of the Ban's swordmasters, perambulating the deck and taking simple pleasure in the sun's rising warmth, the bright rays burning off the mists as we gained the open seas. The Illyrian sailors startled to see me, hands moving in quick warding gestures; I had nearly forgotten how Kazan's men had received me at first. Now one of them trailed behind me, a self-appointed guard. It was Ushak, his prominent ears concealed beneath a conical steel helm. He turned scarlet whenever I glanced back at him, until I laughed aloud and paused to wait for him, giving him my arm which he took, blushing.

"It is a fair day," I mused in Illyrian. "Is it not, Ushak?"

"Y-yes." He was as red as a boiled lobster, and stam-mering with it. "Every day is f-fair, when it is graced with the sight of you!" he said all in a rush.

"Is it?" I halted, gazing at him. "Is that why you came, Ushak?"

His throat worked convulsively. "It is . . . it is one rea-son, my lady," he said stiffly. "I think . . . we do not have such things on Dobrek, such things as you. To die in your name . . . it, it w-would be an honor!"

"To live would be a better one," I said gently. "I am D'Angeline and Naamah's Servant, yes, but beauty is not worth dying for."

He shook his head, blushing and swallowing fiercely. "Not . . . not that alone, my lady. You, you were kind to us, you learned our tongue, you laughed at our jests . . . even, even mine." He swallowed again and added helplessly, "You were kind."

I thought on it, searching the empty blue skies. "Is the world so cruel, then, that that is all that is required to move a man to risk his life? Kindness?"

"Yes." Trembling and gulping, Ushak stood his ground, holding manfully to my arm. "Sometimes . . . y-yes, my lady," he finished firmly.

Ah, Elua! I bowed my head, overwhelmed by nameless emotion. I understood Kazan, and the debt he perceived; I understood the Ban and his kin, weighing merit against risk. Even those of Kazan's men who had been my ship-mates, I understood better; we had forged a bond, we had, during that dreadful flight, and the terrors of the Temenos. But this . . . this came straight from the heart.

Love as thou wilt.

They are fools, who reckon Elua a soft god, fit only for the worship of starry-eyed lovers. Let the warriors clamor after gods of blood and thunder; love is hard, harder than steel and thrice as cruel. It is as inexorable as the tides, and life and death alike follow in its wake.

I spent much time in contemplation during that journey, for there was naught else to be done and I wished to make my peace as best I might with Blessed Elua and his

Companions before entering La Serenissima. Our plan was a simple one, insofar as it went. When we drew nigh unto the harbor, I would conceal myself within the trunk. If the harbor guards' search penetrated my hiding place . . . well and so, it would go no further. If it did not, the tribute ship would continue up the Great Canal to make anchor at the residence of Janàri Rossatos, who was the Illyrian Ambassador to La Serenissima, and thence plot our next move.

It was my hope that the presentation of tribute-gifts to the newly elected Doge would take place before the ceremony of investiture, for it might afford an opportunity for Kazan and his men to get a message to Ysandre. We didn't know, though; not even Pjètri was certain of the protocol, and the exact date of the arrival of the D'Angeline *progressus regalis* was unknown.

I wished I knew what Melisande was planning.

For of a surety, no matter whose hand bore the dagger or the vial of poison, no matter whose mouth uttered the order, the mind that conceived it was hers . . . although there would be no trail easily traced to her doorstep. Of that, I was equally sure. And Marco and Marie-Celeste Stregazza were canny, too; neither of them would risk showing their hands openly when it came to the death of a sitting monarch.

An accident, then? It would have to be very, very well orchestrated – and a sure thing. A greased step, an over-turned gondola; plausible, but uncertain. No, Melisande's plan would have to be foolproof. Which meant . . . what?

It would be easy enough to do it in the Little Court. Poison, an assassin . . . Ysandre's guards will be relaxed, not looking for treachery in Prince Benedicte's court. It was possible; but no, it would reek overmuch of suspicion. Gaining the throne was one thing; Melisande's ability to *hold* it — for surely she looked to long outlive Benedicte and establish her son as heir — depended on the D'Angeline people's acceptance of her blamelessness. Ysandre de la Courcel would not die under that roof.

Then, where?

A public place, I thought. A public place, where the eyes of all La Serenissima can see that Prince Benedicte and his lovely wife, as well as the new Doge, played no hand in the death of the Queen of Terre d'Ange.

Melisande would conceive of something that brilliant, I was sure. The only problem was, I still couldn't guess *what*.

Thus far did I get in my speculation, and no further. There were too many unknown variables, not least of which was the fact that, for all I knew, Ysandre's entourage had arrived and the deed was already done. When my thoughts began to chase themselves in circles, I let be and spent time with Kazan's men, listening to them swap tales with the Ban's Guard and improving my skill at dice. It had begun to rain on the second day at sea; naught to slow our progress, but a cold, relentless drizzle that chilled one to the bone and drove every hand not on duty below decks. Dank and close as it was, it was better than shivering in the open air.

On the fourth day, the weather cleared and, by late afternoon, we passed La Dolorosa.

I went to stand at the railing and watch as soon as I heard the sighting called; the Wailing Rock, they call it in Illyrian. Pjètri Kolcei ordered the ship's captain to steer a wide berth around it. None of the Illyrians would even look in the direction of the black isle. Whistling tunelessly as the sailors aboard the *Darielle* had done, they stared fixedly ahead or eastward, fingering amulets and making warding gestures in the direction they dared not look.

I looked; I had to.

And there it stood, much the same, crags of black basalt rearing skyward, waves crashing at its foot. The fortress where I had been held captive was still nestled atop the isle, stony and silent. I could hear, now that I knew to listen for it, the mournful, maddening winds playing over the crags.

Not until we had almost passed it did I see that the bridge, the hempen bridge that spanned the deadly drop betwixt mainland and isle, hung loose and dangling against La Dolorosa's cliffs. It twisted in the wind, wooden planks being slowly battered to splinters by the rock. On the mainland, the watchtower maintained a hollow vigil. La Dolorosa was abandoned.

Someone had cut the bridge.

Joscelin, I thought, my heart pounding madly in my breast.

"Phèdre." It was Kazan's voice. He touched my arm, breaking my reverie. "It is time."

Sixty-eight

In the hold of the Illyrian ship, lamplight played over the contents of the Ban's tribute-gift, glinting on masses of gold and amber. Two of Pjètri's men glanced at their leader for permission; he gave the nod to proceed. Working quickly, they emptied the trunk of its spoils, a heady pile of treasure. A layer of marten skins followed, soft, lustrous pelts mounded on the cabin floor.

The false bottom of the trunk lay bare.

Pjètri Kolcei knelt, drawing his dagger and working it alongside the seam. It was a tight fit; the Ban's carpenters had wrought well. Wiggling the blade, he prised it upward. The false bottom gave way, raising a hairs-breadth. He reached under it, wedging his fingernails into a narrow groove and lifting with a grimace. It came, though, and he lifted the false bottom clean away from the tiny ridge that supported it.

It was a small space left betwixt the true bottom and the false. It was a very small space.

I gazed at it, drawing a deep breath. Solid and dark and heavy, the trunk was, carved of cypress wood and bound in silver. There were air holes, yes, bored into the centers of the elaborate floral pattern that adorned the base; holes so small no light pierced them. I had not reckoned, until then, how much I feared confinement in that space.

"There is no time, Lady Phèdre," the Ban's middle son said quietly. "The Spear of Bellonus has been sighted. We must make ready for arrival."

I nodded once and took another deep breath – it seemed I could not get enough air into my lungs – and glanced around at Kazan and his men, their faces all at once seeming very familiar and dear. And then, lest my nerve fail me, I climbed into the trunk and forced myself into that terribly, terribly small space, knees drawn tight into my belly, chin tucked, squeezed on all sides by the trunk's walls.

"Now," Pjètri ordered. "Do it quickly!"

Epafras and Oltukh set the false bottom back in place, and that was the last glimpse I had of light and life; their worried faces, quickly obliterated by a solid width of wood. And then the false bottom was pressing down on me and I was in darkness. My shoulders and hips were crushed against it; I shifted, trying to move, but there was no space. It was tight and airless. I heard the soft sound of marten skins being piled atop the false bottom, and fought down a wave of panic. Not airless, no; it only seemed that way. Here, in utter blackness, I could see the air holes; there was one close to my left eye, admitting a faint hint of lamplight.

If light can penetrate, so can air, I told myself. It didn't help. I felt my chest heave, gulping involuntarily for breath, and forced myself to calm, thinking, you are breathing, Phèdre; not dying, not suffocating.

A simple thing, this confinement, and yet horrifying. I

daresay I would have withstood it better when I was younger — before La Dolorosa, and before my near-drowning. As it was, it was all I could do to keep from pounding on the walls of the trunk and begging for release. Instead I shivered and gulped and prayed it went smoothly with the harbor guard — smoothly, and oh, Elua, swiftly!

The sounds that I heard with my ear pressed to the floor of the trunk were strange and stifled, coming through the wood itself. The lapping of water against the hull of the ship, the muffled tread of feet and the deep scrape of oars. And from far away, very far, an occasional shout. On and on it went, until at last I felt the change when we neared the harbor; our progress slowing, the creak of topsails being lowered, and then the back-stroke of oars, bringing us to a halt.

A measure of stillness, then, until the tread of footsteps increased many-fold.

I know, because Kazan told me, that the Serenissiman harbor guard searched the ship with the utmost of thoroughness. The Illyrians were made to drop anchor, and every man on board assembled on deck, relinquishing their swords and standing at attention while the captain of harbor directed the search. Kazan and his men stood among them, unblinking and unwavering, not knowing if they would be recognized as pirates. All of them had daggers concealed somewhere on their persons; if the worst came, they would die fighting.

Every hammock and every bunk was overturned, every cabin tossed, every soldier's kit opened and searched; a stash of silver denari stamped with the likeness of the Ban of Illyria was seized from the best of the dice players. Pjètri Kolcei lodged a furious protest, claiming that they had not sought to use the coin in trade. The captain of harbor ignored him, and gave orders to search the trunk which held the Ban of Illyria's tribute-gift.

All of this I learned later; then, I only heard them enter the cabin, holding myself still as the dead in my cramped hiding-space, scarce daring to breathe. It seemed the very hammering of my heart would give me away. Pjètri Kolcei unlocked the lid of the trunk and lifted it; the squeak of the hinges penetrated the marrow of my bones. And while I lay tight-curled and terrified beneath the false bottom, the Serenissiman harbor guard emptied the trunk one item at a time, making a tally of the Ban's tribute.

How long it lasted, I cannot say; an eternity, it seemed to me. When a Serenissiman guard reached into the trunk to remove the last of the marten-skins, his knuckles rapped the wood directly above my ear. It felt as immediate as a blow and I could not imagine that he was insensible of my presence, so acutely aware was I of his.

They will see, I thought; they will look inside the trunk, and they will look outside of it, and they will see there is a foot of space missing.

This thought ran through my head, over and over, while a methodical voice counted out the goods of the tribute-gift in Caerdicci and a quill scratched against parchment. It took on a rhythm of its own, beating in my mind; they-will-see, they-will-see, they-will-see. I fought to keep from saying it aloud, fought to keep my limbs from shivering, fought to keep my breathing quiet and steady.

I was still concentrating on it when I heard the captain of harbor's muffled voice. "This gift is tallied to the last coin and pelt, Illyrian. If it's short in the Treasury's reckoning, it comes out of your hide."

"It will arrive as you have counted it," Pjètri Kolcei said coldly, his Caerdicci precise and fluent. "If your Treasurer is a thief, I will not be held accountable."

The captain made some reply, lost to me in the thump of martenskins being tossed carelessly back into the trunk. This time, I could have wept with joy at the sense of stifling weight returning. Piece by piece, the Ban's gift was replaced. Someone slammed the lid of the trunk, and the crash of it fair split my skull. I didn't care; it was music to my ears. Footsteps retreated, the cabin door closed. Within the trunk, I let out a long-held breath and gave thanks to Blessed Elua.

If my terror was lessened by a measure, my discomfort only increased. We had reckoned it wisest if I were to stay in concealment until the trunk could be safely unloaded and brought into the Ambassador's residence, and so I remained, cramped and stifling in darkness, while the Ban's ship made its way across the harbor and proceeded up the Great Canal.

I daresay they went as swiftly as they might, but unlike Kazan's vessels, the tribute ship was not built for speed in close quarters and there was a good deal of sea traffic in the harbor and canals. I lay quiet, ignoring the twinges of pain in my contorted limbs, counting my own breaths to time the journey and imagining in memory the sights we passed: the Arsenal; the Palace of the Doge alongside the Campo Grande, where the statue of Asherat-of-the-Sea looked out on the harbor; the Temple of Baal-Jupiter; and, oh, yes, the Little Court, proudly flying the standard of House Courcel. Other houses of the Hundred Worthy Families lined the Great Canal, and then the mighty Rive Alto bridge, and beyond, the warehouses and banking institutions and residences of foreign ambassadors. . . .

And we were there. I heard the oars jostle and splash as the rowers maneuvered the ship into position, the thump of padded bolsters thrown over the side to cushion her against the dock, and the deep plunge of the anchor dropped into murky green waters. The myriad sounds of sailors striking the sails and making fast the ship followed, and then, mercifully, the opening of the cabin door and Illyrian voices, soldiers moving swiftly under Pjètri Kolcei's command.

It took four of them to carry the trunk, heavy on its own and heavier still with my weight added to the tribute-gift. A terrifying feeling, to be thus trapped, lifted and swaying in midair. My panic returned, sweat trickling between my shoulder blades as the trunk rose, jolted awkwardly and began to move. Every time it tilted, my stomach lurched in fear; out of the hold, down the landing plank and, worst of all, up a steep stairway and into the ambassador's residence.

There, at last, they lowered the trunk with a bone-jarring thud. I heard voices, familiar and unfamiliar, exchanging formalities and hurried explanations, and then Kazan's voice cutting through it all. "Pjètri, the key. Get her out *now!*"

A key fidgeted in the lock and the lid was thrown open. For the third time that day the Ban's tribute-gift was unloaded, gold coinage and chunks of raw amber dumped in an unceremonious pile as Kazan's men scooped it out by the armload, hauling the pelts after. I coiled my body tighter, shivering as someone wedged a dagger-blade into the seam very near my unprotected head, prying up the false bottom. It was Kazan; I heard him curse as his finger-nails scrabbled futilely for purchase, seeking the tiny groove.

"Here." Pjètri's voice, quick and impatient. "Move over. Move over, I say! I know how to do it. No, there — pry up on the hilt."

Of a sudden, the pressure atop me was gone and there was light and air, fresh, clean air. I breathed in a great, gulping draught of it, filling my lungs, and drew myself up to kneel in the trunk. A wave of dizziness overcame me, and I had to brace my hands on the sides to remain upright.

"Phèdre?" Kazan's face swam in my vision. "Are you well?"

I nodded, which made the dizziness worse. Beyond Kazan, I saw an older Illyrian nobleman, elegantly attired, his brows arched in astonished surmise. Pjètri moved between us, bowing and extending a letter to the man.

"Ambassador Rossatos," he said politely. "My father will explain in full."

So he did, I trust; I never knew for a surety what the Ban had written. Janàri Rossatos called for an Illyrian manservant he trusted to bring us wine while he read the letter through twice, taking his time about it. We were in his parlor, which was pleasantly appointed, although the furniture was simple by Serenissiman standards. I sat on a couch and sipped my wine, feeling steadier and wondering at the strangeness of seeing reflected canal-light wavering once more on walls and ceiling. Pjètri sat too, and Kazan; four of their men remained standing.

When he had done, Rossatos gazed at me. He had a diplomat's face, smooth and canny despite the lines of age, and one could not read his thoughts in it. "The

Contessa de Montrève, I presume," he said in flawless Caerdicci.

I rose and made him a curtsy. "My lord Ambassador, I am Phèdre nó Delaunay de Montrève. Please accept my thanks for your hospitality."

His eyelids flickered. "I but do the will of the Zim Sokali, my lady. You are welcome here." He tapped the letter. "I am commanded herein to give you such aid as I may, providing it places our position here in no jeopardy. If I understand aright, you seek to prevent the assassination of your Queen, yes? Ysandre de la Courcel of Terre d'Ange?"

"Yes, my lord."

"You have proof of this conspiracy?"

I hesitated. "My lord . . . yes. The woman Prince Benedicte has taken to wife is a condemned traitor, sentenced to execution in Terre d'Ange. He knows this, has deliberately deceived the Queen in this matter. It is all the proof that is needful."

"Ah." Janàri Rossatos imparted great precision to a single syllable. "And are you prepared to make this accusation to the Doge-elect, his own son-in-law?"

"No." I shook my head. "Marco Stregazza is his ally."

"Is he really?" Rossatos leaned back in his chair, looking intrigued. "You know, a month ago, I'd have laughed to hear it, so long had Prince Benedicte and the Stregazza been feuding. 'Twas a strange and wondrous thing, how their feud was resolved nearly on the eve of the election. It is widely agreed that Benedicte's endorsement – and the promise of D'Angeline funds to support fresh dredging and construction – gave Marco the election."

"It was planned thusly," I said.

"Perhaps."

"No. Of a surety." I sighed. "Let me guess, my lord Ambassador. Prince Benedicte repented of his haste in naming his newborn son Imriel heir to his D'Angeline properties, and has restored them to the inheritance of his daughter Marie-Celeste. Do I have the right of it?"

The Ambassador's brows rose. "Near enough. What of it? The boy may inherit the Little Court; the daughter, no. Not in Serenissima."

"The boy will inherit Terre d'Ange," I said softly. "That is their plan. But I cannot prove it to you, my lord, without getting myself killed."

"She speaks the truth," Kazan rumbled impatiently. "I stood on a Serenissiman ship, I, while her captain ordered Phèdre nó Delaunay slain on the Stregazza's orders, eh, Marco Stregazza. I did not let that happen, I. So what is your aid worth, diplomat?"

Rossatos spread his hands helplessly and glanced at Pjètri, his Ban's son. "Little enough, I'm afraid. My word carries little sway with the Doge at the best of times. Now Cesare sees no audiences — due to his health, it is claimed — and as for the Doge-elect . . . Marco claims piety prevents him from receiving foreign embassies until he is rightfully invested as Doge."

"What of Ysandre?" I asked. "Has the D'Angeline *progressus regalis* arrived?"

He shook his elegant head, silver-grey hair neatly barbered. "Tomorrow, it is said; a day before the investiture. Her emissaries arrived today, from Pavento."

"Where are they housed?"

"The Little Court," Rossatos said. "Where else?

Prince Benedicte has been making ready for weeks. It is,"
he added thoughtfully, "a pity that his wife is said to be
unwell, and perhaps unable to attend the festivities."

I'd wondered whether or not Melisande would risk
recognition, veiled or no. "I suspect it is an illness of con-
venience, my lord, in much the same way that I suspect the
Doge's ill health has no natural provenance." I wouldn't
put it past Marie-Celeste Stregazza to have dosed poor old
Cesare with something that gave him a flux. "Can you gain
access to the Little Court?"

"No." Rossatos' voice was curt; no diplomat likes to
admit to such failure. "Last week, yes; next week, perhaps.
Today, tomorrow, the day after . . . no. You must understand, Contessa, that La Serenissima is in turmoil. A Doge
stepping down before his time, a new Doge elected, the
visit of the D'Angeline Queen . . . all of this, and the city
in arms over the riots. Security in the Palace and the Court
is as tight as a drum, and it will remain so until Marco
Stregazza has the Dogal Seal on his finger. He is taking no
risks; nor is Prince Benedicte. It is not only an Illyrian
embassy that would be turned away, for once. There is an
Akkadian ambassador I know, who sought invitation to the
festivities in the Little Court — even his suit was denied,
and he ambassador to the Khalif, whose own son is wed to
the Queen's cousin!"

I blinked, thinking over his words. "Riots?"

"Riots, yes." Janàri Rossatos gave a dismissive shrug.
"Do you know La Serenissima, Contessa? The Scholae,
the craft-guilds? Half of them are on strike, trade ships sit
empty in the harbor, and there is violence in the streets.
Even the market in the Campo Grande has been closed,
since five days past. The salt-panners wrought havoc there,

overturning the stalls of all who dared sell goods. There was a brawl, and two young men whose names are writ in the Golden Book were killed. At night, the Chandlers' Schola sets fires, throwing lighted tapers into the homes of the Hundred Worthy Families."

"Riots," I said again, touching my fingers to my lips in thought. "What does Ricciardo Stregazza say about this?"

"Ricciardo?" Rossatos looked at me in surprise. "It is all his fault, Marco says. His brother has roused the Scholae to strike, in petty revenge for his defeat. Until his investiture, when Marco may hear out the grievances of the leaders of the Scholae, Ricciardo has been confined to house arrest."

"Ricciardo wouldn't rouse the craft-guilds out of vengeance," I said absently. "He had a true care for their concerns. How many of the Scholae are involved?"

"Rumor says a dozen or more," Rossatos said. "Proven?" He shrugged. "At least seven are striking. As for the violence, the Serenissiman Guard has caught members of the salt-panners, the chandlers and the saddlers guilds engaged in acts of civil disturbance. And those young fools from the nobleman's clubs, willing to brawl at the flicker of an eyelash, do but add fuel to the fire."

"Phèdre," Kazan said curiously. "What are you thinking, you?"

He and Pjètri had sat patiently throughout our exchange, listening and offering little or no comment. I glanced at him. "If I were going to stage a public assassination," I said slowly, "I would ensure there was a measure of confusion, that my agent might strike undetected therein. A riot would be the very thing. My lord

Ambassador, where does the ceremony of investiture take place?"

"In the Great Temple of Asherat," Janàri Rossatos replied. "With a progression across the Campo Grande, where the newly invested Doge plights his troth to Asherat-of-the-Sea."

I sat unmoving, hearing the surge pressing on my eardrums, the deep, steady thrumming of the current around La Dolorosa that had born me aloft on the waters and saved my life. I had a promise to keep, and I knew, in the marrow of my bones, where I must keep it. "It will be there," I said, hearing my own voice come hollow and echoing, as if from a great distance. "With Ysandre de la Courcel in attendance and a thousand people pressing into the Square, too many to keep at bay. It will be there."

SIXTY-NINE

İT WAS a frustrating thing, to be so near and so far at once, so sure and so unable to prove it; and even if I could have, there was no merit in it. The Illyrian Ambassador had stated the truth. He had no means of gaining access to Ysandre, nor any of her people.

Pjètri Kolcei quarreled bitterly with him that evening, for he had it in mind to try his hand as the son of the Ban of Illyria, writing to the Little Court to request an audience with Prince Benedicte, thereby enabling him to deliver a message to Ysandre's entourage. Eventually Rossatos despaired of him, and the letter was sent; a reply came swiftly, arriving by morning. Prince Benedicte would be honored to grant his request . . . after the investiture of the Doge.

I had no illusions about the source of these precautions. Marco Stregazza might well believe me dead, slain by the terrible storm that had driven our ship southward before watching Serenissiman eyes. Melisande would take no such chances, and she would ensure that the Stregazza didn't either. No Illyrian suit would be entertained until Ysandre was dead.

I had reached La Serenissima, and the Ban of Illyria's aid had reached its limits.

I needed the impossible.

I needed Joscelin.

"You are mad," Janàri Rossatos said irritably. "You are very beautiful, Contessa, and very easily recognized. If half of what you surmise is true, you place my position in grave danger, very grave indeed. No," he added, shaking his head. "I cannot countenance it, cannot countenance it at all. You must stay here, until the investiture is complete. Do you wish a message sent, I will lend my aid, but if you were to be discovered in the company of Illyrians . . . I cannot be responsible for this."

"I am sorry, my lord Ambassador," I said to him. "But I must go."

"You must certainly *not!*"

It was unwise, I daresay, for Rossatos to take such a forceful tone in Kazan Atrabiades' presence. Lounging in the doorway, Kazan grinned and fingered the hilt of his sword. "I almost think you gave an order, you," he said cheerfully. "It is a good thing I am a pirate, eh, and do not heed such things, I."

Rossatos flushed with helpless anger, casting a glance at Pjètri Kolcei. "You're the Zim Sokali's son, my lord – *do* something! We will all answer to Serenissima's wrath, if these lunatics are caught!"

"Very well," Pjètri said casually, sauntering onto the balcony. Outside, he leaned over the balustrade and whistled sharply; an answering call came from below, and he returned, his grey-blue eyes light and thoughtful. "Pardon, my lord Rossatos, but I do not believe my father intended your discretion to encompass governing our guests' actions, and I judge this aid worth giving. Your gondola is ready," he added to Kazan. "It has a three-sided awning, ought to do the trick. If not . . ." He shrugged, and they clasped wrists in a warrior's grip. "Yarovit's grace on your blade, pirate."

"And yours," Kazan replied. "Phèdre? Are we going to this, this temple of Yosua?"

"Yeshua," I said. "Yes." I turned to the Ambassador. "I am sorry, my lord. Please know that I will deny your role if we are captured." He made no answer, and I crossed the room, pausing to address the Ban's middle son. To him, I said softly, "Thank you, my lord."

Pjètri Kolcei smiled wryly. "I'd go with you, if I dared. I'm glad we got you here safely, at any rate. Rossatos is right, this is the most I can do, and a risk at that, letting you and the pirate roam at will. Good luck to you, my lady."

Leaving the Ambassador's residence was the worst of it. Despite the deep-shadowed hood of my Illyrian cloak and the escort of Kazan and his men blocking me from view, I felt terribly exposed as I ventured into the chill light of dawn. The gondola was a humble affair, weathered but sound, with faded paint and a much-patched awning. Keeping my head low, I stepped onto it with care and settled myself on the burlap sacking laid beneath the awning, surrounded by tented walls. Kazan sat directly in front of me, hiding me further. Like his men, he had exchanged his mail and livery for rude pirate's garb.

If anyone were to inquire, they were mercenary sailors out of work due to the strikes; 'twas plausible enough, for a number of Illyrians had hired on to Serenissiman merchanters, valued for their skill at sea and unable to find employ with trade strangled in Illyria. It would not hold up to close inspection, of course — Rossatos was right, I was hard to disguise — but there was no way around it.

The Great Canal was crowded with ships despite the earliness of the hour; already patrols of the Serenissiman Guard roamed the streets. And beyond the arch of the Rive Alto, a tumult of activity was beginning on the waterways, gilded bissone belonging to Stregazzan supporters vying for position with ships of the Serenissiman navy.

"They are coming this way, Phèdre," Kazan reported to me in whispered Illyrian, poking his head beneath the awning. "I think that they are blockading the main canals, to secure them for your Queen's entrance. We may yet leave safely, but returning is another matter. Are you sure you want to go?"

I shivered, not at all sure; if there was a chance, any chance, of reaching Ysandre upon her entrance, I would be a fool to let it pass. Storming her ship, leaping onto it from a bridge, firing an arrow with a message tied around the shaft . . .

"Do we stand any chance of reaching the Queen from here?" I asked him.

Kazan hesitated, then shook his head. "With seven men? No. We would die."

"Then we go," I replied grimly.

Concealed within my awning, I saw little of our journey. Kazan's men maneuvered the battered gondola with swift efficiency, although I confess our route meandered considerably through the labyrinth of canals and it took some doing to find the Yeshuite quarter. It lay in the impoverished eastward sector of the city, where the buildings were all of simple wooden construction and the muddy streets unpaved. Unfortunate for the Yeshuites, though lucky for us; once we had left the Great Canal and the larger waterways behind, we saw few guardsmen.

It was good that we had left at dawn. By the time we located the Yeshuite quarter, the sun was well above the horizon.

The Yeshuites had done what they might to make their dwelling place a more pleasant one. The houses were sturdily constructed and planked walks had been laid over the mire; the water of the narrow canals themselves was cleaner and lacked the reek of ordure one found elsewhere. Here and there, pots of flowers decorated the wooden balconies. Few people were about in the early morning, but I heard the sound of a resonant voice raised in song coming from somewhere within the quarter.

"That will be the temple," I said to Kazan. "Is it safe to disembark?"

"Safe enough," he said dubiously. "Better if you stay, and I go."

"Can you speak Habiru?" I asked him; he rolled his eyes. "It has to be me, Kazan. If I'm right, if they've sheltered him this long, they wouldn't trust anyone else."

After a few minutes' quarrel, we settled on a compromise. I would go, taking Kazan and three others as my escort; the others would remain with the gondola. We traversed the quarter quickly, the Illyrians watching out on all sides, but no Serenissimans were in sight, not here.

The temple was a modest affair, low-built, of wooden construction with a solid stone foundation. I heard the voice of the chantor grow louder as we approached, rising and falling in ritual song; the Sa'akharit, I thought, recalling somewhat of the Rebbe's teaching. It was regrettable that we had arrived during the morning prayer, but there was nothing for it. I had no time to lose.

There was a *khai* symbol engraved on the wooden door. I pushed it open and entered, flanked by four Illyrian pirates.

We came into an antechamber that opened onto the temple proper, where scores of worshippers were seated. The chantor broke off his song and stared, and their Rebbe stood open-mouthed at his lectern. Everyone in the temple, men and women alike, wore bright yellow hats such as the Yeshuite man I'd seen in the Campo Grande so long ago had worn. One by one, the seated worshippers turned around to look.

All of them looked terrified, and Joscelin was not among their number.

"Barukh hatah Yeshua a'Mashiach, father," I said politely in Habiru; it was hard to get my tongue around the harsh syllables after so long. "For . . . forgive me for disturbing your prayers, but it is a matter of great urgency. I seek the D'Angeline, Joscelin Verreuil."

The congregation looked to the Rebbe; his eyes shifted and he licked his lips, two of the telltales of a man preparing to lie. "I do not know who you mean, child."

"No? Then I shall say it thusly, father," I said, and echoed the words the Yeshuite had spoken in the Campo Grande, after Joscelin had come to his rescue. "I seek the one whose blades shine like a star in his hands."

A voice – a young, male voice – uttered a sound somewhere within the congregation, and I saw a woman put her hand hard on her son's shoulder, forcing him to sit when he would have stood. Kazan shifted, looking to me for direction. The Rebbe stood silent. There was an aisle along the side of the temple. I walked slowly down it, drawing back the hood of my cloak, until I stood before the raised dais.

"Look well at me, father," I said softly, turning my face up for his regard. "I am Phèdre nó Delaunay, and Joscelin Verreuil is my oathsworn companion. With those words and this visage I show to you, I have put my life into your hands."

The Rebbe licked his lips again, and glanced past me toward the Illyrians. He was not old for the position, no more than forty. Behind him, the flickering light of the Ur Tamid, the light that is never extinguished, cast shadows over the sacred ark of scrolls. "I . . . hear your words, child. But this person you seek . . . is not here."

"You can get word to him." I kept my voice steady. "I beseech you, by all you hold sacred, to do so. Tell him I have come. Tell him you have seen a D'Angeline woman, who bears in her left eye a fleck of crimson. The men I am with are friends; I trust them with my life. Tell him I swear it, by Cassiel's Dagger. Until the sun stands high overhead, I will wait for him, at the Inn of Seven Strangers."

No more could I say. Putting up my hood, I turned and made my way back. In the shadowy antechamber, Kazan grinned, teeth gleaming white against the darkness save for the gap where one was missing. "We wait?" he asked; he may not have understood my words, but he read the Rebbe's face well enough and he knew my plan.

"We wait," I said.

The Inn of Seven Strangers had the advantage of being highly disreputable, and an establishment given a wide berth by the Serenissiman Guard unless absolutely necessary. It was a tavern and flophouse recommended with considerable enthusiasm by one of Pjètri Kolcei's sailors, who had sojourned as a mercenary before joining the Ban's service.

Even in the morning hours, it was thronging with out-of-work seafarers from a half-dozen nations; Caerdicci, Ephesians, Akkadians and Umaiyyati, even a few Skaldi, which always gave me an involuntary shiver. No other Illyrians, which I was glad to see. There is privacy in a tongue unshared. Two men stayed with the gondola, and Kazan and Tormos forged a path to the rear of the common room, bulling their way by main force while the others took care to keep me surrounded.

I kept my head down and hooded; there were a few good-natured curses but, for the most part, the other patrons of the inn took no notice, supposing I was a harbor-front whore hired to be shared among Kazan and his men. For once, I was glad of such a mistake.

Kazan secured a table in the farthest, darkest corner of the inn by shifting a sleeping drunkard, who took little notice. We disposed ourselves about the table, and Ushak went to purchase a jug of wine, carefully counting over the Serenissiman coins Kazan gave to him to be sure of the currency's value.

"That's foul stuff!" Tormos proclaimed, drawing in his breath with a sharp hiss as he tasted it. "We make better on Dobrek. I thought it would be all ichor, here in Serenissima."

"That's because you're an idiot," his brother Stajeo said promptly. "My lady Phèdre . . . I will drink bad wine and play dice all day, if you like, but why are we here? I thought we came to kill Serenissimans and save your

Queen! What can this . . . D'Angeline . . ." he pronounced the word with a contempt that I was now spared, ". . . do that we cannot?"

There were grumbled echoes of the query all around, and Kazan raised his brows at me; although he had forborne asking, he was surely wondering.

"I don't know," I answered honestly. "In truth . . . mayhap naught. If nothing else, he will make our count eight men rather than seven; nine, if Elua's mercy is with me, and my chevalier Philippe yet lives."

"Nine will die a little slower than seven," Kazan said. "Not much."

"It may be." I took a breath. "From the age of ten, Joscelin Verreuil was raised a member of the Cassiline Brotherhood, taught fighting skills to ward the scions of Elua and his Companions from harm. My lord Kazan, you and your men are doughty warriors, that much I have seen, but to thwart the assassination of a regent at close quarters . . . this is what Joscelin has trained all of his life to do. If there is a way it may be done, he will find it."

The other Illyrians made disparaging remarks and jests — they had never faced a D'Angeline in battle, let alone a Cassiline — but Kazan's face was thoughtful. "Your Queen," he said. "Does she not already have such guards in her service?"

"Yes," I admitted. "At least two, mayhap more, for the *progressus*. But if aught happens, they will not look to Prince Benedicte's quarter for betrayal." I gave a hollow laugh, remembering Joscelin's once-fierce loyalty to his vow. "Indeed, they are Cassilines; they will protect House Courcel to the death."

"And death it will be," Kazan mused. The wine-jug

went around again, and his men tossed dice to see who would bear the cost of a refill; it fell to Epafras, who went with a grimace. Kazan ignored them and reached out to brush his fingers down a lock of my hair. "You are not afraid of death, you, I think," he said softly in Caerdicci. "But I think, I, you are afraid of dying without seeing this, this Joscelin Verreuil once more."

"What I have said is true," I said to him.

He gave a crooked smile. "This much I believe, eh? I would like to meet the man, I, who assailed the black isle single-handed. I stood with you on the ship, yes, and I saw the tower empty, the bridge dangling. Others did not dare to look, but I did, I. And yet . . . your voice goes soft when you speak his name. I think that you love him, you."

"Yes." I owed him the truth. "I do."

Kazan nodded. "So we will see, eh? If he comes, it is to the good. And if he does not?"

I turned the earthenware wine cup in my hands. "If he does not, we go to Lord Ricciardo Stregazza, and beg his aid. It will alert the Dogal Guard, and likely we will be hunted for it, but mayhap Ricciardo can rouse the other Scholae to counter Marco's attack."

"Good," Kazan said briskly. "It is something, and Serenissimans will die. It is better to try than to surrender."

To that, I made no answer; I could not but help thinking that most of the Serenissimans were merely following orders, knowing no more of Marco's machinations than a babe. It did not please me, to think on their deaths. In the cavern of the *thetalos*, I would be accountable.

Time passed, and another wine-jug was drained; Stajeo and Ushak went to relieve Oltukh and Volos of their guard duty on the gondola. They came in reporting that the sun stood a few degrees shy of noon. Out came the dice, with good-natured quarrels. I began to despair, when the Yeshuite entered the tavern.

He was alone, which marked him, and his eyes scanned the crowd, seeking and discarding. I did not know him for a Yeshuite at first; he did not wear the yellow cap, and his sidelocks were cut. We took no chances. When his gaze fell upon our table, Kazan pulled me onto his lap with a hearty laugh, making pretend indeed that I was a rented doxie for his pleasure.

It would have fooled a casual observer; it did not fool the young man with the dark, intent eyes. He made his way to the table and asked in Habiru, "Be you the Apostate's oath-sworn?"

Volos sprang to his feet and drew his dagger, setting its point at the Yeshuite's throat.

"Let him be," I said in Illyrian, and then added in Caerdicci, that Kazan might understand, "I am Kushiel's Chosen and Servant of Naamah, and Joscelin Verreuil has sworn Cassiel's Oath to protect me. Do you doubt it?" I drew back my hood, and the Yeshuite inhaled sharply.

"No," he said simply and bowed, crossing his forearms in the Cassiline manner. Beneath rough-spun garb, leather vambraces protected his arms. "Do you doubt who has sent me?"

"No." My heart hammered within my breast; Kazan's hands rested lightly on my waist. "Is he here?"

"Not here." The young Yeshuite shook his head. His Caerdicci was faintly accented, and he ignored Volos' hovering blade as if it didn't exist. "I am Micah ben Ximon, and he has sent me to bring you where he is."

I stood up; Kazan's hands fell away. "Then take us."

SEVENTY

A QUARREL broke out as we left the Inn of Seven Strangers; I saw Tormos deliberately jostle the elbow of a tall Umaiyyati holding a pot of ale, and suspected it was staged. Insults were traded, with accompanying gestures; a few blows were exchanged. Kazan hurried me past unnoticed, following Micah ben Ximon, and Tormos caught up with us outside, grinning.

The patrons of the inn might recall a handful of quarrelsome Illyrians leaving, but they would not remember a D'Angeline woman with them, nor a lone Yeshuite.

Micah had a skiff, more disreputable than our hastily purchased gondola. He boarded it and leaned on the oars, waiting. Kazan decided that he and I would travel with the Yeshuite, as well as Oltukh; the rest would follow in the gondola, under Tormos' command. It sat ill with Stajeo, to obey his brother's orders. I saw the Yeshuite go wide-eyed, watching while the Illyrians argued. He was younger than I had thought in the tavern, no more than seventeen or eighteen.

"Go," I said, leaning forward. "They will settle it, and follow."

He glanced once at Kazan, who nodded; Oltukh settled himself on the bench next to Micah and took an oar, and the skiff moved speedily into the center of the canal as they rowed in unison. Before long, the gondola followed, the sound of Illyrian voices raised in quarrel still audible.

Kazan spared a grin.

La Serenissima is built on islands; some large, some small, some reclaimed from the sea and linked by bridges and waterways . . . and some not. It was to one of the latter that Micah ben Ximon guided us, a small hummock of land with a dense pine forest, interlocking roots at the water's edge making landing difficult. It was obvious that some preliminary clearing had been done at the shoreline, but work had been abandoned.

The boats were dragged ashore and concealed under clumps of browning autumn ferns, and we picked our way across the burned swathe of land, roots poking out of the cinders, tripping up my skirts. Although no path was visible, Micah strode boldly into the scrub pines on the verge of the forest as if he knew where he went. I followed doggedly, and Kazan made hand signals to his men, who fanned out to flank us. It was familiar enough terrain to them, Dobrek's hills being much the same, although they glanced warily over their shoulders, looking for *Leskii*.

This time, I was not looking for forest spirits. I was looking for Joscelin.

The pine forest closed in on us, dark-green and forbidding. Here, no workmen's boots had trod. Micah led us unfaltering, pine mast giving way softly beneath his steps. Itching and hot with exertion, I pulled off the hood of my woolen cloak and let the breeze cool me. There was no one to see. I looked at Kazan, who loosened his sword within its sheath, teeth bared in a battle-smile. By the time the forest gave way to an open glade, I was uneasy with misgivings. I had given the Rebbe my name. If the Yeshuites chose to betray me, 'twould be easy enough, and doubtless well rewarded.

Micah halted, Kazan and I beside him. To the right and the left of us, the other Illyrians emerged from the forest, several with short swords already drawn. In the center of the glade, some ten men stood ranged in a loose line, all of them armed and two with crossbows.

My heart was beating like a drum.

I took a step forward. Their leader took a step forward.

He wore rough-spun garb like the rest and his tangled mane of hair was an odd, ashen hue, but steel flashed at his wrists and the hilt of a broadsword rose over his left shoulder and I would have known him anywhere.

"*Phèdre?*"

His voice, Joscelin's voice, cracked on my name and tears blurred my eyes at the disbelief in it, the wondering hope against hope. I took one step and then another and tried to say his name, only my voice broke and caught in my throat, and then he was moving, running, until he was there and his hands came hard around me, solid and living, and I was lifted clean off my feet, gazing down at his incredulous face. Laughing and weeping at once, I cupped his face in both hands and kissed him all over it.

"Oh, Joscelin, Joscelin!" My own voice, breathless with joy. He let me slide through his grip and set me down, burying both hands in my hair and drawing me to him.

"Never again, never, never, never, Phèdre, I swear it,"

he murmured, muffled words punctuated with frantic kisses, "in the name of Blessed Elua, I swear it, I will never leave you again, take a thousand patrons if you want, take ten thousand, wed Severio Stregazza, I don't care, but I will never leave you!"

I raised my face and he kissed me, long and hard, until desire and love, like a dagger in the heart, sent the world reeling around me and I had to cling to the front of his jerkin when he released me, struggling to remain on my feet.

We regarded one another.

"You're *alive*," Joscelin whispered, astonishment in his summer-blue eyes.

"You're . . . your *hair!*" I said idiotically to him, reaching up to touch it, ragged dun streaked with ash-grey. "What did you do to your *hair?*"

"It's walnut dye." It was another voice that spoke, a D'Angeline voice, thready but familiar. "It washes out, in time." I whirled in Joscelin's arms, seeking the speaker; Ti-Philippe grinned at me, thin, worn face beaming under a similarly ragged crop of hair, dyed a flat, dark brown.

"Philippe!" I flung both arms about his neck, kissing his cheek. He held me hard, and I saw tears in his eyes when he let me go.

"We thought you were dead, my lady," he said softly. "Joscelin saw you fall from the cliff."

"No." I smiled through my tears. "Not quite, not yet." I swallowed hard, adding, "Fortun and Remy . . . Fortun and Remy are dead."

"We guessed." Joscelin's voice was quiet. "Phèdre, who are these people?"

He had taken a step back, crossed hands hovering over

the hilts of his daggers. Wiping my eyes and gathering myself, I saw that Kazan and his men had come up to surround me, while the others, Joscelin's folk — Yeshuites, I saw, young men and one woman — had done the same on their side. I realized then that we had been speaking D'Angeline, and none of them knew what had transpired.

"Friends, all of them," I said firmly in Caerdicci, and repeated it in Illyrian for the benefit of Kazan's men. "Friends." I looked at Joscelin, my heart breaking at the sight of his beloved face. "Joscelin Verreuil, this is Kazan Atrabiades. I owe him my life."

They regarded each other; two men, much of a height, some ten years difference between them. What transpired in that silent exchange, I will never know. It was Kazan who broke it, grinning broadly.

"As I owe her mine, I," he said. "I have heard of you, D'Angeline! You have a reputation to live up to, you."

Joscelin bowed, his crossed vambraces flashing in the autumn sun. He smiled as he straightened, a wry, familiar smile, and my heart sang to see it. "Does Phèdre nó Delaunay owe you her life, my lord," he said, "then I owe you my reason for living. Let us be friends."

Thus were we met, Illyrians and Yeshuites and D'Angeline alike, and the bond among us forged. From our meeting-place in the glade, we went to Joscelin's hidden encampment, a rough establishment of tents and shanties where we sat to confer.

To recount all that was told at that conference would take nigh as long as it took to live it, although we spoke swiftly in turns, starting in the middle of the tale, voices tumbling over one another in a myriad of tongues. I told the bare bones of what had befallen me since I had plunged from the cliffs of La Dolorosa, leaving most of the details of our Kritian sojourn for another day, and Joscelin and Ti-Philippe told their end of it.

With many interruptions, I pieced the story together bit by bit. When Benedicte's guardsmen broke into our rented home on the canal, Ti-Philippe had recognized two of them as the veterans of Troyes-le-Mont we had met only days earlier in the barracks of the Little Court. After Phanuel Buonard's murder, he didn't hesitate, plunging over the balcony into the canal below, making his way afterward, sodden and reeking and already shivering with ague, to the Yeshuite quarter, where he knew Joscelin had been training Yeshuites to arms. 'Twas a lucky thing after all that they had been concerned enough to spy him out at it. Marco Stregazza had nearly been right about the pestilence; he'd been sick for two weeks, although he hadn't died of it.

"And I was nearly as sick at heart," Joscelin said grimly, "to think on what had happened. We didn't dare get near the Little Court, or the Palace either — there were guards searching everywhere — but Elua be thanked, they never thought to search the Yeshuite quarter."

"How in the world did you find me?" I asked, bewildered.

"We did," Micah offered in a quiet voice. "We scoured the city, serving as eyes and ears. It took a long time, because we dared not arouse suspicion. One or two of us followed the guardsmen who were looking for D'Angelines. Where they passed, people spoke of it, even to Yeshuites. It was a simple matter to invent a rumor that a D'Angeline noblewoman had been abducted by two of her countrymen, that people might speak of what they had seen."

"But no one in the city saw anything," I said. "How could they?"

Micah smiled. "One did, though. He was hunting geese on the far side of the lagoon and hid himself when he saw a boat land, with D'Angeline soldiers and a woman, hooded and stumbling, a collar of pearls about her neck."

I had forgotten the Doge's gift. It had been enough to convince Joscelin and Ti-Philippe. With the aid of Micah and three others, they had crossed the lagoon hidden in the bottom of a fishing boat and picked up my trail on the mainland. Benedicte's men had been cautious enough, but the guards of La Dolorosa had been less discreet; the bee-keeper who sold honey to the garrison had heard rumor of my existence. With a pang, I remembered Tito licking his fingers, devouring the evidence of his kindness.

As it transpired, Joscelin had not assailed La Dolorosa wholly on his own; Ti-Philippe and the four Yeshuites — who had begged to go, wanting to test their blades and new-won skill — had aided him, securing the watchtower and their retreat. But all had gone for naught when I plummeted over the cliff, and after a fruitless search, they made their way back to La Serenissima, adopting the ragged disguises they wore still and electing to wait for Ysandre's arrival.

"I didn't know what else to do," Joscelin admitted wearily, scrubbing at his tangled hair. "Mayhap 'twas a mistake to return, for it's well-nigh impossible to get out and worse since the riots began. But all I could think was that if we failed, if we missed the *progressus* and ended up chasing over half of Caerdicca Unitas . . ." He shook his

head. "At least we *knew* Ysandre was coming here. If it
hadn't been for your message, we'd be on our way to the
Little Court by now. It's a risk, still, but we stand a chance.
I don't know how many of the guard have turned, but de
Somerville's men don't dare act as openly with the
Queen's entourage in residence. If I can hold them off
long enough . . . mayhap Ti-Philippe can reach Ysandre
with word of de Somerville's betrayal. I didn't dare, when
it was only Prince Benedicte, but Ysandre will know from
whence the message came."

I stared at him, cold with shock. I had lived with it so
long I had forgotten, beginning my story in the middle, at
La Dolorosa. "You don't know," I whispered. "Oh,
Joscelin! Blessed Elua have mercy . . ."

"What?" he asked, frowning. "What is it?"

A peal of wild laughter escaped from me; I pressed my
hands against my face. "Melisande," I gasped. "That's who
Prince Benedicte wed. Melisande Shahrizai."

"*What?*" Joscelin's voice was high and strained; next
to him, Ti-Philippe went white. The Illyrians and the
Yeshuites stared uncomprehending, lost to the politics of
it.

"Oh, yes," I said simply. "That's what I was met with
at my audience at the Little Court. Benedicte de la
Courcel's pious war-bride who fled her homeland to claim
sanctuary in the Temple of Asherat."

"Does he know?" Joscelin asked in a sickened tone.
"Surely he would not . . ."

"He knows." I looked at him with pity, remembering
my own horror. "Joscelin, he gave the order for Remy and
Fortun's deaths. He wants a true-born D'Angeline heir on
the throne. Melisande could give him that . . . and put the

Royal Commander and his army in his hand. She's done both. He knows."

Ti-Philippe cursed steadily and methodically. Joscelin rose to his feet, pacing restlessly, unable to contain his fury at the betrayal. "We thought the guardsmen of Troyes-le-Mont took you," he said aloud. "We thought the summons was a ruse, that there was a plot operating in the Little Court that Benedicte was insensible of. Elua! Phèdre, do you know how many times I thought of trying to gain access to him? If I hadn't chosen to wait for the Queen's arrival . . ." He stopped, realization dawning across his face. "They're going to kill her, aren't they?"

"Yes," I said. Our eyes met in silence.

"Do you know where, and when, and how?"

"I think so." I swallowed. If I were wrong . . . "Or at least where and when. It will be in the Temple of Asherat, at the ceremony of investiture. These riots . . ." I shook my head. "They're being staged. You met Ricciardo Stregazza, Joscelin; he's not behind them, I'd stake my life on it. It has to be done out in the open, where the world can see that neither Benedicte nor Melisande nor Marco Stregazza had a hand in it. That's the only place it could be done convincingly, and they've allies in the Temple. 'Twas a false prophecy bid the Doge to step down."

"And gave Melisande Shahrizai sanctuary," Joscelin said grimly.

"No," I said. "That was fairly done, as far as I know. It is Marie-Celeste Stregazza who suborned the Temple. And I have sworn a promise to Asherat-of-the-Sea to cleanse her worship of corruption. It will be there, Joscelin. Tomorrow."

He sat down and set his head in his hands.

"So we will go there, eh?" Kazan's voice broke the silence, cheerful and fierce. Lounging at his ease, propped on one elbow, he glanced around the seated company. "Seven men may die, or eight or nine, yes, but here we are almost twenty, we. I saw this temple from the ship, I. Twenty men is enough, maybe, to take the door and hold it for a little while."

"No." Joscelin spoke without looking up. "Not the Yeshuites."

"Joscelin." Micah protested, and one or two others. "You risked your safety to aid us, when we had naught to offer in return. It is not for you to say how we will repay it."

"You've done enough, and more." Joscelin lifted his head to give him a level stare. "No, Micah. This is not like taking the watchtower. The odds are bad, very bad, and there is no avenue of retreat. It is near-certain death."

"A warrior's death, yes," Kazan added helpfully.

Micah flushed. "Have you not trained us to be warriors?" he asked Joscelin bitterly. "Then treat us as equals and let us fight."

"I trained you that you might fulfill your prophecy and lead your people north." Joscelin's tone was gentle. "Not die in La Serenissima defending my Queen."

"You'll let the Illyrians fight!" another lad burst out in anger.

I glanced at Kazan, wondering how he would take it; fortunately, he was amused, eyebrows raised at the notion of a D'Angeline determining where and when he was allowed to do battle. All the Illyrians, even Ushak, who had seemed so young and green to me when I thought of him risking his life, looked like seasoned veterans next to the Yeshuites. I listened while Joscelin overrode their objections, hoping they would hear reason.

In the midst of it all, the young woman spoke, knitting her brows.

"Joscelin," she said, a soft trace of a Habiru accent in her voice. "What if it *was* like the watchtower?"

SEVENTY-ONE

IT IS impossible to say when the hands of the gods intervene in the affairs of mortals and to what purpose, but of a surety, there are times when they do. Although the Yeshuites have no tradition of women fighting along-side the men such as one finds among the Albans and the Dalriada, the girl Sarae came of a family of notoriously strong-willed women.

She had chosen to learn to defend herself, that she might travel at the side of her beloved, Micah ben Ximon, when they followed Yeshua's prophecy and journeyed northward. In so doing, she had broken ties with her equally strong-willed mother, who had arranged a different marriage for her.

Sarae was not the first woman in her family to have thus defied her parents' wishes.

"My great-great-aunt Onit," she murmured, suddenly shy at speaking to so many attentive listeners, "ran away rather than marry a fat rag merchant, ran away and joined the Temple of Asherat-of-the-Sea. When she was very old, she came home to die. We children were not allowed to see her lest we be corrupted, but we would sneak into her room, to hear tales of the worship of the terrible goddess Asherat." Glancing around, she cleared her throat. "There is a balcony above the temple where the Oracle stands to give prophecy twice a year to the city entire, facing the altar and the people gathered below. Onit told us how it is staged, with an echo chamber to make her voice mighty and a bronze sheet that is rattled for the sound of thunder. We laughed, to think a goddess would need such tricks. There is a secret passageway, too, so it may seem that the Oracle vanishes without descending, while in truth it leads to a tunnel beneath the canals."

There was silence as we considered the implications, save for the murmur of Kazan translating her words into Illyrian for the benefit of his men.

"Where does the tunnel emerge?" Joscelin asked with reluctant interest.

She pushed her hair back from her face, frowning in thought. "To a warehouse, where some things are stored in winter; oil, dried goods and such. It was only to stay for a little while. When the Temple was empty, the Oracle would come back and descend the stairs. Only the priestesses and the temple eunuchs know about it. It would be lightly guarded, if at all."

"Joscelin," I said.

He looked at me. "No. Oh, no."

"It could work."

"In a temple," he said slowly, "full to bursting with Benedicte's and Marco Stregazza's supporters, with the likelihood of rioters breaking in the doors."

I shrugged. "There is an avenue of escape, and a great many folk present who are *not* their supporters, including Cesare Stregazza, who is still technically the Doge."

"You don't have any idea how they mean to kill Ysandre, do you?"

"No." I shook my head, recalling Melisande's words with regret. I had asked. *You know enough.* "A rioter, like as not. They'll seek to lay it at Ricciardo's doorstep, and get rid of him for good. I'm sure witnesses will be found to testify as much. It doesn't matter, Joscelin. If we're there, we stand a chance of preventing it. If we're not, she will die."

"It is a good plan, D'Angeline," Kazan remarked. "Better than storming the door, eh? If we die . . ." he grinned, ". . . many Serenissimans will die with us, yes."

"He likes that idea, doesn't he?" Joscelin asked me, then turned resolutely to Sarae. "All right, then. Do you know where to find this warehouse?"

"Yes." Her voice was strained, her face pale and stubborn. "I will show you . . . if you take us with you to fight at your side."

Joscelin swore and clutched at his tangled hair. "I said no!"

"It is not your choice, apostate," Micah said calmly. "It is ours."

Joscelin opened his mouth to protest again when Ti-Philippe interrupted him. "Joscelin, he's right; it's not our choice. Let them come if they will, and obey orders. They can ward the tunnel and safeguard our retreat. It's no more risk than La Dolorosa, and," he added, eyeing Micah, "I suspect you'd find them in the Square if you don't let them come. At least this way they'll be out of sight, and less likely to be arrested for bearing arms unlawfully."

In the end, there was nothing else for it. Once it was agreed, Sarae went willingly enough with Ti-Philippe to examine the warehouse's security. I misliked the risk, for 'twas near enough to the Great Canal that there would be guards about, but I had to admit, with his gaunt features, rough-spun garb and a farmer's wide-brimmed hat atop his dyed, cropped hair, Ti-Philippe looked nothing like himself. As for Sarae, no one was looking for Yeshuites.

Like as not, I thought, if aught happens, it will be that they are turned away and forced to make a detour; and even at that, Ysandre should have arrived by now, and the net of security will have drawn tight around the Little Court. Still, I would not rest easy until their return.

Kazan and his men set to making windbreaks for the night's shelter, since it seemed we had little choice but to remain on this nameless isle, at least until the small hours of the night. The Yeshuites aided them warily, and Joscelin and I sat together with too much to say and not enough time to say it.

"I'm so sorry," he said at length. "For everything."

"No." I took his hand. "I am. I hurt you in my actions, and wronged you in my thoughts. I drove you to cruelty, I pushed you to breaking, and I took pleasure in it when you did. Joscelin, the fault was mine."

"I gave you reason," he said dryly. "Phèdre, I fell in love with you with both eyes wide open, and fighting against it every step of the way. When you told me you were returning to Naamah's Service, I thought I had bent as far as I could without breaking. When you began spending so much time with Severio, I was sure of it. And when you disappeared, I realized that I hadn't even begun to fathom what I could endure." Glancing down at the silver *khai* pendant that rested still on his chest, he took it in his free hand and gave a short, sharp jerk, snapping the thin chain. "The Yeshuites will have to wait a while longer for Cassiel the Apostate to bow his head before the Mashiach's throne," he said, holding the bright object in his palm. "Elua's priest spoke truly; I choose the path of the Companion."

I folded his fingers over the pendant and leaned over to kiss his hand. "Keep it. You've done what you could for them. You've given them the means to survive."

"If I can keep them alive long enough." He brushed my hair with his fingertips, saying my name with wonder. "I thought I had lost you, truly."

"And I thought I was truly lost," I said. "More than once. But here we are."

"Until tomorrow, at least." Joscelin gave his faint smile. "Is there any chance I can convince you not to go?"

I shook my head. "No. I began this, after all, and I've faced too many kinds of death and madness not to see it through."

"I thought as much." He pondered our joined hands. "Is there any chance we'll live to see the end, do you think?"

"There's a chance," I said. "If we can turn the tide against Prince Benedicte, even for a little bit, Marco Stregazza may turn with it rather than fall with his ally. If he sees danger and a chance to save himself, he'll take it." I stirred, thinking. "Joscelin, do you think one of your Yeshuites could get word to Ricciardo Stregazza? He's confined to house arrest, but if the Scholae still answer to him, those who aren't in Marco's pocket, they might serve to counter the rioters."

"It might arouse suspicion, if he's guarded," he said thoughtfully.

"What about his wife?" I remembered Allegra Stregazza, seated at her desk in the charming library over-looking their estates, writing out a letter of introduction for me. It had gotten me into the Little Court, where I had walked in the Queen's Garden with Madame Felicity d'Arbos and admired the charming sight of Prince Benedicte's veiled wife and her babe on the balcony. "She has a name for being eccentric, a woman of letters in La Serenissima. Would it arouse suspicion if a young Yeshuite scholar delivered her a scroll?"

"Probably not," Joscelin admitted, grinning involun-tarily. "Your mind still turns out ideas like a Siovalese windmill churns grain."

"It works better when I'm with you," I said. "Do you have pen and paper on this forsaken isle?"

"We might." He rose. "Teppo's scholar enough to have brought it . . . oh, wait, I have something that will serve for paper, at any rate." Disappearing into one of the tents, he reemerged with a packet wrapped in oilskin. "After Ti-Philippe turned up with his tale, I went to Mafeo Bardoni, your factor's man here. I thought if there was any chance you'd left word with him, I should get to him before anyone else did. You'd gotten a letter from home," he said, handing it over. "Eugènie sent it in care of your factor's man, since you'd never written with another address. I looked," he added as I began to open it. "But 'twas naught to do with your disappearance."

It was, in fact, a letter from Micheline de Parnasse, the Royal Archivist, who had at last heard a reply from the Prefect of the Cassiline Brotherhood; one Lord Calval, who had inherited the post when Lord Rinforte passed away at the end of a long illness. In accordance with her long-ago promise, she enclosed a list of those Cassiline Brothers who had attended House de la Courcel, the information excised from the ledger in the Royal Archives.

"You saw what this is?" I asked Joscelin.

He nodded. "You learned as much from Thelesis de Mornay's inquiries," he said, shrugging and adding laconically, "I wrote too, you know. Lord Calval never bothered to answer me."

"The Cassiline Brotherhood has not declared the Royal Archivist anathema," I said absently. "You, they have. Joscelin, this list isn't the same as the one Thelesis gathered."

"No?" He crouched to peer over my shoulder. "What's different?"

My lord Delaunay used to challenge Alcuin and me to exert our powers of observance and memory, quizzing us at unexpected intervals about the most seemingly innocuous of things. It is a habit that has stuck with me all my life. I daresay I would not have scanned the entire list, had it not been for that. But I did, and I came across a name that made my blood run cold with foreboding, my hand rising of its own volition to cover it.

Your Queen, does she not already have such guards in her service?

"Thelesis' list only had the adoptive names of those taken into Lord Rinforte's household, the names such as the Cassiline Brothers themselves offered to her," I whispered. "This comes direct from the Prefect's archives, and gives their names in full. The ledger in the Royal Archives, the one that was desecrated, must have done the same. Oh,

Joscelin! I think I know how they're planning to kill Ysandre."

He knew what I was reading. He looked sick. "Let me see."

I moved my hand to reveal a name: David de Rocaille nó Rinforte.

"De Rocaille," Joscelin said aloud, and swallowed. "David de Rocaille."

"You're Siovalese, and a Cassiline," I said softly. "Joscelin, Ysandre's mother Isabel was responsible for the death of Edmée de Rocaille. I ought to know; it's what began Delaunay's feud with her. Did Edmée de Rocaille have a brother who joined the Brethren?"

"I don't know." He pressed the heels of his hands into his eyes. "I never followed the genealogies of the Great Houses of Siovale; I knew I was bound for Cassiel's service. And if he was among the Cassilines . . . I don't know. He would have left, by the time I began training. Ah, Elua!" He dropped his hands, looking at me with anguish. "That soldier, among the Unforgiven . . . he said he saw it, didn't he? A Cassiline Brother, escorting the woman he thought was Persia Shahrizai."

"Svariel of L'Agnace said it," I murmured. "Fortun had it written in his notes."

"Why would he do it?" Joscelin demanded, slightly wild-eyed. "Why now, after so long? Why take revenge on someone for the crimes of her mother? Even if it's true, if he's been attendant on Ysandre, he could have done it at any time! Why now?"

"I don't know." I made my voice gentle. "Melisande blackmailed Percy de Somerville; mayhap he did the same to de Rocaille, or she did. He hid his name a-purpose, to be sure; the timing suits her needs, and the diversion his; the other Cassilines on guard will be distracted. Mayhap he was waiting for the same thing as Prince Benedicte, a true-born D'Angeline heir — and one untainted by L'Envers blood — to inherit. Mayhap I'm wrong, after all. 'Tis only a guess."

"No," he said dully. "All the pieces are there. It makes too much sense, Phèdre. A riot for distraction, yes; but what assassin could be sure to break through the Queen's guard, Cassilines included? This way, it is certain. And Benedicte and Melisande and Marco . . . as you said, all the world would see their hands were clean."

Perversely, I found myself arguing against it, willing it for Joscelin's sake not to be. "Still, it would be suicide on his part."

He gave a short laugh, raking his hands through his hair. "Yes," he said simply. "If David de Rocaille nó Rinforte is considering killing the Queen of Terre d'Ange, he is preparing to die." I had no words left, and merely knelt, wrapping my arms around him. After a moment, Joscelin shuddered, hands rising to grip mine. "And if that is the case," he whispered, "I will oblige him. All right. Let me go, and I'll see if Teppo has pen and ink to spare."

In a short time, he brought the young Yeshuite, a fine-featured lad whose hands bore calluses and inkstains alike. Teppo stammered out a greeting, laying before me a wealth of scholar's supplies; inkpot and quill, and some good pieces of foolscap. I penned a swift note to Allegra Stregazza. "My lady, you aided me once in kindness with an introduction to your mother's friend. I tell you in turn that Marco Stregazza conspires with Benedicte de la Courcel against your lord, his brother Ricciardo, rousing

the Scholae to blacken his name. Let him order those
guildsmen who are loyal to keep the peace in the Campo
Grande during the investiture ceremony; for if he does not,
he will be named a conspirator in the death of a Queen.
This I swear is true."

I didn't sign it; Allegra Stregazza would know well
enough who I was, and if the letter was intercepted, she
could yet deny it, for all the good it did her. And Teppo,
who rolled the letter carefully between two scrolls, reverence in his inkstained fingers, he would go himself; he
insisted on it.

Another frail barque, I thought, watching him go,
wending his way through the underbrush; another ship of
hope, bearing my words. I wondered if the letters I had
sent to the Lady of Marsilikos and the Duc L'Envers had
arrived, and if they had acted upon them.

There was little time for contemplation, for a commo-
tion had erupted in the encampment. Blades clashed and
shouts rang out, a mix of Illyrian, Caerdicci and Habiru.

"Name of Elua," Joscelin muttered. "What now?"

I should have guessed, if I'd thought on it. Kazan's
men were putting Joscelin's Yeshuites to the test. We
arrived at the center of the camp to find Stajeo and Micah
circling one another. Such will happen, when men who
are strangers to one another hone their weapons together.
The Illyrian had his buckler and short sword, his guard a
trifle high and a broad smile on his face. Micah ben Ximon
held two daggers in the Cassiline fashion, watchful and
wary, his steps tracing the forms Joscelin had drilled into
him with no small measure of competency.

"Kazan," I sighed. "This is foolishness."

He came over to stand beside Joscelin and me, shrugging carelessly. "So you say, you, but my men, they will not like it, to fight beside untrained boys with knives in their hands, no. If he is worthy, let him prove it, eh, and we will all fight better for it."

"Joscelin." I turned to him in appeal.

"Micah can handle himself," he said absently, watching. "He's very good, for coming to it so late. See?"

As we watched, Micah feinted with the left-hand dagger; with a cunning move, Stajeo made to bring the edge of his buckler down hard on his arm. The Yeshuite whirled swiftly, somehow moving beneath the blow to end with the tip of his right-hand dagger pointed at the Illyrian's belly.

Kazan whistled through his teeth. The other Illyrians laughed and applauded, and Stajeo stepped back with a sour look on his face, putting up his sword in acknowledgement of surrender. Micah gave a quick Cassiline bow and sheathed his daggers.

"They will fight," Kazan said, satisfied. He eyed Joscelin. "You taught him that?"

"Yes." Joscelin nodded his approval to Micah, who flushed with pleasure.

"Why without swords, eh? It is clever, this fighting, but on a battlefield . . ." Kazan drew his hand across his throat. "Pfft!"

"Because Yeshuites are forbidden to bear weapons in La Serenissima," Joscelin said in a hard tone. "As elsewhere. And a dagger, a pair of daggers, may be concealed, where a sword may not. It is what I was taught, my lord Atrabiades, because I am trained first and foremost not to take life on the battlefield, but to defend in close quarters, where a sword may be hampered by innocent flesh."

"But you carry a sword, you," Kazan said casually. "Do you know how to use it, eh?"

"Yes," Joscelin said.

I held my tongue at the understatement. "Kazan," I said. "Cassilines draw their swords only to kill. He does. Trust me in this matter."

Kazan Atrabiades looked at me sidelong, and the whole of our history was in that glance. When all was said and done, it was a considerable one. He grinned and made me a sweeping bow. "As you wish. My men will fight beside his, eh, and that is enough. But I am interested, I, to see what happens when this D'Angeline draws his sword!"

He left us, laughing, to join the others in commiserating with Stajeo on his defeat. Joscelin watched him a moment, then turned to me with raised brows.

"You do find interesting companions, Phèdre," was all he said.

"Yes." I looked evenly at him. "A score of his men died who might not have, had they not fought the Serenissimans on my behalf. All who are with him, and Kazan himself, are willing to die at our sides. Do you have a quarrel with that?"

"No." Putting his hands on my shoulders, Joscelin drew me close. "Should I?"

I rather liked this new side of him. It would be nice, I thought wistfully, if we both lived to enjoy it.

SEVENTY-TWO ☉

TI-PHILIPPE AND Sarae returned in the early evening hours, excited and full of talk. It seemed the warehouse was unguarded from the outside, and largely unwatched by Serenissiman guards to boot. If any of us had had doubts, that sealed it. Our plan was set. In the small hours before dawn, we would take the warehouse by stealth, and gain our access to the Temple of Asherat-of-the-Sea.

The young Yeshuite scholar Teppo returned too, albeit with less information. Marco Stregazza's guards set to enforce his brother's house arrest had allowed him to deliver his scrolls without much interest, but they had been taken by a maidservant; whether or not they had found their way into Allegra's hands – and what her reaction – he could not say.

Well and so, I had expected no more, and was glad that all had returned alive.

Pooling our stores of food in common, we put together a tolerable meal of small game – rabbit, and a brace of ducks – dressed with autumn berries, wild greens and a dish of pulses. The Illyrians shared around several skins of wine and there was fresh water in plenty from a spring-fed creek on the isle. Afterward, the hours of the night watch were divided among our company, with considerable arguing over who would take the vital duties.

Dark was falling as the Yeshuites huddled together, quarreling among themselves softly in Habiru. Kazan watched idly, and I knew him well enough to guess that the Illyrians would maintain a separate watch of their own.

"I will take the first watch," Joscelin announced, looking to put an end to it. "And Philippe the last. Settle the middle among yourselves. Will that suffice?"

"But . . . Joscelin." One of the young men – Elazar, his name was – looked flustered. "We thought . . . you are D'Angeline, after all, and you risked your life to rescue her . . ."

Joscelin looked uncomprehendingly at him.

"Your tent," Elazar said lamely. "We . . . well, you will see."

And see we did, how they had set a pair of lighted oil lamps within his humble tent, strewing the bedroll and rough ground with lateblooming wood roses, small and fragrant, painstakingly gathered from the dense undergrowth. I caught my breath and let it out in a gasping laugh. Ti-Philippe grinned with a trace of his old mischief, the Yeshuites shuffled in embarrassment and Oltukh, peering over their shoulders, called back a comment in Illyrian that roused laughter from several of Kazan's men.

"Phèdre . . ." Joscelin said, his voice trailing off and he glanced at me. "This need not . . ."

"No?" I raised my brows at him. "We are D'Angeline, after all."

After a second's pause, Joscelin laughed, a free and

unfettered sound I hadn't heard since Montrève. With one easy motion, he scooped me into his arms. "Micah," he said over his shoulder, ducking to step through the tent flap, "take the first watch. Philippe, wake me when it's time."

And with that, he closed the flap behind us.

Naamah's gift is manifold, and I have known it in many forms; still, I think, none have I cherished so much as that night with Joscelin on an unnamed isle of La Serenissima. After so much had passed, we were nearly strangers to one another, and yet at once so achingly familiar. I had forgotten the sheer, breathtaking beauty of him, gleaming like sculpted marble in the lamplight. Without artistry, without aught but love and simple desire, I relearned his flesh inch by inch. And Joscelin . . . ah, Elua! Whatever had broken in him, it loosed the passion he held in rigid check so much, too much, of the time; his hands and mouth moved on me until I pleaded for release and he took me with a tender fury, autumn roses trapped beneath my body, sharp, cunning thorns pricking my naked skin. It was a goad to my pleasure and he knew it and did not care, a secret smile curving my lips as he lowered his head to kiss me.

Afterward, we lay entangled together without speaking for a long while.

"I've missed you," I murmured at length against the hard curve of his shoulder. "Awfully. For a long time, Joscelin."

"So have I." He ran his fingers through my hair where it lay across his chest. "Is that pirate of yours going to challenge me for this, do you think?"

"No." I kissed his shoulder. "Not likely."

"Good," he said drowsily. "I'd hate to kill him, since you seem rather fond of him."

I thought of all I had not told him yet – the *kríavbhog*, the Kore and the *thetalos*, my bargain with Kazan and his brother's death – all of that, and more. And I laughed softly, because it did not matter; right now, none of it mattered. If there was time, if we lived, Elua willing, I would tell it all to him, yes, and hear his stories too, all that he had left unsaid, including whether or not he had indeed hacked off his hair with a dagger, which is rather what it looked like.

And if there was not . . . we had had this night, and Naamah's gift.

I have been her Servant a long time, I thought. This, I have earned.

So thinking, I fell asleep, and for all the restless nights I had passed, for all the myriad worries that plagued my brain, with Joscelin's arms around me and his breathing steady beneath my ear, I slept dreamless as a babe until Ti-Philippe scratching discreetly at the tent awoke us.

'Tis only my opinion, but I daresay I have seen my share and more of those chill, dank hours before dawn, when the resentful moon begins its descent and the stars grow distant and sullen. I scrambled into my clothing – a Kritian gown, an Illyrian cloak, no trace of my homeland to comfort me – while Joscelin, swift to don his attire, was already out and about in the encampment.

By the time I emerged, our company was mustered, and an ill-assembled lot we were. The Yeshuites looked painfully young, fingering their weapons and doing their best to summon expressions of stern resolve.

"My friends," I said to them. "We go forth this day into certain danger. Pray, if any one of you here is not fully resolved in your heart to do this thing, stand down

now, for it is no quarrel of yours and there is no shame in
quitting it. For the aid you have given us, I will ever be
grateful." I waited in the crepuscular silence. No one
moved. "So be it. Then let us be comrades-in-arms, few
though we may be, and set ourselves against the forces of
greed and ambition that seek to claim by stealth and treachery what is not rightfully theirs. Let us show the world that
honor is not forgotten, and that the gods themselves – the
gods of Illyria, of Terre d'Ange, of the Yeshuites, of La
Serenissima itself – will lend their aid when men and
women seek with utmost courage to do that which is
right."

And with that, I told them my plan. The girl Sarae's
eyes widened and she ducked her head, fidgeting with
the crossbow she held; whether or not she thought it
blasphemous, I could not say. The Yeshuites murmured.
Ti-Philippe swore admiringly. Kazan Atrabiades laughed
so hard he had difficulty translating for his men. Some of
the Illyrians grinned, when they heard it; some made
superstitious gestures to avert evil.

Joscelin looked at me for a long time without comment. "Have you lost your mind?" he said at length. "No."

"What else would you have us do? If we make it
inside, we won't have the option of stealth." I watched the
thoughts flicker behind his eyes. "Joscelin, we're outnumbered. *Ysandre* is outnumbered. Even if we succeed in
gaining access to the warehouse, to reaching the Temple –
what if it's not enough to warn her? Melisande and Marco
have too much to lose, and too many allies at hand. We
need to turn some of them, or at least confuse them. I can't
think of another way. Can you?"

He closed his eyes. "No."

"I have sworn a vow," I said softly, "and this is how I mean to keep it."

He opened his eyes and looked at me. "And if it goes awry?"

I shrugged. "We run like hell, and pray they haven't surrounded the warehouse." I looked around at their watching faces. "Does anyone have a better plan?" No one did. "All right," I said. "Shall we go?"

In that, at least, no one was disagreed; we set out across the rough terrain, scrabbling our way through near-darkness to the water's edge, where our vessels lay concealed. Two skiffs in total, and our hard-won gondola. Dense ferns lay rotting in the water; to this day, the smell of decaying foliage brings that morning back to me in all its nerve-strung anxiety. A thin mist hovered above the river. I took my place beneath the awning of the gondola, as there was no room in the smaller skiffs. With soft splashing and a few muffled curses, we were launched.

It was a tense journey, especially once we were off the sedge-choked river and into the canals proper, wending our path through the waterways of La Serenissima. Once a bissone full of drunken rowdies returning home from the mean tenements of the courtesan's quarter passed nearby to us, voices raised in a ragged, off-key tune, the lantern in their prow casting wavering light over the dark waters. We hid ourselves in the shadows alongside the canal, all of us crouching low and scarce daring to breathe. Once they had gone, the oarsmen set our vessels to gliding silently out once more.

The street on which the warehouse was located was a quiet one; the residences were slightly more modest than those that lined the Great Canal, interspersed with some of the more elegant trade establishments, jewelers and drapers and the like. Beyond the two-storied roofs, I could see the pointed domes of the Temple of Asherat-of-the-Sea looming in the predawn sky to obscure the paling stars.

"There," Sarae whispered, her voice carrying faintly over the water. She pointed to a marble building, long and low, with a single entrance at street level. In the first skiff, Ti-Philippe was already making for it. We came noiselessly alongside and disembarked. One oarsmen stayed in each of the smaller rowboats, and a pair of Illyrians in the gondola.

"Get as near to the harbor as you dare, and turn the boats loose," Joscelin murmured in Caerdicci. "Come back swiftly, but have a care for guards."

I repeated it in Illyrian, and Kazan nodded curt agreement. If we had any hope of going undetected, it would hardly do to have three strange vessels moored in the vicinity. The oarsmen pushed off and headed toward the harbor, quick and stealthy.

It left fifteen of us huddled on the dark street, a motley assortment bristling with arms, dreadfully suspicious and vulnerable to any passers-by. I thought of the looming temple domes and shivered. One outcry was all it would take to bring the Serenissiman Guard down on us.

The door to the warehouse was of solid oaken construction, half again as tall as a man, with Asherat's crown of stars etched in silver. Joscelin and Kazan both felt at it, drawing daggers to pry at the hinges and the massive lock. It was well and truly bolted, secured from within, the hinges set deep and tight. The Illyrians muttered under their breath. I wrapped my cloak around me and shifted from foot to foot, tense and nervous. Kazan swore and struck the marble blocks of the building with the heel of his palm; one of the Habiru made a stifled sound in his throat.

I couldn't stand it any longer. "Name of Elua! Joscelin, get out of the way," I hissed, wrenching loose the silver falcon brooch that clasped my cloak. He stepped aside obligingly and Kazan raised his eyebrows as I stuck the pin between my teeth, bending the tip into a tiny hook. Crouching, I worked it into the lock, feeling my way for the tumbler that would drop the bar on the far side and silently blessing Hyacinthe for having taught me this dubious skill. 'Twas not a difficult lock, but it was a heavy one and I held my breath as I caught the tumbler, maneuvering it with delicacy lest it bend the slender silver pin.

In the midst of my operation came the sound of pelting footsteps, bare feet slapping softly on the wooden walkway; the oarsmen, returning. I didn't dare look up, but I heard a gasping voice. "A squadron of guardsmen coming on foot! Halfway to the corner!"

Illyrian steel scraped as Kazan's men reached for their hilts, and I heard an anxious, murmured prayer in Habiru. "Phèdre?" Joscelin's voice asked calmly.

I closed my eyes and bore down on the pin, levering the tumbler to the left. The pin bent, bent . . . and held. With a solid chunking sound, the bar dropped. Clutching my cloak closed with one hand, I set the other to the handle of the warehouse door and tried it.

It gave, opening onto a wedge of dark interior.

"Go, go!"

We piled inside in a mass, barefoot oarsmen with boots in hand, no order of procedure to our company, and someone closed the door behind us, softly and firmly. Inside, it was wholly dark. There were high windows along the outer wall to admit daylight, but nothing penetrated in these small hours before dawn. Whispering, shuffling bodies jostled me. Someone trod on the hem of my cloak, nearly jerking it from my shoulders. I took it off and wrapped it over one arm.

It would have looked humorous, I imagine, if anyone could have seen us in our tight, milling knot. No doubt it did when a door at the rear of the main chamber was thrown open and a sudden blaze of torchlight fell over us.

"What . . . ?" It was one of the Temple eunuchs, blinking and sleepy-eyed, a torch in one upraised hand and his ceremonial spear held loosely in the other, silver barbed head pointing at the floor. And no more than that did he say, for Sarae, acting on terrified reflex, brought up her crossbow and fired at him.

The barb took him in the throat; he blinked once more, slow and surprised, while his spear fell with a clatter. Still clutching his torch, he sank to his knees and slumped forward, facedown and motionless, the torch now guttering on the floor beside his outstretched hand.

It was Kazan and his men who raced forward instantly, swords drawn and bucklers raised, hurdling the fallen figure to enter the chambers beyond. They were pirates, after all, scourges of the sea, trained to a swarming attack. Sick at heart, I followed, while Joscelin and Ti-Philippe set grimly about retrieving the torch and directing the Yeshuites to search the rest of the building.

There had been four attendants in all set to watch over the warehouse; there were sleeping quarters, a privy chamber and a meager kitchen beyond the door from which the first had emerged. Two more were dead by the time I got there, slain half-naked in their beds, and Tormos had his sword raised for the killing stroke against the fourth.

"No!" I cried. He paused. "Eisheth's mercy, we don't need them dead, Kazan!" I pleaded. "Let him live, and he may show us the passage."

Kazan hesitated, then said shortly, "Do as she says."

They had been young, the attendants of the warehouse; the survivor was no exception. I guessed him no older than Joscelin's Yeshuites, though 'twas harder to tell since he was cut and beardless. He watched with wide, terrified eyes as the Illyrians cleaned their weapons and I drew near.

"What is your name?" I asked softly.

"Cer . . . Cervianus." Shock and fear prompted his stuttering answer.

"Cervianus, aid us and you will live, I promise. There is a passage below the canals to the Temple of Asherat. I need you to show us."

His eyes darted this way and that and his throat moved as he swallowed audibly, but for all his terror, he was no coward. "I know of no such passage."

"Do you fear to betray the goddess?" I asked him, and his eyes fixed on my face, pupils dilating. "Cervianus, I swear to you, Asherat-of-the-Sea has already been betrayed, by one who stands high in her favor, and this night's doings are the fruit of that betrayal. Although I serve another, I have come to avenge her."

Some of Kazan's men grumbled; they had come to kill Serenissimans. I ignored them.

No coward and no fool, Cervianus. He licked his lips, trembling. "And if I do not aid you? What then?"

"You will die," I said. "And we will find it anyway."

He closed his eyes briefly. "It's in the underchamber. The door is hidden. Let me put on clothing, and I will show you."

The Illyrians stepped back, allowing him to rise. Trusting to Kazan to keep order, I returned to the warehouse space. Joscelin and the others were waiting; there had been no one else present, only rows of oil jars and stacks of dried goods, as Sarae had claimed. She was pale-faced and shaky, and Micah was attempting to soothe her. Joscelin met my eyes as I returned.

"She killed a man in cold blood," he said. "It takes one hard."

"I know," I said. "Where did you get crossbows, anyway?"

"We took them from the guards at the watchtower at La Dolorosa." He glanced at her with pity. "I thought it would be safer for her to carry one. We're doomed anyway if we're caught, and she's not skilled with the daggers."

I unfolded my cloak and shook it out, settling it over my shoulders and shoving the bent brooch-pin through the woolen fabric and fastening it. "Her ill luck to be a good shot," I said wryly. "Mayhap 'tis better they know such things, before they choose to battle their way to the northlands. Prophecies never name the blood-price they exact."

"No." Joscelin roused himself with a shake. "The others?"

"Dead, but for one," I said. "He's agreed to show us the passage. I promised him his life for it."

"Let's go, then."

Another torch and a few lamps had been found and kindled, and by their light, Cervianus led us to the rear of the warehouse. He had donned the deep-blue tunic of Asherat's attendants, the emblem of her starry crown worked in silver thread on the breast, rich and glimmering amid the Illyrians who surrounded him, but his eyes looked like dark holes in the mask of his face.

"It is there," he said faintly, pointing at a mammoth clay vessel, shoulder-high to Kazan. "Beneath the jar."

With a doubtful grunt, Kazan set his shoulder to the jar and shoved. It tilted beneath his force, being empty, and two others joined him in rolling it carefully to one side. Cervianus had spoken the truth. Beneath lay a trapdoor, set flush into the stones of the floor. Joscelin grasped the iron ring and hauled up on it; with a faint screech of hinges, the door opened to reveal a gaping square of darkness below, smelling of stale air and mildew. There were worn stone steps leading downward, the first few visible by torchlight.

"And this leads to the Oracle's balcony in the Temple proper, yes?" I asked Cervianus.

"Yes." He turned his hollow gaze on me. "Beneath the canal."

"And the Oracle does not preside from thence over the ceremony of investiture?"

"N . . . no." Cervianus hesitated, and shook his head. "Only twice a year, at the *Fatum Urbanus*. I think. I do not know, for certain. I am only a junior attendant, and a Doge has never been invested in my lifetime. But . . ."

"But they would have told you, were the tunnel to be opened for the Oracle's usage, would they not?" I asked gently. "That you might make ready to receive her, until she could return unseen."

"Yes." He stared at me with bitter hatred in his shadowed eyes. I did not blame him. "It is our duty, to keep the inventory and ward the passage. They would have told us."

"So." Joscelin knelt beside the open trap door, holding a lamp and peering into the darkness below. "Are there guards within the tunnel, or at the other end?"

"There are no other *guards!*" Cervianus spat out the words in fury. "It was our duty, our sacred duty! No one knows of this passage. A thousand and more years ago, the masons who built it were slain to keep it secret."

"Charming," Joscelin murmured. Sarae made an involuntary sound, choked at the realization of the extent to which her great-great-aunt Onit's death-bed tales had betrayed the trade-secrets of the order that had sheltered her for most of her life. I sat on my heels, thinking.

"Cervianus," I asked, "what is happening in the Temple now?"

He gave a sullen shrug, then winced when Kazan Atrabiades prodded his ribs with a dagger. "The Priestess of the Crown and her six Elect hold a vigil, praying that Asherat-of-the-Sea will accept the people's choice as Her Beloved and a true bond may be forged. So I am told. At dawn the preparations begin, and when the sun strikes the crown of Her image which overlooks the harbor, the procession will begin from the Doge's Palace to enter the Temple."

"Then," I said, "we had best make ready."

SEVENTY-THREE

THE STEPS leading down into the tunnel were narrow and treacherous, overgrown with a slick coating of mold. I could well believe this passage was used but twice a year. We went in single file, with Joscelin in the lead. I followed close on his heels and Ti-Philippe behind me; Kazan and his Illyrians followed.

After the bloodshed in the warehouse, the Yeshuites were less loathe to be left behind to secure our retreat. Those who had fought on the mainland at La Dolorosa had done so against armed prison guards; 'twas another matter altogether, this slaying out of hand of innocent attendants, ceremonial spears or no. We found a stack of grain sacks bound with twine and cut the cord, using it to tie Cervianus securely, hand and foot, gagging him with a wad of bed-linen.

It pained me, but there was nothing else for it. I had promised him his life, and we could not risk leaving him free to give an alarm. The gag cut sharply into the corners of his mouth, and his sunken eyes continued to glare hatred at me. I spoke to him before we left.

"For what it is worth," I said to him, "I spoke the truth to you, Cervianus. I am sorry for the deaths of your companions."

His expression never changed. Kazan, passing, caught my arm. "Do not waste such pity on him, you," he advised in a grim tone. "If we had not taken them by surprise, eh, the catamites would have killed us, yes. You heard him speak of the tunnel, eh? They do not hesitate to kill for their goddess."

It was true – and yet. I knew beyond doubt that if I lay coiled once more enduring the agonies of the *thetalos*, I would endure the bloodguilt of their deaths. So be it. I had made my choices, knowing full well I must live with the consequences. 'Twas only pain, after all; and who better equipped to bear it than I? Surely, I thought, though it never be given us to know, the tally of the living must outweigh the dead.

If we did not fail.

Down and down and down went the stairs, growing ever more slippery. Once my heel skidded and I put out a hand to catch myself, finding the walls green with slime, moisture seeping between the solid blocks of stone. We were beneath a city built on water. By the time we reached the floor of the tunnel, the air had grown increasingly dank. The flame of Joscelin's oil lamp guttered, and I felt my lungs working for sustenance. The passage is open at our end, I reminded myself; surely air must be moving in it. Joscelin held up his hand and waited patiently for the flame to steady, growing brighter. Massed behind us, the Illyrians muttered superstitiously, falling silent at Kazan's harsh order.

We proceeded.

I do not know how far it was, that stone-sealed journey
beneath a city built on water. Not far, I suppose; a mere
city block, as the architects would reckon it. Outside, I had
seen the domes of the Temple and shuddered at their near-
ness. Below ground, it seemed a world away. The dense,
sodden stone absorbed the sound of our footfalls until we
seemed a line of shuffling wraiths. I felt a weariness born of
dampness and chill and stone, the never-ending dark eye of
the tunnel opening on and on before us. It came almost as
a shock when Joscelin stopped in front of me and gazed
upward, lifting the lamp.

Another set of stairs, equally steep and narrow, leading
upward to vanish in darkness.

"This is it," Joscelin whispered. "Phèdre, the plan is
yours. What do you will?"

I gazed up the stairs, straining eyes and ears, but I
could not penetrate the darkness and no sound filtered
down to us in the tunnel. "Let me go first and see," I
whispered back. "If the priestesses of Asherat are the only
danger, I'm best equipped to avoid it."

His face tightened. "And if they're not, you're the
worst. I'm coming with you."

"Will you stay three paces behind and wait on the stair
for my signal?"

Joscelin paused, then gave a curt nod.

"Good." I turned to the others. "Wait here. We'll
investigate, and send word."

Ti-Philippe let out a sigh of resignation; he knew
better than to try talking me out of anything. Kazan
frowned. "I do not like it any better than *he* does, I," he
said in a low voice, jerking his chin at Joscelin. "That
you should walk first into danger, no. Better one of us."

I smiled in the dim, lamplit tunnel. "You named me rightly when you named me a spy, my lord, long ago on Dobrek. This is what I am trained to do. I would no more allow you to go in my place than you would allow me to lead your men in battle."

Someone at the rear — Volos, I thought — offered an Illyrian jest under his breath regarding the nature and extent of my training. I was glad of the dim light hiding my blush, and doubly glad that Joscelin spoke not a word of Illyrian. Kazan's mouth twitched in a reluctant smile. "Then be careful, you," he said aloud.

I nodded, took a deep breath, and began to ascend the stair.

It is harder to move silently in utter blackness, which is what I found myself in once the sharply rising walls cut off sight of the tunnel below. All sounds seem magnified, and one is prone to a vertiginous unsteadiness without vision's markers. As well that Delaunay made Alcuin and me train at such things blindfolded. I let my fingertips trail along the slimy walls and climbed steadily, step by noiseless step. True to his word, Joscelin followed several paces behind me. He did a fair job of stealth — Cassilines are trained to move with grace and balance and discretion, all of which stood him in good stead — but I could hear him clearly enough; an occasional scrape or creak of leather, the faint sound of his breathing.

Then again, I am trained to hear such things, too.

As it happens, our stealth on the stair was unnecessary; 'twas sealed at the top with another door. I felt at the slick, mossy wood with both hands and pressed my ear to it, grimacing with distaste. Faintly, very faintly, I could make out the sound of voices beyond, a low, rhythmic chanting.

In the Temple, I thought; not near enough to be immediately on the other side of the door. I tried the handle cautiously. It was locked, of course.

"The eunuch may have a key." Joscelin spoke at my ear, so quietly his breath scarce stirred my hair.

"And he may not," I murmured in reply, reaching for my brooch. " 'Twill be quicker, this way." I found the lock by touch, working the pin in blindly; it does not matter, for such a task. The faint scratching sound rattled loud in my ears.

"I am sorry," Joscelin said almost inaudibly, "we never found a way to free him."

So he thought of Hyacinthe too.

"Don't say never. We're not dead yet." The lock gave and I held my breath at the thundering clatter, going still and listening.

"Did you get it?" Joscelin whispered; he hadn't heard a thing. "Is it open?"

I nodded, forgetting he couldn't see. "Stay back." I turned the handle, opening the door narrowly. Only a dim, ambient light filtered through the crack and I could hear the chanting more clearly now. Four or more voices; it was hard to discern, in unison, but of a surety, it came from a distance, echoing from the dome of the Temple. I listened hard for anything nearer, and heard naught. Repinning my cloak, I drew its hood up and slipped through the door, ducking low to crouch with both hands splayed on the floor.

Nothing before me, and only the door behind. I was in a low-ceilinged hall that slanted upward toward a tall, narrow archway. It framed a balconied alcove, in which sat a three-legged stool. To the right and left of the alcove, clearly visible from behind, were openings onto dark chambers, slanted recesses which, like the hallway, would have been nearly undetectable from the front. Lying flat on my belly, I squirmed forward, positioning myself behind the stool to gaze through its legs and the balustrade beyond into the Temple.

Directly opposite me was the massive visage of Asherat-of-the-Sea, wide-eyed and staring, a crescent moon adorning her brow; old, this goddess was, ancient and mighty! I caught my breath, staring back at her, feeling a cold sweat break out between my shoulder blades. I have come to keep my promise, I reminded her silently; have a care for your children's children, O Asherat!

Below, the Temple was filled with candlelight and the sweet blue smoke of incense. I wormed my way forward to peer down at the sight. Seven women stood before the stone altar and the mighty image of the goddess; seven women clad in robes of flowing blue silk, with silver netting overlaying it and shimmering, crystal-strung veils. The one in the center wore a tiara on her unbound hair, with seven diamonds set in starry silver rays. The Priestess of the Crown, I thought, and her six Elect. One had hair as white as milkweed, upraised hands gnarled with age; old Bianca, who had told my fortune true. This would be her balcony from which I espied, then, for surely she was the rightful Oracle.

I felt a little better, to think on it.

And which had betrayed their goddess for gold or mortal power? Vespasia, I knew; that was the name of Bianca's successor, who had given the Doge false foretelling. Was she one of the Elect? I had no way of guessing. The Priestess of the Crown? Mayhap. If not her, it had to be one or more of the Elect. Such risk, such blasphemy, was not undertaken lightly, without surety of gain. Face-to-face, I might have gauged it; hidden above, I could discern little.

There were two sets of stairs curving down from balcony, leading to the floor below. Slithering like an eel, I checked both and found them empty; only pink-veined marble steps disappearing from my sight where they curved, framed by gilded railings. Well and good; thus far, at least, Cervianus had not lied. I backed my way carefully to gaze inside the hidden flanking rooms.

Echo chambers, both of them; Sarae's great-great-aunt Onit had spoken true, too. I had some little knowledge of such things, by virtue of my friendship with Thelesis de Mornay. Each had sounding boards, cunningly set, to conduct the Oracle's voice into the chamber, and thence into the vaulted ceiling of the central dome, magnifying it vastly. A trick, I thought, to pitch one's voice just so; but it could be done in either direction, to the right or left. One held a flexible sheet of bronze, rigged to a mechanism with lever and cogs. This I guessed to be the thunder machine. The Hellenes had such devices of old.

Save for the bronze sheet and some ceremonial items — incensors and the like — the chambers were empty. Satisfied with my inquiry, I withdrew discreetly and slipped through the door to rejoin Joscelin.

" 'Twill suit, for our needs," I said in lowered tones. "It is as Cervianus said; they maintain a vigil below. Let Ti-Philippe join us, and Kazan's Illyrians wait behind this door, on the stair. I'd sooner they were out of the way, and quiet."

Joscelin nodded, barely visible in the faint, filtered

light. "It's a mad plan, Phèdre," he whispered. "You know that, don't you?"

"Madder than singing Skaldi hearth-songs to the Master of the Straits?" I whispered back.

"No." He grinned in the darkness. "That was mine, wasn't it? Blame it on the Tsingano, then, for putting me in Mendacant's robes, and pray yours works half as well."

"Believe me," I said fervently, "I do." Reaching blindly for him, I brushed his cheek with my fingertips, caught a double handful of his shorn, tangled hair and kissed him hard. "Elua keep you, whatever happens."

"And you," Joscelin whispered against my lips. "And you, my love."

In all the time we had been together, in all that we had endured, I couldn't remember him calling me that. I let him go, breath catching in my throat. "Go on, then, and bring them."

He did, and in short order we were all positioned. With every sense and every nerve on edge, I thought the rustling and creaking and whispering would drive me to distraction, but in truth, they handled it with subtlety. Kazan and his men would wait on the stair, ready to spring into action should need be; Joscelin and Ti-Philippe lurked in the echo chambers, hidden from view to all but me, where I could summon them at a glance.

For my part, I resumed the position I had taken before, lying on my stomach and gazing through the legs of the stool into the Temple below. 'Twas a waiting game, from this point hence.

And wait I did, for yet another seeming eternity, half-lulled by the melodious chanting below. It matters naught, I thought. I have waited, and waited and waited and waited, throughout this long sojourn; waited for information in the City of Elua, waited for events to turn in La Serenissima, waited on my ransom, waited on the *thetalos*, waited on the Archon's answer . . . for months on end, I had done naught but wait.

I could wait this while longer.

At last the Priestess of the Crown brought an end to their litany and she rose with her Elect, clapping her hands. Somewhere, outside, dawn was breaking. I lay hidden, watching as the Temple of Asherat-of-the-Sea scurried to life. Candles were replenished, the incensors refilled, and a great dais of wood brought before the altar in three parts, borne by harried eunuchs. Untouched by it all, the mighty image of Asherat stared forth, hands reaching down to touch the stone-wrought waves.

In all the bustle, I took the measure of the echo chamber's pitch, humming softly in either direction until I was sure I had the angle of it. Ti-Philippe looked at me as if I were mad, though he held his tongue; Joscelin's eyes glinted with an answering wildness. Once he had committed to a thing, he held nothing back. Whether or not he learned it in his brief tenure with Anafiel Delaunay or no, we were alike, in that.

Somewhere, a ray of light struck Asherat's crown alongside the harbor.

I saw sunlight flood into the Temple as the great entrance doors opened in the antechamber; I heard the muted roar of the gathered crowd in the Campo Grande outside. I heard it rise as the procession drew near and the Dogal Guard formed a double line, protest breaking against the wall of shields and spears. I saw the Priestess of the Crown take up her place before the altar, flanked by her chosen, while acolytes and attendants made ready to receive the royal retinue.

I saw them enter the Temple.

Ah, Elua! They were all there, all of them. Cesare Stregazza, still the Doge, and a frail woman at his side who must be his wife; Marco and Marie-Celeste, with Severio proud beside them. Others I knew by sight, knowledge garnered, it seemed, so long ago: Orso Latrigan and Lorenzo Pescaro, once contenders for the Dogal Seat, defeated by Marco's bid, and others, too, members of the Hundred Worthy Families and the Consiglio Maggiore, noblemen from the Six Sestieri, attired in garish splendor, embittered or sycophantic according to their natures.

And there were D'Angelines. Oh yes, there were D'Angelines.

It took me aback, to see Ysandre de la Courcel enter the Temple of Asherat; to see, after so long, all the glory and beauty of Terre d'Ange, my homeland, personified in my Queen. She wore a gown of pale lavender with a cloak of green, Elua's color, laced with gold brocade, and even from my poor view on the floor of the balcony, I could see the workmanship was exquisite. A simple circlet of gold sat atop her pale blonde hair and a gold mesh caul bound it, and her profile was breathtakingly pure.

I had forgotten, somehow, that Ysandre was no older than me.

Along with a handful of D'Angeline nobles and a file of men-at-arms, who took posts at the rear of the Temple, four Cassiline Brothers accompanied her to a place of honor to the right of the Doge and the Doge-elect on the dais. With their ashen-grey attire, hair bound in neat clubs at the napes of their necks, daggers at their waists and swords at their backs, they were nearly identical, all of an age, somewhere betwixt forty and fifty years, I guessed. Any one of the four might have been David de Rocaille . . . or none.

And then Prince Benedicte's party entered.

I hadn't been sure, until then, if Melisande would dare it. I should have known that she would. She came in on the arm of Benedicte de la Courcel, tall and hale in the blue and silver of his House, his erect carriage belying his age. Her gown of deep-blue velvet matched his doublet, and her head was lowered modestly, the shining Veil of Asherat hiding her features; but behind, ah! Her hair hung loose and unbound, falling in gleaming blue-black waves to the small of her back.

Melisande, I thought, laughing silently, tears in my eyes; oh, Melisande!

When all was said and done, there was no one to match her.

My heart beat quickly in my breast and my breath came hard and fast, making my mouth dry. Desire beat in me like a pulse, remembering her hands, her mouth, her scent. But I had been Naamah's Servant for a long time too, twice-dedicated, and I knew what it was to endure yearning as fierce as pain. A coterie of guardsmen surrounded them, clad in the livery of House Courcel. I marked their faces well, and saw many of the veterans of Troyes-le-Mont among them as they took their place amid the jostling throng of noble retinues at the back of the Temple. Benedicte and Melisande mounted the dais to the left of Marco and Marie-Celeste Stregazza, their strong allies and reunited in-laws.

Last to enter was the double line of the Dogal Guard,

securing the doors against an already-roaring crowd in the Campo Grande. I heard crisply shouted orders and injunctions as they did and guessed — rightly, as it happened — that at least one unit of the civic Serenissiman Guard was posted to ward the doors outside.

Inside, it grew quiet, save for the rustle and murmur of several hundred bodies gathered in one place and the hiss of incense burning, the slight crackle of candle flame. From my hidden perch, I gazed down at the gathered tableau. A chair had been provided for Cesare Stregazza; I could see the peaked crimson cap atop his thinning white hair, the Dogal Seal flashing gold on his trembling hands where they rested on the arms of the chair.

He had asked my aid in keeping it, the canny old manipulator. Of a surety, what he had intended was not what I had in mind; but it was the course that had offered itself to me, and I had no other choice.

The ceremony of investiture was about to begin.

SEVENTY-FOUR

AS MOST ceremonies do, this one began with an invocation.

Raising both hands to the effigy of Asherat-of-the-Sea, the Priestess of the Crown uttered a prayer beseeching the goddess to lend her blessing to this day's proceedings, while her Elect came forward with offerings; gleaming ceremonial vessels, gilded baskets of fruits and grains, brown eggs in a silver bowl, a jewel-bedecked wine chalice, all of which were set upon the altar.

I was glad there was to be no blood sacrifice.

A difficult thing, to choose the perfect moment. I considered seizing upon the Priestess of the Crown's invocation, which would have been apt; and yet. It lacked drama. Better it should come at the crux of the matter, when those assembled already watched with bated breath. I wished I could see their faces rather than the backs of their heads. Once the invocation and the offerings were given, the Priestess of the Crown and the Elect turned toward the crowd, but 'twas not their expressions I wished to see.

In the litany that followed, the Priestess of the Crown cited the ancient history of La Serenissima and the role of the Doge within it, enumerating his duties, which were given voice in a call-and-response style by the six Elect. It was a pleasant enough ceremony, if one were not watching it from a hiding place, aquiver with tension. I strained my ears to listen to the noise of the crowd in the Campo Grande, faintly audible at times. It had not reached a breaking point.

No, I thought; nor will it, not until Marco Stregazza wears the Dogal Seal upon his finger. He'll take no risk of having his investiture disrupted. It must be a done thing, before chaos is loosed. Even from above, I could read as much from his posture, at once relaxed and eager. I wondered if Allegra Stregazza had gotten my message, and if her husband Ricciardo had responded by rallying the Scholae.

It went on for a considerable time, this ceremony, until my attention nearly began to wander. I caught myself, worrying; if I were distracted, how much more so were Joscelin and Ti-Philippe, and Kazan and his Illyrians hidden behind the door, who were not trained to attend on tedium? And then the Priestess of the Crown addressed herself to the Doge-elect, and my focus sharpened.

"Marco Plautius Stregazza," she intoned, giving him his full name. "You have heard here enumerated the sacred charges given unto he who would give himself unto the hand of Asherat-of-the-Sea and take up the throne of the Doge of La Serenissima. By the will of the people, the vote of the Consiglio Maggiore and the consent of the Temple of Asherat, you have been so appointed. Is it your will to make this vow?"

"It is," Marco Stregazza said firmly, stepping forward.

"Do you swear on pain of death to execute these charges faithfully?"

"I do."

She bound him, then, in a long and complicated oath which I failed to commit to memory and which Marco repeated letter-perfect, and then summoned him to the altar to anoint his brow with chrism, which I watched in an agony of indecision. Should it be now? It must be done before the sacrament was complete.

"Your Grace," the Priestess of the Crown said to Cesare Stregazza, not quite inclining her head. "Before Asherat-of-the-Sea, the appointed hour has come. It is time for the Dogal Seal to pass to another." I watched his crimson-capped head bow in defeat, his crabbed hands rise from the arms of the chair as his trembling fingers fumbled at the massive gold seal.

Now. Yes.

The moment was now.

Easing backward, I rose to my knees, the very breath shivering in my lungs, rehearsing the Caerdicci words, the pitch and intonation, in my mind. Asherat, I thought, glancing at the image of the goddess, for this you saved me; lend me now your aid. Elua's child I am, Kushiel's Chosen and Naamah's Servant, but you plucked me from the depths of the sea and raised me upon your bosom that I might be here today. If it is your will, then use me now!

In memory I heard once more the mourning, maddening dirge of the winds of La Dolorosa, the sound I had endured through countless days, numberless black nights in my tiny cell, the grieving of a goddess bereft. Loss, endless loss; Asherat's grief for her slain son Eshmun commingling with my own. Joscelin's face by wavering flames, despairing; a torch, falling like a star. Kazan's brother, dying at the end of Kazan's sword. The cavern of the Temenos, the blood-guilt I wore like shackles. A curse undone and cast anew in bitter guise; a lost son, a lost lover.

Bright and gleaming gold, the Dogal Seal slid over Cesare Stregazza's gnarled finger.

Kneeling on the balcony, I pitched my voice toward the echo chamber.

"O my Beloved, why do you forsake me?"

They had wrought well, those masons who died to keep the goddess' secrets; my own words startled me, vast and resonant, echoing from the vaulted dome itself into every corner of the Temple. Somewhere, an earthenware vessel dropped and shattered.

I think there was no one, in that instant, who did not raise their eyes to the apex of the dome, seeking the presence of divinity. And in that moment, two years' worth of careful planning, two years of hard-won allegiances bought and sold, began to unravel.

"It is a sign!" Cesare Stregazza cried in his quavering voice, shoving the Dogal Seal back onto his finger and curling his fist on the chair arm. "A sign!"

"It is a trick!" Marie-Celeste Stregazza hissed, whirling in her finery. I could only guess how her gaze scalded the Priestess of the Crown, the gathered Elect. "A trick, I say! Find it out and make an end to it!"

I had guessed aright when I guessed her the cunning one of the pair.

The Priestess of the Crown, two of her Elect; heads turning, seeking the balcony, slow-dawning comprehension

on their features. Others followed their gazes. Reacting
slowly, the Dogal Guardsmen began to move indetermin-
ately, still unable to see me.

"What trick the truth, Serenissimans?" I called down to
them. *"Whom the goddess has chosen, She does not relinquish
living. You are here under false prophecy, Serenissimans.
Marco Stregazza seeks to seize the Doge's throne to his own
ends, while Benedicte de la Courcel seeks the death of his
Queen."*

And with those words, pandemonium was unleashed.

It was the Priestess of the Crown who reacted first,
swiftly, casting out her arm to point at the balcony. "An
intruder dares blaspheme in the Temple of Asherat!" she
cried. "Get her!"

There was a pause, and then the Temple eunuchs
moved to obey her, several on each side mounting the
curving stairs, ceremonial spears held tentatively before
them.

"Now, Joscelin," I murmured over my shoulder, rising
fluidly to my feet. With a grim smile, he emerged from the
echo chamber, Ti-Philippe on the other side a mere step
behind him. Each of them took a post at the top of the twin
stairs; narrow, winding stairs defensible from above by a
single armed man. The attendants halted at the first curve,
untrained to combat and fearful.

Stepping into the balcony and laying my hands on the
railing, I gazed down into the Temple. Let them see me
now; it no longer mattered. In the milling crowd, the divisions nonetheless showed clearly. The captain of the
Dogal Guard and a full three quarters of his men looked to
Marco Stregazza for guidance, while the others, bewildered, gazed from their commander to Cesare Stregazza to

the other Serenissiman nobles who began to slowly size up the situation, one by one aligning themselves with the Doge, Cesare.

Ysandre stood tall and erect, her face pale as her Cassiline Brothers formed a square around her, vambraces and daggers crossed to defend. The D'Angeline nobles fell in behind, men-at-arms fanning out to protect them.

The old, blind priestess Bianca raised two trembling hands to the effigy of Asherat, her lips moving in prayer; with a shudder, she turned her sightless face to the Priestess of the Crown and began backing away from her, and three others of the Elect followed.

And the D'Angeline guardsmen of the Little Court shifted as if on cue into a tight knot around Prince Benedicte and his lady wife.

Melisande.

She had turned and stood motionless, veiled features lifted toward the balcony, and I knew behind the crystalline shimmer that her eyes were fixed upon my face. I stared down at her, shuddering, my fingers clenched on the marble balustrade.

"Phèdre?" It was Ysandre's voice, at once sharp and perplexed. "What in Elua's blessed name are you doing here, and what are you talking about? I thought you had gone to Ephesium!"

"Your majesty," I said softly, not shifting my gaze. Even without the echo chamber, my voice carried at this height. "You allowed me to go in search of the traitoress Melisande Shahrizai. And I have found her," I said, lifting one arm and pointing directly at Melisande, standing proudly at Benedicte's side. "There."

Although I cannot be sure, I am nearly certain I saw

Melisande's head bow fractionally toward me in a duelist's nod; I *am* certain that I saw her left hand move in a covert gesture, taken up by Marie-Celeste Stregazza and relayed to the Priestess of the Crown, who nodded in the direction of the antechamber. Easy to see, from above, for one trained to it; still, there was naught I could do. My lips shaped a warning shout, but already a nameless hand had slipped the bar of the great doors to the Temple of Asherat. "Rioters!" cried a high male alto from the antechamber, and acolytes and attendants began to fall back into the Temple proper as an onslaught of crudely armed workers and tradesmen poured through the wide-flung entrance doors.

That was when the fighting began.

I daresay 'twas not so great an influx as the conspirators expected. Now that the doors were opened, I heard the clash and roar of quarrel continuing in the Campo Grande and knew with a great surge of hope that Ricciardo had rallied the Scholae. Still, there was a determined core who penetrated the Temple, and 'twas enough to set violence erupting. Enemy or ally; who could say? I watched it all unfold from above, concentrating on Ysandre's Cassilines even as two sets of attackers stormed the balcony stairs below me.

The first, rioters with clubs and homemade weapons, Joscelin and Ti-Philippe turned back easily. The second was the Dogal Guard, and not so easy to disperse.

"Pirate!" Joscelin cried over his shoulder, dodging in narrow quarters and catching a sword-thrust on his crossed daggers. "Now!"

With a whoop of exultation, Kazan Atrabiades led his Illyrians forth from concealment and they pushed their way past Joscelin and Ti-Philippe, bucklers and short swords carving a path down the curving stairs. Blood was flowing, spattering marble and stone. I heard pushing and shouting, the groans of the wounded. One of the Illyrians went down. Cursing, Kazan waded through the fray, shoving one of the Serenissimans and forcing him over the railing of the stair.

And in the center of the Temple, a wedge of armed tradesmen drove steadily toward my Queen's retinue, Dogal Guardsmen loyal to Marco Stregazza falling back carefully before their onslaught. I marked the skill with which they fought and the well-worn swords they bore, and guessed that these were not bribed rioters, but mercenaries with orders to attack Ysandre's party.

The attempt was coming.

No one was watching, though it was happening in plain sight. Marco Stregazza was shouting, trying to make himself heard over the clamor, but my accusation had had its effect; support was beginning to ebb away from him and growing steadily around Cesare. "The Doge!" a voice bellowed, others taking up the cry. "Rally to the Doge!"

Four Cassiline Brothers, a pair fore and aft, moving with uncanny fluid grace, a space around each where steel wove deadly patterns around them.

I watched them fixedly and Joscelin joined me on the balcony, following my gaze while Kazan's men held the stairs. We both heard it the moment Marco cut his losses, gathering his breath and shouting loud enough to quell the fighting for an instant.

"Serenissimans, we are betrayed! I have been deceived! Benedicte de la Courcel has betrayed me!"

In the pause, the members of the Dogal Guard ceased

fighting among themselves and exchanged uncertain stares, their sundered loyalties reunited by Marco's defection. It didn't take long. With grim resolution, the Serenissimans turned as one against the entourage of the Little Court and the surge of violence began anew.

To his credit, Benedicte de la Courcel was no coward. He had been a hero, once, and a valiant warrior — eldest hero of the Battle of Three Princes, where his nephew Rolande had lost his life. I do not think he reckoned to fight again in his twilight years, but he did, wresting his ceremonial sword from its jeweled scabbard and wielding it courageously in defense of his people . . . and his wife.

Forgotten, the Illyrians lowered weapons on the stairs, catching their breath. Those rioters, the true sons of the Scholae with work-stained hands and bewildered faces, began to retreat or flee, sensing their cause abandoned.

Not so with the mercenaries, who continued to fight. I do not think they were skilled or numerous enough to have taken Ysandre's guard. They didn't have to be. It wasn't the point. They were enough to press the D'Angelines, engaging them — even the Cassilines, who had not yet drawn to kill. They wouldn't, in a Serenissiman temple, not without the Queen's order, unless her life was truly threatened. It was enough to maintain a cordon of safety around her.

Ysandre's face was taut with fear and anger; mostly anger. Across the Temple, I stared at her, at her Cassilines. One by one I stared at them all, my gaze returning again and again to one in particular, in the forward left position, as I remembered an afternoon in the Hall of Portraits, where there hung the image of Isabel L'Envers de la

Courcel, my lord Delaunay's enemy, the mother Ysandre so resembled.

And there hung too a portrait of Edmée de Rocaille, Rolande's betrothed, the woman he would have wed if Isabel had not arranged an accident.

My mother was responsible for her death, you know.

I knew; oh, how I knew! That death had shaped my life in ways I could scarce encompass, forging Anafiel Delaunay, a Prince's beloved, into the man his enemies would name the Whoremaster of Spies; turning me, an *anguissette* raised to serve pleasure in the Court of Night-Blooming Flowers, into one of his most subtle weapons.

One death; so many repercussions.

I stared at Edmée de Rocaille's brother.

If I had not been watching him so hard, I might not have seen it, the beginning of that fateful turn in the clear space that surrounded him, graceful and flowing, tossing his right-hand dagger in the air and catching it by the blade to make ready for the throw.

"Joscelin!" I grabbed his arm with one hand, pointing with the other. "There!"

Joscelin had spoken truly; a Cassiline Brother planning to assassinate his sovereign would indeed be prepared to die.

David de Rocaille was performing the *terminus*.

SEVENTY-FIVE

"DAVID DE ROCAILLE!" Given from the balcony, Joscelin's shout echoed from the vaulted dome as he hurtled into motion, wrenching out of my grip and whipping past Kazan's startled Illyrians on the stair. At the far end of the Temple, the grey-clad figure faltered . . . and continued onward with the *terminus*, setting the blade of the left-hand dagger at his own throat while his right arm cocked for the throw.

Directly at Ysandre de la Courcel, the Queen of Terre d'Ange.

She hadn't even seen the danger, gazing instead at the balcony with the frown of an embattled monarch, wondering what new threat the outcry betokened.

At the sharp curve in the staircase, Joscelin leapt onto the railing, catching himself to balance above the fray, flipping the dagger in his right hand to hold it blade-first. David de Rocaille did pause then, and I think for an instant their eyes met across the crowded space. With a death's-head smile, the brother of Edmée de Rocaille looked at the Queen and made to cast his dagger.

And with a prayer that was half-curse, Joscelin threw first.

I do not think it is stretching the truth to say that Cassiel himself guided Joscelin's hand that day, for it was an impossible throw under impossible conditions. I cannot think how else he made it. End over end, the blade flashed over the heads of skirmishing guardsmen.

Ready to die or no, David de Rocaille reacted on instinct, blocking the strike with one vambraced arm. Joscelin's dagger clattered against it and fell harmlessly to the floor. Slow to react, those nearest turned, uncertain what had happened. Closing his eyes briefly, David de Rocaille bowed and sheathed his daggers, reaching over his shoulder to draw his sword.

With a wordless cry, Joscelin launched himself from the railing, scattering members of the Dogal Guard as he landed.

I daresay he would have been slain then and there had he stood still for it, but he took them by surprise and, by the time they responded, he was already halfway through the melee. I stood rigid with fear as he forced his way through them.

In the uncertainty, David de Rocaille attacked – but he had waited a heartbeat too long to seize his advantage. Shock and disbelief writ on their faces, Ysandre's other Cassilines closed ranks around her and faced their comrade.

One died quickly, too slow to raise his guard, thinking somehow, still, that it was all a terrible mistake until David de Rocaille opened his chest with an angled, two-handed blow. The second fought better and might have lived longer if he had drawn his sword instead of trusting to his daggers; he went down when de Rocaille dropped to one knee and leveled a sweeping blow at his legs, finishing him as he fell with a quick cut to the neck.

By that time, Joscelin had arrived, and his sword sang free of its sheath as he drew it. "David de Rocaille," he said softly. "Turn and face me."

The remaining Cassiline backed slowly away, covering Ysandre's retreat. In the stillness, David de Rocaille turned to meet Joscelin Verreuil.

Outside the practice fields of the sanctuary, where they are raised and trained under the eye of the Prefect, no one living has ever seen two Cassiline-trained warriors do battle. It is a spectacle capable of bringing an entire riot to a standstill — and that, in fact, is exactly what it did. D'Angelines, Serenissimans, mercenaries . . . all of them, quarrels laid by as they watched in awe, stepping back to give the combatants room.

I gripped the balcony railing so hard my fingers ached, and watched it happen.

It is to this day one of the deadliest and most beautiful things I have ever witnessed. Their blades flickered and clashed in patterns too complex for the eye to follow, while they moved through form after form, those movements drilled into them from boyhood onward. On his side, Joscelin had the vigor of youth; but D'Angelines are not quick to age. De Rocaille was a man in his prime, his strength not yet faded, fighting with nothing to lose.

"Anathema!" he hissed as their blades locked. "You betrayed the Brotherhood for one of Naamah's pets!"

"I honor my vow to Cassiel," Joscelin said grimly. "How will you answer for yours, oath-breaker?"

David de Rocaille answered him with a clever twist,

slipping his blade loose and stepping back to aim a great blow at Joscelin's head; Joscelin ducked and spun, de Rocaille's blade passing harmlessly above his half-shorn hair, striking on the rise at his opponent's midsection. The other parried ably and they fought onward, whirling and dodging. It was an odd-looking match, David de Rocaille the model of austerity and competence in his grey Cassiline garb and Joscelin in rough-spun attire, his tangled locks still streaked with walnut dye.

In that disparity, however, lay the other difference between them. For all that de Rocaille had twenty years on him, the bitter wisdom of experience was Joscelin's. David de Rocaille had spent his life waiting attendance on the regents of Terre d'Ange.

He had never drawn his sword to kill.

Joscelin had.

I'd been with him when he fought Waldemar Selig's thanes, alone and unaided in a raging Skaldic blizzard, one of his greatest battles still, and one unheralded by poets. I had been there when he fought the Tarbh Cró in Alba, defending with blood and slaughter myself and the family of Drustan mab Necthana, who hailed him as brother for it. And I had been there on La Dolorosa, when he assailed it with bared daggers alone, fighting to win my freedom.

He knew what it was to fight for love's sake.

Slowly, ever so slowly, the tide began to turn against David de Rocaille. He who had nothing to lose had nothing to gain, either, save death. Still the bright blades flashed, wielded in dueling two-handed Cassiline grips, subtle angles and interplay half-lost on the watchers; still they maneuvered around each other in a series of intricate steps and turns too numerous to count. But David de Rocaille had begun to despair, and it showed in his face.

It was hard, Elua knows, harder than many things I have done, to turn away from that fight and gaze out over the Temple. Several hundred people with less invested in that battle could not do it.

I knew who could.

With their strength united under Cesare Stregazza's command, the Serenissiman contingent had surrounded Benedicte's retinue. Most of those had surrendered by now, vastly outnumbered, and I saw a gathered knot around Prince Benedicte himself, fallen and bleeding from many wounds, his chest rising and falling slowly as he labored for breath. I saw the mercenaries who had attacked Ysandre's party slinking backward along the Temple walls, making for the exit. I heard the shouts and curses of the Serenissiman Guard outside the doors, now trying in earnest to keep out the pressing citizenry and tradesfolk. I heard a rising murmur from the Temple and had to look back.

On the floor, David de Rocaille mounted a furious defense, regaining ground, transforming his despair into wild energy, going on the attack; he was smiling, now, with clenched teeth, the way a man will smile facing his death. Step by step, he forced Joscelin backward . . .

This, I saw, and all of La Serenissima watching it. It hurt to look away again, but I did.

And I saw Melisande Shahrizai in her blue gown and shimmering veil, calmly walking toward the antechamber, and no one at all watching her do it.

Whatever happened, she would walk away free.

On the floor, Joscelin retreated warily, alert and aware,

the glinting line of his blade deflecting de Rocaille's blows
out and away, away from his body. He moved with care,
placing his feet with precision, his body coiled and waiting
as David de Rocaille spent his last, furious strength. He
would live; he had to live. He had love at stake. I watched
him with my heart in my throat. Surely, surely, that was
victory writ in his gaze, biding and watchful.

I closed my eyes and chose.

"There is a thing I must do," I murmured unsteadily to
Ti-Philippe, who had joined me in the balcony when
Joscelin went after de Rocaille. "For Fortun, for Remy . . .
for all of us. Will you come with me?"

He nodded once, grim as death, my merry chevalier.
"My lady, I have sworn it."

"Then come."

Trailing him in my wake, I hurried down the staircase,
past Stajeo and Tormos, who had fought side by side at
last, past Oltukh, who asked in a startled voice where I
went, and plunged into the crowd, threading my way
through the throng. There is an art to it, as in many things;
'tis one of the first things we are taught, in the Night
Court, wending our way amid patrons at the grand fêtes. I
took an indirect route, following the openings between
tight-pressed bodies, ignoring exclamations as I passed.
Once, I stumbled over something, and glancing down, saw
'twas Joscelin's fallen dagger, kicked and forgotten by the
spectators. Under cover of the sound of clashing steel, I
stooped quickly and snatched it up, hurrying onward.

I had lost Ti-Philippe somewhere in the crowd, though
I could hear him, by the fervid curses and explanations as
the Serenissimans sought to detain him. If Melisande had
taken a less leisurely pace, the Dogal Guard might have

taken notice, and stopped her . . . or she might have reached the antechamber before me. She did not.

I got there first.

Alone save for a cluster of bewildered acolytes, I put my back to the Temple doors and set myself in Melisande's path, raising Joscelin's dagger between us, low and pointed upward as I had seen him do. Outside the door stood the Serenissiman Guard, keeping back the crowds of the Campo Grande. They would let her through, I thought; like as not, they had orders to do so.

Melisande stopped and regarded me through her veil.

"My lady Melisande," I said, trying to keep my voice level. It seemed impossible that I had spoken with a goddess' echoing tones only minutes ago. "You will not leave this place."

"Phèdre." There was a world of meaning in that one simple word, my name, the entire battle in all its complex knots of enmity and love, hatred and desire, that lay between us, invested with the faint amusement that only Melisande could give it, cutting to the marrow of my soul and dismissing aught else as incidental. "Will you do violence by your own hand to stop me?"

I shut my eyes, not wanting to see how her beauty shone like a torch behind the veil, and then opened them again, not trusting her out of my sight. I could hear, beyond the crowd, a shift in the deadly music of swordplay. Now it was the offensive strokes that rang measured and true, a steady, patient stalking, counterbalanced with desperate, clashing parries. "If I must."

"Then do it," she said simply, and took a step forward.

I was already trembling before she did; I have killed one person only in my life, in my own defense, and he was not Melisande. She reached out one hand, caressing the naked steel of Joscelin's dagger, fingers sliding up to cover mine where I clutched the hilt.

"Will you?" she asked again, glorious eyes grave behind the veil as she twisted the dagger in my grip, turning my strength against me, my knees weakening at the touch of her hand. My breath came in white flashes and I felt my heart beating overhard and cursed my own ill-starred birth that shaped me to give in to the will of Kushiel's most splendid scion. "Will you truly?"

Somewhere, on the Temple floor, Joscelin was pressing his attack. I knew it, knew the sound of his blade-strokes, quickening toward victory. But it was very far away and my world had dwindled to the scant inches that separated me from Melisande Shahrizai. His dagger rose between us, her hand guiding mine, the dagger no longer pointed at Melisande. My limbs did not answer to my wishes, surrendering to hers with a languor against which I struggled in vain. Gently, inexorably, the dagger rose, gripped hard in our linked hands, until its point rested beneath my chin, pricking the tender skin.

"Yes," I breathed, somewhere, distantly, appalled at my own response. Her scent surrounded me, rousing my desire, the warmth of her body devastatingly near. I raised my eyes to hers, feeling the dagger's prick, promise of the final consummation between us. I thought of Anafiel Delaunay, lying in his own gore; of Alcuin, raised as a brother to me. I thought of Fortun and Remy, Phèdre's Boys, slain for their loyalty. And though their shades cried out for vengeance, I could not strike. Not her, not Melisande. In the end, I was what I was, Kushiel's Chosen. Strength was not my weapon; only surrender. Was

Melisande's freedom worth Kushiel's torment to her? I tightened my grip on the dagger beneath her hand, raising my other hand to cover hers, forcing the sharp tip hard beneath my chin, willing to complete the *terminus* begun so long ago on the fields of Troyes-le-Mont. "Will you?"

It only took a moment's hesitation.

Melisande hesitated.

"Immortali!" The name of the nobleman's club rang like a battle cry, and I knew the voice that uttered it; Severio Stregazza, bursting through the gathered ranks of Serenissimans to enter the antechamber with a grinning Ti-Philippe and several of his fellows in tow, swords drawn. "Drop the dagger," Severio said grimly, "and step away from her, Principessa! You have dealt enough poison to my family to last a lifetime; sully it no further."

At the same moment, a wild-eyed Ricciardo Stregazza convinced the Serenissiman Guard to admit him through the Temple doors, backed by an army of tradesmen . . .

. . . and somewhere, at the rear of the Temple, a great cry arose as Joscelin Verreuil's sword entered David de Rocaille's flesh, making an end to a battle I have always regretted missing.

With a gesture of infinite grace, Melisande loosed her grip on the dagger and took a single step backward.

It left me, terribly obviously, holding a dagger beneath my own chin. I cast it down hastily. Mercenaries and rioters fled, an assassin thwarted, allies rallying, Benedicte defeated and Marco turned. I drew a long, shuddering breath. "Thank you," I said to Severio. "I am in your debt, my lord."

"Credit your fast-talking chevalier," he said shortly,

and then nodded to Ricciardo. "Hello, Uncle. Aren't you supposed to be under house arrest?"

Ricciardo was breathing hard; I learned later that he'd fought a pitched battle to win past the guards at his estate. "The riot in the Campo Grande is contained," he said, ignoring the question. "And the instigators in custody. Severio, I'm sorry, but they will swear to your father's part in it."

After a pause, Severio nodded curtly. "You tried to warn me. Thank you." He turned to his fellow Immortali. "Escort my maternal grandfather's *wife* to his side," he said with loathing. "Let her offer comfort in his agony, since she has brought him to this impasse."

Melisande said naught to him. I remembered well his bitterness at Benedicte de la Courcel's regard for his half-breed children and grandchildren; 'twas that cruel regard that Melisande had turned, drop by drop, into the poison of treason. She would find no sympathy here. Without a second glance, she went of her own accord.

Ti-Philippe bent to retrieve Joscelin's dagger, thrusting it in his belt. "My lady," he said to me. "I think it is time we saw our Queen."

Whatever else was true of him, Cesare Stregazza had the stuff of command in him. By the time we made our way to the center of the Temple, he had established the semblance of order. Marco and Marie-Celeste knelt at his feet, pleading clemency for their part in the conspiracy, claiming they had been deceived by Benedicte and his treacherous wife.

His withered eyelids flickered; he did not give an inch. "Is it true?" he demanded of Melisande, who stood tall and straight beside the bleeding form of her royal husband.

"Not in the least, your Grace," she replied calmly. "Your daughter-in-law herself bribed the Priestess of the Crown to ensure the false prophecy and see to it that the rioters were admitted to the Temple. Two votes in the Consiglio Maggiore, I believe was the price. I would not stoop to blasphemy."

Marie-Celeste Stregazza drew a hissing breath and made some sharp reply; I did not stay to hear it, for I had won through at last to Ysandre's retinue. And there . . .

"Joscelin!" I flung my arms around him, assuring myself that he was alive and whole; and so he was, save for a few minor wounds about the arms. He laughed at my onslaught, holding me off only long enough to kiss me.

"You make a dramatic entrance, near-cousin," the Queen of Terre d'Ange said wryly.

Horrified, I let go of Joscelin and knelt swiftly to her. "Your majesty, forgive me—"

"Oh, Phèdre, get up." There was a familiar impatience in Ysandre's voice; only a trace. "I'm sorry I doubted you. You were right, and more, and we will speak of it at length later. Come, you have earned the right to bear witness to this encounter."

I would rather not have gone, but one does not refuse an order from one's sovereign. The throng of Serenissiman nobles and guardsmen parted as Ysandre de la Courcel made her way to her kinsman's side, and even the Doge fell silent. My struggle lay with Melisande, always Melisande; I had nearly forgotten that Benedicte de la Courcel was Ysandre's great-uncle, her nearest living kin on her royal father's side.

She took his betrayal hard.

"Why?" Ysandre asked, disregarding Melisande to kneel beside him. "Why have you done this thing, Uncle?"

Benedicte's eyes rolled in his head; his lined features worked, a bloody froth appearing at the corners of his mouth. They had laid him on a cloak of cloth-of-gold, and he was not long for this world. His roving eye fell on Severio Stregazza, standing close at hand, and contempt suffused his face. "Barbarian . . . blood . . . tainting Elua's line," he spat. "Bad enough here . . . there . . . blue-painted barbarian Picti in your bed . . ."

It was enough; Ysandre straightened even as he seized convulsively, her face hardening. "Tend to him," she said sharply to the Eisandine chirurgeon who travelled with her. "If he lives, he will face our justice." Her gaze fell on Melisande, who had drawn back her veil at last. For a long moment, neither spoke. "Your life," Ysandre said at length, expressionless, "is already forfeit. As for your son . . ." She paused. "As for your son, I will adopt him into my household, and raise him as a member of my own."

"Mayhap," Melisande said calmly.

I laughed; I couldn't help it, a short, choked laugh. And Melisande Shahrizai turned her glorious, unveiled gaze on me, raising her graceful eyebrows. "My lady," I said to her, filled with sorrow and impotent rage at the lives lost, the prices paid, echoing the words she had spoken to me in the throne room of the Little Court. "We played a game. You lost."

In the silence of the watching Temple, Melisande smiled coolly at me. With Ysandre confronting her, with all of La Serenissima watching, with Marco betraying her

and Benedicte dying, Melisande Shahrizai made her reply
with icy precision.

"I'm not finished."

That was when the bells began to ring.

SEVENTY-SIX

THINGS MOVED very swiftly.

I knew, of course; I had to know. 'Twas one of the few things Melisande had divulged to me in my dreadful cell on La Dolorosa. *Four couriers on fast horses will depart La Serenissima the instant the bell tower in the Great Square tolls Ysandre's death . . .*

To his credit, the Doge responded with shrewd celerity, ordering the bells silenced at once and dispatching the civil guard to the mainland to halt the couriers' flight. Though we learned it later I daresay all of us knew it was already too late. In truth, he could have done no more. Melisande laid her plans with skill. It had been too late when the first bell pealed.

Four couriers, with fresh horses on relay all the way to the City of Elua, bearing the spark of war. Ysandre heard my news unflinching; at that point, she was inured to shock.

"So Percy de Somerville will take the City," was all she said.

"Mayhap." I said, glancing at Melisande. "And mayhap

not, my lady." I thought of my own countermove, my Kritian missive, yet to play out, and kept silence for now.

"My dear Queen," Cesare Stregazza offered. "I am grievous sorry at what has befallen here. What may be done to punish those responsible . . ." his quavering voice hardened, ". . .will be done, though my own son pay the price for it."

"I ask only those born to Terre d'Ange for my justice," Ysandre said grimly. "And the woman Melisande Shahrizai in particular."

"It shall be done," the Doge promised.

Melisande's cool defiance had altered not a whit. "And will you violate the sanctuary of Asherat-of-the-Sea, your grace?" she asked him, lifting her chin and regarding him. "For such has been granted to me."

Someone swore; later, I learned it was Lord Amaury Trente, who served as Ysandre's Commander of the Guard on the *progressus,* "Elua's Balls! Surely you jest, lady!"

"No." It took courage for the Elect priestess who spoke to do so. Although she was pale and quivering, she held her ground; not one of those who had stood with the Priestess of the Crown, but one who had recoiled in horror at her blasphemy. "The lady speaks the truth. We granted her sanctuary upon her arrival in La Serenissima. She claims it now, in Asherat's holy presence. I do swear it upon my vows; her claim is valid."

Cesare Stregazza, still, by the grace of Asherat, the Doge, supported her claim, though it pained him to do it. He had little choice, after what had transpired. Profanation of the Temple had brought down Marco and Marie-Celeste; the Doge could not indulge in it.

Ysandre heard him out stone-faced.

"While you linger here, you live," she said to Melisande. "Do you set foot outside Asherat's grounds, your life is forfeit. Your holdings, your possessions, your son – all forfeit. Do you understand?"

"Perfectly." Melisande inclined her head with a faint, secret smile.

It gave me the chills.

By now the situation was well in hand. The Dogal Guard had escorted its D'Angeline prisoners away, and physicians had arrived, tending to the wounded. Ricciardo Stregazza and his tradesmen provided invaluable support that day, quietly and efficiently seeing to much that needed doing; and I was glad to see Severio working at his side. Their esteem rose that day in the eyes of La Serenissima, and rightfully so.

The body of David de Rocaille lay facedown, blood seeping onto the marble floor.

I learned, later, how it had finished. He had known himself beaten, at the end, and stepped into the killing thrust himself. Better if he had lived to be questioned; I daresay he knew it. Joscelin had asked him how he would answer for his oath. He had answered with his life.

Once Ysandre's Eisandine chirurgeon had done all she could for Prince Benedicte, who was removed on a litter into the Doge's custody, I had a quiet word with her, sending her to the balcony where Kazan and his men lurked unobtrusively, forgotten for the moment. It was Volos who had fallen, a deep gash on his brow splitting it near to the bone. Ti-Philippe had already made a hurried trip through the tunnel, ordering the Yeshuites to disperse.

He had less luck with the Illyrians.

I approached Cesare Stregazza, curtsying deeply before him. He was in his glory, restored to a fullness of command he had not enjoyed for many months; his wrinkled, hooded lids flickered to see me, and he looked amused. "So, little spy! You have kept your pledge to me after all. Where is the gift I gave you for it?"

The collar of pearls, I remembered. It had saved my life, in a way, serving to identify me to Joscelin's Yeshuite seekers. "For that, you must ask the warden of La Dolorosa, your grace. If you would, I crave another boon."

His brow creased with curiosity. "Indeed? Well, it seems I must grant it. What is it you ask?"

I took a deep breath, not entirely unmindful of the effect it had upon him. Joscelin stood behind me, one hand upon my shoulder. "Clemency, your grace, for those allies who aided me in securing your throne. Your son Marco sought their deaths. Violence has been done. I would see them pardoned of all wrongdoing."

"Is that all?" The Doge smiled cunningly. "Then it shall be done."

"You do so swear upon the altar of Asherat?" I asked.

Cesare Stregazza waved his hand, the Dogal Seal glinting gold as he summoned witnesses. "I do so swear, Contessa, in the presence of Asherat-of-the-Sea, that I absolve of wrongdoing in the eyes of La Serenissima all who aided you in thwarting this treachery. Does this satisfy?"

"Yes, your grace." I nodded to Ti-Philippe on the balcony, and in short order Kazan appeared, sauntering down the stairs and crossing the Temple floor, grinning fit to split his face. "This is Kazan Atrabiades of Epidauro, your grace, who stands for his men. They will be grateful for your pardon."

The Doge's wrinkled lips pursed with wry displeasure. "The seawolf who has harried our ships these many years," he said sourly. "I know the name. You choose your allies strangely, Contessa. I thought you meant yon blades-master here, who gave us such a show."

"Nevertheless," I said. "It required many allies to save your throne, your grace."

He grunted, liking this no better than he had liked upholding Melisande's claim; mayhap less. But for the same reasons, he had to do it. "I have sworn it."

Kazan made him a sweeping bow, still grinning. "Oh mighty Doge, I am grateful, I! My poor mother, she gives you thanks for your mercy, yes, to see her son come home alive."

"Do not strain the limits of that mercy, pirate," Cesare Stregazza said, eyeing him sardonically. "It erases only the past, and not the future."

"Of course, mighty Doge." Kazan's high spirits knew no bounds, standing free and pardoned in the Temple of Asherat where he'd been given the opportunity to shed Serenissiman blood. "But who knows what the future will bring, eh?"

With Joscelin's aid, I got him out of there before the Doge changed his mind, and made him an introduction to Ysandre de la Courcel, who blinked in startlement at his fearsome appearance. "We are grateful for your aid, Lord Atrabiades," she said formally. "I see by it that Phèdre nó Delaunay has a great deal more to tell me of her adventures."

"It is a long story, yes," Kazan said with considerable

understatement. "Majesty, to your ears alone in this place, I tell you that I have acted, I, with the blessing of the Zim Sokali, the Ban of Illyria. You will remember this, I hope, that my poor vassal nation offered aid to powerful Terre d'Ange in its hour of need, eh?"

"Yes." My Queen looked steadily at him, seeing past his fierce, mustached visage, his topknot and his dangling pirate's eardrops. It was the same clarity of regard that had seen past Drustan mab Necthana's blue-whorled tattoos and clubfoot to envision a King worthy of sharing her throne one day — and worthy of loving. Bearing the weight of a close kin's betrayal, a near-assassination and a realm threatened by siege, Ysandre de la Courcel stood unfaltering and inclined her head to him with dignity and gratitude. "I will remember it, Kazan Atrabiades."

There was a reason, after all, I had risked my life for hers.

Kazan made her a bow before departing, deep and sincere.

The Illyrians withdrew through the tunnels, quick and efficient, two of them carrying Volos between them. The chirurgeon had assured me that he would live, although the gash looked dreadful and he became nauseated when moved. I did not envy them that trip, though I was glad that they would ensure the Yeshuites had well and truly left, and that they would free the poor eunuch Cervianus. I made Kazan promise he would be freed unharmed, since he could do us no damage now.

We said our farewells then and there; I would seek him out at the Illyrian Ambassador's residence if I could, but I feared we would be departing La Serenissima in swiftness, and my duties to Ysandre would keep me well occupied until then. It had all changed so quickly, now that I was back among D'Angelines, despite our politically precarious position.

'Tis a hard thing, to sever ties forged in powerful circumstance. I thanked each of the men in turn – romantic Epafras, sea-loving Oltukh, the ever-quarreling Stajeo and Tormos, Ushak with his jug-ears and poor Volos, who mustered a sickly grin – and gave them all the kiss of parting.

And then Kazan looked wryly at me, running a lock of my hair between his fingers. "Stars caught in the night sky, eh, isn't that what that smooth-tongued son of Minos said? It has been a journey, since I plucked you from the waters, Phèdre nó Delaunay. I will not forget you soon, you."

"Nor I you, my lord Atrabiades," I said softly. "Not soon, nor ever."

"So it ends." He dropped his hand and glanced toward the tunnel. "Best I go. If I do not see you again, may your gods keep you safe. They and that tall D'Angeline, eh?" He flashed his irrepressible grin. "Now that I have seen him use his sword, yes, I think maybe it is not impossible!" At that I laughed, and Kazan bent his head to kiss me farewell. Straightening, he took his leave, disappearing into the tunnel without looking back. For a moment, I heard Illyrian voices echoing in the dark passageway, and then they moved onward, fading.

I turned back to the Temple and my own people.

Marco and Marie-Celeste Stregazza had been escorted out by members of the Dogal Guard whose loyalty had never faltered, under the watchful eye of Lorenzo Pescaro, who bore them no love. They were to be confined in their quarters until such time as the Judiciary Tribunal could meet.

As for the Priestess of the Crown and her two allies among the Elect — Asherat's servants would take care of their own, meting out their own justice. I glanced at her towering effigy and shuddered. I did not think Asherat-of-the-Sea dealt mercifully with those who betrayed her.

But Melisande Shahrizai was under her protection. A bitter irony, that.

In one quarter of the Temple, Ysandre de la Courcel held an impromptu war council with her Commander of the Guard and the rest of her retinue. Joscelin was there, although Ti-Philippe was nowhere to be seen; I learned later that he had slipped back to the nameless isle to confirm that the Yeshuites had gotten safely away.

The plan under discussion was the taking of the Little Court and our swift return to Terre d'Ange, for that, I learned was Ysandre's intention: to send her own Royal Couriers hard on the heels of Melisande's emissaries, to secure the Little Court and custody of Benedicte and Melisande's infant son, and thence to proceed in all haste to Terre d'Ange and the City of Elua, lending proof to her couriers' proclamation that she yet lived and dealing with Percy de Somerville's insurrection.

Word had returned, by now, that Melisande's couriers had gotten away clean. With relays already in place, they might gain as much as a day's lead on pursuers.

"It won't be easy if de Somerville's encamped the Royal Army within the walls of the City." Lord Trente's expression was grim. "He only needs a few hours to take it by treachery. And once it's done, his men might stand by him even with your return, your majesty, if it's a choice between that or hanging."

"And if we offer clemency to all who were duped?" Ysandre inquired thoughtfully.

Lord Trente shrugged. "Mayhap. De Somerville will claim 'tis a trick. And without an army at hand, we'll be hard-pressed to get close enough to give the lie to it. They'll be wary; they'll have Barquiel L'Envers' blood on their hands."

I cleared my throat. "My lady . . . it may prove otherwise. Elua grant it arrived, I sent a message to your uncle the Duc, bidding him hold the City against all claimants, including Percy de Somerville. If he will heed the password of House L'Envers, he may do it."

Ysandre stared at me. "You did what?"

I repeated my words, adding, "It would have been delivered first to the Lady of Marsilikos, by way of a courier-ship from the Archon of Phaistos, my lady."

"Phaistos," Ysandre said blankly. "Phaistos is a city, is it not, on the isle of Kriti?"

"Yes, my lady." I felt a fool, though there was no reason for it. "Do you think he will honor the L'Envers' password?"

Ysandre's lips moved soundlessly. "The password," she said at last. "Where did you — no, never mind. Yes. He might. He should. It will make him harder to kill, at any rate." She stood a little straighter, as if the burden on her shoulders had lessened. "Amaury, how many men will it require to secure the Little Court?"

"A hundred more than we have here," Lord Trente replied promptly.

"Good. We shall ask the Doge. And then," the Queen said, "we shall proceed."

With the situation under control, Cesare Stregazza willingly lent the aid of several squadrons of the Dogal Guard, and it was with these that Ysandre's forces swept the Little Court, securing it from bottom to top. I was there, along with Ysandre's ladies-in-waiting and other non-combatants, because in the end, there was no place in La Serenissima anyone reckoned safer. And we had Joscelin to ward us.

It was a small garrison that held the palace; many had accompanied their lord and lady to the ceremony of investiture, and were already under guard. Although I saw none of it, some of Benedicte's D'Angelines fought and were slain. It was a clean death, I suppose, which is why they chose it. Others surrendered, placing themselves at Ysandre's mercy rather than submit to the Doge's. These were held in secure quarters in the Little Court, which included a dungeon cell outfitted as a luxurious pleasure-chamber with tapestried walls, plush pillows strewn on thick rugs and a well-stocked flagellary.

I went to see it; I had to, although I could not say why. Joscelin went with me and looked at me without speaking as I stood in the hallway and shivered, watching as a half a dozen guardsmen were herded inside.

"This was meant for me," I said eventually.

"Melisande." He said it quietly; I nodded. "But she sent you to La Dolorosa instead."

"Yes." I gazed at the torchlight gleaming on rich fabrics; soft, pleasurable textures. "In order that this would seem paradise by comparison. And it would have." I touched my bare throat where her diamond had once hung and shivered again. "I'd made up my mind to take her offer, Joscelin. The very night you came. This is what you spared me."

Wisely, he said nothing more, but only took my arm and drew me away.

Once the palace of the Little Court was safely held, a pair of Royal Couriers was dispatched to be carried by swift gondolini to the mainland, where another, smaller portion of the Queen's retinue was encamped and the horses pastured.

Still, the search of Benedicte's palace continued, supervised by Amaury Trente. Even after the Dogal Guardsmen were dismissed with thanks, the search continued until at last Lord Trente reported to Ysandre, now ensconced in Prince Benedicte's throne room.

I had returned from my sojourn to view Melisande's dungeon and waited attendance on the Queen, along with Joscelin and a handful of other D'Angeline nobles. I saw the taut futility etched in Lord Trente's face as he made his report, shaking his head.

"I am sorry, your majesty," he said. "But the babe is not here."

SEVENTY-SEVEN

SOMETIME IN the middle of the night, word arrived
from the Dogal Palace that Prince Benedicte de la Courcel
had died of his injuries.

Ysandre heard out the news with no more than a nod,
and what she thought of it, I never knew. It was a mark of
her character that she bore out these dreadful betrayals
without succumbing to the desire for vengeance. Over
furious protest, she had made arrangements for the body of
David de Rocaille to be returned home by ship and buried
on his family estate.

"He sought my life in exchange for his sister's death,"
she said implacably. "Let it end here." And insofar as I
know, it did, save for those events already in motion.

Ysandre's search for Benedicte and Melisande's son
was another such mark of character, although there are
those who claimed — and always will be — that she sought
the child's life. It was not so. At a little over two years wed,
Ysandre and Drustan had not yet conceived. With Prince
Benedicte dead and his daughters by his Serenissiman wife
disgraced, the lines of succession were clear. Barquiel

L'Envers, however much she trusted him, whatever his ambition, had not a drop of Courcel blood in his veins; and House Courcel held the throne of Terre d'Ange.

Until the Queen conceived, the infant Imriel de la Courcel was her heir.

I do not think Ysandre intended him to inherit — she was young, and had every hope of yet bearing children of her own — but she had spoken truly in the Temple of Asherat-of-the-Sea. Rather than allow another blood-feud to fester, she would take the child into her household and see him raised with honor and respect, thwarting whatever hopes Melisande Shahrizai harbored of her son eventually cleaving House Courcel in twain.

It might even have worked.

The babe's nursemaid gave her testimony in stammering D'Angeline, over and over. All she knew was that she'd been given orders to see him made ready to be taken to the ceremony of investiture, fed and rested ere dawn and swaddled in cloth-of-silver. One of the Princess' attendants, a man she knew by sight, but not name, had come for the babe, and she'd given him into his custody. Neither man nor child were seen again.

We had a clear description of the infant from numerous sources: a babe of some six months' age, with fair skin, a dense crop of black hair and eyes the hue of blue twilight. By all accounts, Imriel de la Courcel was a beautiful babe — unmistakably, his mother's son.

And just as unmistakably, he was missing.

The following day bore strange, familiar echoes of the aftermath of the battle of Troyes-le-Mont as the denizens of the Little Court were brought before Ysandre for hard questioning. A few were detained, but most appeared genuinely ignorant of Melisande's identity and Benedicte's betrayal. None of them had knowledge of the missing heir. Last time, I had faced questioning too; this time, I stood beside Ysandre's throne, watching and listening for the telltales of a lie. In the matter of the child, I saw none. Melisande's contingency plan was cloaked in secrecy.

Ti-Philippe returned quietly in the small hours of the morning, reporting with weary relief that all the Yeshuites had gotten out safely; I was glad to hear it, and Joscelin all the more so. One day, a party of Serenissiman Yeshuites would indeed depart for the far northern lands, where the sun never sets in summertime but shines day and night upon the snowy vistas, and they would be led by a young man named Micah ben Ximon, who fought with crossed daggers that shone like a star in his hands — but that is a story for another day, and not mine to tell.

I was just glad it was not Joscelin's.

A long night, and a long day to follow it. I made a report in full to Ysandre at one point, detailing all I could remember from my arrival in La Serenissima to my return and my appearance in the balcony. It took the better part of two hours, and Ysandre's Secretary of the Presence, the Lady Denise Grosmaine, wrote furiously the entire time, quill scratching against the parchment. I'm not sure which of us was more tired when I had finished. Ysandre merely looked at me with her brows raised.

"Blessed Elua and his Companions surely watch over you, Phèdre," she remarked. "For I cannot think how else you are alive to tell me this."

"Nor can I, my lady," I said wearily. "Nor can I."

She took my hand, her gaze turning sober. "And over

me, Phèdre nó Delaunay, to have given me such a servant as no mortal deserves. Anafiel Delaunay swore an oath to my father out of love. I did not ask you to keep it in his name. Nonetheless, know that I am grateful for it, beyond the telling of words. His memory lives in your deeds. I will not forget either."

I nodded, unable to speak for the tears that choked me. Ysandre smiled gently, squeezed my hand and released it, and I gave silent thanks to Blessed Elua that he had sired a line that had begotten this scion, worthy of serving.

If not for the incipient war unfolding at home, we would have lingered longer in La Serenissima. There were a good many affairs to be set in order, not the least of which was the inheritance of the Little Court. With Benedicte's daughters both accused of treason and his infant son missing, the lines of succession pointed clearly to Severio. I spoke on his behalf, for I reckoned I owed him as much – he had saved my life, after all – but in the end, Ysandre elected to appoint a member of her own entourage, the Vicomte de Cherevin, to serve as steward of the estate until the matter was settled.

'Twas a dangerous post, and he accepted it with equanimity, knowing full well the risks entailed. De Cherevin was a man who had served under Ganelon de la Courcel as Ambassador to Tiberium, and he was unwaveringly loyal and wise to the ways of Caerdicci politics.

Even so, it took two full days to take care of the business of securing the Little Court and gain the Doge's approval of the arrangements. On the second day, Ricciardo and Allegra Stregazza came to call upon the Queen of Terre d'Ange.

Ysandre received them unhesitatingly, based on their

own actions and my advice as well, if I may say so. Ricciardo's prestige and that of the entire Sestieri Scholae had risen since the melee at the Temple; he was accorded a popular hero, for defying his brother to put down the riots. Ysandre dealt graciously with them, and it did my heart good to see Allegra Stregazza's face alight at being thanked for her role – for it was she who had received my message hidden in the Yeshuite scroll and persuaded Ricciardo to action.

"Comtesse de Montrève." They paused upon leaving the audience, and Ricciardo stooped to kiss me in gratitude. "You have preserved my life, and more," he said fervently. "If there is aught I can do for you, name it."

"There is, actually," I said, glancing at Allegra. "My lord, in Terre d'Ange, the Servants of Naamah are protected by secular guild-laws. I have noted in La Serenissima how the courtesans' quarter is despised, one of the meanest sections of the city. If you would honor me for what I have done, mayhap the courtesans of La Serenissima might be brought within the fold of the Sestieri Scholae. If it is their will to pursue this occupation, let them be trained and educated, and accorded guild-laws for their own protection and benefit."

Ricciardo responded with open-mouthed surprise, but I saw a glimmer of daring and comprehension in Allegra's eyes. She had studied the ways and manners of Terre d'Ange, envying our freedom in matters of love; if there was any woman in La Serenissima who would be willing to undertake the elevation of the courtesan class, it was Allegra Stregazza.

"Teach them to read and write, the gentle arts of poesy

and conversation?" she asked, smiling a little. "Those skills reckoned unfit for noblewomen?"

"Yes, my lady." I smiled back at her, inclining my head. "Precisely."

Ricciardo closed his mouth and swallowed, looking at his gracious and capable wife. "Comtesse," he then said to me. "In your honor, I shall so endeavor."

"I am glad to hear it."

And indeed, in this matter, Ricciardo Stregazza kept his word, creating a legacy that lived on after his death. Although no courtesan of La Serenissima would ever rival the Servants of Naamah — even in its decline, the Court of Night-Blooming Flowers remained unparalleled — they became in time a byword for wit and elegant pleasure in Caerdicca Unitas. Or at least the women did, I should say, for no self-respecting Caerdicci man would prostitute himself.

Once it became evident that the search for Imriel de la Courcel was fruitless, Ysandre sent to the Temple of Asherat to arrange for a meeting with Melisande Shahrizai. To my dismay, it was her will that I attend. Her reasoning was that I knew Melisande's mind better than anyone else; my recalcitrance had much to do with that same fact.

Nonetheless, I went.

Some of my possessions had been recovered from the quarters of Marie-Celeste Stregazza; not what I had lost at La Dolorosa — those things I never saw again, including the great collar of pearls given me by the Doge — but the items seized from my rented house on the canal. It included a portion of my wardrobe, some of which had been altered to fit Marie-Celeste, ever greedy for the latest of D'Angeline fashion, and some of which had not, for lack of matching fabric. There was considerably less of me to cover.

My *sangoire* cloak was among the items retrieved, too. That I did not wear, but folded carefully at the bottom of my trunk. I could no more bring myself to discard it than could Marie-Celeste Stregazza. Anyway, it had been a gift from Delaunay.

Also included was the signet ring of Montrève, which I reclaimed with no little relief, not so much for its own sake as for the memory of my lord Delaunay, who never wore it as was his right. It was fortunate that I never wore it either, the ring being too massive for my finger, or it too would have been lost at La Dolorosa. The ring, Marie-Celeste had kept out of practicality and not greed, using it to set my seal to a handful of forged letters such as the one, I had learned, which convinced Ysandre that I had gone to Ephesium in pursuit of the rumor of Melisande's presence. Ti-Philippe had a jeweler in the Little Court repair the chain on which Joscelin's *khai* pendant had hung, and had the signet of Montrève strung on it that I might wear it about my neck. I wept when he showed me what he'd done.

Thus was I garbed in my own attire, one of those splendid gowns made for me by Favrielle nó Eglantine, and bore the insignia of my title against my skin when I faced Melisande Shahrizai. It helped, a little, to remind me that I was indeed the Comtesse de Montrève.

Not that it mattered much, where Melisande was concerned. But it helped.

The mood within the Temple was somber and well it might be, for we had heard the rumors filtering through the

Little Court. The Priestess of the Crown and the two Elect who had aided her in blasphemy were dead, executed in accordance with Temple ritual. Asherat's vengeance was swift and sure, and their blood had darkened her altar. Passing her effigy, I averted my eyes. By their laws it was just, but I did not like to think on it.

We were escorted into a salon within the rear of the Temple; a pleasant room set about with couches, with a small fountain lending the sound of falling water. Flanked by priestesses and attendants, adorned in blue robes and the shimmering veil, Melisande received us like a Queen in her own right.

Ysandre de la Courcel took a seat opposite her without being asked. The rest of us — which included myself, Joscelin, Lord Trente, Lady Grosmaine, two guardsmen and Ysandre's surviving Cassiline — remained standing.

"Your majesty." Melisande made a graceful gesture of acknowledgment, her tone pleasant and unconcerned. "To what do I owe this honor?"

"I want the child," Ysandre said calmly. "What have you done with him?"

"Ah." Behind the veil, Melisande smiled, and I knew her face was alight with intelligence. "My son. He is safe, your majesty. I thank you for your concern."

"I am not playing a game, Lady Shahrizai." The Queen's voice hardened. "I am not playing *your* game. I am acting in the interests of the realm; no more, and no less. Where is the child?"

"The realm," Melisande said wryly. "Indeed. Is it in the interests of the realm that a single monarch hold the throne? Blessed Elua did not think so; 'twas his Companions who parceled the realm in jealous pieces. You seek to hold a prize given you by accident of birth, Ysandre de la Courcel. I seek to claim it by right of the wits with which I was born. Even the Doges of La Serenissima can point to the mandate of popular election to justify their power. Do not tell me you do not play my game."

Ysandre paled; I do not think she had truly crossed wits with Melisande before. Nonetheless, she retained her composure. "I have neither the time nor the will to engage in sophistry. If it was your wish to reform the D'Angeline system of governance, you have gone about it in a passing strange manner. The penalty for what you have done, you know full well. I am offering to spare your son the taint of it and see him raised to the honor that is his due."

"My wish? No. I merely observe that what we seek is not so different. Now you seek to claim my son for your household." Melisande leaned back against the couch, relaxed. "And what do you offer for him, your majesty? My freedom? The restoration of my titles and estates?"

The Lady Grosmaine's quill scratched on parchment as she recorded their exchange. Amaury Trente made a noise deep in his throat. "No," Ysandre said finally. "Neither."

Melisande's brows rose beneath her veil. "No?" she asked, mocking. "You offer . . . nothing? Then does it surprise you that I offer nothing in response?"

"Do you care so little for your own flesh and blood?" Ysandre asked harshly. "You are bound here until you leave or die, Melisande Shahrizai, and it is already decreed that those things are one and the same. I will make no bargains with condemned traitors; and yet you are a mother, are you not? To your son, I offer stature, honor in the eyes of the realm, his rightful role at court. Will you

damn him to a lifetime as a pawn? Will you hide behind
Asherat's altar and watch while he is made a playing piece
for lesser hands seeking to seize the same prize you
sought?" Her mouth curled in contempt. "*Love as thou wilt.*
The precept of Blessed Elua is lost on one such as you."

"Do not presume to teach me to love!"

There was an echo of power in those words, sending a
jolt the length of my spine. I took a sharp breath, glad of
Joscelin's hand resting on the small of my back, steadying
me. I was aware, horribly aware, of the way Melisande's
veiled eyes flashed with passion.

"Do you truly think I would allow you to raise my
only child and turn him against me, Queen of Terre
d'Ange?" she asked softly, rising from her couch with
deadly grace. "No. Oh, no. There has been no animosity
between us. I have always understood, if you have not,
that we played a game. Do you take my son, we become
enemies."

Ysandre drew back, but did not quail, answering
steadily. "You have sought to tear the realm asunder,
Melisande Shahrizai. I have always considered you an
enemy."

"Have you?" Melisande gave her a cutting smile. "For
two years, I have held your life in my hand. If it was only
that I wanted . . ." turning her head, she reached out to
touch the breast of Ysandre's surviving Cassiline Brother
with elegant fingers, ". . . I could have taken it at any time.
But I sought the prize, your throne. And for that, I needed
to choose a time when I could control the events that followed." Her smile froze in place. "Believe me, your
majesty," she said, "you do not want me to regard you as
my enemy."

The Cassiline, whose name was Brys nó Rinforte, breathed hard, hands twitching above his daggers, sweat beading his brow as he struggled to remain impassive. Like Joscelin, he had witnessed one of his Brethren betray his oath in the most incredible fashion, and he knew full well Melisande was the reason, if not the cause.

"*Let him be.*" Joscelin's sword rang free of its sheath and he pointed it full at her, yes grim and implacable. "I have faced damnation from more angles than you can number, Kushiel's scion. One more is of no account. Leave be."

"Cassiline." Melisande regarded him coolly, fingertips still resting on the Brother's heaving chest. "Have you faced the loss of your beloved Phèdre's affection? For surely you will earn it, if you take my life."

He looked at me; they all looked at me, even the priestesses and attendants, and I could not think for the clamor in my head, the sound of my blood beating in my ears. I pressed my fingers to my temples and shouted, "Sit down!"

No one sat, but Melisande took a step back and lowered her hand, gesturing for me to speak. Brys nó Rinforte exhaled; the Secretary's pen scratched. Ysandre watched without speaking. I looked at Melisande.

"My lady," I whispered. "You know what we seek. Is there any price not named that you will accept?"

I had not planned it, this offer; if I had thought on it, I would have faltered. And yet it was a bargain that had lain on the table between us since those dreadful days and nights when I languished in the prisons of the black isle.

They treated her as royalty, here in the Temple of Asherat — and how not, for she was, noble-born, with a courtier's deadly skill and a mother bereft of her son besides. I had spent many a dark night on La Dolorosa; I knew the extent of Asherat-of-the-Sea's grief. I knew what it meant to those who served the goddess. They would shelter her, for so long as she desired. And they would accommodate her, if she wanted me. Not a small price, no; but mayhap worth it, if it bought peace.

It would bring an end, at last, to the chain of blood-guilt I had seen my life's course forging in the cavern of the *thetalos*.

There was that.

Slowly, regretfully, Melisande Shahrizai shook her head, setting the blue-black curtain of her hair rippling down her back. "No," she said softly. "Not for this. Not for my son."

I heard Joscelin release a long-pent breath and I straightened, turning to face my Queen. "You have asked." My composed voice sounded like a stranger's to me. "You have been answered, your majesty. Will you hear my counsel?"

"I would," Ysandre said.

"Go home, your majesty," I said simply. "There is a game being played out whether you will it or no, and naught to be won here. Percy de Somerville moves against your throne, even now awaiting word that flies to him on winged hooves. Go home, and defend it."

Ysandre heard me out expressionlessly, and nodded once, rising. "My offer stands," she said to Melisande. "For now. Remember that I have made it." And without waiting for a response, she swept out of the salon, members of her retinue falling in behind her. Melisande remained standing, watching her go, thoughtful behind her gleaming veil.

I gazed at her one last time before I turned to follow

my Queen, and what she was thinking, I could not say. Even in defeat, Melisande was unhumbled. Wrenching my gaze away, I followed the departing retinue, and Joscelin's hand rested on my elbow, guiding me when my feet stumbled, anchoring me, his love the dagger by which I fixed the compass of my heart.

In the Temple proper, Lord Amaury Trente railed against the newly annointed Priestess of the Crown, she who had spoken in defense of Melisande's claim of sanctuary and stood now in the place of her predecessor. "Her life is forfeit by D'Angeline law!" he shouted, venting futile anger. "How can you defend such a one, whose honey-eyed tongue has shed more blood than a warrior's blade?"

Although she was young enough to tremble, she was old enough to stand her ground, raising her chin. "Only those who transgress against the Goddess may we punish, and that we have done in accordance with Her laws. Asherat's regard favors the cobra as well as the lion, my lord. By what authority do you claim otherwise?"

Caught up in my own turmoil, I turned away without awaiting his answer, nearly fetching up against another priestess. This one I knew, old Bianca with her milk-white eyes. Joscelin, hard on my heels, plowed into me from behind as I halted.

"Ah," the ancient woman said, satisfaction in her tone as she raised her hand to feel at my features. "Elua's child, who did his Mother's bidding and cleansed Her household. Truly, you bear Their fingerprints on your soul, child!" She chuckled to herself. "The gods themselves cannot keep Their hands off you. And your faithful shadow, bound to you in light and darkness. Shall I tell your fortune, since you have stood in the place of the Oracle and wrought ours?"

Shivering under her touch, I welcomed the solidity of Joscelin's presence behind me. "Keep your pomegranates, old mother! Let the gods choose some other vessel for a change, and look to their own. I have done my share."

"Neither the fruits of the soil nor the flesh are needed to tell your fate," Bianca said complacently, withered fingertips resting on my skin. "Serve true, and remember what others have named you; ten years' respite shall be yours if you do." Her hand fell away and she blinked like a child, sightless and bewildered. "Thus I am vouchsafed to say, and no more."

"Thank you," I whispered; what else was I to say? Stooping — for age had wizened her so that her head reached no higher than my chin — I embraced her, feeling her bones as frail as a grasshopper. "Blessed Elua keep thee, old mother. It is time for me to go home."

So it was that our audience ended and I left the Temple of Asherat-of-the-Sea for the last time, following my Queen out of the shadow of its domes into the waiting sunlight. I had kept my vow, made in the watery depths. It was finished, and I felt no victory, only loss and confusion. Members of the Queen's party were tired and frustrated, balked by the Temple's protection of Melisande and fearful of what lay before us.

And yet, with undaunted strength, Ysandre de la Courcel raised her head, gazing unerringly in the direction of home.

"You spoke truly," she said. "We ride for Terre d'Ange."

SEVENTY-EIGHT

IT TOOK yet another day to make ready our departure.

There was no time for me to seek out Kazan at the Illyrian Ambassador's; I had guessed aright, on that score. I did see Severio Stregazza, who was present at the Little Court to consult with the Vicomte de Cherevin. Although Ysandre had deferred judgement on the matter, it was tacitly assumed that the claim would eventually be settled in Severio's favor.

It was an awkward meeting, though I was glad he requested it.

"I cannot exactly thank you for bringing destruction to my family, Phèdre nó Delaunay."

"I know," I murmured. "I would that it had been otherwise, Severio. But——"

He cut me off with a gesture. "I know. What my father did was treason. What my mother did was blasphemy. By the grace of Asherat or Elua or Baal-Jupiter, or whosoever watches over me, I am enough unlike them to hate them for it. And yet they are my parents, and I was raised to honor them." He sighed. "You did what was right and necessary. I only wish it had not been."

"What will happen to them?"

"Imprisonment is likely." Severio shrugged. "Perhaps exile. It depends on the Judiciary Tribunal's findings, on the mood of the people and the Consiglio Maggiore, my grandfather's wrath, and too," he added quietly, "it depends on Terre d'Ange."

I knew what he was thinking, although neither of us said it. Marco and Marie-Celeste were not accused of plotting to kill the Doge, merely to supplant him. Their part in the conspiracy to assassinate the Queen of Terre d'Ange was a graver charge. But if matters went ill at home . . . if Ysandre lost the throne, no D'Angeline voice would call for Serenissiman justice. It would be Percy de Somerville who ruled, in the name of the rightful heir, Prince Benedicte's son. And if he called for anything, it would likely be the freedom of the infant heir's wrongfully accused mother. 'Twas no wonder Melisande was prepared to wait.

"Terre d'Ange stands under the rule of Ysandre de la Courcel," was all I said.

"Truly, I hope so. I am weary of intrigue tearing my loyalties asunder." Severio took my hand, face somber. He had grown a great deal from the rough-tongued young nobleman I'd met at the Palace. "Phèdre, I do not know if events to come will make enemies or allies of us. If Ysandre falls . . . I must stand with La Serenissima, and the city will follow where profit lies. Whosoever rules Terre d'Ange, trade must continue. But know that I will always think fondly of you, and I am sorry for what passed between us before."

"I owe you my life," I said to him. "For that, among other things, I will always be grateful, Prince Severio."

At that he smiled, a little bit. "You taught me to be proud of my D'Angeline heritage, Phèdre nó Delaunay, and to gaze at those parts of myself I despised without fear. It would not, I think, have been so ill a marriage." Bowing, Severio released my hand. "Luck to you, my lady," he said softly. "And warn your Queen not to look to the Doge overlong for support. Once she's left Serenissiman soil, Grandfather will wait to see how matters play out."

I'd never doubted it; but then, Severio was a slow learner in the family business of intrigue. I prayed he remained thus, for he was a better person for it. "Thank you, my lord, and Blessed Elua keep you in his regard."

This was my final farewell in the city of La Serenissima, for we departed the next day at dawn, escorted on the Doge's mighty ships to the D'Angeline encampment on the mainland. My heart swelled to see the bright silken tents with all their pennants fluttering, glossy-hided horses at pasture, hundreds of D'Angeline faces waiting expectantly!

So many . . . and yet so few, when one reckoned the odds. The entourage of the *progressus regalis* numbered a mere seven hundred, of which nearly two hundred were household attendants, cooks, grooms, seamstresses, hairdressers, poets, musicians and the like. Two dozen noble peers, men and women alike, accompanied the Queen; the number set down in ritual centuries ago. Some had brought their families and men-at-arms. It made me nervous to see children in the entourage – for there were several – knowing the danger we were leaving behind, and the danger that lay ahead.

The *progressus* has never been intended as a show of D'Angeline force in Caerdicca Unitas; it is an act of respect and mutual trust. No monarch has undertaken it when the city-states were at war — which is one reason it had not been done in so long — and no monarch has undertaken it without being secure in the knowledge of D'Angeline loyalties being united behind them, promising dire retribution on any nation that dared threaten the *progressus*. Although there were valid political reasons behind it, most especially the need to rebuild the Caerdicci alliances whose absence was evinced during Selig's invasion, I do not think Ysandre would have done it if it had not been for the steady urgings of Benedicte de la Courcel.

The Queen's Guard — the Queen's Guard numbered only five hundred men. And one hundred of these would remain in La Serenissima to secure the Vicomte de Cherevin's stewardship of the Little Court.

If there was a good face one could put on it, it meant that we would be able to move swiftly, retracing a course across the Caerdicci peninsula strung with alliances solidified mere days and weeks before. Elua willing, they would provide us with aid in the matter of supplies and fresh horses.

Ysandre held a brief meeting with her Captain of the Guard and his four remaining lieutenants, her Bursar and the Master of Horse. Whatever transpired, it did not fare well — a tent affords poor insulation for voices raised in heated argument. I know that Ysandre left the meeting in considerable temper, a flush of color on her high cheekbones, and Amaury Trente stormed angrily about the tents, calling for the encampment to be struck.

It was done in record speed, supply wagons loaded,

train ordered and formed. One of the Master of Horse's assistants found mounts for Joscelin, Ti-Philippe and me; there were riderless horses aplenty, since the guardsmen remaining in La Serenissima would have little use for them. There were carriages for some few members of the party, but most rode astride, as Ysandre preferred to do on the road.

We were assigned a position in the ranks of peers behind the Queen, surrounded by a cordon of her Guard. No one had bothered to tell us the plan of action; the chain of command had slipped by us, having never included us in the first place. Ti-Philippe tolerated this for all of a half-hour's march before he began querying the guards and learned that we were headed to inland Pavento, two days away. The Queen's emissaries had already ridden ahead to alert the Principe of the city.

It was Ysandre's intention to leave the non-essential members of the entourage quartered safely in Pavento, and acquire stores to proceed with all speed to Terre d'Ange by way of Milazza. Lord Trente's quarrel was not with this, it seemed. According to the rumors Ti-Philippe garnered, the Queen was refusing to consider his adamant advice that she raise a Caerdicci army to accompany us into Terre d'Ange.

In truth, I didn't know what to think; I was glad enough, for a change, to have no decisions on my head. We travelled briskly along the well-built Tiberian road, wrapped in cloaks against the autumn chill. Despite everything, I could not help but feel a certain joy. I was young and alive, and I had Joscelin and Ti-Philippe at my side. As much as we had lost — and I grieved anew every time I thought of Remy and Fortun — none of us had thought to set out on this homeward journey. Whatever lay at the end, every step of it was a blessing.

For Ysandre de la Courcel, it was another matter.

"It will be a risk just crossing the border," Joscelin murmured to me that night, as we lay together in the small soldiers' tent allotted to us; there was a sufficiency of those, too. "With four hundred men? It wouldn't take much for de Somerville to lay a trap."

"De Somerville doesn't know she's alive," I reminded him. "Though I wouldn't put it past Melisande to have thought of it anyway."

"No." He propped himself up on one elbow, regarding me in the faint light our campfires cast through the oiled silk of the tent. "Would you truly have gone with her, if she had asked it?"

I heard the change in his voice; we hadn't talked about it since that fruitless meeting in the Temple of Asherat. There had been little privacy and less time. I laid my hand on his warm chest, feeling his strong heart beat beneath it. "I don't know," I said truthfully. "Joscelin, it would have made an end to it and laid the foundation for peace. For that . . . mayhap, yes."

There was more to it, for it had to do with what happened on Kriti; I had seen the darkness of my own soul, and I could never close my eyes to it. And I am an *anguissette*, when all is said and done. For these things, I lacked words. One cannot speak of mysteries. Still, Joscelin had been a priest in his own right – and he knew me.

He was silent for a moment, winding a lock of my hair about his fingers. "The Yeshuites promise it," he said at length. "Complete absolution. I thought about it. In the end . . ." He smiled wryly. "In the end, I chose as I will always choose. It frightens me to think that one day she will ask, and you do not know what you'll choose."

"When you threatened her, Melisande named a price you would not pay," I said. "I set one that she will not. She would play the game of thrones with Kushiel himself; she was willing to risk sacrificing all her plans to do it. Not her son. The child is a double-edged weapon, Joscelin. It is knowledge, and worth having."

"Phèdre nó Delaunay," he whispered, drawing me closer, "does your mind never cease?"

"Sometimes," I admitted. "If you—"

I didn't need to tell him that, either, for although it too is a mystery in its own right, it is Naamah's mystery and its knowledge is vouchsafed to all lovers if they will but accept it. In the old days, we would have quarrelled bitterly over what had happened in the Temple. Now, Joscelin heeded Naamah's wisdom rather than Cassiel's logic, and silenced me with a kiss, setting about doing those things which caused my mind to cease working altogether.

On the second day, we reached Pavento and were met outside the city walls by an honor guard sent by the Principe, Gregorio Livinius. While an encampment was set up in the fertile fields surrounding the city, Ysandre and a hand-picked company of nobles — which included me — were escorted inside.

It is a pleasant city, Pavento, although I saw little enough of it. We rode straightaway to the palace of the Principe, wrought of grey stone quarried from the mountains to the north, but softened by brightly woven tapestries; they are famous, in Pavento, for their dyes.

Gregorio Livinius was a robust, energetic man in his mid-forties. He had been eager to secure ties with Ysandre, hoping to better his city's fortunes through increased trade with Terre d'Ange. It had fallen off in the years of Skaldic raiding threatening the overland routes, but since the defeat of Waldemar Selig, the Skaldi had withdrawn their aggressions.

It was to our fortune that Principe Gregorio remained eager to support this fresh alliance, although he bargained hard for the price of his aid. Most of what he demanded, Ysandre gave unhesitatingly. In exchange, he would provide stores for our journey and open the city to her entourage, giving safe haven to nigh onto two hundred folk — "Anyone who cannot hold a sword," Ysandre said grimly.

There were exceptions, of course; as the Secretary of the Presence, the Lady Denise Grosmaine was bound to accompany the Queen, and some few of the grooms, attendants and cooks were reckoned vital, as was the chirurgeon.

And there was me, although I was not reckoned vital.

In the end, it was sheer pleading that swayed her; two others among her ladies-in-waiting accompanied her, too, for she could scarce refuse their pleas having heeded mine. Ysandre would fain have left us all. Fewer to endanger; fewer to protect.

"My lady," I begged, kneeling before her. "I have been deceived, imprisoned, bludgeoned, near-drowned, abducted, storm-lost, driven nigh out of my wits and held at knife-point. If you grant me nothing else, *let me go home!*"

"Phèdre," Ysandre sighed. "The more I try to set you out of harm's way, the deeper in it I find you. All right. Like as not, you'd only turn up with an army of brigands at your back if I tried to leave you. You may come." She cast an acerbic eye at the high-spirited Baronesse Marie de

Flairs, already moving to add her plea to mine, and the Lady Vivienne Neldor a step behind her. "Elua, enough! My lord Cassiline, will you take responsibility for their safety?"

At her side, Brys nó Rinforte looked queasy; but it was Joscelin the Queen had meant. He took a step forward, bowing deeply with crossed vambraces. I had washed most of the dye from his hair at the Little Court, and trimmed the ends so that he looked somewhat presentable. "Your majesty," he said calmly. "I will."

So it was decided, and Joscelin Verreuil placed in command of those men-at-arms attendant on the Queen's ladies. If I feared they would balk at it, I was wrong, for his battle in the Temple with David de Rocaille was already spoken of in hushed murmurs. Ti-Philippe bore it with amusement when he learned of Joscelin's appointment. The days of animosity were long gone between them, replaced by bonds of mutual respect.

Ysandre asked no military aid of Principe Gregorio, and if Lord Trente bridled at it, he held his tongue; Pavento was small, and had few troops to spare. His hopes were pinned on Milazza, and the argument remained open between them.

The other piece of good news to come from our sojourn there was that Melisande's couriers had not stopped to spread word of Ysandre's supposed assassination. 'Twould have slowed their course, but it would have made ours more difficult in turn, taking the time to lay the rumors to rest and convince potential allies that our position remained tenable. As it was, Ysandre needed to offer no explanation save that rumor of a minor rebellion at home had reached her ears, necessitating a speedy return.

That was the good news.

The bad news was that Principe Gregorio had received notice that a pair of D'Angeline riders had been found slain on the road slightly west of Pavento, apparently the victims of robbers. Although they had been stripped of their belongings and apparel, we knew them by description — Royal Couriers, the both of them.

Plans within plans and traps within traps; Melisande had anticipated well. No one bore word ahead of us save her hand-picked couriers.

And their lead had lengthened to a good five days.

SEVENTY-NINE

WE LEFT Pavento in haste, unburdened of wagons and carriages, pushing our mounts as fast as we dared go. In consultation with the Master of Horse, Lord Trente had determined that we were better off conserving our own animals than seeking fresh mounts for four hundred and some riders.

There was no longer any hope of averting treachery. Whatever would happen, would happen; Melisande's couriers would deliver word to Percy de Somerville well ahead of our return. If the Kritian ship had arrived safely, Roxanne de Mereliot had a full report of de Somerville's betrayal — what she could do about it, I could not say, save pass on my warning to Barquiel L'Envers and other known allies of the Queen, and mayhap begin preparing for war. Quintilius Rousse would lend his aid, but there was little enough the Navy could do on land.

It was no simple matter, for de Somerville held the Royal Army at his command, and was the sovereign Duc of L'Agnace as well. Without proof — and a considerable force at their disposal — they could not arrest him out of hand. And if Ghislain was with him, it meant Azzalle was in rebellion. With Azzalle threatening Namarre's borders, Barquiel would have no support from his own province; indeed, with the news of Ysandre's death, he would find little aid forthcoming from any quarter. The City of Elua would be islanded in the heart of de Somerville's forces.

Of course, if the Kritian ship had not arrived, he would be dead.

The reality of the threat awaiting us upon our return had come home with the death of the two Royal Couriers. At best, we faced a nation on the brink of civil war. We made good speed across the Caerdicci peninsula during that wild journey, and a mood of grim determination united our company.

Many years later, I learned that there are stories still told of the ride of Ysandre de la Courcel's company along the old northern route in Caerdicca Unitas. It was in truth a sight to behold. The Queen's Guard wore gleaming armor with silver inlay, and surcoats of deep-blue with the swan insignia of House Courcel; a dozen and more pennants fluttered in the breeze above us, marking the noble Houses that rode with Ysandre, and the gold lily of Elua on a field of green above them all. 'Twas where we passed without pause that rumor grew, telling of a fell company with a dire light shining on their faces, riding fey and terrible without need for sustenance or sleep, and the beautiful Queen who led them ever onward, onward.

I daresay I laughed when I heard these tales; the commonfolk do not tell them where we made camp for the night, the Bursar bartering with shrewd farmers for use of their fields and streams while four hundred weary and saddle-sore D'Angeline soldiers waited impatiently for orders to dismount, cursing the packhorses milling about and fouling their lead-lines. And yet there is a truth to it, after all.

It took us a week's time to reach Milazza, and our supplies from Pavento held out long enough. Amaury Trente misliked our bypassing cities along the route, forsaking the possibility of raising a Caerdicci army; that much was clear. He had great hopes of Milazza, which lies closest to the inland D'Angeline border of all the great city-states.

Ysandre remained adamant.

"No," she said succinctly. "Whatever else I do, I will *not* bring a foreign army onto D'Angeline soil, Amaury."

He disheveled his hair, frustrated. By midday tomorrow, we would reach Milazza, and he had counted on convincing the Queen ere now. "Majesty, with a thousand additional men, you can march safely into Eisande – and the Duke of Milazza can spare them, easily. In Blessed Elua's name, will you not hear reason?"

"Reason this, my lord Trente," Ysandre said in an implacable voice. "Percy de Somerville cannot hope to sway the whole of the Royal Army and the people of Terre d'Ange against me unless he makes them believe me a traitor. A Caerdicci army would give him that proof."

"He doesn't even know you're alive!" Amaury shouted, clutching his hair.

"But he will," Ysandre said softly. "He will hear the reports and he will know, though he may deny it and name me an imposter. Shall I be so naïve to assume de Somerville has not planned for the contingency of failure?"

Amaury Trente sighed and dropped his hand to rest on the map spread on the camp-table beside the central fire where Ysandre held her war council. "All right," he said. "All right. Then let us at least make haste to Liguria, and travel by ship to Marsilikos, where we will find safe harbor and allies aplenty."

"My lord Trente." Ti-Philippe cleared his throat apologetically at his glare. "Forgive me, but I have been a sailor all my life, and I tell you this: it is perilous late in the season to make that crossing. You will be hard-pressed to find sufficient ships willing to make the journey."

I shuddered inwardly at the thought of yet another dangerous sea voyage, and held my tongue. Amaury pounded his fist, making the map jump.

"Is there no other way?" he demanded. "Surely, there must be some means of crossing onto D'Angeline soil that is both feasible and acceptable, Ysandre!"

The Queen's face was set and stubborn in the firelight, and I knew that she would hear no arguments that did not involve riding straight for the City of Elua to set matters aright. Edging around her advisors, I gazed at the map beneath Amaury's clenched fist.

Remember what others have named you . . .

"My lady," I said. "There is a way, if you will hear it."

Ysandre gave me a sharp look and inclined her head. "I am listening, Phèdre."

"If we travel north from Milazza and cross the border here, in the foothills," I said, tracing a path with one finger, "we enter Camlach, under the warding of the Unforgiven. See, here lies the garrison of Southfort."

"Camlach!" Amaury Trente said in disgust. "The Black Shields have betrayed the Queen once already, Comtesse. What makes you think they will be less swift than de Somerville's forces to do it again?"

"I will stand surety for it with my life, my lord," I said steadily. "Whatever politics de Somerville has played with them, the Unforgiven have sworn an oath unto the death to redeem the sin of that betrayal. And because they have sworn to the way of expiation . . ." I cleared my throat, ". . . they have sworn to obey my lord Kushiel and his chosen."

Beside me, Joscelin stirred, remembering. Ysandre looked hard at me.

"You would offer your sovereign Queen and rightful ruler of Terre d'Ange the protection of soldiers sworn to obey an *anguissette*?" she inquired dryly. I felt color rise to my cheeks.

"My lady—" I began in a faint voice.

"Well and good." Ysandre cut me off, gazing into the distance, and I understood then that she had not spoken in mockery of me – and I saw, too, that 'twas no mere stubbornness that held her to this course. It is said, at times, the Scions of Elua could hear his call; I do believe Ysandre heard it then, calling her home to his City. "It is my pride and folly that has brought us to this pass. If I had heeded your fears long ago, I would not have gone trusting to La Serenissima. Let us choose the way of expiation, and place ourselves in Kushiel's hand. The Unforgiven shall form our point guard, and escort us to the City of Elua."

"The Unforgiven have sworn on Camael's sword to ward the borders of Camlach for all time!" Amaury Trente sighed again. "And you granted them that right, Ysandre. If they prove loyal, do you think they will be lightly forsworn?"

"Sometimes," Joscelin murmured, "one must break one oath to uphold a higher."

"Yes." Ysandre turned her gaze back to me. "What do you say, Phèdre nó Delaunay? It is you who shall command them, and not I. Kushiel's chosen has the right to ask what the Queen of Terre d'Ange does not. Will the Unforgiven obey?"

I saw in my mind Tarren d'Eltoine's face washed by firelight, calm and implacable. Kushiel's hand need not know its master's bidding, he had said to me; but I had endured the mysteries of the Temenos since then. I knew what I did, when I asked men to break their oaths and march toward death. Kushiel's hand, they had called me; but in Phaistos, a slave-girl had named me *lypiphera*, the pain-bearer. "Yes, my lady," I said softly. "They will obey."

Thus it was decided that we would ask only hospitality of the Duke of Milazza, and a replenishment of our stores. There, we were received with much fanfare, and our entire party ushered into the gates of the city, a gilded canopy borne over the head of Ysandre de la Courcel as we paraded through the streets to enter the mighty keep of the Castello. It is a vast, walled fortress encompassing an entire park, with tall, sturdy towers at every corner.

The Duke of Milazza was a slow, shrewd man, and I could see he wondered at Ysandre's haste and her story. I will say that she faced him down magnificently, cool gaze and raised chin giving not an inch before his suspicion; and I thought, too, that she had chosen wisely in refusing to ask him for troops. It was his Duchess, who was a noblewoman of an ancient Tiberian line, who intervened, calling upon the laws of hospitality to uphold Ysandre's request.

So we were feasted in the Castello, and the Duke

opened his stores and promised guides to show us the quickest way through the foothills of the Camaelines. I think Amaury Trente repented his eagerness to rely on Caerdicci forces that day, though he never admitted as much. Still, 'twas there for all to see, how swiftly the proffered hand of an ally may be withdrawn when one's fortune turns.

In the morning, we departed for Camlach.

Of that journey, I will say little. I have crossed the Camaelines before, at their highest peak in the depths of winter. It was a dreadful journey, and one on which I thought I might die or simply give up several times daily. If this was considerably less harsh, it was by no means pleasant. I dug my *sangoire* cloak out of my bags and wore it atop the woolen Illyrian cloak, shivering under both. I daresay we all would have flagged on that journey, were it not for Ysandre de la Courcel, who endured the same hardships and ignored them all, gazing westward with the fixed intensity of a sailor following the Navigator's Star. Like the others, I huddled atop my mount and followed after her, blowing on my near-frozen fingers. I'd have laid down with Selig himself for a pair of Skaldi mittens on that journey.

Joscelin, of course, was bright-eyed and alert, breathing in the mountain air and looking about him. He was born and bred to the mountains of Siovale, which are at least as rugged as these foothills. I hated him a little for that, and took comfort in knowing that Ti-Philippe did too.

Our Milazzan guides — hill-folk themselves, fur-clad and silent — melted away as we drew near the border, pointing out the last pass with quick bows. Ysandre's

Bursar tossed them some silver coins, which they caught adeptly before disappearing.

We filed through the pass in a long line, our tired horses stumbling.

Terre d'Ange, I thought. I was home. No matter what else happened, we had at least come this far. Others felt the same, for I heard more than one voice offer a breathed prayer of thanks.

It was only minutes before a lone sentry spotted us. Amaury Trente rode after him, shouting, but too late; the sentry mounted at lightning speed and set off on his fresh horse. Lord Trente was soon left wallowing in his wake and drew up. I leaned on my pommel, glad of a moment's rest, and looked up to find Ysandre gazing at me.

"It is your plan, Phèdre," she said. "What would you have us do?"

"Follow him," I replied wearily. "And let me ride at the fore, my lady. I have promised to stand surety for this plan."

Ysandre paused, and nodded; Amaury Trente's advance guard parted to make a passage. I rode to take my place at the front of the party, with Joscelin at my side, my Cassiline shadow, pausing only to give a few words of instruction to Ti-Philippe and the other men-at-arms who warded Ysandre's ladies.

So we rode onward.

It was late afternoon when the scouting party found us, and the sun slanted low and orange through the pines. They had chosen their spot with care; a narrow bottleneck in the stony path, leaving our party strung out in a straggling line behind us. Twenty of them, crossbows at the ready, in well-worn armor with black shields hanging at their sides. I knew how skilled their formations were. A dozen men would suffice to hold us here for the better part of an hour, while the others raced to report; doubtless the garrison had already been turned out and was on its way.

"Who are you, who have entered unbidden onto D'Angeline soil?" one of the foremost asked, his voice muffled by the visor of his helm. "Name yourselves!"

I nudged my horse forward, fearfully aware of the barbed quarrel of his crossbow pointed directly at my heart. "My lord guardsman, I am Phèdre nó Delaunay de Montrève," I said aloud. "I ask safe passage among the Unforgiven for her majesty Ysandre de la Courcel, the Queen of Terre d'Ange."

There was no echo of Kushiel's bronze-edged thunder to my words, no hint of scarlet haze to my vision; only my voice, thin and tired in the cold air. Nonetheless, the leader checked, putting up his crossbow. A murmur arose, before and behind. He lifted his visor and rode forward, setting his horse sideways to me as he leaned in the saddle, peering at me. Beside me, Joscelin tensed, his hands edging for his daggers. Low sunlight glanced off his vambraces, and one of the Unforgiven exclaimed.

"My lady!" The leader of the scouting party's eyes widened; he had seen my dart-stricken gaze. Before I could speak he had dismounted, kneeling in the snow-dusted pine mast. "Kushiel's chosen," he murmured. "We are yours to command."

Once again, I sat bewildered as, one by one, the Unforgiven dismounted and bowed their heads, kneeling to me, and this second time was no less strange than the first. I turned in the saddle to meet the steady, violet gaze of my Queen, who had chosen to risk her very throne at my word. I turned back to face the Unforgiven.

"Take us to Southfort," I said. "I have a favor to ask Captain d'Eltoine."

EIGHTY

TARREN D'ELTOINE received us with hospitality and no little awe.

"Majesty," he said bluntly, going to one knee and bowing his head to Ysandre. "Forgive my surprise, but we did not look to see you alive. I received word two days past that you were slain in La Serenissima, and your uncle the Duc L'Envers had seized the throne and sealed the City."

Tears of relief stung my eyes. "It's true?" I asked, heedless of protocol. "Barquiel L'Envers holds the City of Elua?"

D'Eltoine opened his mouth to reply, then glanced at Ysandre, who gave a brief nod. "Rise, Captain, and tell us what you know," she bid him.

This he did, in the crowded council room of the Southfort garrison, while members of the Queen's party and the Unforgiven alike pressed close to hear the news. "Majesty, I don't vouch for the truth of it, but this is what I was told. Six days ago, Prince Benedicte's couriers brought the news that there had been rioting in La Serenissima, and you had been foully murdered as part of a conspiracy headed by the newly elected Doge's brother, with the aid of a Cassiline traitor. They carried orders to his grace the Duc de Somerville to secure the City's safety, for Prince Benedicte would be following in all haste. Lord Percy immediately began to move his troops from Champs-de-Guerre, and, begging your pardon, majesty, your uncle Barquiel used his authority as Regent to stage a coup and seal the City against him."

"And now?" Ysandre asked grimly.

The Unforgiven Captain shrugged, spreading his hands. "L'Envers had a fair number of his own men in the City, and it seems the Palace and City Guards are loyal to him. Enough to hold, for a time. The Royal Army is encamped at the very walls of the City; Lord Percy is reluctant to use siege engines against the jewel of Terre d'Ange. It is his hope that the City will surrender and give over your uncle when Prince Benedicte arrives."

"Prince Benedicte isn't coming, my lord," I said softly. "You guessed rightly when you guessed I went hunting traitors. I found them."

He was silent for a moment, and when he spoke, his voice was heavy. "Prince Benedicte?"

"Yes." I felt pity for him; he would take it hard, having served already under one traitor. "He was one. I sought the missing guardsmen of Troyes-le-Mont, do you remember? I found them in La Serenissima, in the Little Court of Benedicte de la Courcel."

Tarren d'Eltoine was not a slow-witted man. He looked at me with a flat gaze. "Who sent his couriers to Lord Percy, the Royal Commander, and not the Queen's chosen regent."

"Yes, my lord," I said. "I am sorry."

"You are certain?"

"We are certain," Ysandre interposed in her cool voice, though there was compassion in her expression. "It was Percy de Somerville who enabled Melisande Shahrizai's escape." And she told him, then, the whole of the story, beginning with de Somerville's complicity in the schemes of Lyonette de Trevalion, all the way through Melisande's blackmail, her deception in La Serenissima, Prince Benedicte's betrayal, the plots of the Stregazza, David de Rocaille's attempted revenge for his sister's long-ago death, and the missing heir, Imriel de la Courcel.

D'Eltoine's mien grew stony with gathering anger, reflected in the faces of all the Unforgiven. "Majesty," he said when she had finished. "My couriers are at your disposal. They will carry this story the length of Camlach, and to Eisheth, to Namarre, to Siovale, that you might begin raising an army to move against Lord Percy—"

"No." Ysandre shook her head. "While I am Queen, I will not instigate civil war in Terre d'Ange. I ride to the City of Elua, Captain, to claim my throne."

He stared at her; behind me, I could hear Amaury Trente heave a sigh. "What would you have me do, majesty?" d'Eltoine asked, bewildered.

I stepped forward. "My lord Captain," I said formally. "You told me once that the Unforgiven had sworn to obey Kushiel's chosen. This thing I ask, in Kushiel's name: That your company lead her majesty the Queen to the City of Elua."

"Leave the borders?" Tarren d'Eltoine blanched. "Comtesse, we have sworn an oath to Camael as well, to ward the passes against the Skaldi for as long as we shall live. Do you ask us to abandon this trust?"

"You have other recruits to man the garrisons, and the Skaldi have retreated far from our borders," I said to him. "The threat to the realm lies now at its heart, my lord, and the path to your redemption lies in facing betrayal, not the Skaldi."

He looked away from me, murmuring, "What you ask is hard, *anguissette*."

"Yes." Though I ached for his pain, I did not waver. "I know."

For a long moment, he said nothing, then gave at last a brusque nod. "Majesty," he said to Ysandre. "Grant me a day, to assemble the Unforgiven. We will escort you to the City of Elua."

So it was decided, and riders set out within the hour, racing north to carry word to the garrisons' relay stations. I knew well how swiftly the Black Shields could muster. For our part, we took our ease as best we could in the confines of Southfort and beyond, establishing a campsite for the bulk of Amaury Trente's guard.

With a decision made and a plan to implement – even a foolhardy one – our spirits were strengthened. It was, after all, somewhat of a homecoming; and we were D'Angeline. Kegs of wine were brought forth and heated in vast kettles above the hearth, mulled with spices, to be shared among guardsmen and soldiers alike, and those few of us who were neither. One of the grey-haired ex-soldiers who served as a steward to the garrison brought out a lap-harp in fairly good tune, and Marie de Flairs and Vivienne Neldor took turns at singing and playing. Ysandre's ladies-in-waiting had endured the journey without complaint, and I had come to admire them both. I daresay their efforts did a good deal to raise the spirits of the Camaeline soldiery, still reeling from our news. We who had been on the road had had longer to become accustomed to it.

Ysandre was closeted with Captain d'Eltoine, Lord Trente and their various subcommanders, plotting a detailed course of action. I did not regret being excluded from these strategies, being content to leave it to the heads of state for once.

As the evening wore on, the dice emerged, as is wont to happen when wine and soldiers are gathered in the same place. I watched Ti-Philippe relieve one of the Unforgiven of a month's pay, chuckling as he threw the winning roll. He looked almost as he had in earlier days, when Remy and Fortun were alive, and it heartened me to see it. I said as much to Joscelin, who agreed.

"I never reckoned him much more than a brash fool, before," he said soberly. "I thought he entered your service for a lark. But I was wrong, he's steadier than I ever guessed. He was the one who kept the Yeshuites together when we attacked La Dolorosa, and he de-serves most of the credit for getting us back alive, at that; I was half out of my wits, thinking my attempt to rescue you might have caused your death. It nearly did, too."

I thought of Melisande's luxurious dungeon beneath the Little Court and shivered. "Saved me from a fate worse than death, more like. Elua knows what would have happened if you hadn't come that night. I don't, and I'm glad of it."

Ti-Philippe scooped up his winnings, stuffing coins into the bulging purse at his belt. A silver regal tumbled free, rolling across the floor. It glinted in the torchlight like those coins the Bursar had thrown to our Milazzan guides. I bent to retrieve it. 'Twas a new-minted coin, one of the

first of Ysandre's regency, depicting her seated in profile
with the lily of Elua on the reverse. It was a good likeness;
D'Angeline artisans are skilled at such things. I gazed at it,
remembering Kazan and his men casting coins bearing the
proscribed image and arms of the Ban of Illyria into silver
ingots. After having met him, I do not think I would have
recognized Vasilii Kolcei from his face on those coins.

But I would recognize Ysandre de la Courcel from this
one. I remembered the Master of Ceremonies preparing
for Drustan mab Necthana's entrance into the City, and
how I had ridden in a merry party with Nicola L'Envers y
Aragon, who handed coins to children along the way and
bid them to hail the Cruarch with flowers, while I taught
them a greeting in Cruithne.

"My lady Phèdre." Ti-Philippe gave me an amused
bow and held out his hand. "My winnings, if you please."

"Philippe!" Startled out of my reverie, I glanced at
him. "May I keep this for a while?"

He tossed his dice in one hand, grinning. "Will you
play me for it, my lady?"

I raised my eyebrows and smiled. "If you wish."

I daresay it was luck as much as anything else that won
me the roll, although Kazan's men had taught me well. Ti-
Philippe surrendered the coin graciously and the soldiers
laughed as I tucked it in my kirtle.

Joscelin looked quizzically at me. "Phèdre nó
Delaunay, what are you about now?" he asked, stroking
my hair.

"Oh, nothing." I leaned against him, enjoying the
warmth and solidity of him. "I have an idea, that's all."

"It seems I've heard those words before," he said
wryly.

In the morning, I sought an audience with Ysandre and her now-joint Captains of War. Amaury Trente clutched his hair and stared at me in disbelief. Ysandre made no response, but looked inquiringly at Tarren d'Eltoine. And d'Eltoine, in turn, paced back and forth in the council chamber, scowling.

"You know this is insane?" he demanded, fetching up before me.

"It's merely a thought, my lord," I said, subdued. "It was my understanding that one of the chief difficulties lay in establishing the Queen's identity before de Somerville can brand her an imposter."

"It is." The Unforgiven Captain closed his eyes. "It's just . . ."

"Will it work?" Ysandre asked.

He opened his eyes. "It might."

"Open the treasuries." Her voice brooked no argument. "Turn out the guards' purses. As many coins as you have with my likeness, I shall repay at double their worth. Captain, any means of succeeding without bloodshed, I will attempt, including this."

"As you wish, majesty."

It was a considerable haul, all told, for the garrisons of Camlach were not poor, and the soldiery had little on which to spend their pay during the cold months. I felt a little sick watching the preparations, for this was wholly mine own idea. If it failed, I could not blame it on the promptings of any god. Then again, if it failed, likely enough we were doomed anyway. A mere six hundred, riding against the whole of the Royal Army, who numbered into the thousands — and no one knew yet whether or not Ghislain de Somerville was involved, or how. The Unforgiven had no news out of Azzalle.

For all his protests, Lord Amaury Trente implemented Ysandre's orders with dogged efficiency, and I could see why she had chosen him as Captain of the Guard for her *progressus*. Ysandre was never one to seek unquestioning obedience, merely loyalty. He had that, and to his credit, not one of his guardsmen faltered in following, though I am sure many of them thought it folly.

I worried more about Brys nó Rinforte, her Cassiline guard, who followed her like a haggard grey shadow. David de Rocaille's actions had shocked him to the core, and I did not think he had recovered from it; those who are too rigid in their beliefs will break rather than bend with fortune's blows. I know it worried Joscelin too, but there was naught he could say that the man was willing to hear.

By contrast, the Unforgiven grew steadily firmer in their resolve as more and more of them poured into Southfort throughout the day, ultimately accepting the dire news and the hard task I had set them with fierce Camaeline determination. Although I understand little enough the desire to seek glory in battle, I understood the hunger for redemption which drove them. My lord Kushiel is a harsh master, but his worship has ever served a purpose.

Tarren d'Eltoine had his day, and when the sun rose on the following day, the full company of Black Shields had assembled at Southfort. It was in itself a heroic effort, though they have their own means of communicating and travelling at speed through the foothills of the Camaelines, a system laid down by Isidore d'Aiglemort when he formed the Allies of Camlach.

It was a cold, crisp morning when we departed from Southfort, still and windless, the sky a brilliant blue overhead, our breath emerging in gusts of frost. Ysandre de la Courcel gave a short speech ere we departed, seated astride her favorite grey palfrey, her purple cloak flowing over its haunches and the morning sun gilding her fair hair.

"It is our purpose to ride hence to the City of Elua and reclaim the throne to which we were born!" she said in her clear, carrying voice. "Not for power nor wealth do I seek to do this thing, but for love. Blessed Elua bid us, *Love as thou wilt*. Terre d'Ange, my first and greatest love, is threatened by those who would tear her asunder to possess her. As I am a Scion of Elua's lineage and the rightfully crowned Queen of Terre d'Ange, I will not permit this to come to pass. Let no man or woman among you set forth this day by aught save his or her free will! Let no one among you ride with me save for love of Blessed Elua, and this glorious nation he begot!"

We cheered her then until our throats were ragged, and the Unforgiven pikemen hefted the points of their weapons heavenward. Ysandre's face was flushed and brilliant, and I think that all there assembled that day saw what I had seen outside Milazza; that the bright shadow of Elua lay upon her like a mantle.

Thus did we depart.

EIGHTY-OΠE

IT WAS four days' ride to the City of Elua, and rumor raced before us like a brushfire.

We had known it would happen; indeed, we encouraged it. Even in the small villages of Camlach, they had heard that the Queen was dead and Percy de Somerville and Barquiel L'Envers strove for mastery of the City. D'Angelines are not known to sit idle on news of such moment. I am happy to say that word that Ysandre de la Courcel yet lived was received with overwhelming joy.

I had seen it when I rode to Southfort in the spring; Terre d'Ange had prospered under Ysandre's rule, and her marriage to Drustan mab Necthana had brought further wealth and trade to the nation. If the nobles bridled at the unprecedented alliance with a foreign power and the mingling of Elua's lineage with barbarian blood — for Prince Benedicte and Percy de Somerville had not been alone in that sentiment — the commonfolk knew that their beautiful Queen had wed for love. They remembered too that her barbarian king was a hero of the realm, and they had known only peace and prosperity under this union.

Here and there, we handed out silver coins along the way, and those who received them marked well the resemblance. There would be no doubt, in Camlach, that the woman styling herself Ysandre de la Courcel was not an imposter.

In L'Agnace, it grew more difficult.

There was no way to prevent the spread of rumor, unless we marched day and night, and both Tarren d'Eltoine and Amaury Trente had reckoned that mere folly. Thus had we chosen to exploit it, letting word race ahead from village to village whenever we paused for an evening's rest. If the citizens of Terre d'Ange awaited us with hope and joy in Camlach, some few leagues into L'Agnace, we encountered rebounding denial.

Word of Ysandre's survival had reached Percy de Somerville's ears, and he had responded in the only manner he could, naming her an imposter.

It hurt her, to see simple farmers and humble folk turned out to jeer, children clutching clods of frozen earth to hurl at her retinue. The Unforgiven formed the vanguard, pikemen marching four abreast, cavalry following behind, their black-painted shields grim and foreboding. They glanced neither to the right nor the left at the jeers, nor did Ysandre, riding between Tarren d'Eltoine and the Captain of Northfort's garrison, with her Cassiline guard a half-pace behind. It fell to those of us who followed after to give the lie to de Somerville's claim, heralding Ysandre as the true-born Queen of Terre d'Ange and naming the Duc de Somerville's actions as lies and treason.

I daresay it was the coins that turned the tide, although

Amaury Trente would never admit to it. At first it was the children who shouted and scrambled after them, quarreling in the fallow fields over gleaming bits of silver; the adults would not be bought so easily, reckoning D'Angeline pride at a higher price. But when one or two of the children stood and stared, pointing at Ysandre, they began to take notice.

And we began to acquire a following.

Some of it, doubtless, was due to the mere fact that we were literally throwing money away; not all of it, I think. They looked, and they believed, grasping the truth that here lay a drama unfolding worthy of the poets' songs. And they were D'Angeline. By twos and threes, a trickle swelling to a flood, they came to join their Queen.

How many came, I cannot say. There were farmers and cartwrights and weavers, chandlers, beekeepers and cheese-makers; no town or village but contributed a few. Some were old enough to have lined visages, though hale enough to march; some few were young, not yet out of childhood. Those we sent back, when we could, though more replaced them down the road. I saw the tears that stood in Ysandre's eyes as she set her face determinedly toward the City of Elua.

So did they. And their numbers continued to grow.

It was at the crossroads of Eisheth's Way that a unit of de Somerville's cavalry intercepted us; five hundred soldiers, mounted and armed. I learned later that they had been stationed in Eisande along the road from Milazza, poised to thwart any incursion – and indeed, it was Melisande's cunning that had suggested the precaution, although it was de Somerville's orders that called them back at the rumor of the Queen's return and set them in our path. I do not think he had reckoned on the whole of the Unforgiven accompanying us.

I know he did not count on the hundreds of unarmed commonfolk.

It was a standoff. The soldiers of the Royal Army were strung in a broad arc across the road and the bordering fields. Our company halted, and Tarren d'Eltoine gave a single command; the Unforgiven responded like a well-oiled machine, pikemen spreading out in a double line to face de Somerville's soldiers, the cavalry bunched behind, poised like an arrow to pierce the Royal Army's lines. We were secure behind them, bolstered on both sides and behind by the Queen's Guard under Lord Trente's command.

Ysandre's herald, who had been chosen no less for his bravery than his ringing voice, made his way to the fore-front of the party, bearing a standard from which flew both the Lily and Stars of Elua and his Companions, and the Silver Swan of House Courcel.

"Make way!" he cried, his voice echoing across the shorn fields. "Make way for Ysandre de la Courcel, the Queen of Terre d'Ange!"

There was a pause, and I knew the commander of de Somerville's cavalry was assessing the situation. He could not identify the Queen at that distance, but he could count our numbers and he was no fool. In a moment, he nudged his tall mount forward, wheeling it in the road. "Imposter!" he shouted. "Vile impersonator! We will meet you and your Black Shield traitors at the gates of the City!"

With that he raised one hand and uttered a command, and the outspread wings of the Royal Army cavalry collapsed, folding in upon themselves as they whirled in an ordered retreat, showing us the flying haunches and tails of their mounts. Some of our D'Angeline followers ran after them, yelling, but soon gave up the chase.

"Well," Tarren d'Eltoine remarked thoughtfully. "We know they will be awaiting us."

In a few short hours, he was proved right.

I had not been there in the field, when Drustan mab Necthana, Ghislain de Somerville and Isidore d'Aiglemort assailed the vast might of the Skaldic army with a few thousand men. I had seen it happen, from atop the ramparts of Troyes-le-Mont; still, that was not the same thing. This day, though, I knew how they must have felt. The white walls of the City of Elua gleamed in the distance, and between us and the City lay the whole of the Royal Army. Although the standing army was only four thousand strong, we numbered a mere six hundred, and the odds were much the same.

Percy de Somerville would not make Waldemar Selig's mistake; he kept a portion of his troops in reserve, relentlessly guarding the egresses from the City. If Barquiel L'Envers had the means to mount a counterattack, he would not be given the opportunity.

The bulk of his forces were awaiting us, and they were in such a formation that let us know de Somerville had taken our measure from his cavalry's report, and prepared to meet us. Even as we drew nigh, a row of archers kneeling in the forefront with L'Agnacite longbows loosed a volley.

"Up shields!" Captain d'Eltoine shouted; and up they rose, a wall of black-painted steel warding the skies. It is an old Tiberian tactic and a good one, effective with infantry;

it was not designed for use with cavalry. A rain of arrows fell hissing, and I heard the skittering of metal on metal as they glancing off shields, and cries of pain where they found flesh, the awful sound of the wounded horses. Someone nearby was moaning. Peering out from behind Joscelin's arms — for he had leaned over to grab me hard, pulling me half out of the saddle to ward me with both vambraces — I saw a boy of no more than twelve to the side of our column, green with pain as he put an uncomprehending hand to the shaft protruding from his chest. He'd run on ahead, to get a better view.

"Ah, no," I murmured. "Elua, no!"

Ysandre saw it too; her throat moved as she swallowed. It was almost in a whisper that she gave the command to Tarren d'Eltoine: "Advance."

And we did.

It must have been a fearsome sight, that wall of Black Shields moving forward undaunted. Not all of them did, for some of Percy de Somerville's L'Agnacite archers had found their targets. It took me like a spear to the belly, to guide my mount around the body of a slain Camaeline cavalryman, lying in the road with glazed eyes still open, his hand clutching his shield's grip. I, who did not even know his name, had sent him here to die.

Still we marched, and a second volley of arrows fell from the sky, and a third. A dozen men took grievous wounds despite their shields, until we drew close enough that Percy de Somerville ordered his archers to retreat through the ranks and sent his own pikemen, a thousand strong, to square off against our approaching forces while he moved two-thirds of his cavalry round to flank and enfold us. The countryfolk who had marched so boldly at our side huddled close behind the Queen's Guard, uncertain and fearful.

Somewhere, on the distant white walls of the City of Elua, there was shouting and the sound of horns, but it was faint and far away, and our tiny company was islanded amidst de Somerville's soldiers, a bristling forest of pikes facing us. In the stillness, Ysandre de la Courcel gave a silent prayer, only her lips moving.

"Herald," she said faintly, then. "Give the proclamation."

The inner ranks of the Unforgiven shifted, allowing him a space in the vanguard from which to deliver his message to the Royal Army. He drew a breath that must have strained his lungs to bursting, shouting, "Make way for Ysandre de la Courcel, the Queen of Terre d'Ange!"

With a roar, the pikemen of Percy de Somerville's army attacked, surging forward in a vast wave; surged forward, and broke, against the implacable wall of Black Shields, the Unforgiven of Camlach. All around and behind us it was chaos, de Somerville's cavalry forced into milling confusion by the presence of unarmed citizens fouling their course.

"Ys-and-dre! Ys-and-dre!"

The pikemen of the Unforgiven drove a wedge into de Somerville's infantry and the cavalry pushed from behind, widening it, and the Queen of Terre d'Ange rode into the gap. Amaury Trente, shouting orders, paused to glance around wild-eyed. "Queen's Guard!" he cried. "Now!"

They had fewer coins left than I would have wished; but enough. Each man among them had hoarded a cache. They spent them now, pressing close behind Ysandre and the ranks of the Unforgiven, jostling the knot of nobles they enclosed – including me – and hurling their remaining stores with slings of homespun cloth. Showers of silver coins burst into the air, scattering over the assembled forces of the Royal Army, who checked themselves out of sheer surprise at this unprecedented rain from heaven.

I had hoped for nothing more.

In the startlement that followed, Ysandre de la Courcel's party pushed forward, surrounded by the riders of the Unforgiven . . . and the ragged chant of the villagers began to make itself heard.

"Ys-and-dre! Ys-and-dre!"

At the outer edges of our company, the skirmishing slowed to a halt. The hurled coins, the cries of the commonfolk and the black shields of the Unforgiven had opened an aisle into the heart of the Royal Army.

"I cannot do it!" It was Brys nó Rinforte who spoke, the Cassiline, his voice strung tight and frantic. His hands trembled on the reins and his mount shifted nervously beneath him. "Your majesty, I have failed you once; I will fail you again! Do not ask me to do this thing!"

"Stand down, Cassiline," Ysandre said gently. "I do not ask it."

I heard Joscelin's indrawn breath; he caught my eye, deadly sober. I nodded. We had learned to speak without words, he and I, a long time ago. I knew what he intended. "Your majesty—" he began.

"No." Ysandre held up one hand. "No, Joscelin," she said, quietly. "It is mine to do alone."

He checked himself, pausing. The Unforgiven held their position, faces grim with resolve. A murmur like a swelling current passed through the vast forces of the Royal Army, drawing near to the ears of Percy de

Somerville. Brys nó Rinforte dismounted on shaking legs and pressed his face against his horse's neck. Joscelin bowed from the saddle, vambraced arms crossed before him. Like the others, I watched.

And Ysandre de la Courcel rode forth alone between the ranks of the Unforgiven.

The Queen of Terre d'Ange.

It was a broad aisle the Unforgiven had opened for a single rider, and Ysandre traversed it slowly, an eternity of suspense in every step her palfrey took. Her chin was upraised, her violet eyes wide and seemingly fearless. I heard Amaury Trente somewhere near me, muttering prayers and love-words like a curse. The dying and the wounded moaned with pain, and the soldiers of the Royal Army stood curiously still, staring past the Black Shields.

When Ysandre was two-thirds of the way down the cordon, Tarren d'Eltoine gave the command, a single, clipped word. "March!"

With the immaculate precision for which they trained, the Unforgiven put up their pikes and sheathed their swords, marching into the throng of the Royal Army, toward the City of Elua.

I, who was there, have no words to describe the sight; how the ranks of soldiers parted, falling away before the advance of the Queen of Terre d'Ange and her tiny vanguard. How knots of protest surged and fell silent, how awe dawned and settled on their faces, and stillness spread across the battlefield. Some glanced down at silver coins held in sword-calloused hands. Some merely stared, and some knelt. It is a grave and mighty thing, to see an army part like the ocean in a Yeshuite tale.

Ysandre never faltered.

The path that they opened led straight to Lord Percy, Duc de Somerville, the Royal Commander. We followed behind, a half-organized handful trailing in her wake, dazed commonfolk wandering between the mounted members of the Queen's Guard. Behind us, hundreds upon hundreds of de Somerville's soldiers came in close.

And ahead of us, always, was the tiny cordon of Black Shields, and in the aisle between them, the lone figure of the Queen, uncrowned, her fair hair falling in ripples down her back, her cloak in sculpted folds over her palfrey's crupper as she closed the distance between her and Percy de Somerville at a slow, even pace.

I will take credit for the coins; 'twas my idea, and it made a difference, that I will maintain. But it accounted only for the first blink of surprise, that opened the door. My skin prickled the whole of that terrible, fearful distance, awaiting the touch of steel.

That it did not come — that is due wholly to the courage of Ysandre de la Courcel.

He was waiting, Lord Percy, with the most loyal of his soldiers about him, unmounted, standing with legs solidly planted like some ancient, mighty tree. His gold-inlaid armor gleamed, though he held his helmet in the crook of his arm. I daresay he had known it, the moment his army turned. He was a good commander; the best, for many years, near as long as I had lived.

Ysandre halted before him. "Do you know who I am, my lord?" she asked softly.

"Yes." His expression never changed as he raised his voice in answer. A scent of apples hung in the chill autumn air, faint and sweet as a sun-warmed orchard. "You are Ysandre de la Courcel, the Queen of Terre d'Ange."

A sound like a vast sob of pain swept the field; soldiers who had not done so sheathed their weapons, shields falling with a clatter, knowing beyond doubt what they had done. Alone among the thousands who knelt in shame, Percy de Somerville remained standing, his gaze locked with his Queen's.

"Percy de Somerville," she said. "I place you under arrest for high treason."

EIGHTY-TWO·

IT WAS atop the walls of the City that the cheering began.

They had witnessed it all from the high white walls, the defenders of the City of Elua under the command of Barquiel L'Envers; indeed, it is his description that Thelesis de Mornay used in her epic when she set these events to verse. It was easy to pick out his figure, a surcoat of L'Envers' purple over his armor, raising his sword in salute. The wintry sun flashed on its length, and Ysandre's herald hoisted her standard in reply.

I saw joy and relief on the faces of many near me as they gave back the shouts of the defenders, but my own heart was too heavy for rejoicing. I saw the stricken grief in the faces of the soldiers of the Royal Army, struggling to understand what they had done. I saw Brys nó Rinforte, trembling with shame. I saw the stern resolve in the faces of the Unforgiven, who would never be done atoning for their own crime, and I saw Ysandre's chirurgeon and her assistant moving among the ranks, beginning the business of attending to the wounded and dying. I saw the glazed eyes of the Camaeline cavalryman I'd ridden around, and the hand of the village boy clutching in disbelief at the arrow shaft emerging from his flesh. I saw the shadow that haunted Ti-Philippe's smile, and remembered how my heart had been like a stone after Remy and Fortun were slain.

These things should not be.

And this sorrow, too, I saw in the face of Ysandre de la Courcel, who gazed at a man she had trusted since birth, her Royal Commander, a hero of the realm, sovereign Duc of L'Agnace, kin to her and a Prince of the Blood on her grandmother's side.

I think he felt it, too; what would have transpired next between them, I cannot say, for shouting of a different tenor arose from the walls. I looked up to see them pointing toward the north, and a ripple of sound coming from the outlying verge of the Royal Army, resolving sighting into words.

Ghislain was coming.

"Let him pass," Ysandre said.

He came armed for battle, bearing the colors and standard of House Trevalion, deep-blue with three ships and the Navigator's Star, and some three hundred men rode with him. The Royal Army parted ranks to allow his company through as he rode unerringly toward us. Ysandre watched him calmly, ordering the Unforgiven to stand aside.

They had ridden hard, their horses lathered and near-spent. Ghislain de Somerville drew rein before Ysandre and his company halted behind him, motionless to a man as he removed his helmet and pressed a clenched fist to his breast.

"My Queen," he said, a catch in his voice; his face was strained with emotion.

Ysandre inclined her head. "My lord de Somerville."

"Name me not thusly, majesty." Ghislain turned his head to his father, mingled hatred and love suffusing his features. "Is it true?"

Percy de Somerville did not look away, although there was a dreadful anguish in his eyes. Whatever else he was, he was no coward. "Yes."

Ghislain flinched as if at a blow, then extended his closed fist and opened it. A length of green cloth fell to the trodden ground, and I glimpsed the embroidered branches of an apple tree, the insignia of the de Somerville line. "In the name of Elua and Anael," he said harshly, "I renounce my House. Ghislain de Somerville is no more."

I felt tears stand in my eyes, and the blood beat hard in my head, a rush of bronze-winged sound, a tinge of crimson washing over my blurred vision. Percy de Somerville bowed his head in grief, his broad shoulders hunched, and I knew something had broken in him.

My lord Kushiel is cruel and just.

"It is heard and acknowledged," Ysandre said quietly, and there was compassion in her gaze. "My lords and ladies of Terre d'Ange, let us go home."

Barquiel L'Envers met us at the gates of the City, where something of a sombre mood had begun to settle after the initial rejoicing; there would be no triumph to celebrate this victory, only a low murmur as they exchanged the kiss of greeting. I do not know what words they spoke. When they parted, L'Envers glanced at me, a trace of the old, familiar irony glinting in his eye.

"Delaunay's *anguissette*," he acknowledged me. "You send a timely message."

"I am glad you heeded it, my lord," I said politely.

"Your wording was rather persuasive." He raised his brows. "Ysandre, will you reclaim your throne? I find the stewardship of it an onerous task."

Thus did the Queen of Terre d'Ange return to the City of Elua. The streets were thronged with people, and many of them wept openly as she passed. They had believed her dead these many days, for de Somerville had kept the rumor of her return from reaching the beleaguered City. It is a profound testament to the will and leadership of Barquiel L'Envers that he managed to maintain order in the City and hold the loyalty of the Palace and City Guards throughout the siege. My Kritian message had arrived scant days before Melisande's couriers, but it had come accompanied by a contingent of Eisandine troops sent by Roxanne de Mereliot, who urged him in strongest terms to act swiftly to secure the City. This he had done, sending to Namarre for a company of his own Akkadian-trained men and setting a watch on Champs-de-Guerre. When the Royal Army began to mobilize, L'Envers' spies fled to the City at breakneck pace and the gates were closed and sealed.

All these things I learned over time; then, there was simply too much to be done for the stories to unfold. Percy de Somerville was taken into custody, along with his chief lieutenants and subcommanders, for of a surety, some few of them must have known. Ysandre appointed Barquiel L'Envers to serve as Royal Commander *pro tem*, and supervise the military trials of the officers; being a peer of the realm, de Somerville would be tried before the assembled Parliament, like the family of House Trevalion long ago.

It was Marc de Trevalion, I learned, who had suspected Lord Percy's complicity when word of the Queen's death and the siege mounted against the City had reached Azzalle, and it was he who told his son-in-law Ghislain as much. He had known what Melisande had known, though he'd had no proof of it; that Percy de Somerville had vowed to support Lyonette de Trevalion's bid to place Prince Baudoin on the throne. Would that he had spoken of it sooner, for it would have saved a great deal of grief. I suppose at the time he thought it was ancient history and would have caused only pain, with his daughter wed to de Somerville's son. He would have been right, too, if not for Melisande.

Whether or not it ever occurred to Marc de Trevalion to suspect de Somerville in her escape, I cannot say. He was not there, at Troyes-le-Mont. He says it did not, and Ghislain believes him. After all, he would have had no reason to suspect Melisande even knew of de Somerville's complicity — save the fact that she is Melisande. It would have been enough for me . . . but then, I know her too well. Ysandre accepted his word; I do not know if she believed it. Enough to let it rest, I daresay.

Ysandre held an audience for those L'Agnacite villagers who had followed our company, learning their names, thanking each in person; to each one, she gave a gift, a gold ducat stamped with her image, sewn in a velvet purse with the Courcel insignia. There are cynics who claim she did it out of political expedience, for there was bound to be unrest in L'Agnace with the arrest of its much-loved Duc de Somerville, but I, who had seen the tears in her eyes when they came to join us, knew otherwise.

There was a private ceremony commending the service of the Unforgiven. Ysandre would have done more, for they were deserving — and too, it would aid in restoring the good name of the former Allies of Camlach — but they refused it to a man. I was there, when she gave them her thanks and blessing, and offered prayers for the dead. Ten had died, one in twenty. It had not been an entirely bloodless victory.

"Was it well done, Kushiel's chosen?" Tarren d'Eltoine asked me.

"It was well done, my lord," I replied.

And I thought on old Bianca's foretelling in the Temple of Asherat-of-the-Sea, and prayed her words held true. I had done as she bid, remembering what they had named me among the Unforgiven. Ten years' peace, she had promised; one, I thought, for every man I sent to his death outside the City of Elua.

Messengers rode out day and night, royal couriers proclaiming the news throughout the realm, laying to rest false rumors and potential uprisings. Ghislain nó Trevalion — for so he was called, now, formally adopted into his father-in-law's household — rode to Azzalle, vowing to see a ship across the Straits to carry a letter and full report to Drustan mab Necthana at Bryn Gorrydum. 'Twould be no mean feat, for the winter crossing was dangerous, but no one knew if the rumor had reached Alba's shores and Ysandre feared Drustan might believe her dead. It was a hardship on her to be parted from him at this time.

I felt it keenly, for I had never been more glad to

have Joscelin at my side. It had been a bittersweet pain, returning to my charming little house. My kitchen-mistress Eugènie embraced me like a mother and wept over our return; for joy at our safety, and again for sorrow at the loss of Remy and Fortun. We felt their absence deeply there, all of us. I missed hearing Remy's voice lifted in song from unexpected quarters of the house, missed seeing Fortun in the sitting room, dark, steady eyes glancing up from the map of Troyes-le-Mont on which he'd worked so hard. They had been my solace and my comrades, my chevaliers, during those days.

It was hardest of all on Ti-Philippe, who had lost his dearest friends. I offered to release him from my service, after paying him many months' wages in arrears, but he refused.

"Who could I possibly serve after you, my lady?" he asked with a ghost of a smile. "I've enough stories to tell, I won't need spend coin in the wineshops for years to come. Anyway, *they* wouldn't like it if I did. Phèdre's Boys are loyal, after all."

So I sent him to Montrève to see how my lamentably neglected estate was faring; of course, it was thriving in my absence, under the able care of my seneschal and his wife. But they fêted him and made much of him, begging him for news, and it did him a great deal of good to play at being lord of the manor for a time.

There were other, more joyous reunions, of course; Thelesis de Mornay, whom I accounted a dear friend, and my old mentor, Cecilie Laveau-Perrin, whom I loved equally well. It took Cecilie all of a heartbeat's time to assess the change in Joscelin's and my relationship and grasp our hands in hers, glowing with heartfelt approval.

"Oh my dears, you *have* set aside your differences! Nothing could make me happier."

Joscelin raised his eyebrows, smiling at her with genuine fondness. "Are you a sorceress, my lady Cecilie, to see as much?"

"No, beautiful man." Cecilie patted his cheek affectionately. "I am a Servant of Naamah, who rewards those who serve her true with vision to see what others would hold concealed in their hearts. Remember it well, if ever you are tempted to leave Phèdre again."

"It will not be soon," Joscelin said softly. "That much, I may promise."

We went too to see the Rebbe, Nahum ben Isaac. The number of Yeshuites in the City of Elua had grown thinner; several hundred had departed during the summer months, seeking their destiny in a far northern land. There had been some trouble in the City; not much, for Ysandre had heeded my plea and ordered the young Yeshuite hot-bloods to be dealt with gently so long as they were not in clear violation of the law. We were not Serenissimans. No, they had gone voluntarily, and it left the Yeshuite community older and sadder. What the Rebbe feared had come to pass; the Children of Yisra-el were divided.

"I am sorry, Master," I said to the Rebbe, sitting on a stool at his feet.

"So am I, young Phèdre nó Delaunay," he said sadly. "So am I. Adonai alone knows which of us is right, and betimes I pray it is not I." He looked unsmiling at Joscelin. "It is said that in La Serenissima, you put weapons in their hands, apostate, and taught them to fight."

"True words, Father." Joscelin met his gaze, unflinching.

"And yet you have forsaken the path of Yeshua."

Joscelin shook his head. "I do not disdain the teachings of Yeshua, Father. What I have learned, I value greatly. But I am D'Angeline, and Cassiel's chosen. Though it lead to perdition and beyond, I must follow my heart, and not the Mashiach." Reaching into a purse at his belt, he withdrew the *khai* pendant and held it forth. "Take it, if you will, and return it to she who gave it me. I am not worthy of bearing it."

"Hanna is gone, apostate." The Rebbe's tone was remorseless. "She has gone north, with the others. She would have given her heart to you, would you have accepted it, but you chose your own course instead."

"I didn't know," Joscelin whispered, paling slightly. For all that I loved him, he could be a bit of an idiot about some things. The Rebbe sighed, jerking his bearded chin at the pendant in Joscelin's hand.

"Keep it, then, and remember, how we do injury unwitting to those around us," he said sternly. "You Children of Elua are too quick to forget how the love you invoke may cut like a blade; even you, apostate. Still," he added, smiling faintly, deepset wrinkles about his eyes, "it gladdens my heart to see the both of you alive."

It made Joscelin thoughtful, and I was not sorry for it; I remembered the pain we had dealt each other in those days. How much of it was my doing, I knew full well; I had not forgotten aught that I had undergone in the *thetalos*. But I had spoken with the Kore, too, and I knew we each of us bear our own careless guilts, too seldom acknowledged.

I saw also Quintilius Rousse in the days after Ysandre's return, for he had been in Marsilikos when my letter arrived, making ready to winter his fleet; instead, he had brought them up the Aviline River to lie some few leagues south of the City, prepared to assail de Somerville's troops by water if necessary, while Roxanne de Mereliot raised an army in Eisande and Siovale. The Royal Admiral was blessedly unchanged, haranguing me mercilessly for the risks I'd taken, and hugging me in a bone-cracking embrace.

"La Serenissima will pay," he said ominously. "See if they don't!"

"My lord Admiral," I wheezed, still trying to catch my breath. "Despite what has happened, La Serenissima continues under the rule of Cesare Stregazza, who has pledged his alliance to Ysandre de la Courcel. It is a delicate situation, and I suspect the Queen might take it amiss if you were to exact vengeance against her orders."

Rousse scowled at me under his brows. "I'd have razed their mother-sodding Arsenal if they'd harmed you, child, make no mistake. Besides, La Serenissima is no friend to us while they hold Melisande Shahrizai in health and comfort – there's that, eh!"

"Yes," I said softly. "There is that."

For it was true, and would remain so; Melisande Shahrizai – Melisande Shahrizai de la Courcel – remained alive and well in the custody of the Temple of Asherat-of-the-Sea. Letters were carried back and forth from the City of Elua and La Serenissima that winter. The wily old Doge professed his great joy at learning that Ysandre had retained sovereignty of the realm, but he pleaded impotence in light of her repeated requests for Melisande's extradition.

I know, because Ysandre spoke candidly of these

matters with me, and I received letters also from Severio Stregazza, and betimes his aunt, Allegra. Always, the news was the same: Melisande remained at the Temple, attended like a queen and seemingly content to continue thusly.

Of her son Imriel, there was no trace.

"How should I proceed, Phèdre?" Ysandre asked me once in a rare moment of frustration. "You tried to warn me against her, and I failed to give credence to your fears. You, who know her best — tell me now what I may expect from Melisande Shahrizai!"

"My lady, I cannot say," I said helplessly, spreading my hands. "Melisande's plans failed, save this last avenue of retreat. If she is content to remain in the Temple — for I think it could hold her no more than Troyes-le-Mont; indeed, a good deal less — it is because whatever further plans she might spin have not yet come to fruition. It is beyond my guessing to know what those might be."

Ysandre gave me a wry look. "The boy stands in line for my throne. You cannot guess?"

"To guess *what* is simple," I said, meeting her eyes. "The problem lies in discerning *how*. I swear to you, my lady, I will maintain every vigilance and report to you aught that I learn. But I make no promise."

"It would be nice," Ysandre said mildly, "if you found the child."

One day I would remember those words with a deep and bitter irony; then, I merely bowed my head, acknowledging my Queen's wishes. I did not offer to return to the Service of Naamah to pursue the search. I had made no decision on that score, and any mind, I didn't think

Melisande would involve any current or likely patrons of mine where her son's safety was concerned. I had seen the passion that flashed in her eyes when Ysandre had challenged her care for the babe. No, Melisande would not risk the boy, not even for the sake of our deep-laid game; and if Naamah desired her Servant's return, let her summon me herself.

Thus did the winter pass, and the realm slowly healed from the second shock of betrayal in as many years. Parliament was convened out of season, and a trial held for Percy de Somerville. I had to testify, as did Ti-Philippe, who had heard the words of Phanuel Buonard's widow; the conclusion was foregone, as one of de Somerville's lieutenants had already made a full confession in the military hearings presided over by Barquiel L'Envers. I have heard some dubious comments about the Duc L'Envers' method of questioning, but no complaints were filed, and the majority of the army command was exonerated. I held my tongue; Barquiel L'Envers had earned my forbearance. Like his chief lieutenant, Percy de Somerville was convicted of high treason and sentenced to death, given his choice of means. A good soldier to the end, the one-time Royal Commander fell on his sword.

The City did not grieve for him as it had for Baudoin de Trevalion, another hero of the realm who had died the same way. That plot had died stillborn, aborted by Melisande's schemes; this one had hatched in full, and the memory of the Royal Army surrounding the City of Elua was too fresh. Still, I do not think anyone rejoiced, either. For my part, I was merely glad it was over.

Early spring I spent immersing myself in my resumed

studies in Habiru lore, patiently retracing the steps I had begun a year earlier. I had not forgotten my Prince of Travellers, or given up hope of finding a key to his freedom. I bought some Illyrian books as well, mindful that I did not lose that skill, and practiced by composing a letter to Kazan Atrabiades. Quintilius Rousse would be sailing to Epidauro when the weather cleared, carrying an emissary to discuss trade negotiations. Ysandre had not forgotten her promise, either; and Rousse would be sailing on to Kriti afterward, bearing a very generous gift for the Archon of Phaistos. I wrote letters to Demetrios Asterius also, and his cousin Pasiphae, Kore of the Temenos, whom I thought of often.

When the last of spring's gales had blown themselves out, the shipping routes were open. Rousse's fleet departed from Marsilikos . . . and once more, riders from Azzalle vied to be the first at the Palace with the news that the flagship of the Cruarch of Alba had been sighted on the Strait. Ysandre's face brightened at the news, and when she declared it was time at last for a celebration, I agreed wholeheartedly.

"We have had the winter to remember and sorrow, my lady," I said. "It is spring, and a time for joy. I can think of no better reason for celebration than my lord Drustan's return."

"Which we shall do, in abundance, but there is one reason yet lacking, near-cousin." Ysandre looked at me with quizzical amusement; I fear I bewildered her at times, though she loved me well enough. We were very different people, Ysandre and I. "Phèdre nó Delaunay de Montrève, it has not escaped my awareness that I owe my life and my throne to you, you and your companions. I have been awaiting a fitting time to make formal acknowledgment of your deeds. Did you truly think I would let it pass without a fête?"

"Actually," I said, "I did."

Eighty-three

"BUT WHAT is she planning to *do?*" Joscelin demanded.

"I don't know!" I retorted, irritated. "She won't say. Make a speech and toast us in front of the assembled peers of the realm, I imagine. Don't laugh." I pointed at Ti-Philippe, returned this spring from Montrève. "You're included in this, chevalier."

"Oh, I wouldn't miss it." He raised his eyebrows and grinned. "I want to see the faces of those of your patrons in attendance when they learn the whole of what you've done. I don't think many of them truly reckoned they were bedding a genuine tales-of-the-poets heroine."

To his credit, Joscelin merely responded by shying a grape at Philippe's head; Ti-Philippe dodged it, laughing. A great deal had changed between them since La Serenissima. I thought on Ti-Philippe's words, which held a certain truth. 'Tis a strange thing, to be lauded by one's peers, when a number of them have known one naked and pleading. I never set out to be aught but a courtesan. It is an odd quirk of fate that made me otherwise.

"Delaunay's *anguissette*," Joscelin said aloud, his

thoughts following the same course as my own. "He would be proud beyond words, Phèdre; I knew him long enough to know that. Let Ysandre honor you. You've earned it."

"We all have, and you will go too, my lord Cassiline, without fussing." I cocked my head, considering him. "A trip to the barber wouldn't be amiss, either."

Since La Serenissima, Joscelin's hair had grown out in ragged wheat-gold profusion; I do not think he'd had it trimmed since my efforts, but merely bound it back in a braid, wisps escaping down the cabled length of it. I swear he was as careless of his beauty as a rich drunkard with his purse. In the end, I ordered him into Ti-Philippe's custody to be properly shorn, and commissioned new attire for all three of us.

Favrielle nó Eglantine had prospered in my absence; impossible to believe, but her year's tenancy at Eglantine House had already passed, and she had opened a salon of her own in the clothiers' district. It was small, but thriving, occupying the ground floor of a building there. Three assistants she had already – draper, a cutter and a second seamstress – and looked to add more in short order.

"Comtesse," she greeted me, curling her scarred lip; I found myself, oddly, reassured by her unchanged demeanor. "You come at a poor time, as usual. I have a number of commissions on short order, a good many of which seem to be for *your* gala. I suppose you think I shall make time for you, merely because I am beholden to you?"

"No," I said cheerfully. "You'll make time because it *is* my gala and you are a shrewd businesswoman, and because I will tell you in detail what they are wearing in the court of the Archon of Phaistos on Kriti. Also, if you wish, about a gown that was made for me based on an ancient poem in Illyria."

Favrielle paused, narrowing her green eyes at me. "Tell me."

I did, while she made sketches and notations, pacing the room, muttering to herself and hauling out swatches of fabric. When I had done, she called crossly for more foolscap and sat for a time sketching furiously and dabbling pigment, showing me the results at length — a gown of sheerest green, pleated and gathered under the breasts in the Kritian style, nigh-transparent over a close-fitting sheath of deep bronze silk. On paper, the effect was of an ancient Hellene statue veiled in thin drapery.

"Very nice," I said, and smiled to see her scowl. "Can you make it in time for the fête?"

She could and did, of course; it was too splendid not to, and Favrielle nó Eglantine had the pride of her genius. In addition, she had powers of persuasion beyond my ken, sufficient to coax Joscelin out of his usual drab Cassiline-inspired greys. It took me aback to see him in a doublet of forest green and breeches to match, sober and elegant. As was his wont, Ti-Philippe wore more festive garb, echoing the same colors, with a close-fitting vest striped green and bronze over dark breeches and a full-sleeved white shirt, and we all of us looked quite fine.

The fête was held in the vast Palace ballroom, with an immense dining table echoing the banquet depicted on the gorgeous murals of Elua and his Companions at banquet; truly, Ysandre spared no expense. Sprays of blossoming branches laced the slender colonnades — peach, cherry and apple — and the tiny glass lamps were filled with clear water that night, shimmering with white light. A fountain played

in the grotto, lending its liquid music to the musicians'
tunes, while finches in gilt-filigree cages sang sweetly
above it all. I thought that we had arrived late, although
it was the hour appointed by the Queen's invitation, for it
seemed the flower of D'Angeline nobility had already
assembled. It was not until the chamberlain announced us
that I understood.

"The Comtesse Phèdre nó Delaunay de Montrève,
Messire Joscelin Verreuil, the chevalier Philippe Dumont,"
he called in ringing tones.

Save for the birdsong and fountain, silence fell over the
vast space as the music ceased; and then a soft ripple of
applause, D'Angeline heads inclined in bows. I had not
fully grasped, until then, that we were the guests of honor
and the fête awaited on our entrance. Ysandre received us
personally, extending both hands in greeting, Drustan mab
Necthana at her side.

I had seen him, of course, when he entered the City in
procession, but there had been time only for a brief
exchange of pleasantries. It gladdened my heart to see him
again; his quiet smile, dark eyes calm and steady in his
blue-whorled face.

"It is good," he said softly in Cruithne, a tongue we
shared, "that we gather to celebrate your courage, Phèdre
nó Delaunay."

I thought of Ysandre's ride between the black shields
of the Unforgiven, her upraised profile defying the troops
of Percy de Somerville, and shook my head. "If I have
seen aught of courage, my lord Cruarch, I have seen it in
your lady wife, who is my liege and sovereign."

Drustan's dark eyes crinkled with amusement. "Do not
say it, or she will be vexed with you; it is her wish to give

you your due." He turned to Joscelin, clasping his fore-arms. "My brother," he said simply. "If you were less skilled with blades, my heart would have died within me that day."

"And the heart of Terre d'Ange with it," Joscelin murmured, returning his grip hard. "I am passing glad to be here today, my lord Cruarch."

With that, Drustan turned to Ti-Philippe; I did not hear what he said, for I was caught up in a whirl of greet-ings, hands proffered, cheeks pressed close to give the kiss of greeting. There were people there I had not seen for nearly a year — indeed, faces I had last seen gloating over the falling-out I had staged with Ysandre and Drustan. Such is politics. While the fate of the realm hangs in the balance, these things continue. It seemed much longer than a year gone by. I saw the faces of those who knew — Lord Amaury Trente, Lady Vivienne, others who had been present on our terrible race across Caerdicca Unitas — and saw the same knowledge reflected in their eyes, how near a thing it had been. They had been there, in the Temple of Asherat-of-the-Sea, where Benedicte de la Courcel nearly gained the throne of Terre d'Ange.

For the rest, it was merely a poet's tale.

A ten-day siege laid to the City; how quickly and easily people forget! Ysandre's ride had done that, had rendered the whole of Melisande's vast and intricate scheme no more than a misunderstanding, one man's treasonous folly, a footnote in the annals of history. Now, seeing the ease and merriment of the D'Angeline nobles, I understood the true import of her actions.

Not all had forgotten, for Barquiel L'Envers was there. Our eyes met in the crowded ballroom and he inclined his

fair-cropped head, according me my due. We had gauged
each other wrongly, he and I, and both of us knew it. If
our methods were unorthodox, still, our ends had been the
same. Nicola L'Envers y Aragon had tried to tell me as
much, and I would not hear her; I had learned that much in
the *thetalos*, the cost of my pride and the ghost of
Delaunay's ancient enmity. Small wonder, thinking on it,
that I half-thought I had conjured her image between us.
But I was wrong, for Nicola was there, amused at my
blinking startlement across the crowd; I could not help that
my blood beat faster in my veins at it.

   I'd no time, though, to speak with Nicola or any number of other guests before the bell rang to summon us to
the table. Ysandre and Drustan presided at either end. As
her nearest kin and a ranking Duc, Barquiel L'Envers sat at
the Queen's right hand and I was across from him at her
left in the place of honor; it would have made me nervous,
save that Joscelin was seated beside me and Ti-Philippe
across from him, alit with unabashed merriment. It was an
exceedingly fine repast and the liveried servants circulated
with flawless efficiency, pouring wine like water. Course
upon course was served; lark and pheasant in delicate pastries, smoked eel, a rack of lamb stuffed with currants and
a crumbling white cheese, roasted bream, quivering jellies
flavored with nutmeg and bay leaves . . . I cannot remember all we ate nor all we discussed, save that the conversation sparkled and the plates and goblets gleamed, and
there is a glow on that night that endures in memory.

   When the last course had been served and the last
dinner platter cleared, Ysandre de la Courcel clapped her
hands. Servants came round again to fill our glasses of cordial and set out dishes filled with candied orange and lemon

peel, arranged to resemble bunches of flowers with sugared violets at their centers. Part-way down the table,
Thelesis de Mornay rose and bowed, commanding our
attention as she announced the entrance of Gilles Lamiz,
her gifted apprentice-poet. We dipped our hands in the
finger bowls of rosewater before applauding politely.

I had seen the young man before in Thelesis' quarters;
he assisted her in many things, and had taken notation for
her when I related the long tale of my adventures. 'Twas
for her work on the Ysandrine Cycle, I had assumed, only
partially correct. Thelesis' dark, lovely eyes glowed with
pleasure as her surprise was revealed – Gilles Lamiz was
working on his own, more modest offering, too.

'Twas a poem based upon my exploits, and those of my
companions.

It was not a bad effort and he recited it well, in a clear
tenor voice that owed its richness to his mentor's training.
I rested my chin in my palm and listened, amazed to hear
my own deeds recounted thusly, if not wholly as I remembered them. Young Gilles had listened well and captured
the grieving madness of La Dolorosa, but he omitted the
stench and tedium. My retort to Melisande Shahrizai's offer
resounded with dignity, and not the skull-splitting reality
of the desperate defiance I recalled. I thought the
magnificent daring of Joscelin's attack on the black isle
was well rendered, and Ti-Philippe's heroic marshaling
of their scarce-trained Yeshuite allies to hold the tower,
but both of them laughed afterward, saying there was
a considerable measure of panic and terror that went
unmentioned.

So it went, and I must own, it sounded a good deal
more impressive when set into verse. The sea-flight, the

kríavbhog and the storms were all fearful, which was no more than the truth. Kazan Atrabiades came off as rather dashing, which made me smile; it would have pleased him, I think. In Gilles' version, Demetrios Asterius, the Archon of Phaistos, rendered his aid out of adoration for my beauty. I reckoned that did poor justice to his shrewd trader's wiles, but the D'Angeline nobles around the table glanced at me from the corners of their eyes and nodded sagely, more than willing to believe it true.

One tale missing was that of the *thetalos*, for that I had not told, even to Thelesis de Mornay. It is a mystery, and of such things one cannot speak to the uninitiated; it sufficed to say that there was a ritual, and Kazan Atrabiades of Epidauro was cleansed of blood-guilt.

Gilles Lamiz' poem ended in the Temple of Asherat, with my proclamation from the Oracle's balcony and Joscelin's heart-stopping duel with the Cassiline traitor David de Rocaille. I daresay the latter read well enough without embellishment, and even Joscelin did not argue with it. Although all the realm knows his name because of it, it is not a deed in which he takes pride. No longer do two Cassiline Brothers attend the ruler of Terre d'Ange at all times. Ysandre broke with seven centuries' tradition after La Serenissima and Brys nó Rinforte's defection on the battlefield, dismissing them from her service.

It is an irony that the Cassiline Brotherhood swelled in popularity after Gilles Lamiz' poem became famous, peers demanding Cassiline guards, families who had abandoned the tradition for generations sending their middle sons to foster with the Brethren. Joscelin only smiles wryly when people speak to him of it, and changes the subject.

There was applause when Gilles Lamiz finished; a great, resounding deal of it, and much of it aimed my way. I felt myself flush hotly. The young poet bowed repeatedly, and Thelesis de Mornay beamed with pride. Ysandre raised her hand for silence, swiftly obeyed.

"As you have heard their deeds," she said clearly, "so do we gather to honor them."

Rising to stand as Queen, flanked on one side by Drustan mab Necthana and the other by Barquiel L'Envers, she called first Philippe, my chevalier Ti-Philippe, presenting to him the Medal of Valor, a heavy gold medallion embossed with Camael's sword and the lily of Elua, strung on a thick, green ribbon. Tears sprang to my eyes as I watched the last of Phèdre's Boys kneel before Ysandre, unwontedly sober, fingering the dense medal as she bid him rise.

Afterward, she summoned Joscelin, and whether he welcomed it or no, my heart ached with pride to see his grave beauty as he gave his Cassiline bow, so much a part of him no one dared question it, and knelt to the Queen. To him too she gave the Medal of Valor, receiving it from the hand of Barquiel L'Envers, who served still as Royal Commander; and somewhat else beside. "It is an ancient tradition for a ruling Queen to appoint a Champion to do battle in her name," Ysandre declared, lifting a finely wrought wreath of vines from a pillow proffered by a waiting servant. "I have not done so, Joscelin Verreuil, but I give thanks to Blessed Elua for choosing you to fulfill that role when it was needful. I could not have chosen better."

With that, she placed the wreath on his fair, bowed head.

It would have been enough, for me, to see those I loved thus honored; it was not enough for Ysandre de la Courcel, who summoned me to stand before her. This I did, and when I would have curtsied and sunk to kneel, she shook her head and caught my wrist, keeping me upright.

"Comtesse Phèdre nó Delaunay de Montrève." Ysandre gave my name and title with a gleam in her eye; I daresay she'd had as much wine as the rest of us. "Like your patrons, who prize you above gold, I shall take pleasure in challenging your uniquely indomitable will. For those deeds which we heard lauded this night in verse, for your unfathomable courage, and for the memory of your lord Anafiel Delaunay, who taught us all what it truly means to keep an oath sworn in love, I present you with the Companion's Star."

I stared uncomprehending as Drustan mab Necthana, smiling, held forth an object — a brooch, a many-rayed gold star, set in the center with a single faceted diamond, Elua's sigil etched on the face of it in delicate lines, the work of a master jeweler. Ysandre took the brooch from him and fastened it onto my gown with deft fingers.

"This grants you the right," she said softly, "to address me in public or private as an equal, and bend your knee to no Scion of Elua throughout the realm; indeed, to fail to do so is to belittle the honor I bestow upon you this night. Do you show this to the least of my guards, they will admit you unto an audience without question. And I swear to you, whatever you may say, I will hear it." Taking a step back, Ysandre surveyed her handiwork. "It carries also," she added, "a boon. Aught that you might request of me that is in my power and right to grant, I will do. Do you wish it, ask now."

"There is nothing, my la—" Catching her warning glance, I swallowed. "Ysandre."

"Well, then." The Queen of Terre d'Ange smiled. "Accept it with my thanks, near-cousin, and save the boon for the day you require it. Until then, let us drink your health, and give thanks to Blessed Elua we are all alive to do so."

That, at least, I could do and did, returning to my seat and waiting until the glasses were refilled, the toast given and drunk, before tossing back a measure of cordial, feeling the fiery burn of it scald my insides to match my flushed skin. And with that, mercifully, Ysandre's tribute was done, and she was content to order the musicians to strike up a dancing tune and declare the fête open to celebration.

It was with a full heart that I watched Ysandre and Drustan begin the first dance, shortly joined by many other couples. Their duties done, they had eyes only for each other, locking glances and smiling deeply; two realms, two rulers, united in love and a shared dream. It is my thought that this is the deeper meaning of the Precept of Blessed Elua; in love, howsoever it is manifest, we are greater than the sum of our parts.

Little enough time I had to think on it, for Barquiel L'Envers claimed a dance of me, and I joined him with good will, glad of a chance to lay our quarrels to rest before the eyes of the realm. I looked for Joscelin afterward, but he was partnering Thelesis de Mornay; Gilles Lamiz approached me, an unexpected nervous stammer threading his poet's voice. In the dance, he held me so lightly one might have thought I was made of porcelain. It made me smile, to think I would break so easily, after all I had endured. I drank a toast to his poem when we had done, for the mischievous pleasure of seeing him redden and stammer all the harder. The cordial tasted heady, and it seemed to me that the lamps burned brighter for it.

There is a wild and piercing sweetness in celebrating life after a long sorrow; all of us felt it that night. Spring is ever a time of renewal, and it seemed fit, after so long, to rediscover pure, unalloyed happiness.

"Phèdre nó Delaunay." I turned at the voice, recognizing it; Nicola L'Envers y Aragon regarded me with amusement. "It is no easy task to gain your ear this evening," she said, giving me the kiss of greeting.

"Nicola." I took her hand, having too much to say, and no words to say it. "You were right, in what you tried to tell me. I owe you a greater debt than I can repay."

"Mmm." She shrugged and gave her lazy smile, setting my heart to speed its pace, remembering our dalliances. "You could try, of course. I have heard that you've not returned to the Service of Naamah, but there's naught to prevent you from taking a lover." Her violet gaze drifted over my shoulder, and she inclined her head in greeting. "Well met, my lord Cassiline."

"My lady Nicola."

I fair jumped at the sound of Joscelin's voice, craning my head around to see his expression. Nicola laughed, reaching out to stroke my burning cheek.

"Think on it," she said lightly, moving away.

I opened my mouth to speak, and Joscelin cut me off. "Phèdre, if you're going to think of taking lovers—"

"I'm *not*—"

"—I think it would be a good idea if you declared me your official consort, first."

"Joscelin, I'm not . . ." I stopped, staring at him. He wore a crooked smile and his green-leaved wreath sat askew on his head, making him look rather like a young, drunken god. "Do you mean it?"

"I told you in La Serenissima, I don't care if you take a thousand patrons—"

"Not *that*," I interrupted him. "About declaring you my consort."

"Oh, *that*." Joscelin laughed. "Phèdre nó Delaunay, we are mismatched in more ways than I can count, and like as not, we'll find ways to hurt each other neither of us have even dreamt yet. The only thing I can imagine worse than spending my life with you is being without you – I've done it, and I never want to experience the like again. If you can find your way back to my side through besotted pirates, murderous Serenissimans and deadly storms, I'm not going to waste time worrying about a few ambitious patrons. Besides . . ." he grinned, ". . . I reckon I ought to claim the role before you find a way to get that damned Tsingano off his forsaken island, and—"

He didn't get any further, for at that moment I threw both arms around his neck and kissed him hard enough to make both our heads reel.

Somewhere in the Temple of Asherat, Melisande Shahrizai was likely spinning a new and deadly plot; somewhere, Elua only knew where, a babe was being raised, with her blood in his veins and a claim to the throne of Terre d'Ange. Somewhere in Illyria, in La Serenissima, in Terre d'Ange, in Alba, the kindred of those slain by events I had set in motion continued to mourn their dead, and somewhere in the Strait, the Prince of Travellers pursued his lonely destiny. None of these things did I forget, for somewhere in a cavern in the Temenos, the knowledge was ever awaiting me. But there is a limit to how much pain we mortals can bear, even I, and in that moment, my world was bounded by joy, encompassed in Joscelin's beautiful face that I held between my hands, his summer-blue eyes smiling down at me.

"Did I mention," I whispered to him, "that I love you?"

"Yes," he whispered back, kissing me. "But it bears repeating."

Hand in hand, we threaded our way through the revelers to find Ysandre de la Courcel, seated once more at the long table next to Drustan, while one of her courtiers related an amusing tale. She glanced up at our approach, and the courtier broke off his story, mindful of the pre-eminence the Companion's Star granted me.

"Yes?" Ysandre asked mildly.

"Your maj—" I broke off the words and cleared my throat. "Ysandre. Before Blessed Elua and all here assembled, I wish to present Joscelin Verreuil as my consort."

Drustan mab Necthana laughed, and the Queen of Terre d'Ange raised her eyebrows.

"It's about time."

JACQUELINE CAREY

Kushiel's Dart

TOR

A massive fantasy tale about the violent death of an old age and the birth of a new one. Here is a novel of grandeur, luxuriance, sacrifice, betrayal and deeply laid conspiracies.

Born with a scarlet mote in her left eye, Phèdre nó Delaunay is sold into indentured servitude as a child. When her bond is purchased by an enigmatic nobleman, she is trained in history, theology, politics, foreign languages and the arts of pleasure. Above all, she learns the ability to observe, remember and analyse. An exquisite courtesan, yet a talented spy, she may seem an unlikely heroine . . . but when Phèdre stumbles upon a plot threatening her homeland, Terre d'Ange, she has no choice but to act.

Betrayed into captivity in the barbarous northland of Skaldia, and accompanied only by a disdainful young warrior-priest, Phèdre make a harrowing escape and an even more harrowing journey, to return to her people and deliver them a warning of the impending invasion. And that proves only the first step in a quest that will take her to the edge of despair and beyond.

'A very sophisticated fantasy, intricately plotted and a fascinating read' Robert Jordan

'Making a marvellous debut, Carey spins a breathtaking epic starring an unflinching yet poignantly vulnerable heroine' *Booklist*

OTHER PAN BOOKS
AVAILABLE FROM PAN MACMILLAN